METAL HURLANT

SELECTED WORKS

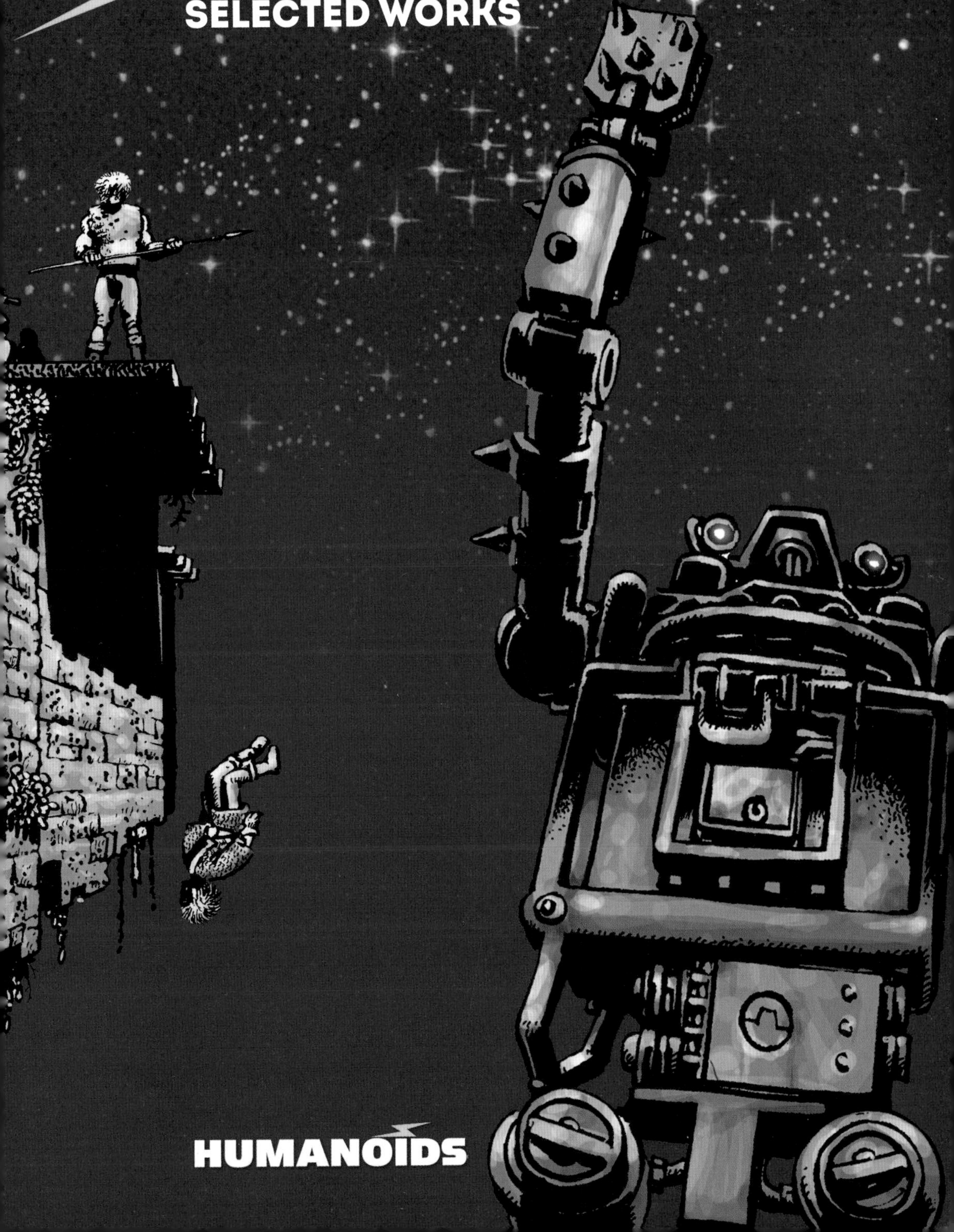

HUMANOIDS

CAZA
Cover Artist

RICHARD CORBEN
Title Page Illustration

RYAN SOOK
Back Cover Illustration

**SAMANTHA DEMERS FOR WORLD
LANGUAGE COMMUNICATIONS
SASHA WATSON
QUINN AND KATIA DONOGHUE
NATACHA RUCK AND KEN GROBE
BENJAMIN CROZE**
Translators

**ROB LEVIN
ALEX DONOGHUE**
US Edition Editors

AMANDA LUCIDO
Assistant Editor

**PAUL BENJAMIN
MAXIMILLIEN CHAILLEUX
JEAN-PIERRE DIONNET
PHILIPPE HAURI
BRUNO LECIGNE**
Original Edition Editors

JERRY FRISSEN
Senior Art Director

FABRICE GIGER
Publisher

Rights and Licensing - licensing@humanoids.com
Press and Social Media - pr@humanoids.com

METAL HURLANT: SELECTED WORKS.
This title is a publication of Humanoids, Inc. 8033 Sunset Blvd. #628, Los Angeles, CA 90046. Copyright © 2002, 2020 Humanoids, Inc., Los Angeles (USA). All rights reserved. Humanoids and its logos are ® and © 2020 Humanoids, Inc. Library of Congress Control Number: 2019916117

3 ON A MATCH

Story by R.A. JONES
Art by RYAN SOOK
Colors by DAVE STEWART

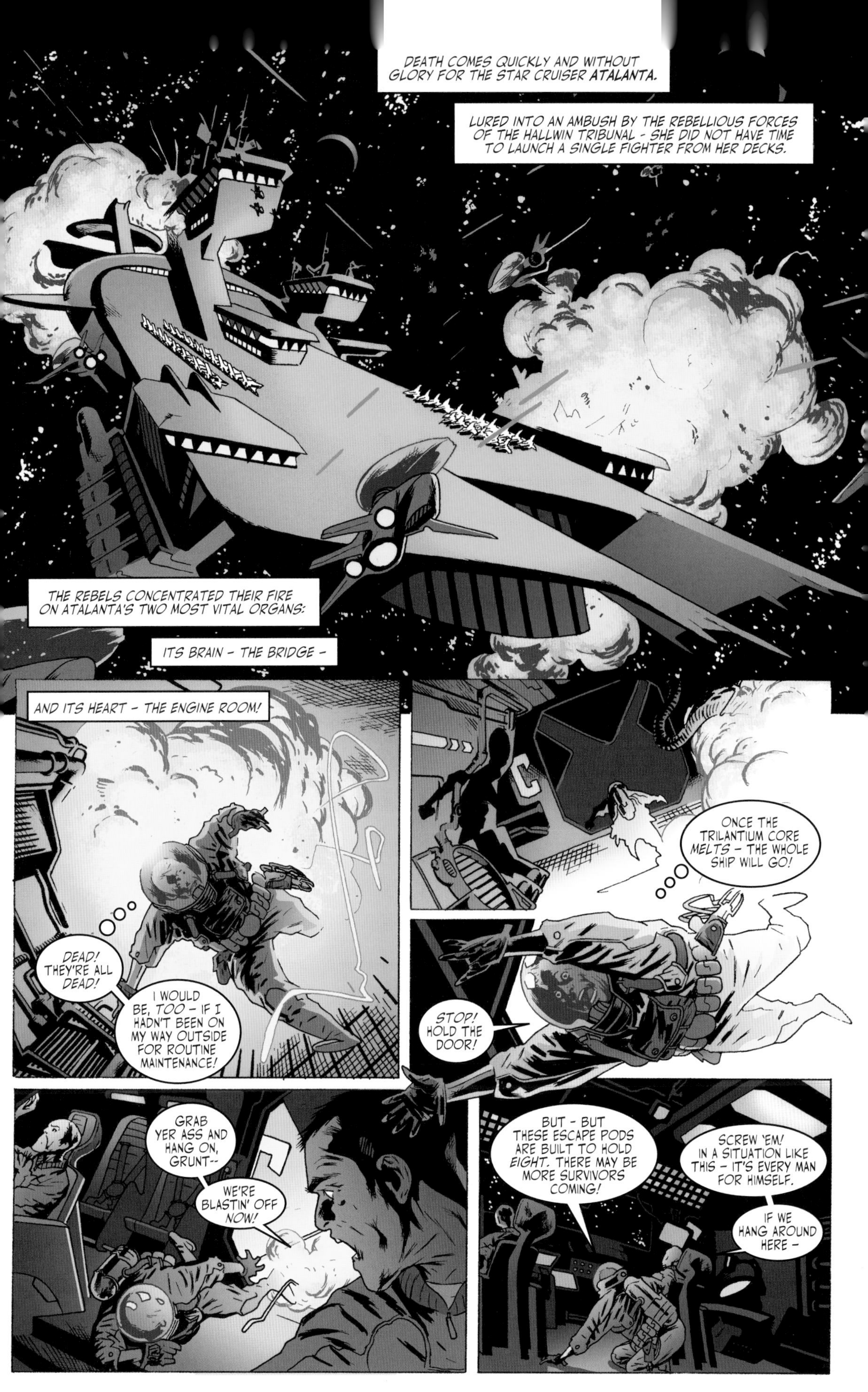
DEATH COMES QUICKLY AND WITHOUT GLORY FOR THE STAR CRUISER ATALANTA.
LURED INTO AN AMBUSH BY THE REBELLIOUS FORCES OF THE HALLWIN TRIBUNAL - SHE DID NOT HAVE TIME TO LAUNCH A SINGLE FIGHTER FROM HER DECKS.
THE REBELS CONCENTRATED THEIR FIRE ON ATALANTA'S TWO MOST VITAL ORGANS:
ITS BRAIN - THE BRIDGE -
AND ITS HEART - THE ENGINE ROOM!
DEAD! THEY'RE ALL DEAD!
I WOULD BE, TOO - IF I HADN'T BEEN ON MY WAY OUTSIDE FOR ROUTINE MAINTENANCE!
ONCE THE TRILANTIUM CORE MELTS - THE WHOLE SHIP WILL GO!
STOP! HOLD THE DOOR!
GRAB YER ASS AND HANG ON, GRUNT--
WE'RE BLASTIN' OFF NOW!
BUT - BUT THESE ESCAPE PODS ARE BUILT TO HOLD EIGHT. THERE MAY BE MORE SURVIVORS COMING!
SCREW 'EM! IN A SITUATION LIKE THIS - IT'S EVERY MAN FOR HIMSELF.
IF WE HANG AROUND HERE -

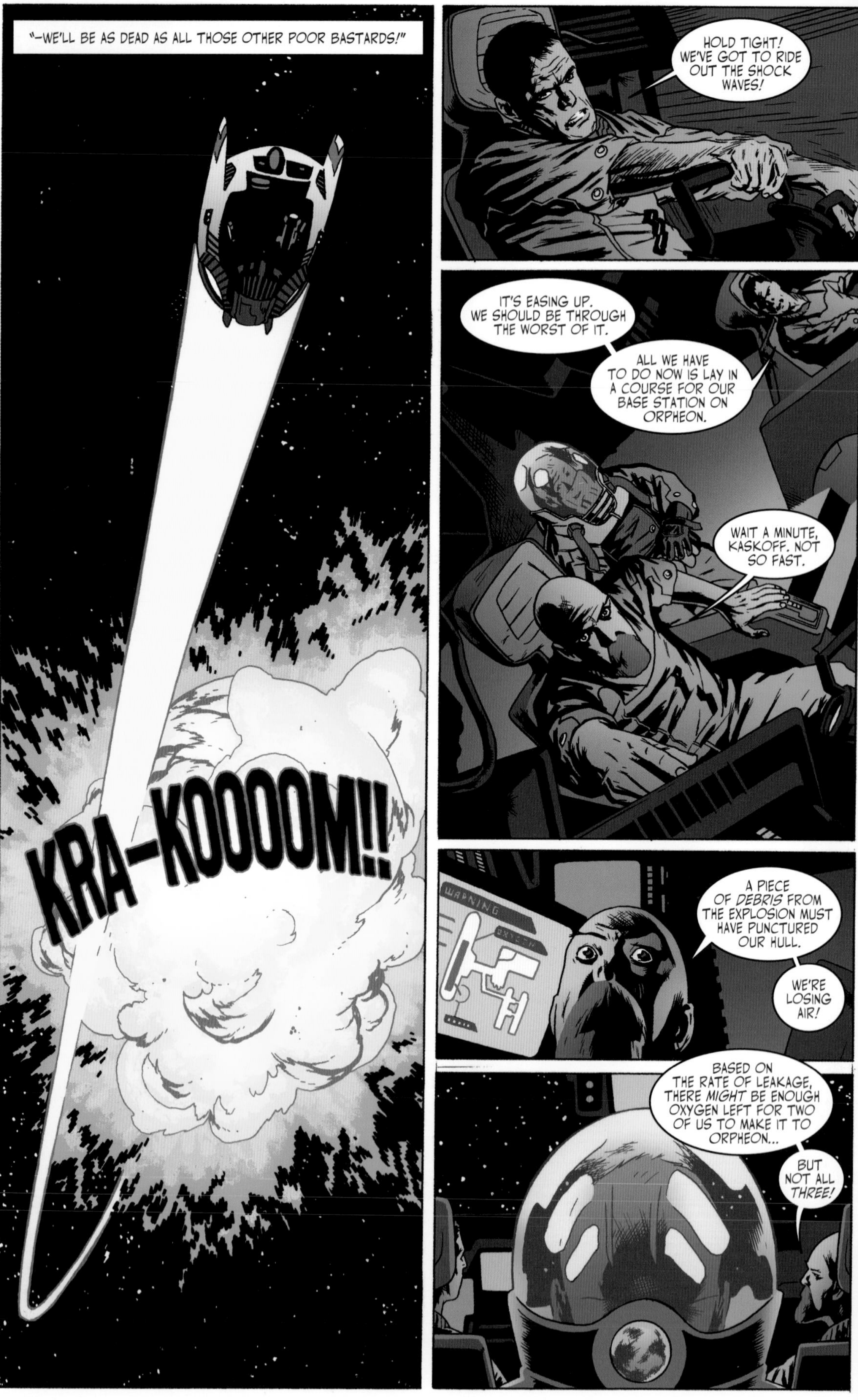
"—WE'LL BE AS DEAD AS ALL THOSE OTHER POOR BASTARDS!"
KRA-KOOOOM!!
HOLD TIGHT! WE'VE GOT TO RIDE OUT THE SHOCK WAVES!
IT'S EASING UP. WE SHOULD BE THROUGH THE WORST OF IT.
ALL WE HAVE TO DO NOW IS LAY IN A COURSE FOR OUR BASE STATION ON ORPHEON.
WAIT A MINUTE, KASKOFF. NOT SO FAST.
WARNING
OXYGEN
A PIECE OF DEBRIS FROM THE EXPLOSION MUST HAVE PUNCTURED OUR HULL.
WE'RE LOSING AIR!
BASED ON THE RATE OF LEAKAGE, THERE MIGHT BE ENOUGH OXYGEN LEFT FOR TWO OF US TO MAKE IT TO ORPHEON...
BUT NOT ALL THREE!

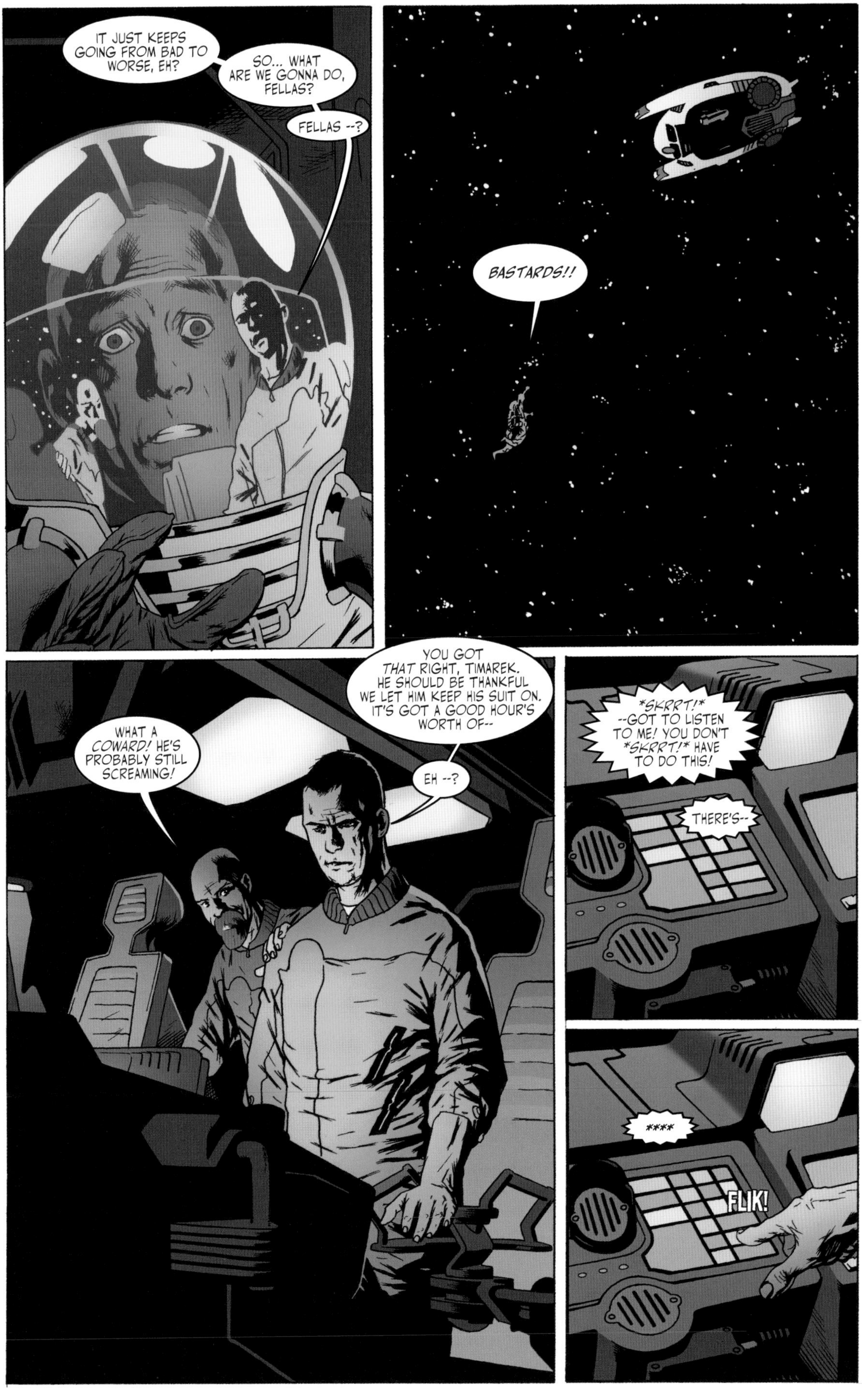

IT JUST KEEPS GOING FROM BAD TO WORSE, EH?
SO... WHAT ARE WE GONNA DO, FELLAS?
FELLAS --?
BASTARDS!!
WHAT A COWARD! HE'S PROBABLY STILL SCREAMING!
YOU GOT THAT RIGHT, TIMAREK. HE SHOULD BE THANKFUL WE LET HIM KEEP HIS SUIT ON. IT'S GOT A GOOD HOUR'S WORTH OF--
EH --?
SKRRT! --GOT TO LISTEN TO ME! YOU DON'T *SKRRT!* HAVE TO DO THIS!
THERE'S--
****
FLIK!

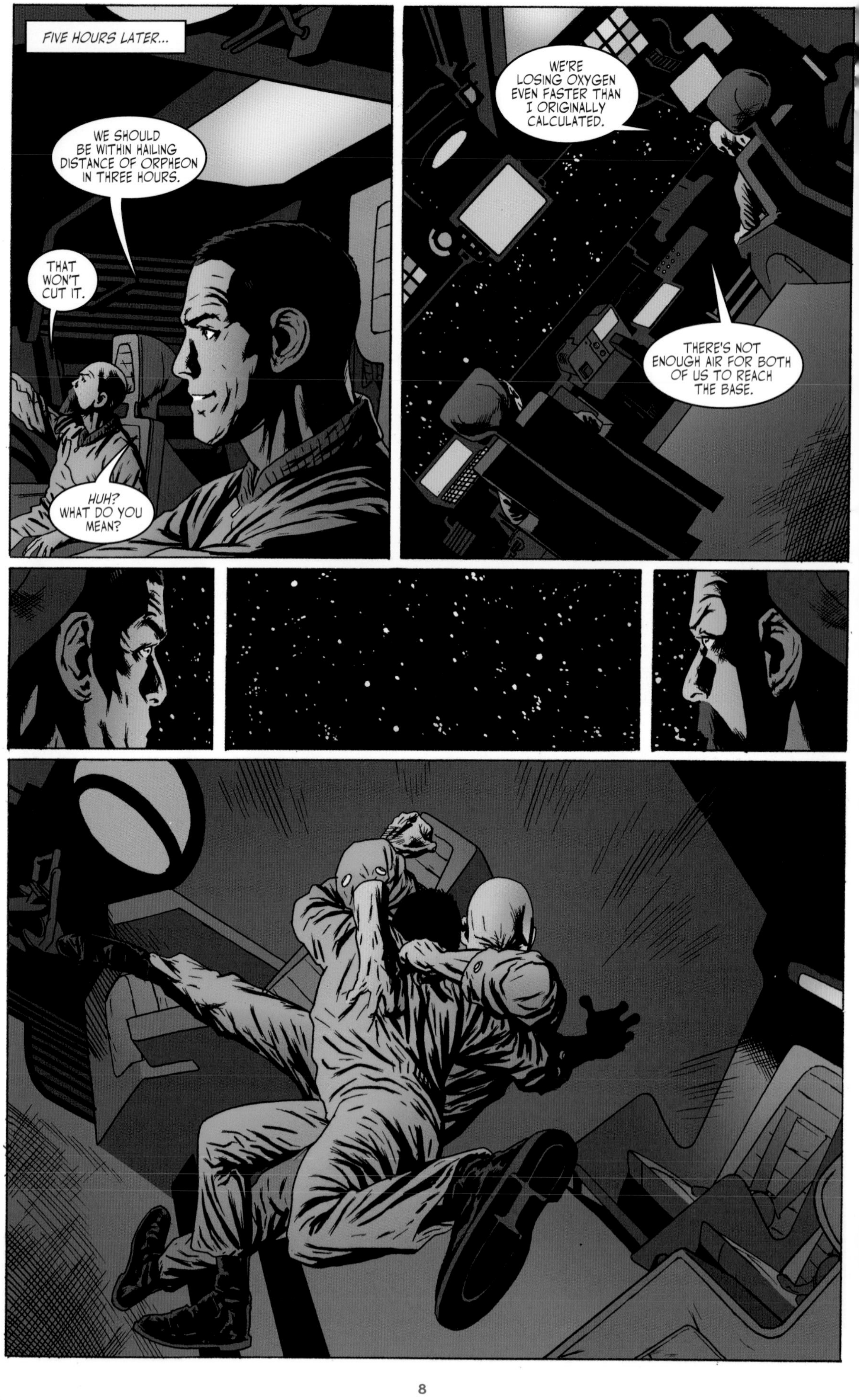
FIVE HOURS LATER...
WE SHOULD BE WITHIN HAILING DISTANCE OF ORPHEON IN THREE HOURS.
THAT WON'T CUT IT.
HUH? WHAT DO YOU MEAN?
WE'RE LOSING OXYGEN EVEN FASTER THAN I ORIGINALLY CALCULATED.
THERE'S NOT ENOUGH AIR FOR BOTH OF US TO REACH THE BASE.

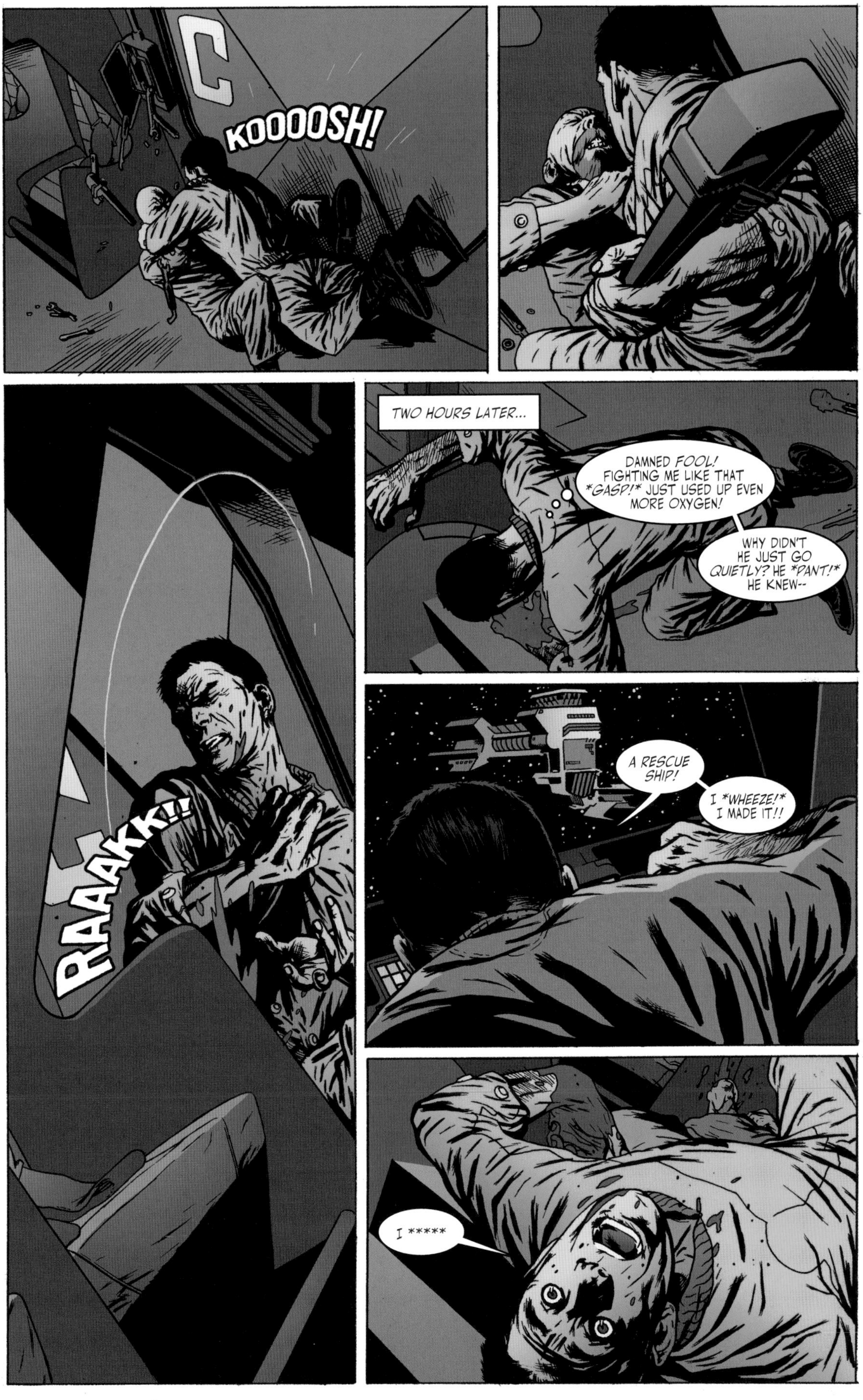
KOOOOSH!
RAAAKK!!
TWO HOURS LATER...
DAMNED FOOL! FIGHTING ME LIKE THAT *GASP!* JUST USED UP EVEN MORE OXYGEN!
WHY DIDN'T HE JUST GO QUIETLY? HE *PANT!* HE KNEW--
A RESCUE SHIP!
I *WHEEZE!* I MADE IT!!
I *****

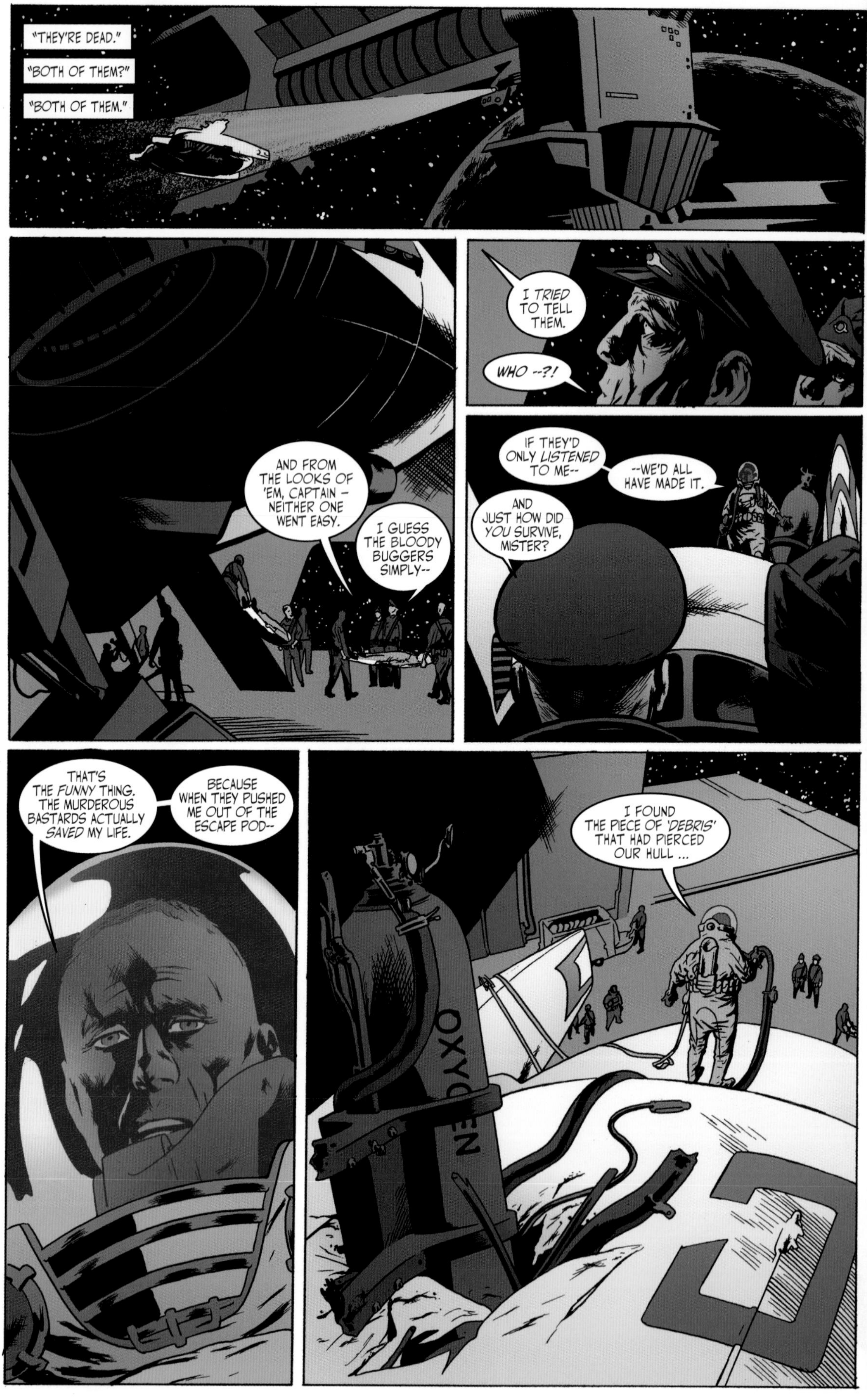
"THEY'RE DEAD."
"BOTH OF THEM?"
"BOTH OF THEM."
AND FROM THE LOOKS OF 'EM, CAPTAIN – NEITHER ONE WENT EASY.
I GUESS THE BLOODY BUGGERS SIMPLY--
I TRIED TO TELL THEM.
WHO --?!
IF THEY'D ONLY *LISTENED* TO ME--
--WE'D ALL HAVE MADE IT.
AND JUST HOW DID *YOU* SURVIVE, MISTER?
THAT'S THE *FUNNY* THING. THE MURDEROUS BASTARDS ACTUALLY *SAVED* MY LIFE.
BECAUSE WHEN THEY PUSHED ME OUT OF THE ESCAPE POD--
I FOUND THE PIECE OF *'DEBRIS'* THAT HAD PIERCED OUR HULL ...
OXYGEN

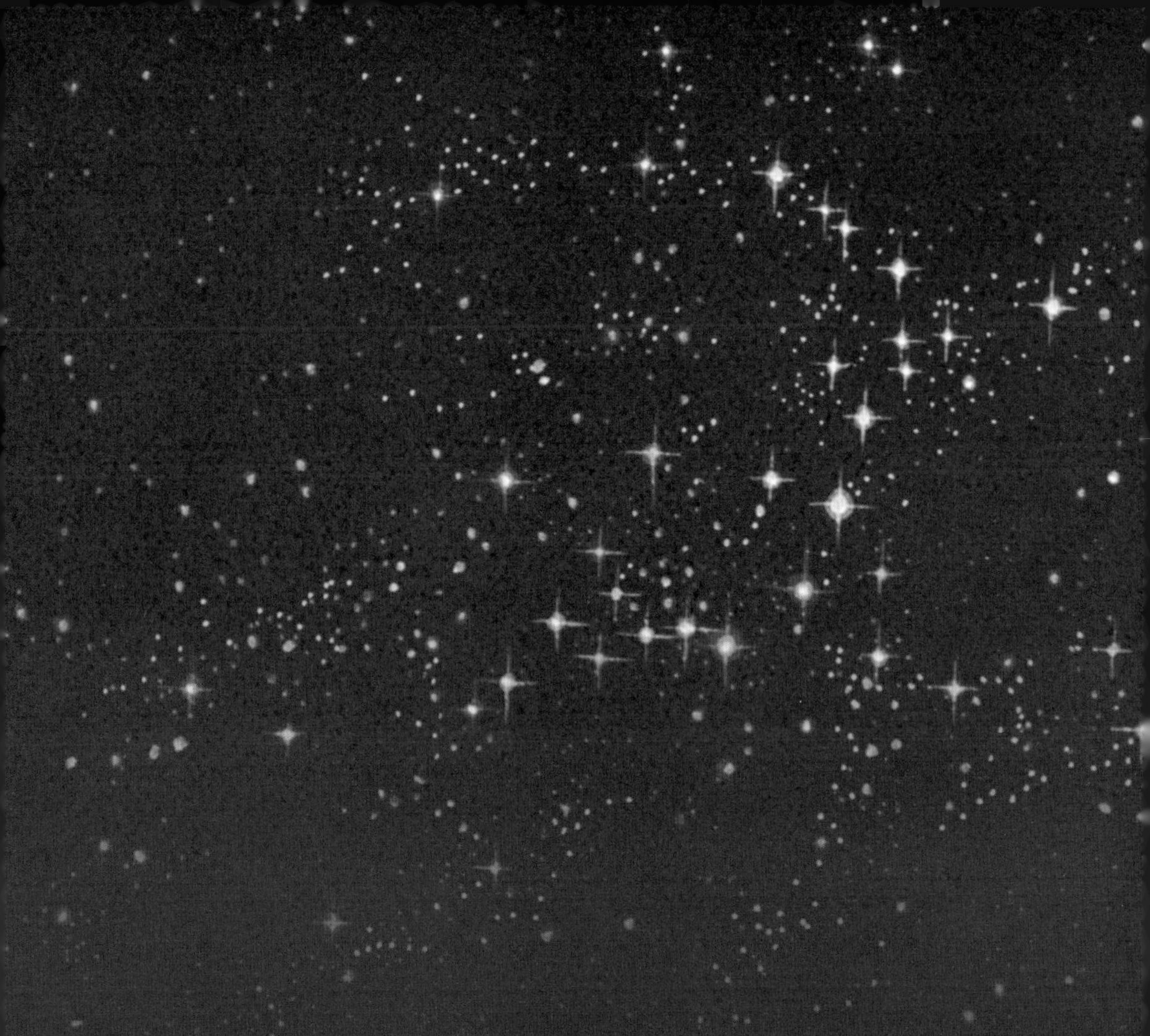

HUNTER'S MOON

Story by KURT BUSIEK
Art by GERALD PAREL

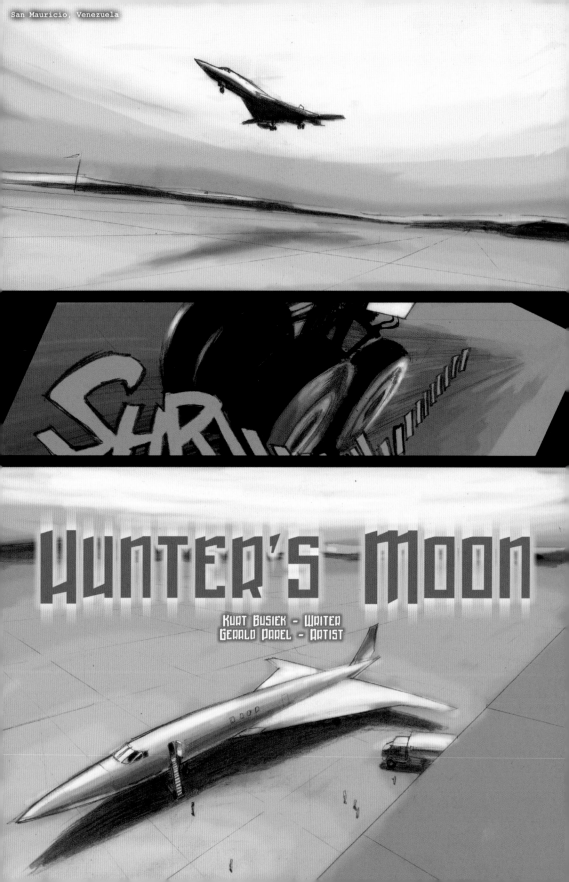

San Mauricio, Venezuela

HUNTER'S MOON

KURT BUSIEK - WRITER
GERALD PAREL - ARTIST

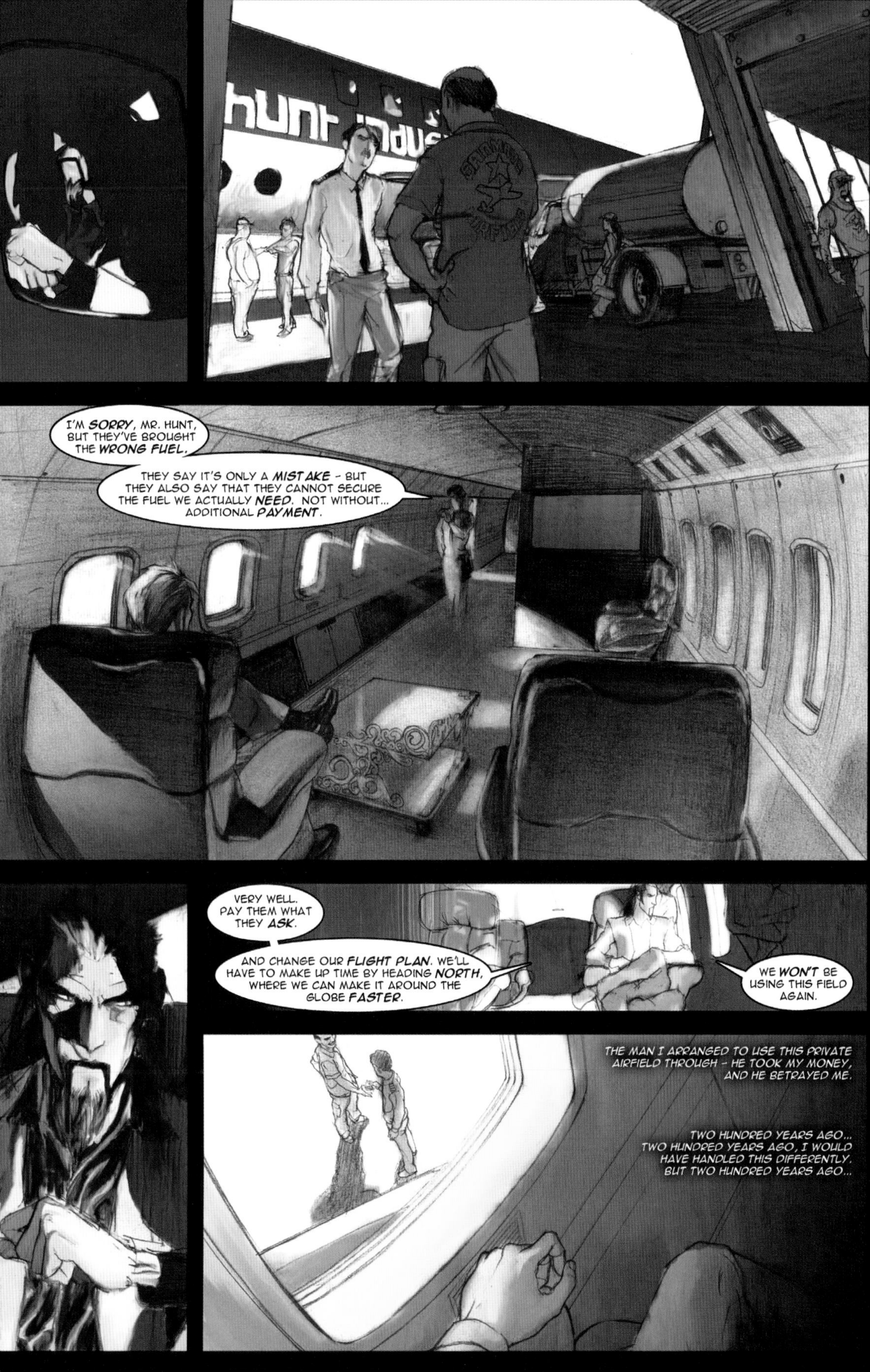
hunt indus
I'M SORRY, MR. HUNT, BUT THEY'VE BROUGHT THE WRONG FUEL.
THEY SAY IT'S ONLY A MISTAKE - BUT THEY ALSO SAY THAT THEY CANNOT SECURE THE FUEL WE ACTUALLY NEED. NOT WITHOUT... ADDITIONAL PAYMENT.
VERY WELL. PAY THEM WHAT THEY ASK.
AND CHANGE OUR FLIGHT PLAN. WE'LL HAVE TO MAKE UP TIME BY HEADING NORTH, WHERE WE CAN MAKE IT AROUND THE GLOBE FASTER.
WE WON'T BE USING THIS FIELD AGAIN.
THE MAN I ARRANGED TO USE THIS PRIVATE AIRFIELD THROUGH - HE TOOK MY MONEY, AND HE BETRAYED ME.
TWO HUNDRED YEARS AGO...
TWO HUNDRED YEARS AGO, I WOULD HAVE HANDLED THIS DIFFERENTLY.
BUT TWO HUNDRED YEARS AGO...

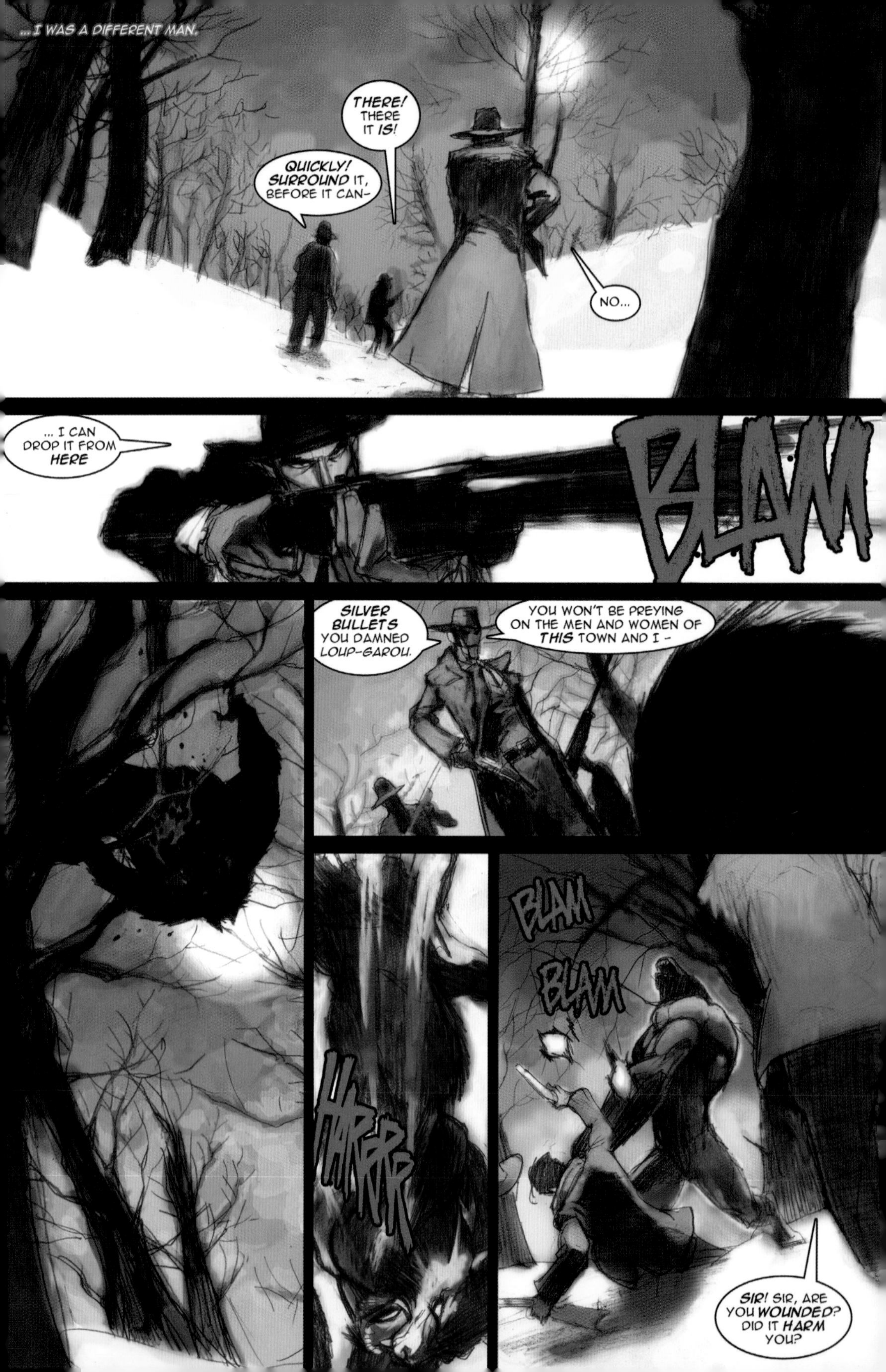
...I WAS A DIFFERENT MAN.
THERE! THERE IT IS!
QUICKLY! SURROUND IT, BEFORE IT CAN-
NO...
... I CAN DROP IT FROM HERE
BLAM
SILVER BULLETS YOU DAMNED LOUP-GAROU.
YOU WON'T BE PREYING ON THE MEN AND WOMEN OF THIS TOWN AND I -
HARRR
BLAM
BLAM
SIR! SIR, ARE YOU WOUNDED? DID IT HARM YOU?

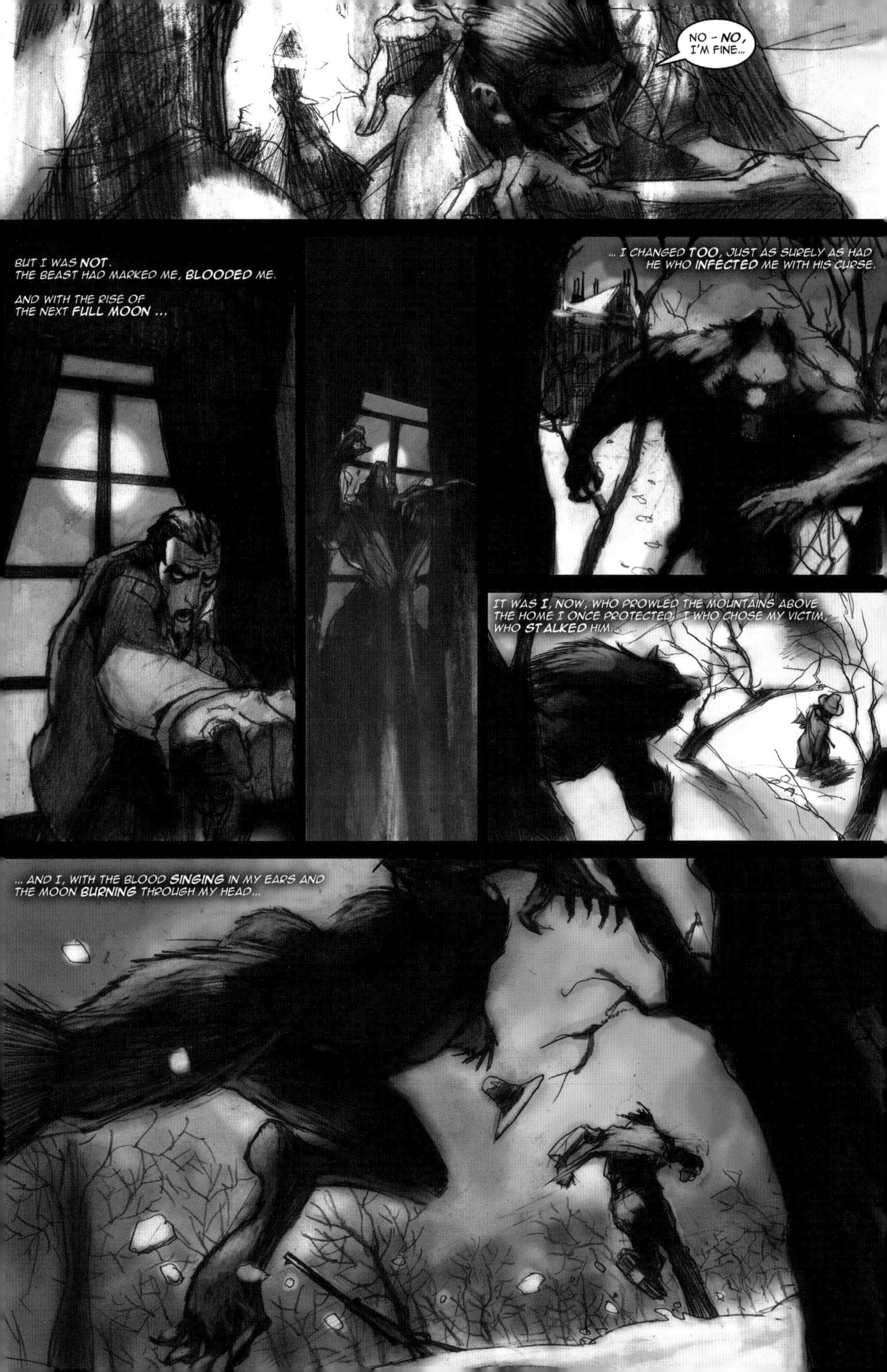
NO - NO, I'M FINE...
BUT I WAS NOT. THE BEAST HAD MARKED ME, BLOODED ME.
AND WITH THE RISE OF THE NEXT FULL MOON ...
... I CHANGED TOO, JUST AS SURELY AS HAD HE WHO INFECTED ME WITH HIS CURSE.
IT WAS I, NOW, WHO PROWLED THE MOUNTAINS ABOVE THE HOME I ONCE PROTECTED. I WHO CHOSE MY VICTIM, WHO STALKED HIM...
... AND I, WITH THE BLOOD SINGING IN MY EARS AND THE MOON BURNING THROUGH MY HEAD...

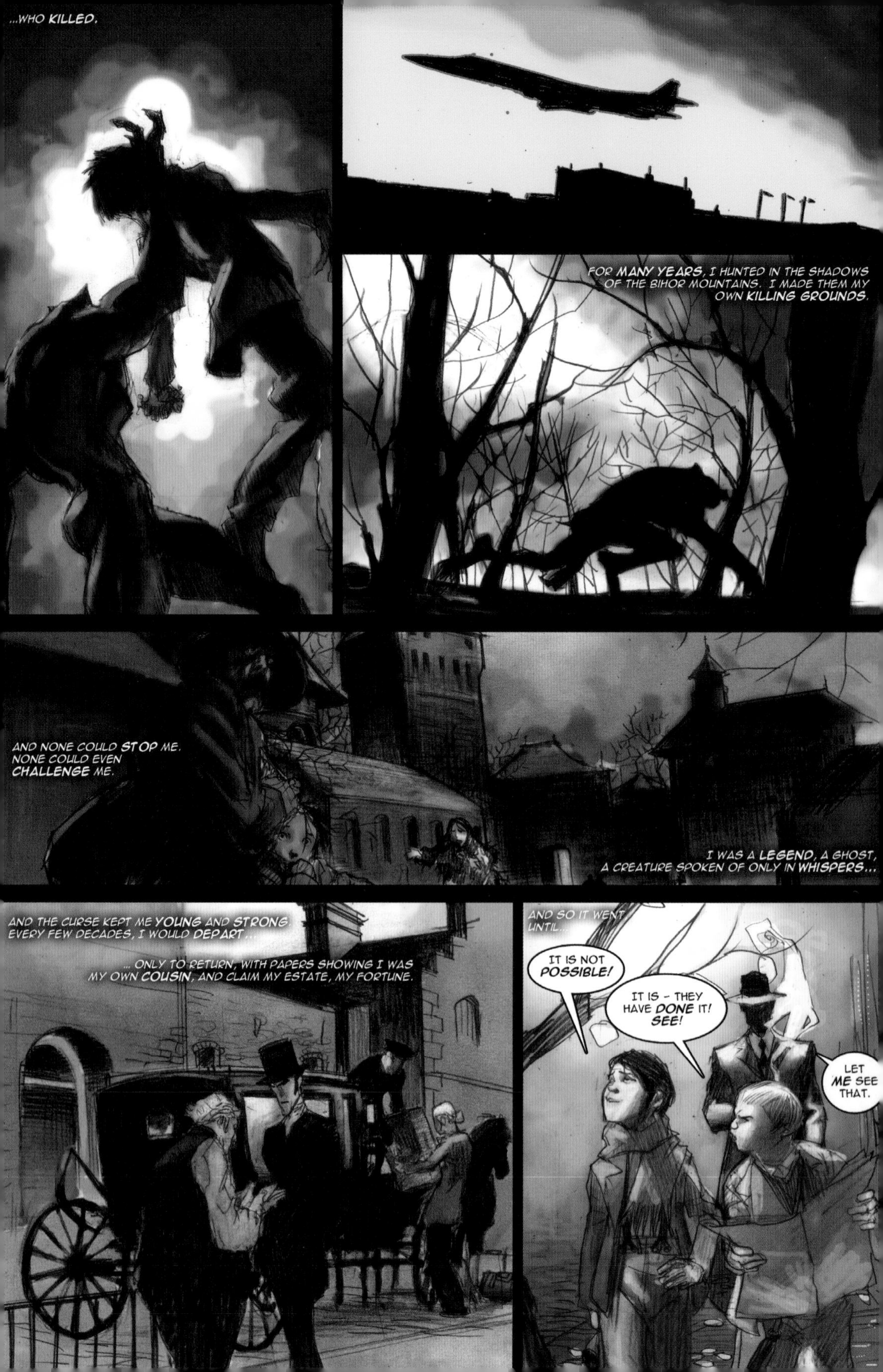
...WHO KILLED.
FOR MANY YEARS, I HUNTED IN THE SHADOWS OF THE BIHOR MOUNTAINS. I MADE THEM MY OWN KILLING GROUNDS.
AND NONE COULD STOP ME. NONE COULD EVEN CHALLENGE ME.
I WAS A LEGEND, A GHOST, A CREATURE SPOKEN OF ONLY IN WHISPERS...
AND THE CURSE KEPT ME YOUNG AND STRONG. EVERY FEW DECADES, I WOULD DEPART...
... ONLY TO RETURN, WITH PAPERS SHOWING I WAS MY OWN COUSIN, AND CLAIM MY ESTATE, MY FORTUNE.
AND SO IT WENT UNTIL...
IT IS NOT POSSIBLE!
IT IS - THEY HAVE DONE IT! SEE!
LET ME SEE THAT.

IN AMERICA THEY HAD BUILT A *MACHINE* THAT FLEW.
THAT FLEW LIKE A *BIRD.*

AND THEY WOULD BUILD BETTER ONES.
FASTER ONES.

AMERICAN VICTOR
ZBOR TEST APART

BEGAN TO *THINK*, FOR THE FIRST
TIME, OF A *NEW HUNT*...A *NEW PREY.*

MY OLDEST *ENEMY.*
MY *CONSTANT* ENEMY.

Oahu, Hawaii.

I WOULD NEED TO BE *PREPARED*, HOWEVER. I WOULD NEED
MONEY — MORE THAN I HAD EVER *DREAMED* OF. BEFORE.

AND SO I ROBBED, AS WELL AS KILLED...

I MOVED TO THE WEST, AND
BEGAN A *BUSINESS*...

HUNT & COM

AND I IGNORED THE FINANCIAL *FLUCTUATIONS* OF THE DAY,
ALWAYS TAKING THE *LONG VIEW*, ALWAYS LOOKING *AHEAD*...

BUT SIR,
THE
MARKET...

NO! WE HOLD THE COURSE!
LET THOSE FOOLS CHASE *ILLUSIONS.*
WE PUT OUR FAITH IN WHAT WE CAN FEEL,
WHAT WE CAN...

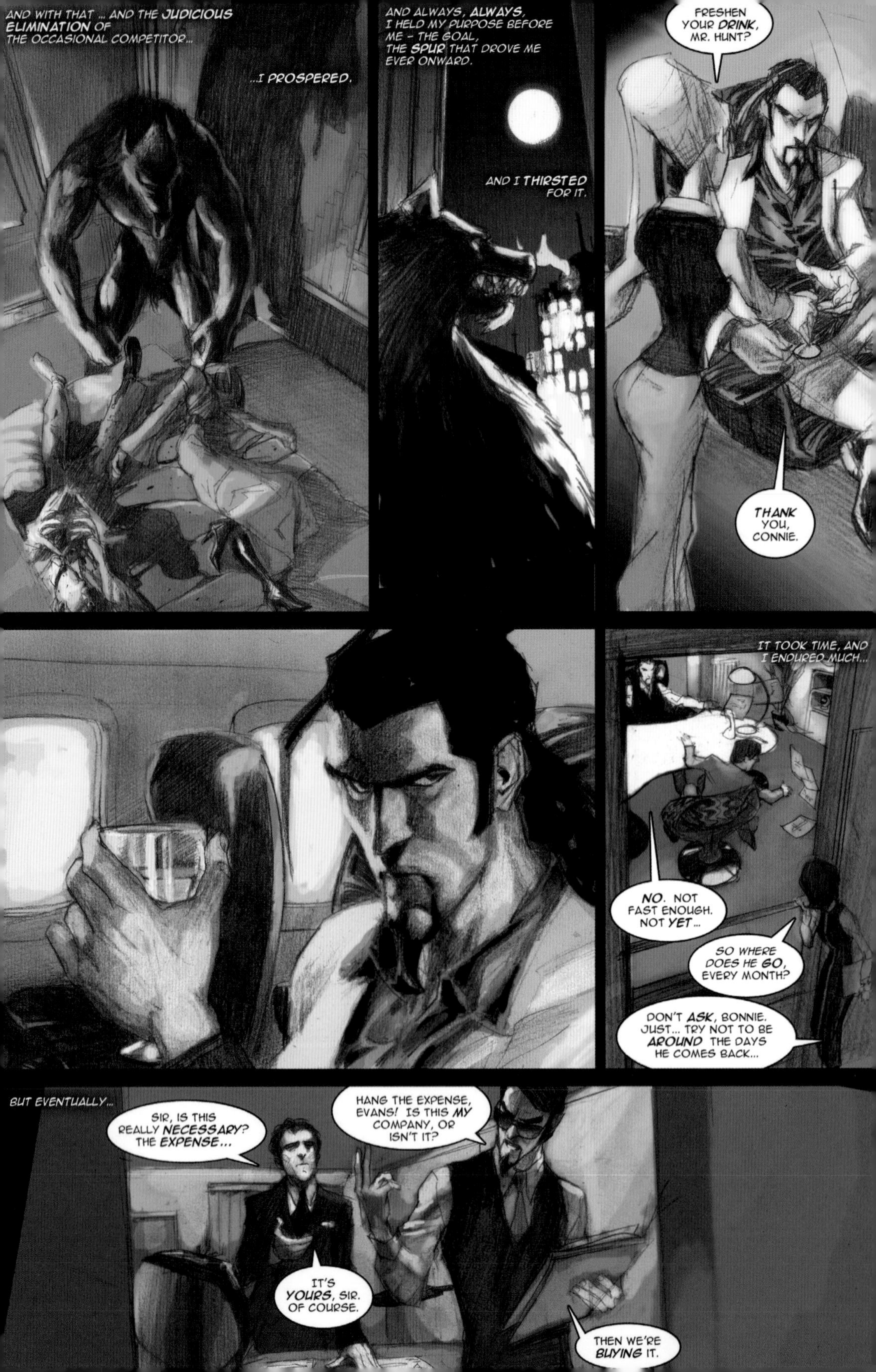

AND WITH THAT ... AND THE JUDICIOUS ELIMINATION OF THE OCCASIONAL COMPETITOR...
...I PROSPERED.
AND ALWAYS, ALWAYS, I HELD MY PURPOSE BEFORE ME - THE GOAL, THE SPUR THAT DROVE ME EVER ONWARD.
AND I THIRSTED FOR IT.
FRESHEN YOUR DRINK, MR. HUNT?
THANK YOU, CONNIE.
IT TOOK TIME, AND I ENDURED MUCH...
NO. NOT FAST ENOUGH. NOT YET...
SO WHERE DOES HE GO, EVERY MONTH?
DON'T ASK, BONNIE. JUST... TRY NOT TO BE AROUND THE DAYS HE COMES BACK...
BUT EVENTUALLY...
SIR, IS THIS REALLY NECESSARY? THE EXPENSE...
HANG THE EXPENSE, EVANS! IS THIS MY COMPANY, OR ISN'T IT?
IT'S YOURS, SIR. OF COURSE.
THEN WE'RE BUYING IT.

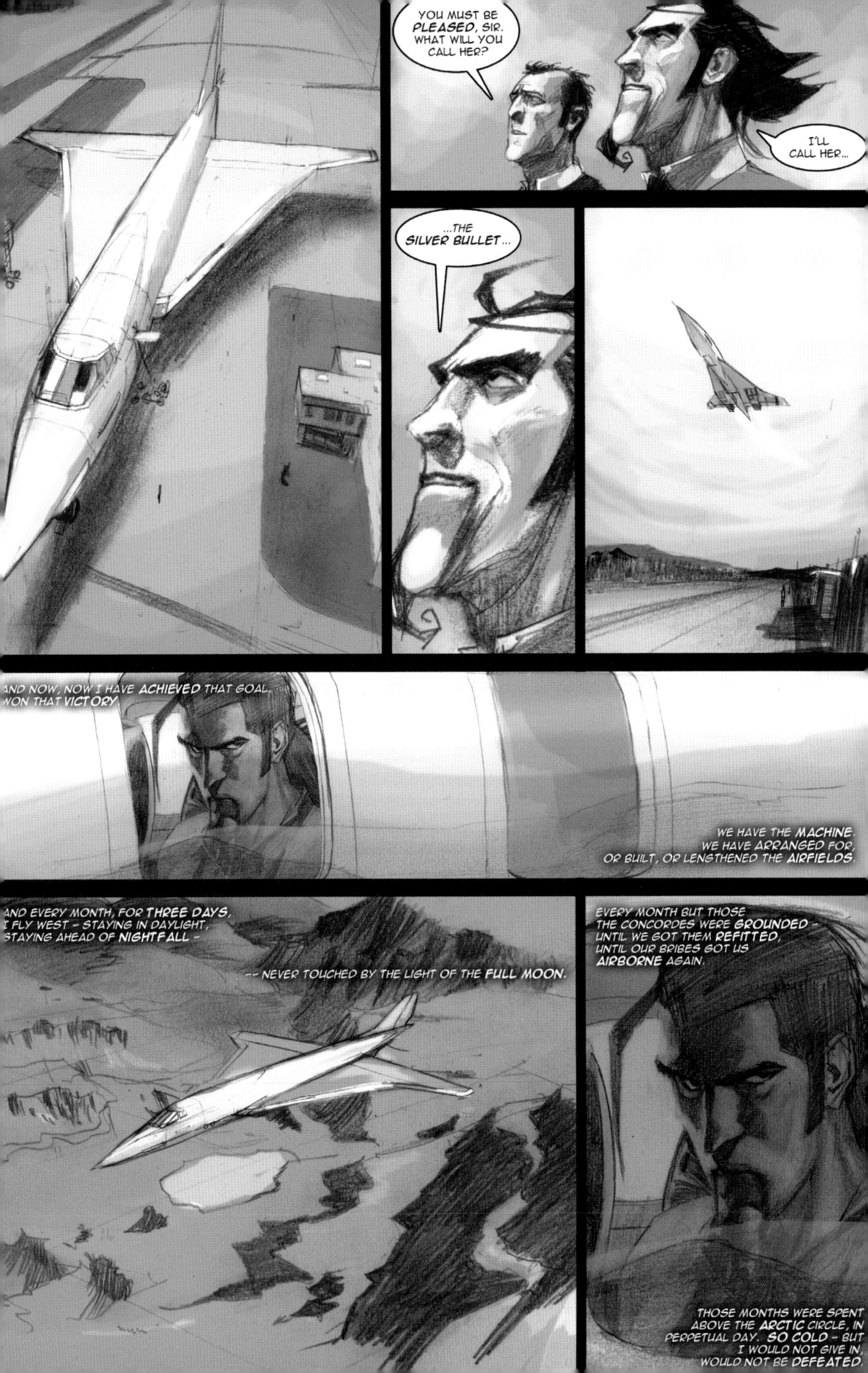
YOU MUST BE PLEASED, SIR. WHAT WILL YOU CALL HER?
I'LL CALL HER...
...THE SILVER BULLET...
AND NOW, NOW I HAVE ACHIEVED THAT GOAL, WON THAT VICTORY.
WE HAVE THE MACHINE. WE HAVE ARRANGED FOR, OR BUILT, OR LENGTHENED THE AIRFIELDS.
AND EVERY MONTH, FOR THREE DAYS, I FLY WEST - STAYING IN DAYLIGHT, STAYING AHEAD OF NIGHTFALL -
-- NEVER TOUCHED BY THE LIGHT OF THE FULL MOON.
EVERY MONTH BUT THOSE THE CONCORDES WERE GROUNDED - UNTIL WE GOT THEM REFITTED, UNTIL OUR BRIBES GOT US AIRBORNE AGAIN.
THOSE MONTHS WERE SPENT ABOVE THE ARCTIC CIRCLE, IN PERPETUAL DAY. SO COLD - BUT I WOULD NOT GIVE IN, WOULD NOT BE DEFEATED.

AND EVERY MONTH I FLY OVER MY OLD HOMELAND, AND I REMEMBER HOW IT WAS.

AND I CANNOT HELP BUT LOOK BEHIND ME –

-- AND ALL I CAN THINK IS, "IS IT GETTING CLOSER? DID WE LOSE TOO MUCH TIME?"

"WILL WE WIN THE RACE AGAIN?"

AND I CANNOT HELP BUT WISH –

-- THAT ONCE, JUST ONCE, I COULD LET IT CATCH ME.

SHRACK

-- AND BE THE HUNTER ONCE AGAIN TO KNOW THAT STRENGTH, THAT SPEED, THAT POWER.

TO FEEL THAT HUNGER – FEEL THE LIFE FLOWING THROUGH MY HANDS --

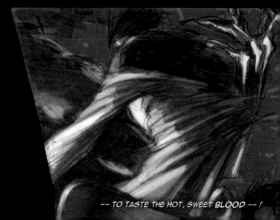

-- TO TASTE THE HOT, SWEET BLOOD --!

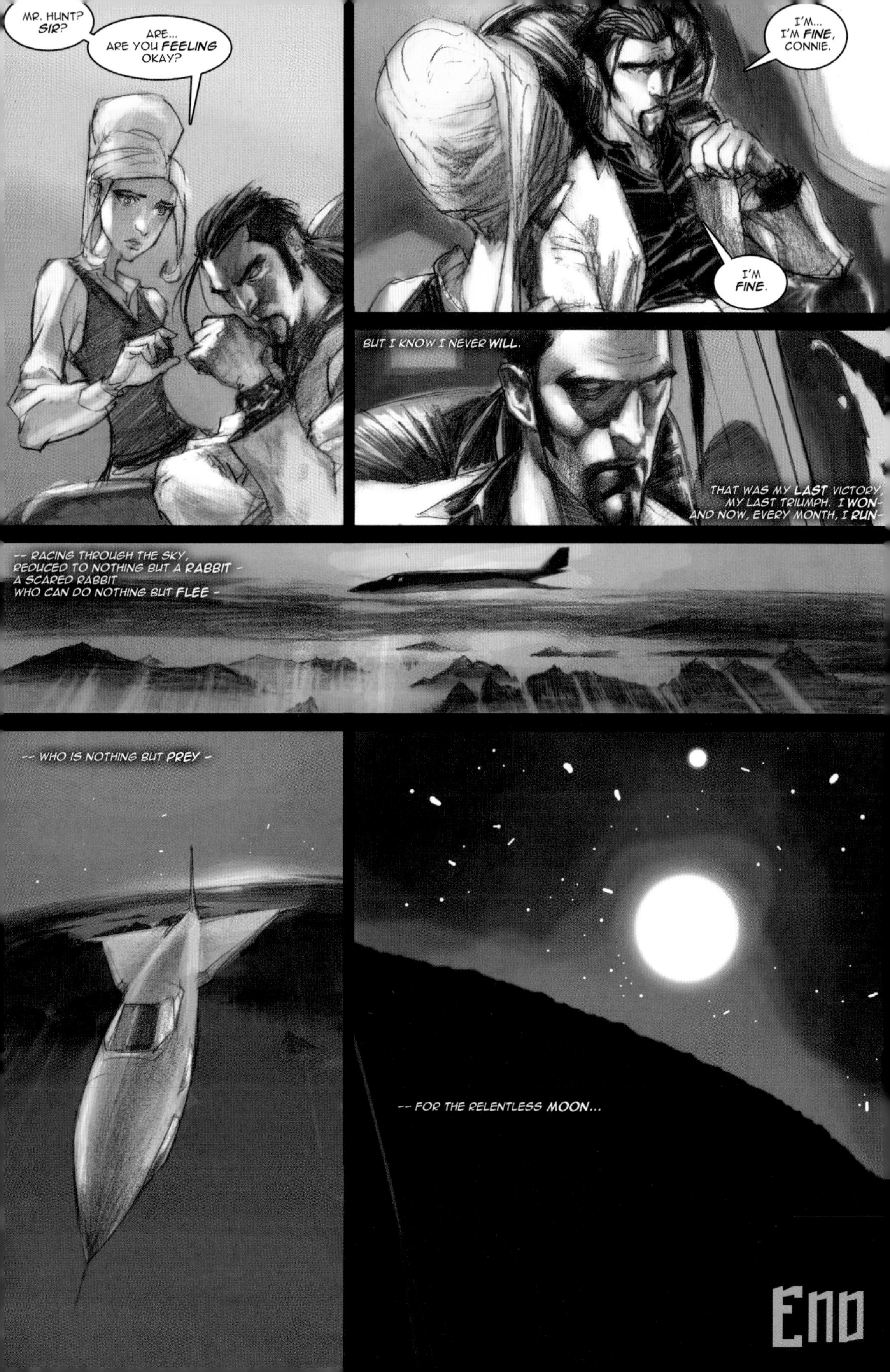

MR. HUNT? SIR?
ARE... ARE YOU FEELING OKAY?
I'M... I'M FINE, CONNIE.
I'M FINE.
BUT I KNOW I NEVER WILL.
THAT WAS MY LAST VICTORY, MY LAST TRIUMPH. I WON- AND NOW, EVERY MONTH, I RUN-
-- RACING THROUGH THE SKY, REDUCED TO NOTHING BUT A RABBIT - A SCARED RABBIT WHO CAN DO NOTHING BUT FLEE -
-- WHO IS NOTHING BUT PREY -
-- FOR THE RELENTLESS MOON...
END

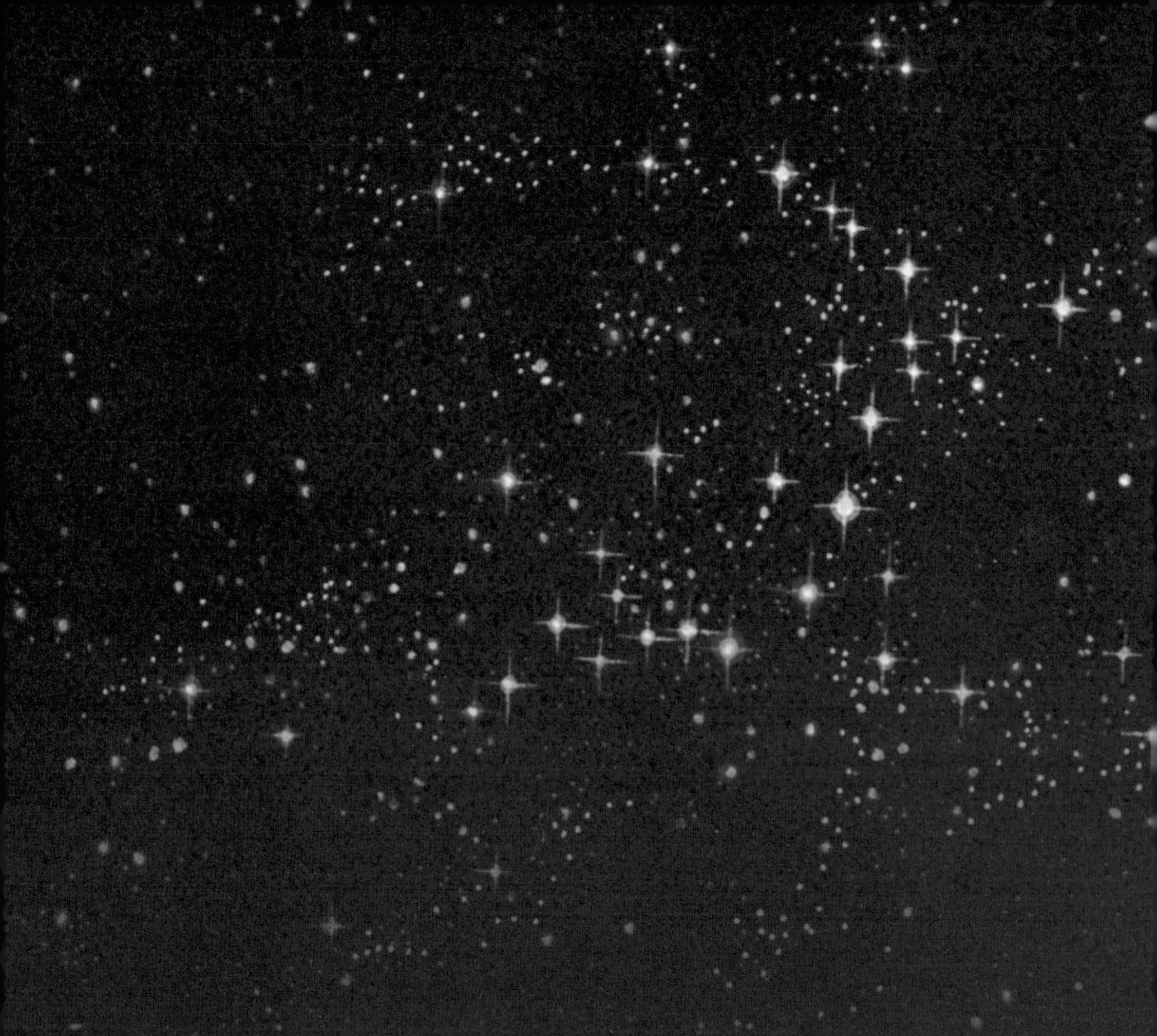

RED LIGHT

Story by GEOFF JOHNS
Art by CHRISTIAN GOSSETT
Colors by SNAKEBITE

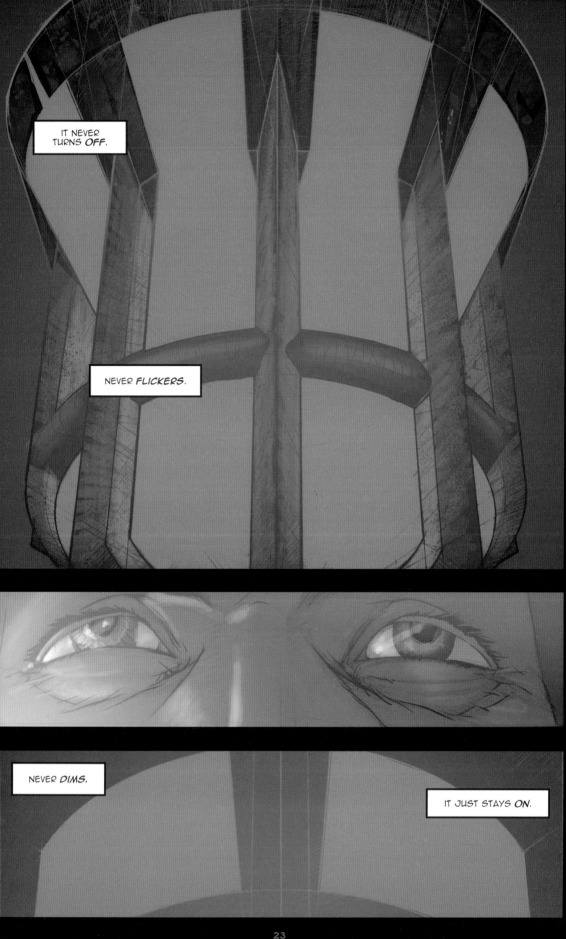

IT NEVER TURNS *OFF.*

NEVER *FLICKERS.*

NEVER *DIMS.*

IT JUST STAYS *ON.*

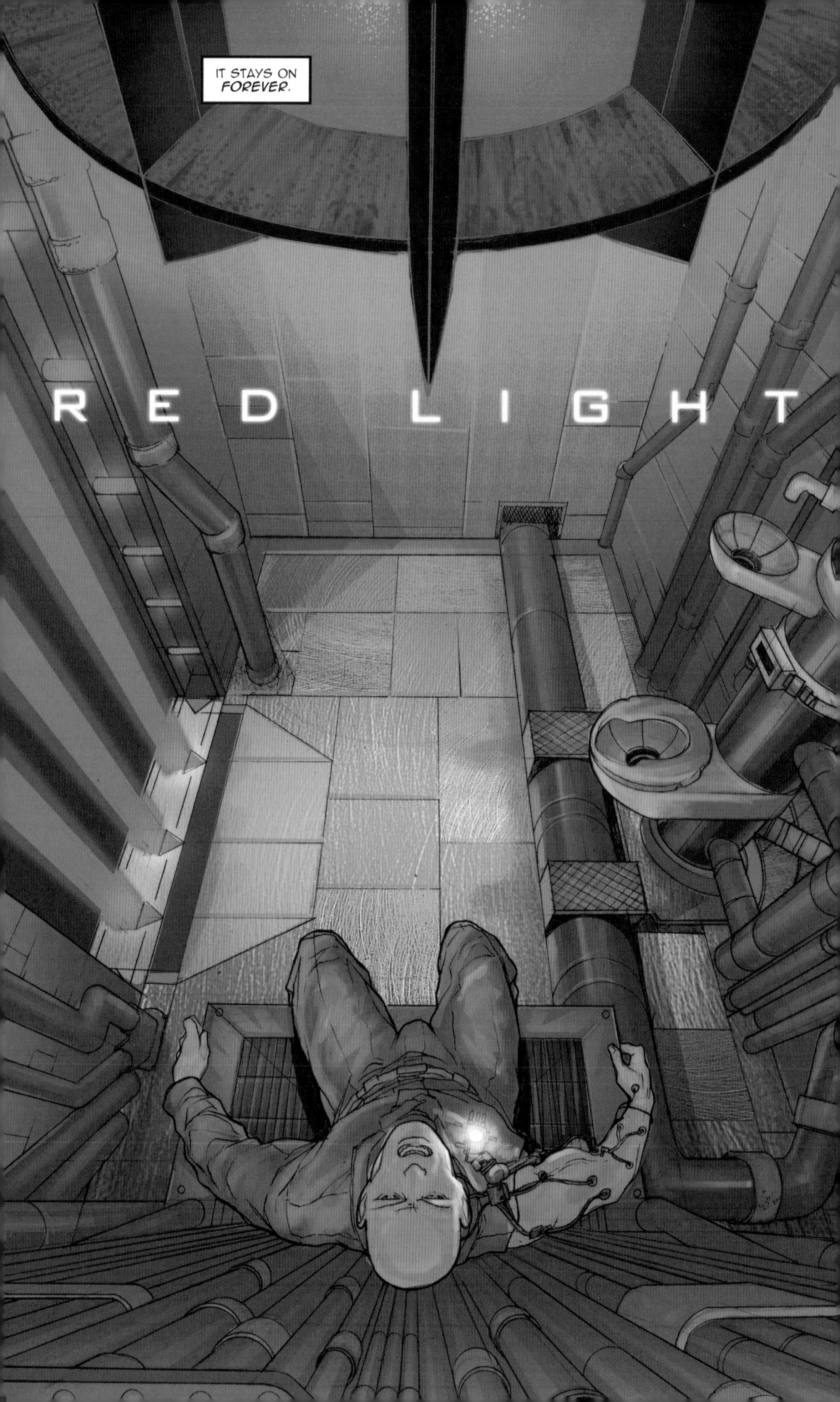
IT STAYS ON FOREVER.
RED LIGHT

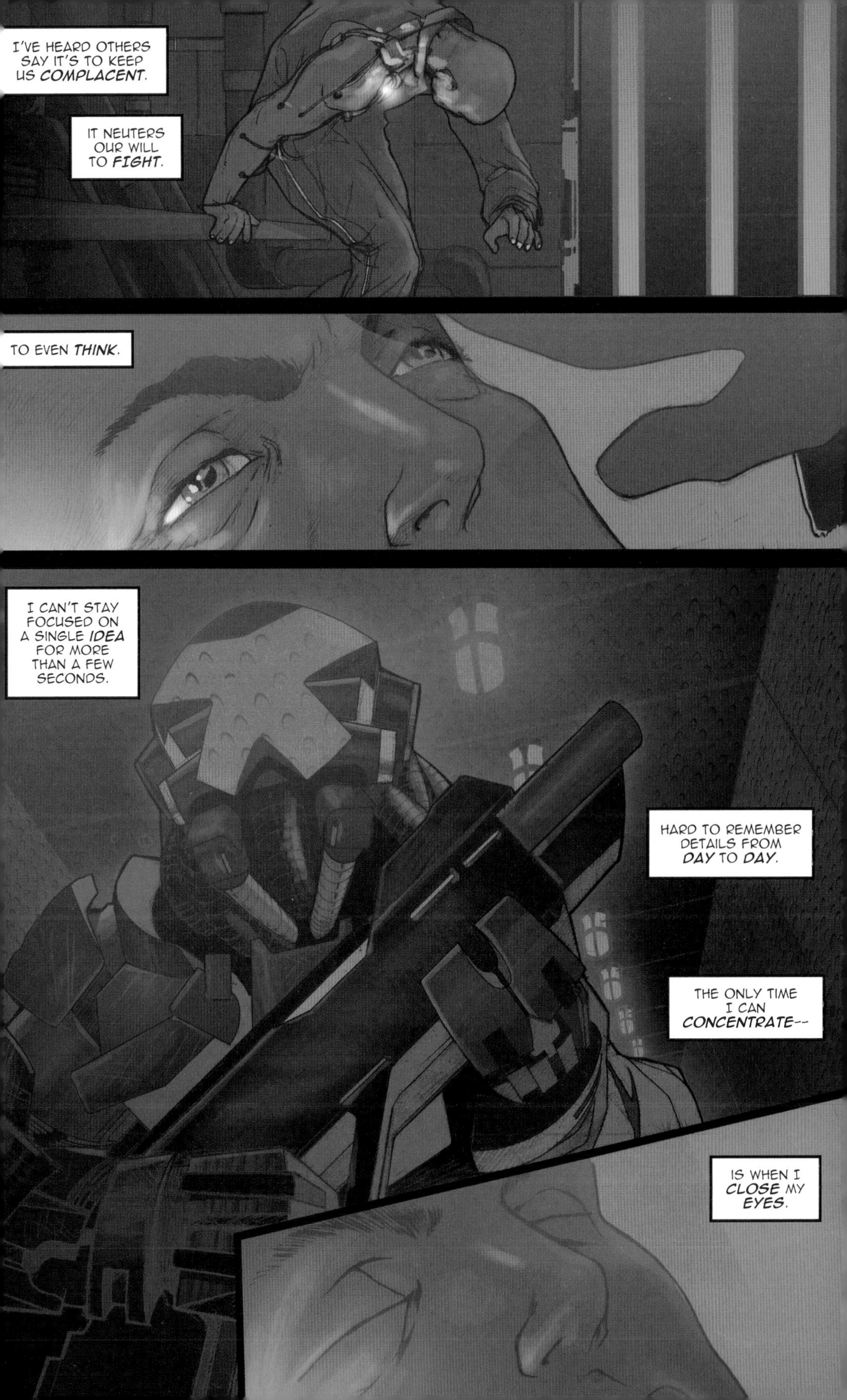

I'VE HEARD OTHERS SAY IT'S TO KEEP US *COMPLACENT*.
IT NEUTERS OUR WILL TO *FIGHT*.
TO EVEN *THINK*.
I CAN'T STAY FOCUSED ON A SINGLE *IDEA* FOR MORE THAN A FEW SECONDS.
HARD TO REMEMBER DETAILS FROM *DAY* TO *DAY*.
THE ONLY TIME I CAN *CONCENTRATE*--
IS WHEN I *CLOSE* MY *EYES*.

I CLOSE THEM AND I TRY TO REMEMBER WHAT IT WAS LIKE.

WHEN I LIVED IN A WORLD *FULL* OF *COLOR*.

BEFORE THE *COLONISTS* FROM THE *STARS* CAME.

THE COLONISTS PROMISED OUR LEADERS UNIMAGINABLE *FIREPOWER*.

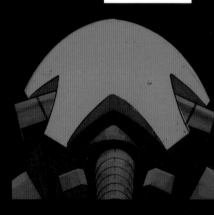

WEAPONS THAT WOULD END THE GREAT *WAR* AND VIOLENCE.

THEY SAID THEY *BELIEVED* IN OUR "*NOBLE CAUSE*."

BUT THERE WAS *ONE* PROBLEM.

THE COLONISTS GAVE THE WEAPONS TO *BOTH* SIDES.

WE NEARLY WIPED EACH OTHER *OUT*--

--AND THEN THEY CAME IN. PICKING UP THE PIECES.

AFTER THEY SOAKED OUR *PLANET* IN *BLOOD*.

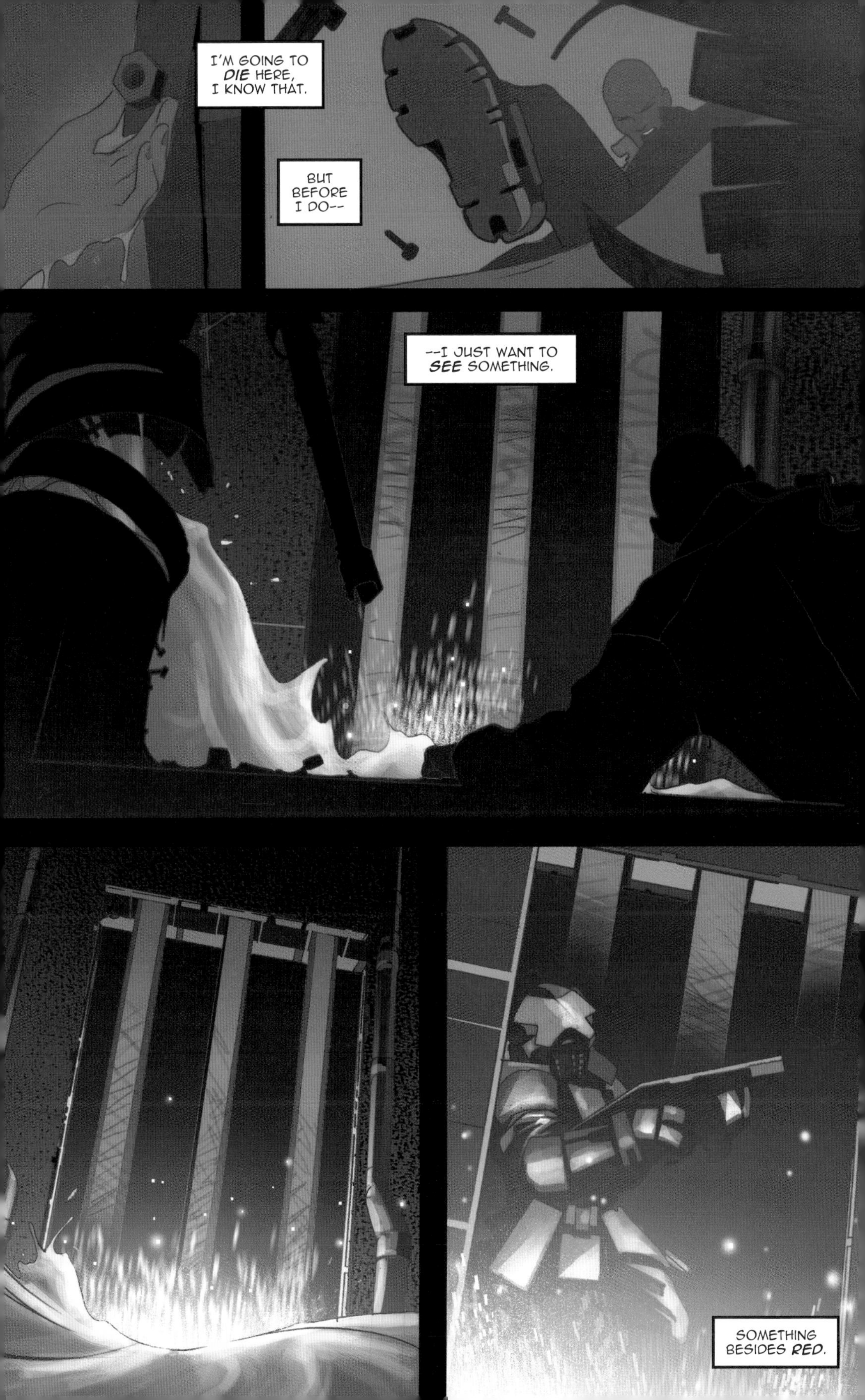
I'M GOING TO DIE HERE, I KNOW THAT.
BUT BEFORE I DO--
--I JUST WANT TO SEE SOMETHING.
SOMETHING BESIDES RED.

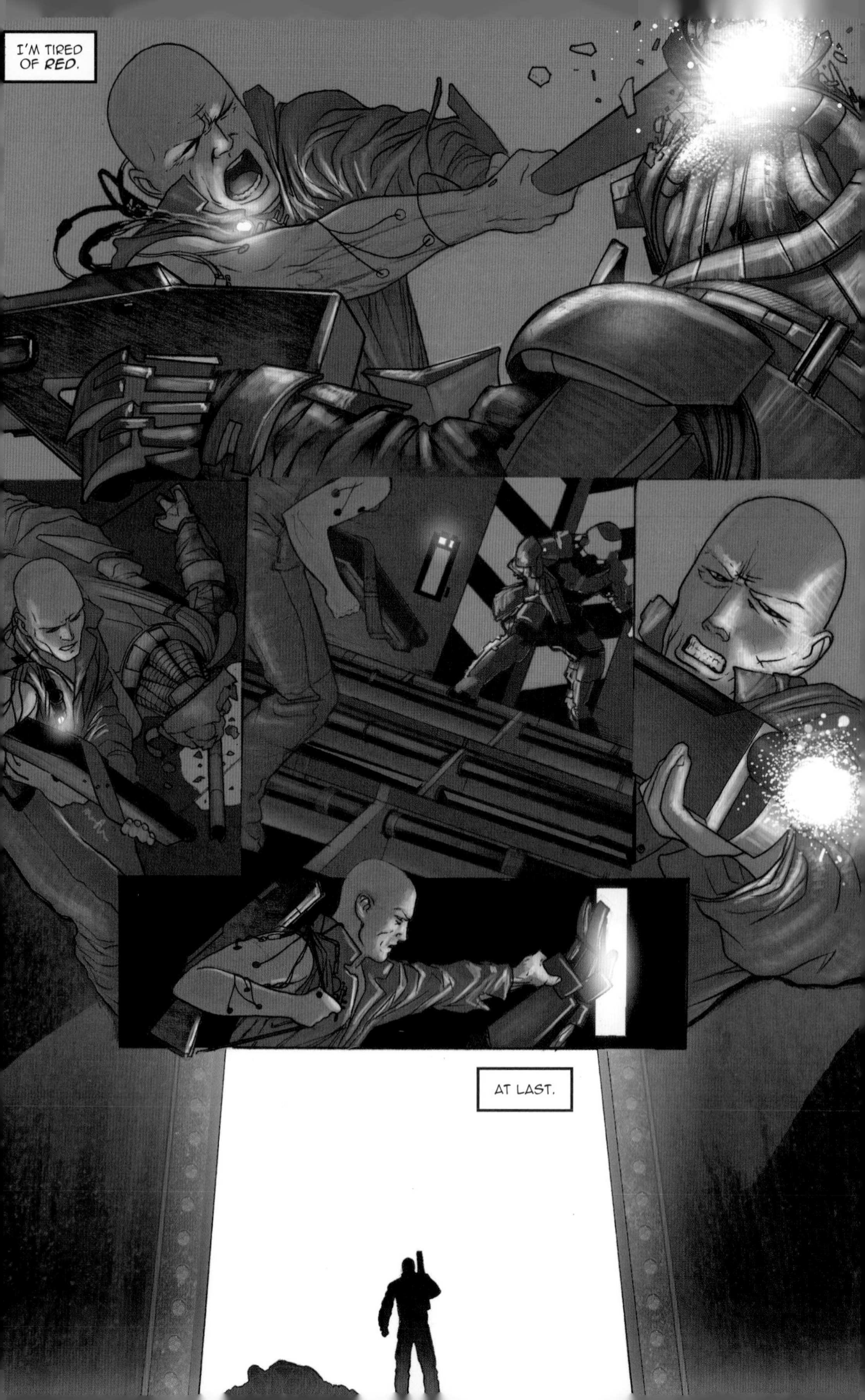
I'M TIRED OF RED.
AT LAST.

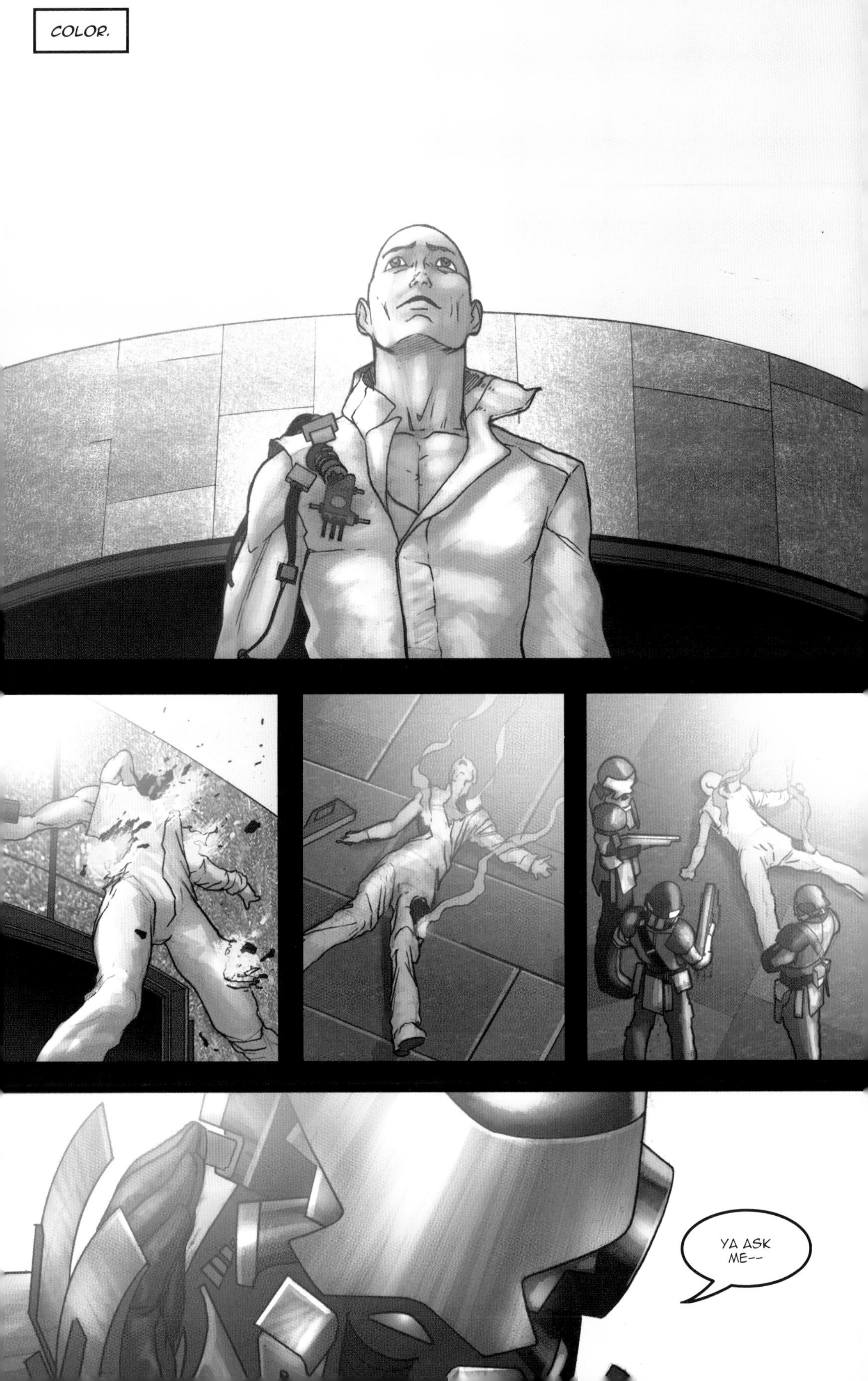
COLOR.
YA ASK ME--

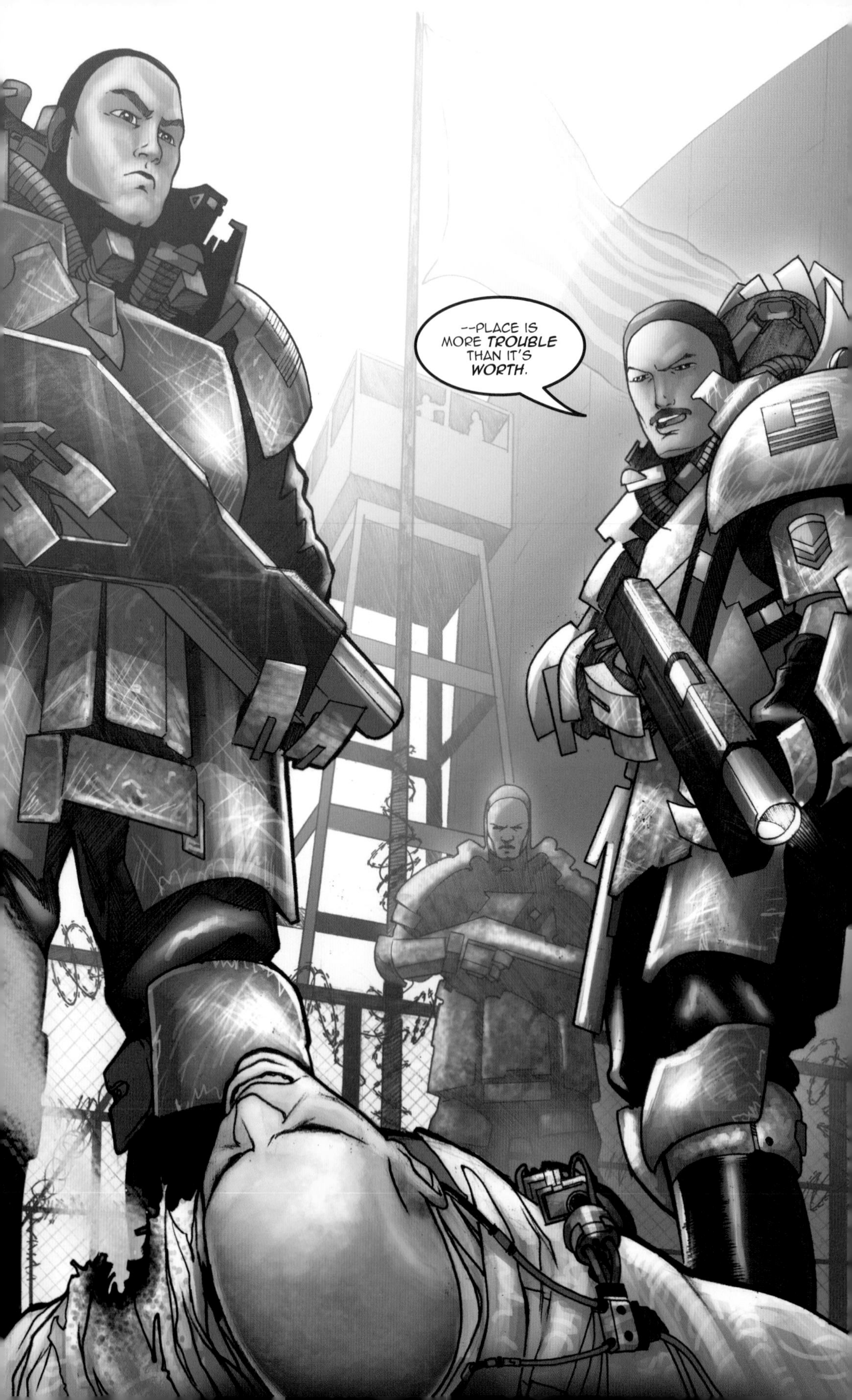
--PLACE IS MORE TROUBLE THAN IT'S WORTH.

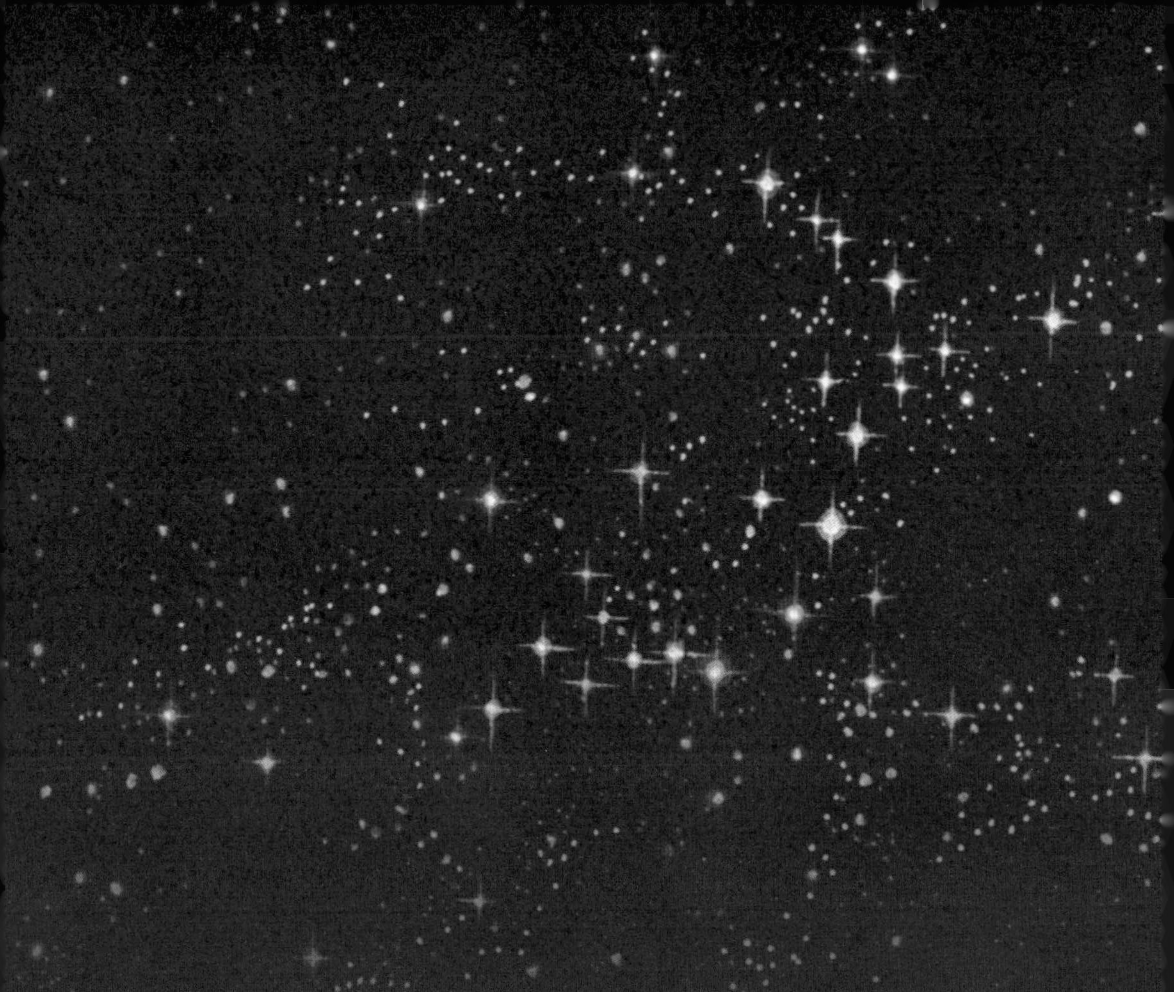

MONSTER POLICE DEPARTMENT

Story by JIM ALEXANDER
Art by PASCAL ALIXE

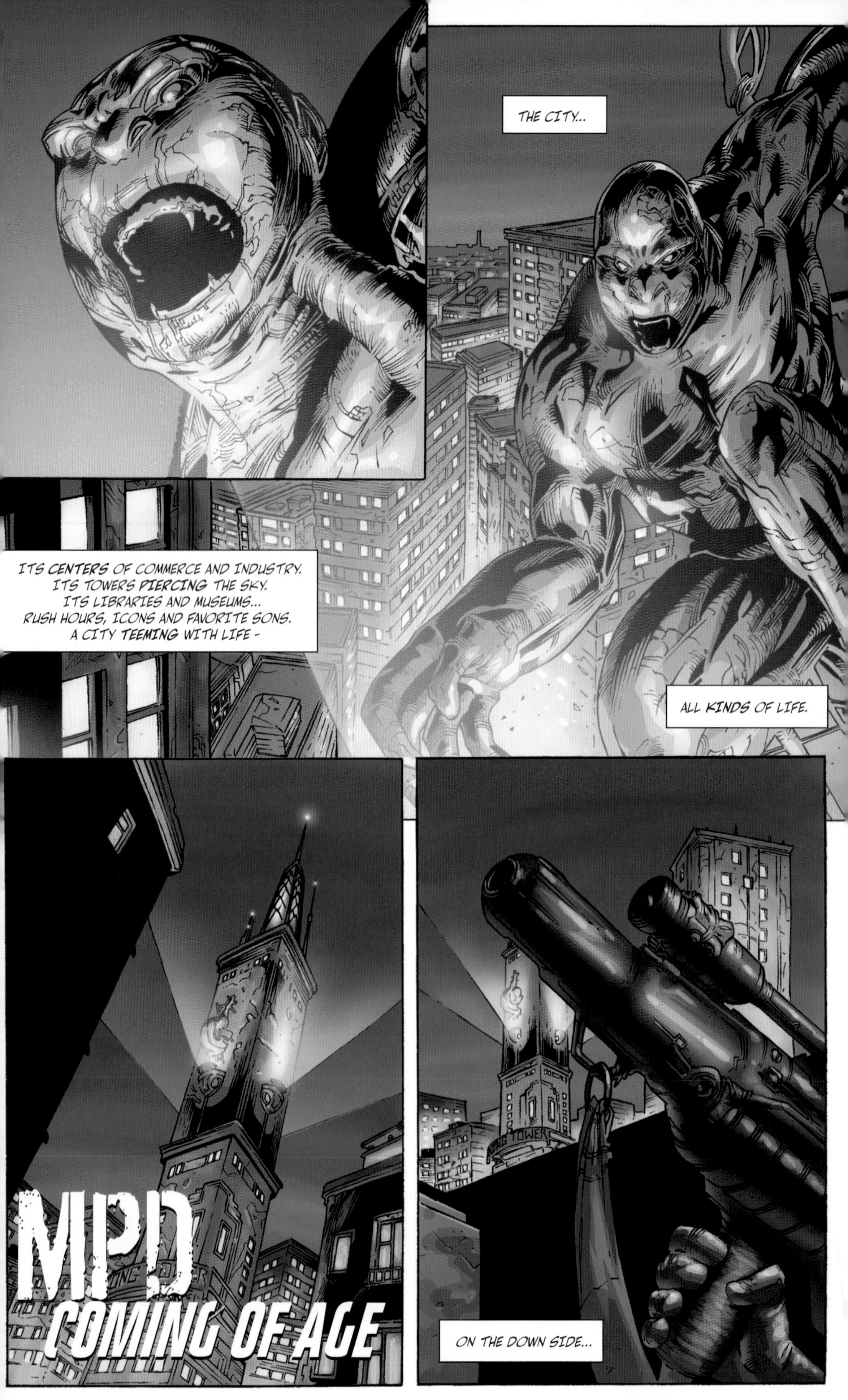
THE CITY...
ITS CENTERS OF COMMERCE AND INDUSTRY. ITS TOWERS PIERCING THE SKY. ITS LIBRARIES AND MUSEUMS... RUSH HOURS, ICONS AND FAVORITE SONS. A CITY TEEMING WITH LIFE -
ALL KINDS OF LIFE.
MPD
COMING OF AGE
ON THE DOWN SIDE...

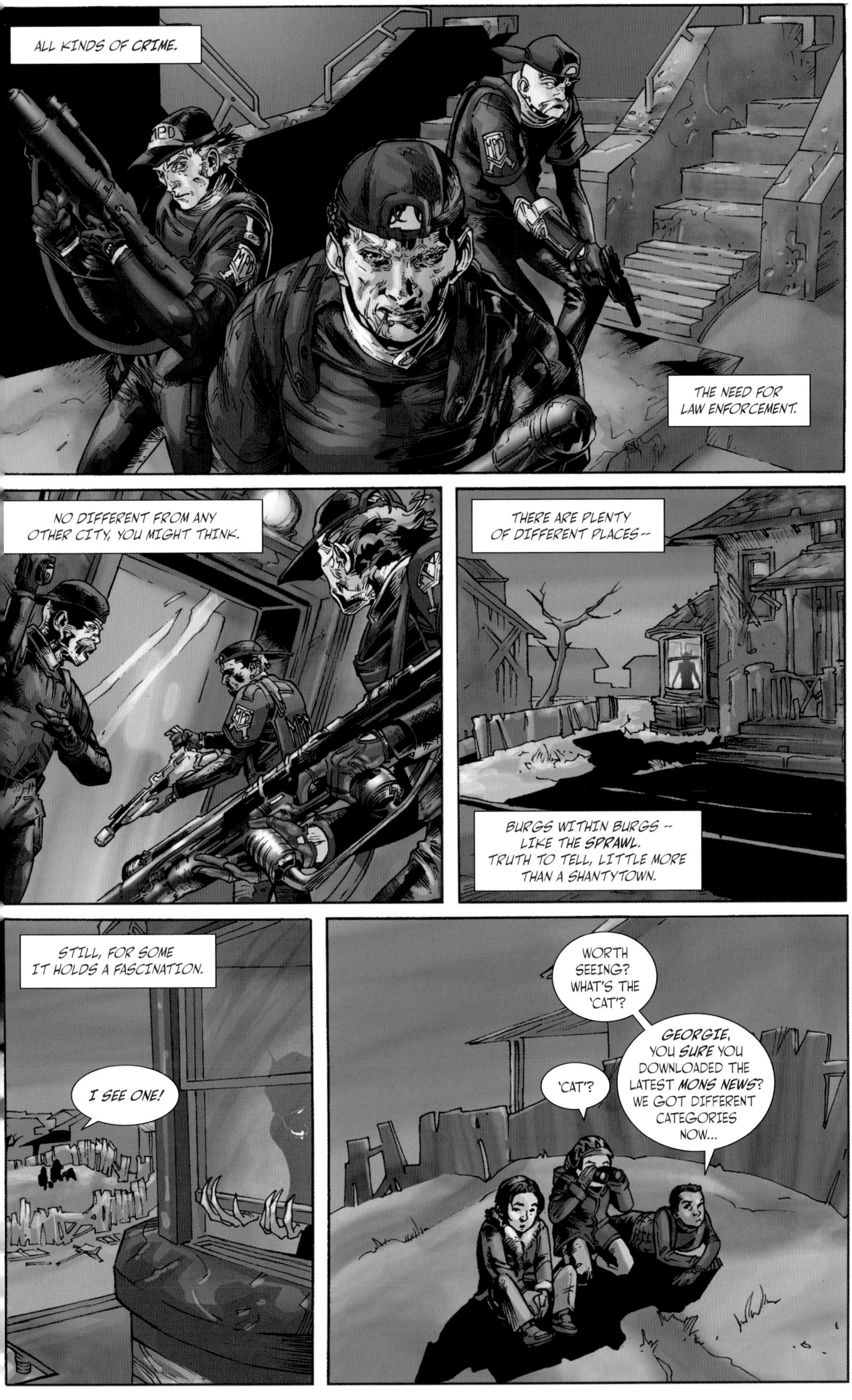
ALL KINDS OF CRIME.
THE NEED FOR LAW ENFORCEMENT.
NO DIFFERENT FROM ANY OTHER CITY, YOU MIGHT THINK.
THERE ARE PLENTY OF DIFFERENT PLACES--
BURGS WITHIN BURGS -- LIKE THE SPRAWL. TRUTH TO TELL, LITTLE MORE THAN A SHANTYTOWN.
STILL, FOR SOME IT HOLDS A FASCINATION.
I SEE ONE!
WORTH SEEING? WHAT'S THE 'CAT'?
'CAT'?
GEORGIE, YOU SURE YOU DOWNLOADED THE LATEST MONS NEWS? WE GOT DIFFERENT CATEGORIES NOW...

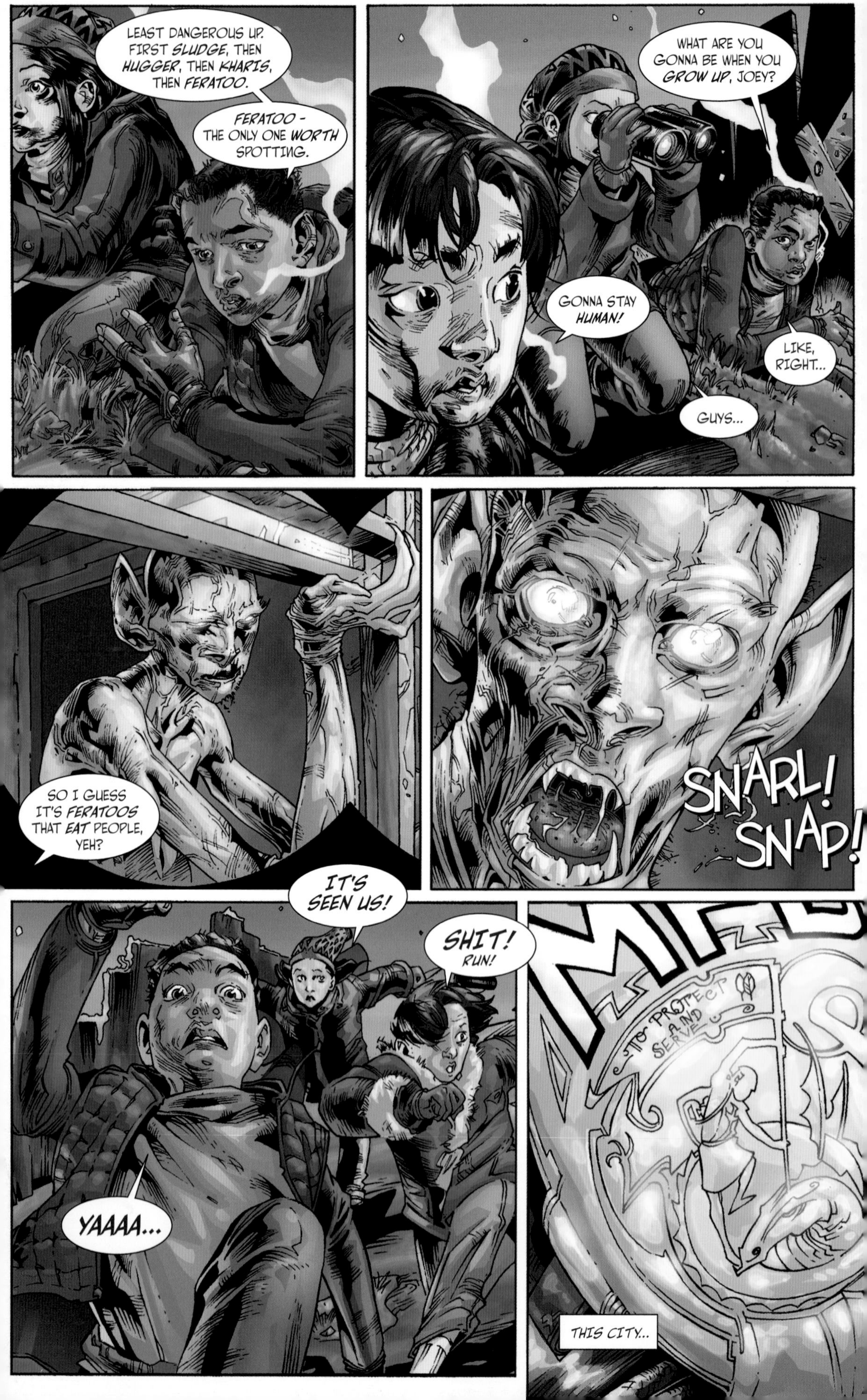
LEAST DANGEROUS UP. FIRST SLUDGE, THEN HUGGER, THEN KHARIS, THEN FERATOO.
FERATOO - THE ONLY ONE WORTH SPOTTING.
WHAT ARE YOU GONNA BE WHEN YOU GROW UP, JOEY?
GONNA STAY HUMAN!
LIKE, RIGHT...
GUYS...
SO I GUESS IT'S FERATOOS THAT EAT PEOPLE, YEH?
SNARL! SNAP!
IT'S SEEN US!
SHIT! RUN!
YAAAA...
TO PROTECT AND SERVE
THIS CITY...

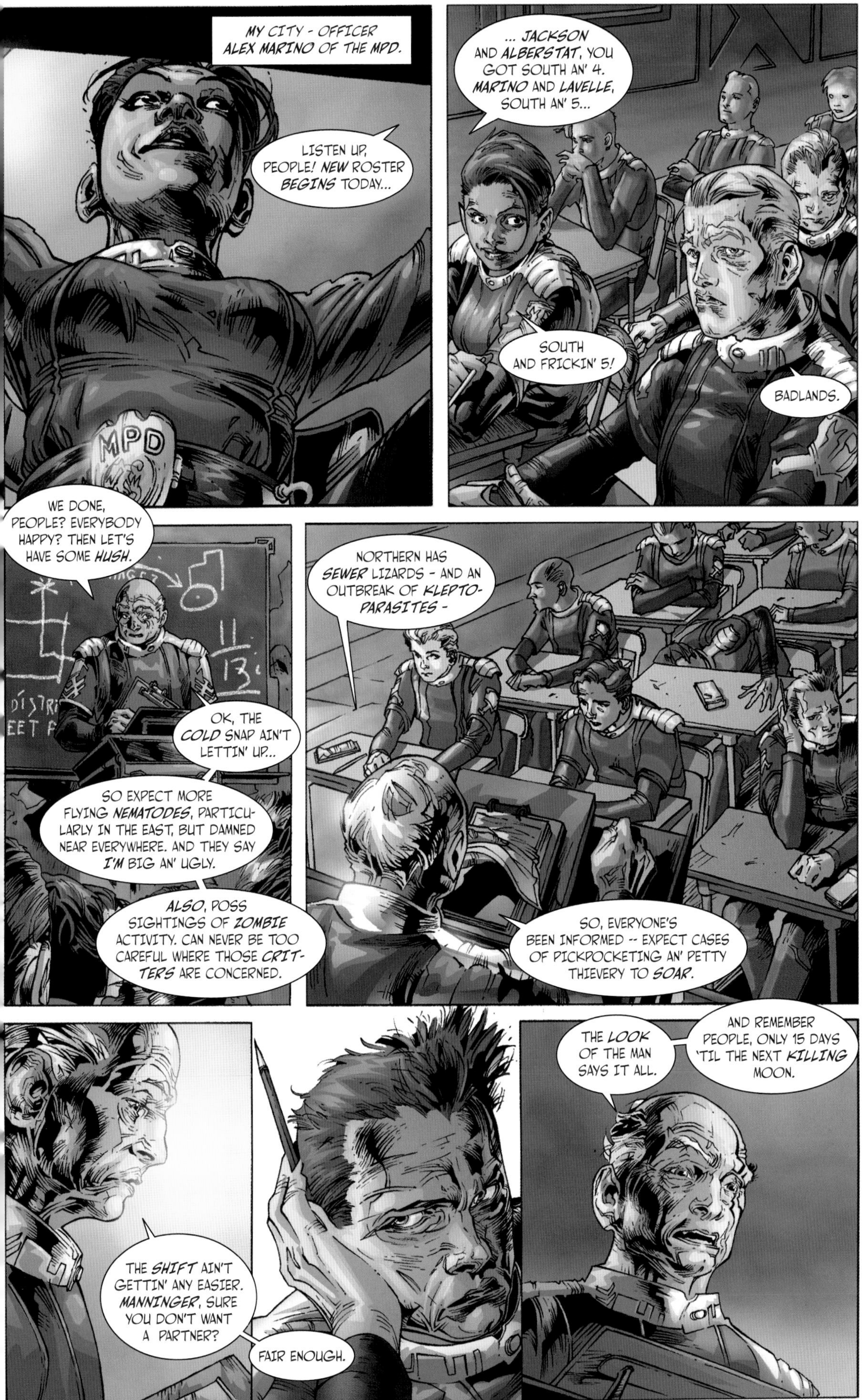
MY CITY - OFFICER ALEX MARINO OF THE MPD.
LISTEN UP, PEOPLE! NEW ROSTER BEGINS TODAY...
MPD
... JACKSON AND ALBERSTAT, YOU GOT SOUTH AN' 4. MARINO AND LAVELLE, SOUTH AN' 5...
SOUTH AND FRICKIN' 5!
BADLANDS.
WE DONE, PEOPLE? EVERYBODY HAPPY? THEN LET'S HAVE SOME HUSH.
OK, THE COLD SNAP AIN'T LETTIN' UP...
SO EXPECT MORE FLYING NEMATODES, PARTICU-LARLY IN THE EAST, BUT DAMNED NEAR EVERYWHERE. AND THEY SAY I'M BIG AN' UGLY.
ALSO, POSS SIGHTINGS OF ZOMBIE ACTIVITY. CAN NEVER BE TOO CAREFUL WHERE THOSE CRIT-TERS ARE CONCERNED.
NORTHERN HAS SEWER LIZARDS - AND AN OUTBREAK OF KLEPTO-PARASITES -
SO, EVERYONE'S BEEN INFORMED -- EXPECT CASES OF PICKPOCKETING AN' PETTY THIEVERY TO SOAR.
THE SHIFT AIN'T GETTIN' ANY EASIER. MANNINGER, SURE YOU DON'T WANT A PARTNER?
FAIR ENOUGH.
THE LOOK OF THE MAN SAYS IT ALL.
AND REMEMBER PEOPLE, ONLY 15 DAYS 'TIL THE NEXT KILLING MOON.

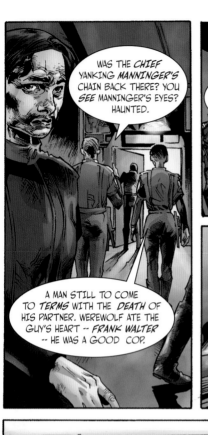

WAS THE *CHIEF* YANKING *MANNINGER'S* CHAIN BACK THERE? YOU *SEE* MANNINGER'S EYES? HAUNTED.

A MAN STILL TO COME TO *TERMS* WITH THE *DEATH* OF HIS PARTNER. WEREWOLF ATE THE GUY'S HEART -- *FRANK WALTER* -- HE WAS A GOOD COP.

MANNINGER'S GOING THROUGH THE 'STRICT LONER' STAGE. CHIEF ISN'T EXACTLY *SENSITIVE* TO IT.

NOW, IF THE *SAME* THING HAPPENED TO *MY* PARTNER, GUESS *I'D* GET OVER IT.

GEE, THAT'S REASSURING.

HOW LONG SINCE YOU WERE A CADET, LAVELLE? 6 MONTHS, GIVE OR TAKE?

MAYBE IT *WOULD* BE A SHAME, YOU SHUFFLING OFF THIS MORTAL COIL.

HEY, NO PLANS ON "SHUFFLING OFF" *ANYWHERE!* MARINO, WHAT'S WITH THE *MORBID* TALK, ANYWAY?

SOUTH AND 5, LAVELLE. AND *ZOMBIE* SIGHTINGS.

VRUMMM

I *HATE* THOSE BASTARDS.

ANTDEC APARTMENT BLOCK

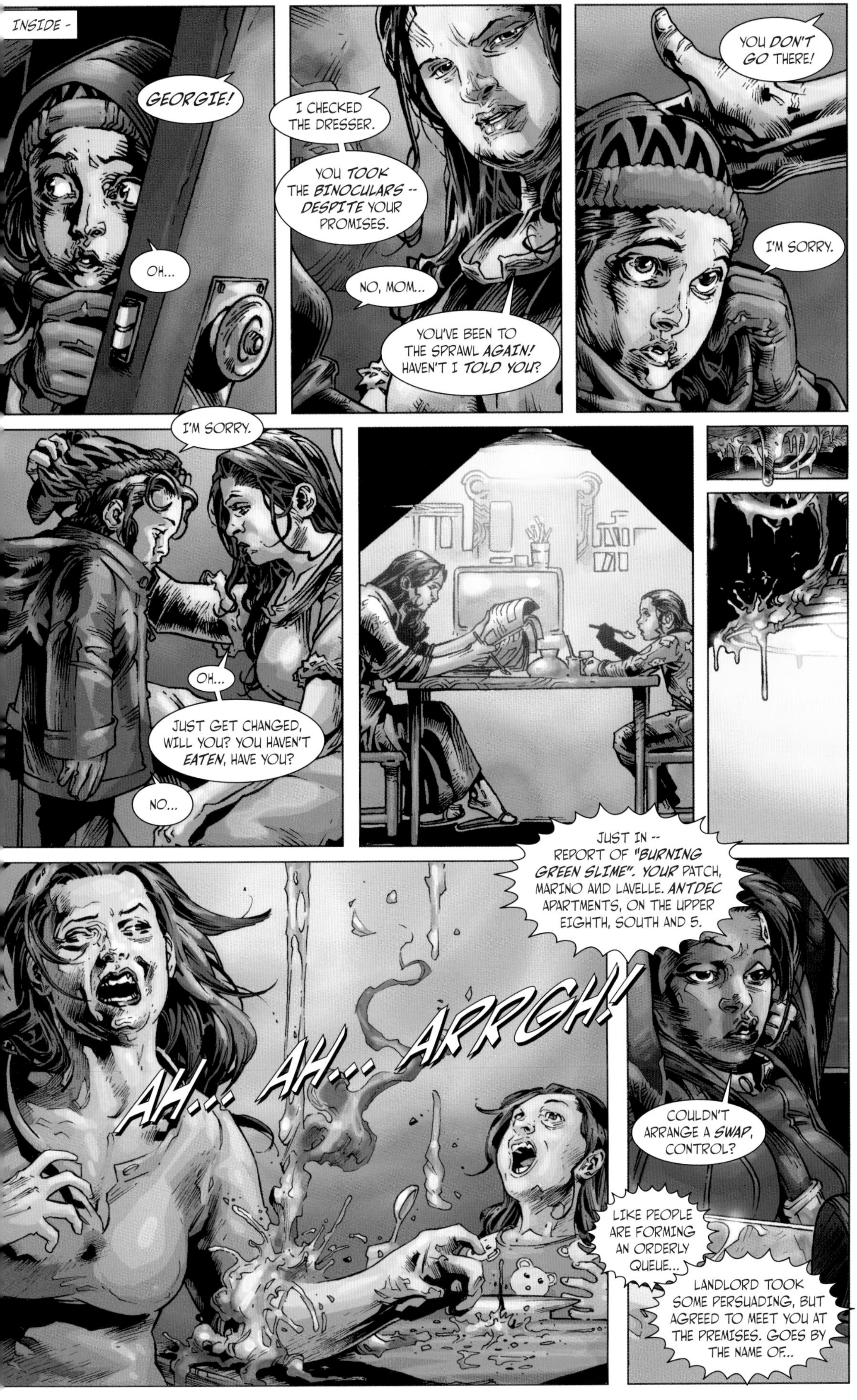
INSIDE -
GEORGIE!
OH...
I CHECKED THE DRESSER.
YOU TOOK THE BINOCULARS -- DESPITE YOUR PROMISES.
NO, MOM...
YOU'VE BEEN TO THE SPRAWL AGAIN! HAVEN'T I TOLD YOU?
YOU DON'T GO THERE!
I'M SORRY.
I'M SORRY.
OH...
JUST GET CHANGED, WILL YOU? YOU HAVEN'T EATEN, HAVE YOU?
NO...
AH... AH... ARRGH!
JUST IN -- REPORT OF "BURNING GREEN SLIME". YOUR PATCH, MARINO AND LAVELLE. ANTDEC APARTMENTS, ON THE UPPER EIGHTH, SOUTH AND 5.
COULDN'T ARRANGE A SWAP, CONTROL?
LIKE PEOPLE ARE FORMING AN ORDERLY QUEUE...
LANDLORD TOOK SOME PERSUADING, BUT AGREED TO MEET YOU AT THE PREMISES. GOES BY THE NAME OF...

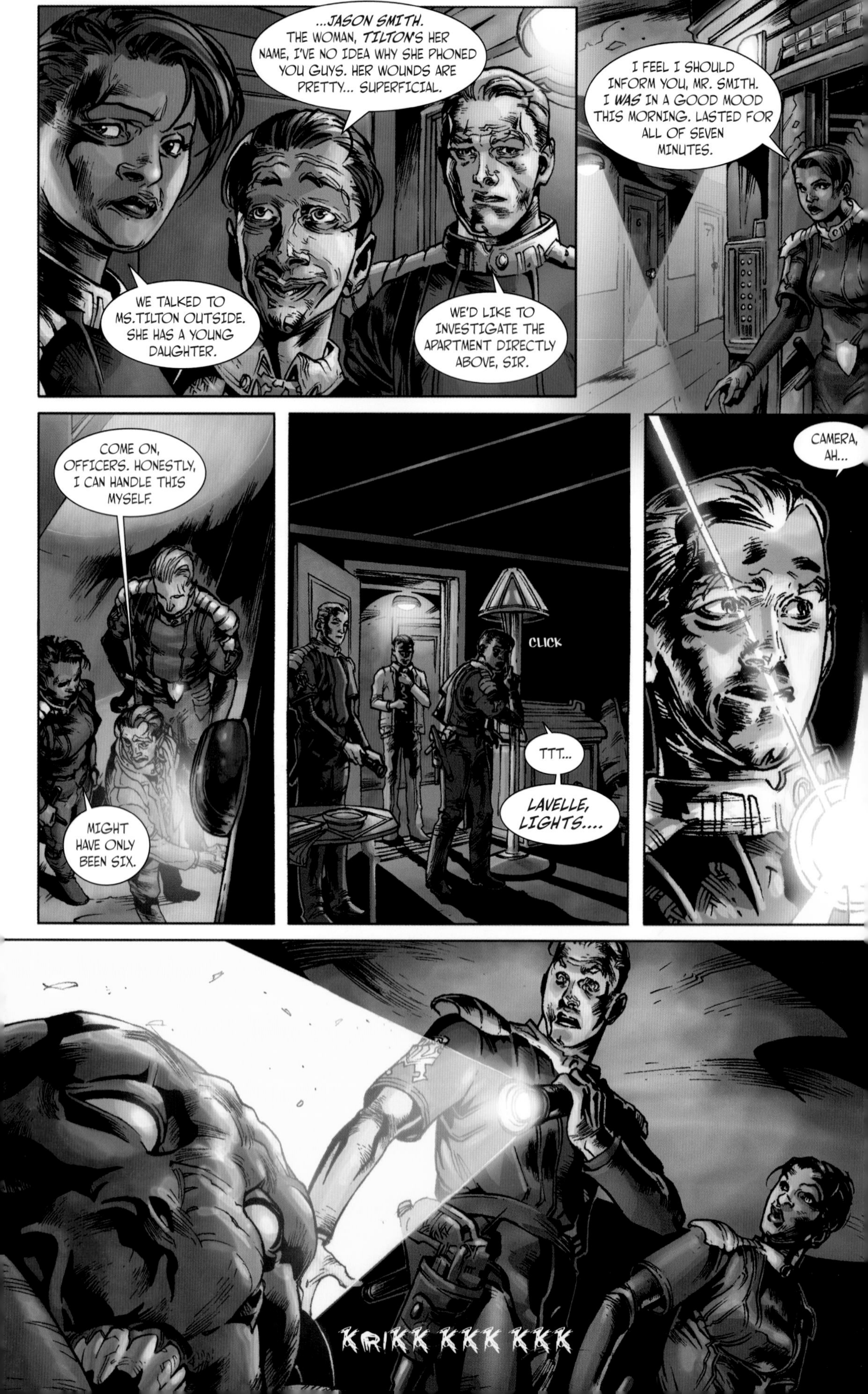
...JASON SMITH. THE WOMAN, TILTON'S HER NAME, I'VE NO IDEA WHY SHE PHONED YOU GUYS. HER WOUNDS ARE PRETTY... SUPERFICIAL.
WE TALKED TO MS.TILTON OUTSIDE. SHE HAS A YOUNG DAUGHTER.
WE'D LIKE TO INVESTIGATE THE APARTMENT DIRECTLY ABOVE, SIR.
I FEEL I SHOULD INFORM YOU, MR. SMITH. I WAS IN A GOOD MOOD THIS MORNING. LASTED FOR ALL OF SEVEN MINUTES.
COME ON, OFFICERS. HONESTLY, I CAN HANDLE THIS MYSELF.
MIGHT HAVE ONLY BEEN SIX.
CLICK
TTT...
LAVELLE, LIGHTS....
CAMERA, AH...
KRIKK KKK KKK

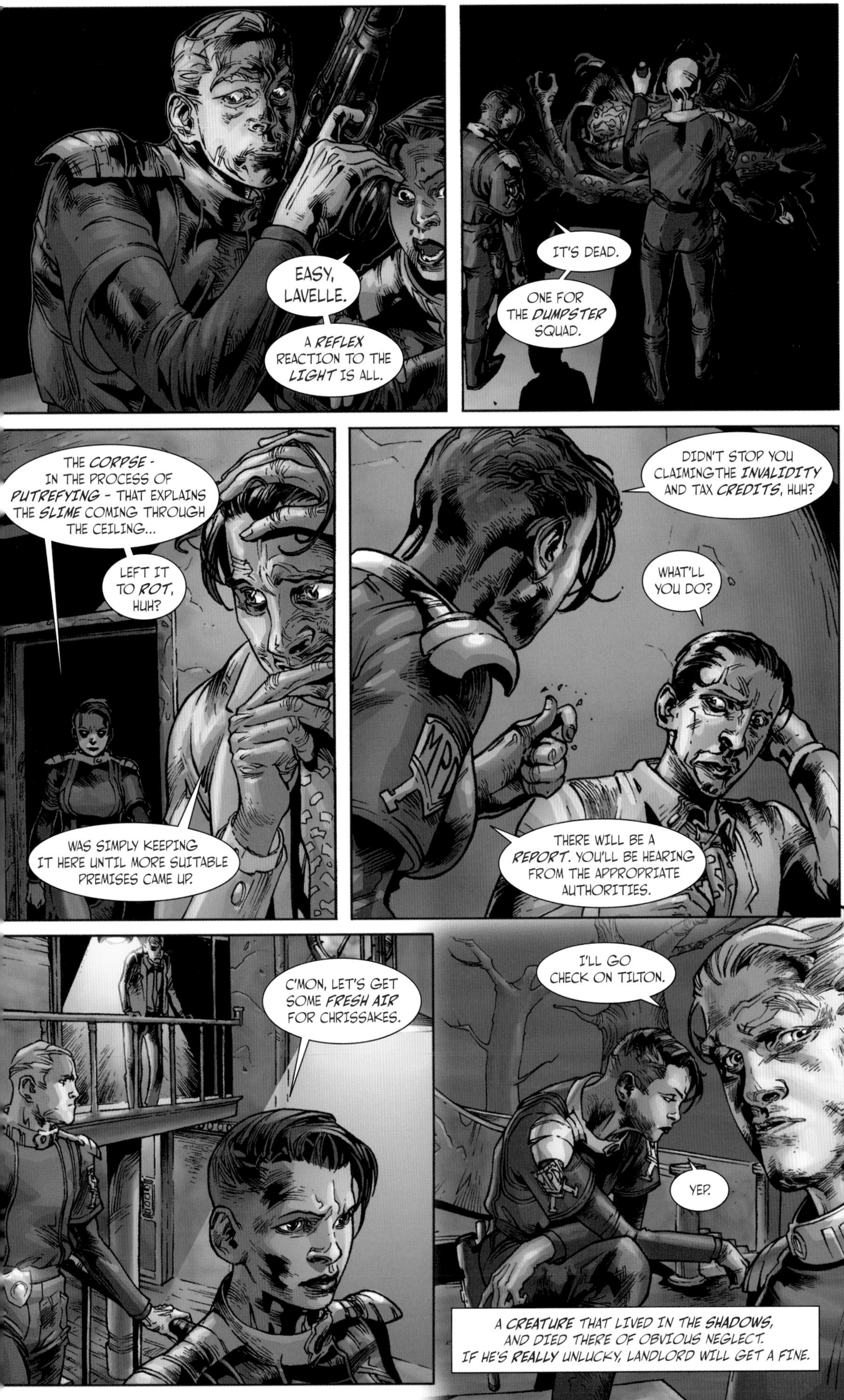
EASY, LAVELLE.
A REFLEX REACTION TO THE LIGHT IS ALL.
IT'S DEAD.
ONE FOR THE DUMPSTER SQUAD.
THE CORPSE - IN THE PROCESS OF PUTREFYING - THAT EXPLAINS THE SLIME COMING THROUGH THE CEILING...
LEFT IT TO ROT, HUH?
WAS SIMPLY KEEPING IT HERE UNTIL MORE SUITABLE PREMISES CAME UP.
DIDN'T STOP YOU CLAIMING THE INVALIDITY AND TAX CREDITS, HUH?
WHAT'LL YOU DO?
THERE WILL BE A REPORT. YOU'LL BE HEARING FROM THE APPROPRIATE AUTHORITIES.
C'MON, LET'S GET SOME FRESH AIR FOR CHRISSAKES.
I'LL GO CHECK ON TILTON.
YEP.
A CREATURE THAT LIVED IN THE SHADOWS, AND DIED THERE OF OBVIOUS NEGLECT. IF HE'S REALLY UNLUCKY, LANDLORD WILL GET A FINE.

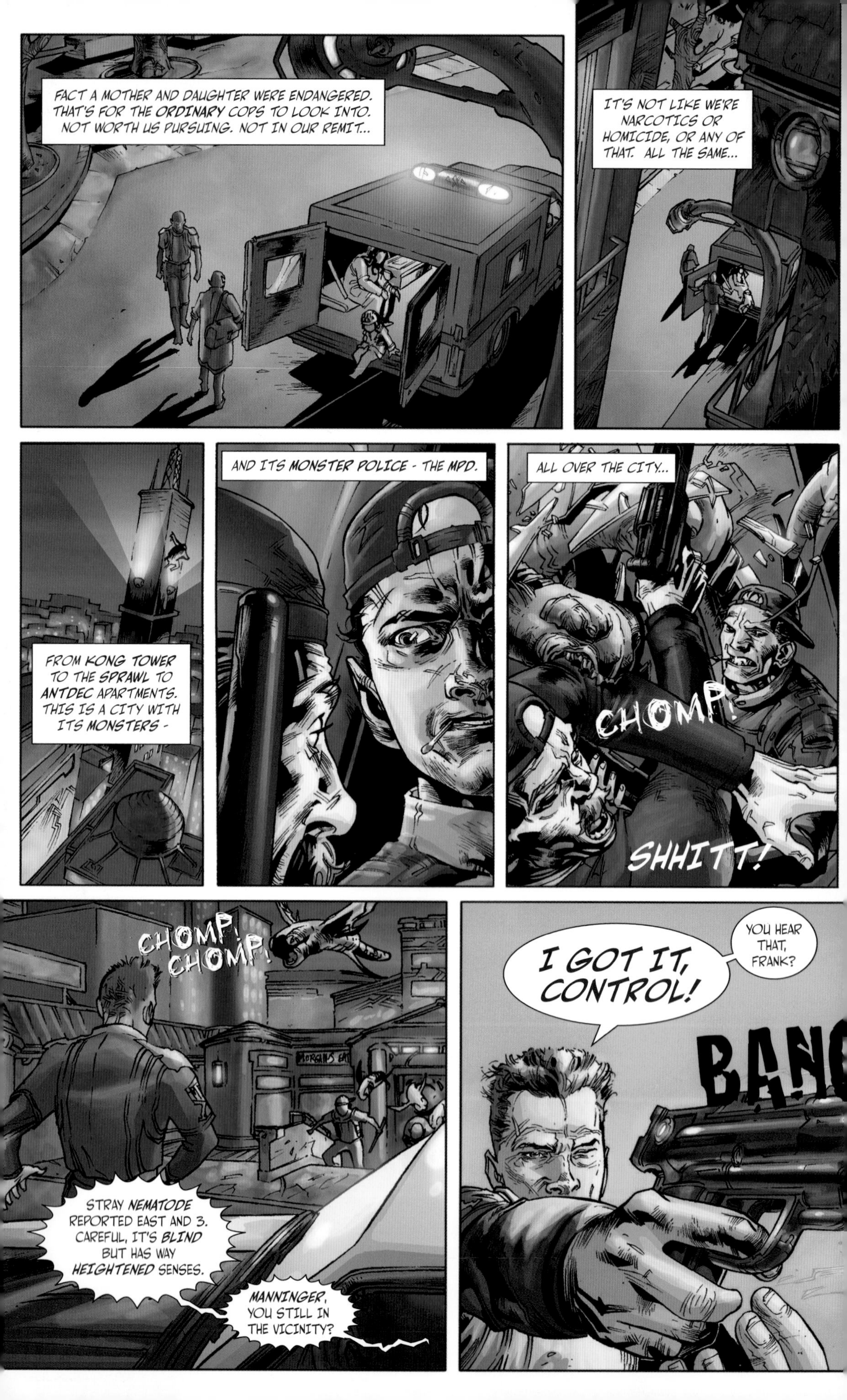
FACT A MOTHER AND DAUGHTER WERE ENDANGERED. THAT'S FOR THE ORDINARY COPS TO LOOK INTO. NOT WORTH US PURSUING. NOT IN OUR REMIT...
IT'S NOT LIKE WE'RE NARCOTICS OR HOMICIDE, OR ANY OF THAT. ALL THE SAME...
FROM KONG TOWER TO THE SPRAWL TO ANTDEC APARTMENTS. THIS IS A CITY WITH ITS MONSTERS -
AND ITS MONSTER POLICE - THE MPD.
ALL OVER THE CITY...
CHOMP!
SHHITT!
CHOMP! CHOMP!
STRAY NEMATODE REPORTED EAST AND 3. CAREFUL, IT'S BLIND BUT HAS WAY HEIGHTENED SENSES.
MANNINGER, YOU STILL IN THE VICINITY?
YOU HEAR THAT, FRANK?
I GOT IT, CONTROL!
BANG

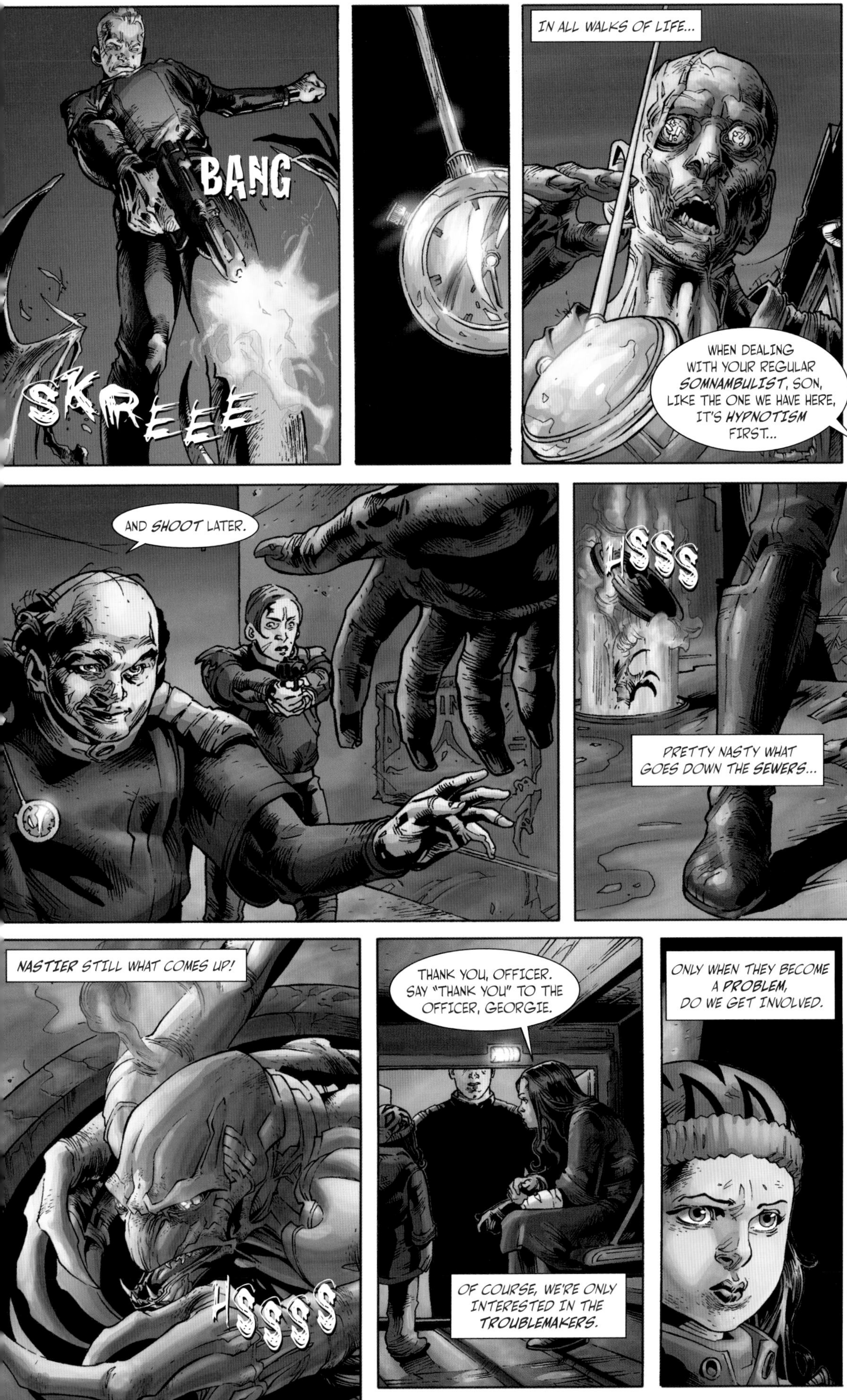
BANG
SKREEE
IN ALL WALKS OF LIFE...
WHEN DEALING WITH YOUR REGULAR SOMNAMBULIST, SON, LIKE THE ONE WE HAVE HERE, IT'S HYPNOTISM FIRST...
AND SHOOT LATER.
HSSS
PRETTY NASTY WHAT GOES DOWN THE SEWERS...
NASTIER STILL WHAT COMES UP!
HSSSS
THANK YOU, OFFICER. SAY "THANK YOU" TO THE OFFICER, GEORGIE.
OF COURSE, WE'RE ONLY INTERESTED IN THE TROUBLEMAKERS.
ONLY WHEN THEY BECOME A PROBLEM, DO WE GET INVOLVED.

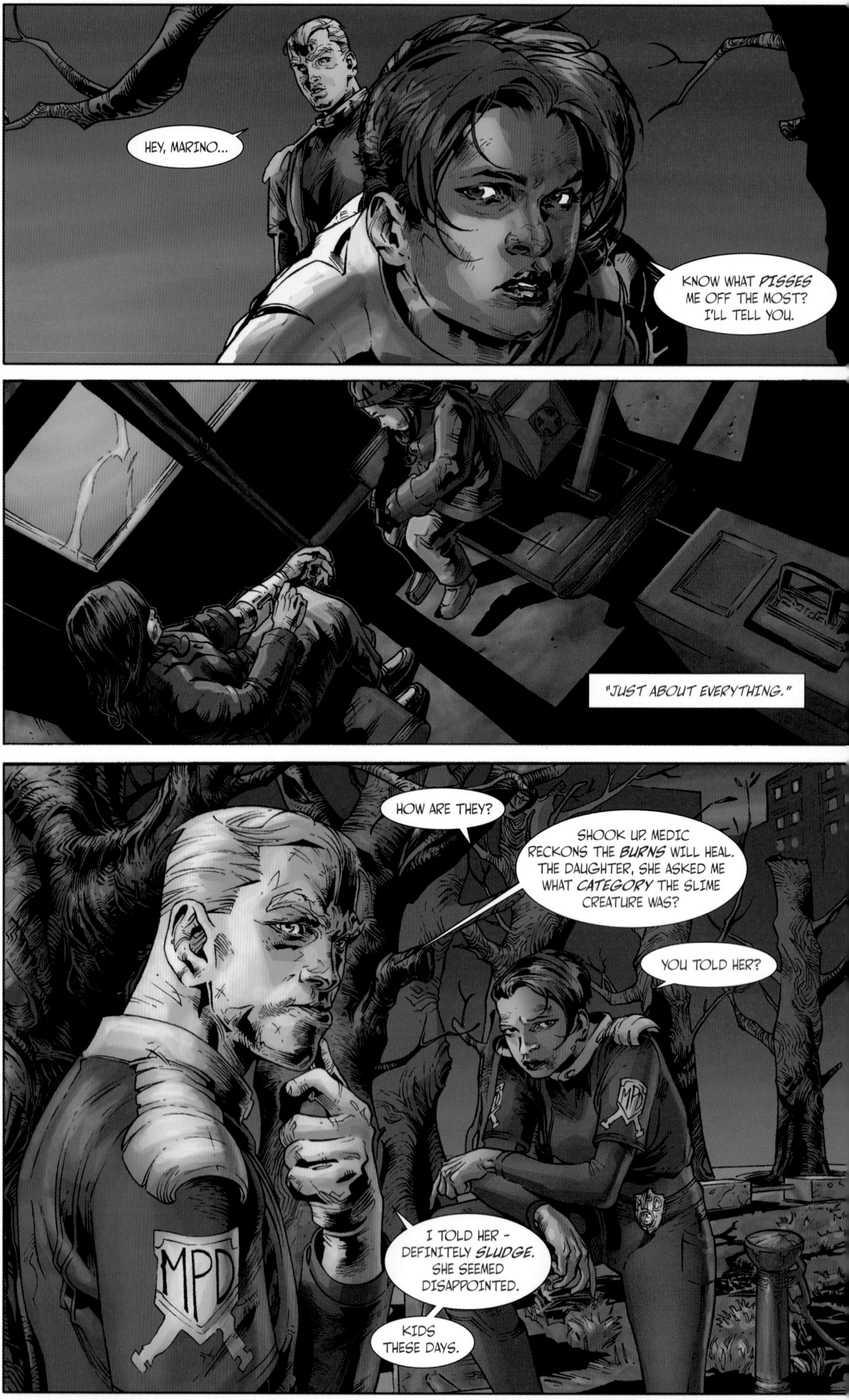
HEY, MARINO...
KNOW WHAT PISSES ME OFF THE MOST? I'LL TELL YOU.
"JUST ABOUT EVERYTHING."
HOW ARE THEY?
SHOOK UP. MEDIC RECKONS THE BURNS WILL HEAL. THE DAUGHTER, SHE ASKED ME WHAT CATEGORY THE SLIME CREATURE WAS?
YOU TOLD HER?
I TOLD HER - DEFINITELY SLUDGE. SHE SEEMED DISAPPOINTED.
KIDS THESE DAYS.
MPD

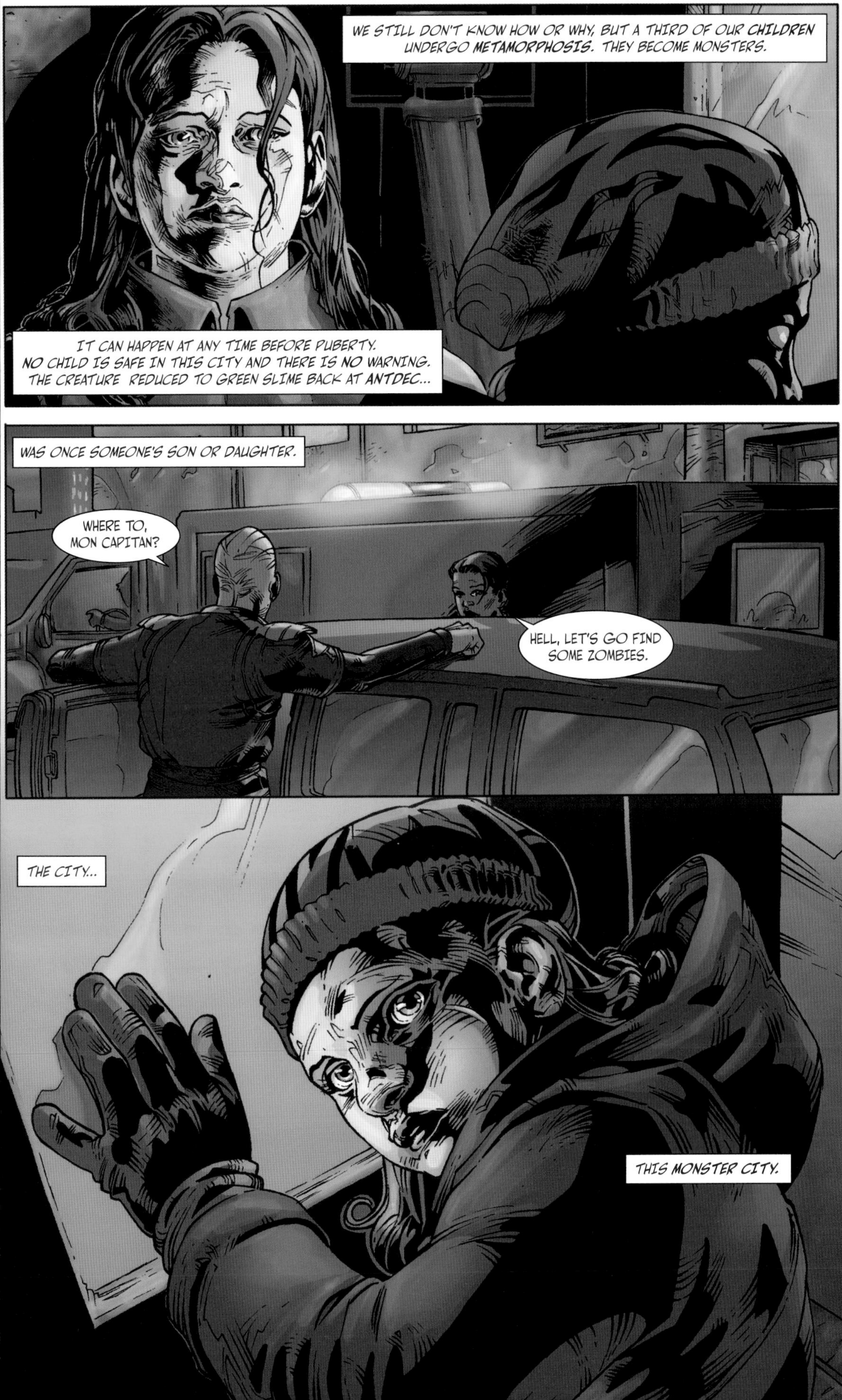
WE STILL DON'T KNOW HOW OR WHY, BUT A THIRD OF OUR CHILDREN UNDERGO METAMORPHOSIS. THEY BECOME MONSTERS.
IT CAN HAPPEN AT ANY TIME BEFORE PUBERTY. NO CHILD IS SAFE IN THIS CITY AND THERE IS NO WARNING. THE CREATURE REDUCED TO GREEN SLIME BACK AT ANTDEC...
WAS ONCE SOMEONE'S SON OR DAUGHTER.
WHERE TO, MON CAPITAN?
HELL, LET'S GO FIND SOME ZOMBIES.
THE CITY...
THIS MONSTER CITY.

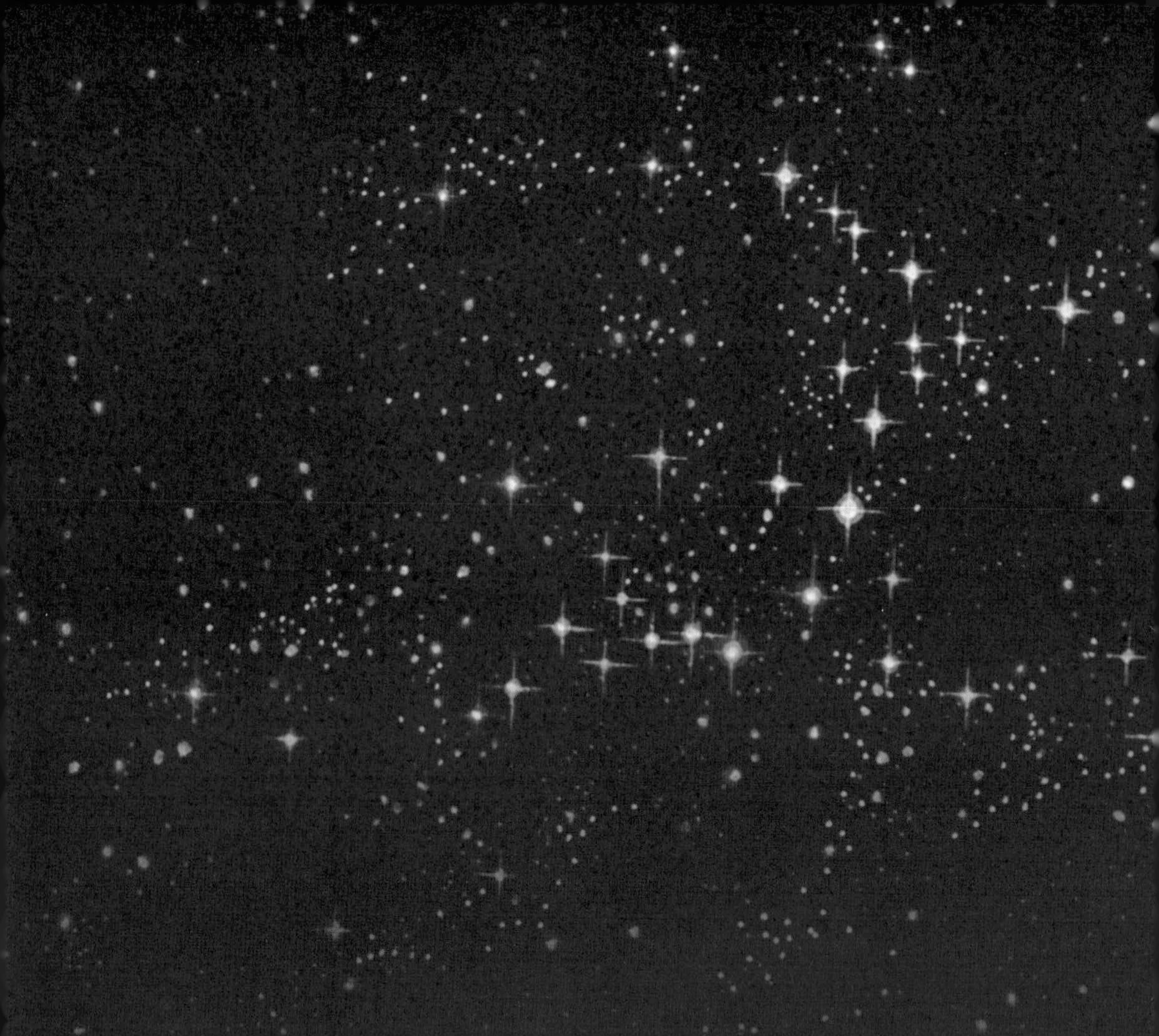

SECOND CHANCES

Story by JIM MACDONALD
Art by JORGE LUCAS
Colors by DAN BROWN

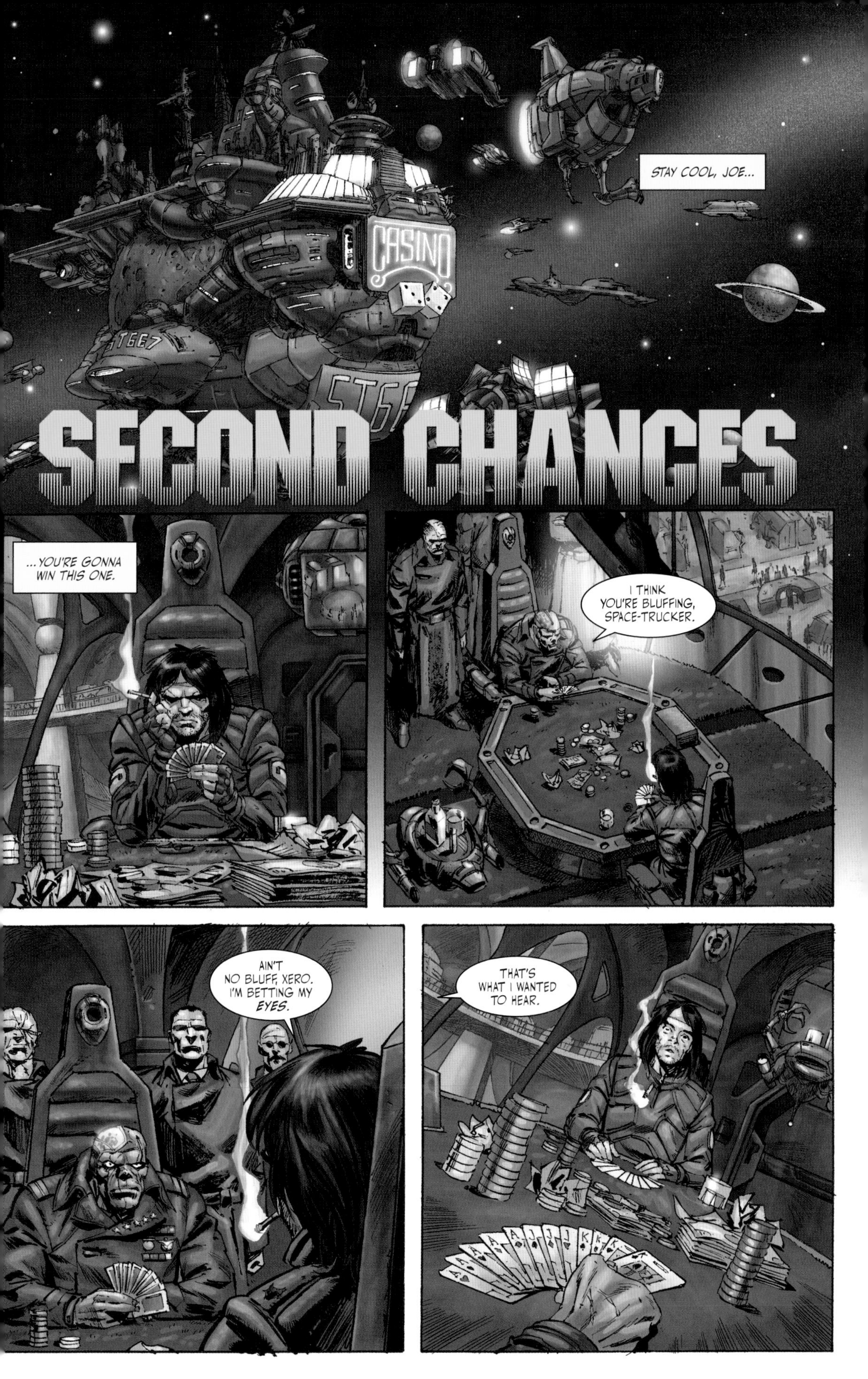
STAY COOL, JOE...
CASINO
SECOND CHANCES
...YOU'RE GONNA WIN THIS ONE.
I THINK YOU'RE BLUFFING, SPACE-TRUCKER.
AIN'T NO BLUFF, XERO. I'M BETTING MY *EYES*.
THAT'S WHAT I WANTED TO HEAR.

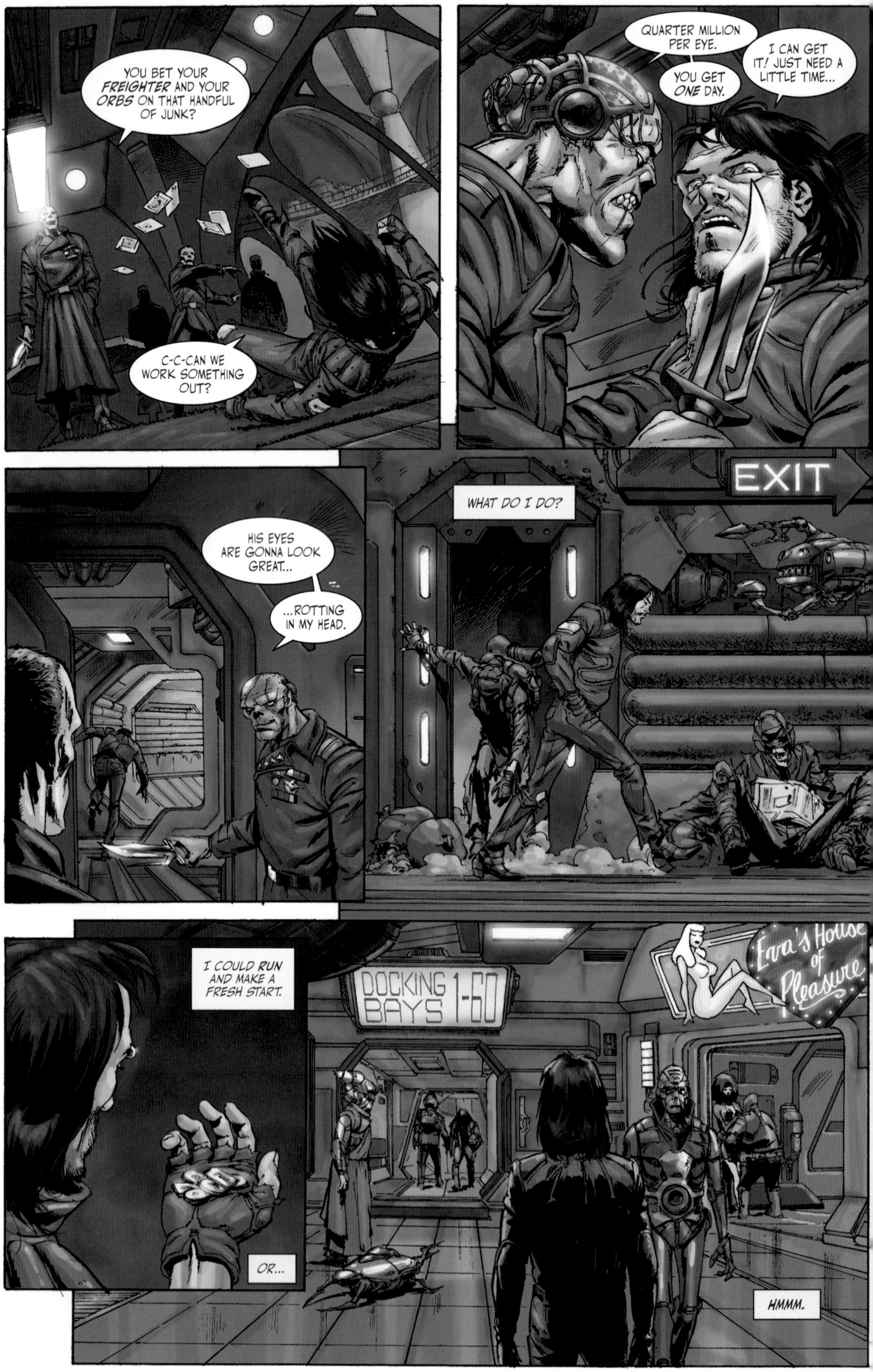
YOU BET YOUR FREIGHTER AND YOUR ORBS ON THAT HANDFUL OF JUNK?
C-C-CAN WE WORK SOMETHING OUT?
QUARTER MILLION PER EYE.
YOU GET ONE DAY.
I CAN GET IT! JUST NEED A LITTLE TIME...
EXIT
WHAT DO I DO?
HIS EYES ARE GONNA LOOK GREAT...
...ROTTING IN MY HEAD.
I COULD RUN AND MAKE A FRESH START.
OR...
DOCKING BAYS 1-60
Eva's House of Pleasure
HMMM.

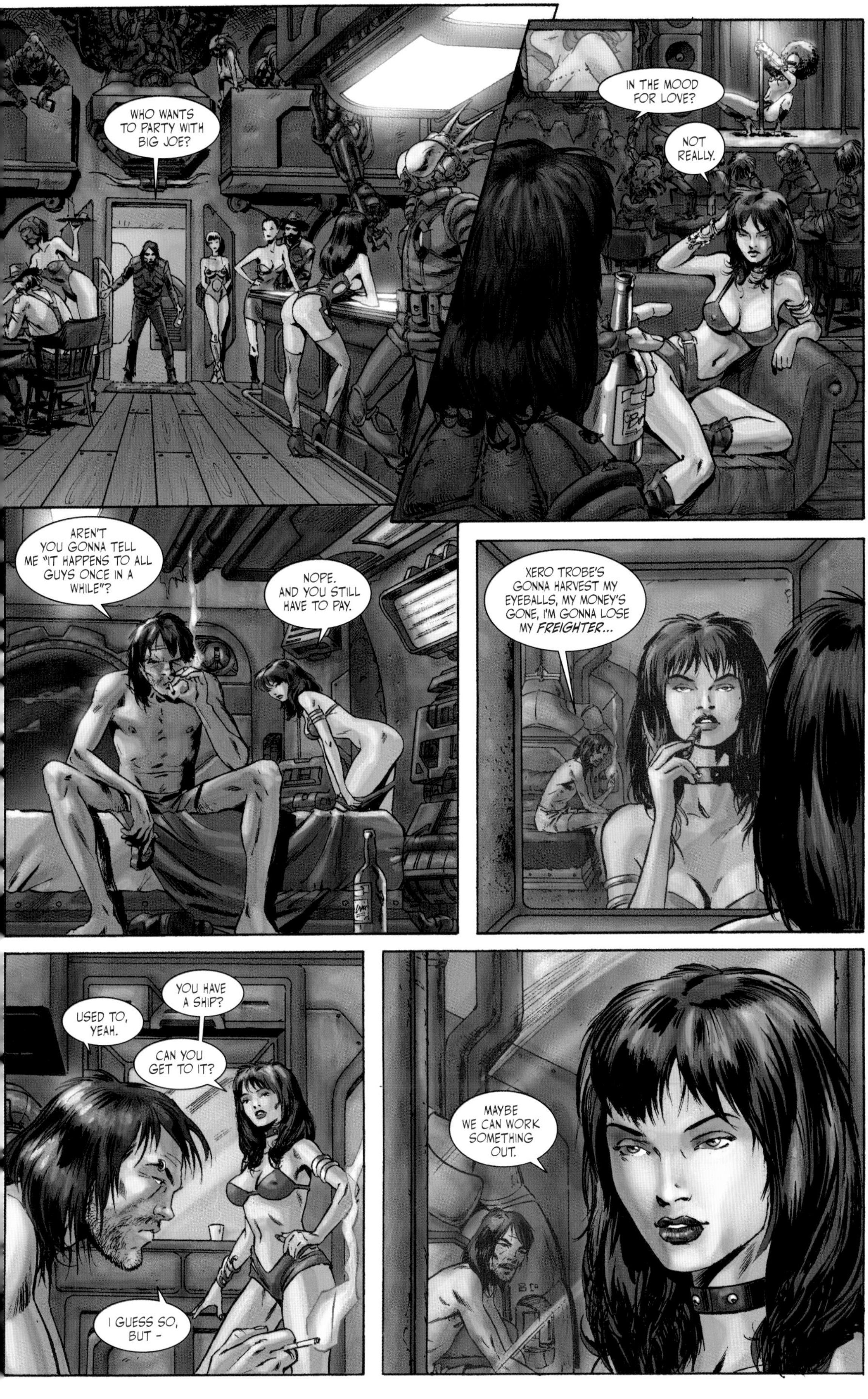
WHO WANTS TO PARTY WITH BIG JOE?
IN THE MOOD FOR LOVE?
NOT REALLY.
AREN'T YOU GONNA TELL ME "IT HAPPENS TO ALL GUYS ONCE IN A WHILE"?
NOPE. AND YOU STILL HAVE TO PAY.
XERO TROBE'S GONNA HARVEST MY EYEBALLS, MY MONEY'S GONE, I'M GONNA LOSE MY *FREIGHTER*...
USED TO, YEAH.
YOU HAVE A SHIP?
CAN YOU GET TO IT?
I GUESS SO, BUT -
MAYBE WE CAN WORK SOMETHING OUT.

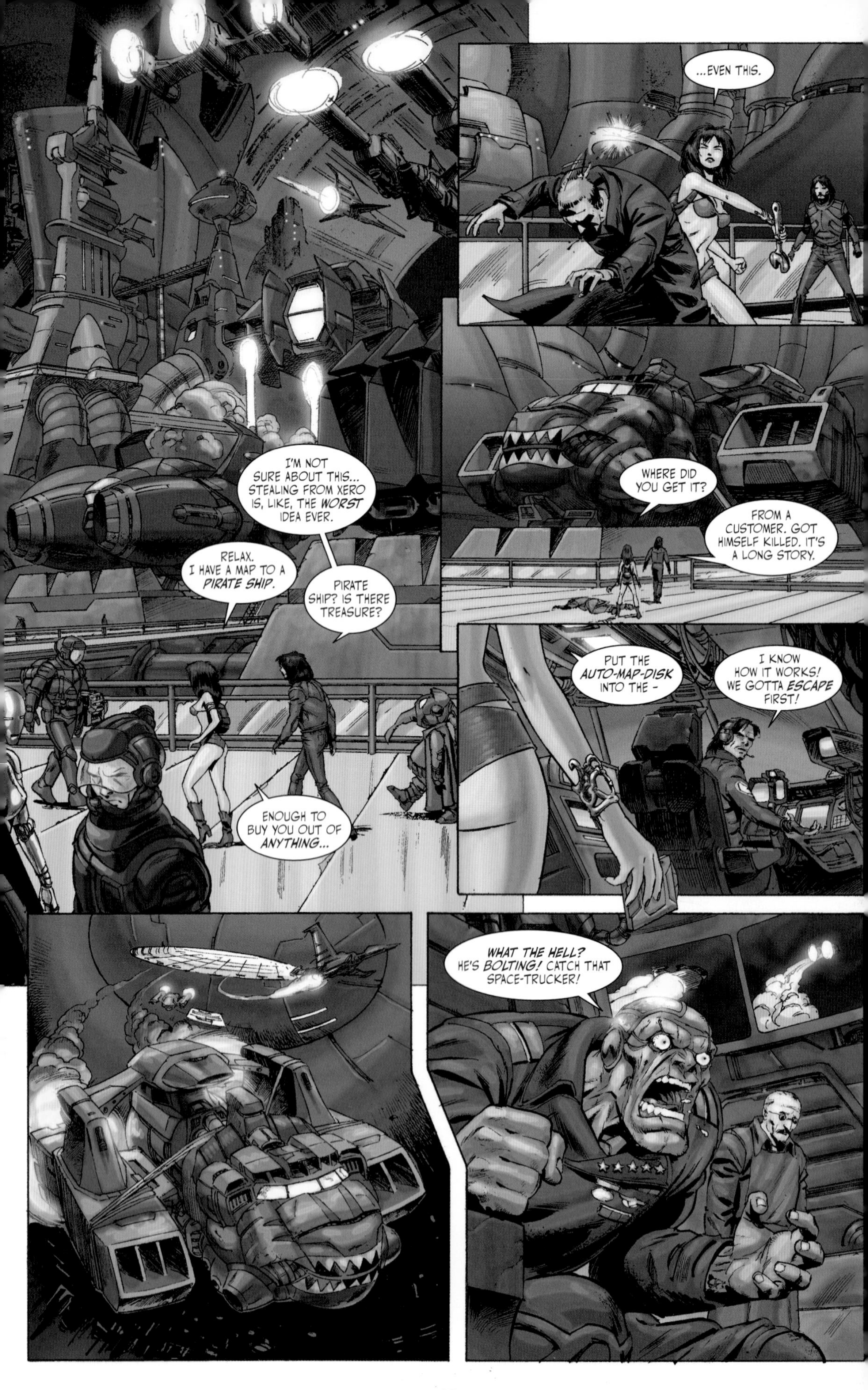
...EVEN THIS.
I'M NOT SURE ABOUT THIS... STEALING FROM XERO IS, LIKE, THE *WORST* IDEA EVER.
RELAX. I HAVE A MAP TO A *PIRATE SHIP*.
PIRATE SHIP? IS THERE TREASURE?
ENOUGH TO BUY YOU OUT OF *ANYTHING*...
WHERE DID YOU GET IT?
FROM A CUSTOMER. GOT HIMSELF KILLED. IT'S A LONG STORY.
PUT THE *AUTO-MAP-DISK* INTO THE -
I KNOW HOW IT WORKS! WE GOTTA *ESCAPE* FIRST!
WHAT THE HELL? HE'S *BOLTING!* CATCH THAT SPACE-TRUCKER!

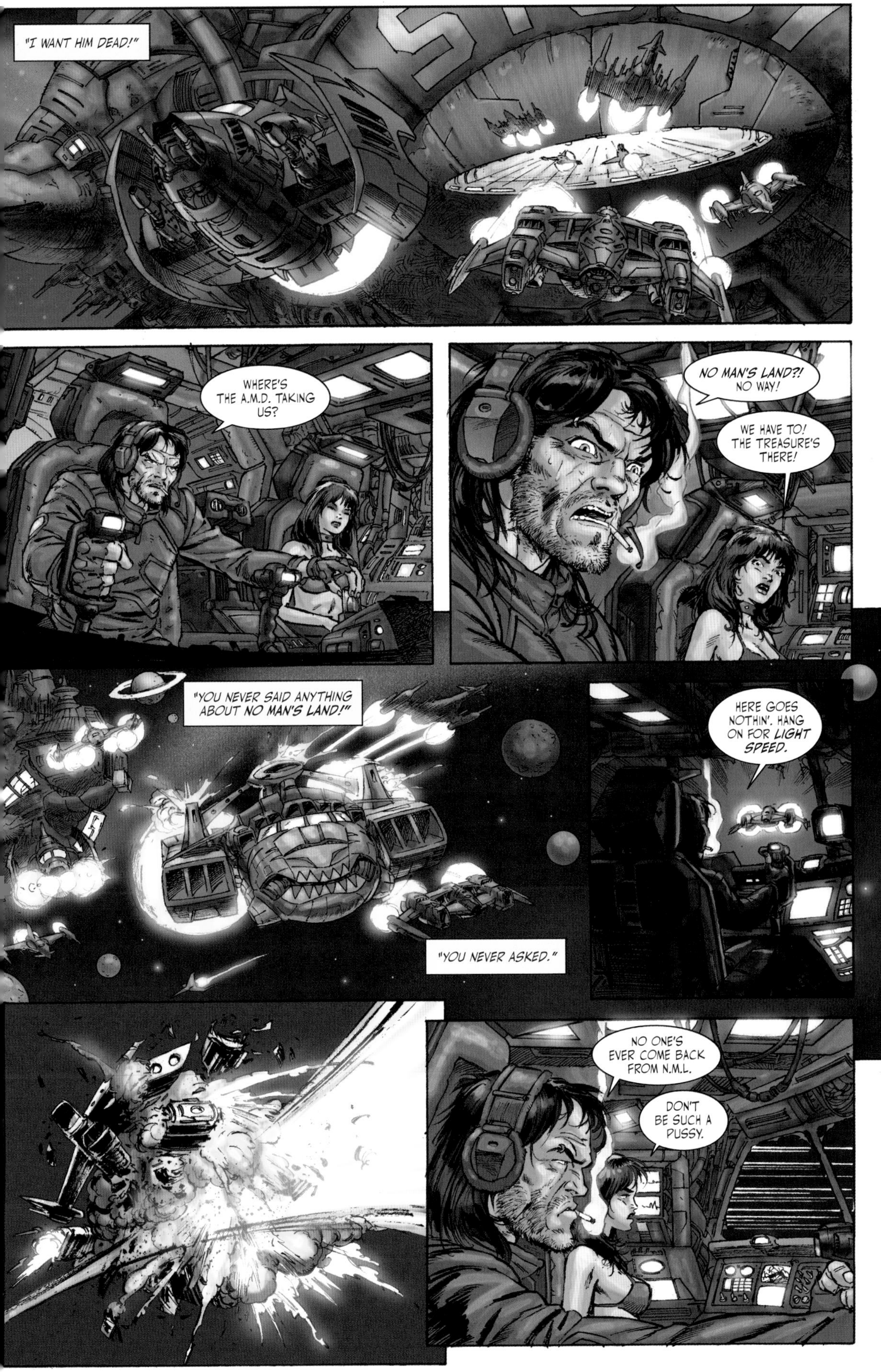
"I WANT HIM DEAD!"
WHERE'S THE A.M.D. TAKING US?
NO MAN'S LAND?! NO WAY!
WE HAVE TO! THE TREASURE'S THERE!
"YOU NEVER SAID ANYTHING ABOUT NO MAN'S LAND!"
"YOU NEVER ASKED."
HERE GOES NOTHIN'. HANG ON FOR LIGHT SPEED.
NO ONE'S EVER COME BACK FROM N.M.L.
DON'T BE SUCH A PUSSY.

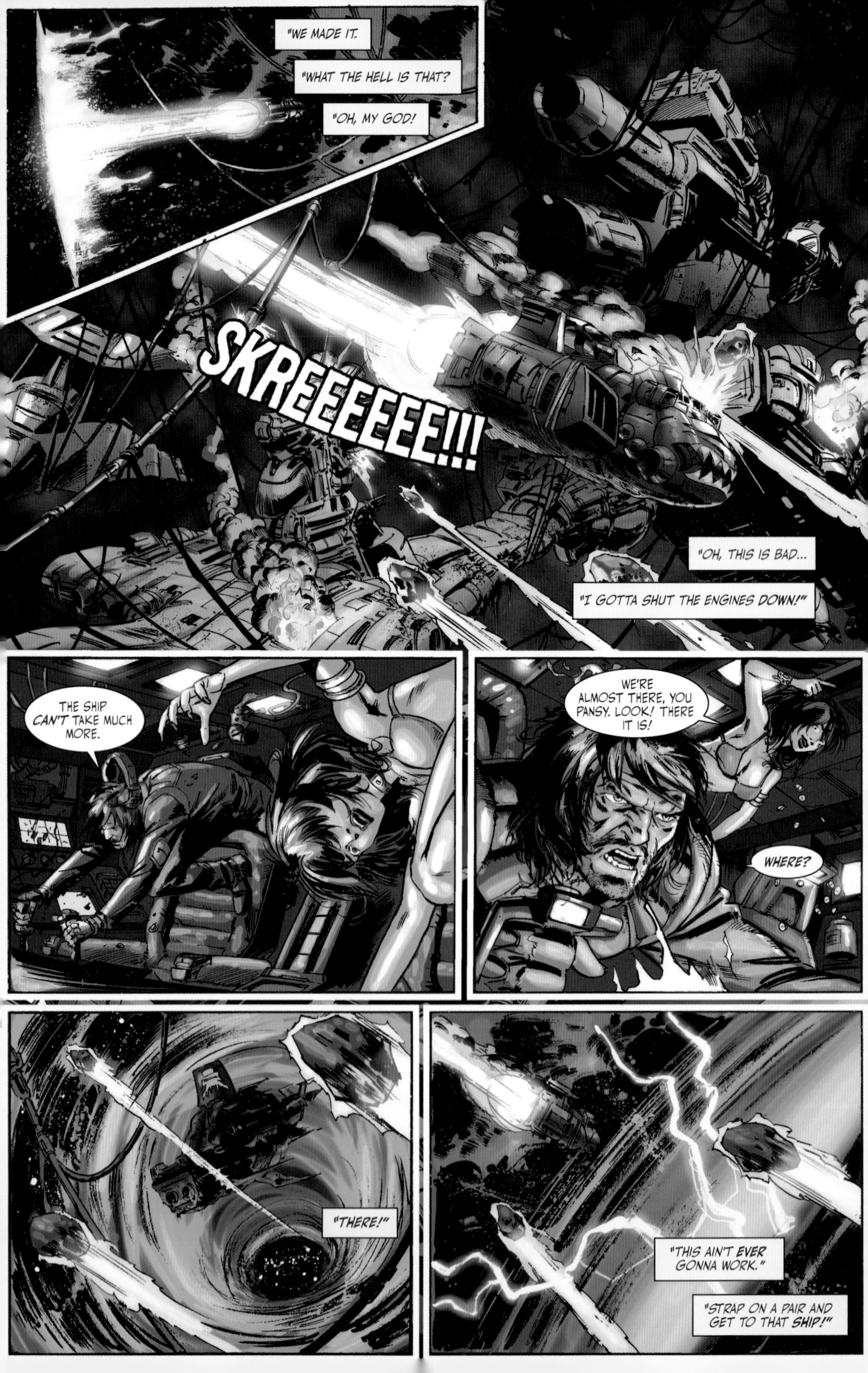
"WE MADE IT.
"WHAT THE HELL IS THAT?
"OH, MY GOD!
SKREEEEEEE!!!
"OH, THIS IS BAD...
"I GOTTA SHUT THE ENGINES DOWN!"
THE SHIP CAN'T TAKE MUCH MORE.
WE'RE ALMOST THERE, YOU PANSY. LOOK! THERE IT IS!
WHERE?
"THERE!"
"THIS AIN'T EVER GONNA WORK."
"STRAP ON A PAIR AND GET TO THAT SHIP!"

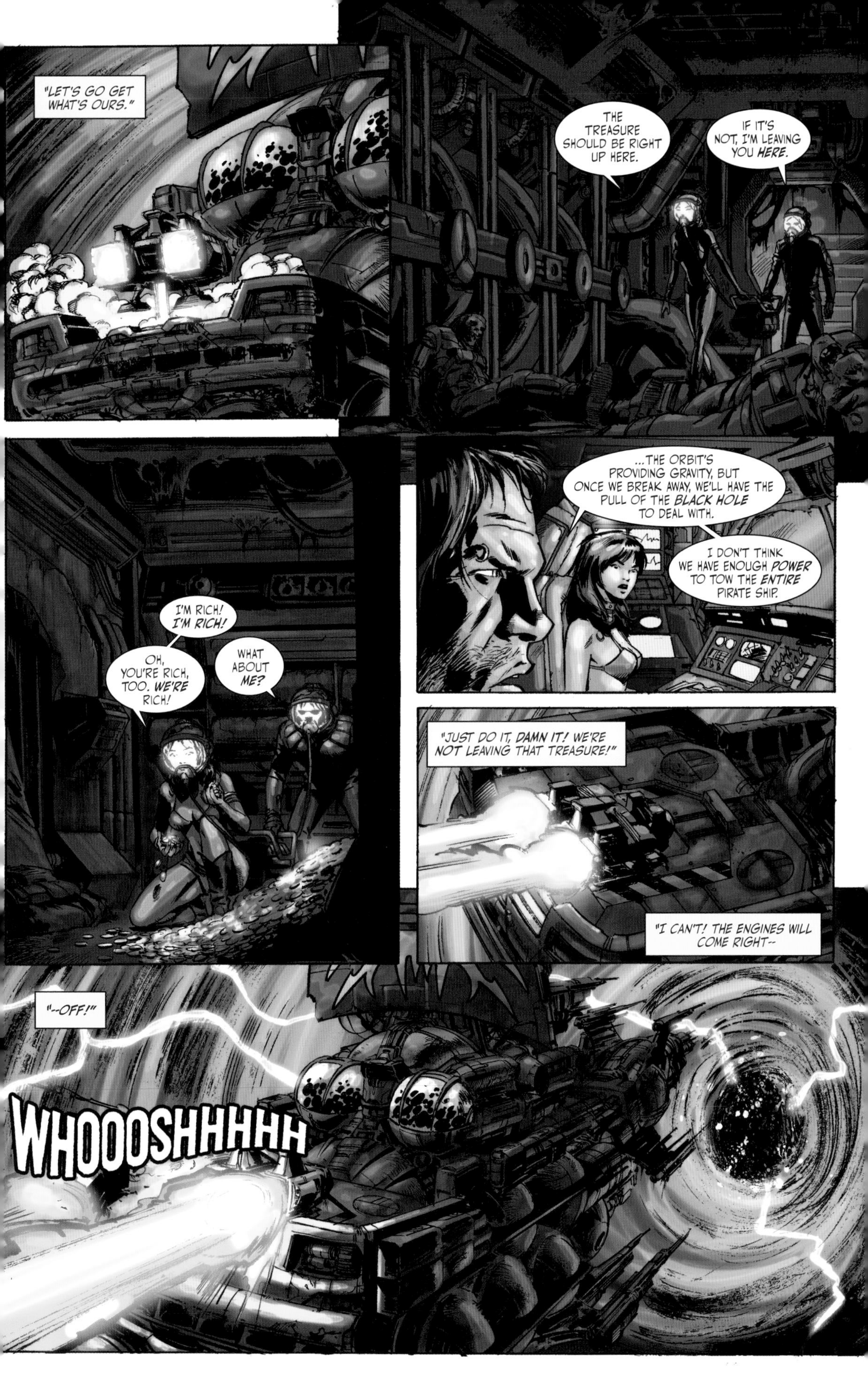
"LET'S GO GET WHAT'S OURS."
THE TREASURE SHOULD BE RIGHT UP HERE.
IF IT'S NOT, I'M LEAVING YOU HERE.
I'M RICH! I'M RICH!
OH, YOU'RE RICH, TOO. WE'RE RICH!
WHAT ABOUT ME?
...THE ORBIT'S PROVIDING GRAVITY, BUT ONCE WE BREAK AWAY, WE'LL HAVE THE PULL OF THE BLACK HOLE TO DEAL WITH.
I DON'T THINK WE HAVE ENOUGH POWER TO TOW THE ENTIRE PIRATE SHIP.
"JUST DO IT, DAMN IT! WE'RE NOT LEAVING THAT TREASURE!"
"I CAN'T! THE ENGINES WILL COME RIGHT--
"--OFF!"
WHOOOSHHHHH

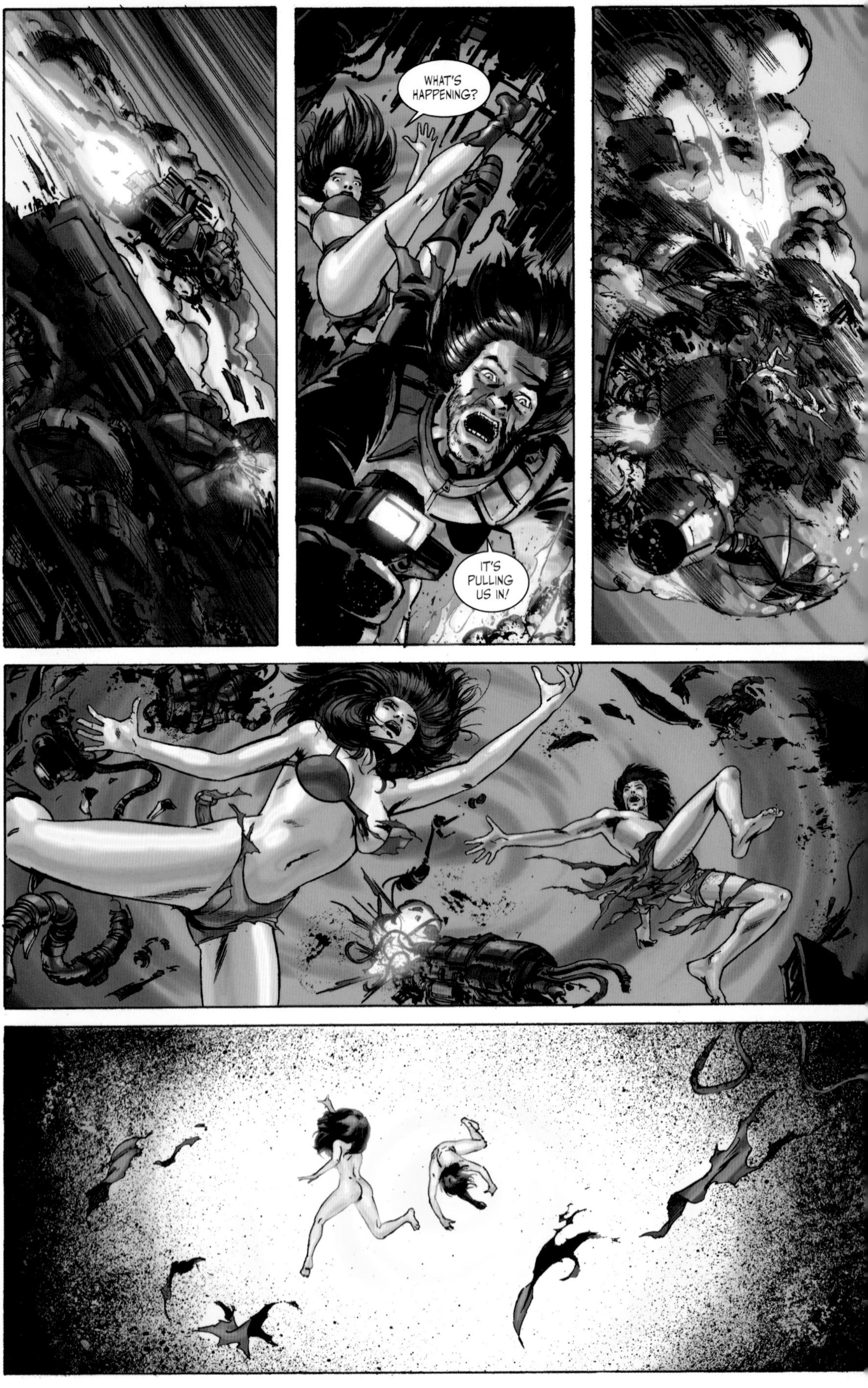
WHAT'S HAPPENING?
IT'S PULLING US IN!

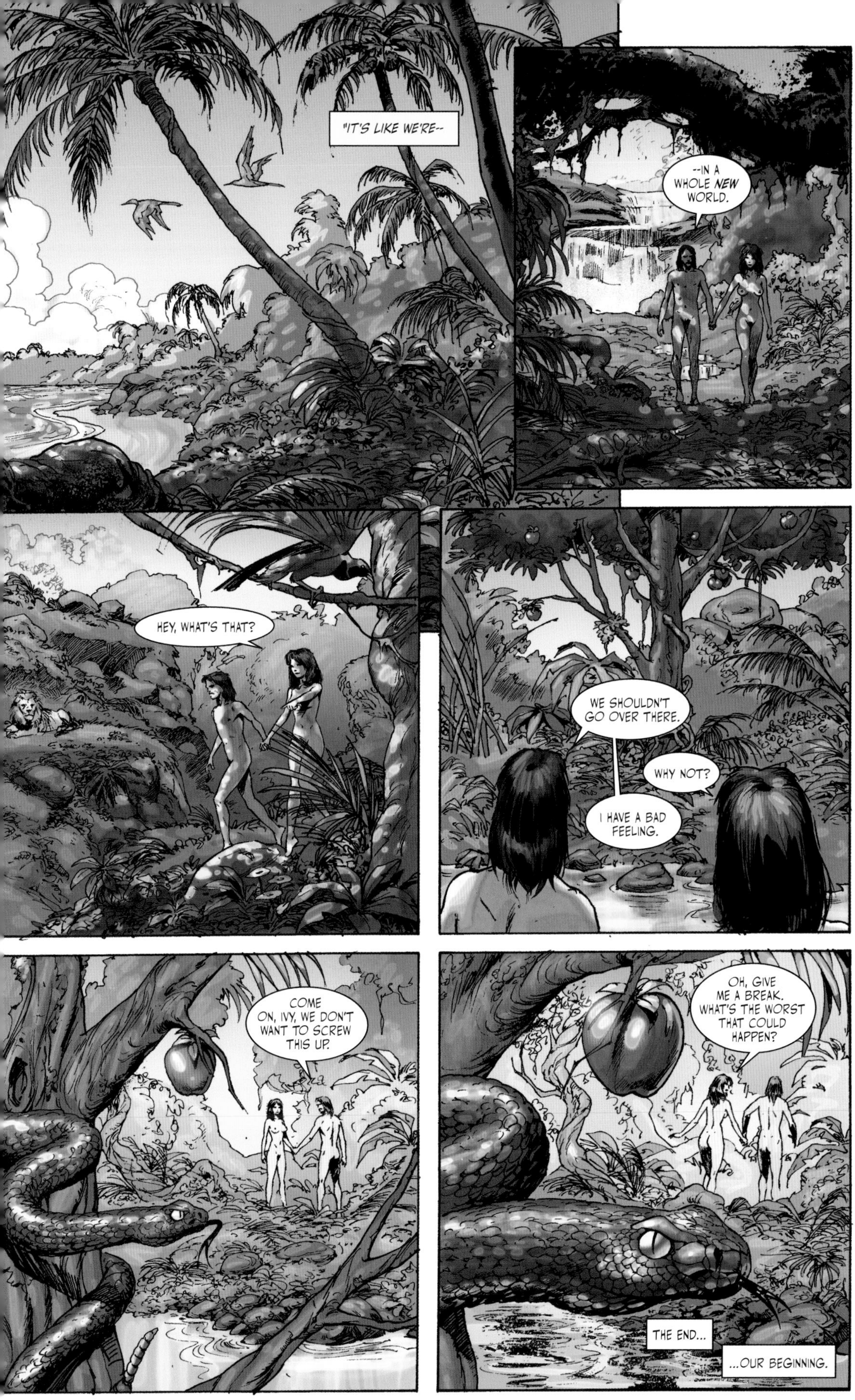
"IT'S LIKE WE'RE--
--IN A WHOLE *NEW* WORLD.
HEY, WHAT'S THAT?
WE SHOULDN'T GO OVER THERE.
WHY NOT?
I HAVE A BAD FEELING.
COME ON, IVY, WE DON'T WANT TO SCREW THIS UP.
OH, GIVE ME A BREAK. WHAT'S THE WORST THAT COULD HAPPEN?
THE END...
...OUR BEGINNING.

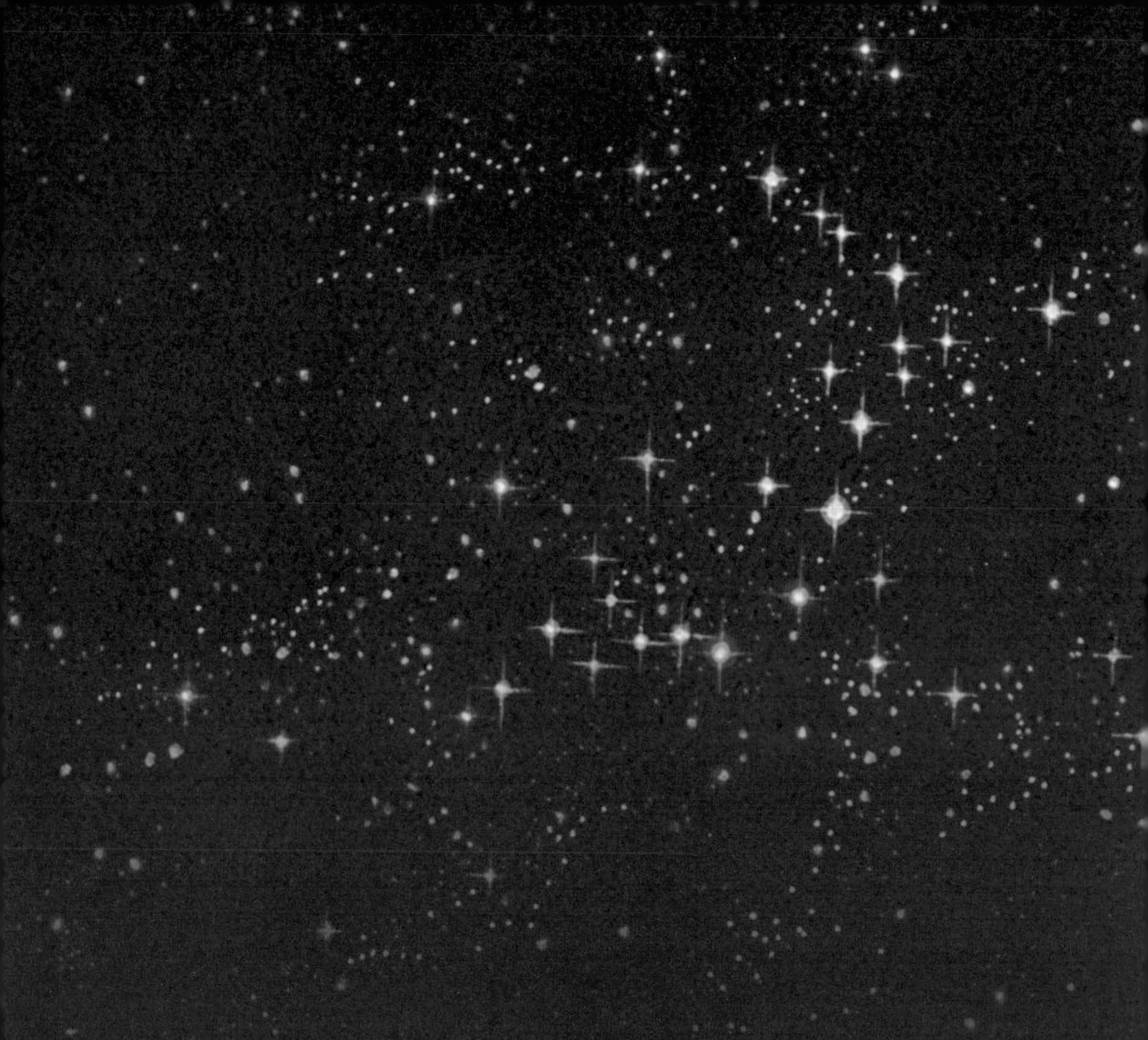

SHAME ON YOU!

Story and Art by FRANÇOIS BOUCQ
Colors by ISABELLE BUSSCHAERT

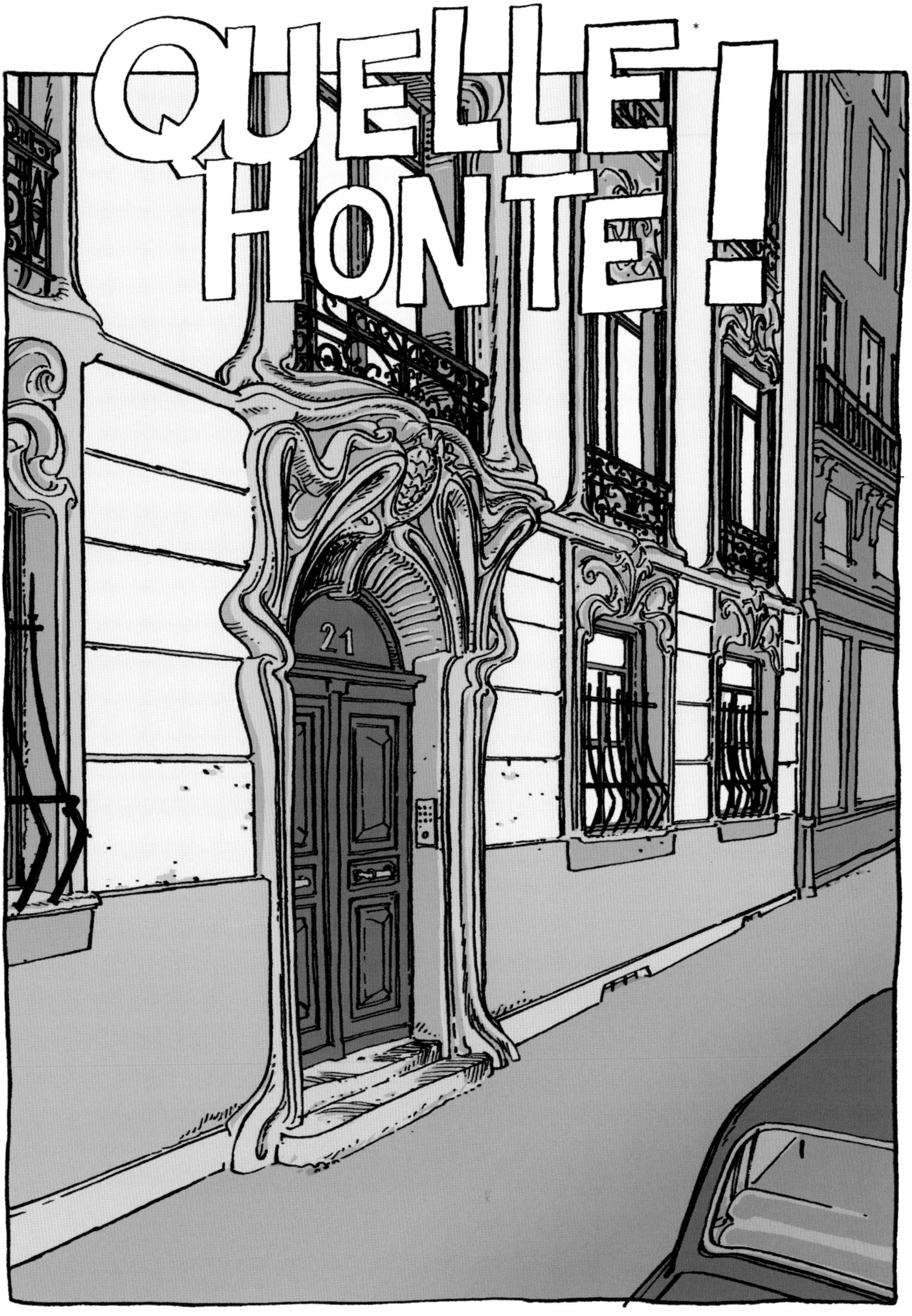
QUELLE HONTE!*
21

*SHAME ON YOU!

MRS. SIMONEAU IS A THOROUGHLY RESPECTABLE LADY...

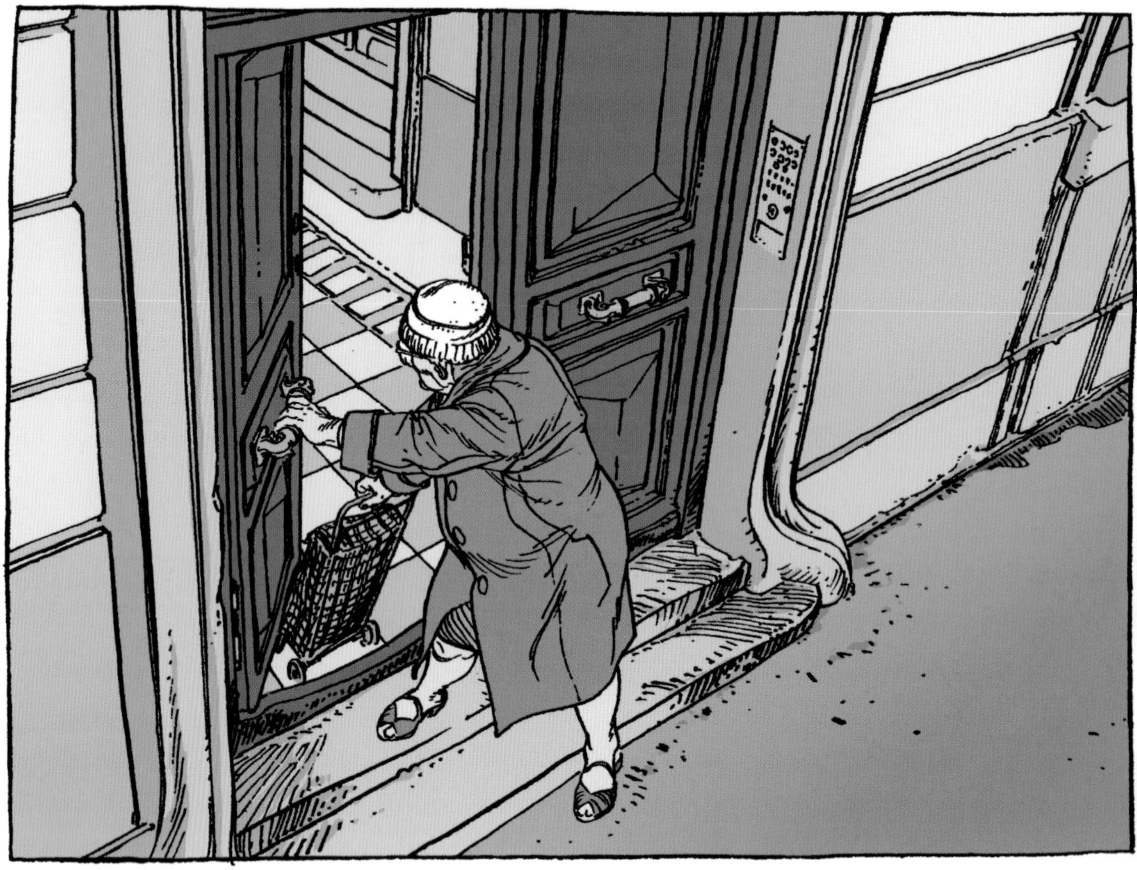

HER LIFE PLAYS OUT AS PRECISELY AS SHEET MUSIC. A TUNE AS CLEAN AS A POLISHED HARDWOOD FLOOR AND TIGHT AS A GIRDLE.

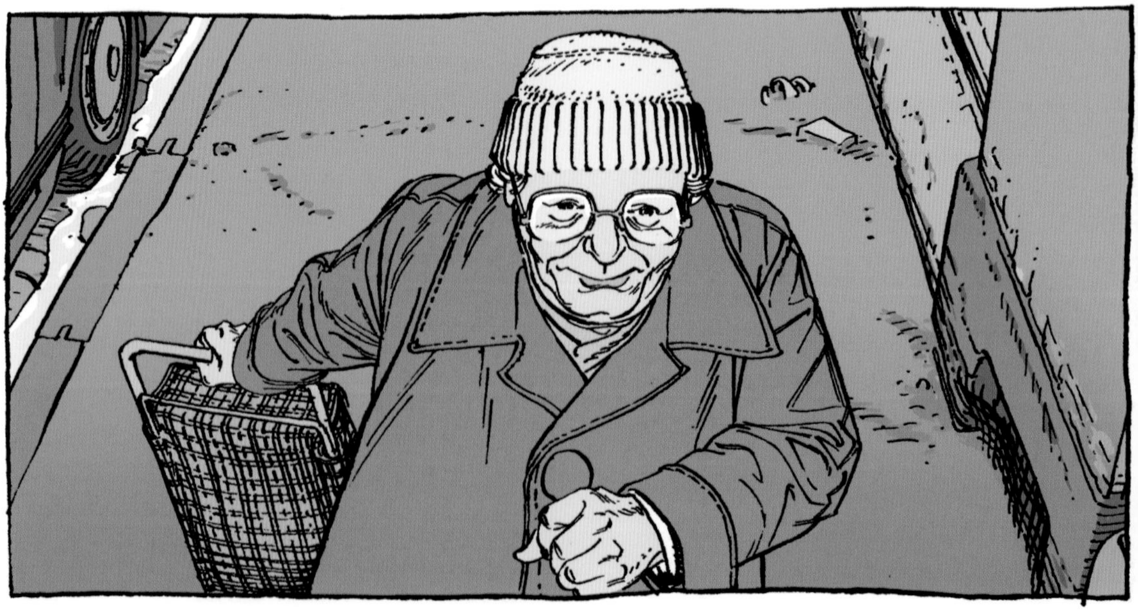

EACH DAY GOD GRACES US WITH HER PRESENCE AS SHE WALKS THROUGH HER NEIGHBORHOOD, SPORTING A COAT WITH LARGE BUTTONS. THE UNIFORMITY AND PUNCTUALITY OF HER WALKS HAS A TENACIOUSLY STUBBORN QUALITY.

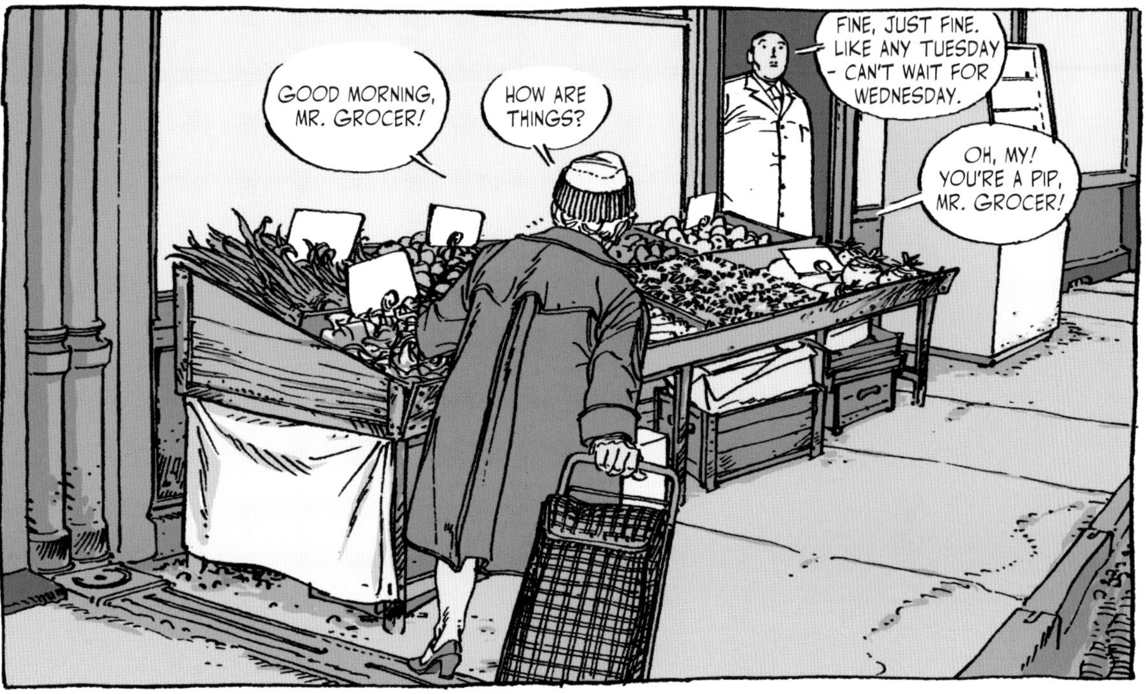
GOOD MORNING, MR. GROCER!
HOW ARE THINGS?
FINE, JUST FINE. LIKE ANY TUESDAY - CAN'T WAIT FOR WEDNESDAY.
OH, MY! YOU'RE A PIP, MR. GROCER!

SHE ONLY BUYS THINGS THAT OTHER PEOPLE BUY, JUST TO AVOID UPSETTING ANYONE.

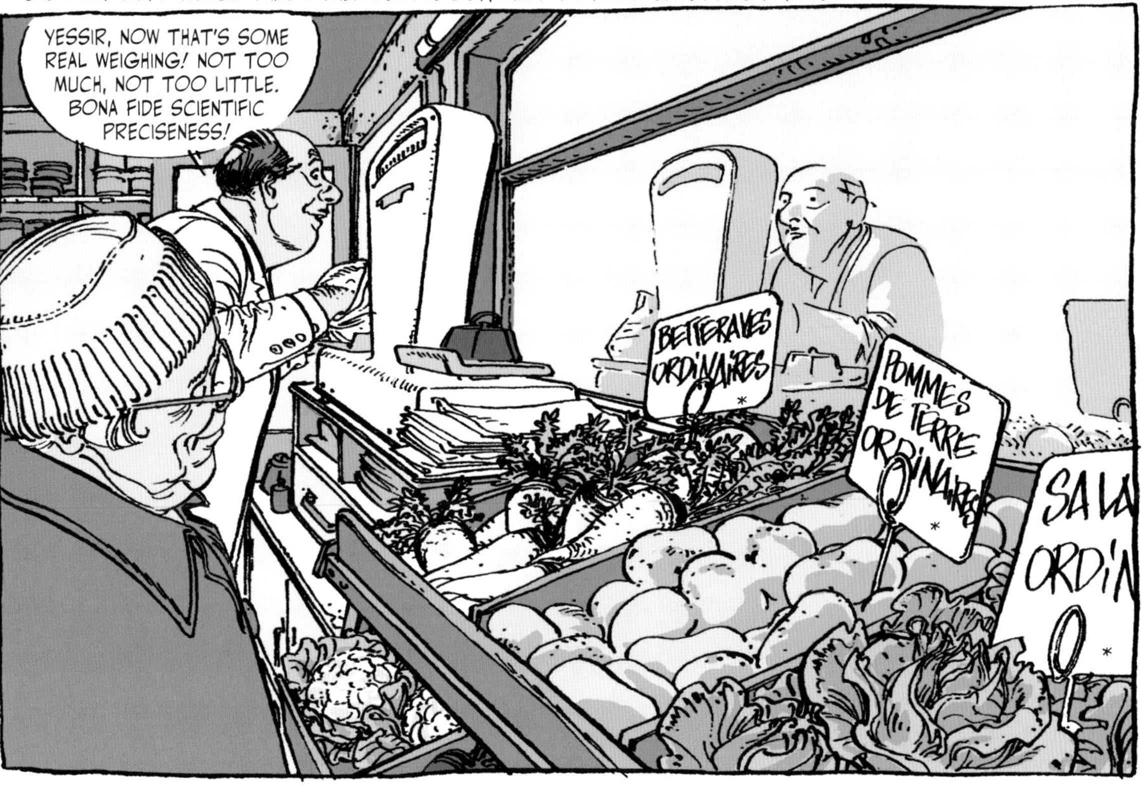
YESSIR, NOW THAT'S SOME REAL WEIGHING! NOT TOO MUCH, NOT TOO LITTLE. BONA FIDE SCIENTIFIC PRECISENESS!
BETTERAVES ORDINAIRES *
POMMES DE TERRE ORDINAIRES *
SALA ORDIN *

*PLAIN BEETS / PLAIN POTATOES / PLAIN LETTUCES

SHE RESUMES HER SELF-APPOINTED ROUNDS, SPRINKLING "GOOD MORNINGS" LIKE BREADCRUMBS ALONG HER PATH...

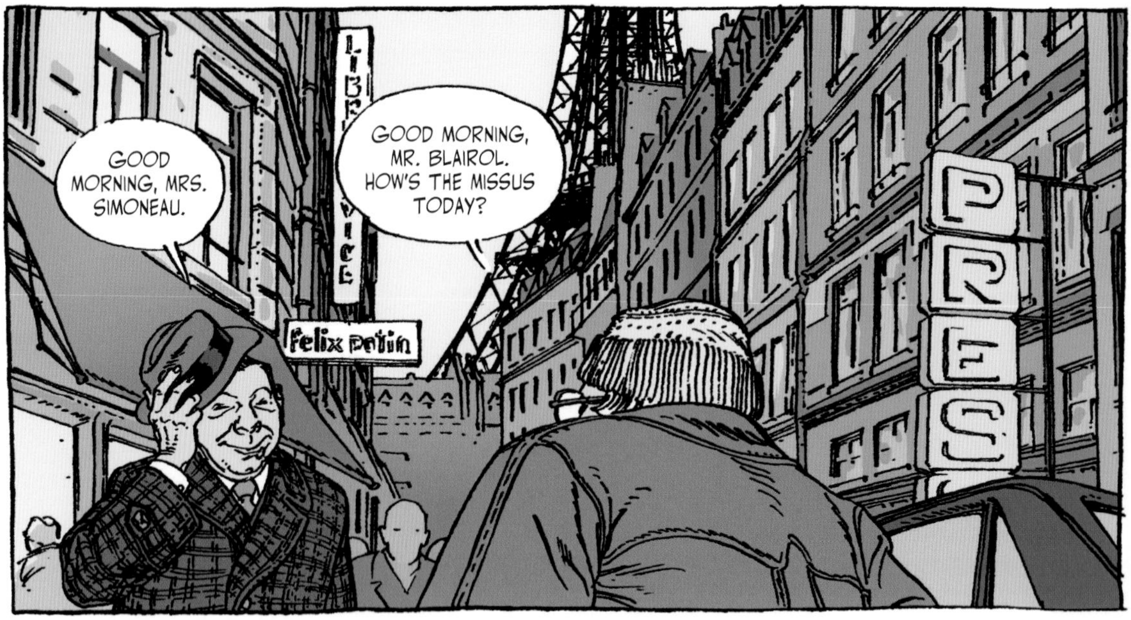
GOOD MORNING, MRS. SIMONEAU.
GOOD MORNING, MR. BLAIROL. HOW'S THE MISSUS TODAY?
felix potin
PRES

NOW, IT'S THE BAKER'S TURN FOR HER DAILY VISIT.

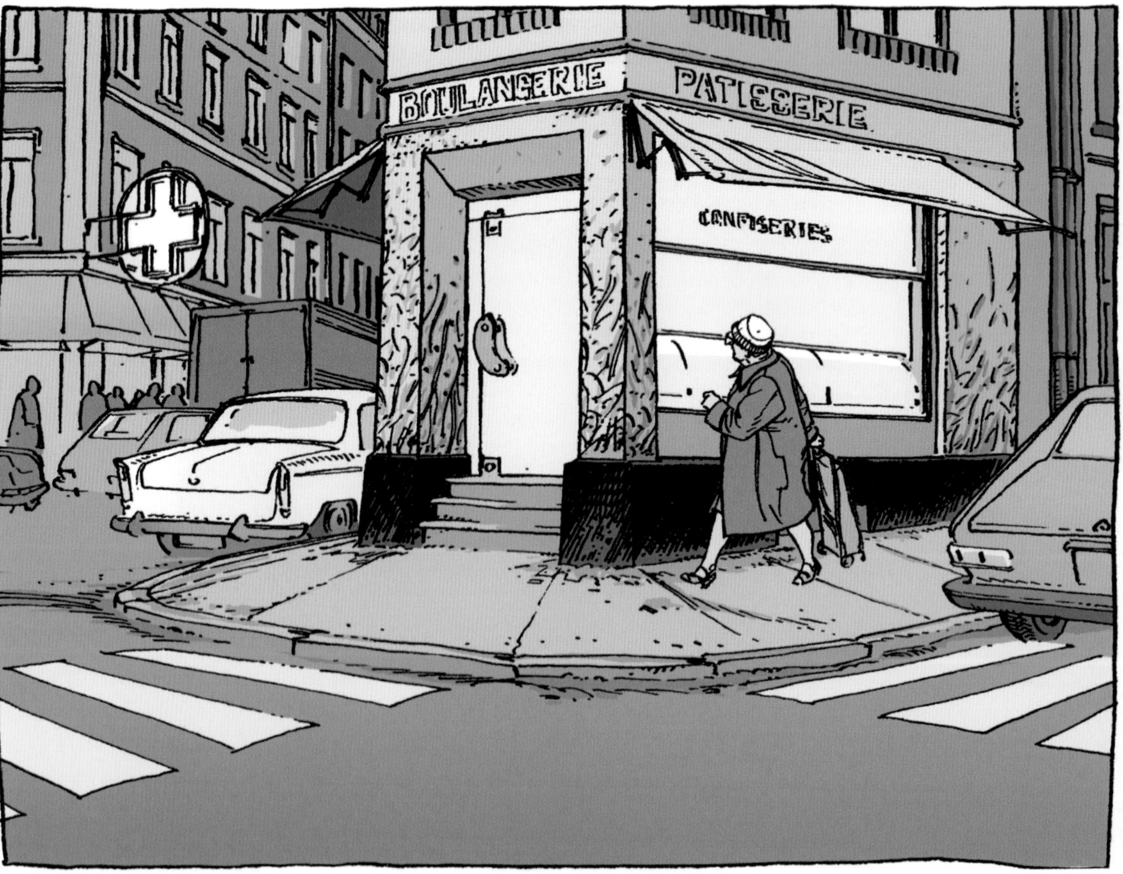
BOULANGERIE
PATISSERIE
CONFISERIES

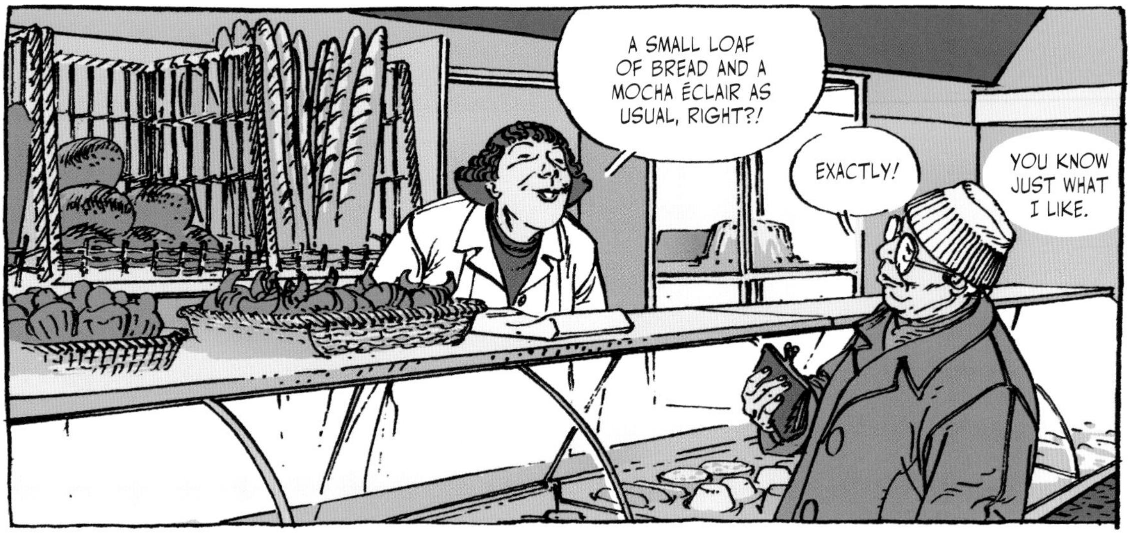
A SMALL LOAF OF BREAD AND A MOCHA ÉCLAIR AS USUAL, RIGHT?!
EXACTLY!
YOU KNOW JUST WHAT I LIKE.

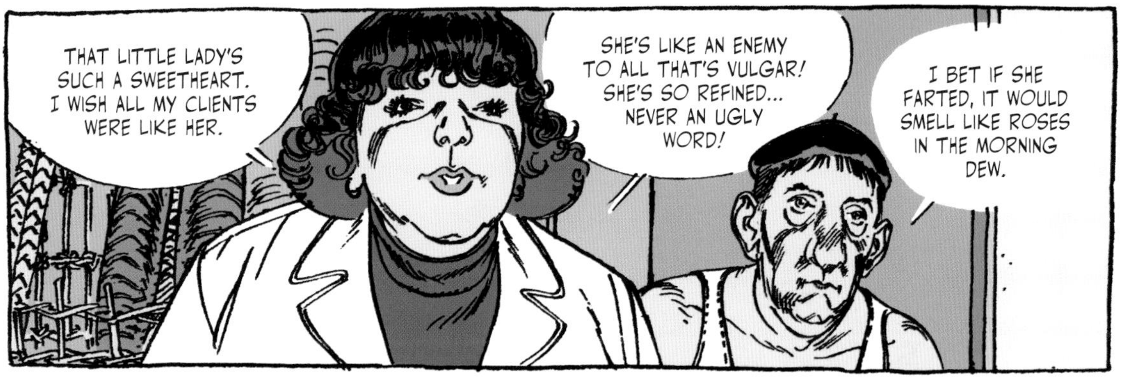
THAT LITTLE LADY'S SUCH A SWEETHEART. I WISH ALL MY CLIENTS WERE LIKE HER.
SHE'S LIKE AN ENEMY TO ALL THAT'S VULGAR! SHE'S SO REFINED... NEVER AN UGLY WORD!
I BET IF SHE FARTED, IT WOULD SMELL LIKE ROSES IN THE MORNING DEW.

SHE CONTINUES TO TREAD HER PERPETUAL PATH WITH A SURGEON'S PRECISION.

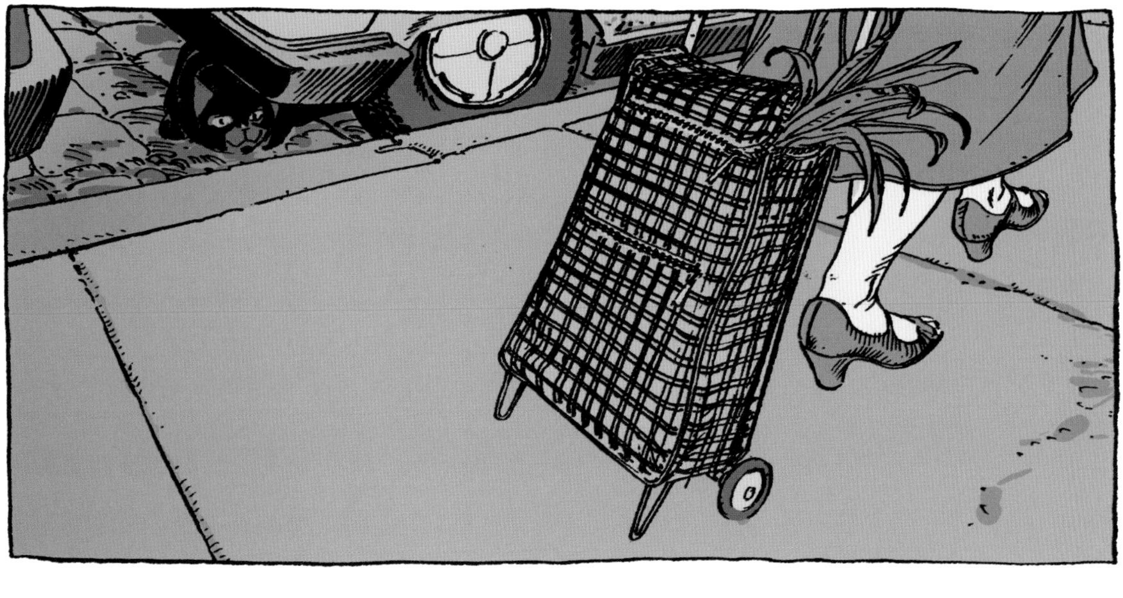

BUT MRS. SIMONEAU IS NOT THE ONLY ONE. MR. ROLIN SHARES THE SAME CURIOUS QUIRKS.

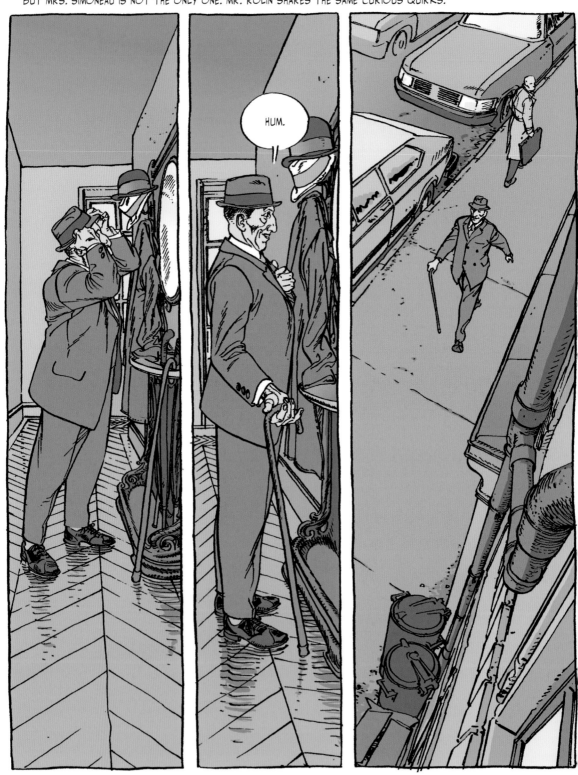

HIS ROUTE STARTS AT MARECHAL FOCH PARK.

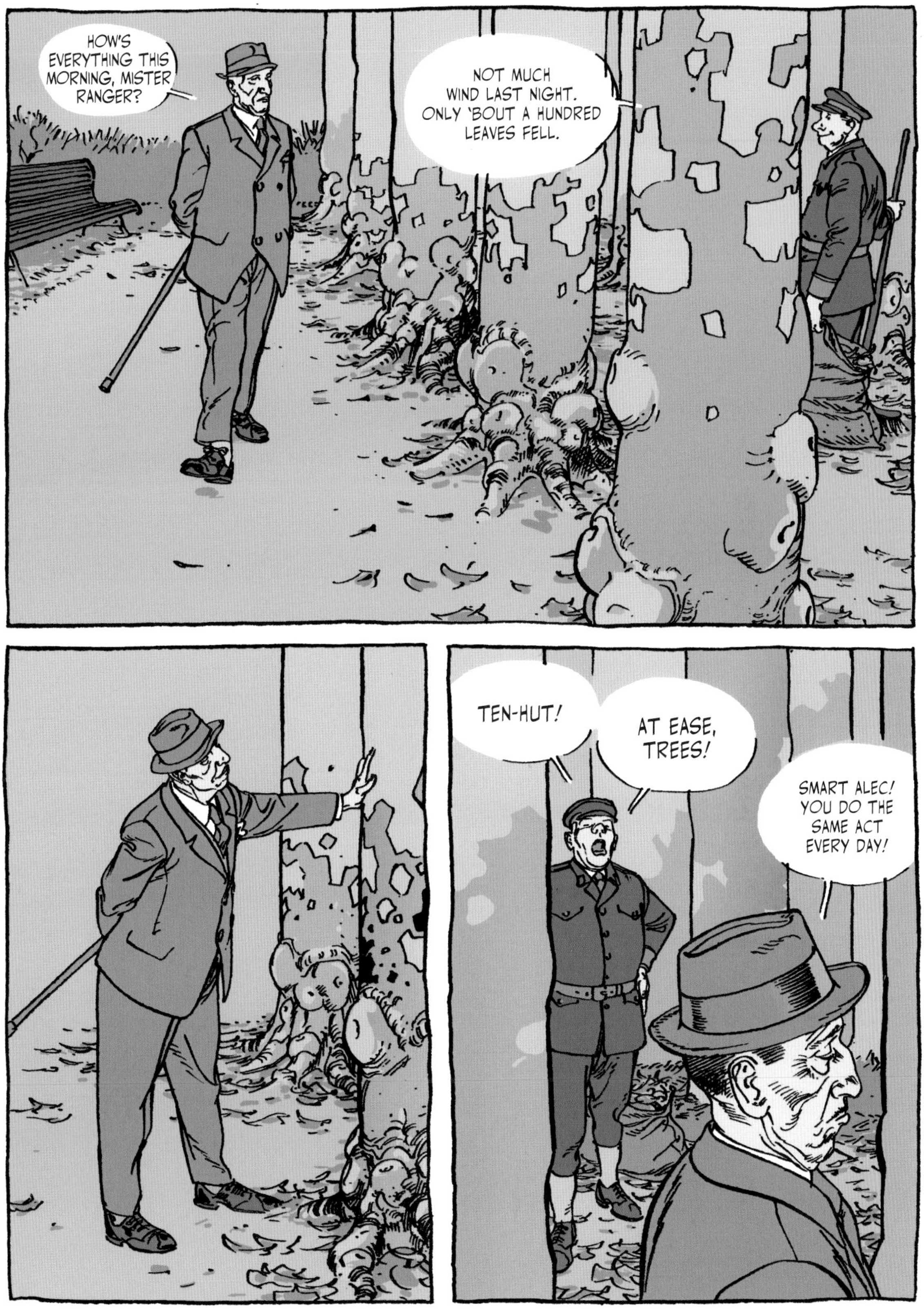
HOW'S EVERYTHING THIS MORNING, MISTER RANGER?
NOT MUCH WIND LAST NIGHT. ONLY 'BOUT A HUNDRED LEAVES FELL.
TEN-HUT!
AT EASE, TREES!
SMART ALEC! YOU DO THE SAME ACT EVERY DAY!

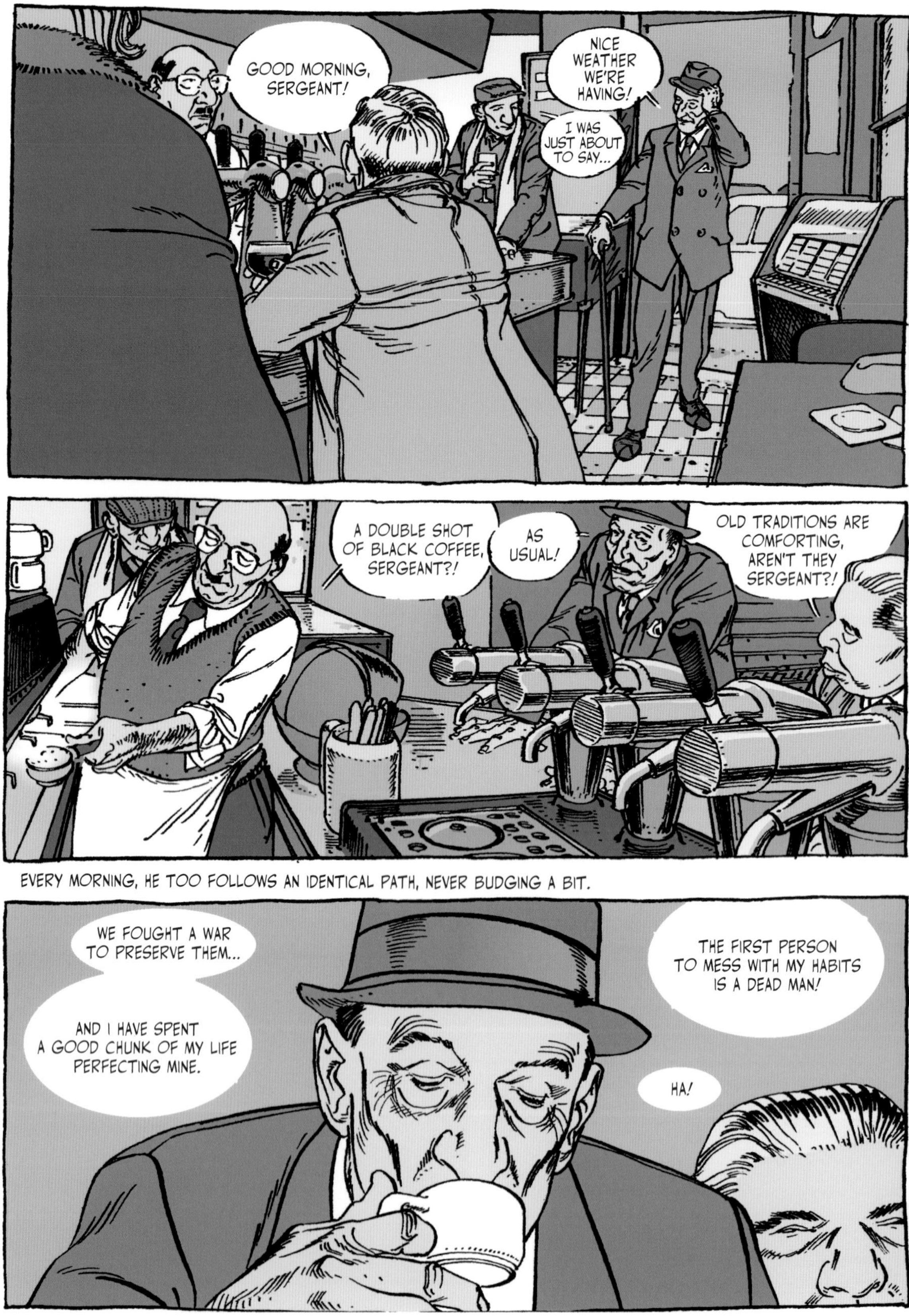
GOOD MORNING, SERGEANT!
NICE WEATHER WE'RE HAVING!
I WAS JUST ABOUT TO SAY...
A DOUBLE SHOT OF BLACK COFFEE, SERGEANT?!
AS USUAL!
OLD TRADITIONS ARE COMFORTING, AREN'T THEY SERGEANT?!
EVERY MORNING, HE TOO FOLLOWS AN IDENTICAL PATH, NEVER BUDGING A BIT.
WE FOUGHT A WAR TO PRESERVE THEM...
AND I HAVE SPENT A GOOD CHUNK OF MY LIFE PERFECTING MINE.
THE FIRST PERSON TO MESS WITH MY HABITS IS A DEAD MAN!
HA!

SOMETIMES, MRS. SIMONEAU AND MR. ROLIN SHAMELESSLY CROSS PATHS.

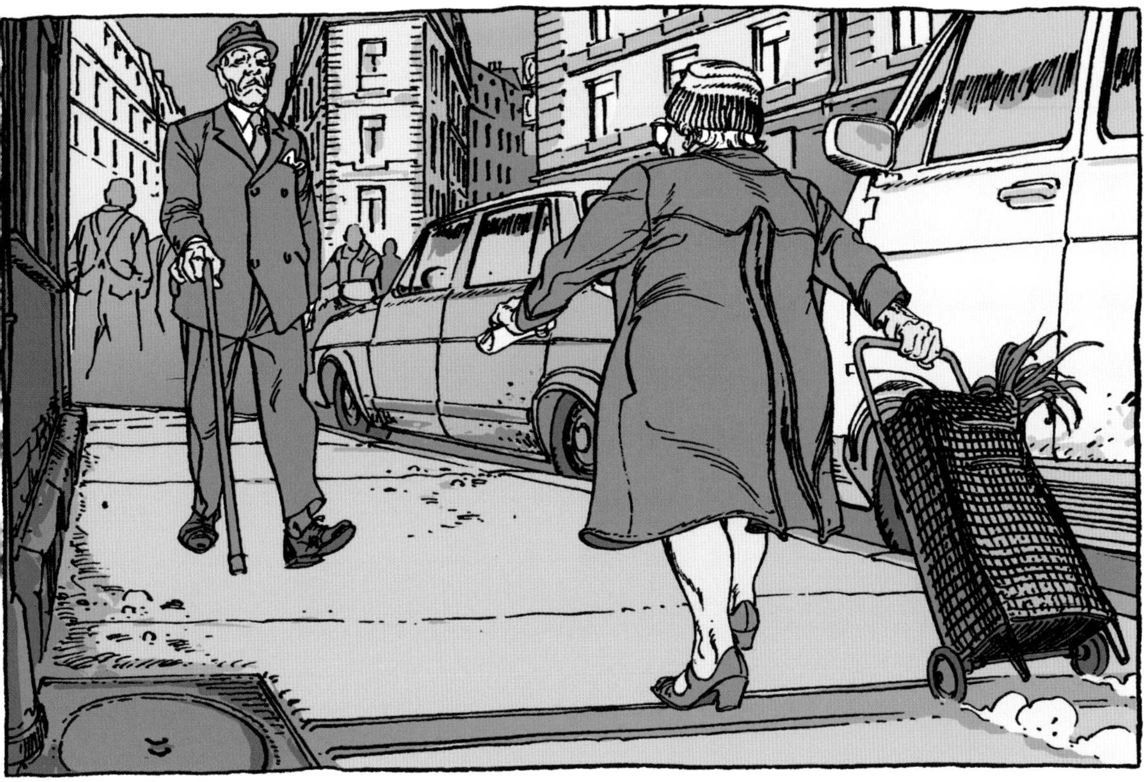

THEY EXCHANGE PERFECTLY DIGNIFIED SALUTATIONS, AS IF NOTHING WAS GOING ON...

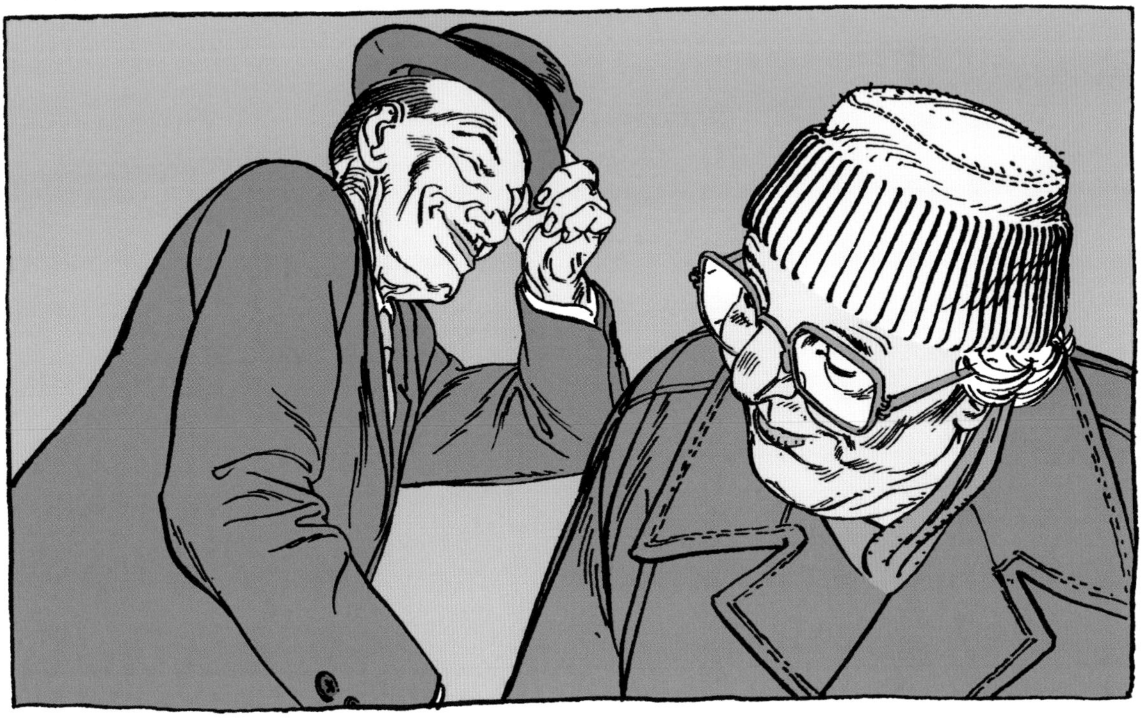

BUT LET'S STEP AWAY FROM THIS SCENE...AND CHECK OUT A BIRD'S EYE VIEW OF THE NEIGHBORHOOD.

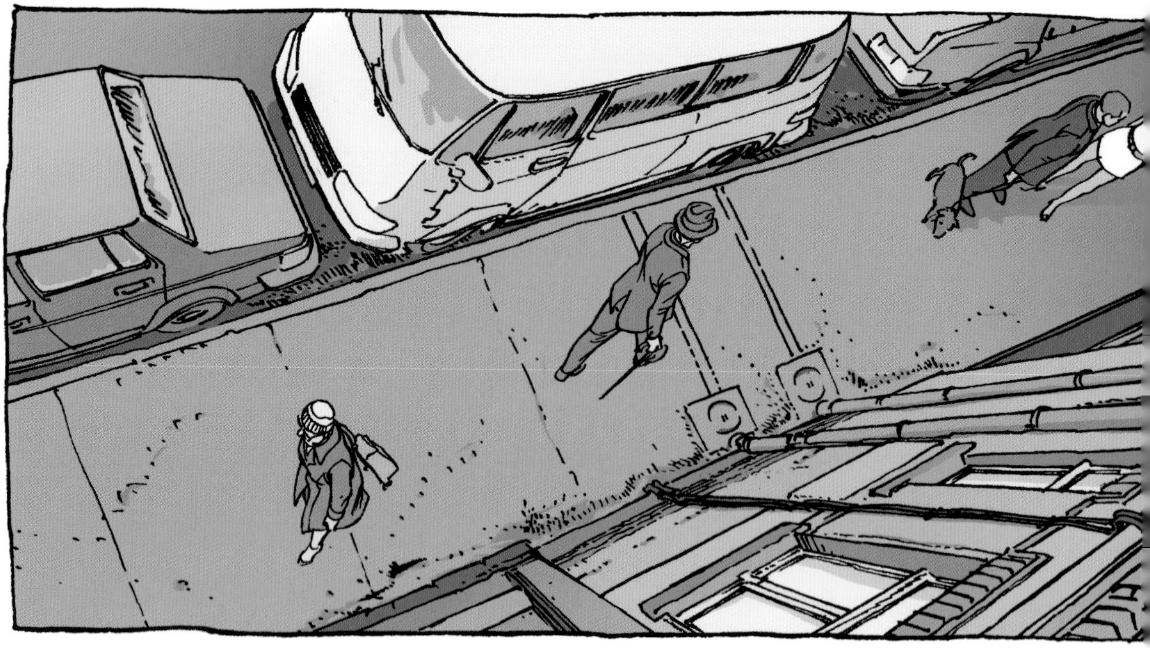

TO AVOID ANY COMPLICATIONS ASSOCIATED WITH LAWS SPECIFIC TO THE UNITED STATES OF AMERICA, WE KINDLY ADVISE THE READER TO GRAB A PEN AND USE IT TO CONNECT THE DOTS IN NUMERIC ORDER IN THE FOLLOWING PANELS.

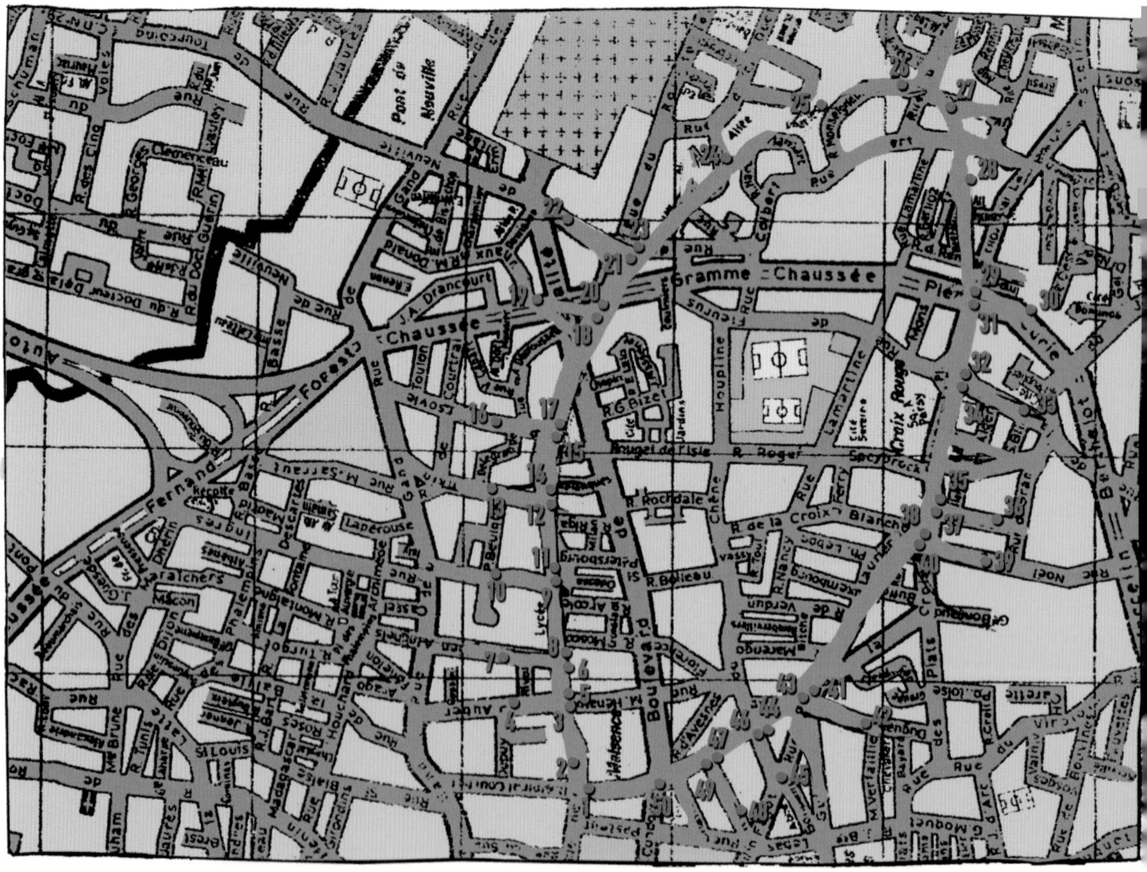
Pont de Neuville
Rue Colbert
Gramme
Chaussée
Rue Lamartine
R. Rochdale
R. de la Croix Blanche
Boulevard

IF WE FOLLOW MRS. SIMONEAU'S PATH ON A MAP, WE'RE STRUCK BY THE PECULIAR SHAPE IT TAKES: A SHAPE IMPOSSIBLE TO SEE FROM GROUND LEVEL. YET ONE THAT BRINGS TO MIND ANOTHER SHAPE THAT THE READER IS WELL ACQUAINTED WITH.

NOW, LET'S LOOK AT MR. ROLIN'S MOVEMENTS.

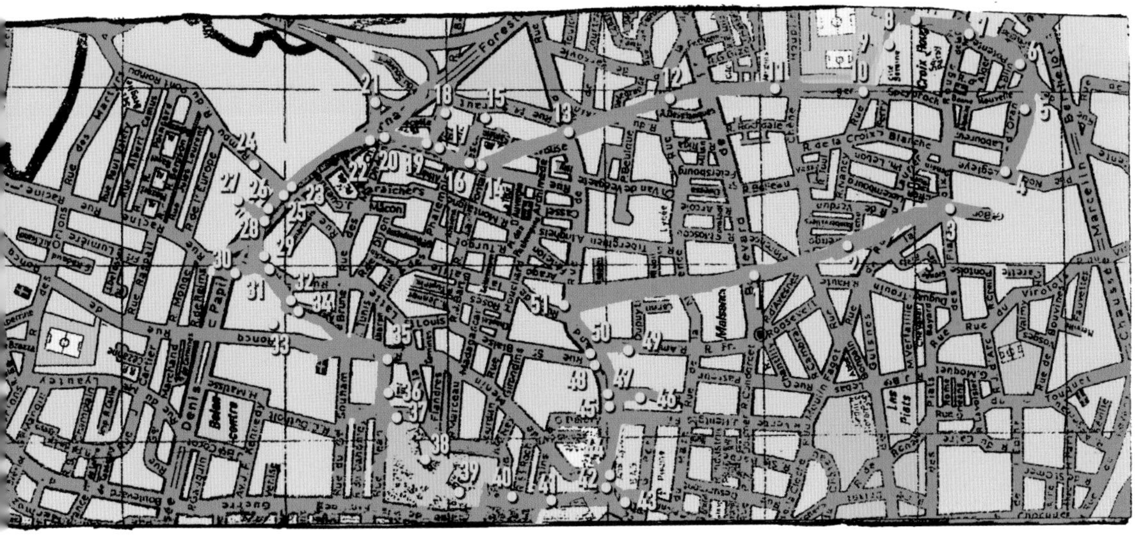

YEP, PRETTY OBVIOUS!

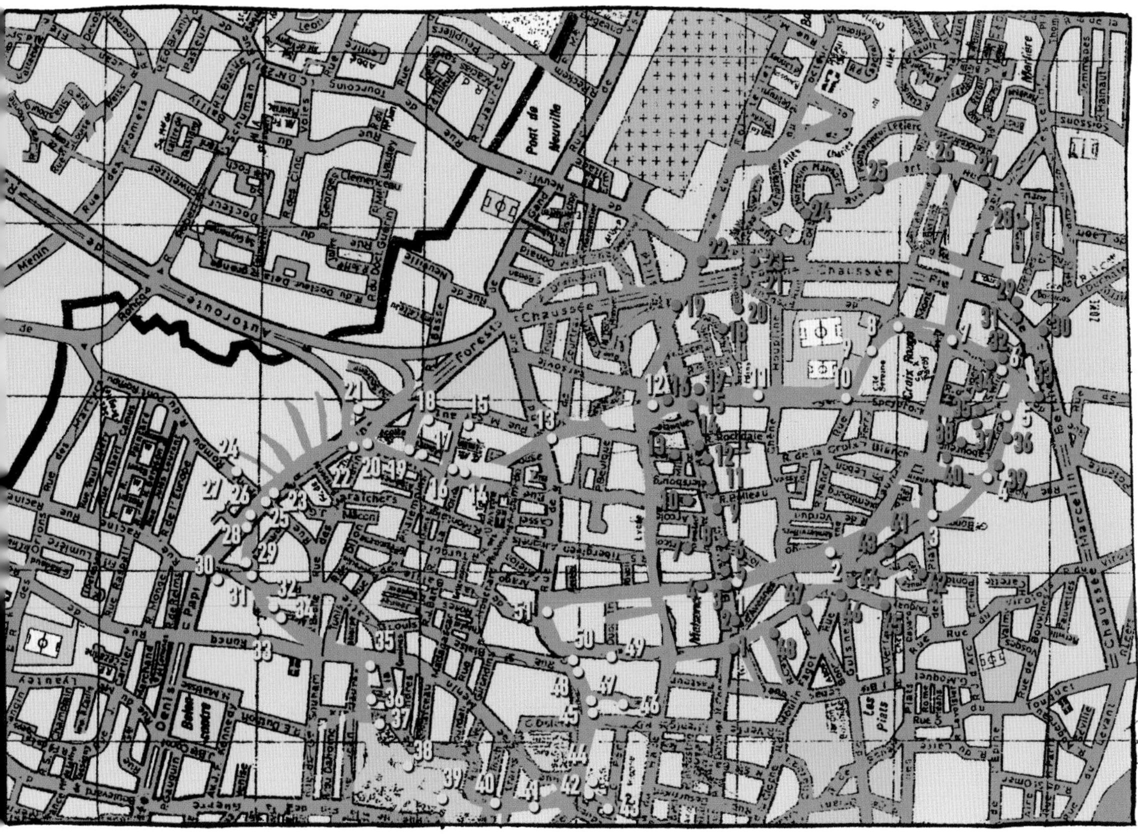

ALL THAT'S LEFT IS TO SUPERIMPOSE THE TWO SHAPES. THEY FIT TOGETHER PERFECTLY.

IMAGINE THE STATE OF OUR PLANET IF OTHER WACKOS DECIDED TO PLAY THE SAME GAME. OUR PLANET WOULD BECOME A CANVAS FOR FILTHY VIRTUAL GRAFFITI...

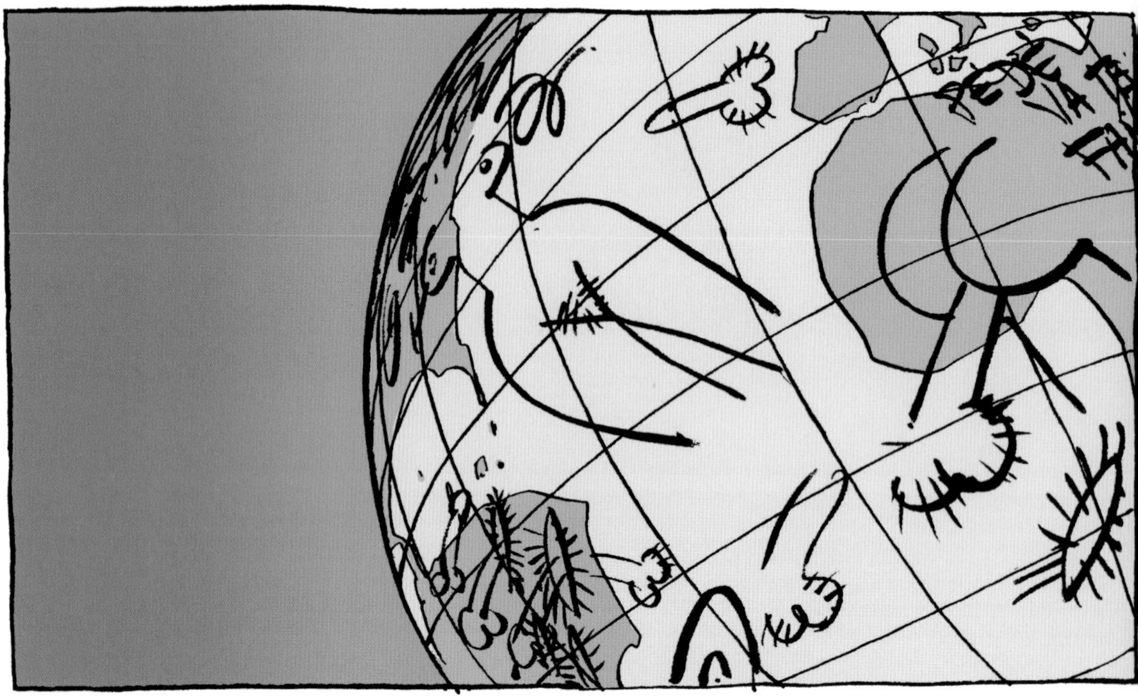

SHAME ON YOU TWO, TO HIDE SUCH PERVERSION BENEATH YOUR GOOD MANNERS!

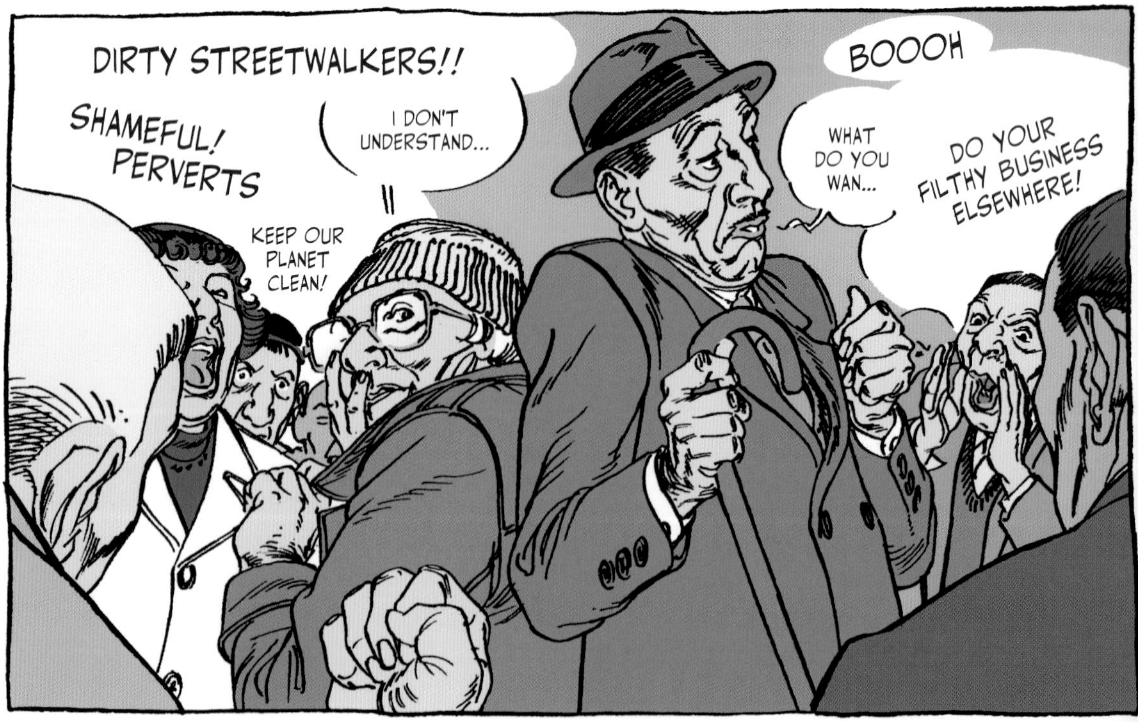
DIRTY STREETWALKERS!!
SHAMEFUL! PERVERTS
I DON'T UNDERSTAND...
!!
KEEP OUR PLANET CLEAN!
BOOOH
WHAT DO YOU WAN...
DO YOUR FILTHY BUSINESS ELSEWHERE!

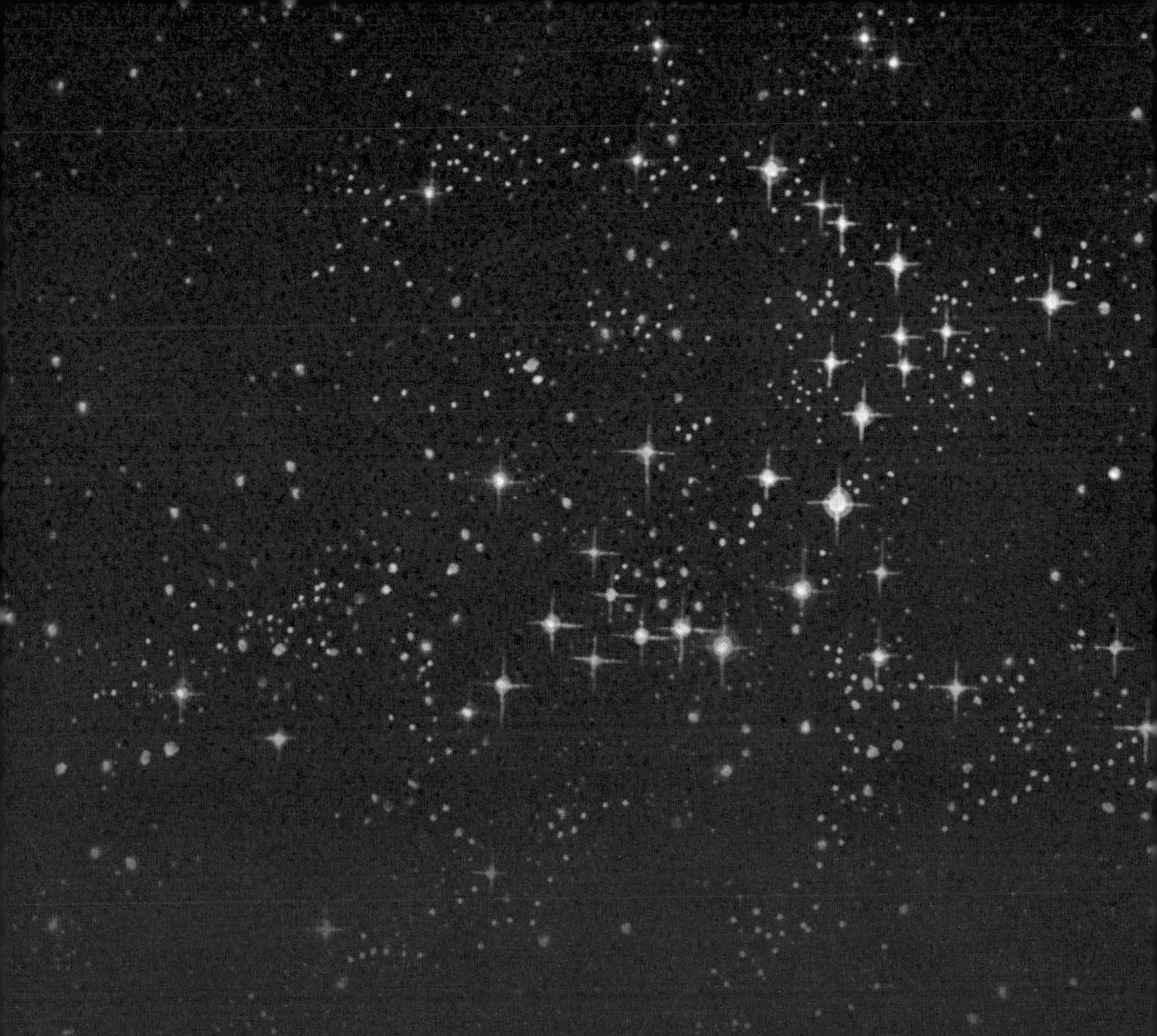

CALL TO ARMS

Story by RICK SPEARS
Art by ROB G.

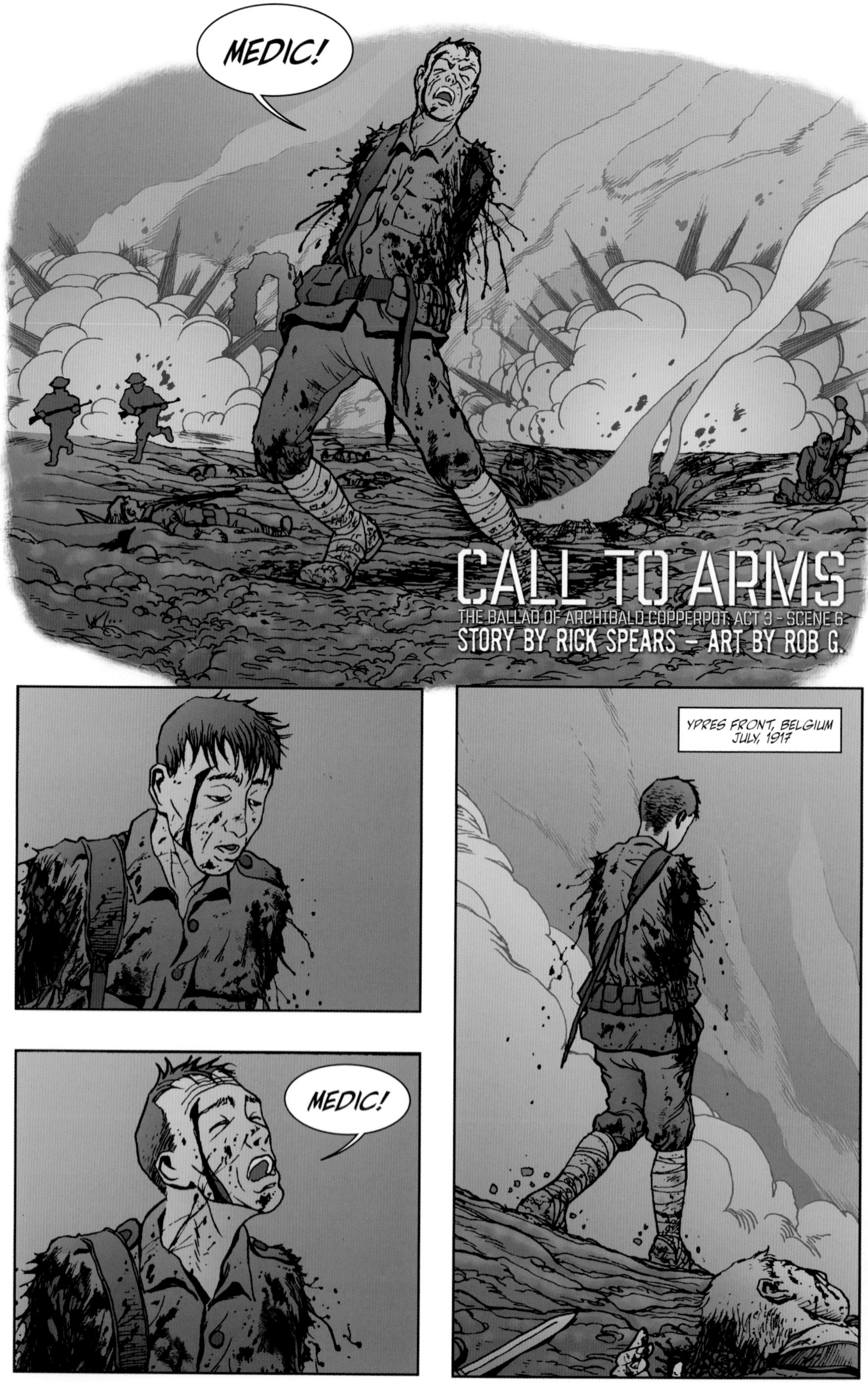

MEDIC!
CALL TO ARMS
THE BALLAD OF ARCHIBALD COPPERPOT: ACT 3 - SCENE 6
STORY BY RICK SPEARS – ART BY ROB G.
YPRES FRONT, BELGIUM JULY, 1917
MEDIC!

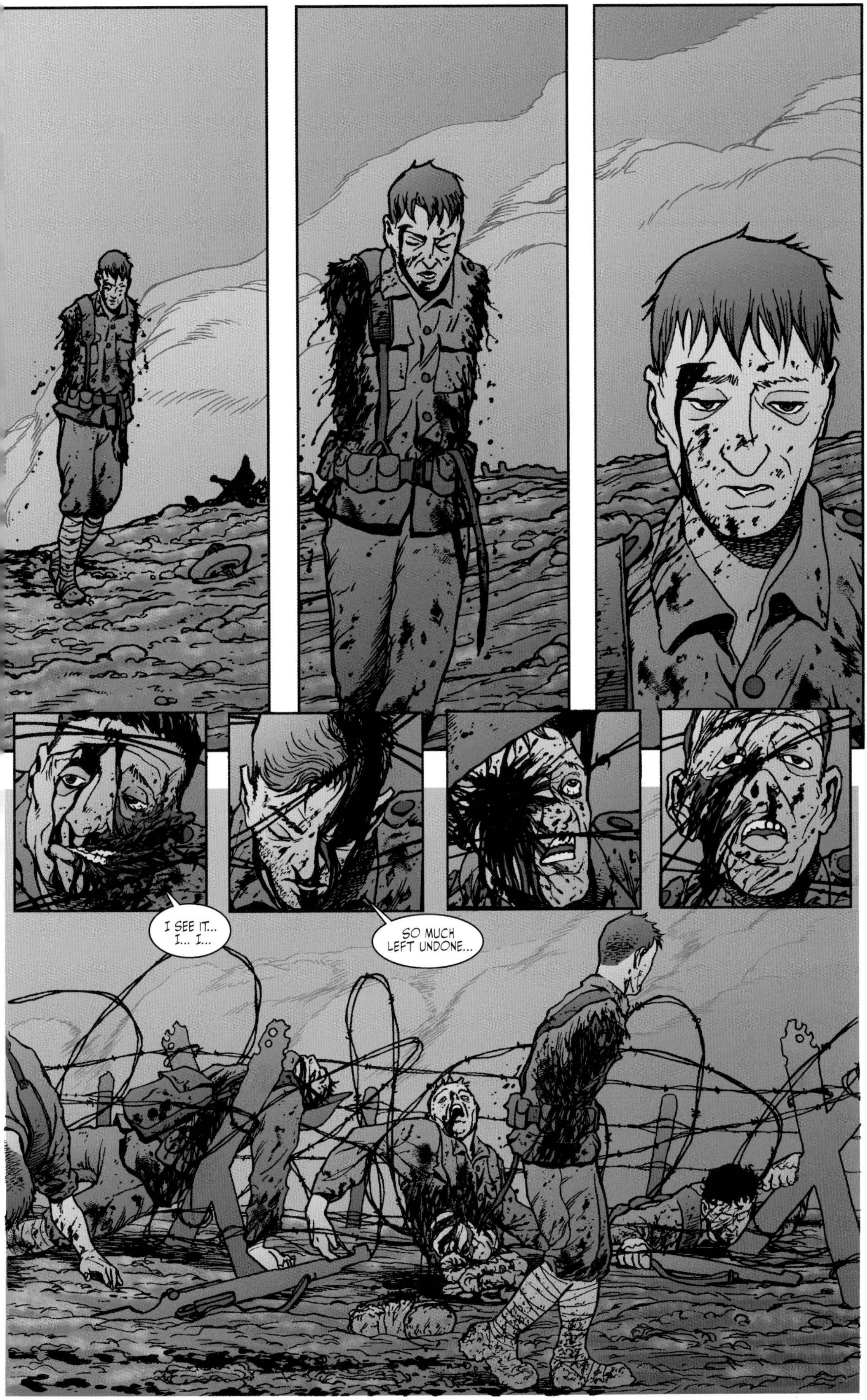
I SEE IT...
I... I...
SO MUCH
LEFT UNDONE...

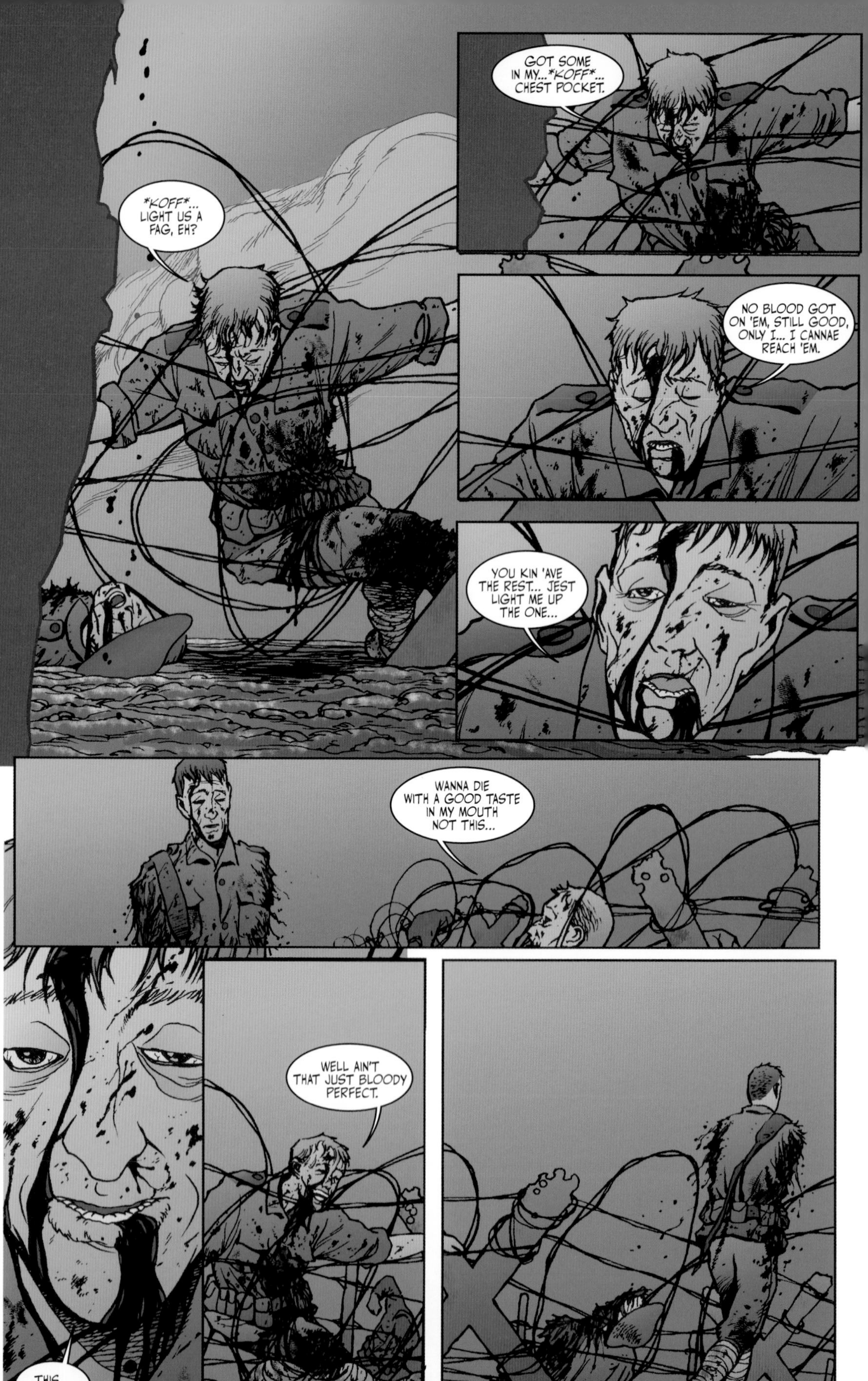
KOFF... LIGHT US A FAG, EH?
GOT SOME IN MY...*KOFF*... CHEST POCKET.
NO BLOOD GOT ON 'EM, STILL GOOD, ONLY I... I CANNAE REACH 'EM.
YOU KIN 'AVE THE REST... JEST LIGHT ME UP THE ONE...
WANNA DIE WITH A GOOD TASTE IN MY MOUTH NOT THIS...
THIS... SHITE.
WELL AIN'T THAT JUST BLOODY PERFECT.

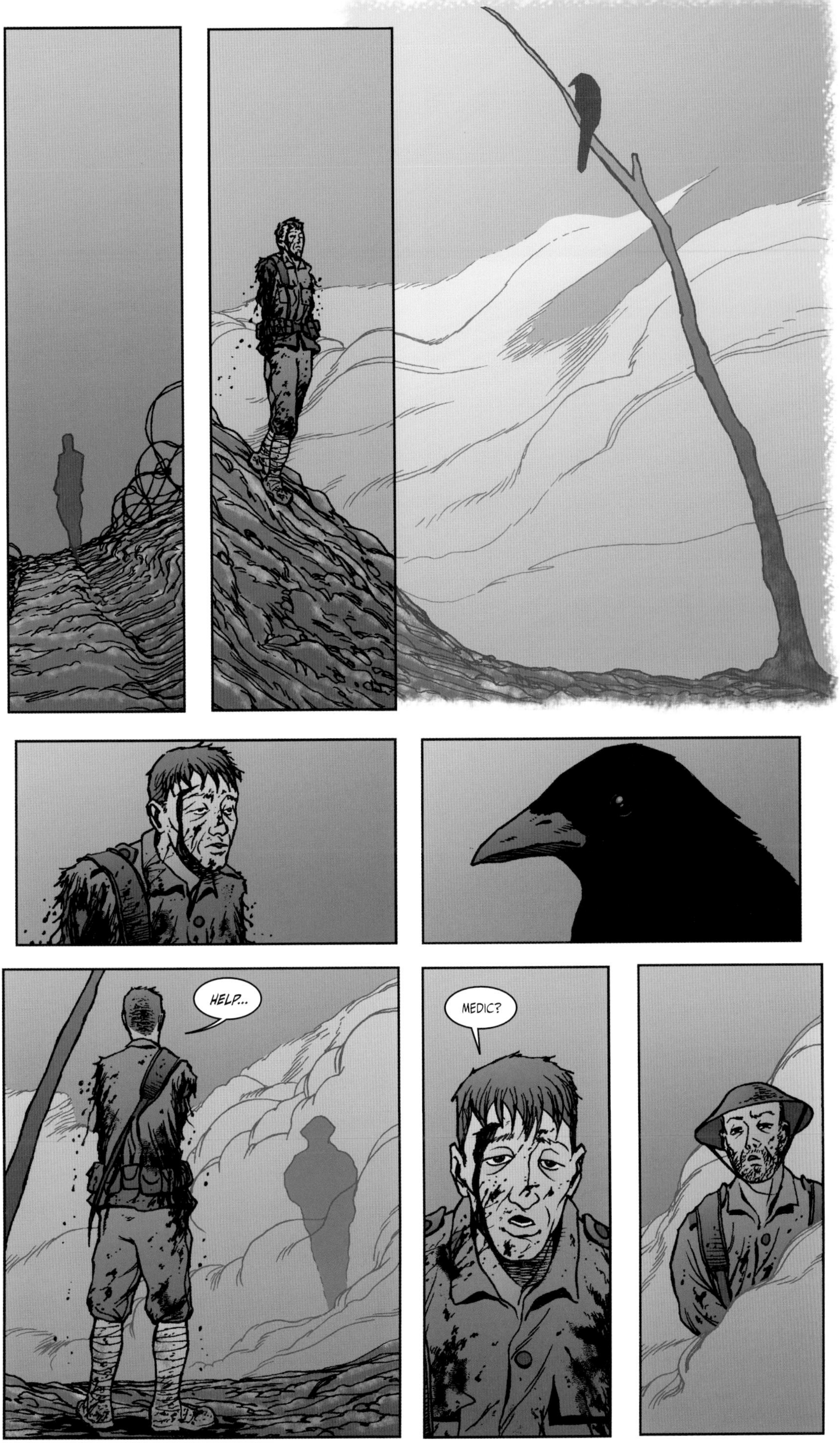
HELP...
MEDIC?

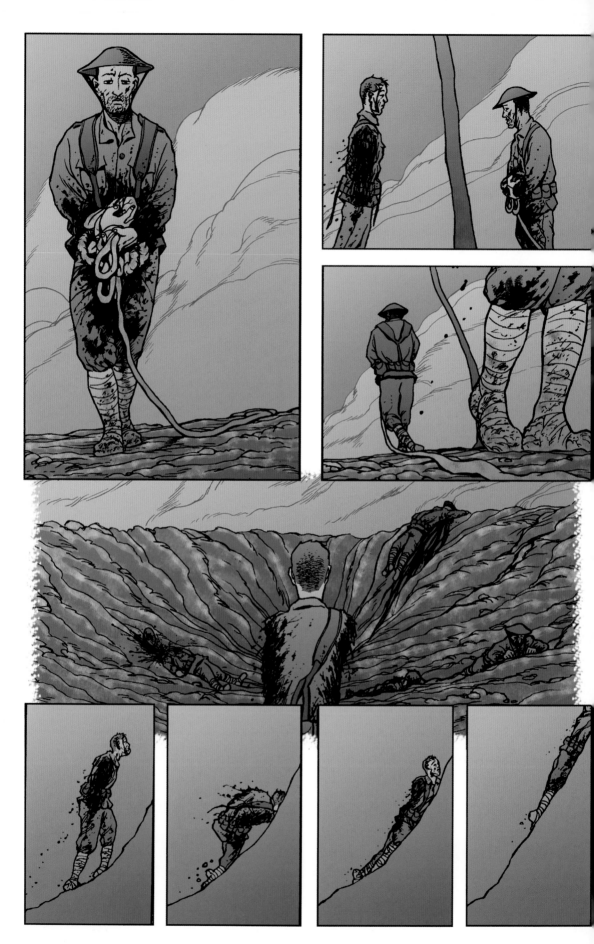

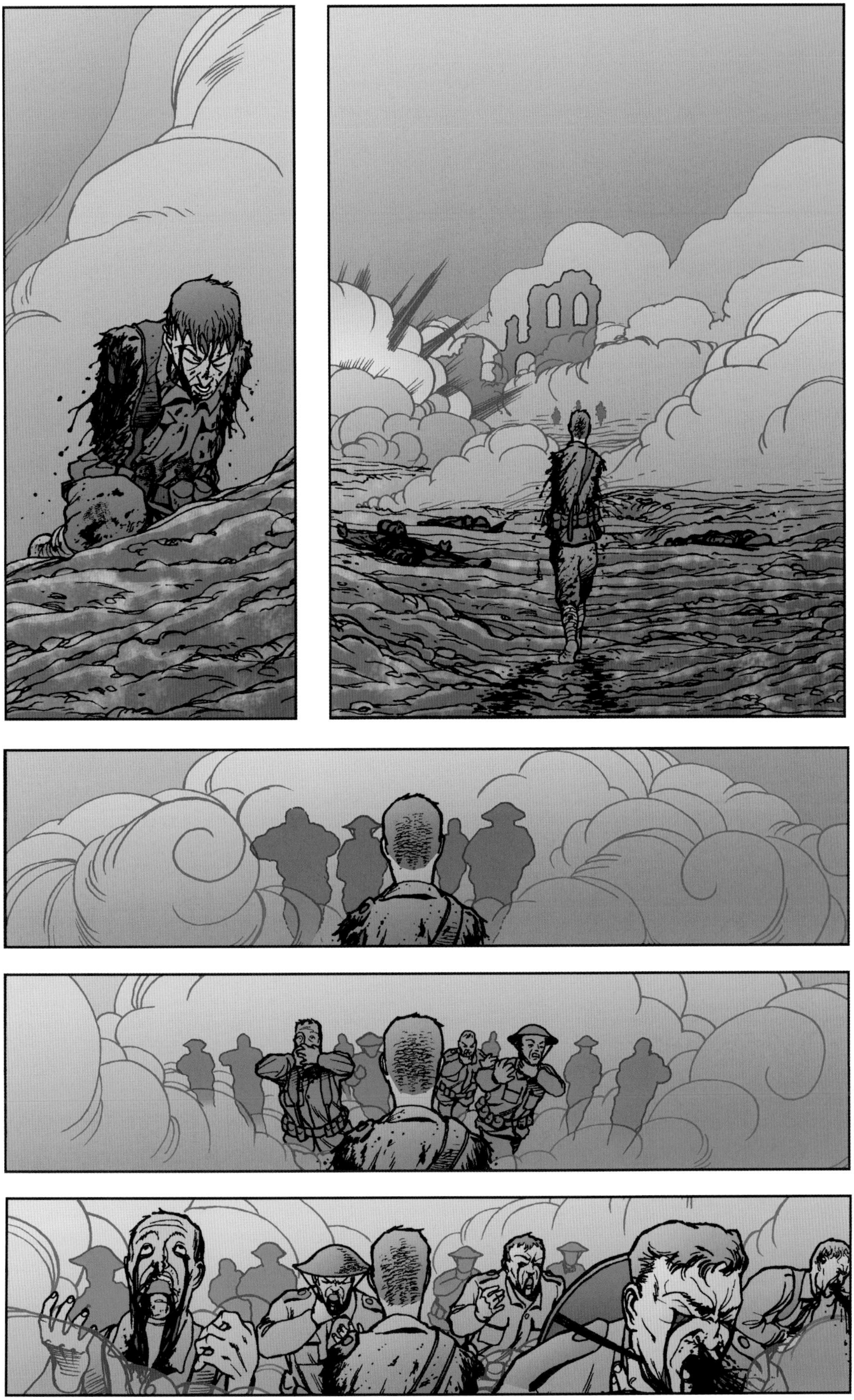

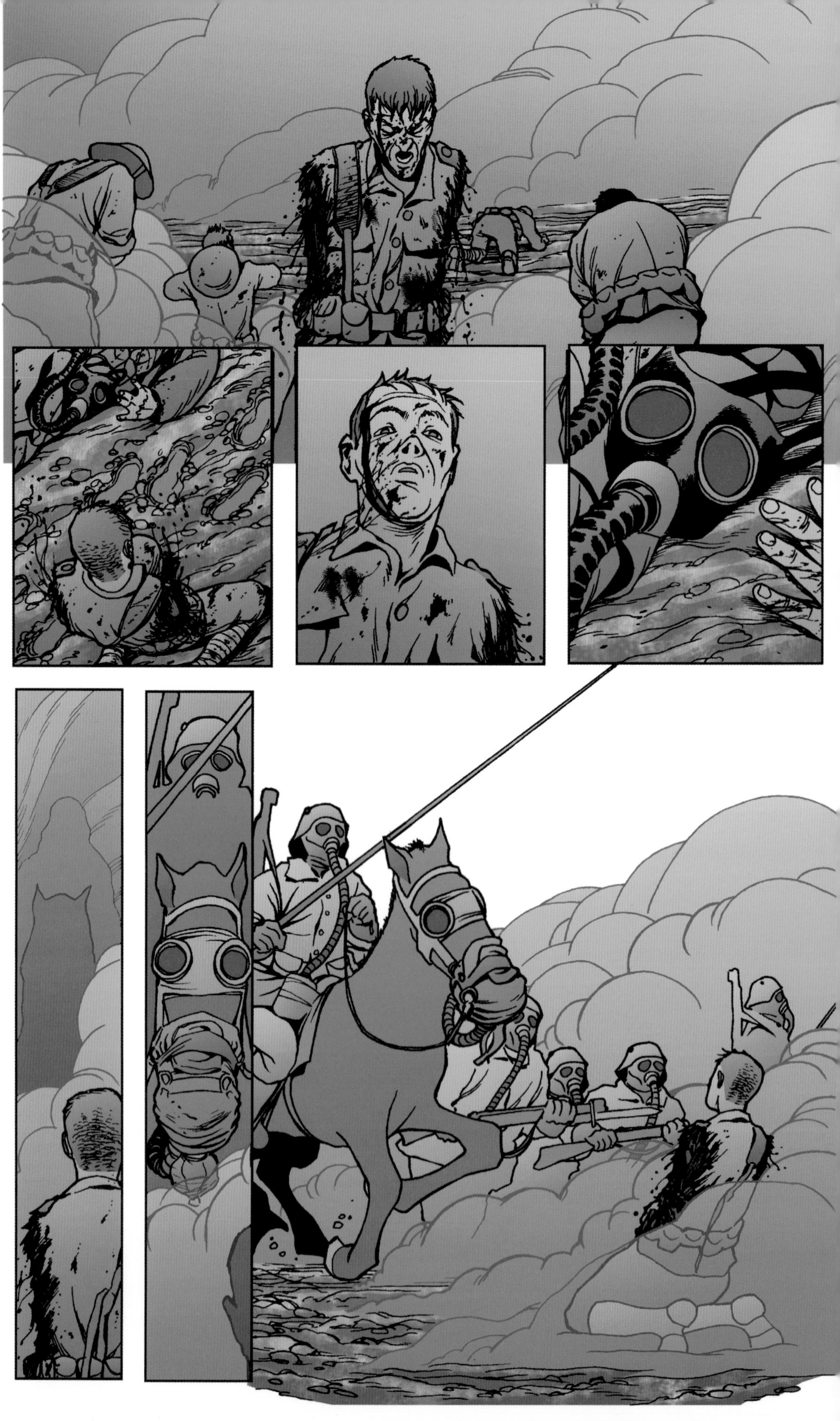

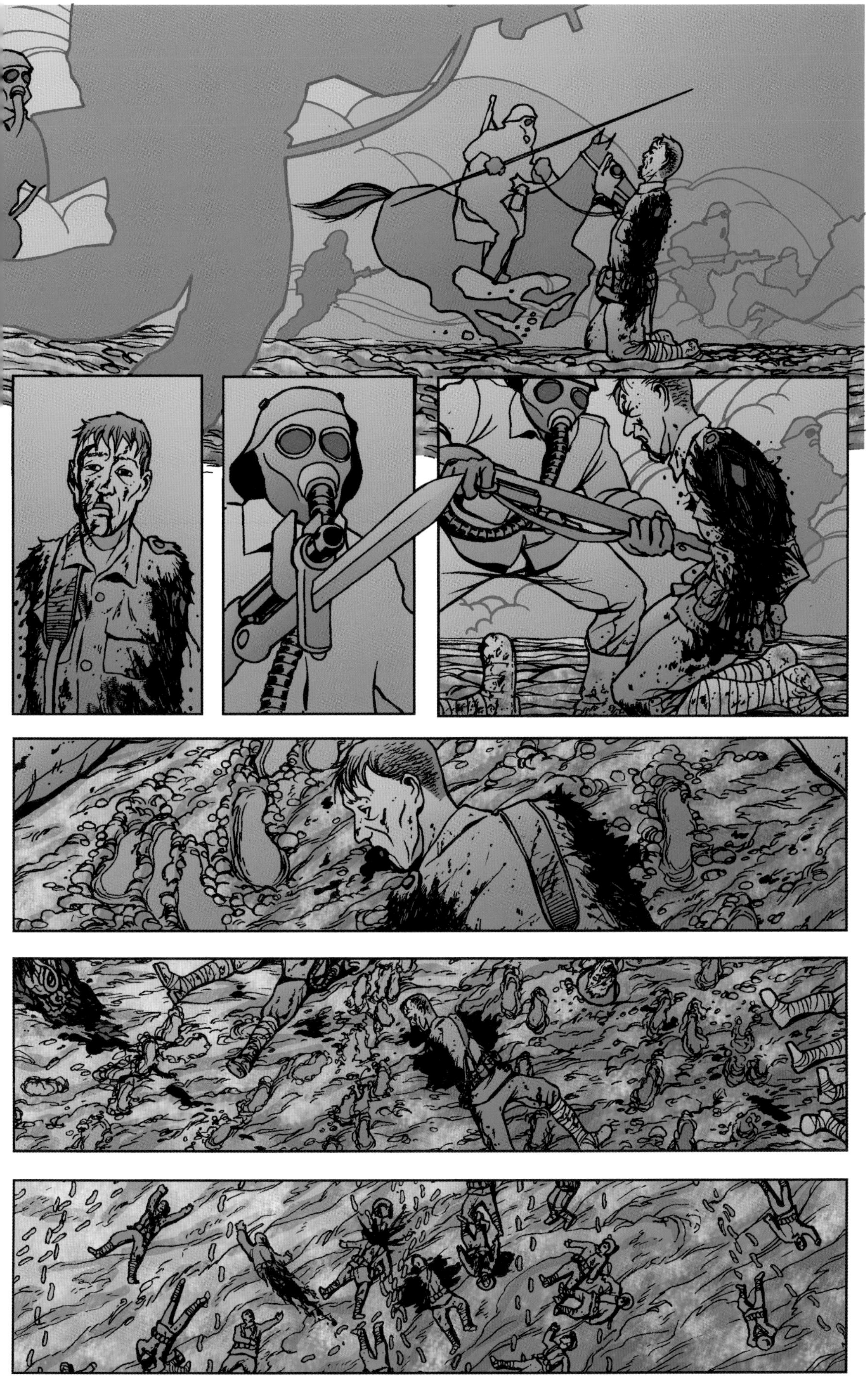

DRAGON OF THE NORTHERN PASS

Story by DAN WICKLINE
Art by JASEN RODRIGUEZ
Pencils by SCOTT BENEFIEL
Colors by CHARLIE KIRCHOFF

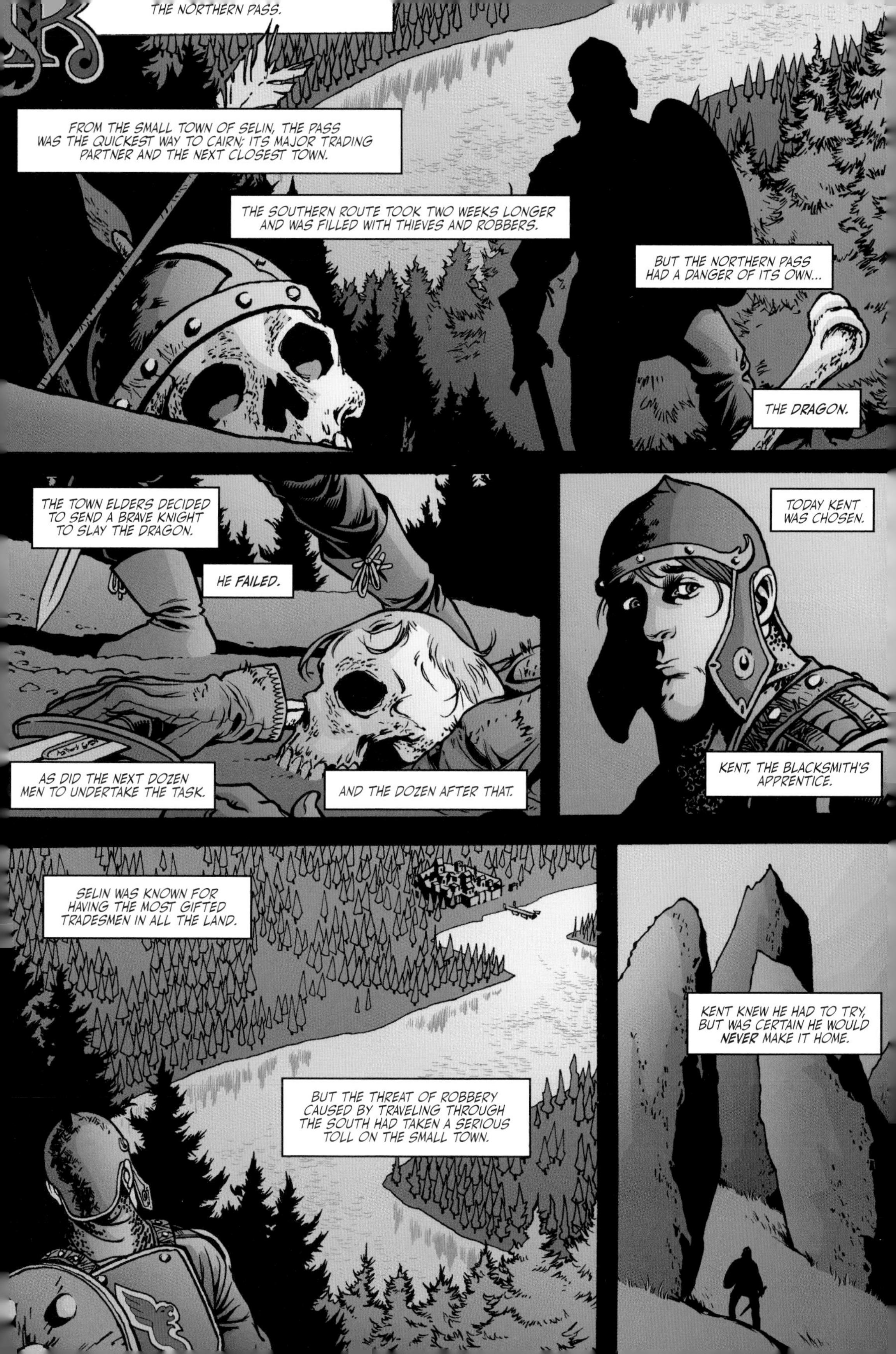

THE NORTHERN PASS.
FROM THE SMALL TOWN OF SELIN, THE PASS WAS THE QUICKEST WAY TO CAIRN; ITS MAJOR TRADING PARTNER AND THE NEXT CLOSEST TOWN.
THE SOUTHERN ROUTE TOOK TWO WEEKS LONGER AND WAS FILLED WITH THIEVES AND ROBBERS.
BUT THE NORTHERN PASS HAD A DANGER OF ITS OWN...
THE DRAGON.
THE TOWN ELDERS DECIDED TO SEND A BRAVE KNIGHT TO SLAY THE DRAGON.
HE FAILED.
AS DID THE NEXT DOZEN MEN TO UNDERTAKE THE TASK.
AND THE DOZEN AFTER THAT.
TODAY KENT WAS CHOSEN.
KENT, THE BLACKSMITH'S APPRENTICE.
SELIN WAS KNOWN FOR HAVING THE MOST GIFTED TRADESMEN IN ALL THE LAND.
BUT THE THREAT OF ROBBERY CAUSED BY TRAVELING THROUGH THE SOUTH HAD TAKEN A SERIOUS TOLL ON THE SMALL TOWN.
KENT KNEW HE HAD TO TRY, BUT WAS CERTAIN HE WOULD NEVER MAKE IT HOME.

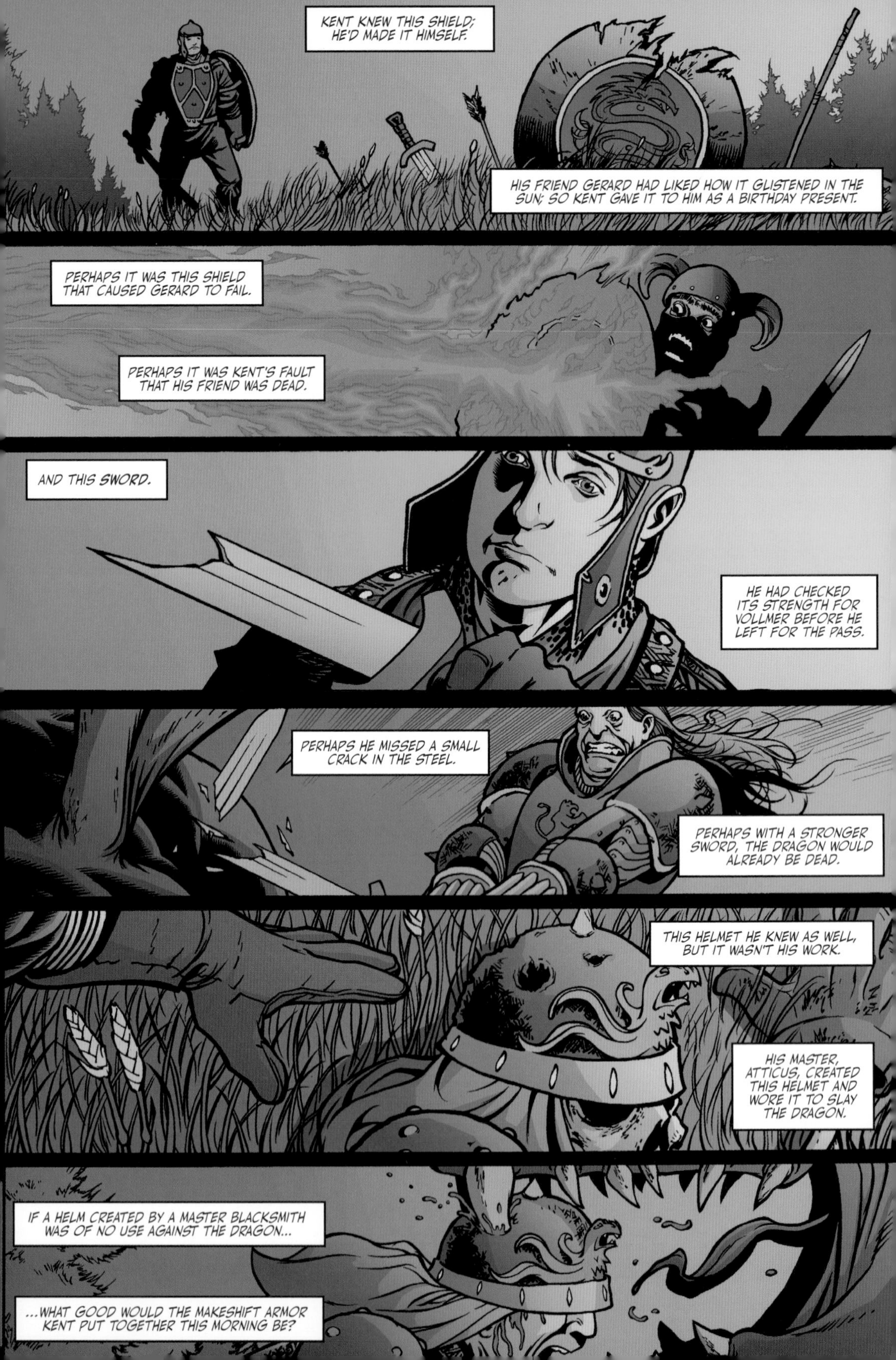
KENT KNEW THIS SHIELD; HE'D MADE IT HIMSELF.
HIS FRIEND GERARD HAD LIKED HOW IT GLISTENED IN THE SUN; SO KENT GAVE IT TO HIM AS A BIRTHDAY PRESENT.
PERHAPS IT WAS THIS SHIELD THAT CAUSED GERARD TO FAIL.
PERHAPS IT WAS KENT'S FAULT THAT HIS FRIEND WAS DEAD.
AND THIS SWORD.
HE HAD CHECKED ITS STRENGTH FOR VOLLMER BEFORE HE LEFT FOR THE PASS.
PERHAPS HE MISSED A SMALL CRACK IN THE STEEL.
PERHAPS WITH A STRONGER SWORD, THE DRAGON WOULD ALREADY BE DEAD.
THIS HELMET HE KNEW AS WELL, BUT IT WASN'T HIS WORK.
HIS MASTER, ATTICUS, CREATED THIS HELMET AND WORE IT TO SLAY THE DRAGON.
IF A HELM CREATED BY A MASTER BLACKSMITH WAS OF NO USE AGAINST THE DRAGON...
...WHAT GOOD WOULD THE MAKESHIFT ARMOR KENT PUT TOGETHER THIS MORNING BE?

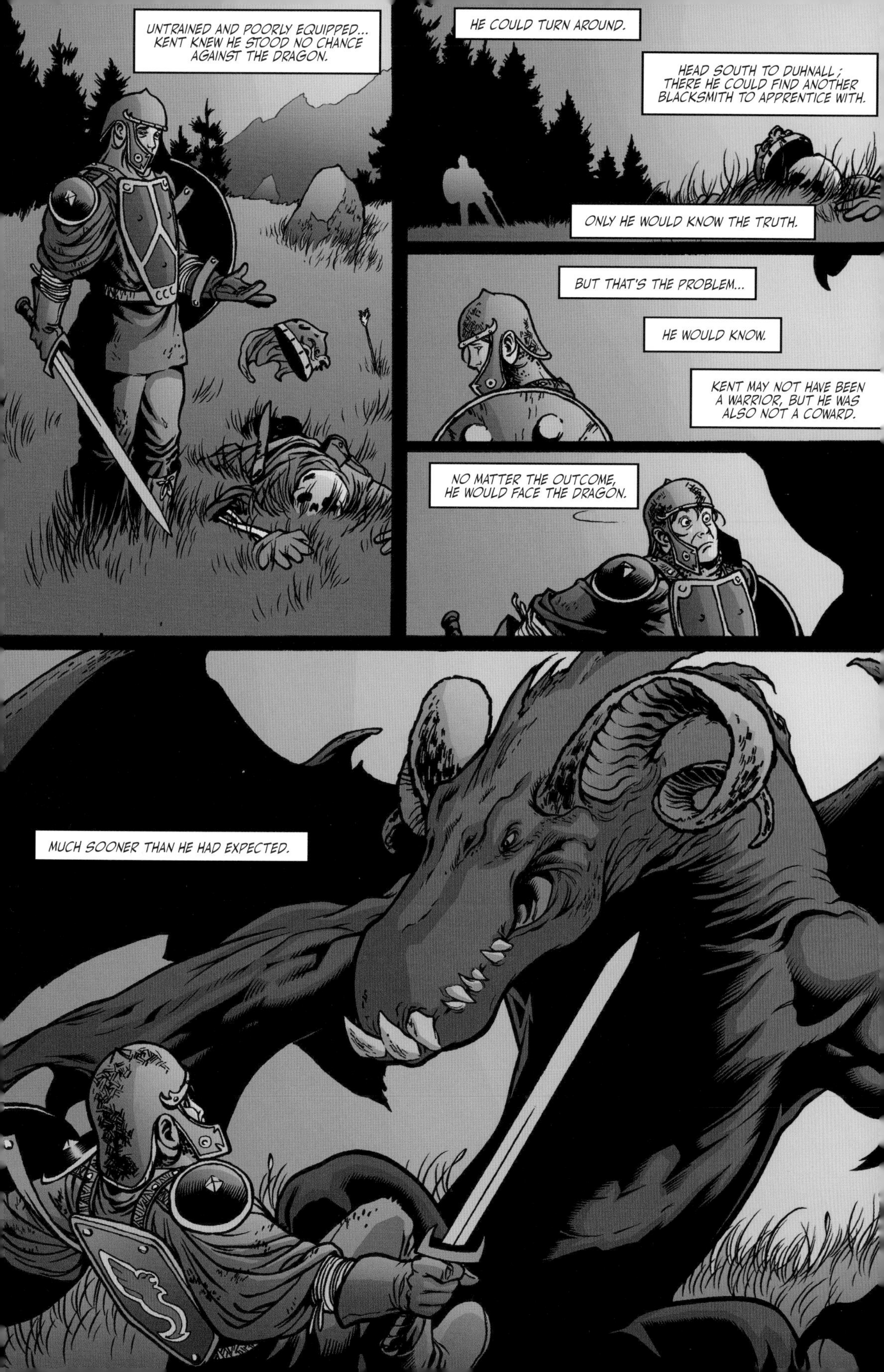
UNTRAINED AND POORLY EQUIPPED... KENT KNEW HE STOOD NO CHANCE AGAINST THE DRAGON.
HE COULD TURN AROUND.
HEAD SOUTH TO DUHNALL; THERE HE COULD FIND ANOTHER BLACKSMITH TO APPRENTICE WITH.
ONLY HE WOULD KNOW THE TRUTH.
BUT THAT'S THE PROBLEM...
HE WOULD KNOW.
KENT MAY NOT HAVE BEEN A WARRIOR, BUT HE WAS ALSO NOT A COWARD.
NO MATTER THE OUTCOME, HE WOULD FACE THE DRAGON.
MUCH SOONER THAN HE HAD EXPECTED.

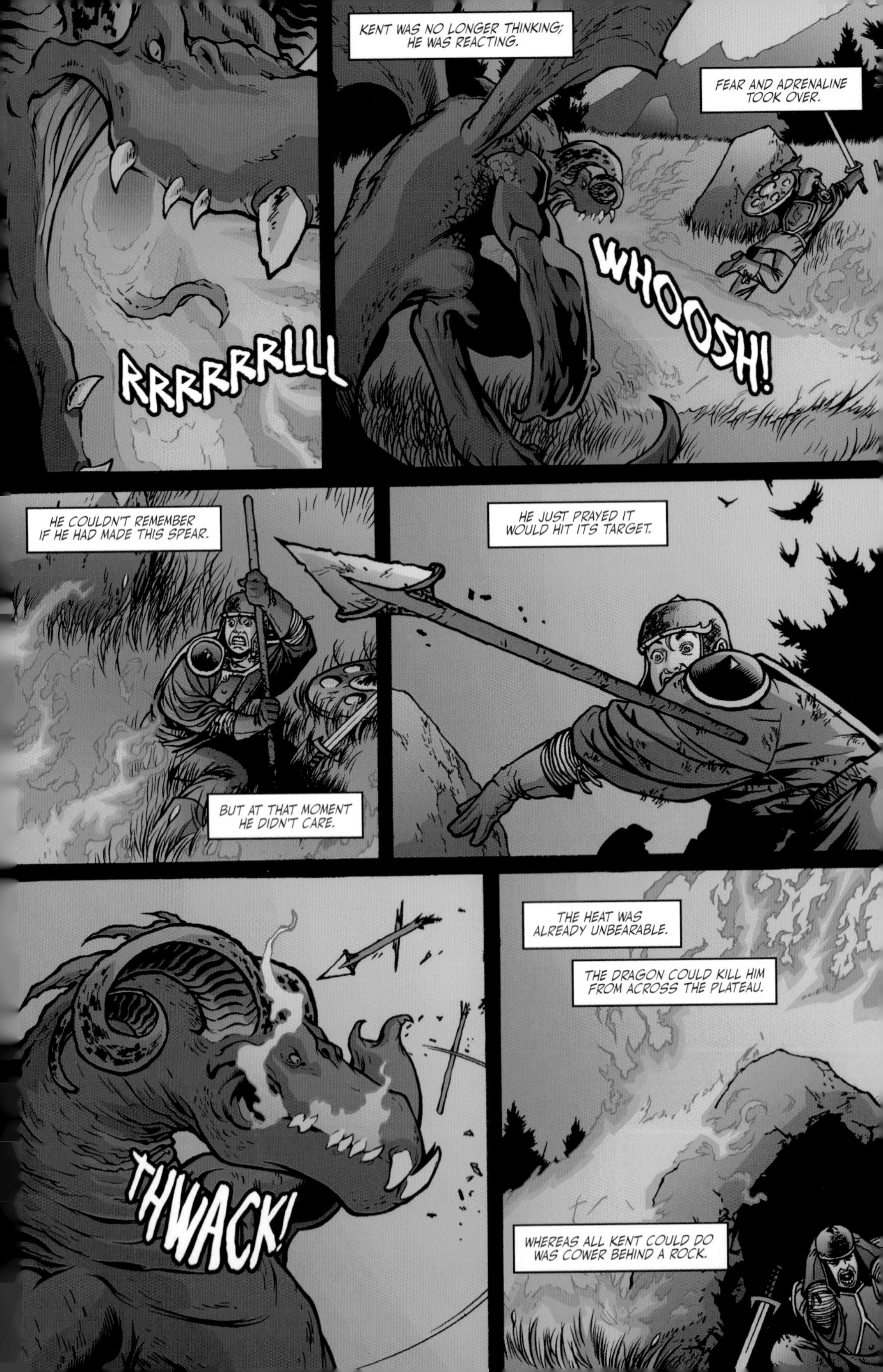

RRRRRLLL
KENT WAS NO LONGER THINKING; HE WAS REACTING.
FEAR AND ADRENALINE TOOK OVER.
WHOOSH!
HE COULDN'T REMEMBER IF HE HAD MADE THIS SPEAR.
BUT AT THAT MOMENT HE DIDN'T CARE.
HE JUST PRAYED IT WOULD HIT ITS TARGET.
THWACK!
THE HEAT WAS ALREADY UNBEARABLE.
THE DRAGON COULD KILL HIM FROM ACROSS THE PLATEAU.
WHEREAS ALL KENT COULD DO WAS COWER BEHIND A ROCK.

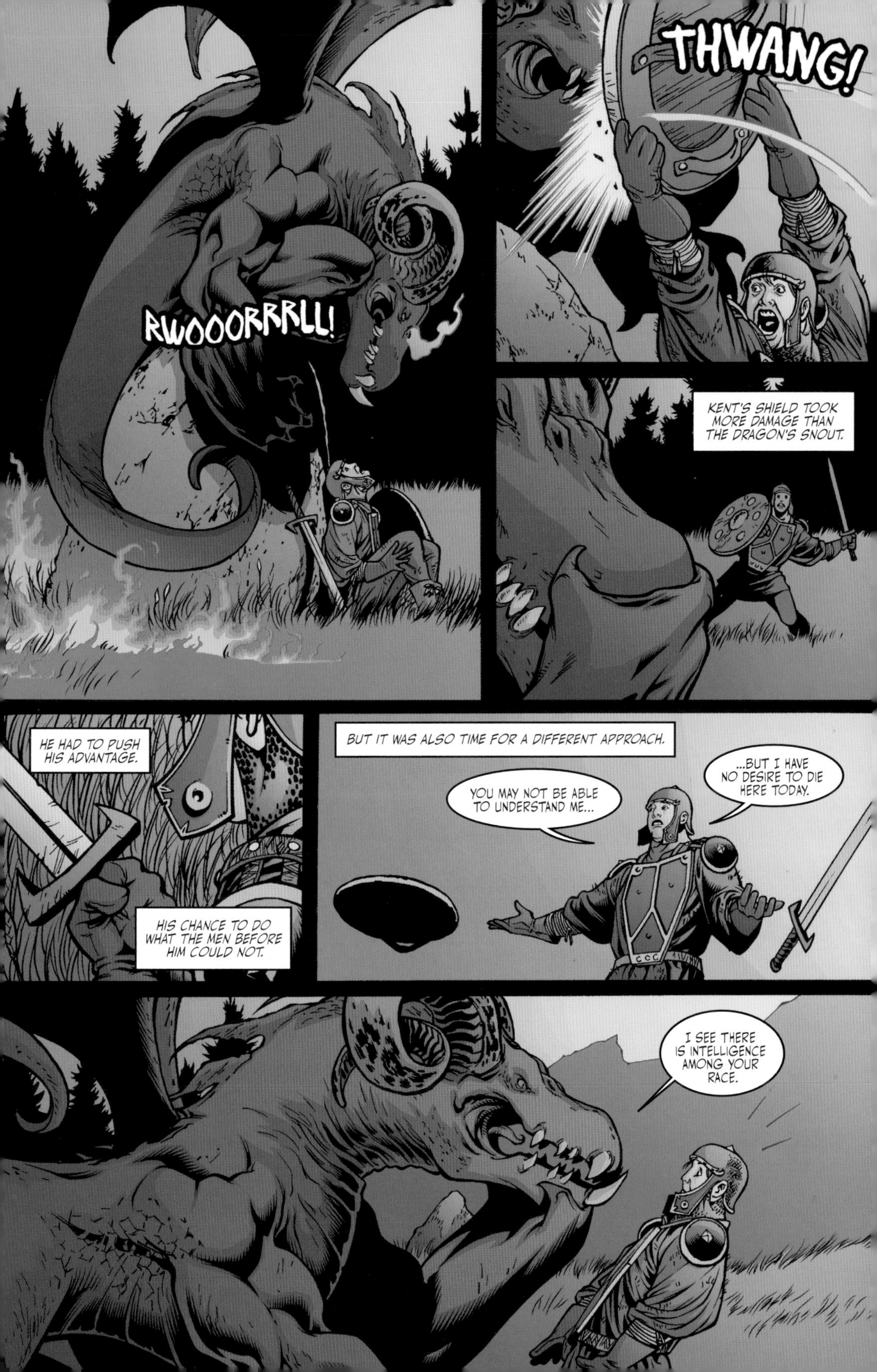
RWOOORRRLL!
THWANG!
KENT'S SHIELD TOOK MORE DAMAGE THAN THE DRAGON'S SNOUT.
HE HAD TO PUSH HIS ADVANTAGE.
HIS CHANCE TO DO WHAT THE MEN BEFORE HIM COULD NOT.
BUT IT WAS ALSO TIME FOR A DIFFERENT APPROACH.
YOU MAY NOT BE ABLE TO UNDERSTAND ME...
...BUT I HAVE NO DESIRE TO DIE HERE TODAY.
I SEE THERE IS INTELLIGENCE AMONG YOUR RACE.

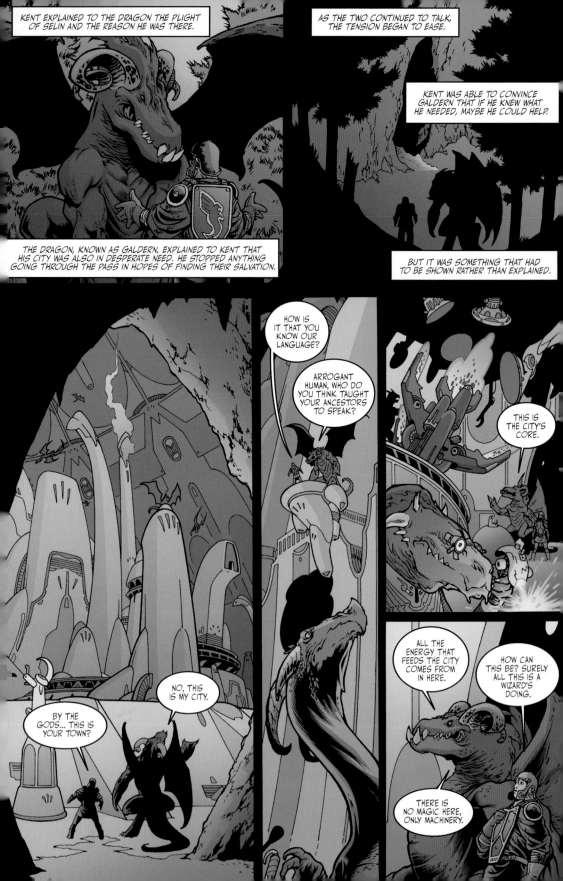

KENT EXPLAINED TO THE DRAGON THE PLIGHT OF SELIN AND THE REASON HE WAS THERE.

AS THE TWO CONTINUED TO TALK, THE TENSION BEGAN TO EASE.

KENT WAS ABLE TO CONVINCE GALDERN THAT IF HE KNEW WHAT HE NEEDED, MAYBE HE COULD HELP.

THE DRAGON, KNOWN AS GALDERN, EXPLAINED TO KENT THAT HIS CITY WAS ALSO IN DESPERATE NEED. HE STOPPED ANYTHING GOING THROUGH THE PASS IN HOPES OF FINDING THEIR SALVATION.

BUT IT WAS SOMETHING THAT HAD TO BE SHOWN RATHER THAN EXPLAINED.

HOW IS IT THAT YOU KNOW OUR LANGUAGE?

ARROGANT HUMAN, WHO DO YOU THINK TAUGHT YOUR ANCESTORS TO SPEAK?

THIS IS THE CITY'S CORE.

ALL THE ENERGY THAT FEEDS THE CITY COMES FROM IN HERE.

HOW CAN THIS BE? SURELY ALL THIS IS A WIZARD'S DOING.

NO, THIS IS MY CITY.

BY THE GODS... THIS IS YOUR TOWN?

THERE IS NO MAGIC HERE, ONLY MACHINERY.

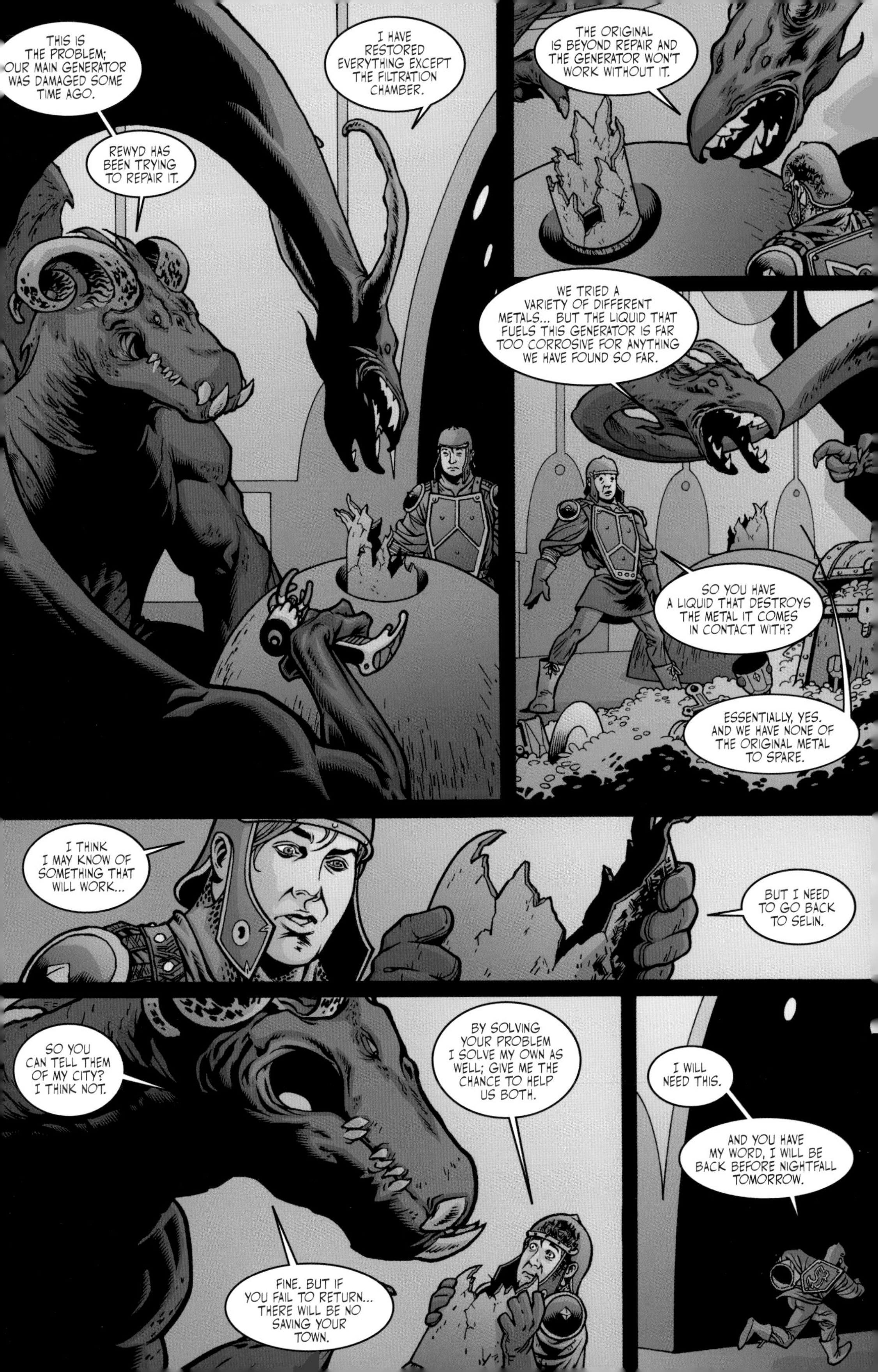

THIS IS THE PROBLEM; OUR MAIN GENERATOR WAS DAMAGED SOME TIME AGO.
REWYD HAS BEEN TRYING TO REPAIR IT.
I HAVE RESTORED EVERYTHING EXCEPT THE FILTRATION CHAMBER.
THE ORIGINAL IS BEYOND REPAIR AND THE GENERATOR WON'T WORK WITHOUT IT.
WE TRIED A VARIETY OF DIFFERENT METALS... BUT THE LIQUID THAT FUELS THIS GENERATOR IS FAR TOO CORROSIVE FOR ANYTHING WE HAVE FOUND SO FAR.
SO YOU HAVE A LIQUID THAT DESTROYS THE METAL IT COMES IN CONTACT WITH?
ESSENTIALLY, YES. AND WE HAVE NONE OF THE ORIGINAL METAL TO SPARE.
I THINK I MAY KNOW OF SOMETHING THAT WILL WORK...
BUT I NEED TO GO BACK TO SELIN.
SO YOU CAN TELL THEM OF MY CITY? I THINK NOT.
BY SOLVING YOUR PROBLEM I SOLVE MY OWN AS WELL; GIVE ME THE CHANCE TO HELP US BOTH.
FINE. BUT IF YOU FAIL TO RETURN... THERE WILL BE NO SAVING YOUR TOWN.
I WILL NEED THIS.
AND YOU HAVE MY WORD, I WILL BE BACK BEFORE NIGHTFALL TOMORROW.

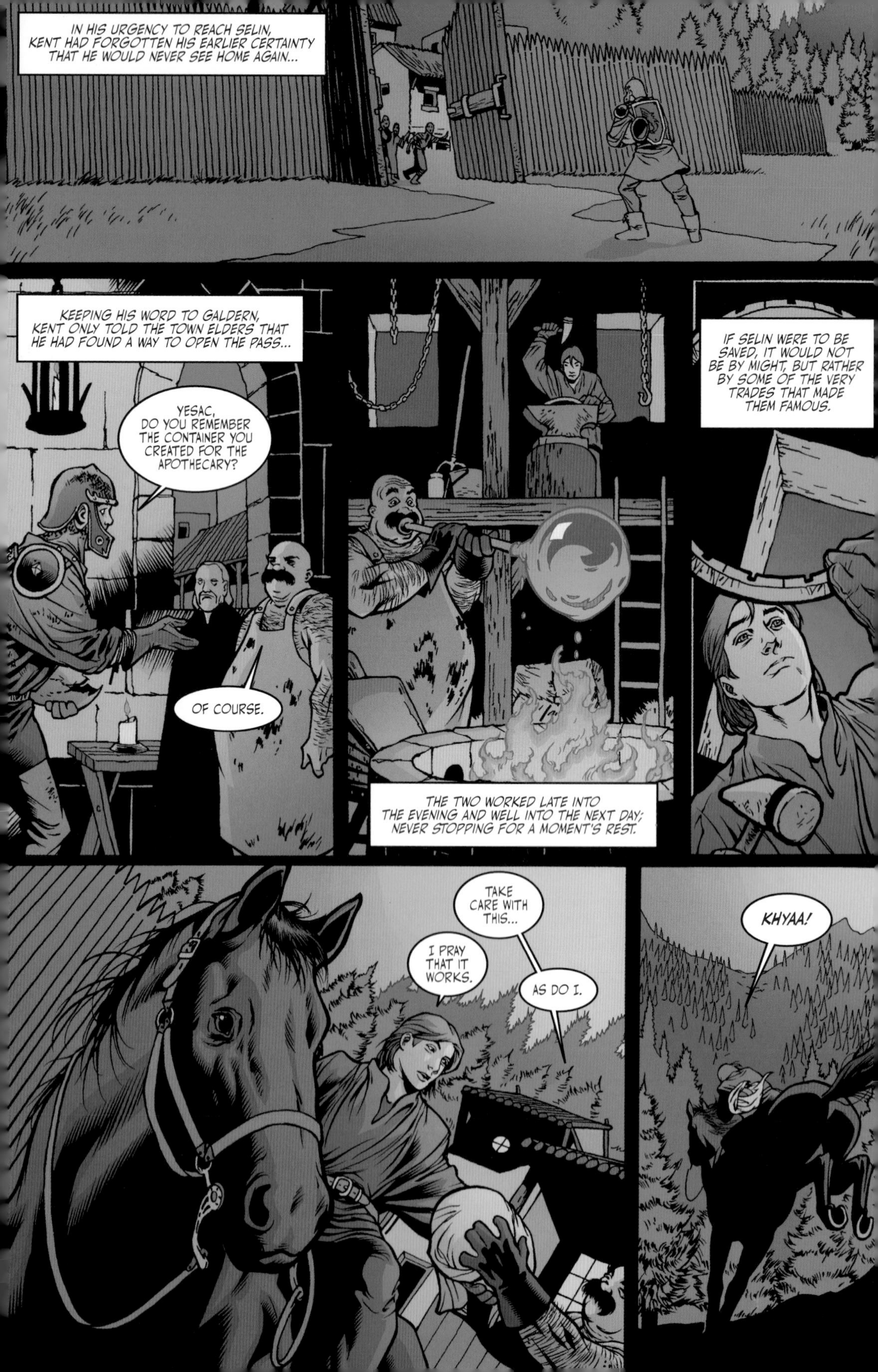
IN HIS URGENCY TO REACH SELIN, KENT HAD FORGOTTEN HIS EARLIER CERTAINTY THAT HE WOULD NEVER SEE HOME AGAIN...
KEEPING HIS WORD TO GALDERN, KENT ONLY TOLD THE TOWN ELDERS THAT HE HAD FOUND A WAY TO OPEN THE PASS...
YESAC, DO YOU REMEMBER THE CONTAINER YOU CREATED FOR THE APOTHECARY?
OF COURSE.
THE TWO WORKED LATE INTO THE EVENING AND WELL INTO THE NEXT DAY; NEVER STOPPING FOR A MOMENT'S REST.
IF SELIN WERE TO BE SAVED, IT WOULD NOT BE BY MIGHT, BUT RATHER BY SOME OF THE VERY TRADES THAT MADE THEM FAMOUS.
TAKE CARE WITH THIS...
I PRAY THAT IT WORKS.
AS DO I.
KHYAA!

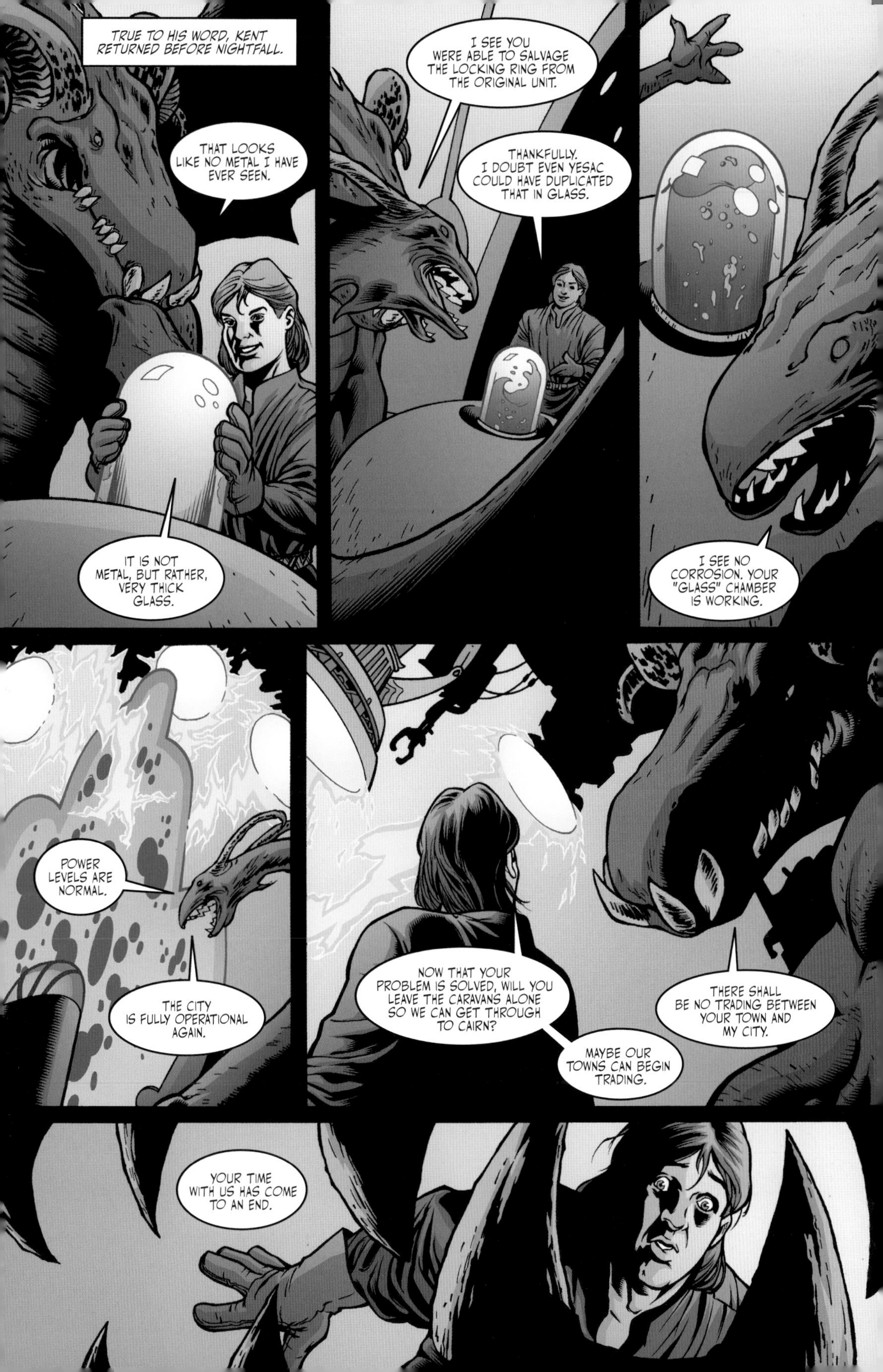
TRUE TO HIS WORD, KENT RETURNED BEFORE NIGHTFALL.
THAT LOOKS LIKE NO METAL I HAVE EVER SEEN.
IT IS NOT METAL, BUT RATHER, VERY THICK GLASS.
I SEE YOU WERE ABLE TO SALVAGE THE LOCKING RING FROM THE ORIGINAL UNIT.
THANKFULLY. I DOUBT EVEN YESAC COULD HAVE DUPLICATED THAT IN GLASS.
I SEE NO CORROSION. YOUR "GLASS" CHAMBER IS WORKING.
POWER LEVELS ARE NORMAL.
THE CITY IS FULLY OPERATIONAL AGAIN.
NOW THAT YOUR PROBLEM IS SOLVED, WILL YOU LEAVE THE CARAVANS ALONE SO WE CAN GET THROUGH TO CAIRN?
MAYBE OUR TOWNS CAN BEGIN TRADING.
THERE SHALL BE NO TRADING BETWEEN YOUR TOWN AND MY CITY.
YOUR TIME WITH US HAS COME TO AN END.

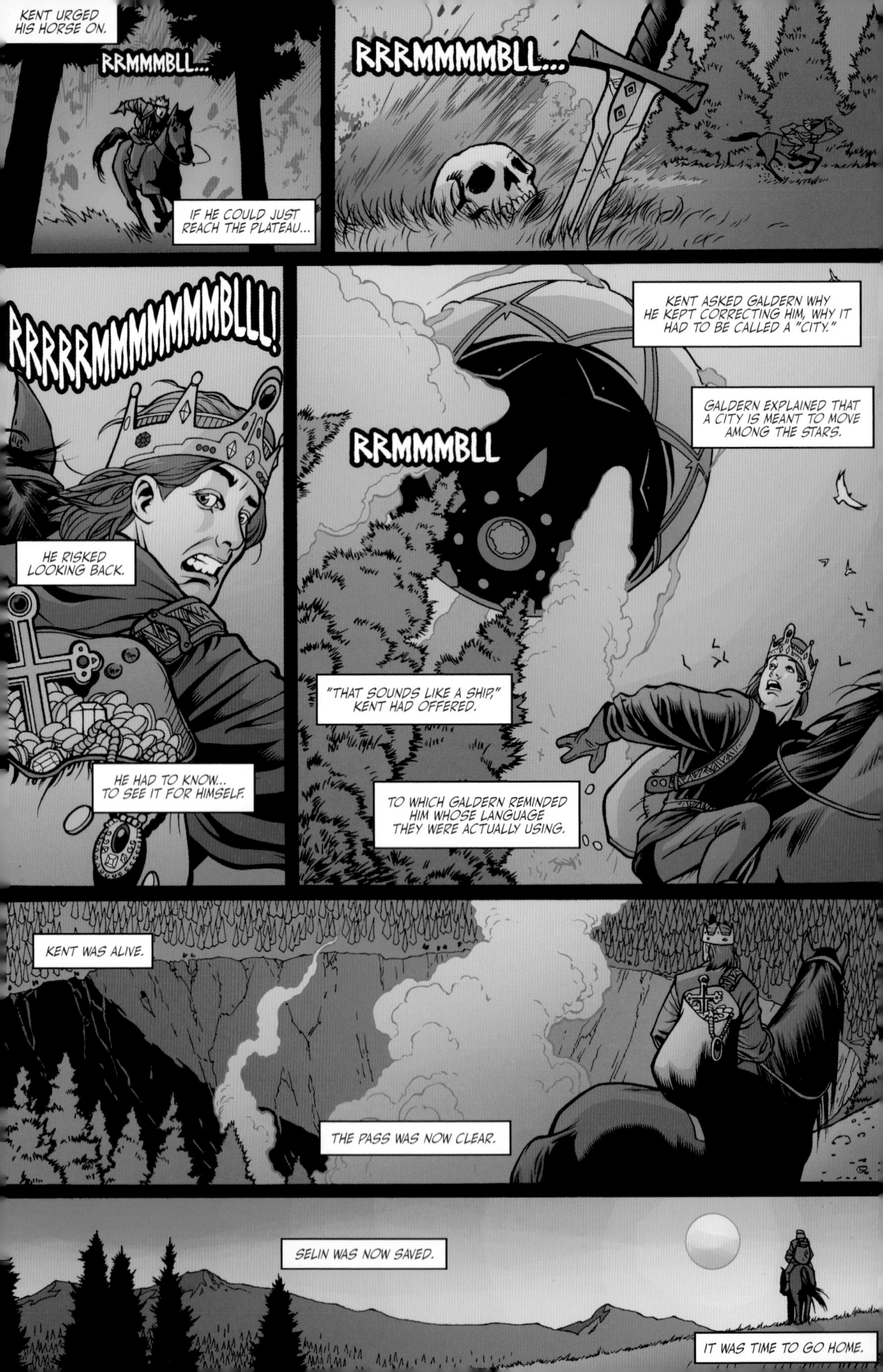
KENT URGED HIS HORSE ON.
RRMMMBLL...
IF HE COULD JUST REACH THE PLATEAU...
RRRMMMMBLL...
RRRRRMMMMMMMBLLL!
HE RISKED LOOKING BACK.
HE HAD TO KNOW... TO SEE IT FOR HIMSELF.
KENT ASKED GALDERN WHY HE KEPT CORRECTING HIM, WHY IT HAD TO BE CALLED A "CITY."
GALDERN EXPLAINED THAT A CITY IS MEANT TO MOVE AMONG THE STARS.
RRMMMBLL
"THAT SOUNDS LIKE A SHIP," KENT HAD OFFERED.
TO WHICH GALDERN REMINDED HIM WHOSE LANGUAGE THEY WERE ACTUALLY USING.
KENT WAS ALIVE.
THE PASS WAS NOW CLEAR.
SELIN WAS NOW SAVED.
IT WAS TIME TO GO HOME.

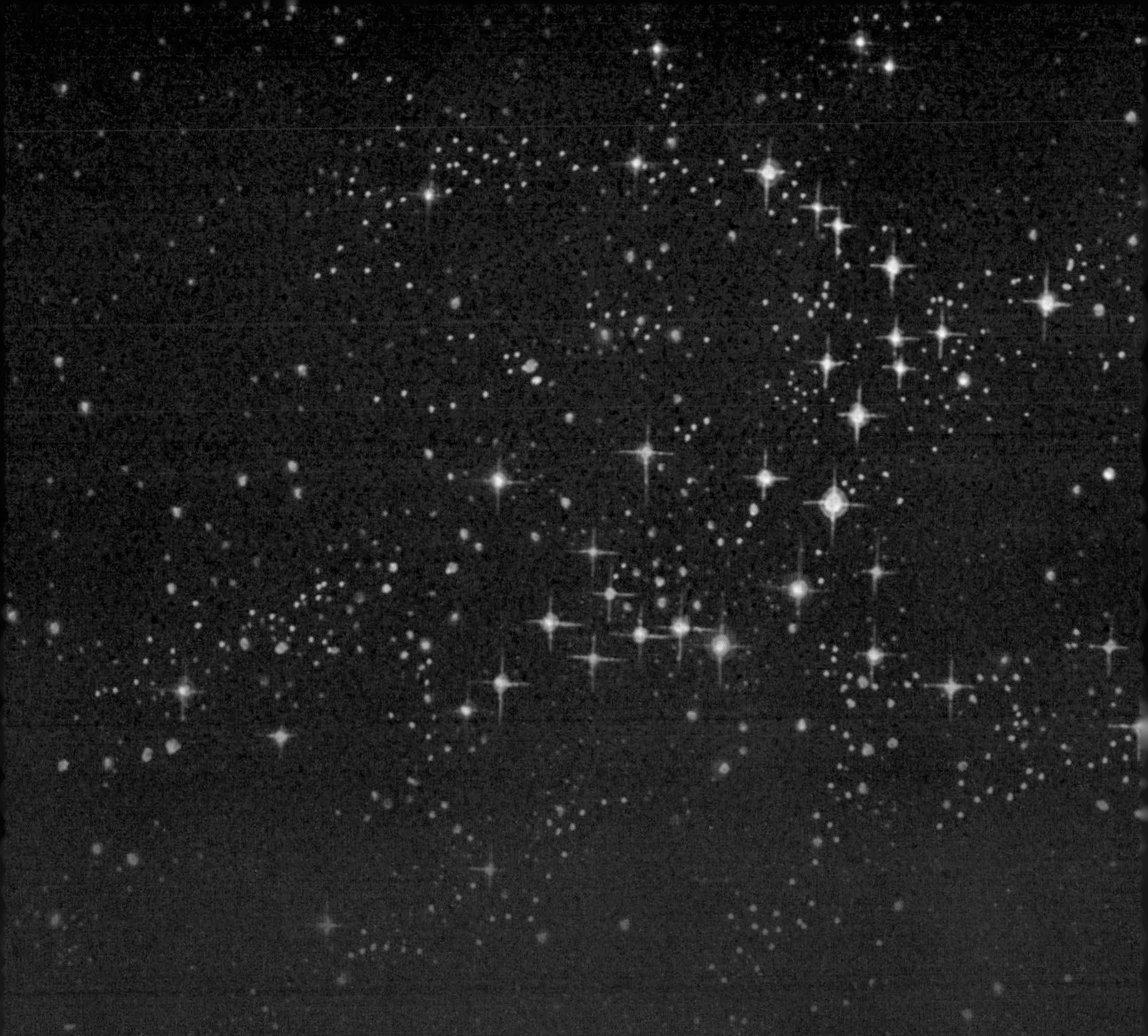

JOSHUE

Story by JULIEN BLONDEL
Art by JEROME OPEÑA
Colors by PATRICE LARCENET

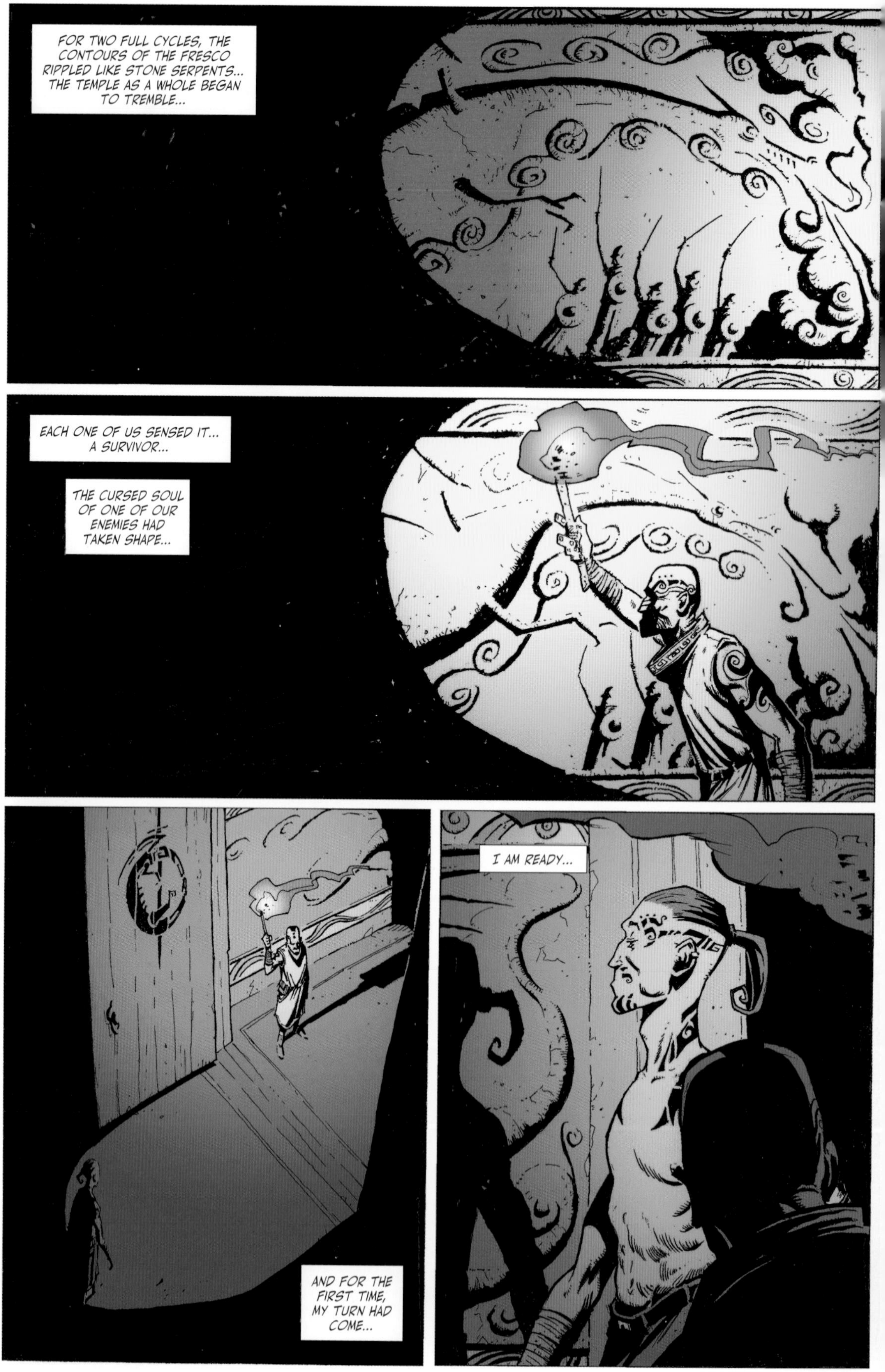
FOR TWO FULL CYCLES, THE CONTOURS OF THE FRESCO RIPPLED LIKE STONE SERPENTS... THE TEMPLE AS A WHOLE BEGAN TO TREMBLE...
EACH ONE OF US SENSED IT... A SURVIVOR...
THE CURSED SOUL OF ONE OF OUR ENEMIES HAD TAKEN SHAPE...
AND FOR THE FIRST TIME, MY TURN HAD COME...
I AM READY...

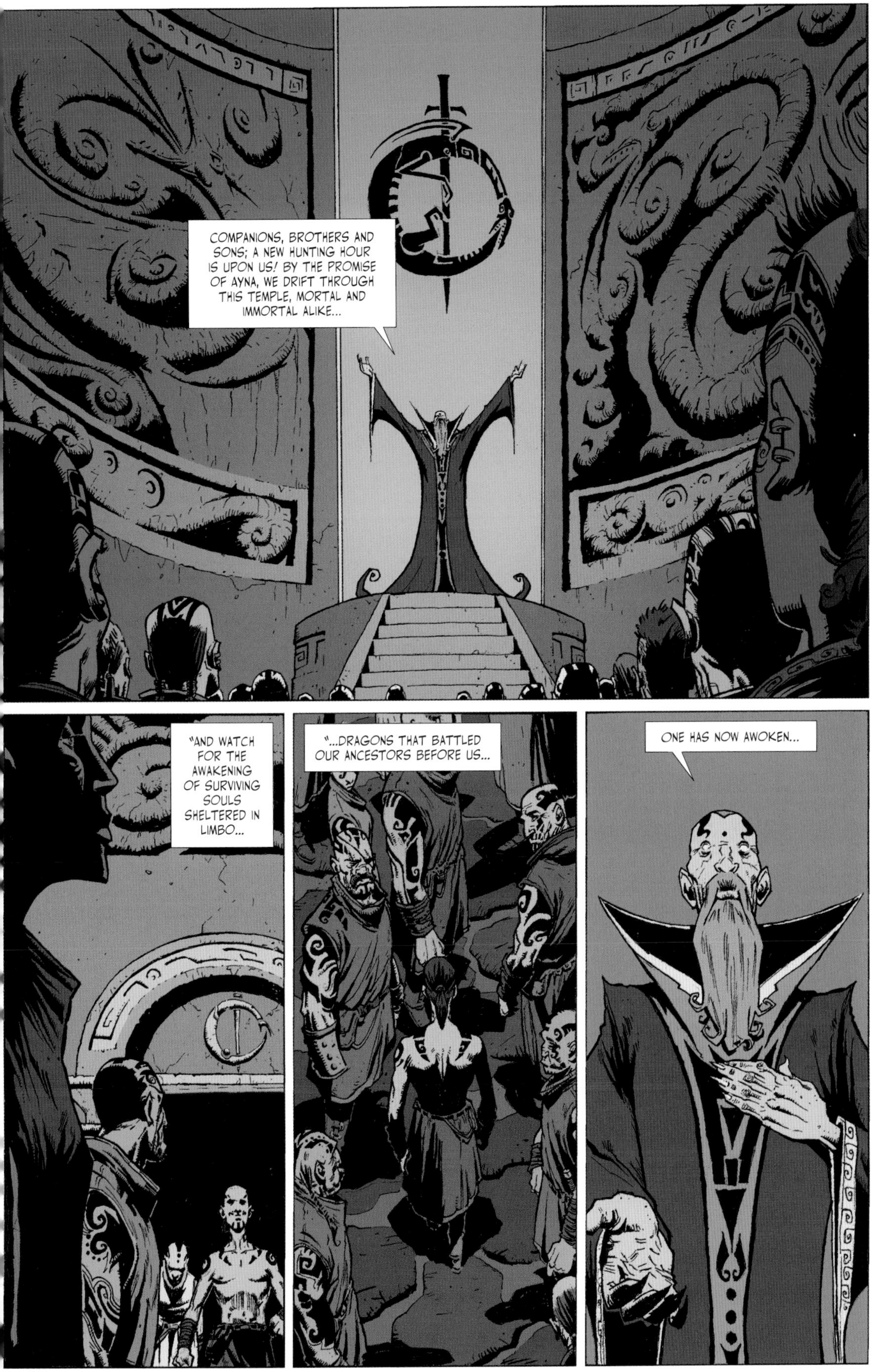
COMPANIONS, BROTHERS AND SONS; A NEW HUNTING HOUR IS UPON US! BY THE PROMISE OF AYNA, WE DRIFT THROUGH THIS TEMPLE, MORTAL AND IMMORTAL ALIKE...
"AND WATCH FOR THE AWAKENING OF SURVIVING SOULS SHELTERED IN LIMBO...
"...DRAGONS THAT BATTLED OUR ANCESTORS BEFORE US...
ONE HAS NOW AWOKEN...

AND ONE AMONG US READIES TO HONOR OUR PLEDGE...

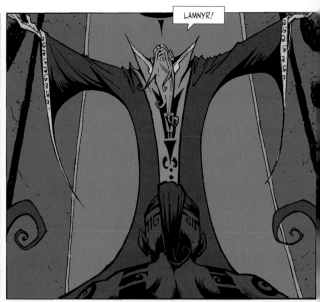

LAMNYR!

"SAINT JUSTICE!

"BY THE PROMISE OF AYNA, OUR VENERABLE MOTHER...

"MAY LAMNYR GUIDE YOU BEYOND THE BOUNDARIES!"

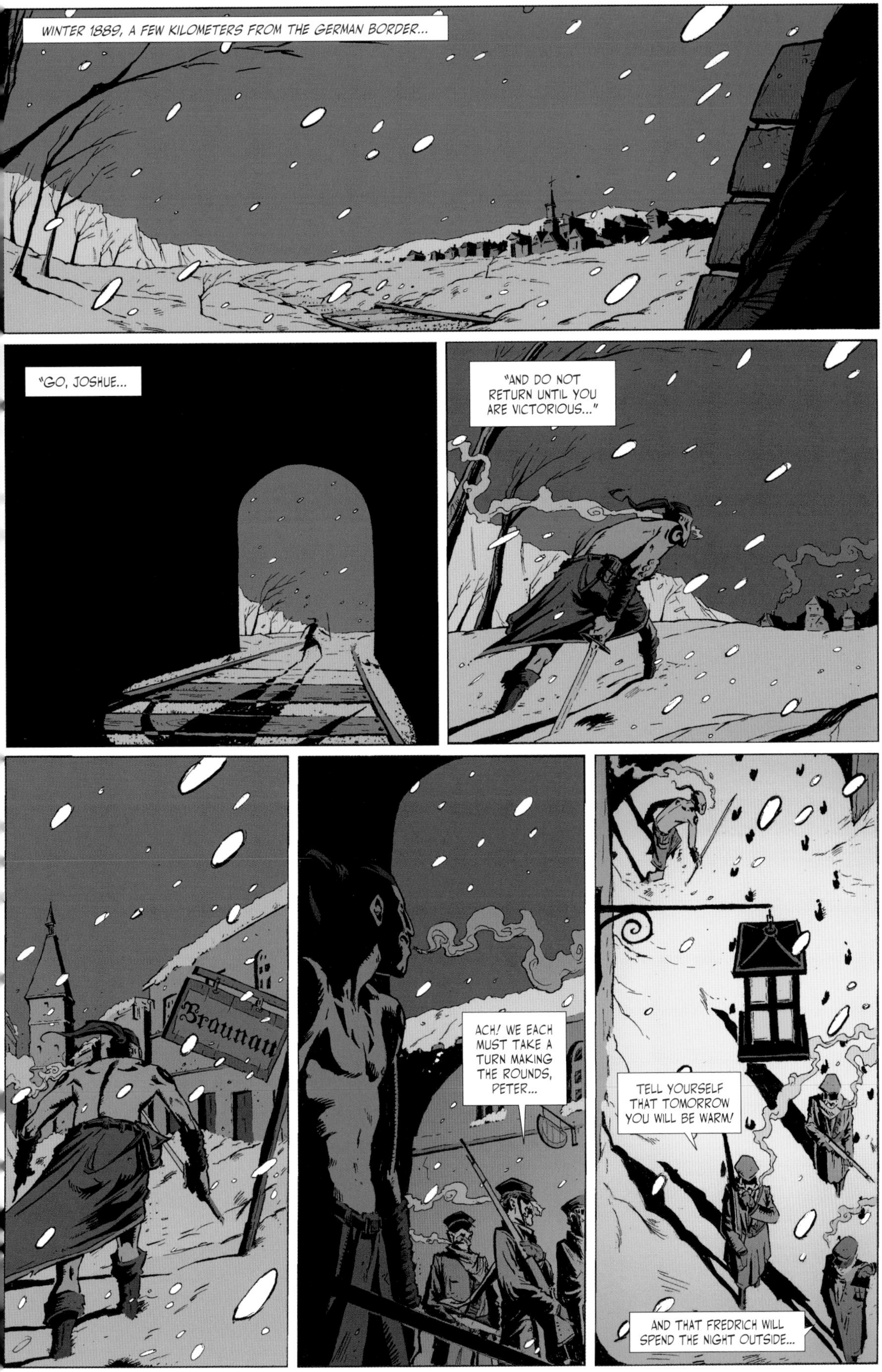
WINTER 1889, A FEW KILOMETERS FROM THE GERMAN BORDER...
"GO, JOSHUE...
"AND DO NOT RETURN UNTIL YOU ARE VICTORIOUS..."
Braunau
ACH! WE EACH MUST TAKE A TURN MAKING THE ROUNDS, PETER...
TELL YOURSELF THAT TOMORROW YOU WILL BE WARM!
AND THAT FREDRICH WILL SPEND THE NIGHT OUTSIDE...

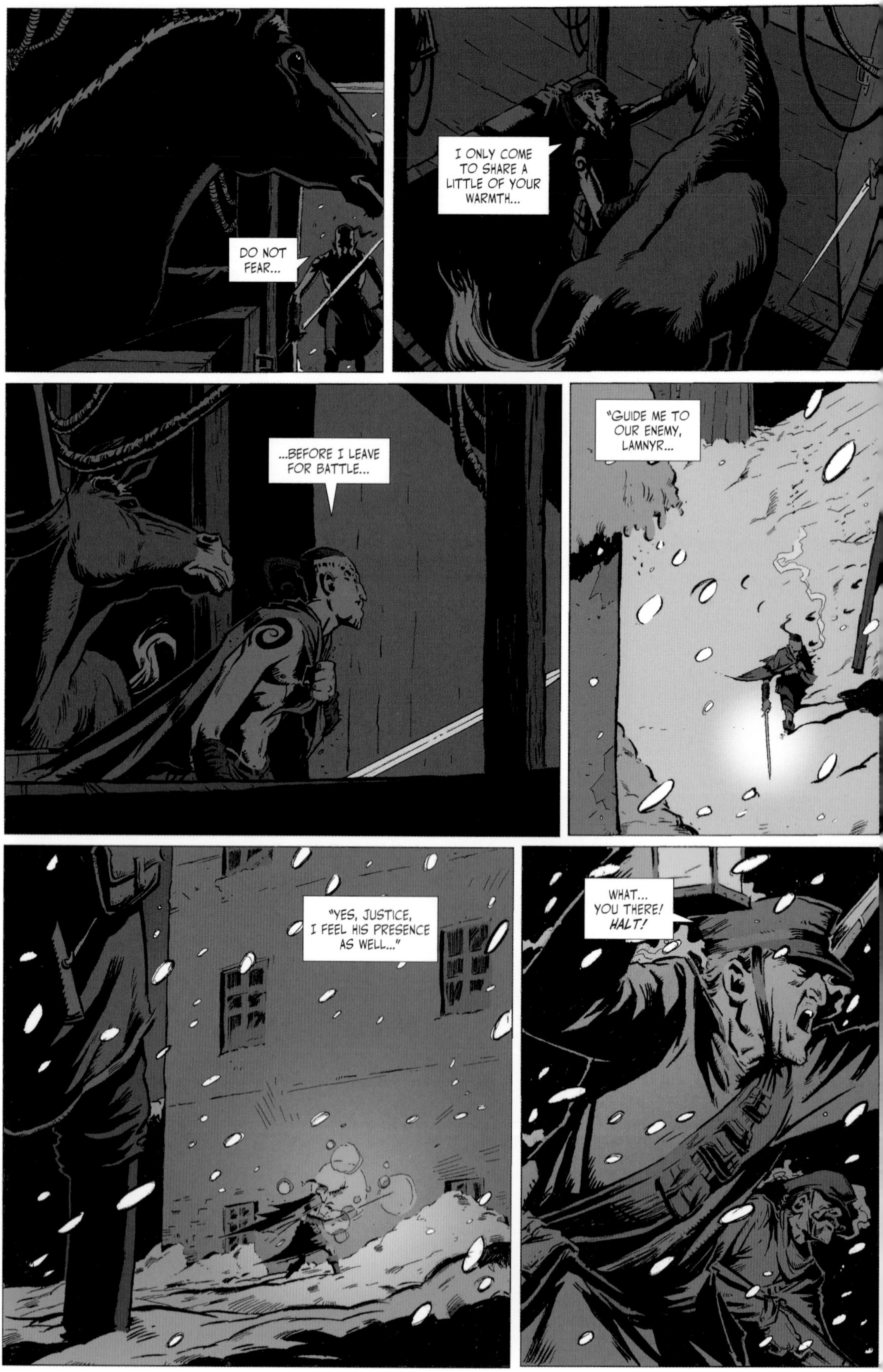
DO NOT FEAR...
I ONLY COME TO SHARE A LITTLE OF YOUR WARMTH...
...BEFORE I LEAVE FOR BATTLE...
"GUIDE ME TO OUR ENEMY, LAMNYR...
"YES, JUSTICE, I FEEL HIS PRESENCE AS WELL..."
WHAT... YOU THERE! *HALT!*

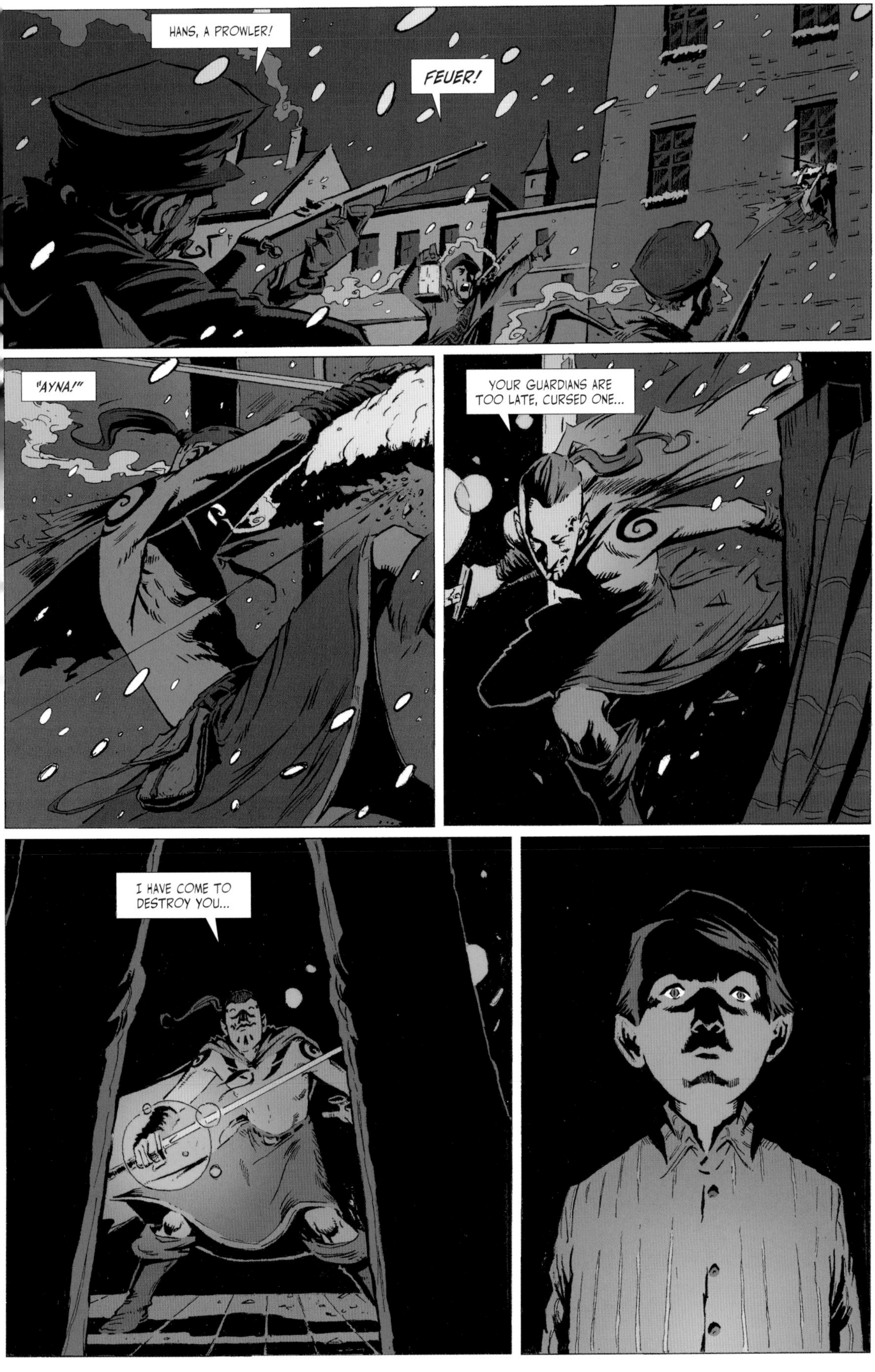
HANS, A PROWLER!
FEUER!
"AYNA!"
YOUR GUARDIANS ARE TOO LATE, CURSED ONE...
I HAVE COME TO DESTROY YOU...

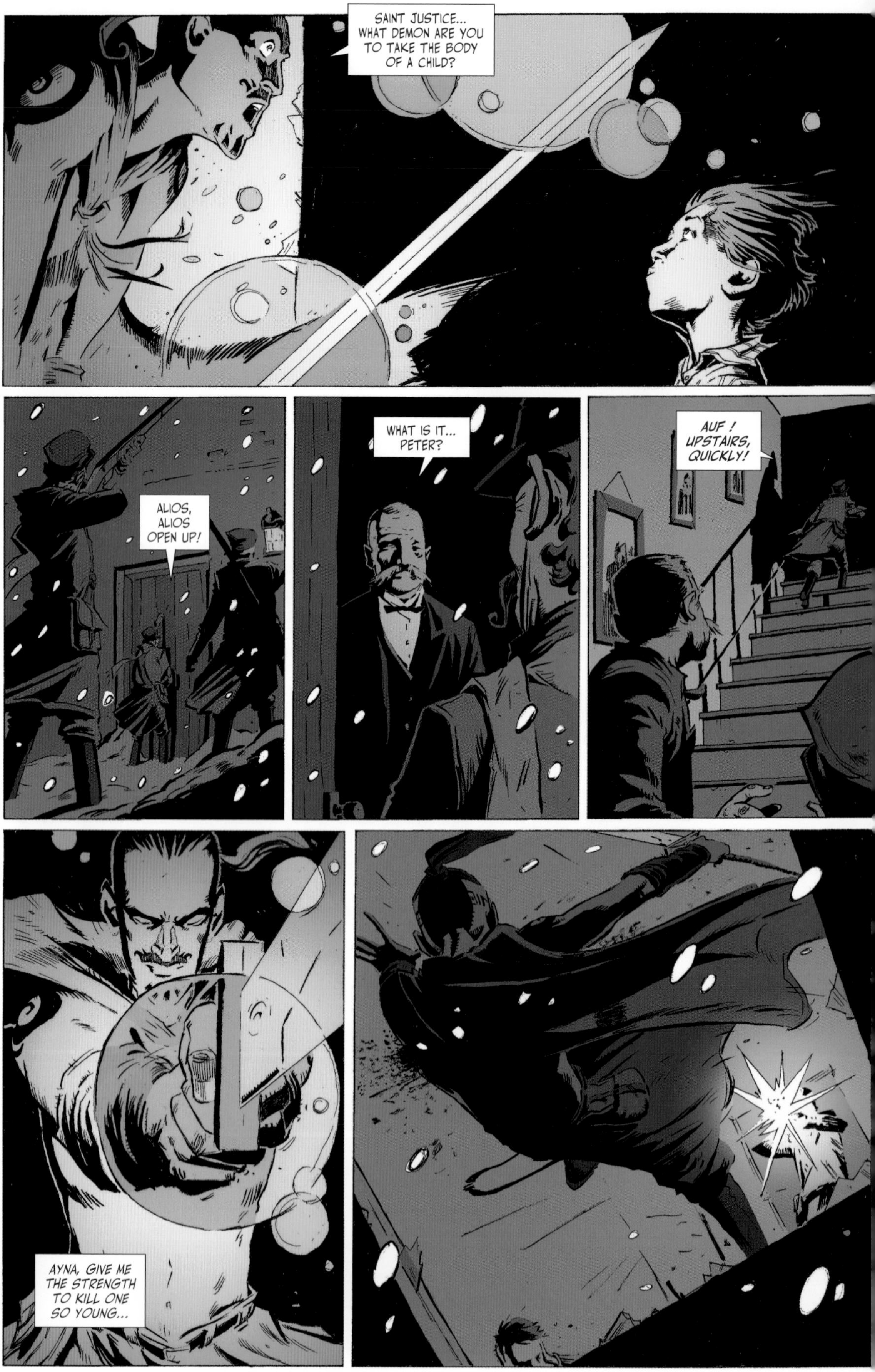
SAINT JUSTICE... WHAT DEMON ARE YOU TO TAKE THE BODY OF A CHILD?
ALIOS, ALIOS OPEN UP!
WHAT IS IT... PETER?
AUF ! UPSTAIRS, QUICKLY!
AYNA, GIVE ME THE STRENGTH TO KILL ONE SO YOUNG...

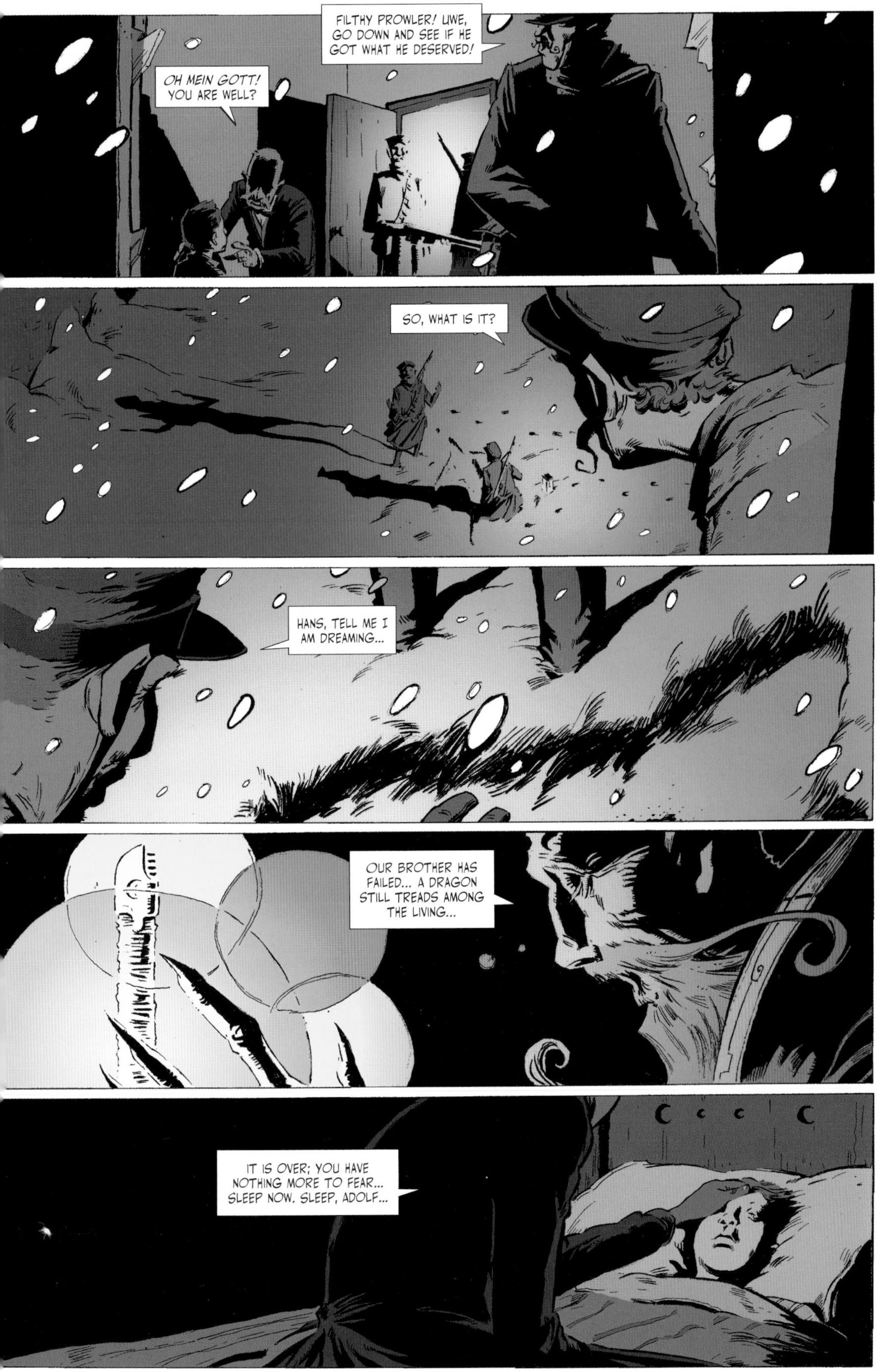
FILTHY PROWLER! UWE, GO DOWN AND SEE IF HE GOT WHAT HE DESERVED!
OH MEIN GOTT! YOU ARE WELL?
SO, WHAT IS IT?
HANS, TELL ME I AM DREAMING...
OUR BROTHER HAS FAILED... A DRAGON STILL TREADS AMONG THE LIVING...
IT IS OVER; YOU HAVE NOTHING MORE TO FEAR... SLEEP NOW. SLEEP, ADOLF...

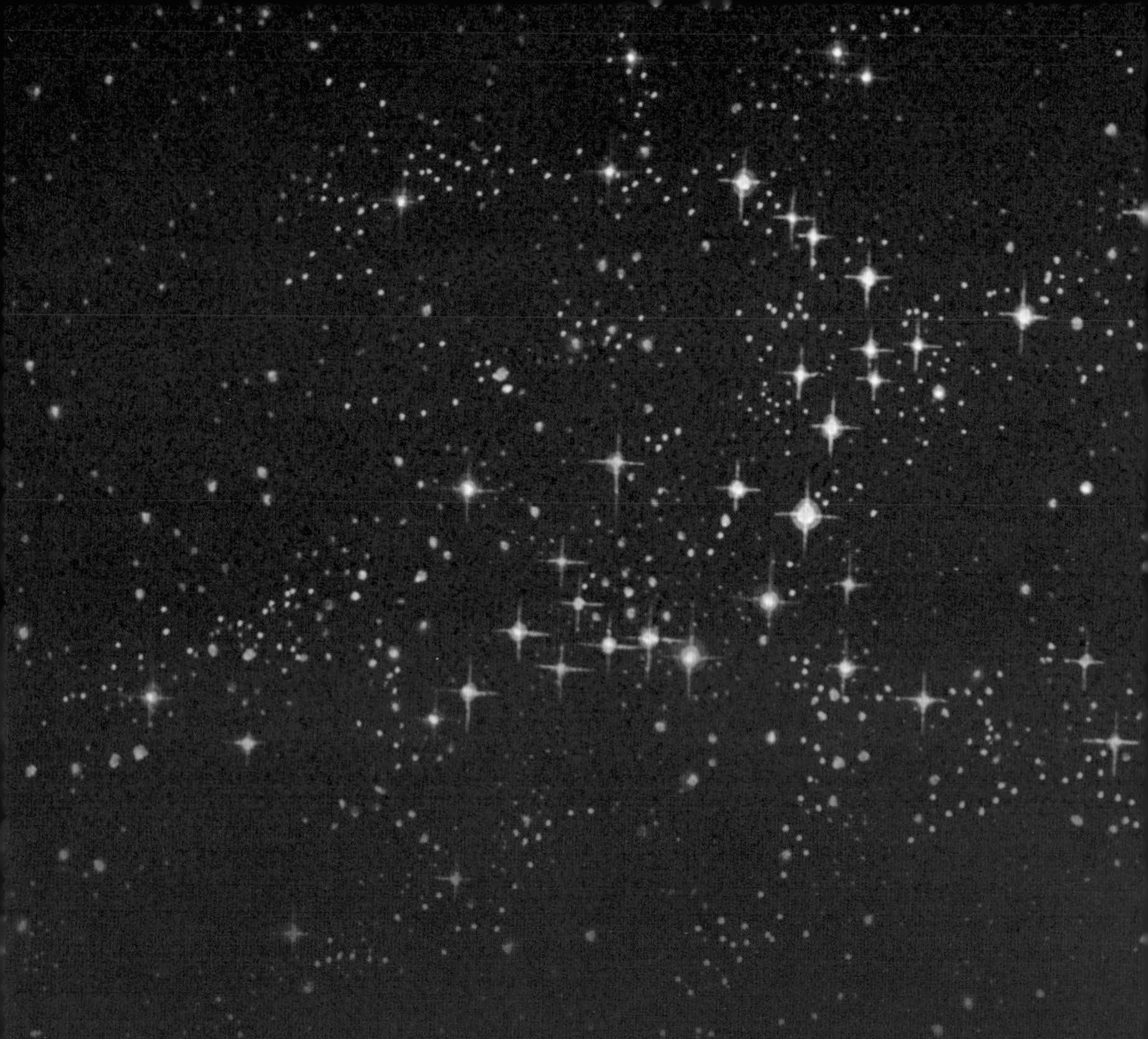

ENDOMORPH

Story and Art by STÉPHANE LEVALLOIS

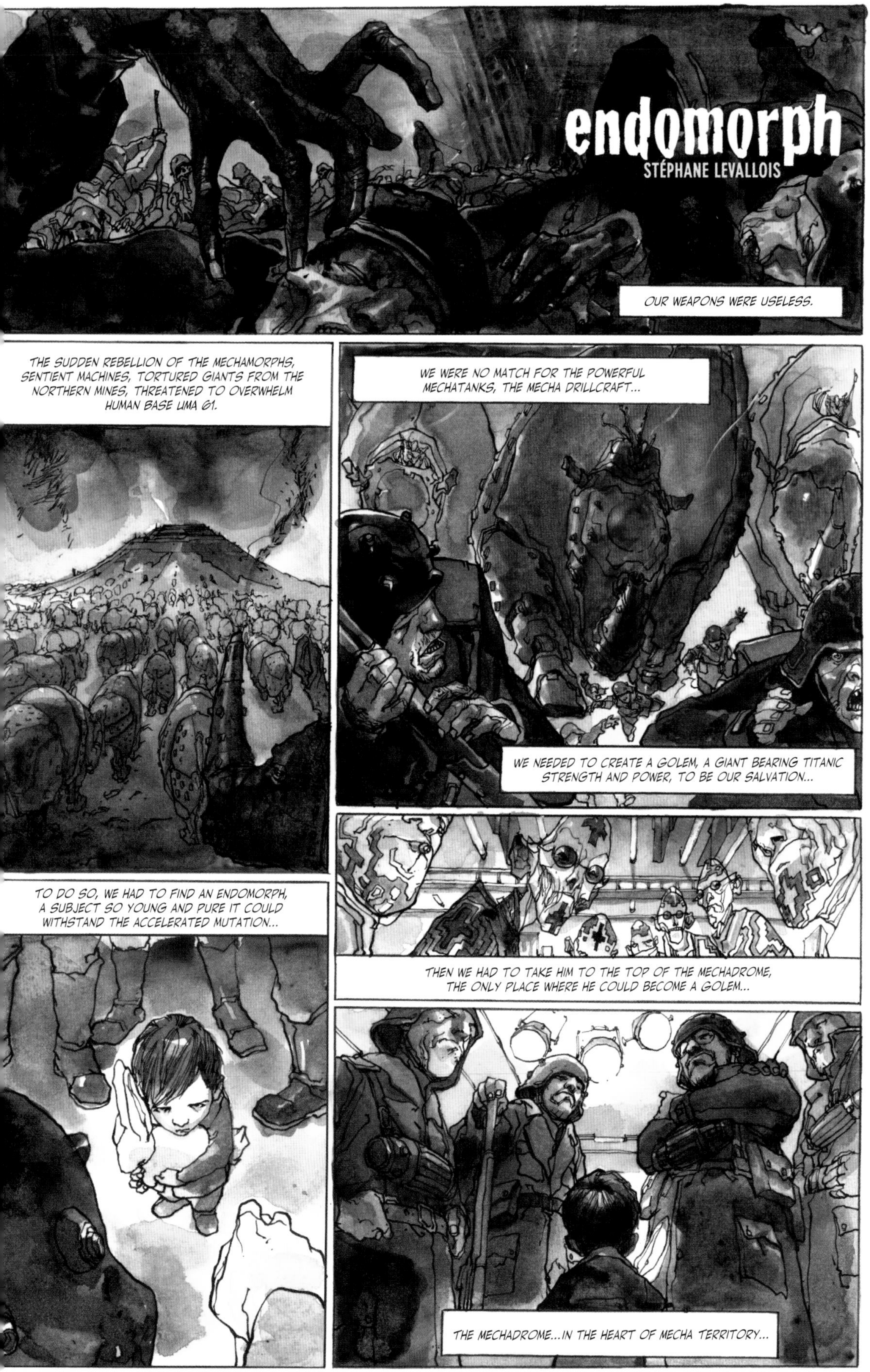
endomorph
STÉPHANE LEVALLOIS
OUR WEAPONS WERE USELESS.
THE SUDDEN REBELLION OF THE MECHAMORPHS, SENTIENT MACHINES, TORTURED GIANTS FROM THE NORTHERN MINES, THREATENED TO OVERWHELM HUMAN BASE UMA 61.
WE WERE NO MATCH FOR THE POWERFUL MECHATANKS, THE MECHA DRILLCRAFT...
WE NEEDED TO CREATE A GOLEM, A GIANT BEARING TITANIC STRENGTH AND POWER, TO BE OUR SALVATION...
TO DO SO, WE HAD TO FIND AN ENDOMORPH, A SUBJECT SO YOUNG AND PURE IT COULD WITHSTAND THE ACCELERATED MUTATION...
THEN WE HAD TO TAKE HIM TO THE TOP OF THE MECHADROME, THE ONLY PLACE WHERE HE COULD BECOME A GOLEM...
THE MECHADROME...IN THE HEART OF MECHA TERRITORY...

THE ENDOMORPH WAS FEARFUL...

...AND FRAGILE...

THERE WERE TEN OF US WHEN WE LEFT OUR BASE...TEN MEN RUNNING UNDER HEAVY FIRE FROM THE MECHATANKS...

AFTER A NINE-DAY CHASE, ONLY FIVE OF US WERE STILL ALIVE WHEN WE MADE IT, AT LAST, TO THE SOURCE OF THE MECHAMORPHS...

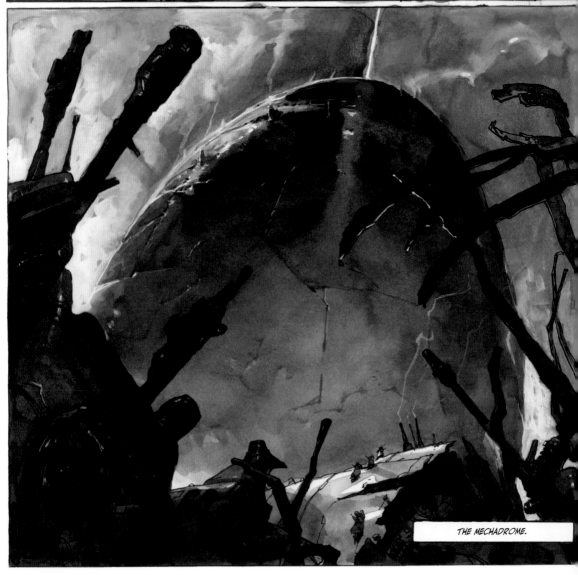

THE MECHADROME.

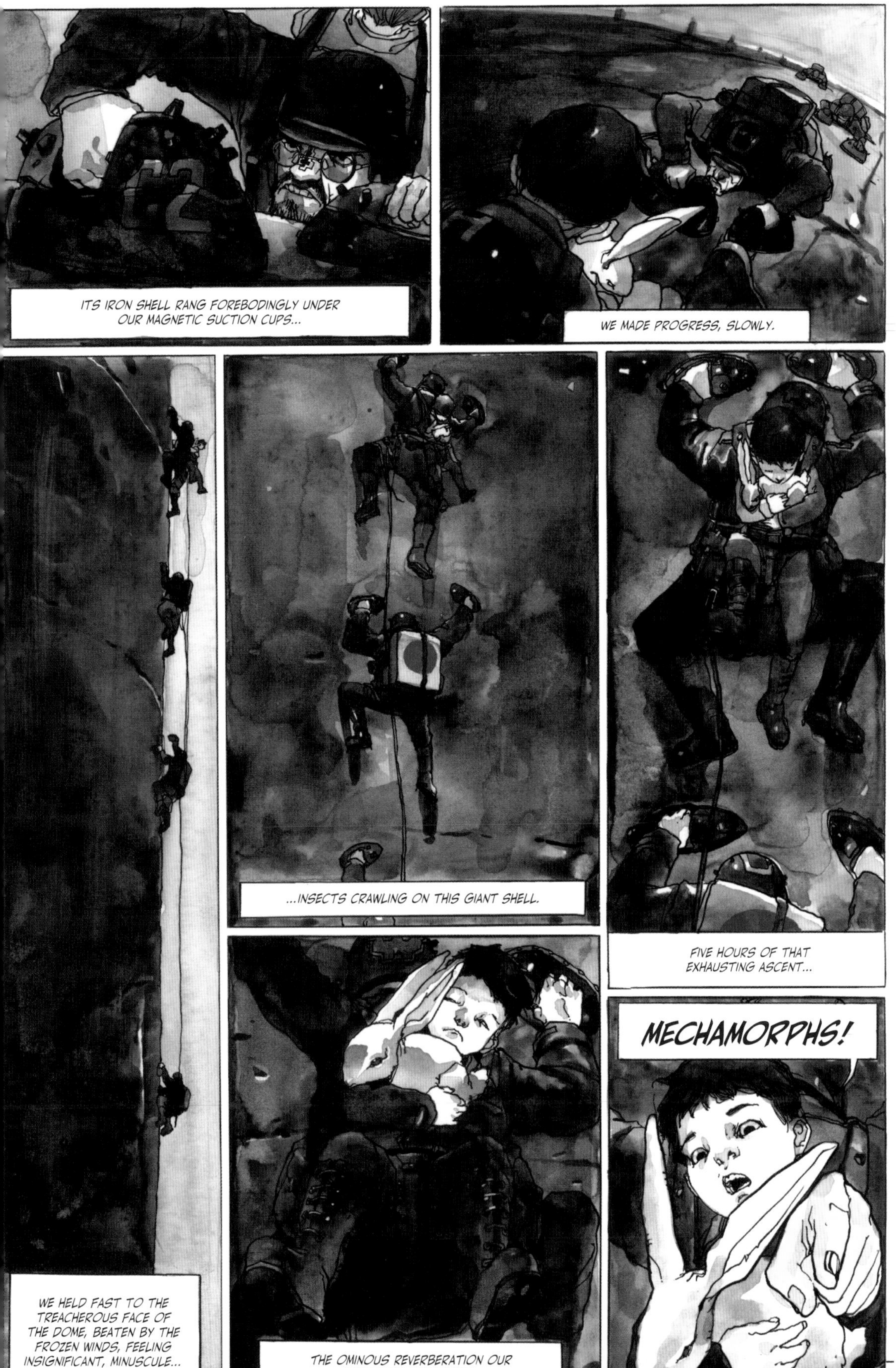
ITS IRON SHELL RANG FOREBODINGLY UNDER OUR MAGNETIC SUCTION CUPS...
WE MADE PROGRESS, SLOWLY.
WE HELD FAST TO THE TREACHEROUS FACE OF THE DOME, BEATEN BY THE FROZEN WINDS, FEELING INSIGNIFICANT, MINUSCULE...
...INSECTS CRAWLING ON THIS GIANT SHELL.
FIVE HOURS OF THAT EXHAUSTING ASCENT...
THE OMINOUS REVERBERATION OUR CONSTANT COMPANION...
MECHAMORPHS!

FOUR MECHATANKS COMING FROM THE EAST HAD SPOTTED US...

AN ARTILLERY BLAST...

THEN A WHISTLING SOUND...

MISSILES!!!

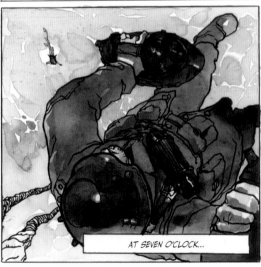

AT SEVEN O'CLOCK...

SQUID MISSILE COMING STRAIGHT FOR US!!!

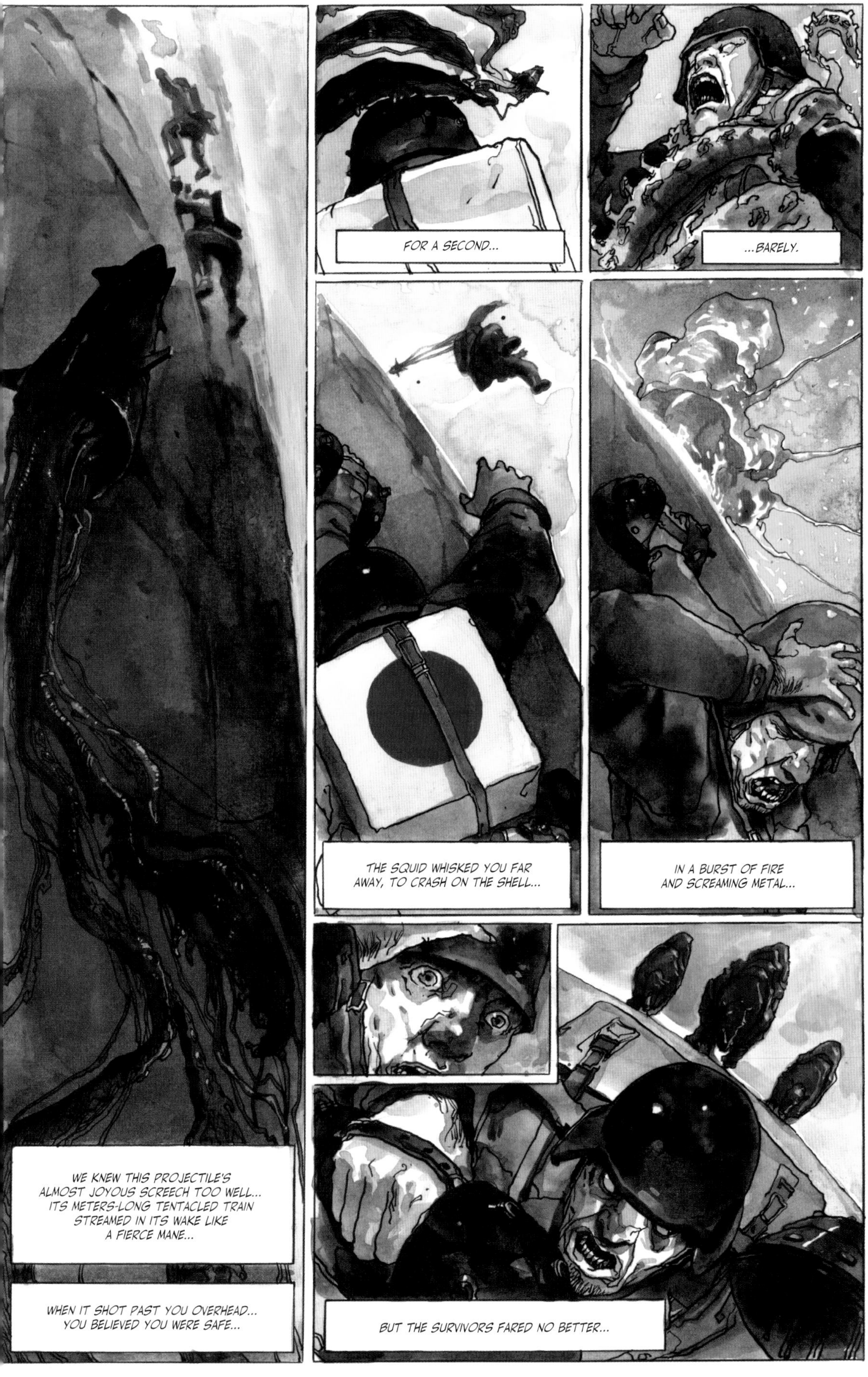
WE KNEW THIS PROJECTILE'S ALMOST JOYOUS SCREECH TOO WELL... ITS METERS-LONG TENTACLED TRAIN STREAMED IN ITS WAKE LIKE A FIERCE MANE...
WHEN IT SHOT PAST YOU OVERHEAD... YOU BELIEVED YOU WERE SAFE...
FOR A SECOND...
...BARELY.
THE SQUID WHISKED YOU FAR AWAY, TO CRASH ON THE SHELL...
IN A BURST OF FIRE AND SCREAMING METAL...
BUT THE SURVIVORS FARED NO BETTER...

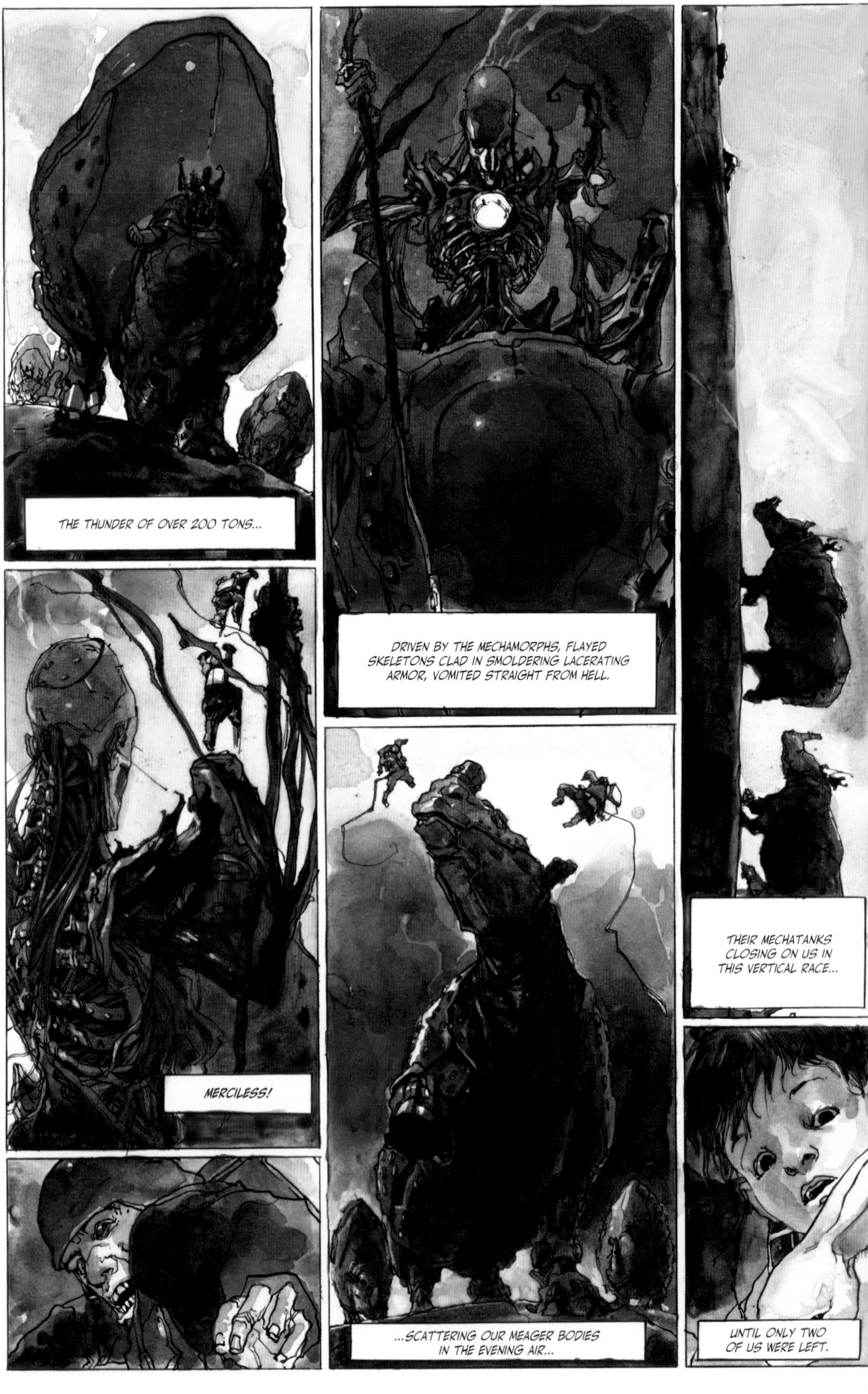
THE THUNDER OF OVER 200 TONS...
DRIVEN BY THE MECHAMORPHS, FLAYED SKELETONS CLAD IN SMOLDERING LACERATING ARMOR, VOMITED STRAIGHT FROM HELL.
THEIR MECHATANKS CLOSING ON US IN THIS VERTICAL RACE...
MERCILESS!
...SCATTERING OUR MEAGER BODIES IN THE EVENING AIR...
UNTIL ONLY TWO OF US WERE LEFT.

AT LAST, THE TOP OF THE MECHADOME.

AT ITS CENTER, THE MUTATION-ACCELERANT BEAM CRACKLED AND BLAZED.

DESPERATELY, THE SOLDIER RAN...

UNTIL HE WAS STOPPED SHORT.

I LANDED LESS THAN TWO METERS FROM THE ENERGY BEAM...

...WHEN I FACED THE MECHAMORPH, ITS TORN MUSCULATURE FLAPPING IN THE WIND...

ENDOMORPH, YOU WILL DIE. THERE WILL BE NO GOLEM. THE FATE OF THE HUMAN RACE ENDS HERE, WITH YOU!!!

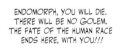

LOOK!

WHAT MAKES YOU THINK I AM THE ENDOMORPH?

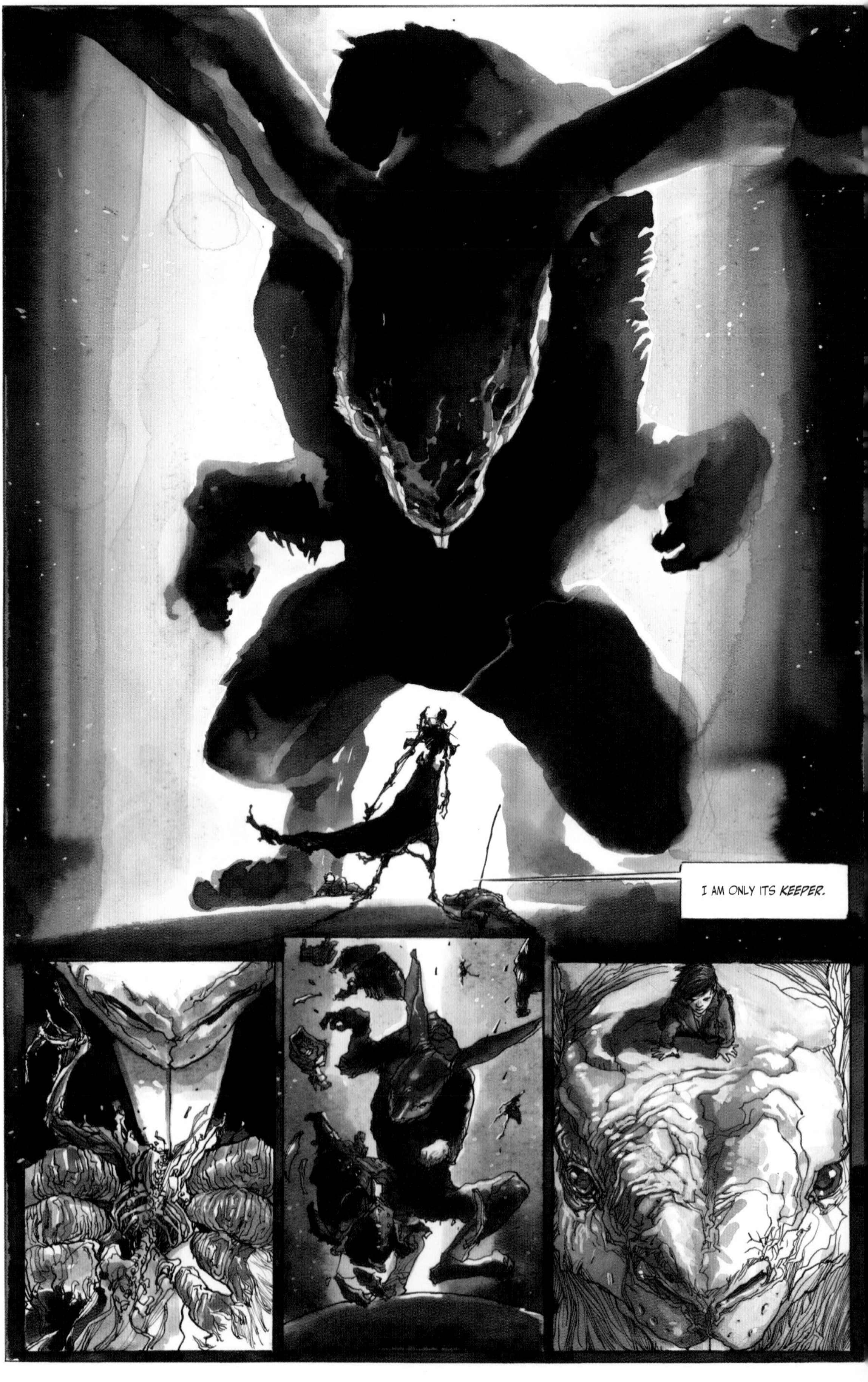
I AM ONLY ITS KEEPER.

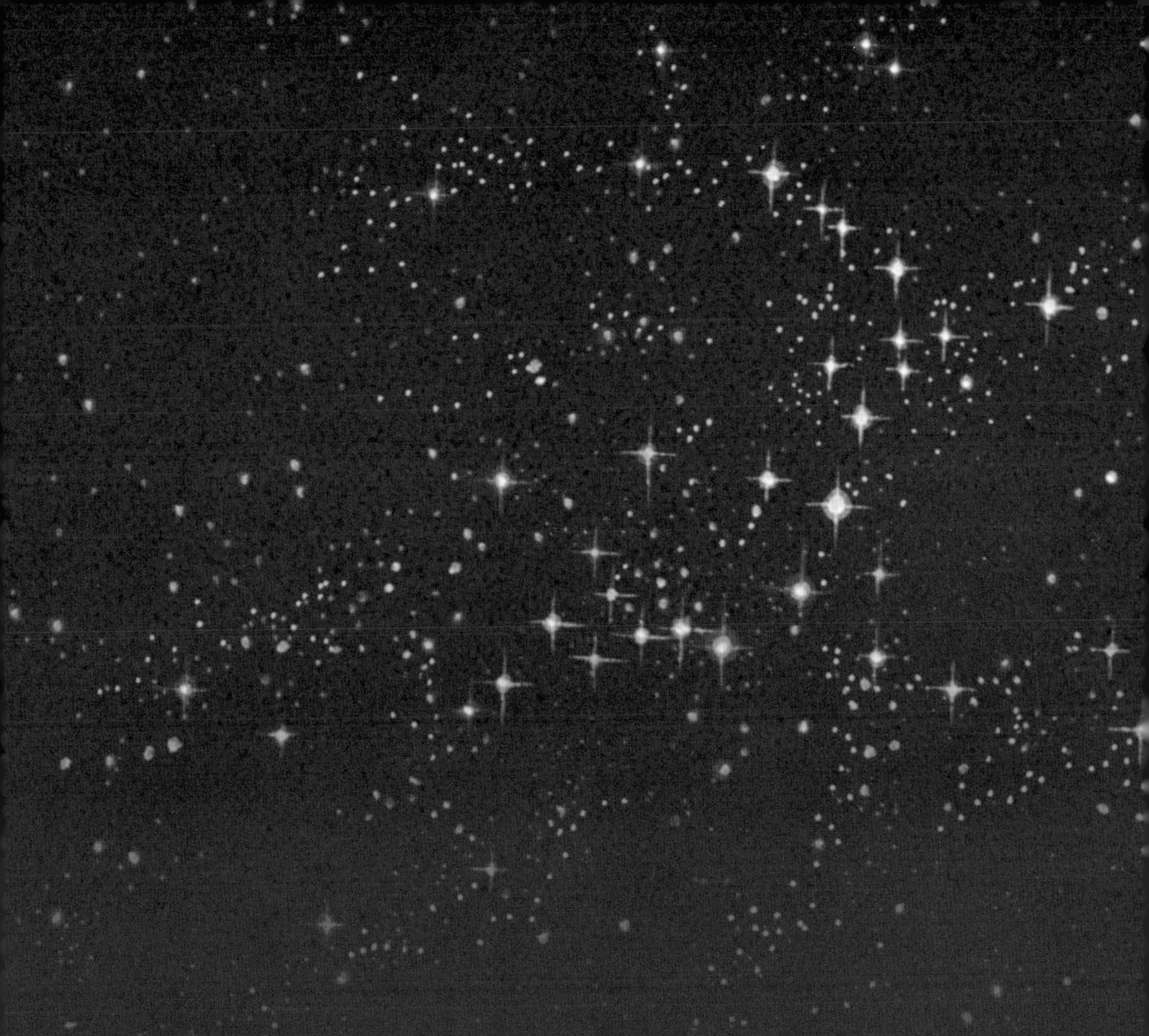

REALITY CHECK

Story by JIM MACDONALD
Art by FRANCIS TSAI

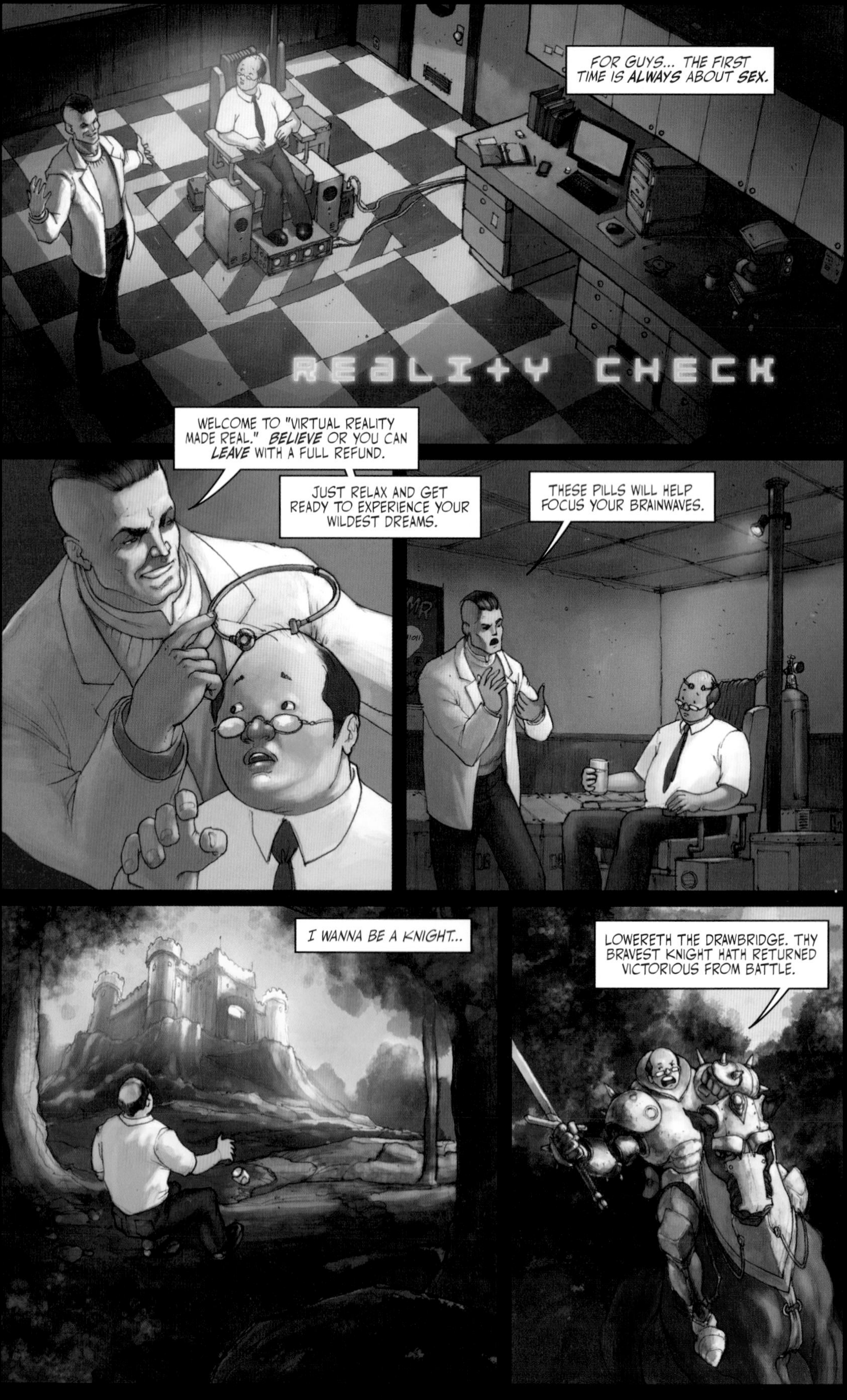
FOR GUYS... THE FIRST TIME IS ALWAYS ABOUT SEX.
REALITY CHECK
WELCOME TO "VIRTUAL REALITY MADE REAL." BELIEVE OR YOU CAN LEAVE WITH A FULL REFUND.
JUST RELAX AND GET READY TO EXPERIENCE YOUR WILDEST DREAMS.
THESE PILLS WILL HELP FOCUS YOUR BRAINWAVES.
I WANNA BE A KNIGHT...
LOWERETH THE DRAWBRIDGE. THY BRAVEST KNIGHT HATH RETURNED VICTORIOUS FROM BATTLE.

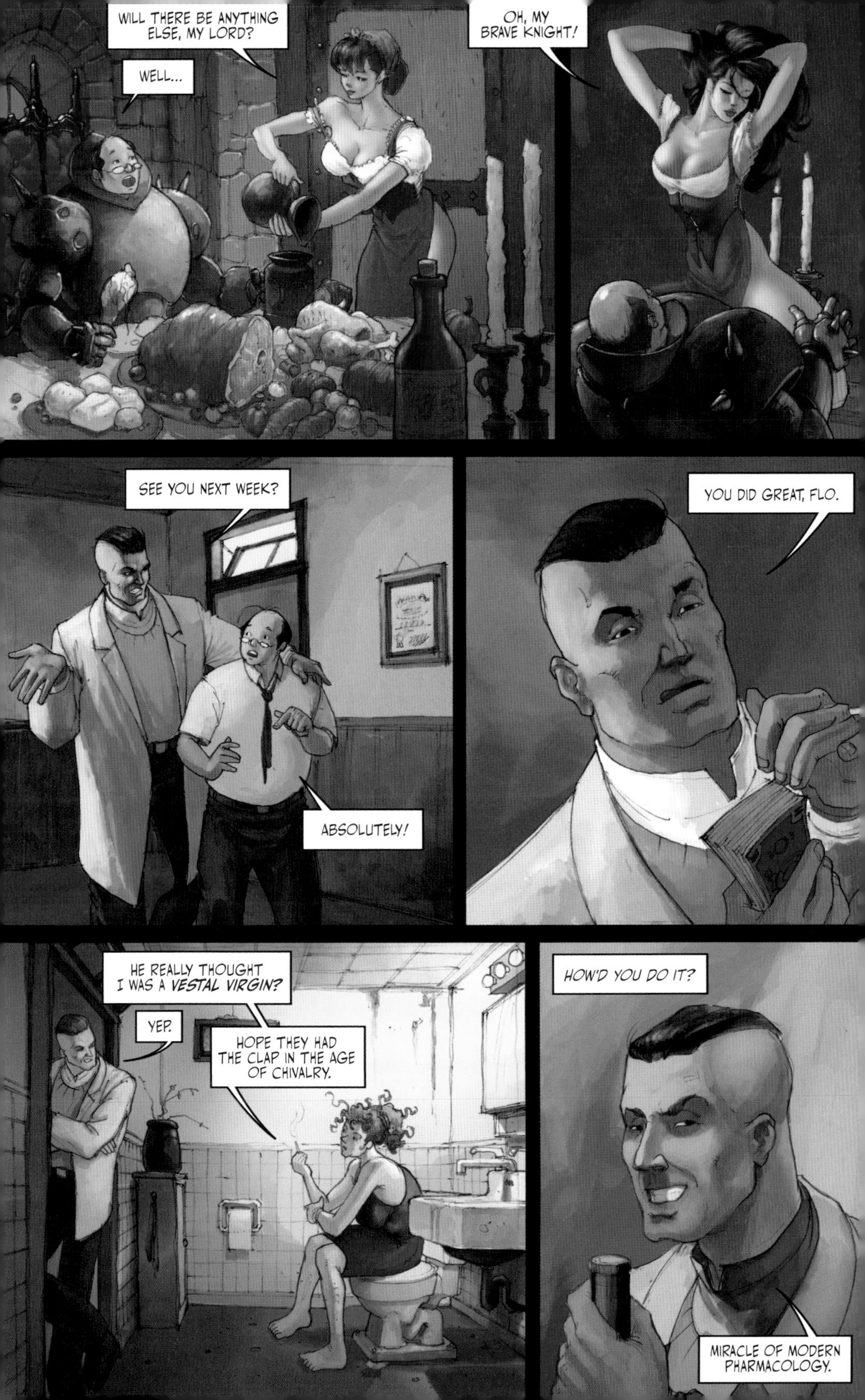
WILL THERE BE ANYTHING ELSE, MY LORD?
WELL...
OH, MY BRAVE KNIGHT!
SEE YOU NEXT WEEK?
ABSOLUTELY!
YOU DID GREAT, FLO.
HE REALLY THOUGHT I WAS A *VESTAL VIRGIN?*
YEP.
HOPE THEY HAD THE CLAP IN THE AGE OF CHIVALRY.
HOW'D YOU DO IT?
MIRACLE OF MODERN PHARMACOLOGY.

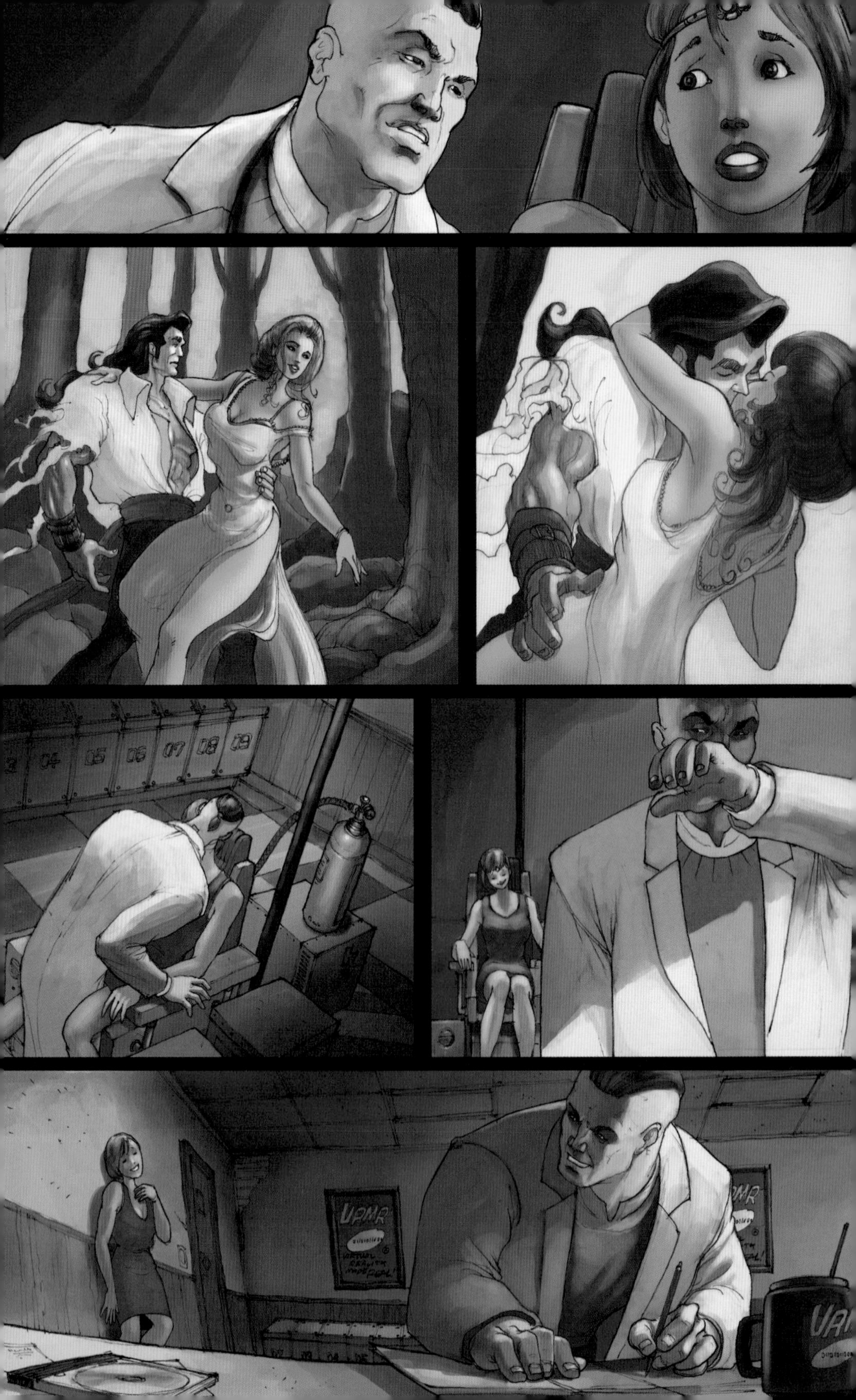
04 05 06 07 08 09
VRMR
VIRTUAL REALITY MADE REAL!

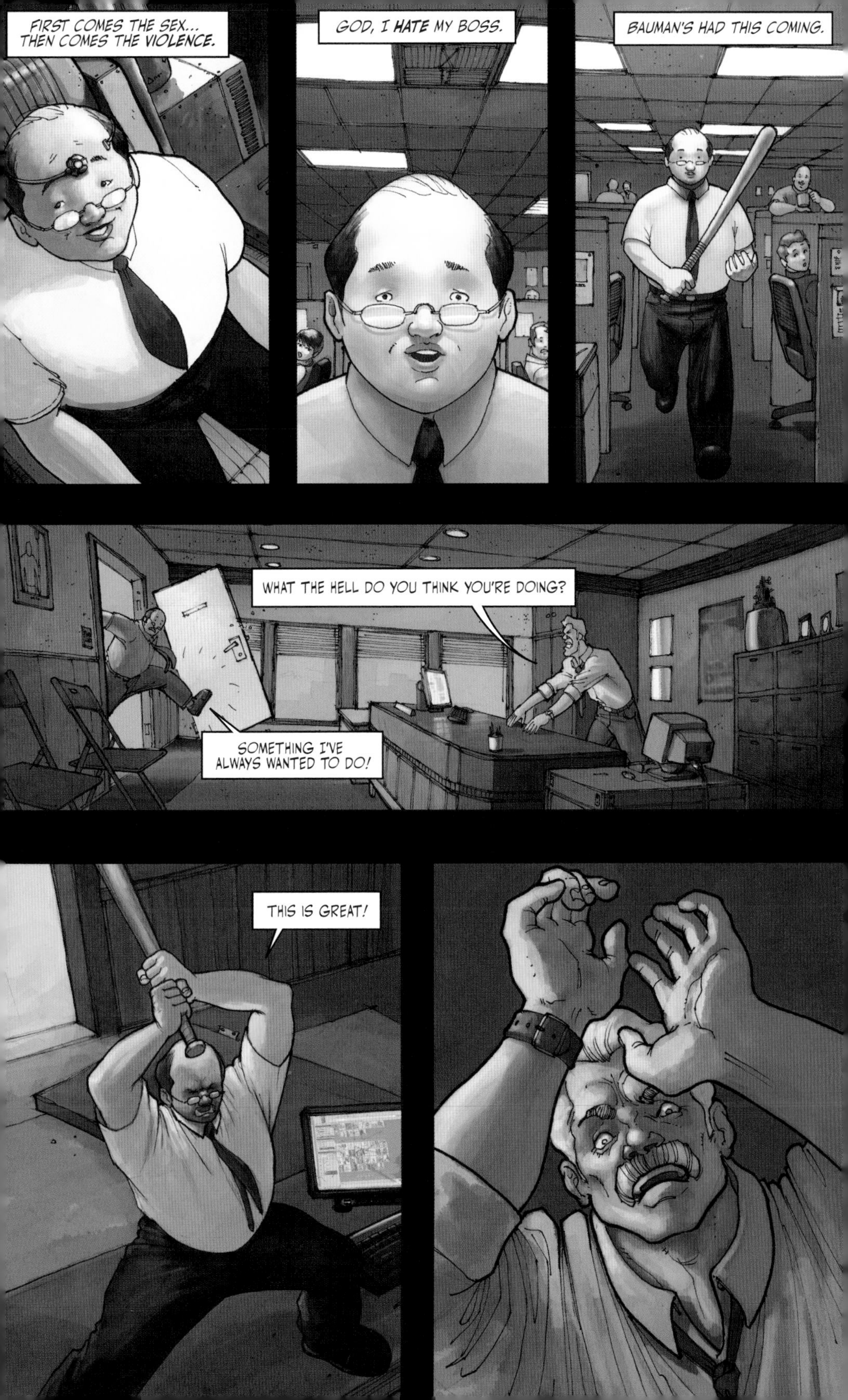
FIRST COMES THE SEX... THEN COMES THE VIOLENCE.
GOD, I HATE MY BOSS.
BAUMAN'S HAD THIS COMING.
WHAT THE HELL DO YOU THINK YOU'RE DOING?
SOMETHING I'VE ALWAYS WANTED TO DO!
THIS IS GREAT!

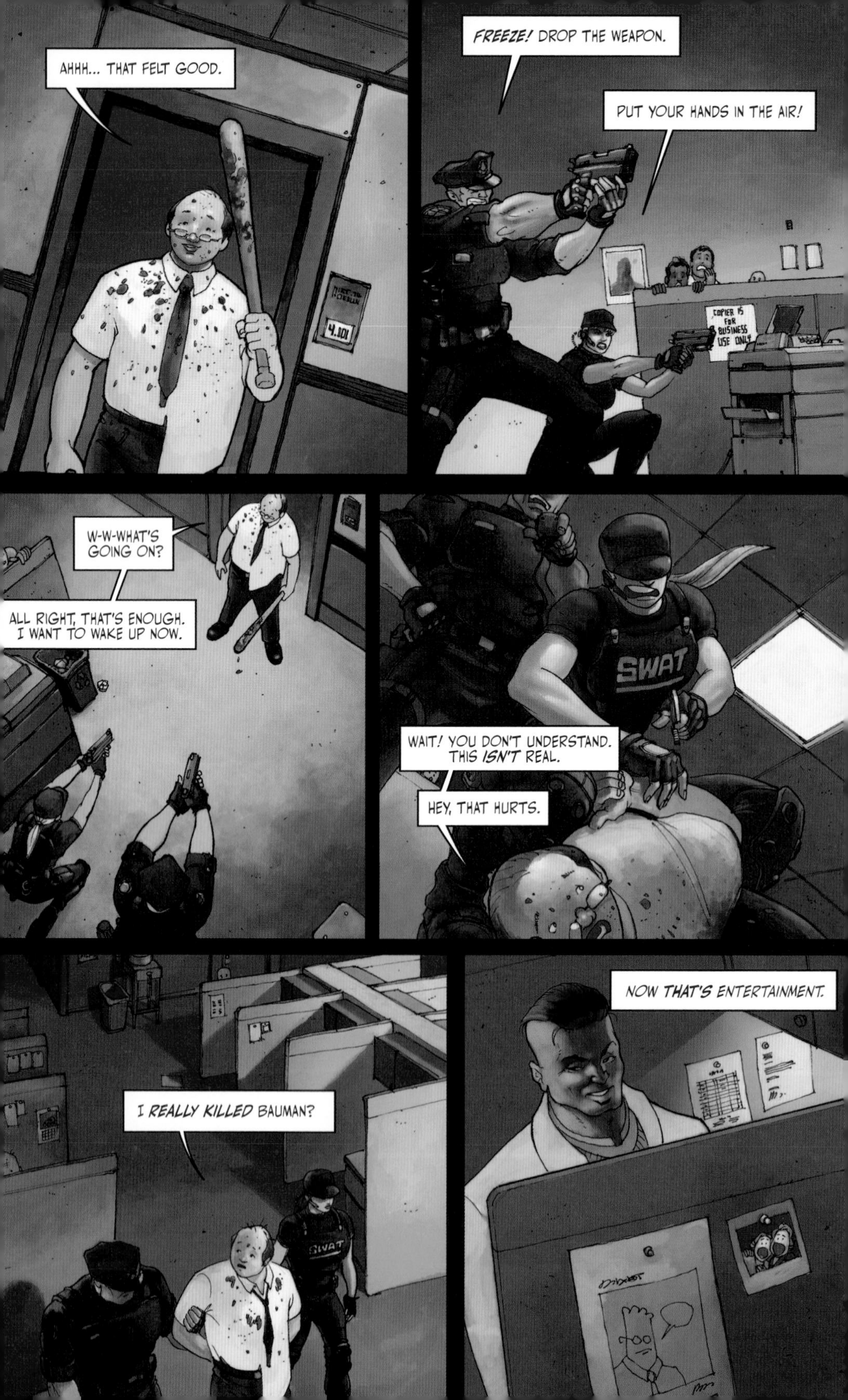
AHHH... THAT FELT GOOD.
4.101
FREEZE! DROP THE WEAPON.
PUT YOUR HANDS IN THE AIR!
COPIER IS FOR BUSINESS USE ONLY
W-W-WHAT'S GOING ON?
ALL RIGHT, THAT'S ENOUGH. I WANT TO WAKE UP NOW.
SWAT
WAIT! YOU DON'T UNDERSTAND. THIS ISN'T REAL.
HEY, THAT HURTS.
I REALLY KILLED BAUMAN?
SWAT
NOW THAT'S ENTERTAINMENT.

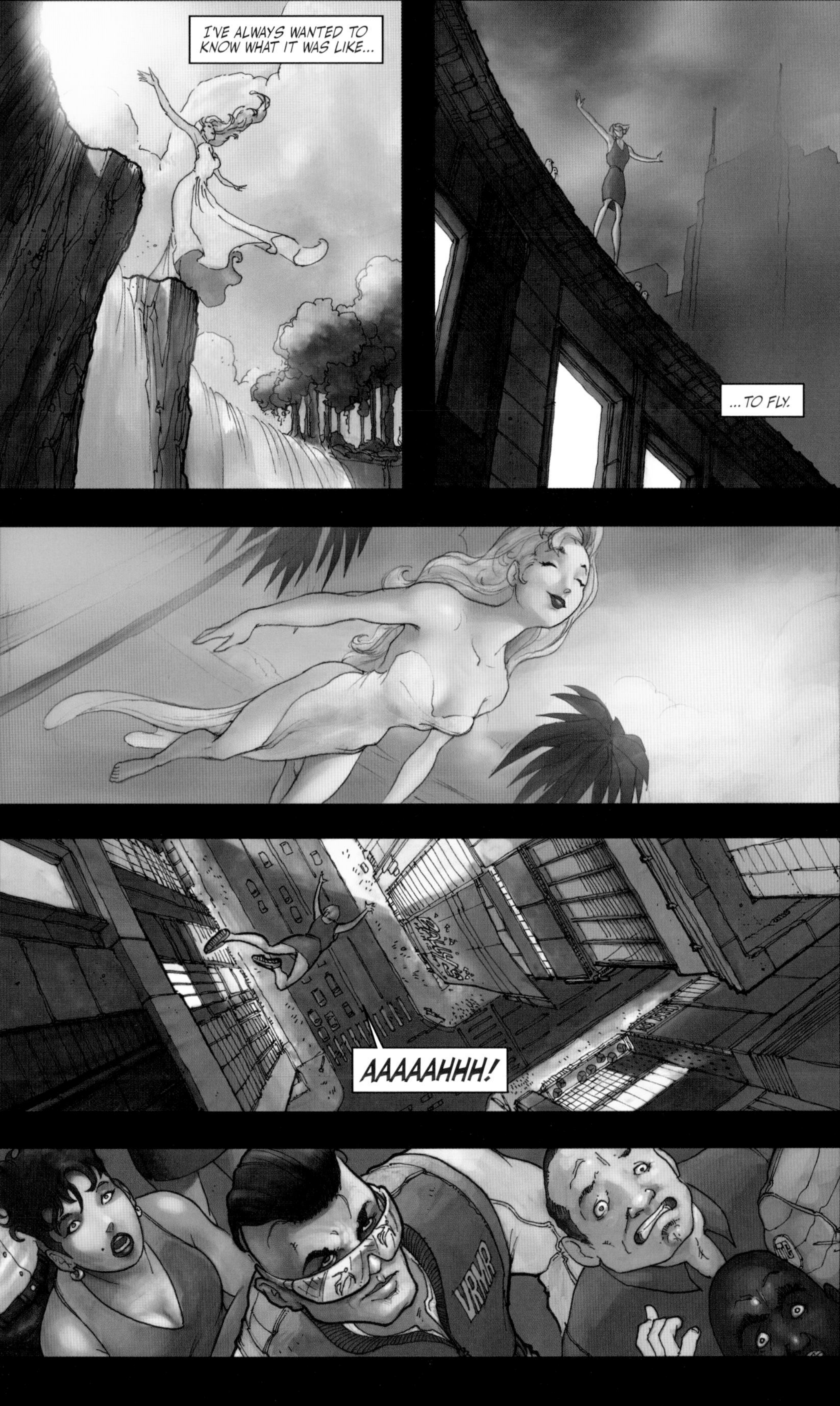
I'VE ALWAYS WANTED TO KNOW WHAT IT WAS LIKE...
...TO FLY.
AAAAAHHH!
VRMR

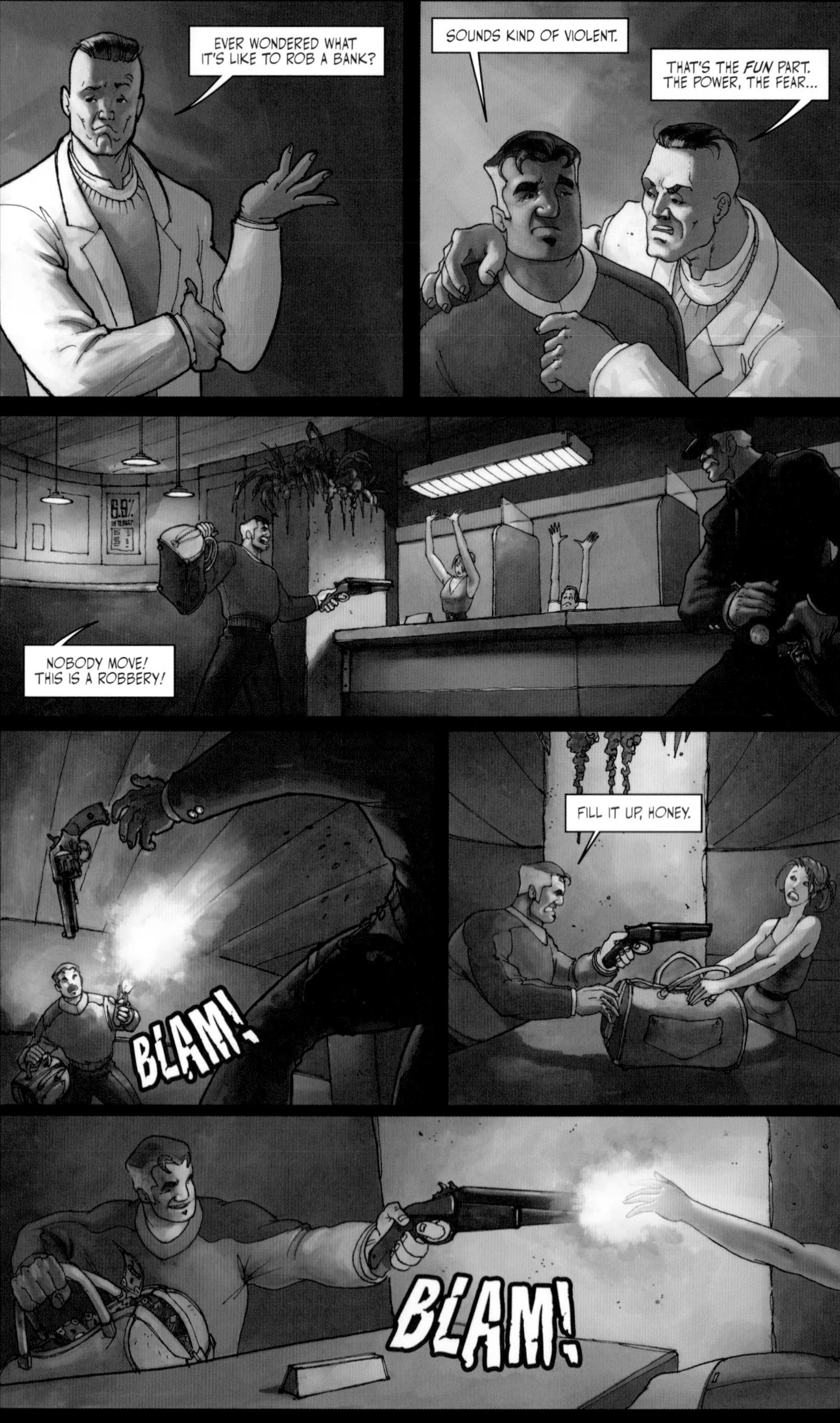
EVER WONDERED WHAT IT'S LIKE TO ROB A BANK?
SOUNDS KIND OF VIOLENT.
THAT'S THE *FUN* PART. THE POWER, THE FEAR...
6.9% INTEREST
NOBODY MOVE! THIS IS A ROBBERY!
BLAM!
FILL IT UP, HONEY.
BLAM!

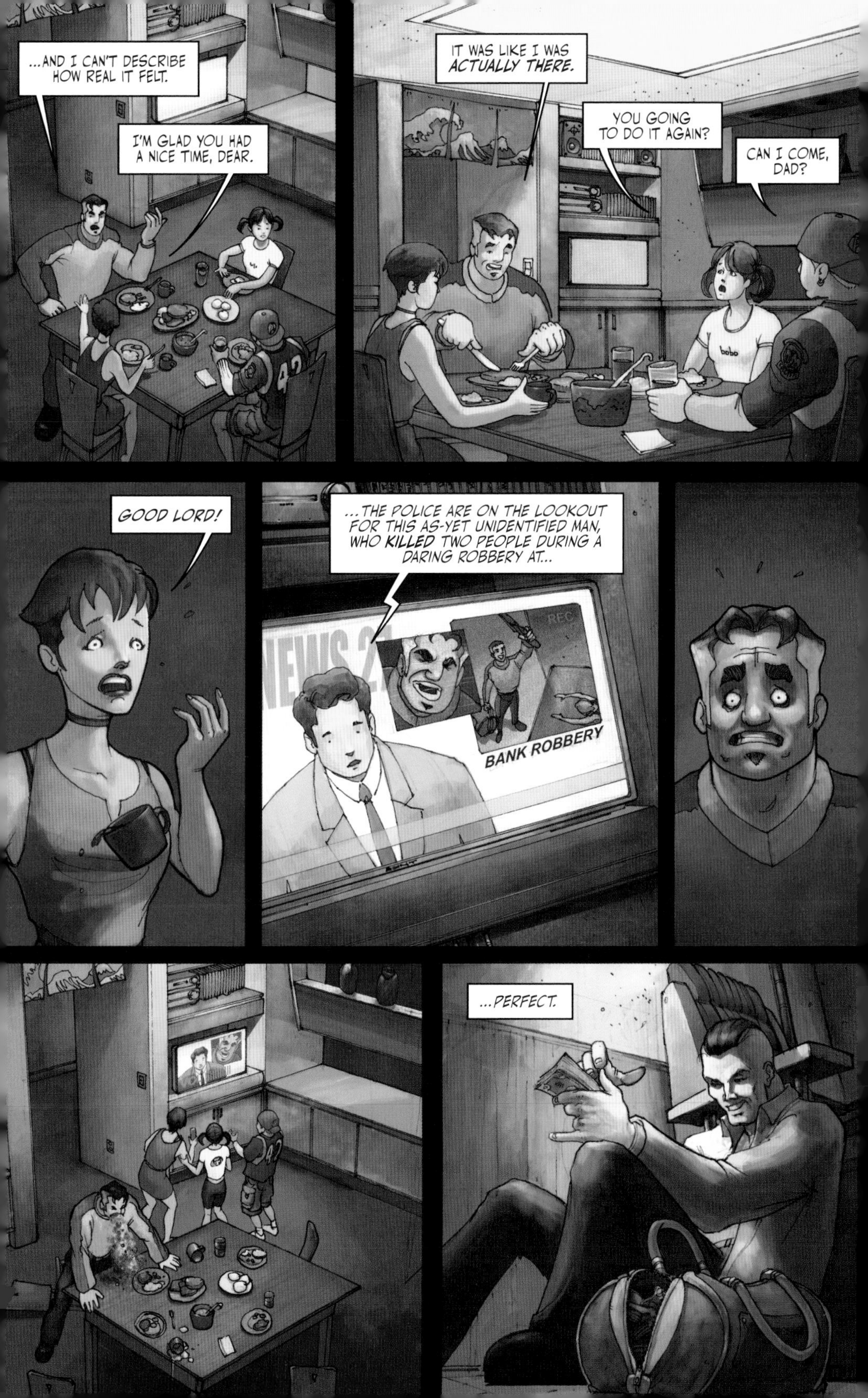
...AND I CAN'T DESCRIBE HOW REAL IT FELT.
I'M GLAD YOU HAD A NICE TIME, DEAR.
IT WAS LIKE I WAS *ACTUALLY THERE.*
YOU GOING TO DO IT AGAIN?
CAN I COME, DAD?
GOOD LORD!
*...THE POLICE ARE ON THE LOOKOUT FOR THIS AS-YET UNIDENTIFIED MAN, WHO **KILLED** TWO PEOPLE DURING A DARING ROBBERY AT...*
REC
BANK ROBBERY
...PERFECT.

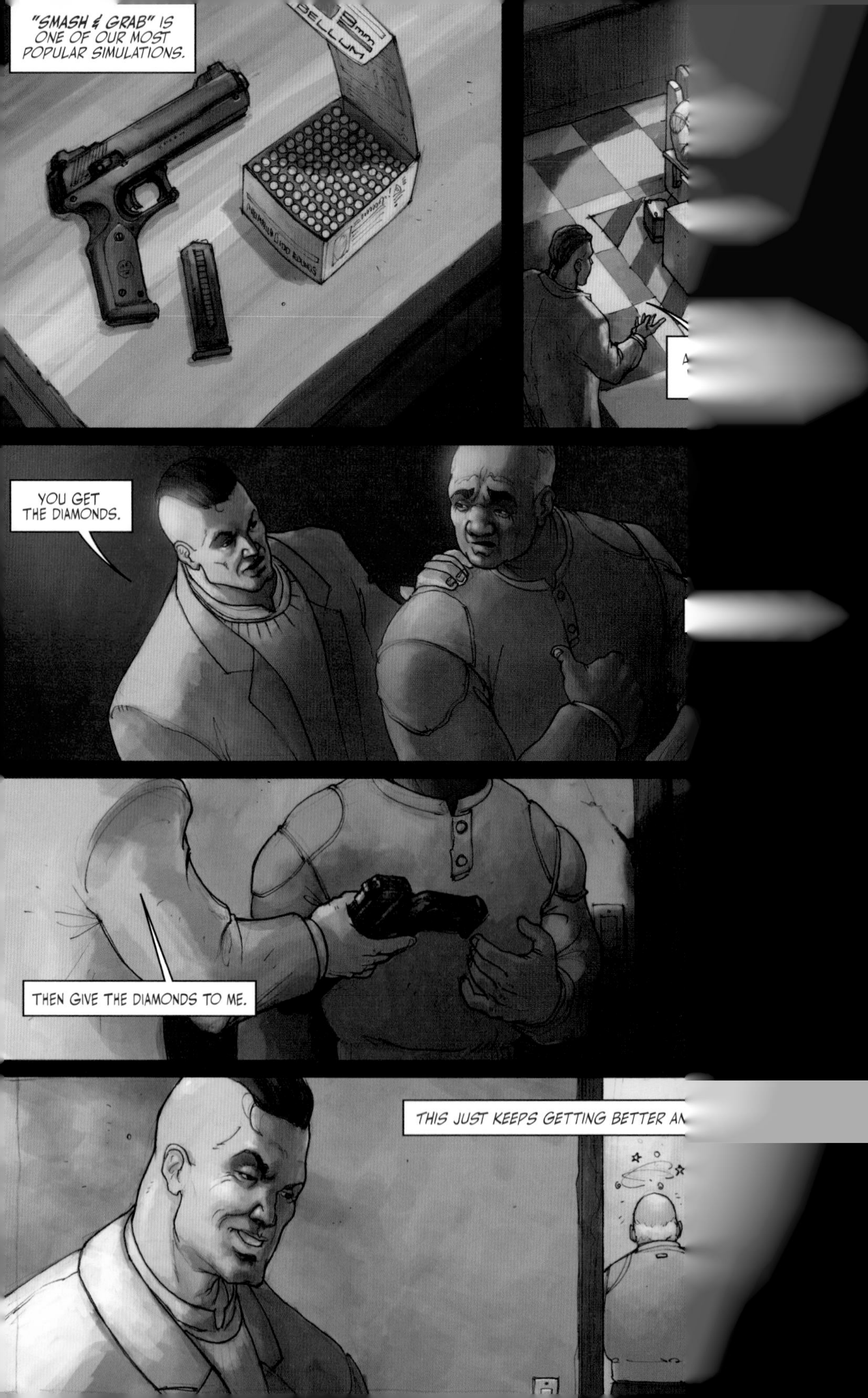
"SMASH & GRAB" IS ONE OF OUR MOST POPULAR SIMULATIONS.
9mm
BELLUM
YOU GET THE DIAMONDS.
THEN GIVE THE DIAMONDS TO ME.
THIS JUST KEEPS GETTING BETTER AN

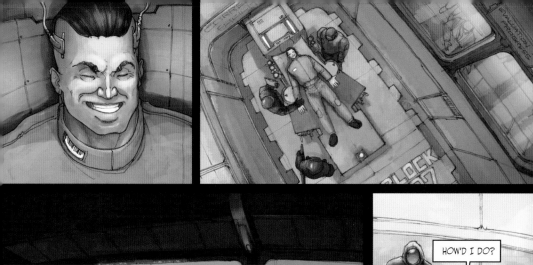

IT DOESN'T LOOK GOOD FOR YOUR CLIENT, COUNSELOR.

WARDEN, THE *FREEDOM SIMULATION* IS STILL UNPROVEN...

HOW'D I DO?

PAROLE DENIED.

NO!

THIS ISN'T FAIR!

HOW MANY MORE OF THESE DO WE HAVE TODAY?

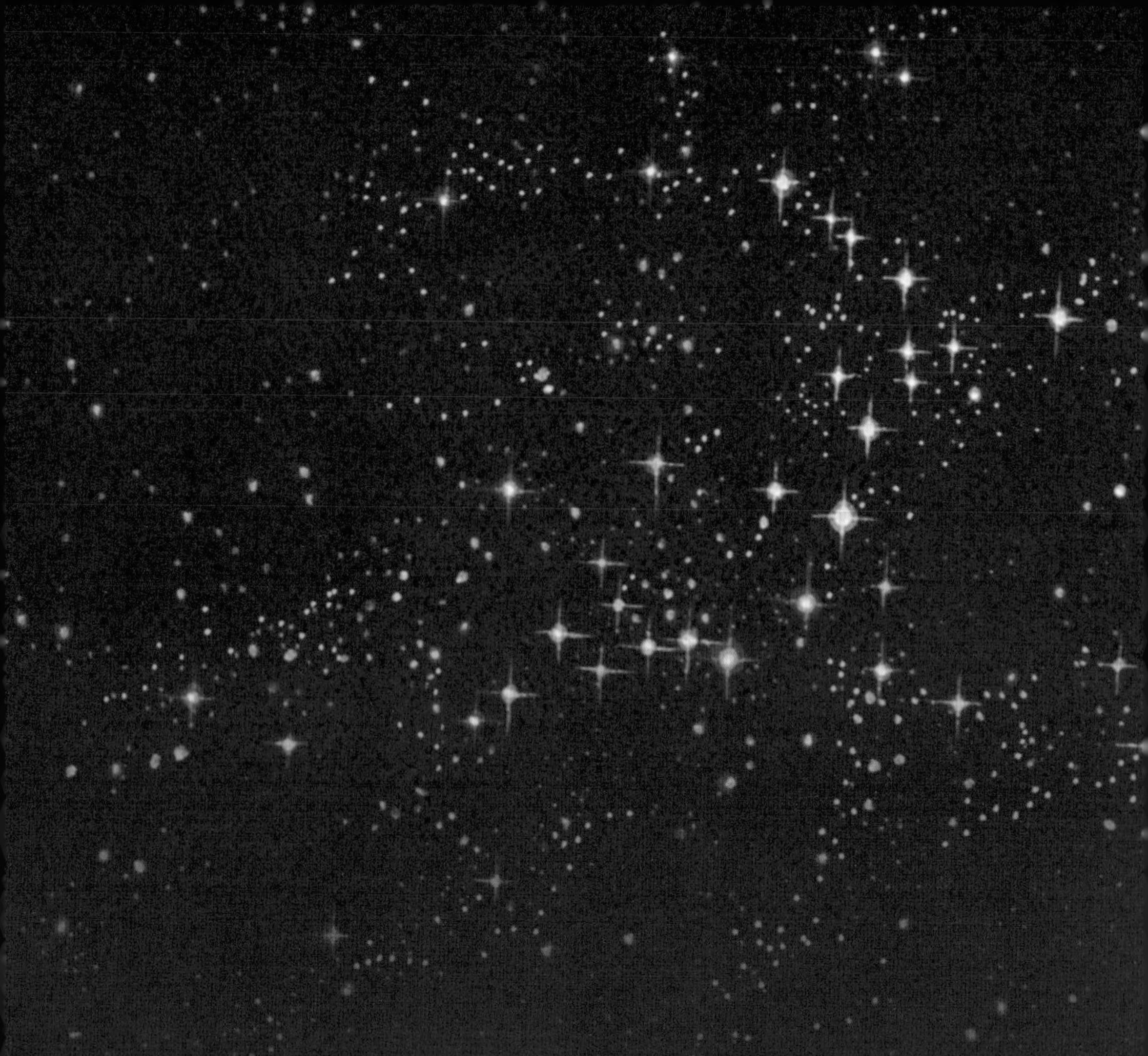

SPARE PARTS

Story by STUART MOORE
Art by CULLY HAMNER
Colors by CLÉMENCE

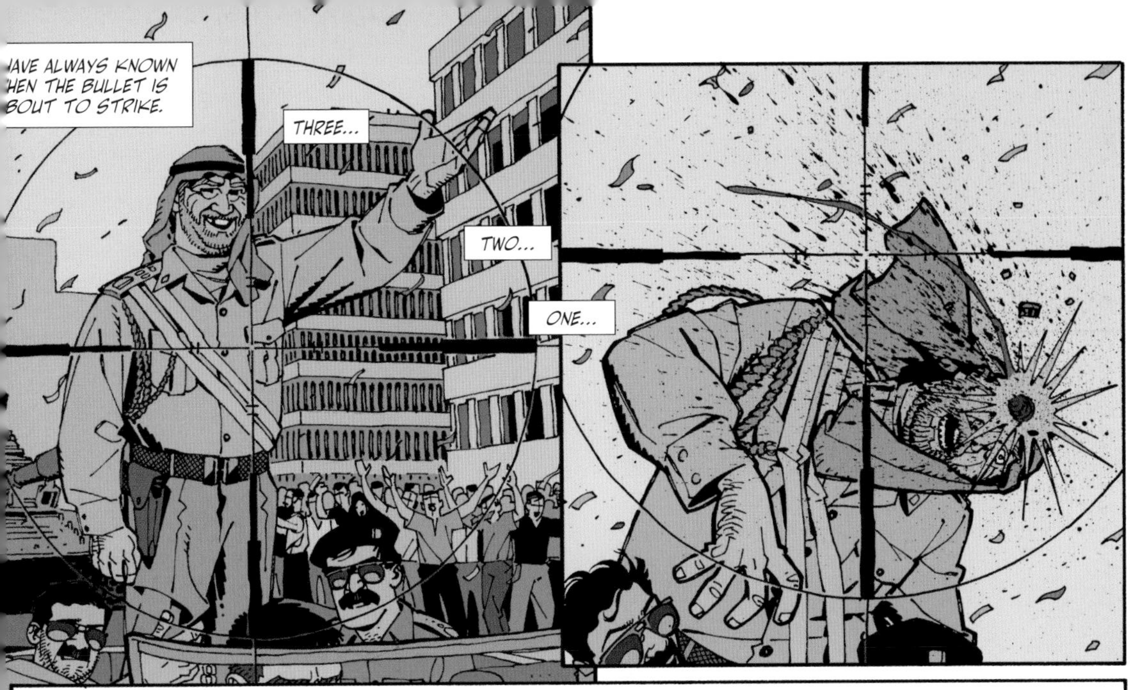

AVE ALWAYS KNOWN HEN THE BULLET IS BOUT TO STRIKE.
THREE...
TWO...
ONE...

SPARE PARTS

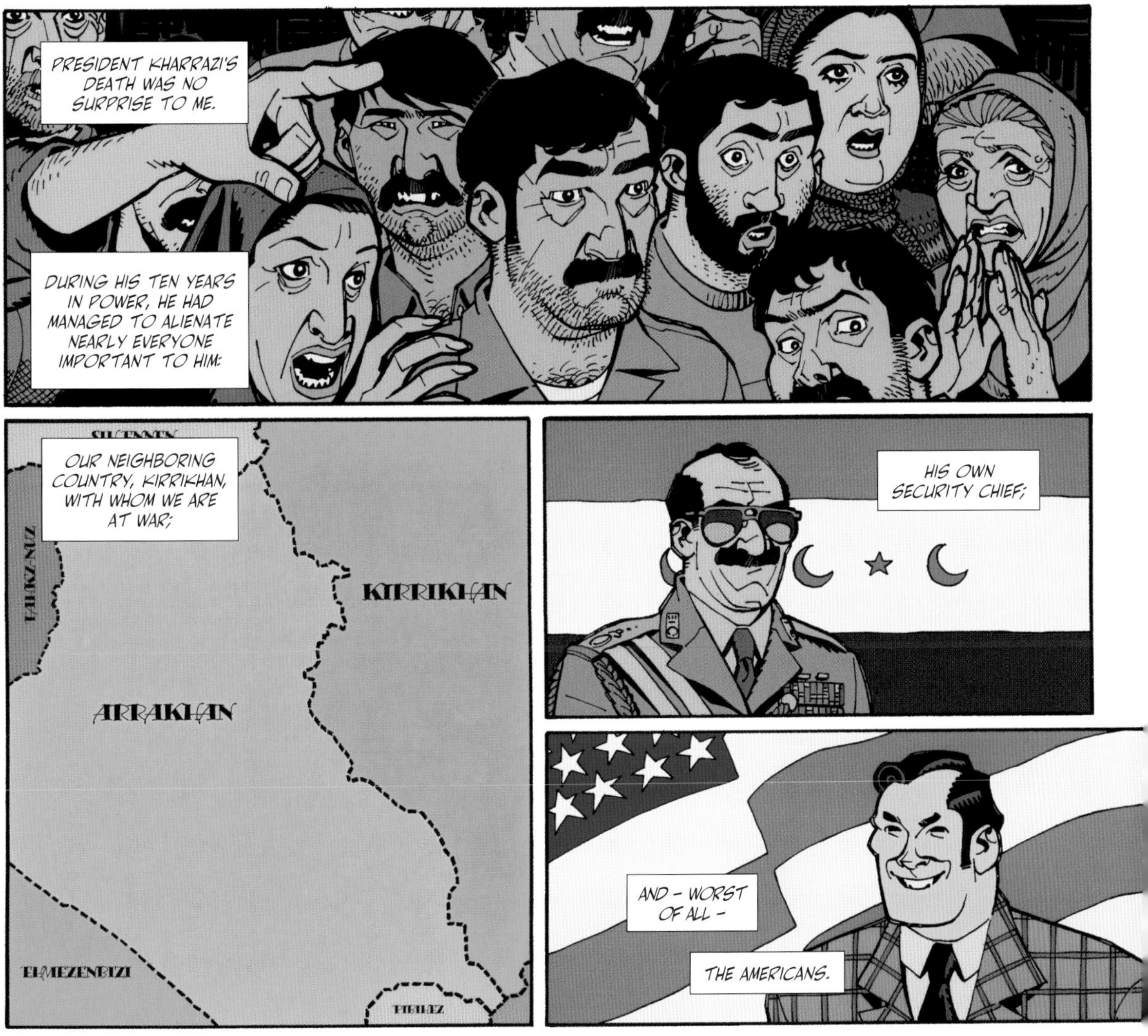

PRESIDENT KHARRAZI'S DEATH WAS NO SURPRISE TO ME.
DURING HIS TEN YEARS IN POWER, HE HAD MANAGED TO ALIENATE NEARLY EVERYONE IMPORTANT TO HIM:
OUR NEIGHBORING COUNTRY, KIRRIKHAN, WITH WHOM WE ARE AT WAR;
KIRRIKHAN
ARRAKHAN
HIS OWN SECURITY CHIEF;
AND - WORST OF ALL -
THE AMERICANS.

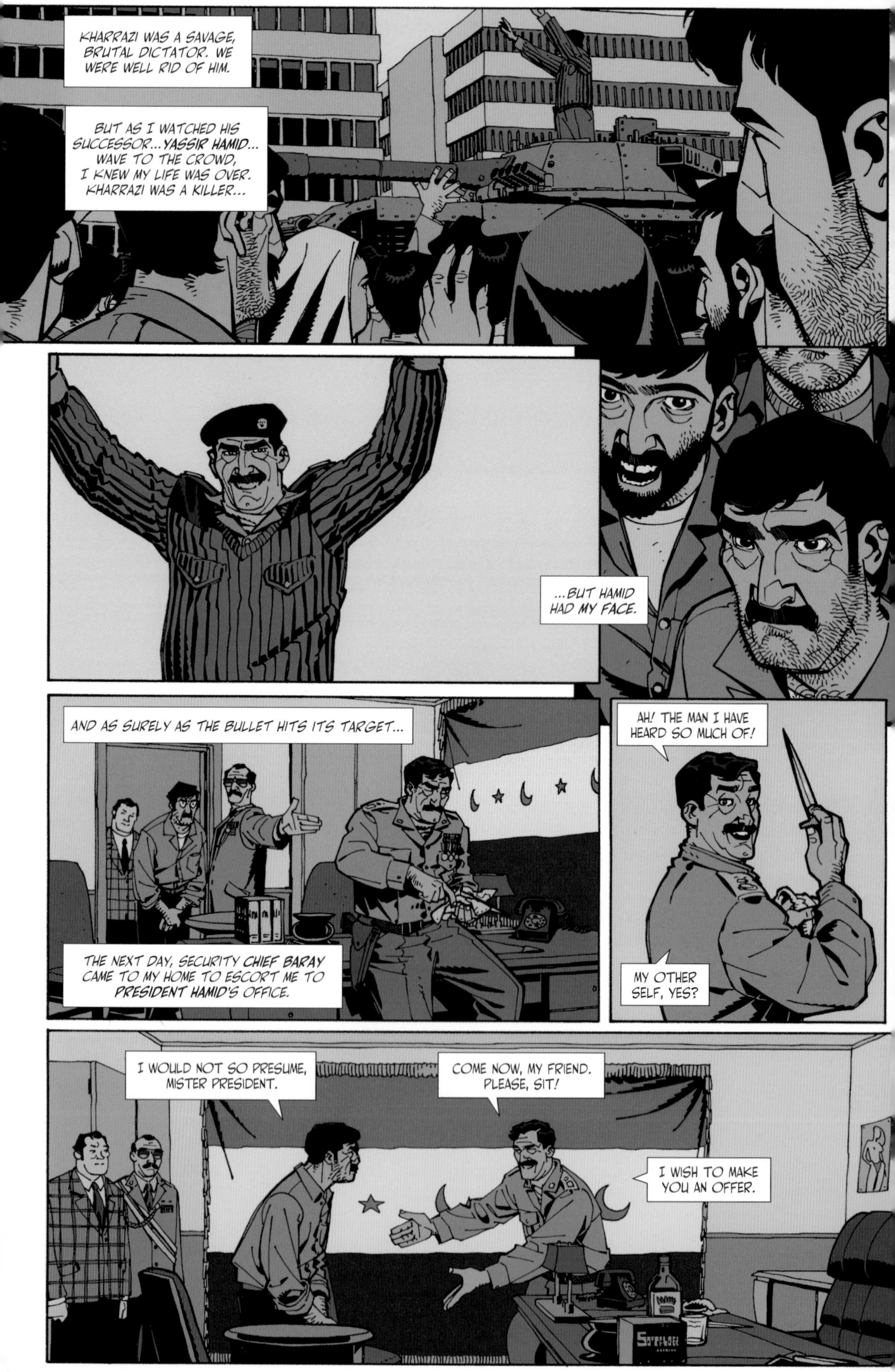
KHARRAZI WAS A SAVAGE, BRUTAL DICTATOR. WE WERE WELL RID OF HIM.
BUT AS I WATCHED HIS SUCCESSOR...YASSIR HAMID... WAVE TO THE CROWD, I KNEW MY LIFE WAS OVER. KHARRAZI WAS A KILLER...
...BUT HAMID HAD MY FACE.
AND AS SURELY AS THE BULLET HITS ITS TARGET...
THE NEXT DAY, SECURITY CHIEF BARAY CAME TO MY HOME TO ESCORT ME TO PRESIDENT HAMID'S OFFICE.
AH! THE MAN I HAVE HEARD SO MUCH OF!
MY OTHER SELF, YES?
I WOULD NOT SO PRESUME, MISTER PRESIDENT.
COME NOW, MY FRIEND. PLEASE, SIT!
I WISH TO MAKE YOU AN OFFER.

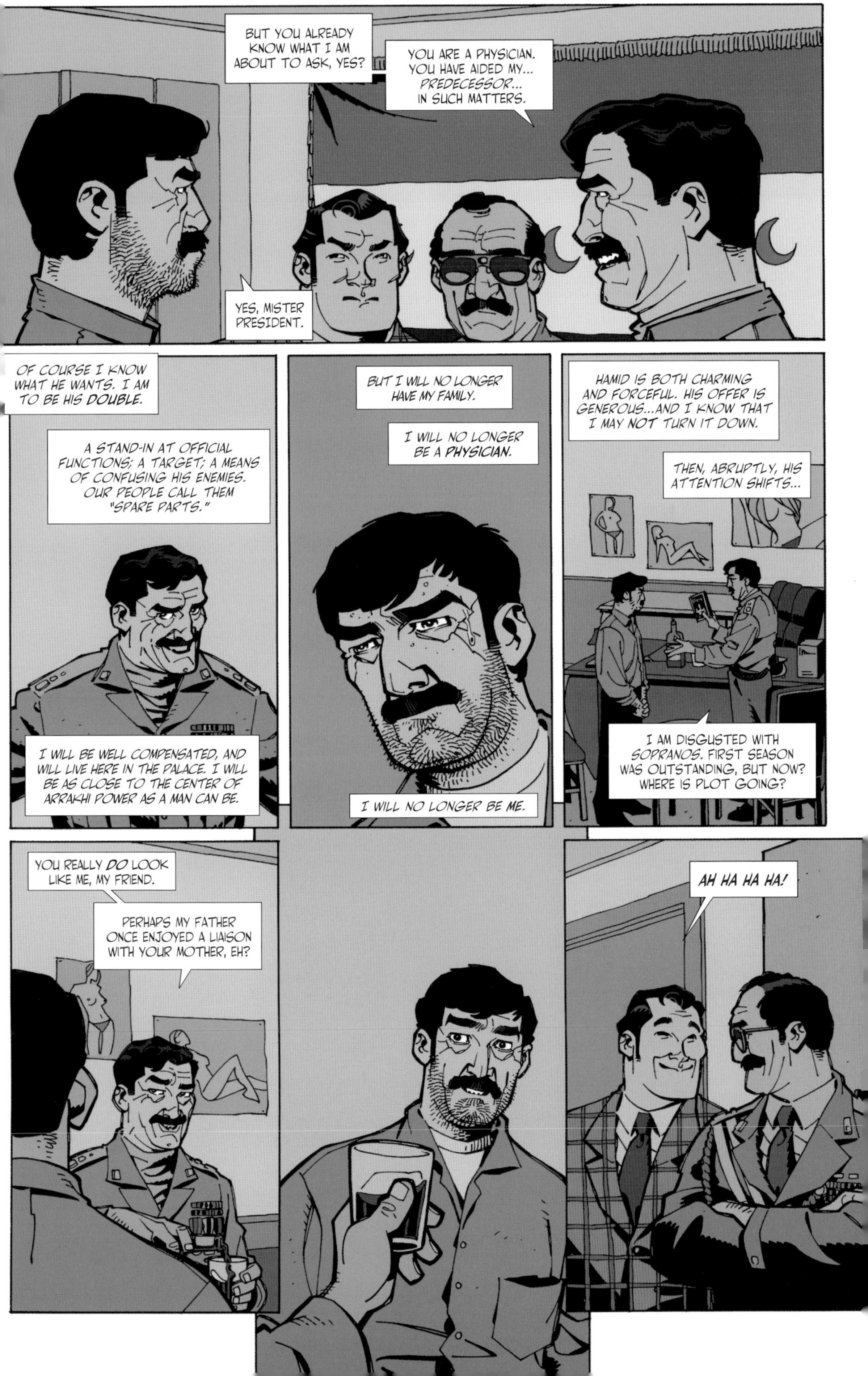
BUT YOU ALREADY KNOW WHAT I AM ABOUT TO ASK, YES?
YOU ARE A PHYSICIAN. YOU HAVE AIDED MY... PREDECESSOR... IN SUCH MATTERS.
YES, MISTER PRESIDENT.
OF COURSE I KNOW WHAT HE WANTS. I AM TO BE HIS DOUBLE.
A STAND-IN AT OFFICIAL FUNCTIONS; A TARGET; A MEANS OF CONFUSING HIS ENEMIES. OUR PEOPLE CALL THEM "SPARE PARTS."
I WILL BE WELL COMPENSATED, AND WILL LIVE HERE IN THE PALACE. I WILL BE AS CLOSE TO THE CENTER OF ARRAKHI POWER AS A MAN CAN BE.
BUT I WILL NO LONGER HAVE MY FAMILY.
I WILL NO LONGER BE A PHYSICIAN.
I WILL NO LONGER BE ME.
HAMID IS BOTH CHARMING AND FORCEFUL. HIS OFFER IS GENEROUS...AND I KNOW THAT I MAY NOT TURN IT DOWN.
THEN, ABRUPTLY, HIS ATTENTION SHIFTS...
I AM DISGUSTED WITH SOPRANOS. FIRST SEASON WAS OUTSTANDING, BUT NOW? WHERE IS PLOT GOING?
YOU REALLY DO LOOK LIKE ME, MY FRIEND.
PERHAPS MY FATHER ONCE ENJOYED A LIAISON WITH YOUR MOTHER, EH?
AH HA HA HA!

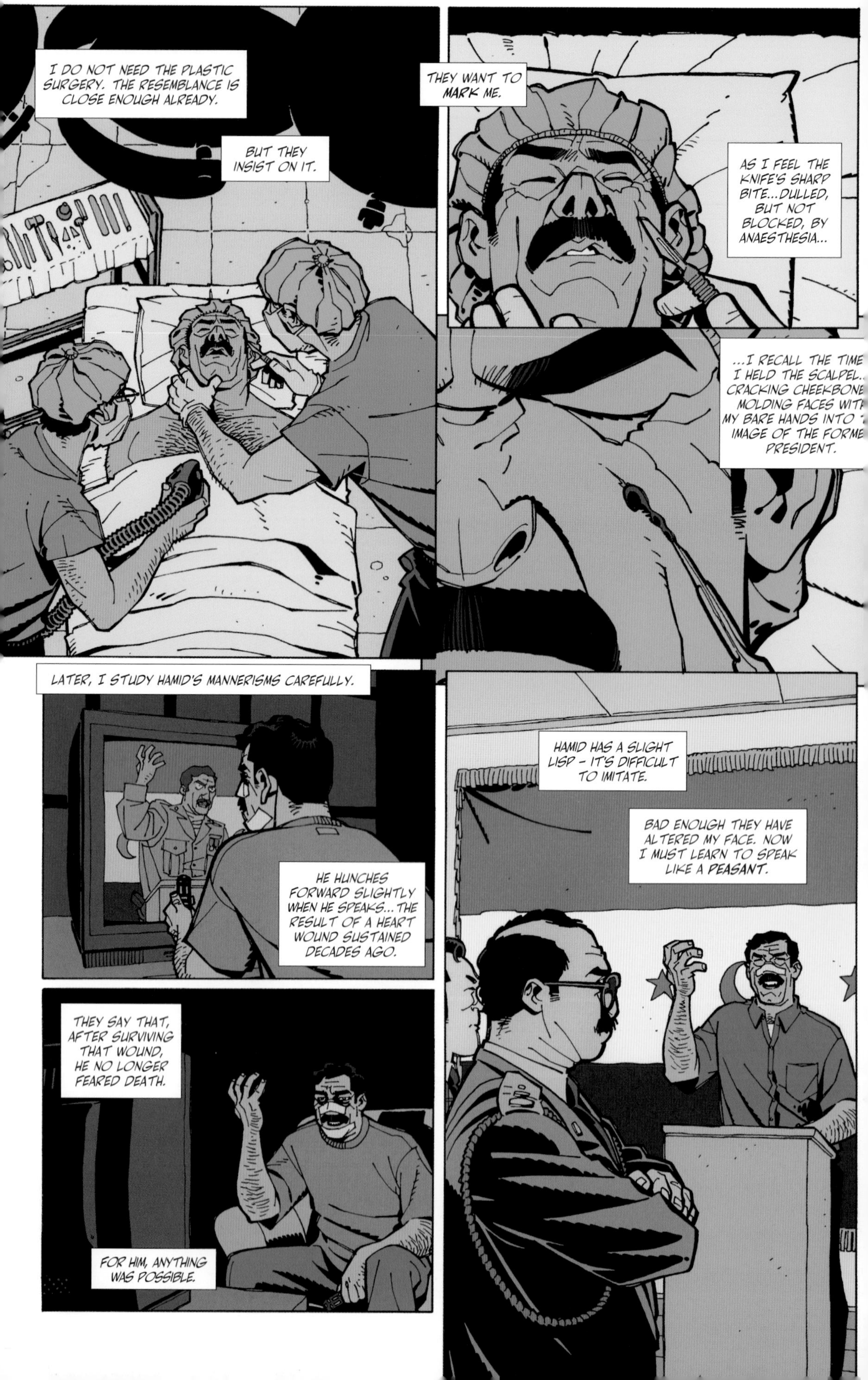
I DO NOT NEED THE PLASTIC SURGERY. THE RESEMBLANCE IS CLOSE ENOUGH ALREADY.
BUT THEY INSIST ON IT.
THEY WANT TO MARK ME.
AS I FEEL THE KNIFE'S SHARP BITE...DULLED, BUT NOT BLOCKED, BY ANAESTHESIA...
...I RECALL THE TIME I HELD THE SCALPEL.. CRACKING CHEEKBONE MOLDING FACES WITH MY BARE HANDS INTO IMAGE OF THE FORME PRESIDENT.
LATER, I STUDY HAMID'S MANNERISMS CAREFULLY.
HE HUNCHES FORWARD SLIGHTLY WHEN HE SPEAKS... THE RESULT OF A HEART WOUND SUSTAINED DECADES AGO.
THEY SAY THAT, AFTER SURVIVING THAT WOUND, HE NO LONGER FEARED DEATH.
FOR HIM, ANYTHING WAS POSSIBLE.
HAMID HAS A SLIGHT LISP – IT'S DIFFICULT TO IMITATE.
BAD ENOUGH THEY HAVE ALTERED MY FACE. NOW I MUST LEARN TO SPEAK LIKE A PEASANT.

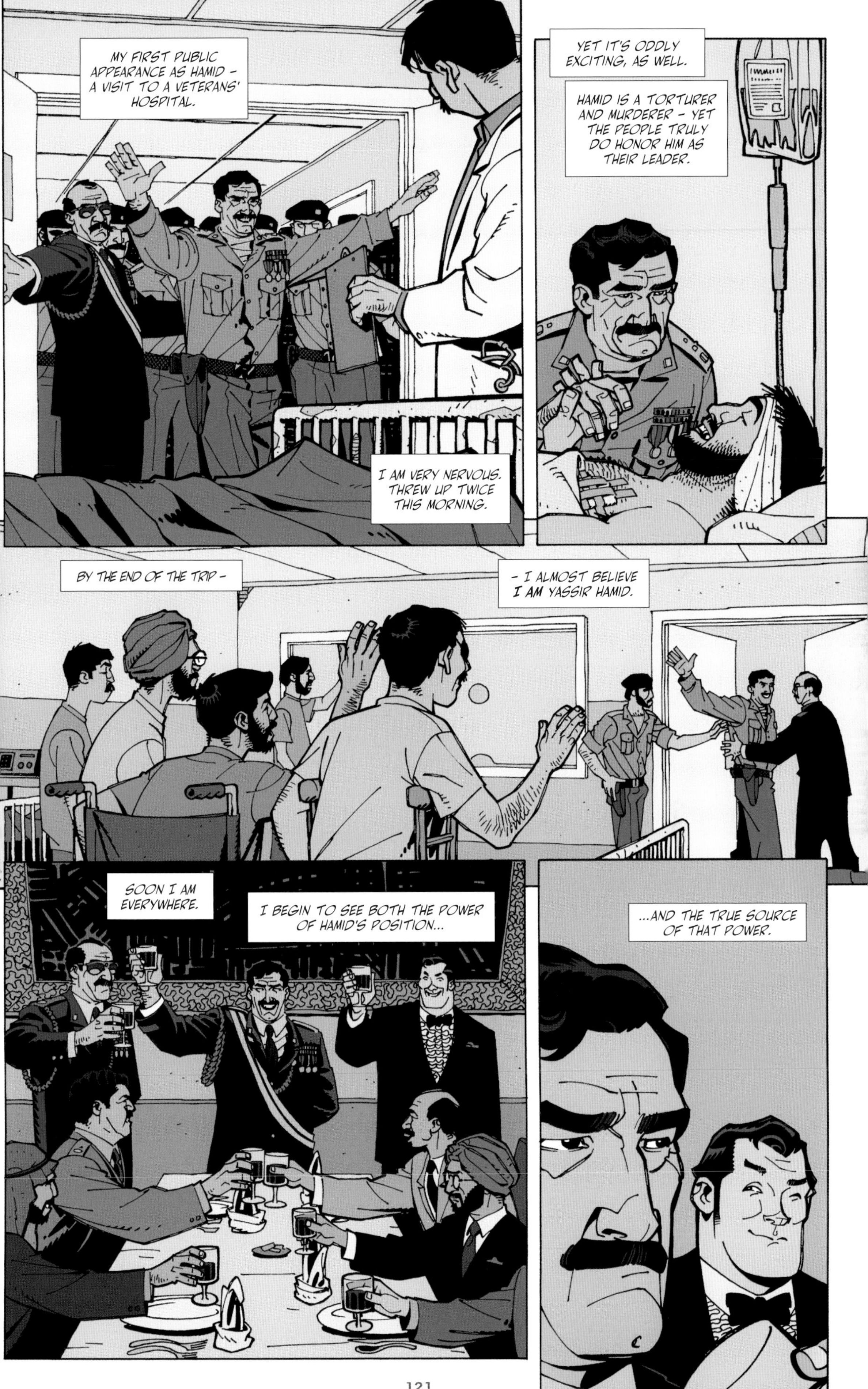
MY FIRST PUBLIC APPEARANCE AS HAMID – A VISIT TO A VETERANS' HOSPITAL.
I AM VERY NERVOUS. THREW UP TWICE THIS MORNING.
YET IT'S ODDLY EXCITING, AS WELL.
HAMID IS A TORTURER AND MURDERER – YET THE PEOPLE TRULY DO HONOR HIM AS THEIR LEADER.
BY THE END OF THE TRIP –
– I ALMOST BELIEVE **I AM** YASSIR HAMID.
SOON I AM EVERYWHERE.
I BEGIN TO SEE BOTH THE POWER OF HAMID'S POSITION...
...AND THE TRUE SOURCE OF THAT POWER.

JUST AS HAMID'S SURGEONS RESHAPED MY FEATURES...

...SO THE AMERICANS ARE COLD-BLOODEDLY RESHAPING OUR WORLD TO SUIT THEIR PURPOSES.

TO SATISFY THEIR BOUNDLESS LUST FOR OIL.

STE ENNEN

FALIKI-NUZ

KIRRIKHAN

ARRAKHAN

EL-MEZEN-BIZI

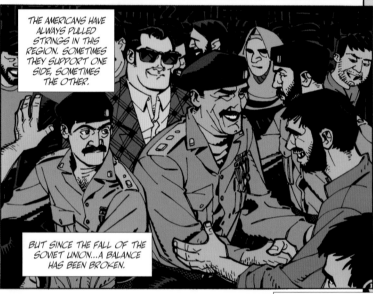

THE AMERICANS HAVE ALWAYS PULLED STRINGS IN THIS REGION. SOMETIMES THEY SUPPORT ONE SIDE, SOMETIMES THE OTHER.

BUT SINCE THE FALL OF THE SOVIET UNION...A BALANCE HAS BEEN BROKEN.

THEY HAVE BECOME GREEDY.

HAMID FREQUENTLY CALLS ME IN JUST TO CHAT.

HE NEVER DISCUSSES POLITICS...YET IN ALL OTHER AREAS, HE IS ASTONISHINGLY OPEN AND KIND.

I THINK, AT TIMES, HE FORGETS THE BOUNDARY BETWEEN US.

HE SAYS HE BELIEVES WE SHARE THE SAME MIND -- THAT MY THOUGHTS ARE A REFLECTION OF HIS OWN.

SOMETIMES...I ALMOST BELIEVE IT. BUT DOES THAT ALSO MEAN...

...THAT HIS THOUGHTS ARE A REFLECTION OF MINE?

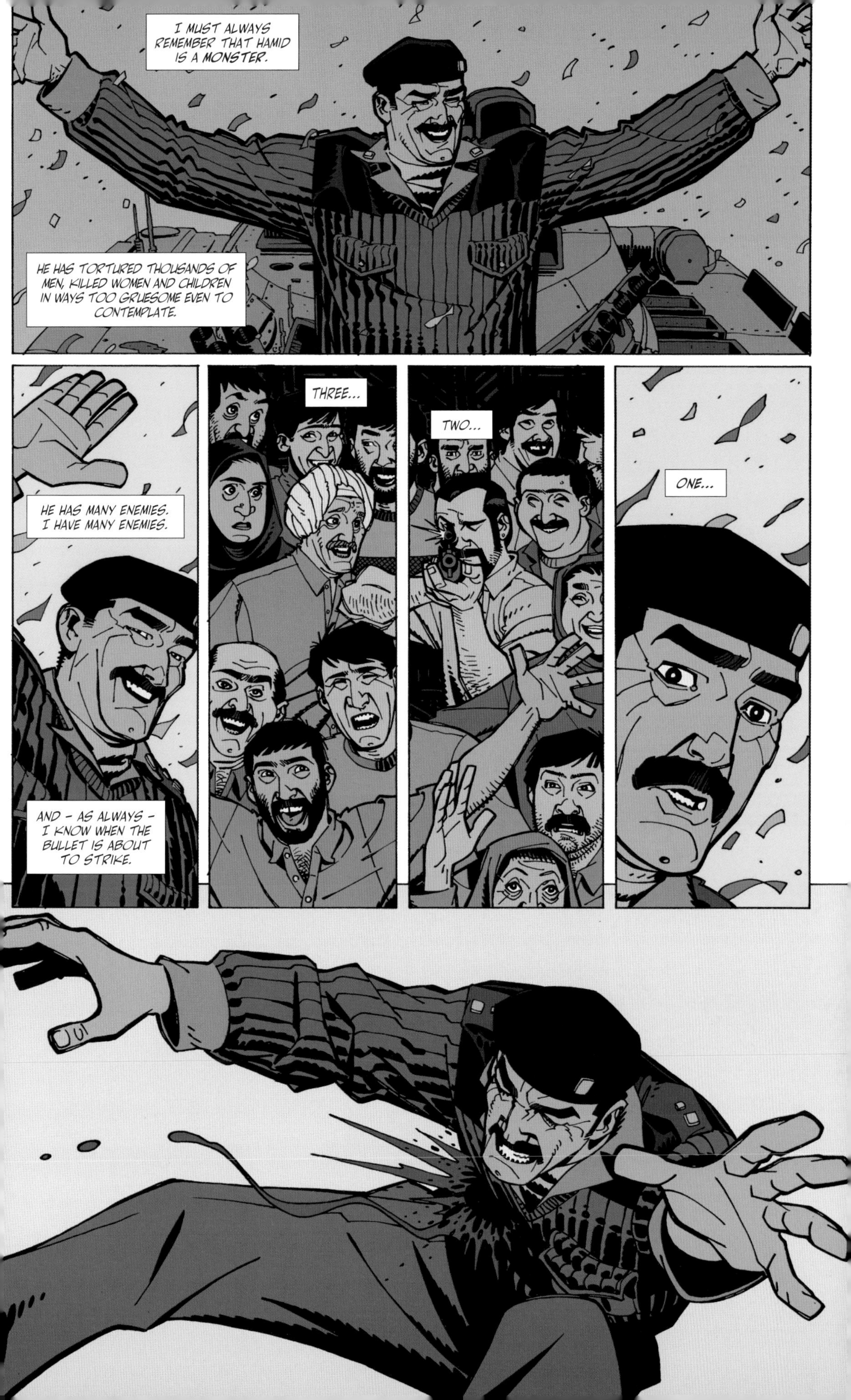
I MUST ALWAYS REMEMBER THAT HAMID IS A MONSTER.
HE HAS TORTURED THOUSANDS OF MEN, KILLED WOMEN AND CHILDREN IN WAYS TOO GRUESOME EVEN TO CONTEMPLATE.
HE HAS MANY ENEMIES. I HAVE MANY ENEMIES.
AND – AS ALWAYS – I KNOW WHEN THE BULLET IS ABOUT TO STRIKE.
THREE...
TWO...
ONE...

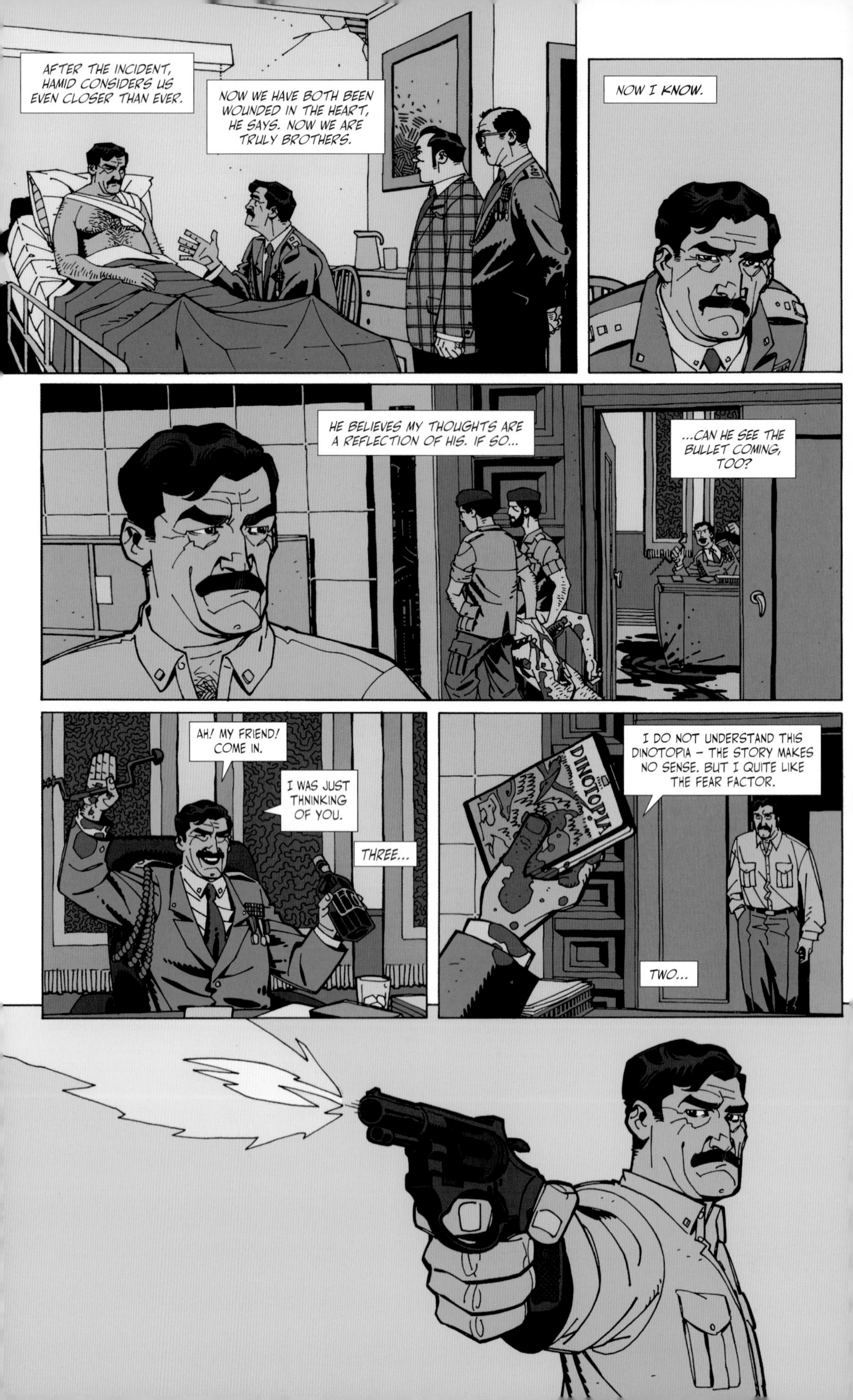
AFTER THE INCIDENT, HAMID CONSIDERS US EVEN CLOSER THAN EVER.
NOW WE HAVE BOTH BEEN WOUNDED IN THE HEART, HE SAYS. NOW WE ARE TRULY BROTHERS.
NOW I KNOW.
HE BELIEVES MY THOUGHTS ARE A REFLECTION OF HIS. IF SO...
...CAN HE SEE THE BULLET COMING, TOO?
AH! MY FRIEND! COME IN.
I WAS JUST THNINKING OF YOU.
THREE...
I DO NOT UNDERSTAND THIS DINOTOPIA – THE STORY MAKES NO SENSE. BUT I QUITE LIKE THE FEAR FACTOR.
DINOTOPIA
TWO...

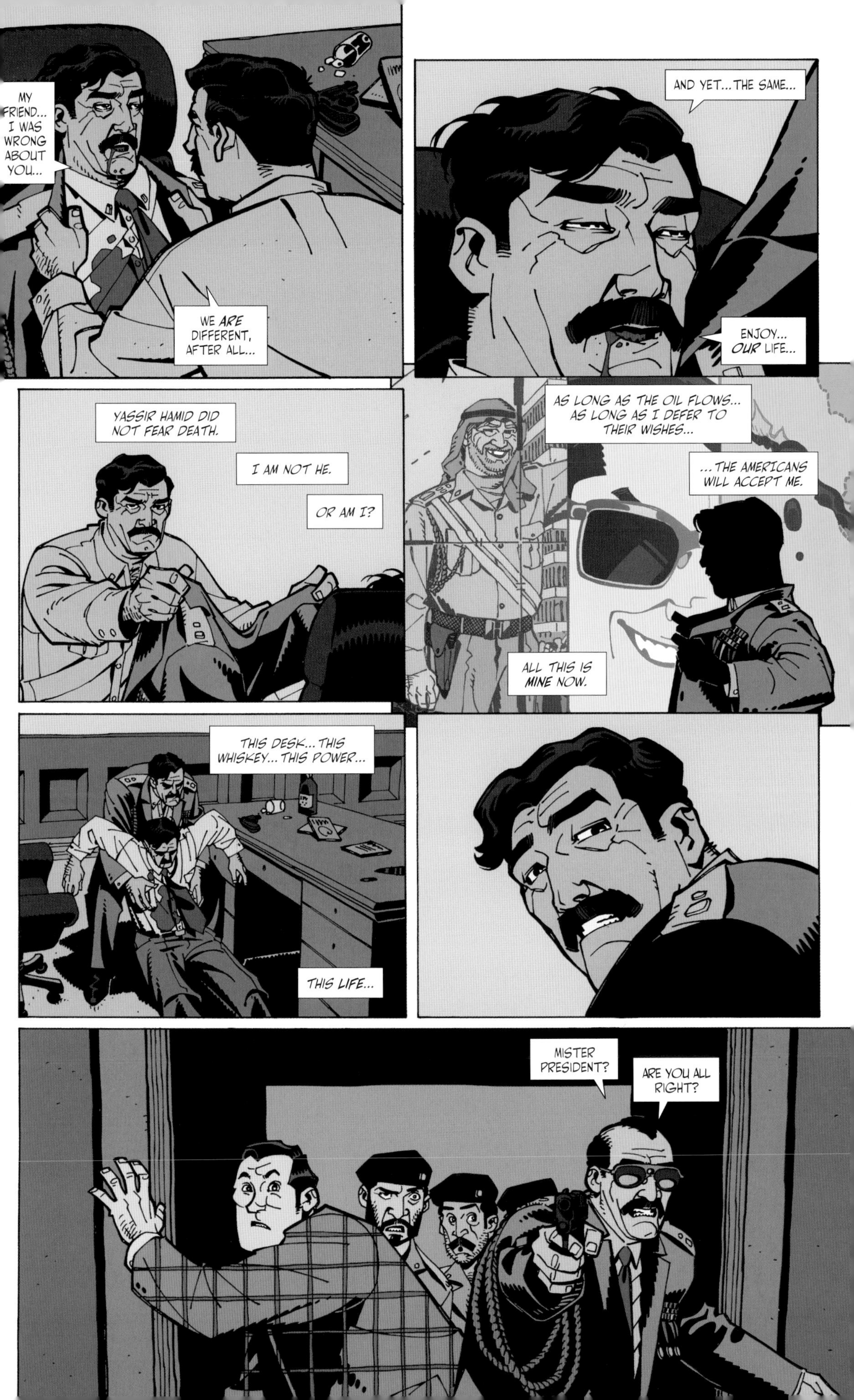
MY FRIEND... I WAS WRONG ABOUT YOU...
WE ARE DIFFERENT, AFTER ALL...
AND YET... THE SAME...
ENJOY... OUR LIFE...
YASSIR HAMID DID NOT FEAR DEATH.
I AM NOT HE.
OR AM I?
AS LONG AS THE OIL FLOWS... AS LONG AS I DEFER TO THEIR WISHES...
...THE AMERICANS WILL ACCEPT ME.
ALL THIS IS MINE NOW.
THIS DESK... THIS WHISKEY... THIS POWER...
THIS LIFE...
MISTER PRESIDENT?
ARE YOU ALL RIGHT?

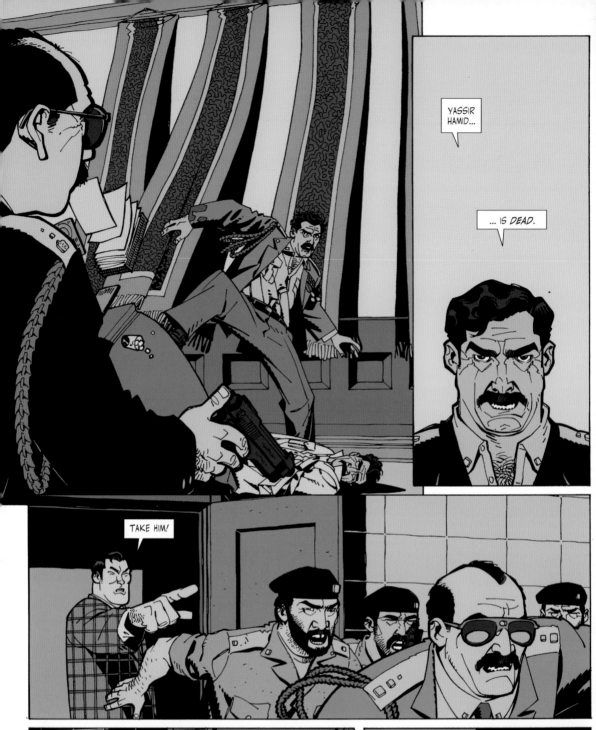

YASSIR HAMID...

...IS DEAD.

TAKE HIM!

I GO NOW.

I HOPE MY END WILL BE SWIFT. THE AMERICANS HAVE LITTLE TO GAIN BY TORTURING ME.

BUT EITHER WAY...WHEN I GO...

I GO AS MYSELF.

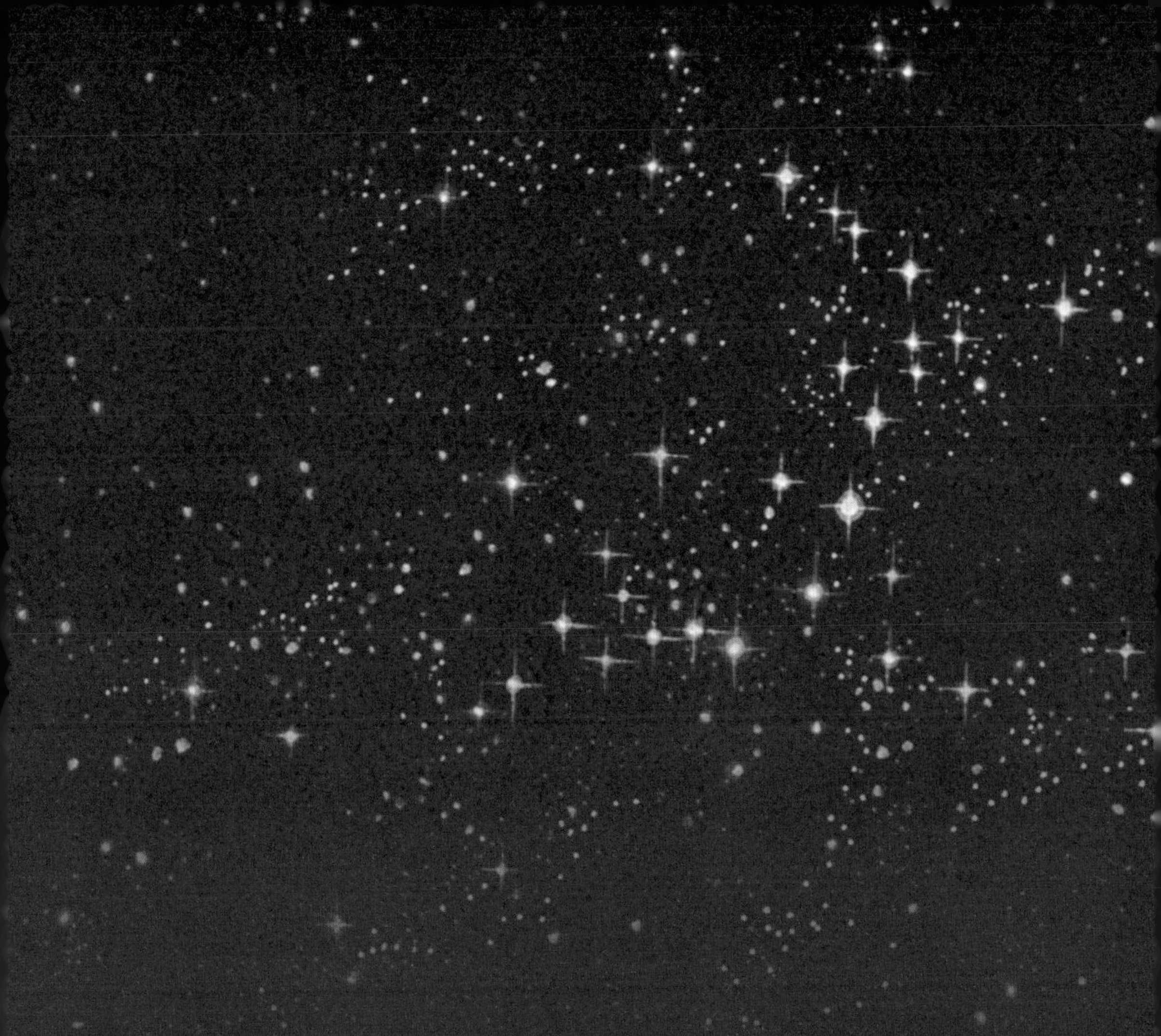

OVERDOSE

Story by JIM MACDONALD
Art by D-PI

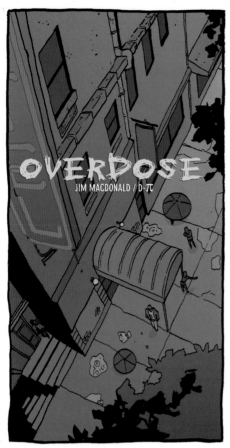

OVERDOSE

JIM MACDONALD / D-π

YOU GET THE H?

ONLY IF YOU GOT US A ROOM.

YOU WENT FIRST LAST TIME, CLARA.

JUST *HURRY UP!*

YOU OKAY, GEEZE?

OH, HELL--

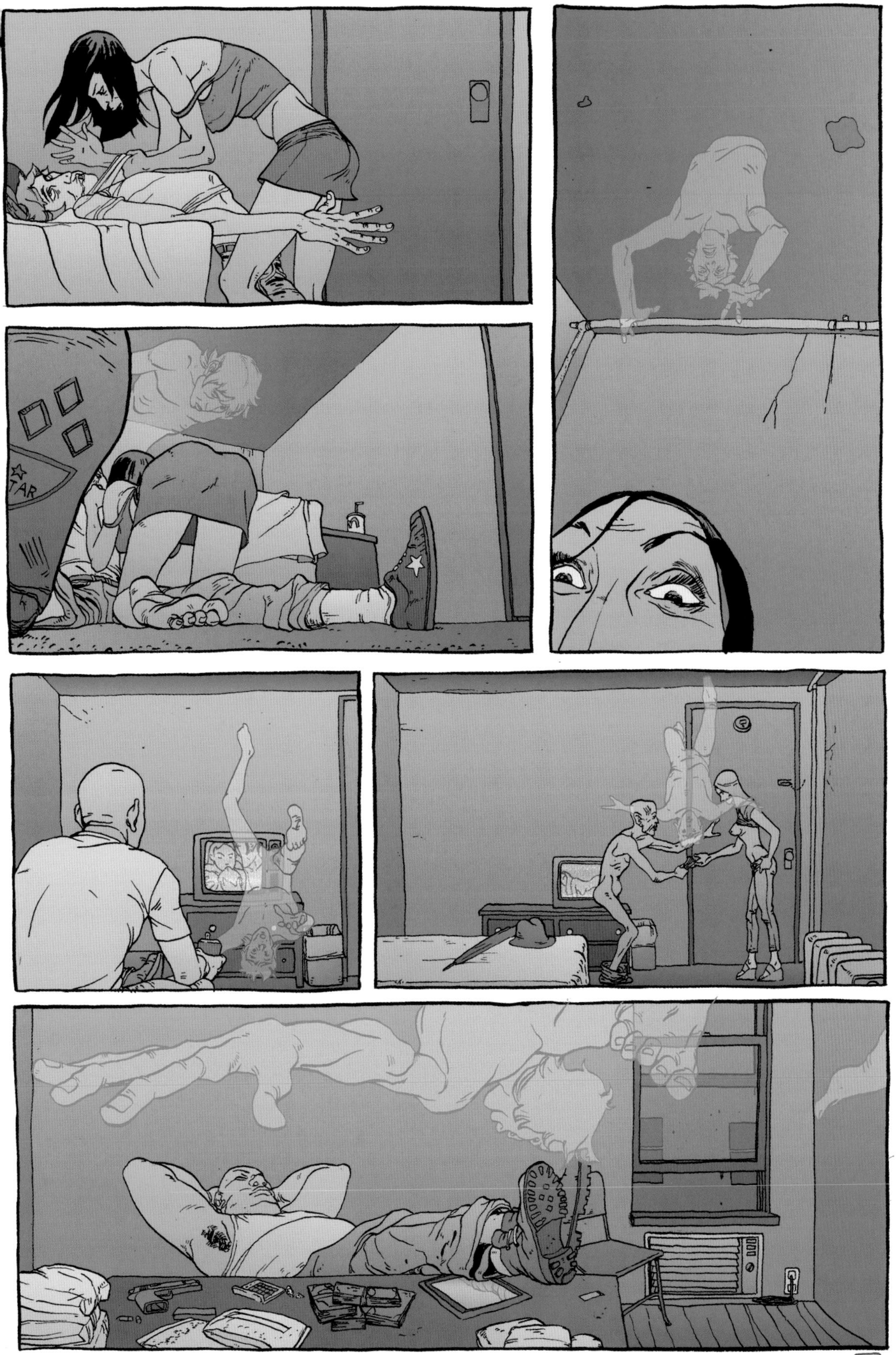
TAR

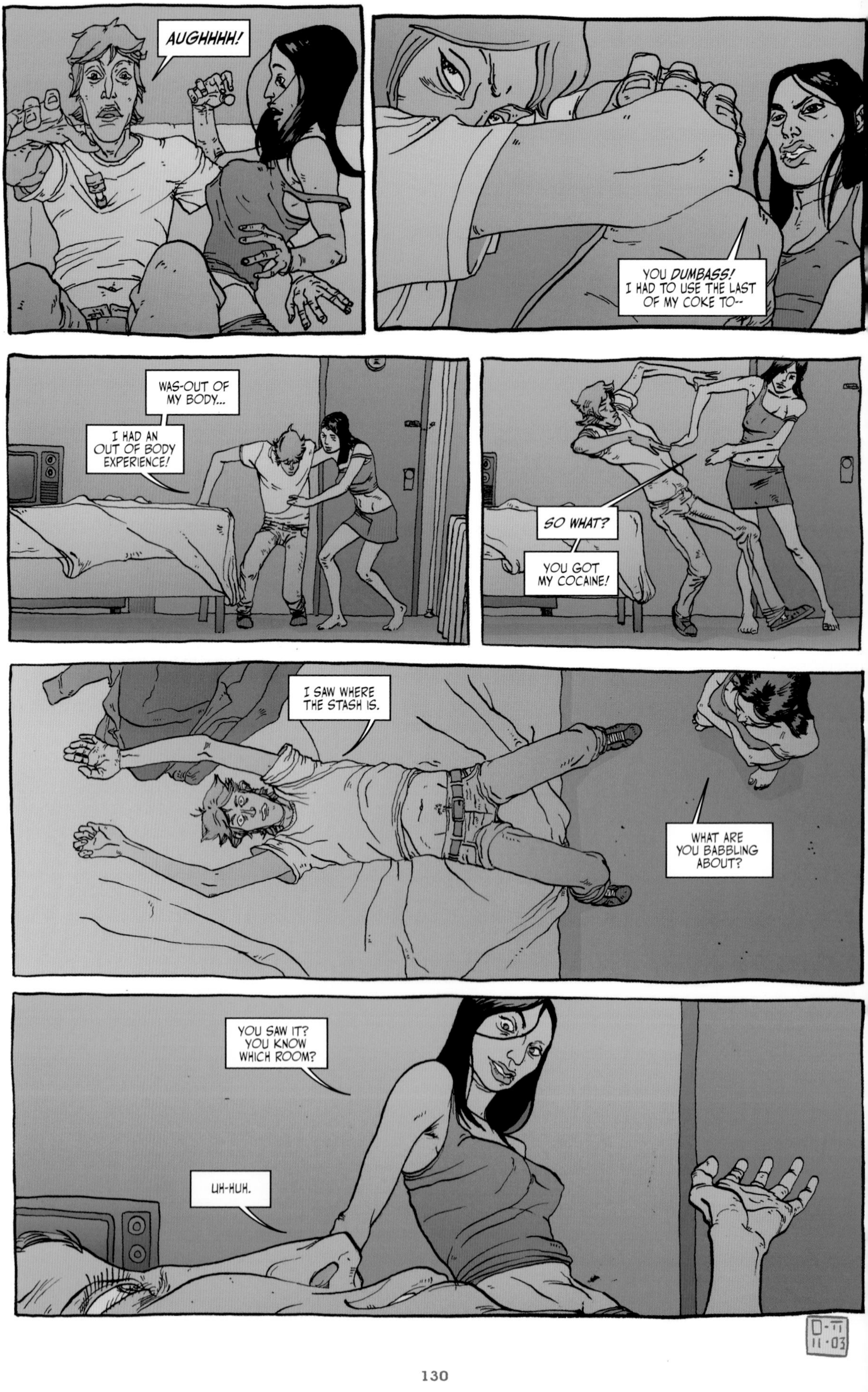
AUGHHHH!
YOU DUMBASS! I HAD TO USE THE LAST OF MY COKE TO--
WAS-OUT OF MY BODY...
I HAD AN OUT OF BODY EXPERIENCE!
SO WHAT?
YOU GOT MY COCAINE!
I SAW WHERE THE STASH IS.
WHAT ARE YOU BABBLING ABOUT?
YOU SAW IT? YOU KNOW WHICH ROOM?
UH-HUH.
D-TT
11·03

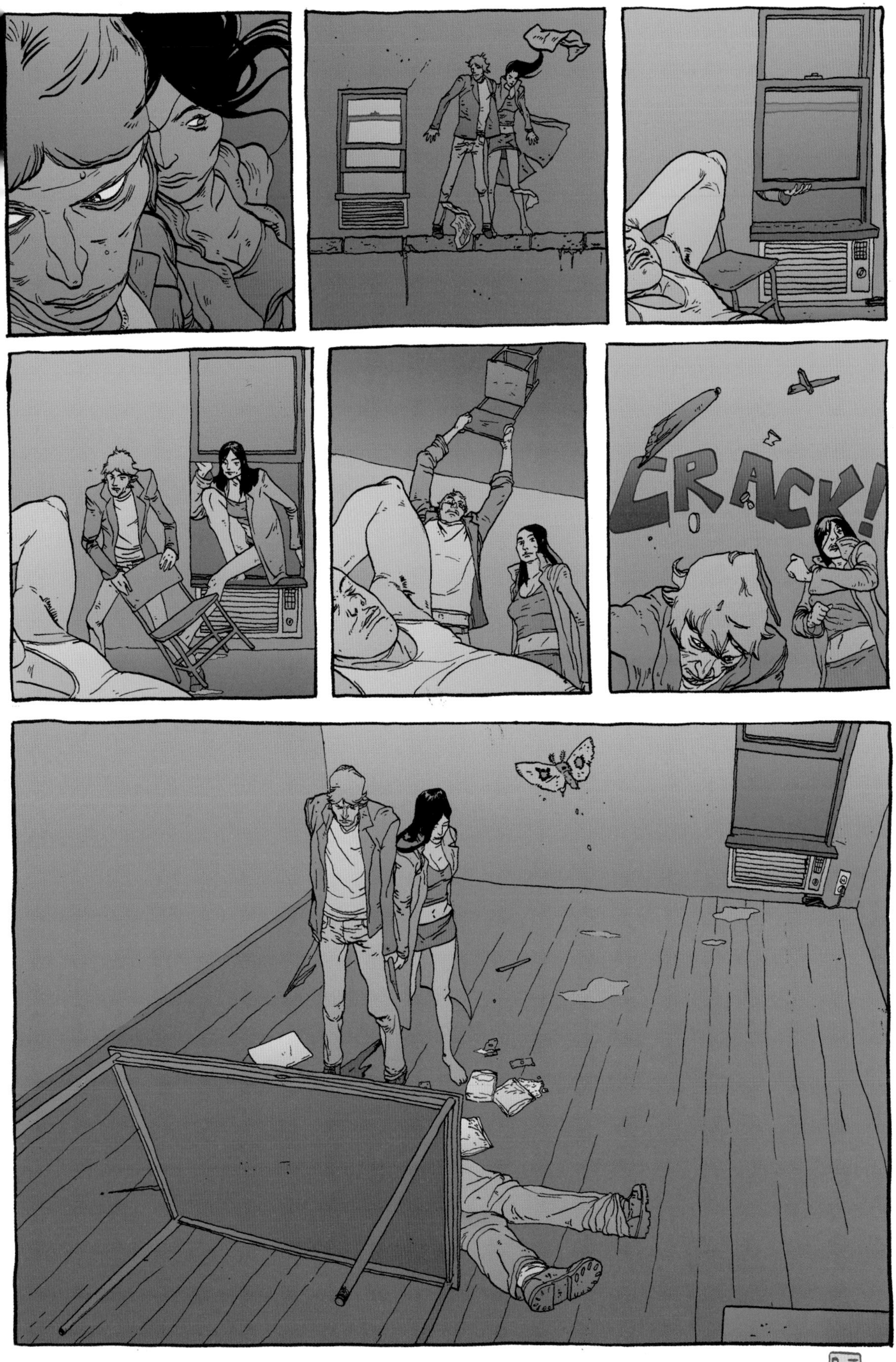
CRACK!
D-π
11-03

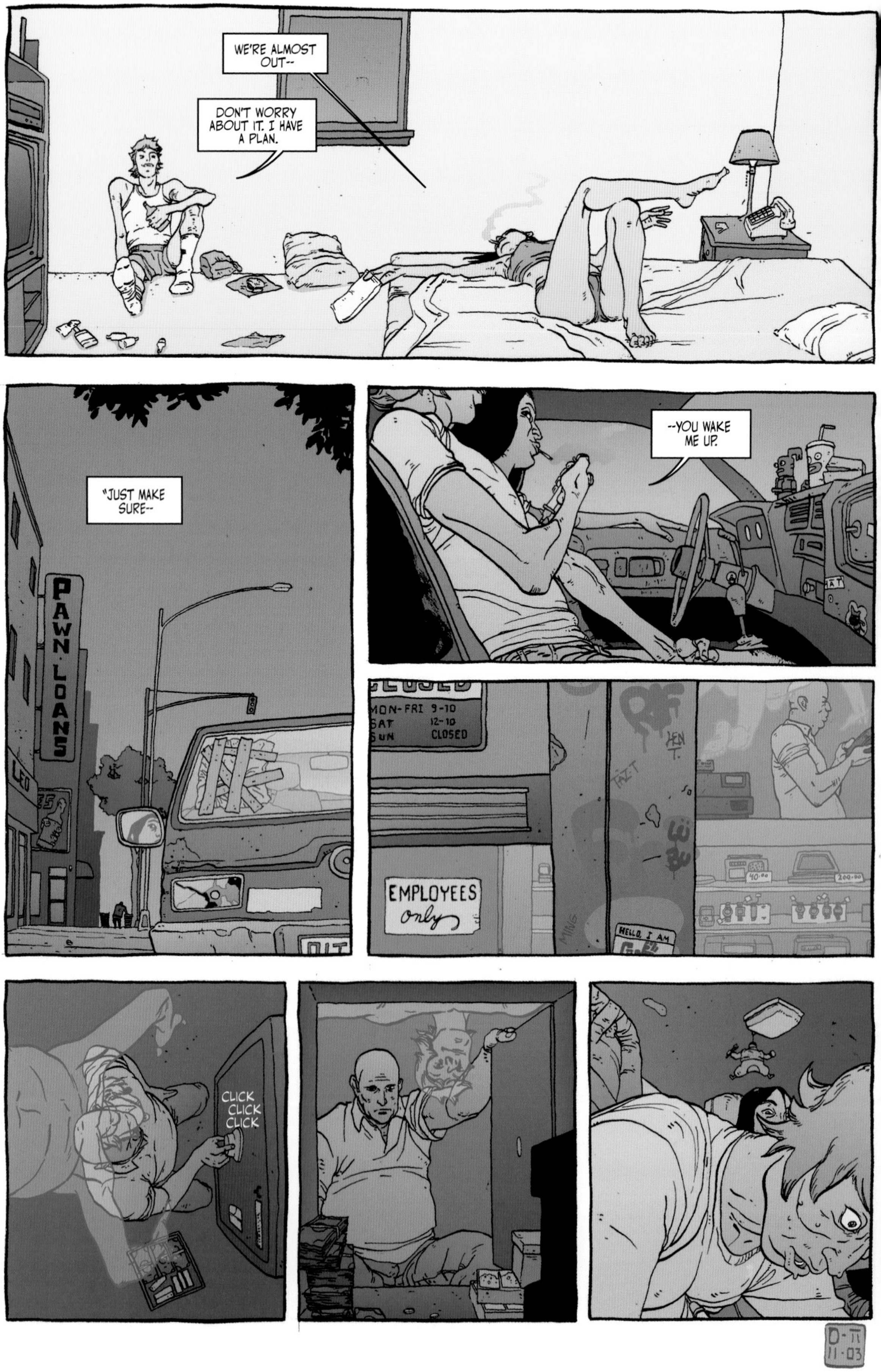
WE'RE ALMOST OUT--
DON'T WORRY ABOUT IT. I HAVE A PLAN.
"JUST MAKE SURE--
PAWN LOANS
--YOU WAKE ME UP.
MON-FRI 9-10
SAT 12-10
SUN CLOSED
EMPLOYEES only
HELLO, I AM
CLICK CLICK CLICK
D-TI 11-03

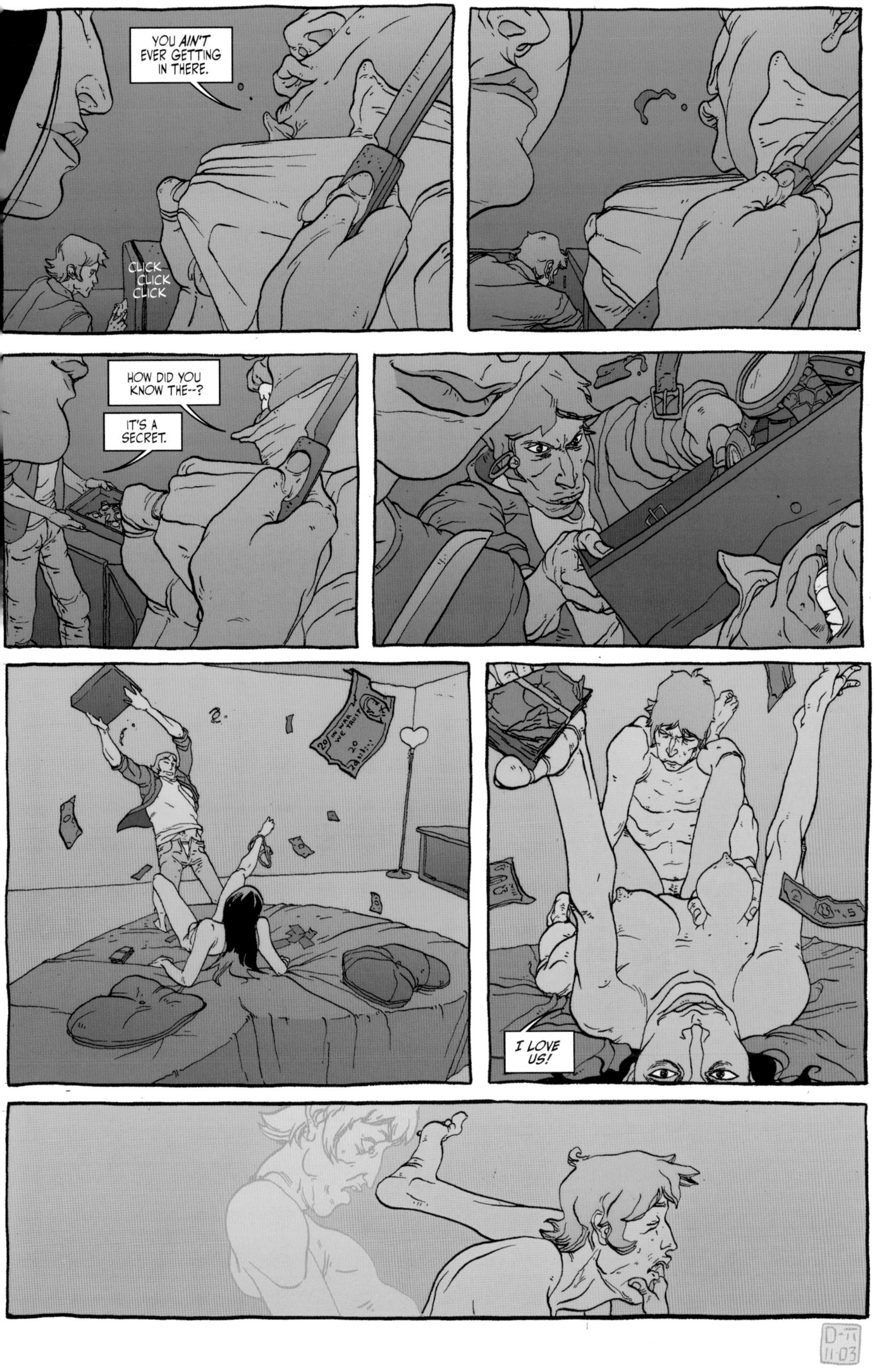
YOU *AIN'T* EVER GETTING IN THERE.
CLICK CLICK CLICK
HOW DID YOU KNOW THE--?
IT'S A SECRET.
I LOVE US!

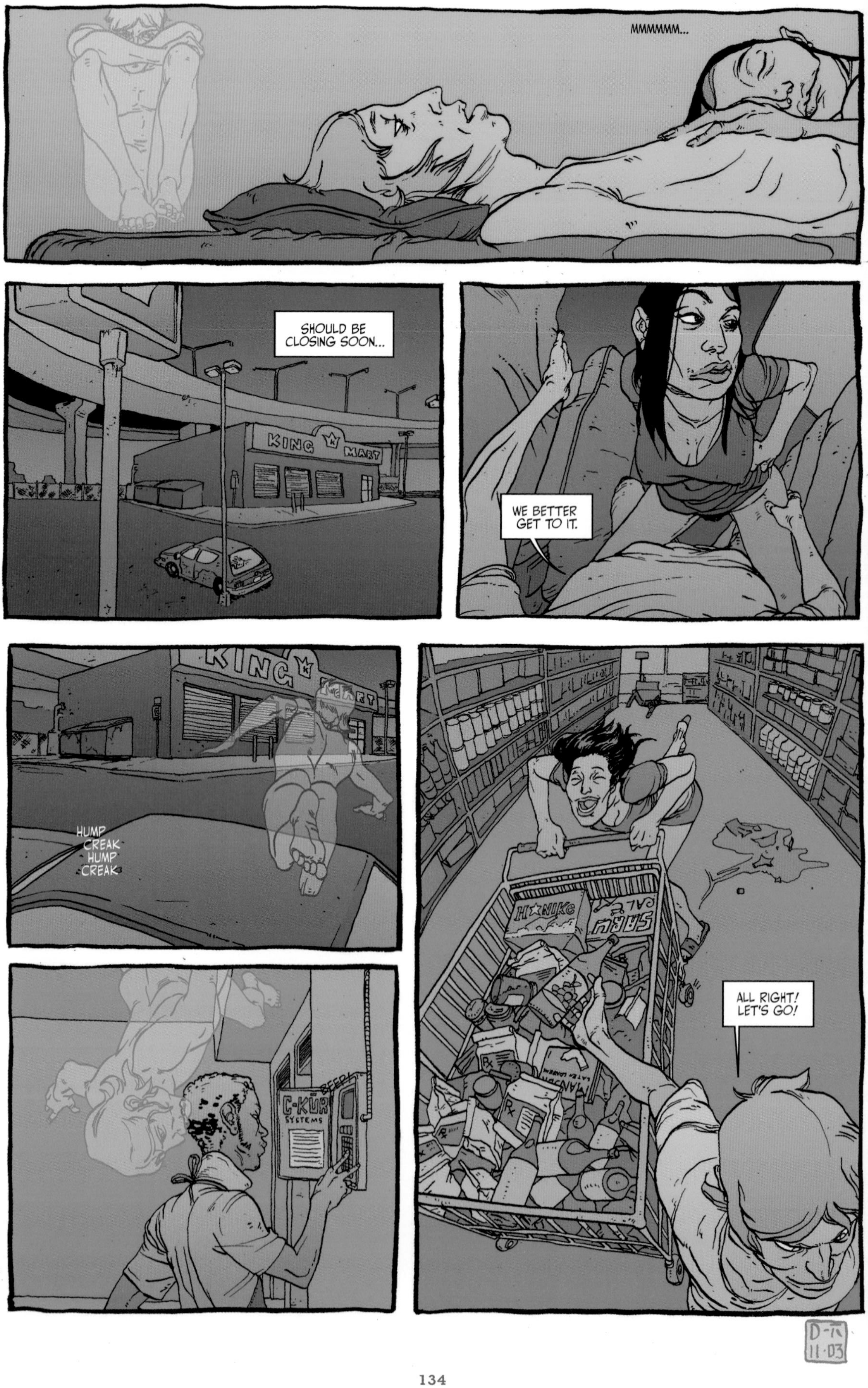
MMMMMM...
SHOULD BE CLOSING SOON...
KING MART
WE BETTER GET TO IT.
KING
HUMP
CREAK
HUMP
CREAK
C-KÜR SYSTEMS
BEEP!
ALL RIGHT! LET'S GO!
D-六 11·03

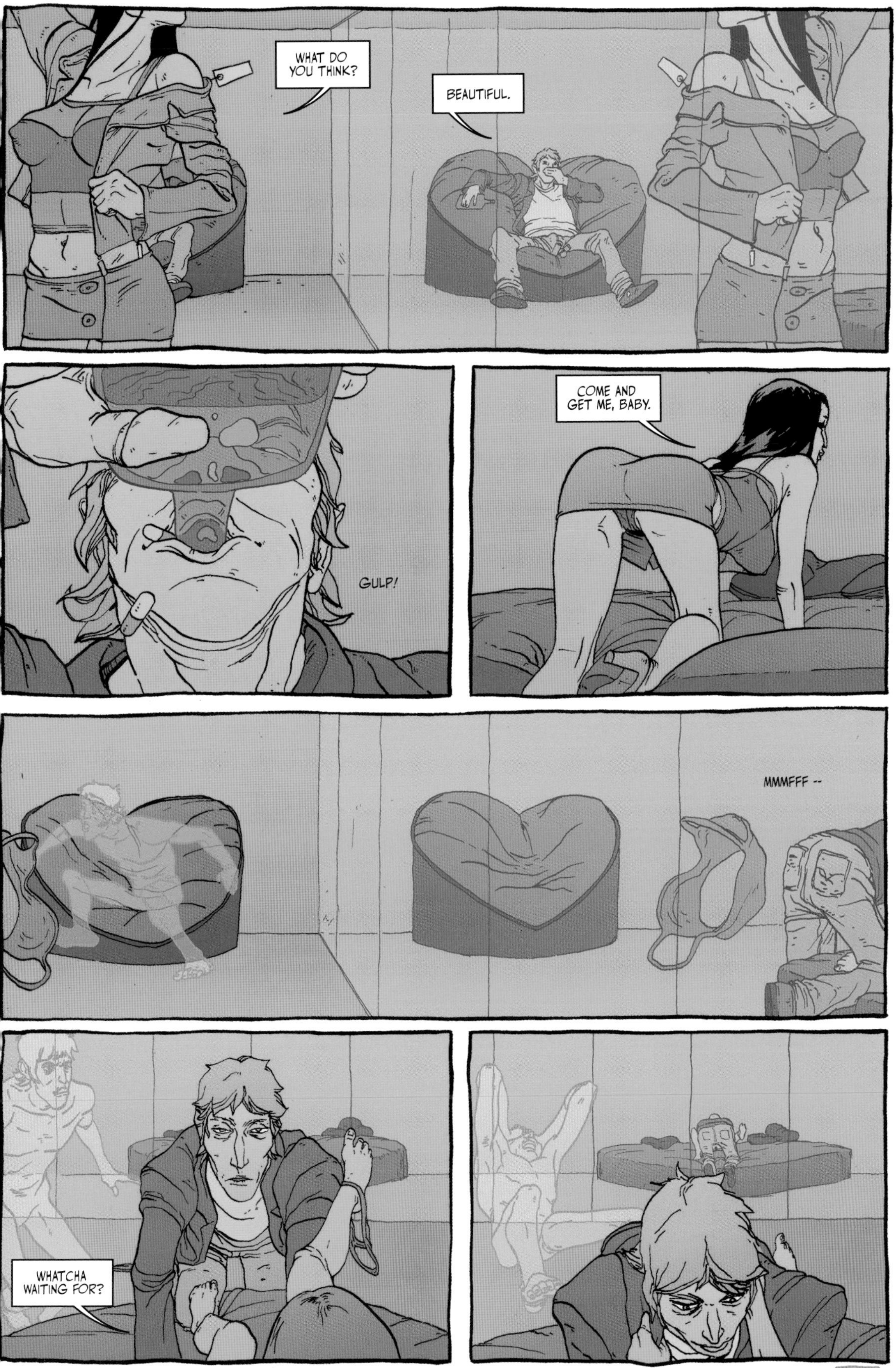
WHAT DO YOU THINK?
BEAUTIFUL.
GULP!
COME AND GET ME, BABY.
MMMFFF --
WHATCHA WAITING FOR?

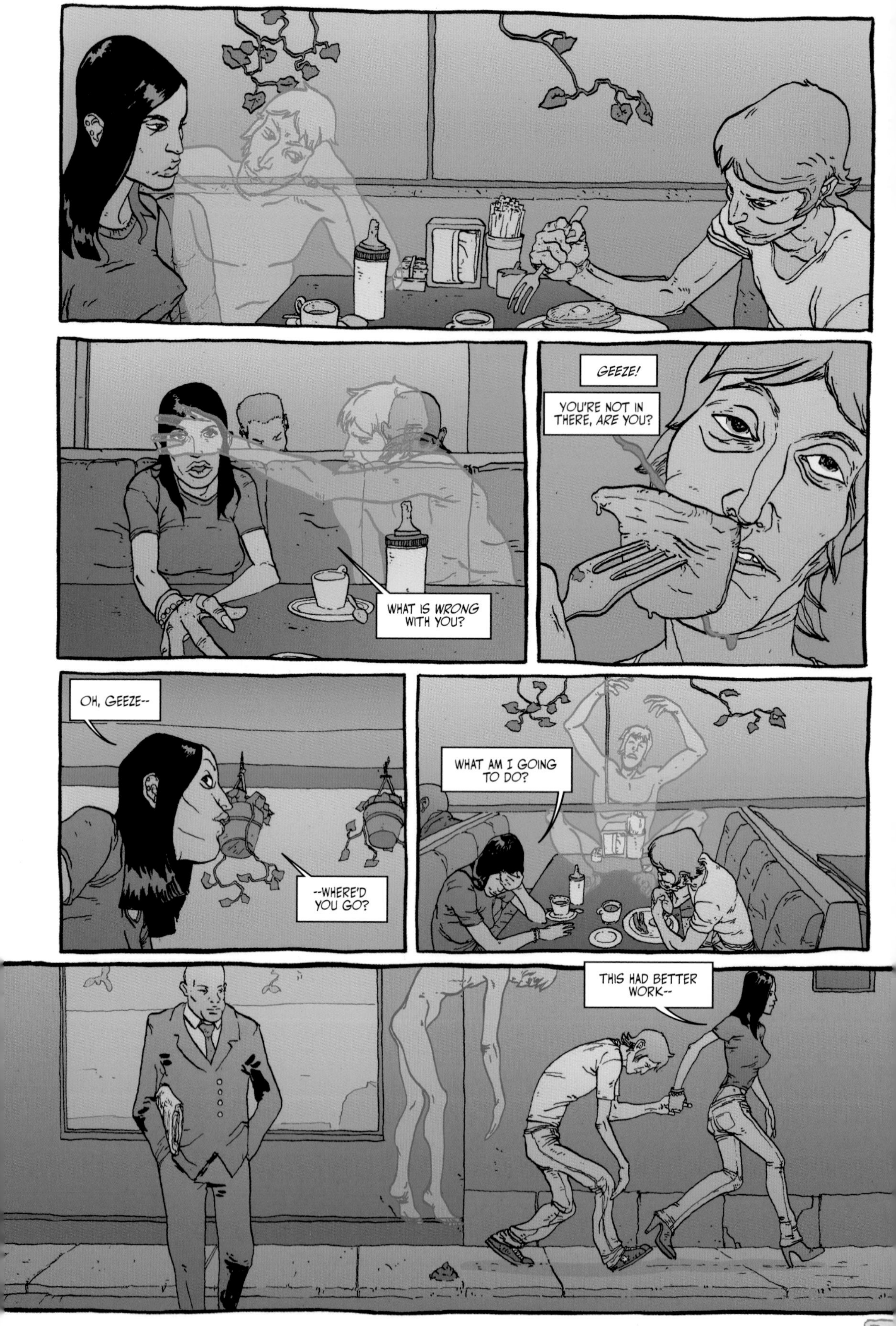
GEEZE!
YOU'RE NOT IN THERE, ARE YOU?
WHAT IS *WRONG* WITH YOU?
OH, GEEZE--
--WHERE'D YOU GO?
WHAT AM I GOING TO DO?
THIS HAD BETTER WORK--

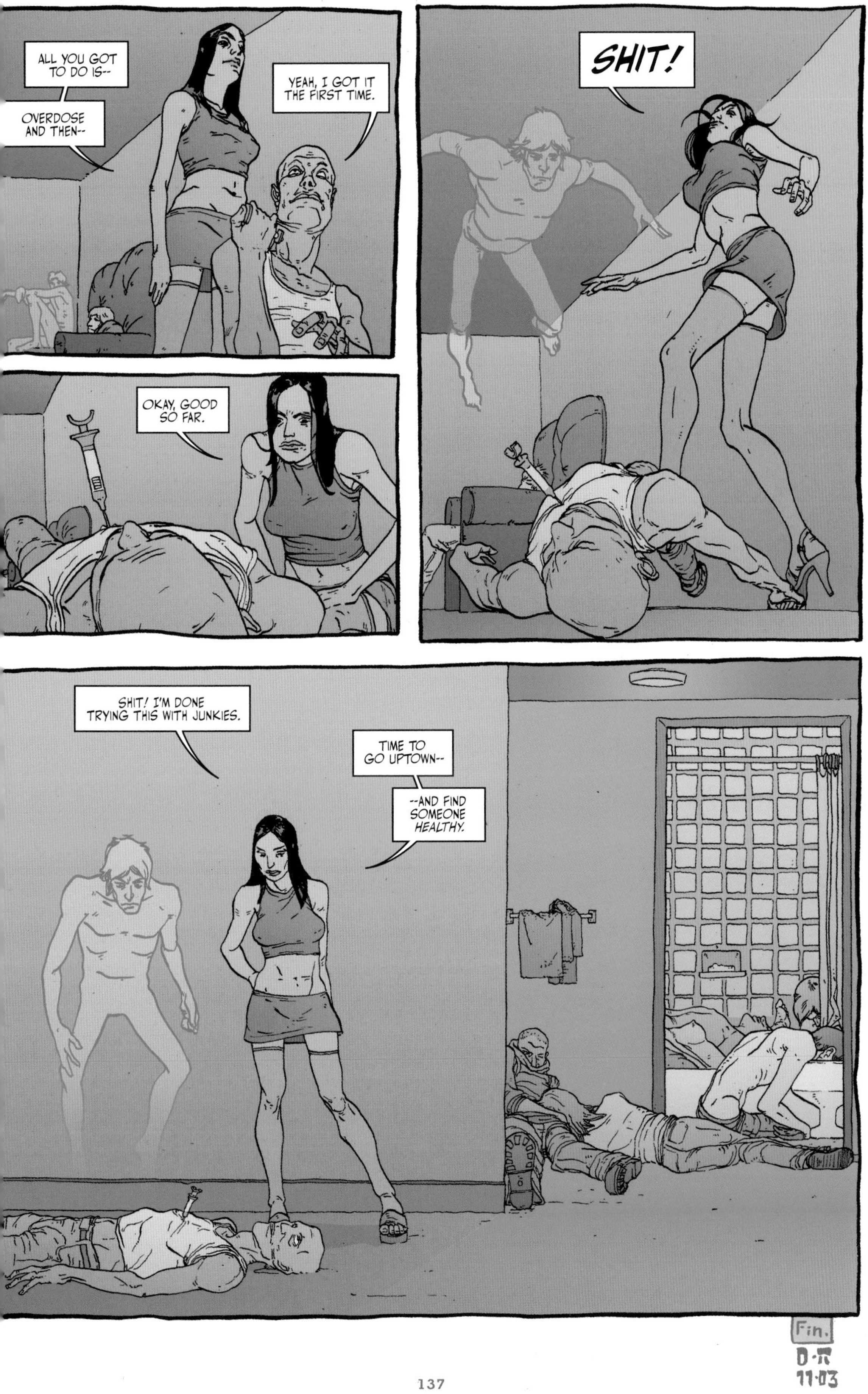
ALL YOU GOT TO DO IS--
OVERDOSE AND THEN--
YEAH, I GOT IT THE FIRST TIME.
OKAY, GOOD SO FAR.
SHIT!
SHIT! I'M DONE TRYING THIS WITH JUNKIES.
TIME TO GO UPTOWN--
--AND FIND SOMEONE *HEALTHY.*
Fin.
D·π 11·03

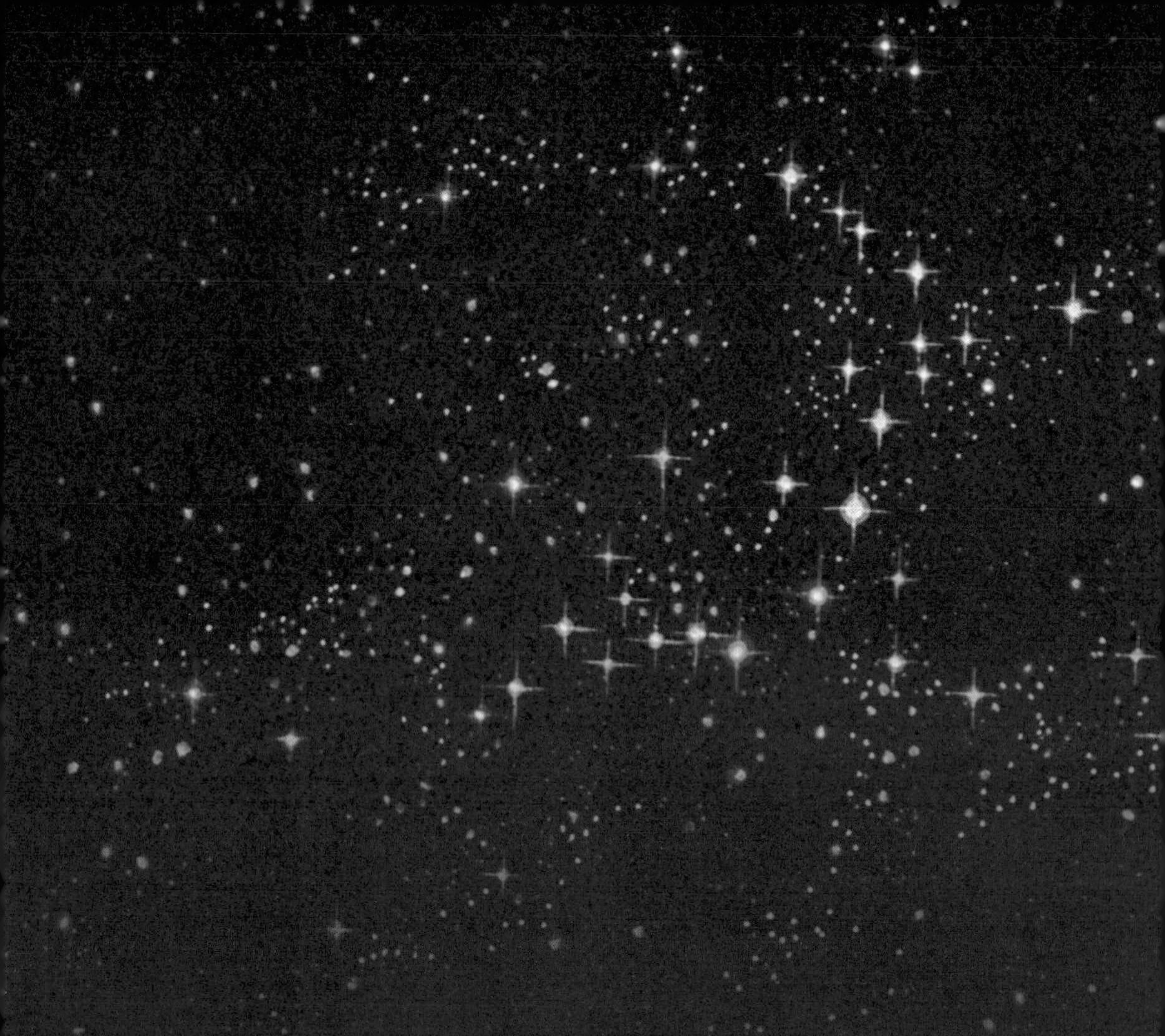

THE PHOTOTAKER

Story and Art by GUY DAVIS
Colors by JERRY FRISSEN

The Phototaker

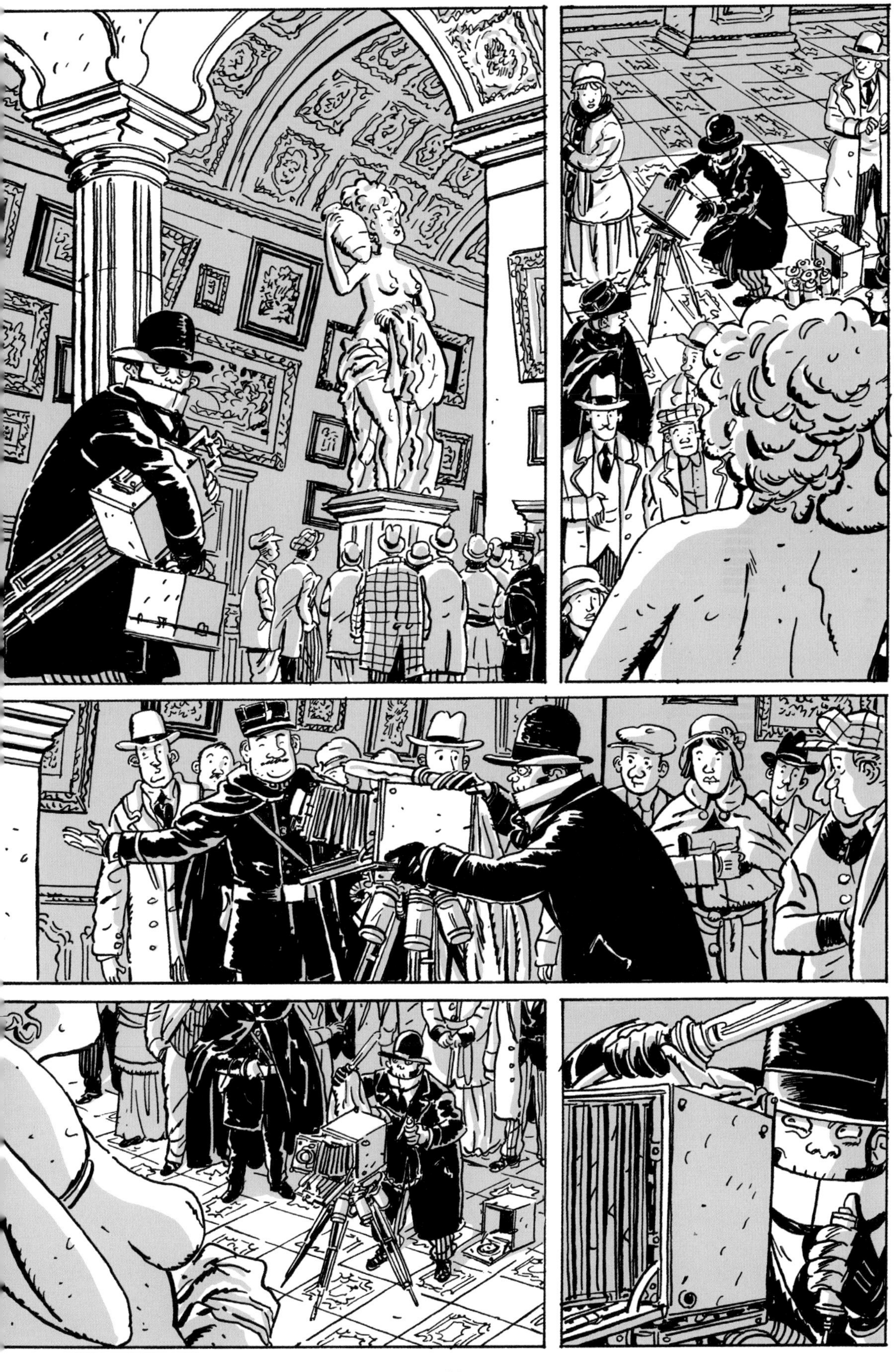

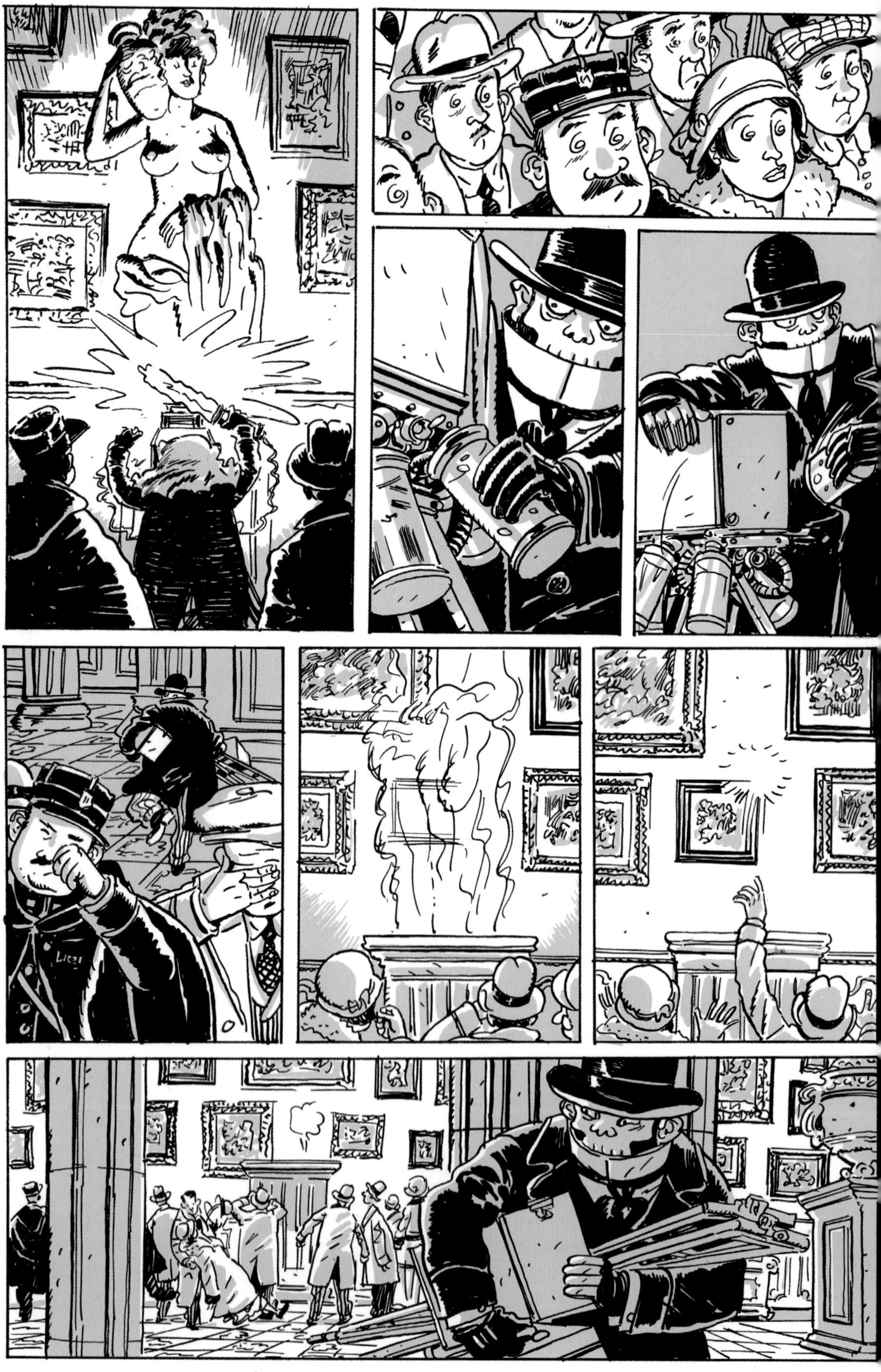

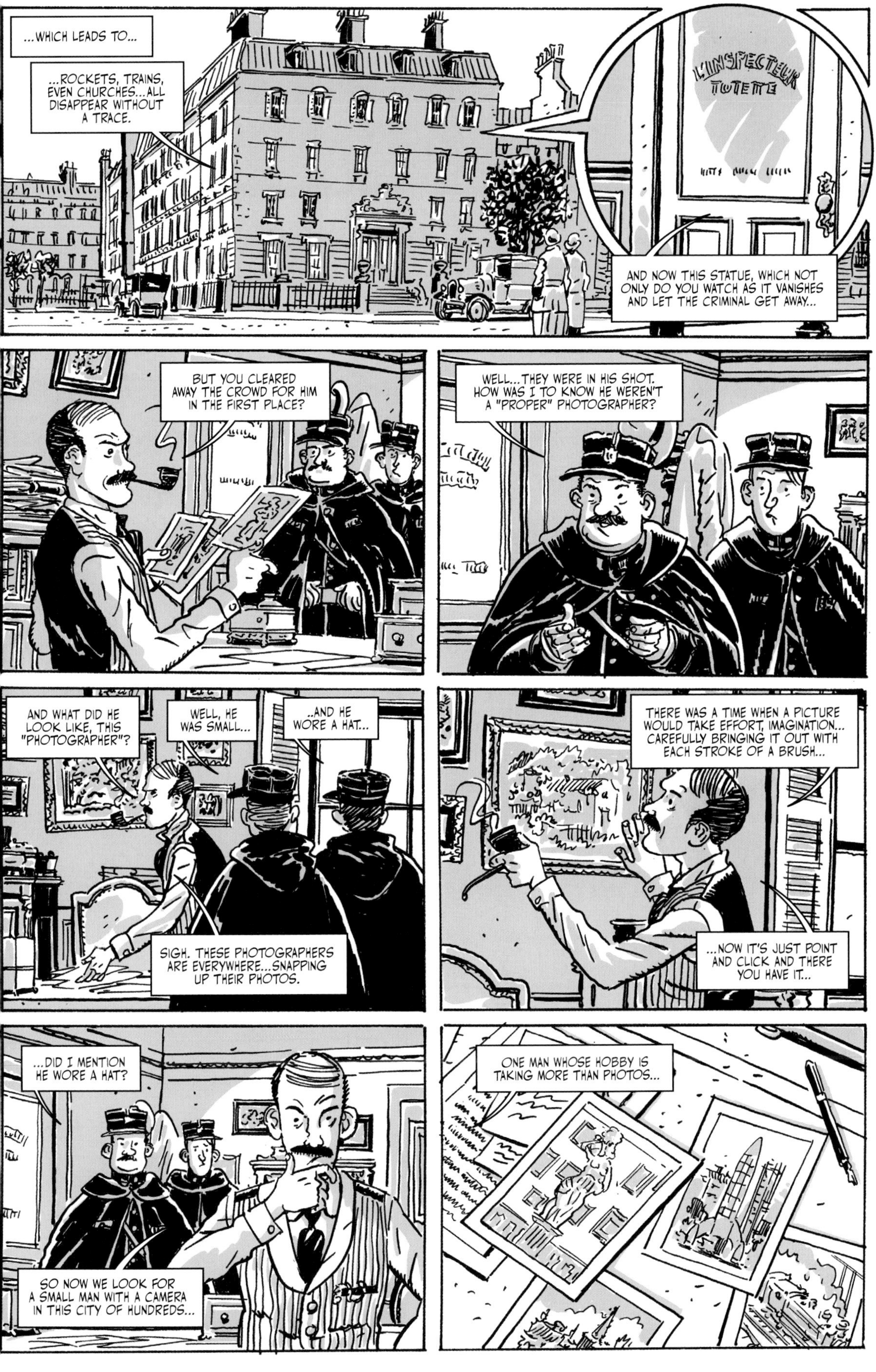

...WHICH LEADS TO...
...ROCKETS, TRAINS, EVEN CHURCHES...ALL DISAPPEAR WITHOUT A TRACE.
L'INSPECTEUR TUTETTE
AND NOW THIS STATUE, WHICH NOT ONLY DO YOU WATCH AS IT VANISHES AND LET THE CRIMINAL GET AWAY...
BUT YOU CLEARED AWAY THE CROWD FOR HIM IN THE FIRST PLACE?
WELL...THEY WERE IN HIS SHOT. HOW WAS I TO KNOW HE WEREN'T A "PROPER" PHOTOGRAPHER?
AND WHAT DID HE LOOK LIKE, THIS "PHOTOGRAPHER"?
WELL, HE WAS SMALL...
..AND HE WORE A HAT...
SIGH. THESE PHOTOGRAPHERS ARE EVERYWHERE...SNAPPING UP THEIR PHOTOS.
THERE WAS A TIME WHEN A PICTURE WOULD TAKE EFFORT, IMAGINATION... CAREFULLY BRINGING IT OUT WITH EACH STROKE OF A BRUSH...
...NOW IT'S JUST POINT AND CLICK AND THERE YOU HAVE IT...
...DID I MENTION HE WORE A HAT?
SO NOW WE LOOK FOR A SMALL MAN WITH A CAMERA IN THIS CITY OF HUNDREDS...
ONE MAN WHOSE HOBBY IS TAKING MORE THAN PHOTOS...

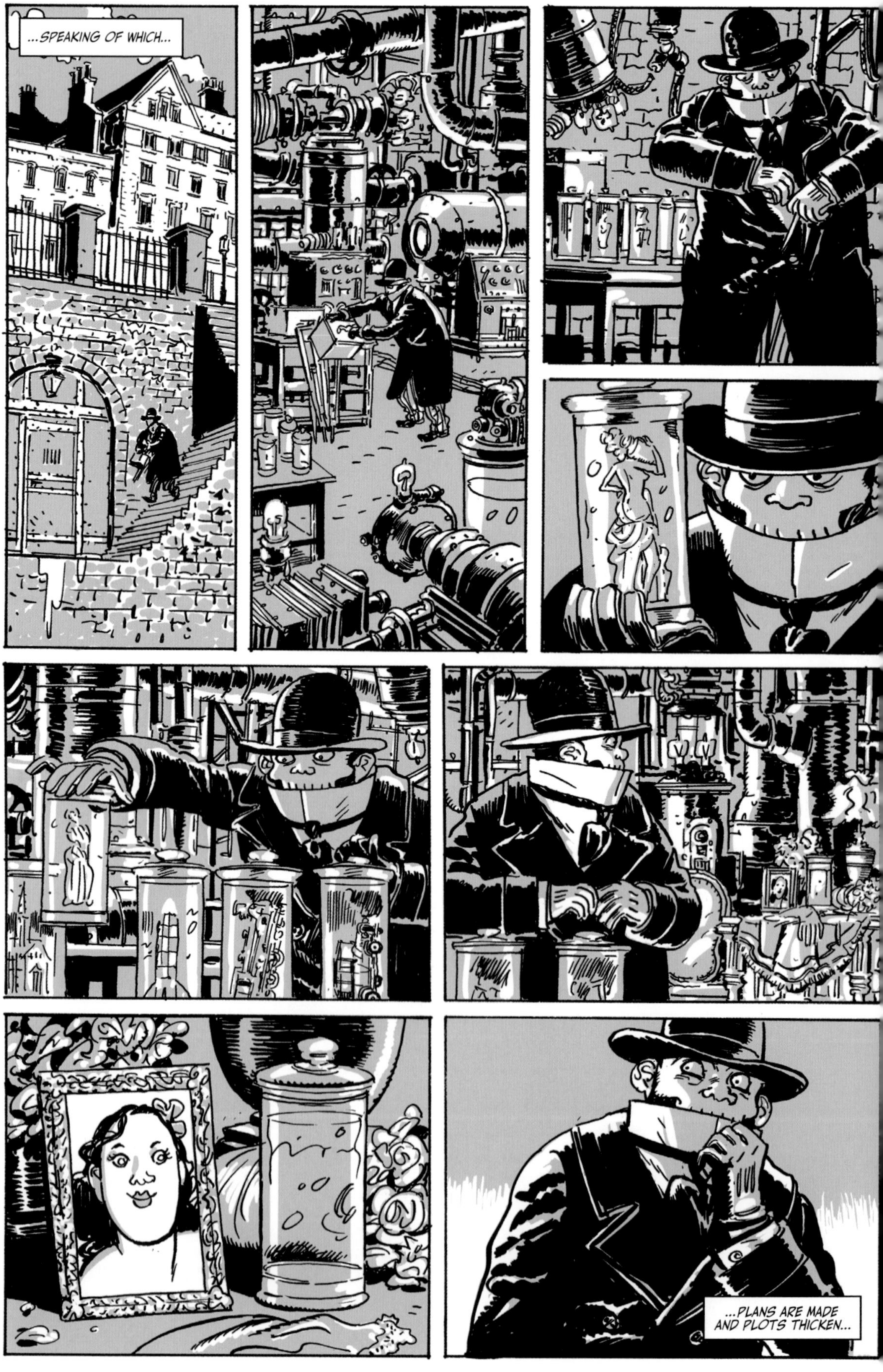
...SPEAKING OF WHICH...
...PLANS ARE MADE AND PLOTS THICKEN...

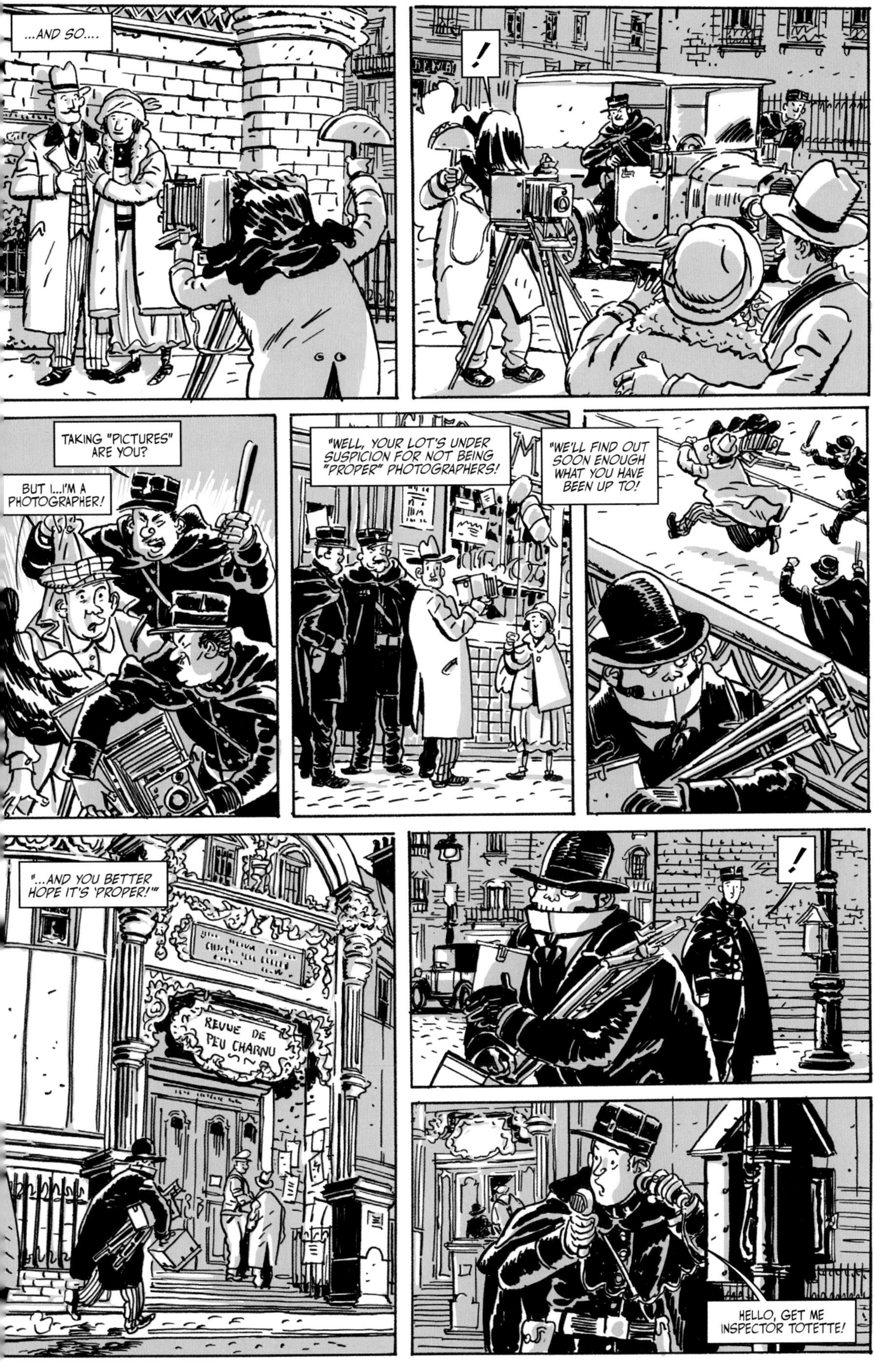
...AND SO....
!
TAKING "PICTURES" ARE YOU?
BUT I...I'M A PHOTOGRAPHER!
"WELL, YOUR LOT'S UNDER SUSPICION FOR NOT BEING "PROPER" PHOTOGRAPHERS!
"WE'LL FIND OUT SOON ENOUGH WHAT YOU HAVE BEEN UP TO!
"...AND YOU BETTER HOPE IT'S 'PROPER!'"
REVUE DE PEU CHARNU
!
HELLO, GET ME INSPECTOR TOTETTE!

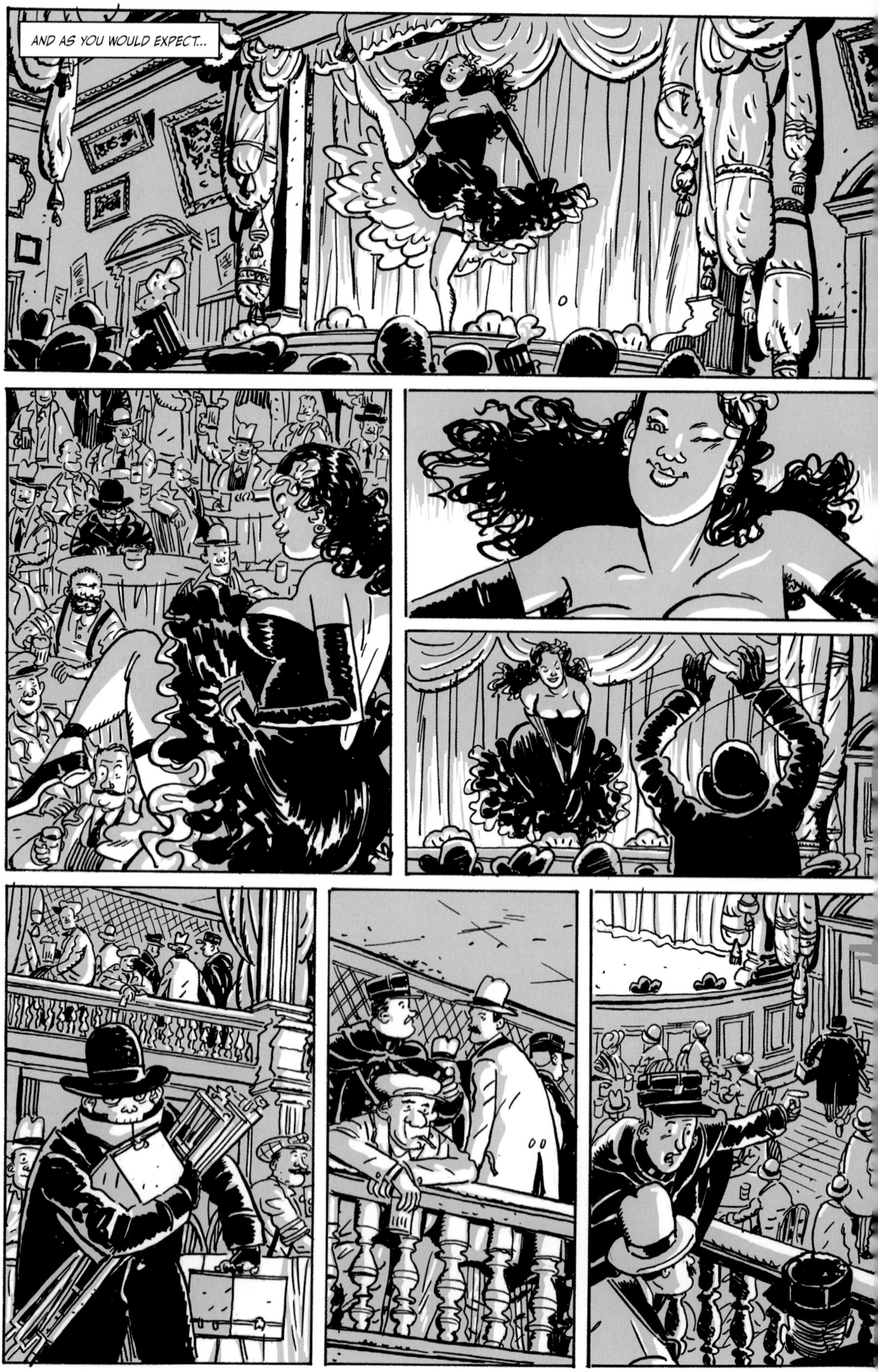
AND AS YOU WOULD EXPECT...

YES? OH!

TAKE, TAKE.

"PROFESSOR"? OF WHAT?

"PHOTO-TAKING," YES?

THE PROFESSOR

COLLECTIVE ACADEMIE OF SCIENTIFIC PHOTOGRAPHIES

PHOTOS? YOU WANT TO TAKE A PICTURE OF ME? REALLY? HOW FUN...

I'VE ONLY SAT FOR A PAINTING ONCE BEFORE...IT WAS SO BORING... THEY SAY PICTURES ARE WHAT CAPTURES THE REAL YOU, DON'T THEY?

COME... SIT, SIT.

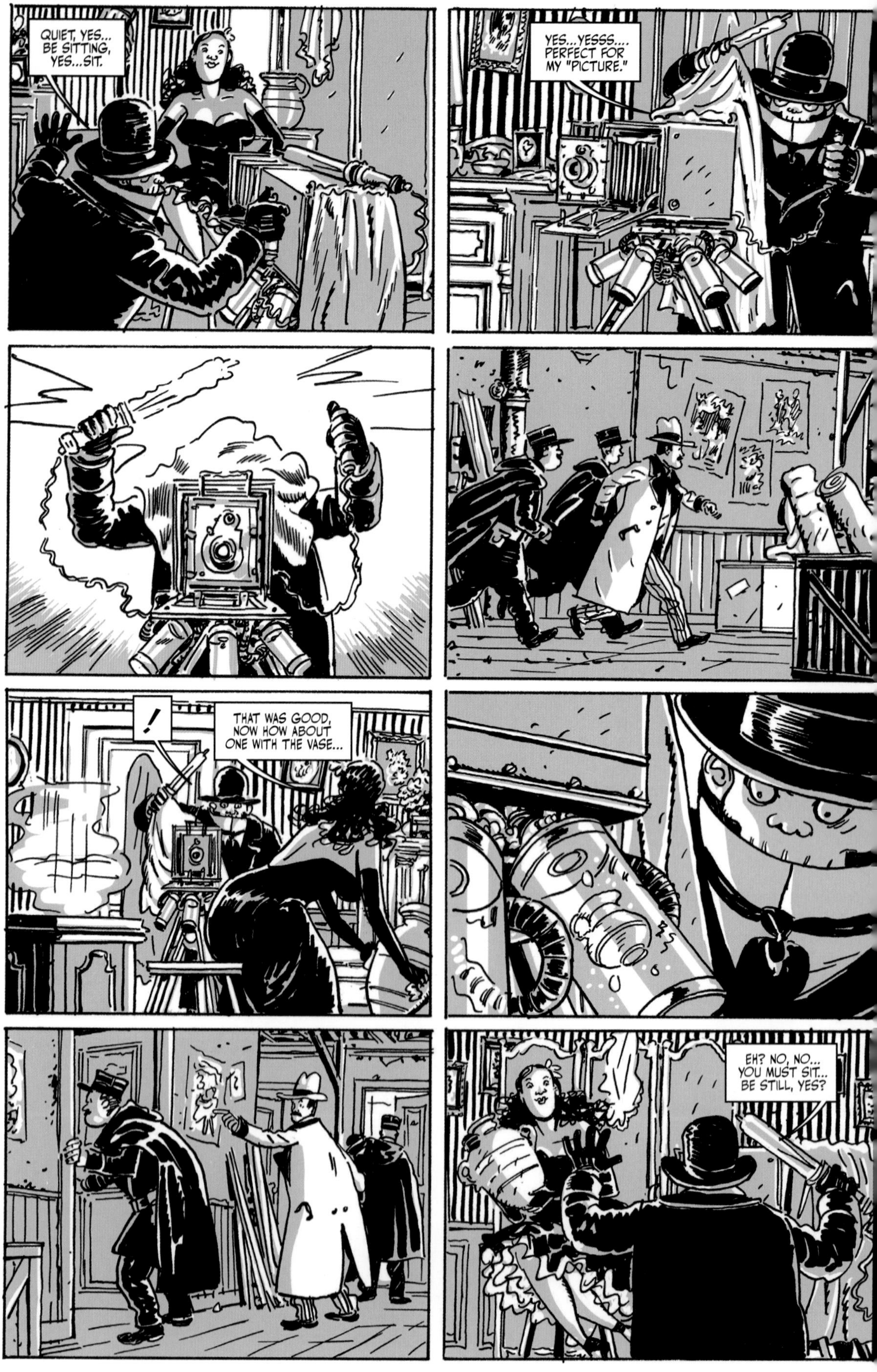
QUIET, YES...
BE SITTING,
YES...SIT.
YES...YESSS....
PERFECT FOR
MY "PICTURE."
!
THAT WAS GOOD,
NOW HOW ABOUT
ONE WITH THE VASE...
EH? NO, NO...
YOU MUST SIT...
BE STILL, YES?

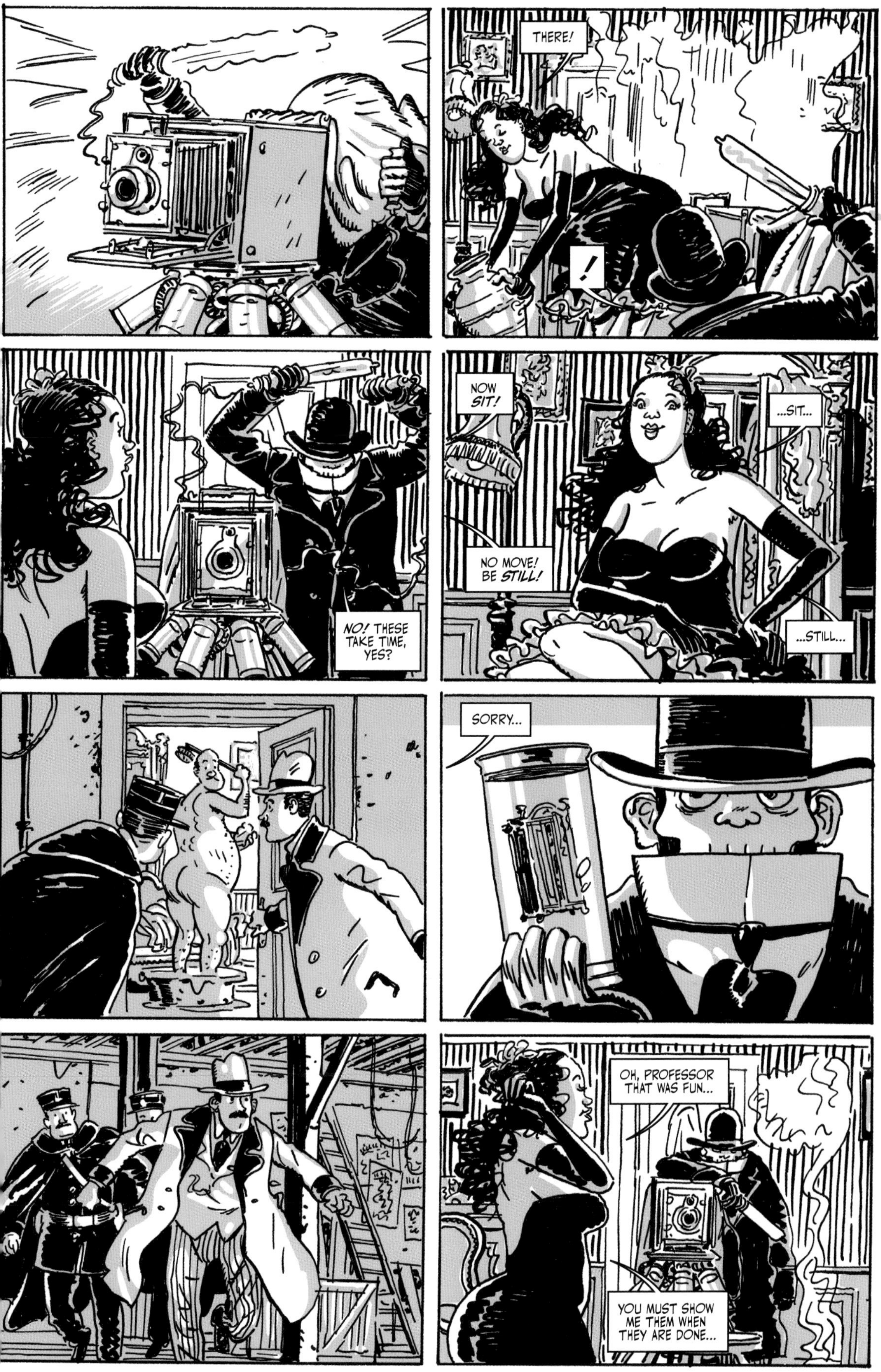
THERE!
!
NO! THESE TAKE TIME, YES?
NOW SIT!
...SIT...
NO MOVE! BE STILL!
...STILL...
SORRY...
OH, PROFESSOR THAT WAS FUN...
YOU MUST SHOW ME THEM WHEN THEY ARE DONE...

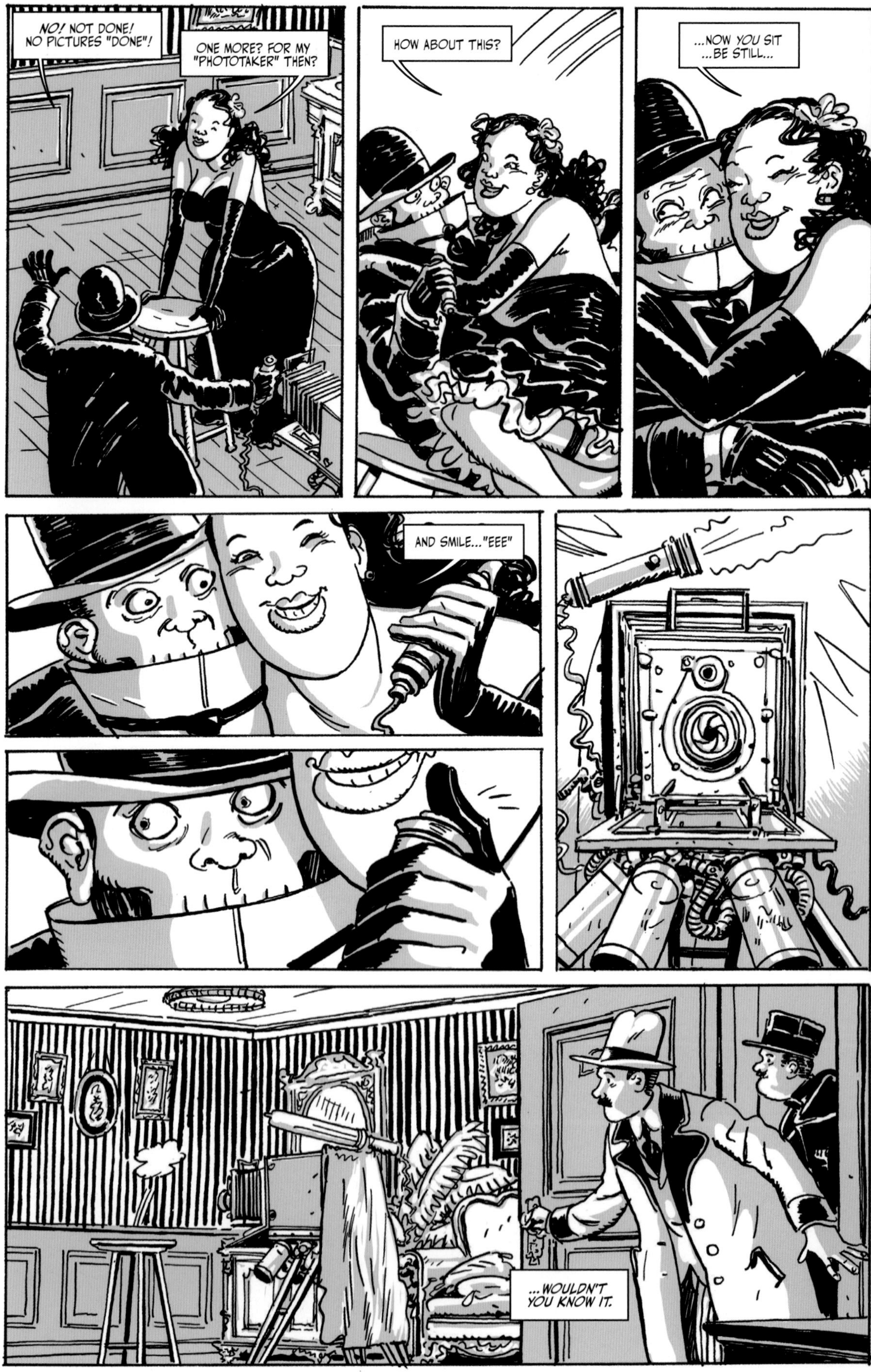
NO! NOT DONE! NO PICTURES "DONE"!
ONE MORE? FOR MY "PHOTOTAKER" THEN?
HOW ABOUT THIS?
...NOW YOU SIT ...BE STILL...
AND SMILE..."EEE"
...WOULDN'T YOU KNOW IT.

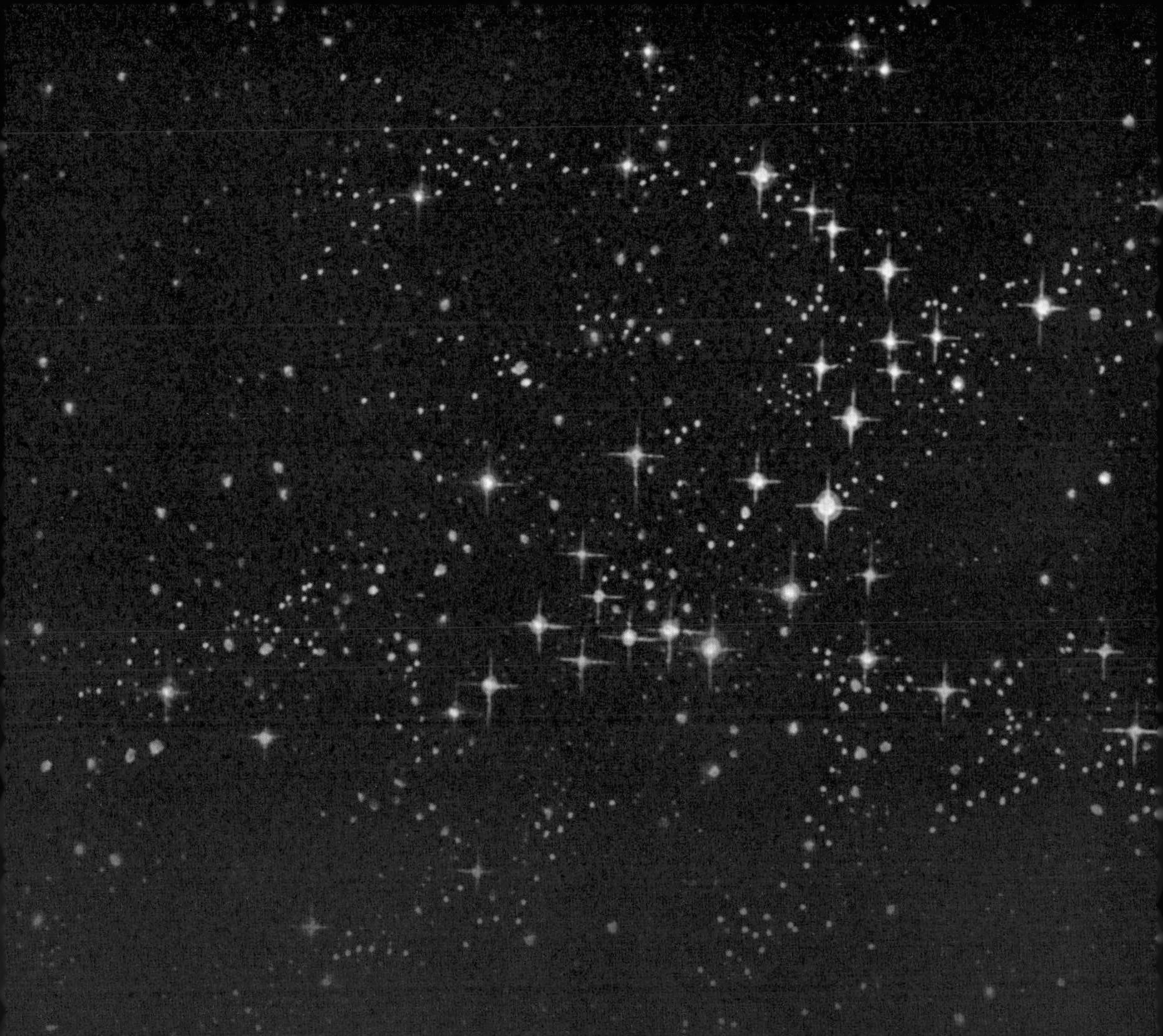

DUST DEVILS

Story by NICOLAS BURNS
Art by TOMMY LEE EDWARDS

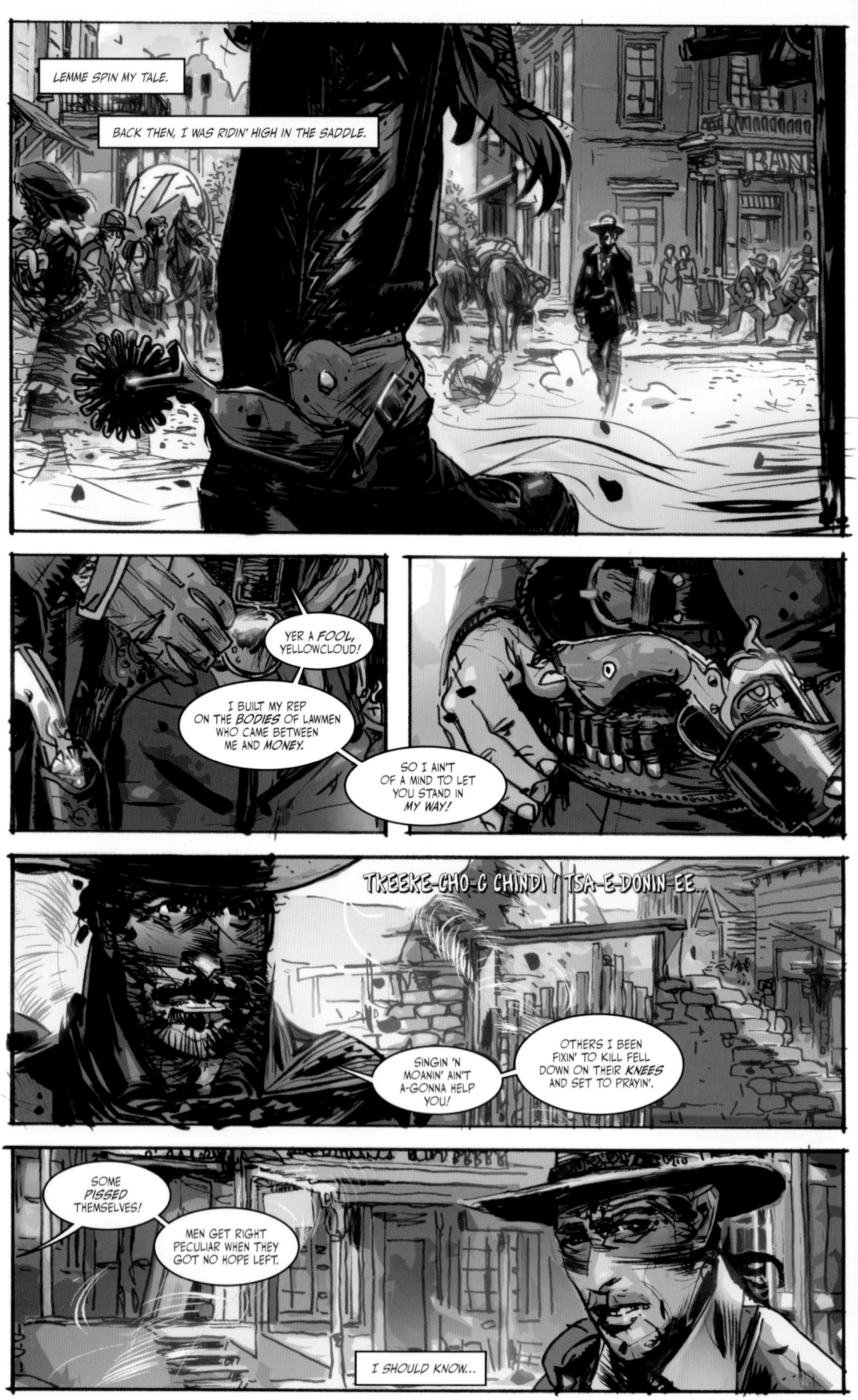
LEMME SPIN MY TALE.
BACK THEN, I WAS RIDIN' HIGH IN THE SADDLE.
YER A FOOL, YELLOWCLOUD!
I BUILT MY REP ON THE BODIES OF LAWMEN WHO CAME BETWEEN ME AND MONEY.
SO I AIN'T OF A MIND TO LET YOU STAND IN MY WAY!
TKEEKE-CHO-G CHINDI! TSA-E-DONIN-EE...
SINGIN 'N MOANIN' AIN'T A-GONNA HELP YOU!
OTHERS I BEEN FIXIN' TO KILL FELL DOWN ON THEIR KNEES AND SET TO PRAYIN'.
SOME PISSED THEMSELVES!
MEN GET RIGHT PECULIAR WHEN THEY GOT NO HOPE LEFT.
I SHOULD KNOW...

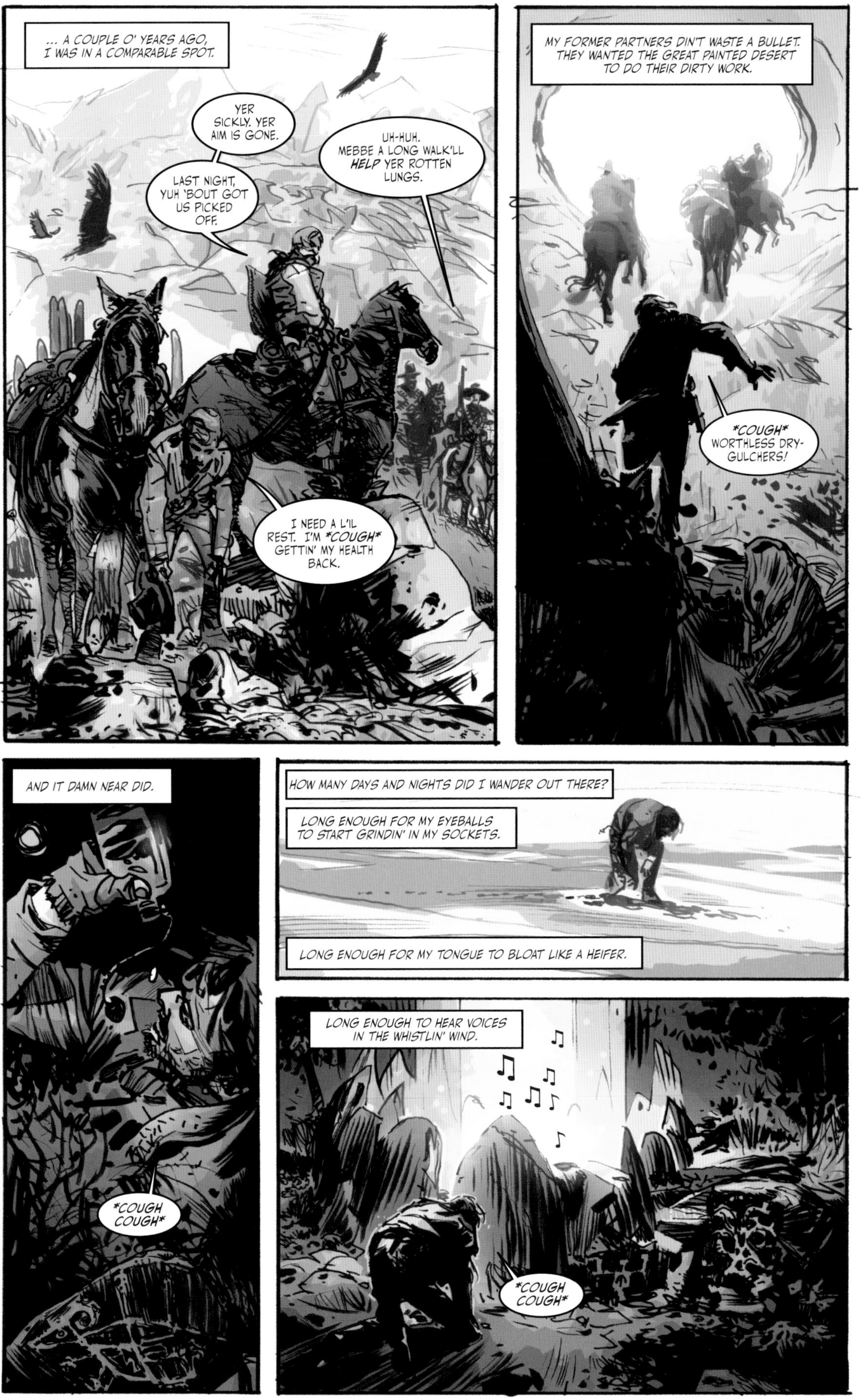
... A COUPLE O' YEARS AGO, I WAS IN A COMPARABLE SPOT.
YER SICKLY. YER AIM IS GONE.
LAST NIGHT, YUH 'BOUT GOT US PICKED OFF.
UH-HUH. MEBBE A LONG WALK'LL HELP YER ROTTEN LUNGS.
I NEED A L'IL REST. I'M *COUGH* GETTIN' MY HEALTH BACK.
MY FORMER PARTNERS DIN'T WASTE A BULLET. THEY WANTED THE GREAT PAINTED DESERT TO DO THEIR DIRTY WORK.
COUGH WORTHLESS DRY-GULCHERS!
AND IT DAMN NEAR DID.
COUGH COUGH
HOW MANY DAYS AND NIGHTS DID I WANDER OUT THERE?
LONG ENOUGH FOR MY EYEBALLS TO START GRINDIN' IN MY SOCKETS.
LONG ENOUGH FOR MY TONGUE TO BLOAT LIKE A HEIFER.
LONG ENOUGH TO HEAR VOICES IN THE WHISTLIN' WIND.
COUGH COUGH

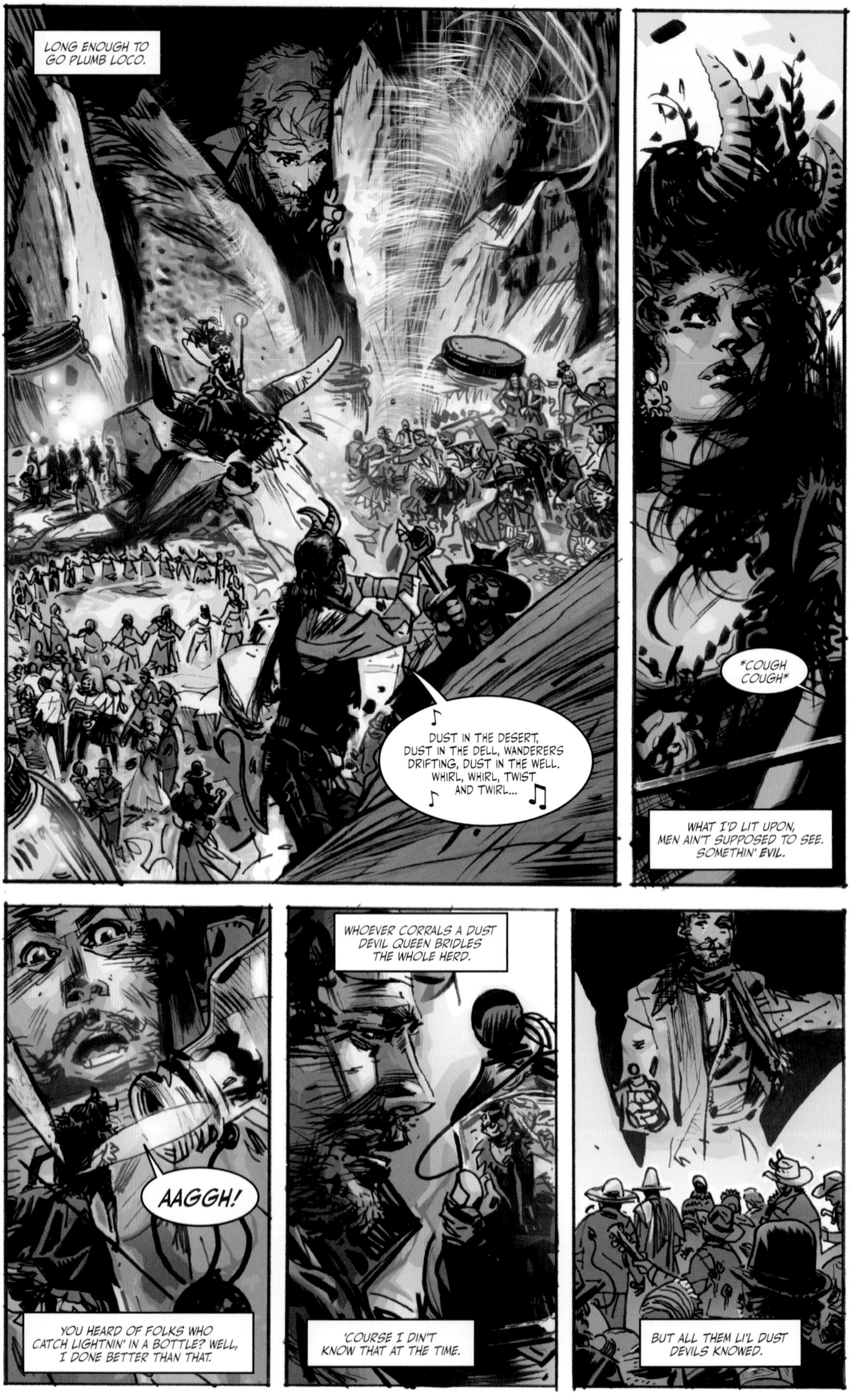
LONG ENOUGH TO GO PLUMB LOCO.
DUST IN THE DESERT, DUST IN THE DELL, WANDERERS DRIFTING, DUST IN THE WELL. WHIRL, WHIRL, TWIST AND TWIRL...
COUGH COUGH
WHAT I'D LIT UPON, MEN AIN'T SUPPOSED TO SEE. SOMETHIN' EVIL.
AAGGH!
YOU HEARD OF FOLKS WHO CATCH LIGHTNIN' IN A BOTTLE? WELL, I DONE BETTER THAN THAT.
WHOEVER CORRALS A DUST DEVIL QUEEN BRIDLES THE WHOLE HERD.
'COURSE I DIN'T KNOW THAT AT THE TIME.
BUT ALL THEM LI'L DUST DEVILS KNOWED.

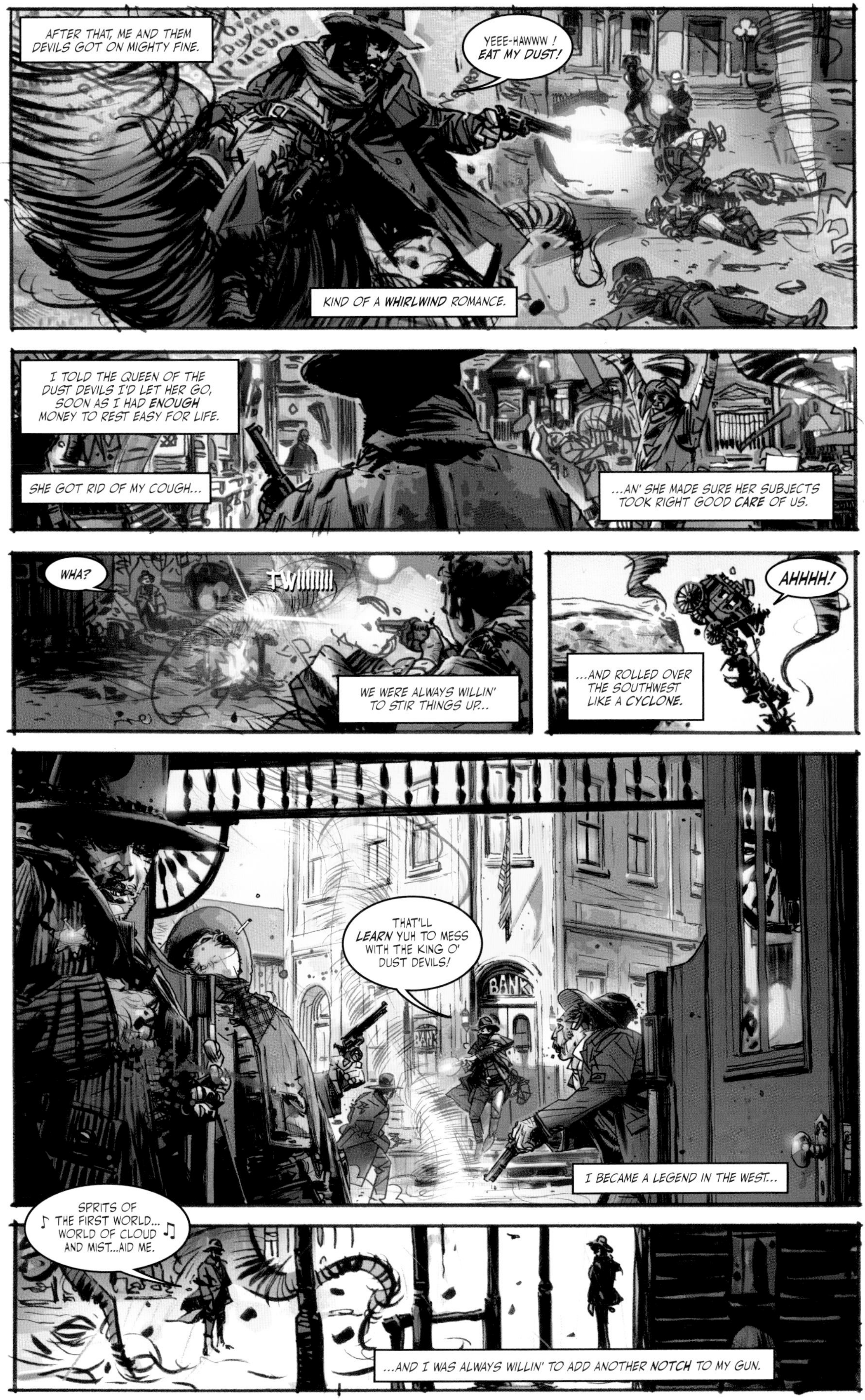

AFTER THAT, ME AND THEM DEVILS GOT ON MIGHTY FINE.
YEEE-HAWWW ! EAT MY DUST!
KIND OF A WHIRLWIND ROMANCE.
I TOLD THE QUEEN OF THE DUST DEVILS I'D LET HER GO, SOON AS I HAD ENOUGH MONEY TO REST EASY FOR LIFE.
SHE GOT RID OF MY COUGH...
...AN' SHE MADE SURE HER SUBJECTS TOOK RIGHT GOOD CARE OF US.
WHA?
TWIIIIIII
WE WERE ALWAYS WILLIN' TO STIR THINGS UP...
AHHHH!
...AND ROLLED OVER THE SOUTHWEST LIKE A CYCLONE.
THAT'LL LEARN YUH TO MESS WITH THE KING O' DUST DEVILS!
BANK
I BECAME A LEGEND IN THE WEST...
SPRITS OF ♪ THE FIRST WORLD... WORLD OF CLOUD ♫ AND MIST...AID ME.
...AND I WAS ALWAYS WILLIN' TO ADD ANOTHER NOTCH TO MY GUN.

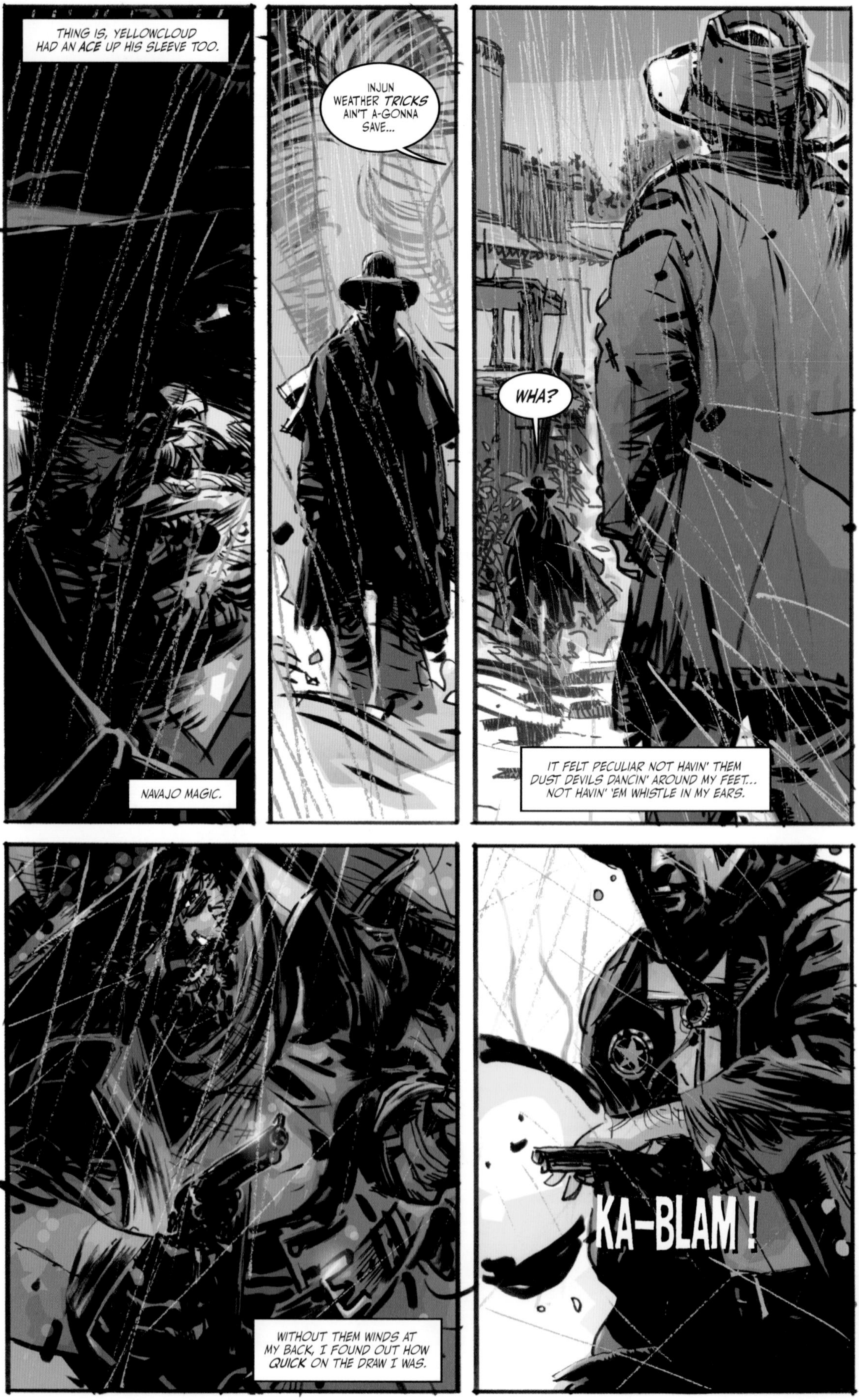
THING IS, YELLOWCLOUD HAD AN ACE UP HIS SLEEVE TOO.
NAVAJO MAGIC.
INJUN WEATHER TRICKS AIN'T A-GONNA SAVE...
WHA?
IT FELT PECULIAR NOT HAVIN' THEM DUST DEVILS DANCIN' AROUND MY FEET... NOT HAVIN' 'EM WHISTLE IN MY EARS.
WITHOUT THEM WINDS AT MY BACK, I FOUND OUT HOW QUICK ON THE DRAW I WAS.
KA-BLAM !

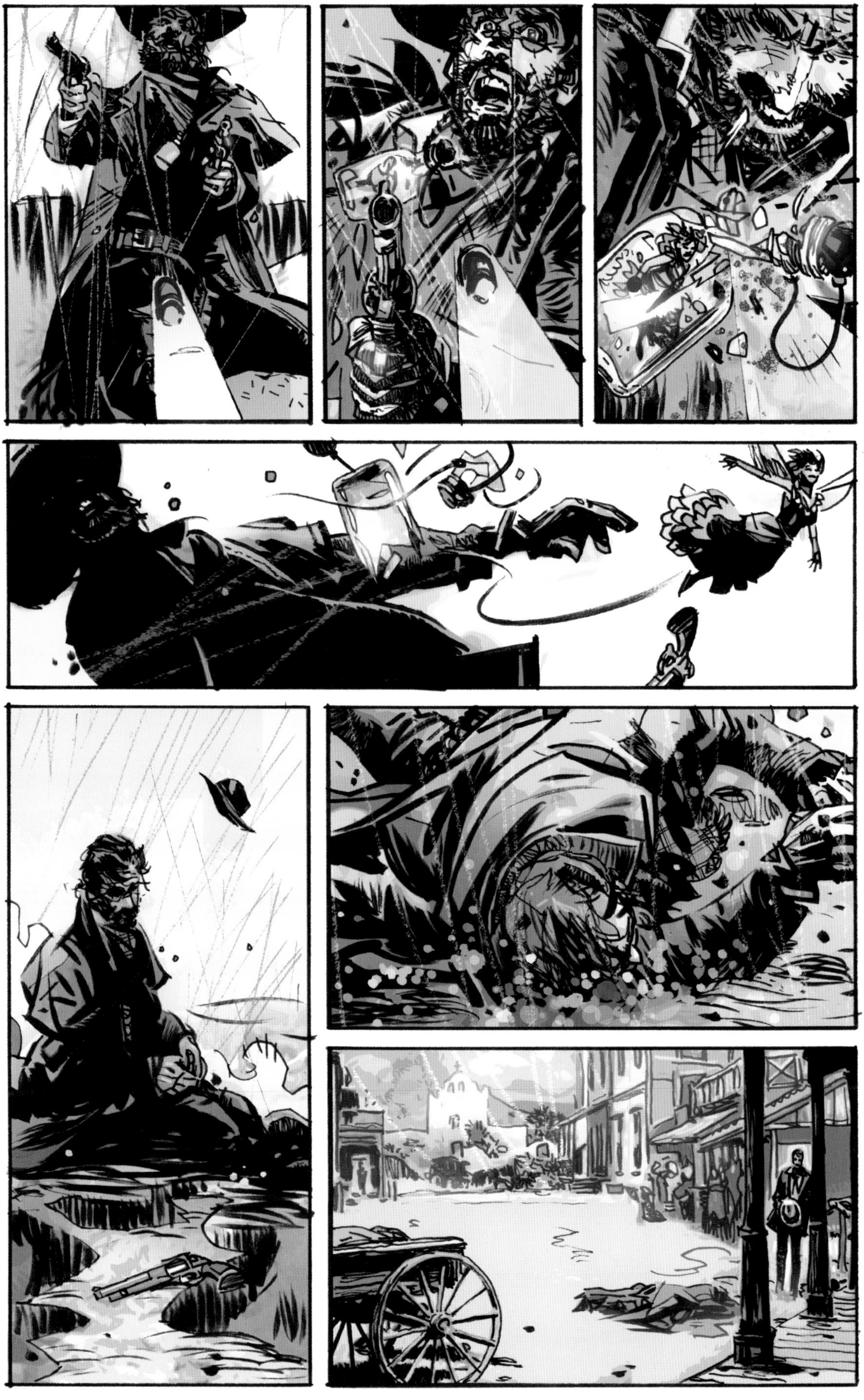

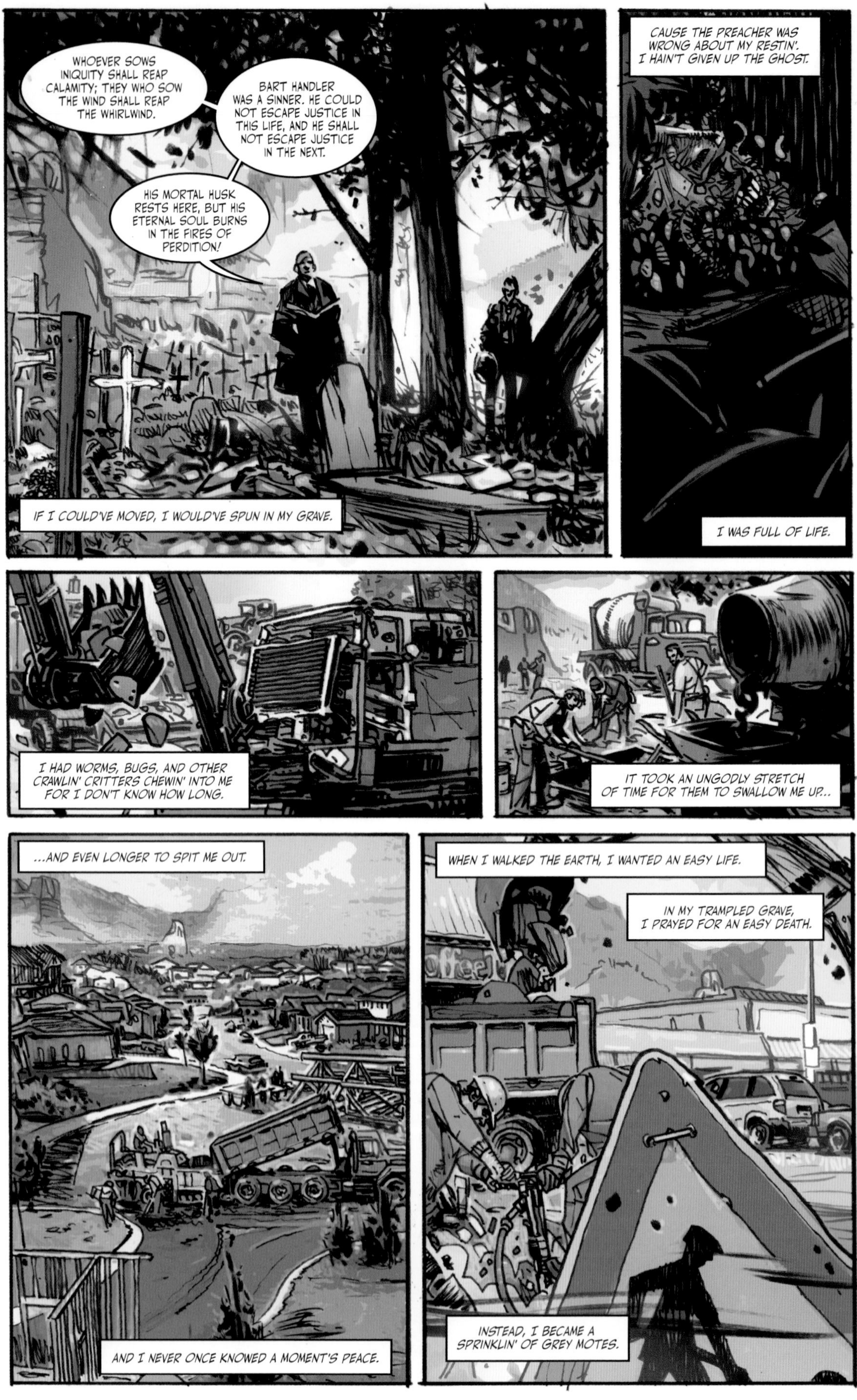
WHOEVER SOWS INIQUITY SHALL REAP CALAMITY; THEY WHO SOW THE WIND SHALL REAP THE WHIRLWIND.
BART HANDLER WAS A SINNER. HE COULD NOT ESCAPE JUSTICE IN THIS LIFE, AND HE SHALL NOT ESCAPE JUSTICE IN THE NEXT.
HIS MORTAL HUSK RESTS HERE, BUT HIS ETERNAL SOUL BURNS IN THE FIRES OF PERDITION!
IF I COULD'VE MOVED, I WOULD'VE SPUN IN MY GRAVE.
CAUSE THE PREACHER WAS WRONG ABOUT MY RESTIN'. I HAIN'T GIVEN UP THE GHOST.
I WAS FULL OF LIFE.
I HAD WORMS, BUGS, AND OTHER CRAWLIN' CRITTERS CHEWIN' INTO ME FOR I DON'T KNOW HOW LONG.
IT TOOK AN UNGODLY STRETCH OF TIME FOR THEM TO SWALLOW ME UP...
...AND EVEN LONGER TO SPIT ME OUT.
AND I NEVER ONCE KNOWED A MOMENT'S PEACE.
WHEN I WALKED THE EARTH, I WANTED AN EASY LIFE.
IN MY TRAMPLED GRAVE, I PRAYED FOR AN EASY DEATH.
INSTEAD, I BECAME A SPRINKLIN' OF GREY MOTES.

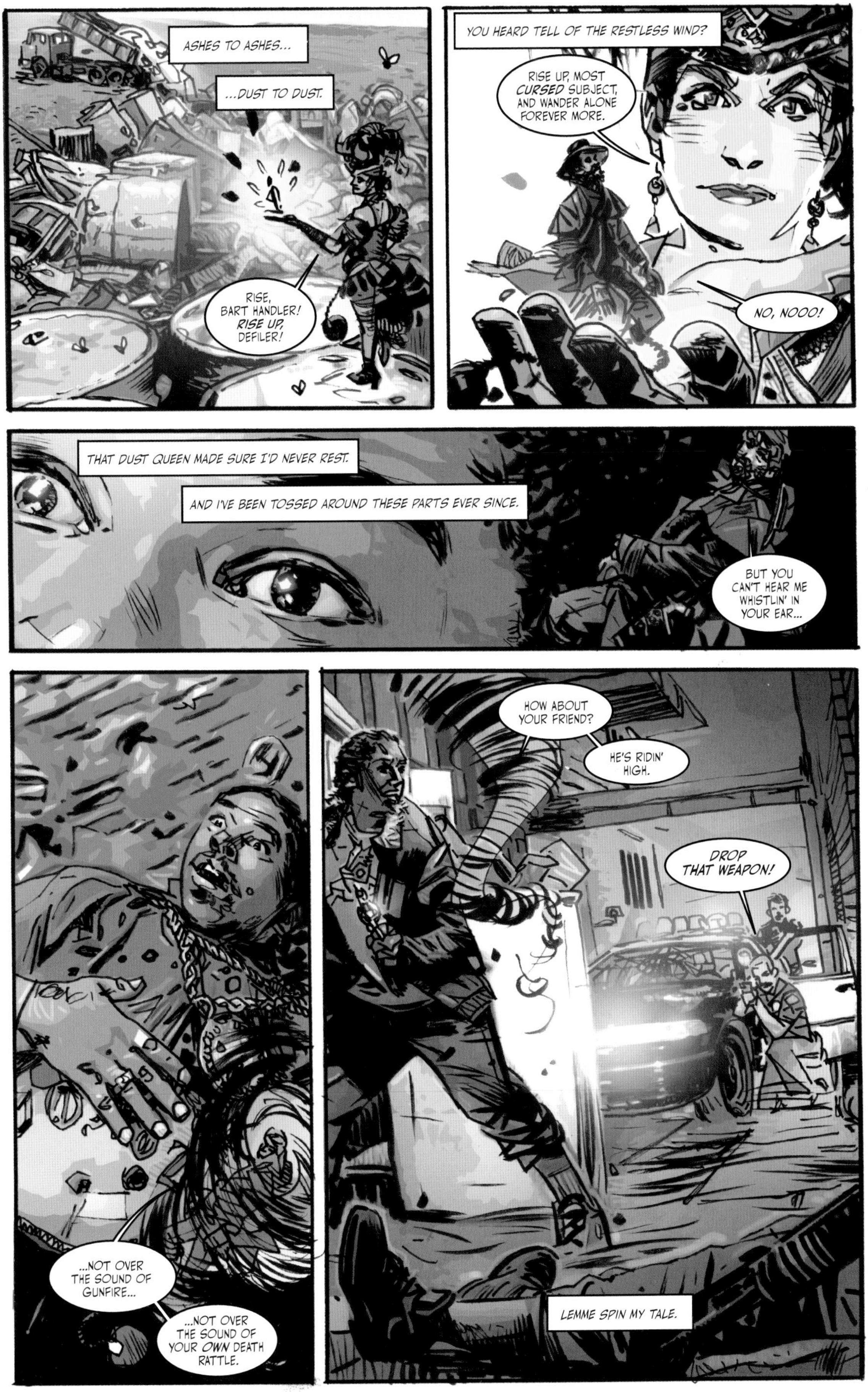
ASHES TO ASHES...
...DUST TO DUST.
RISE, BART HANDLER! RISE UP, DEFILER!
YOU HEARD TELL OF THE RESTLESS WIND?
RISE UP, MOST CURSED SUBJECT, AND WANDER ALONE FOREVER MORE.
NO, NOOO!
THAT DUST QUEEN MADE SURE I'D NEVER REST.
AND I'VE BEEN TOSSED AROUND THESE PARTS EVER SINCE.
BUT YOU CAN'T HEAR ME WHISTLIN' IN YOUR EAR...
...NOT OVER THE SOUND OF GUNFIRE...
...NOT OVER THE SOUND OF YOUR OWN DEATH RATTLE.
HOW ABOUT YOUR FRIEND?
HE'S RIDIN' HIGH.
DROP THAT WEAPON!
LEMME SPIN MY TALE.

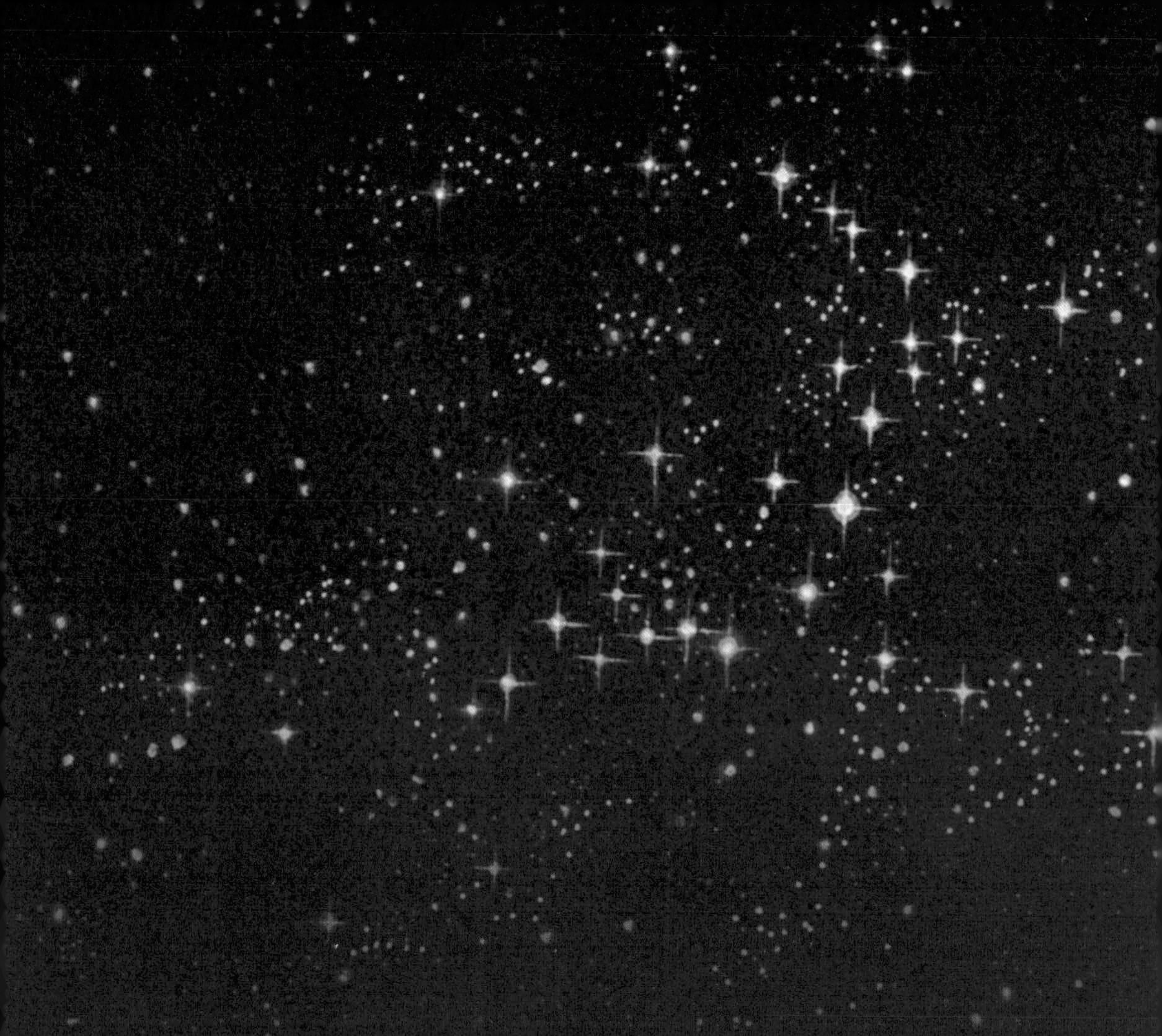

ELEMENTAL

Story by JIM ALEXANDER
Art by DAVID LLOYD
Colors by SNAKEBITE

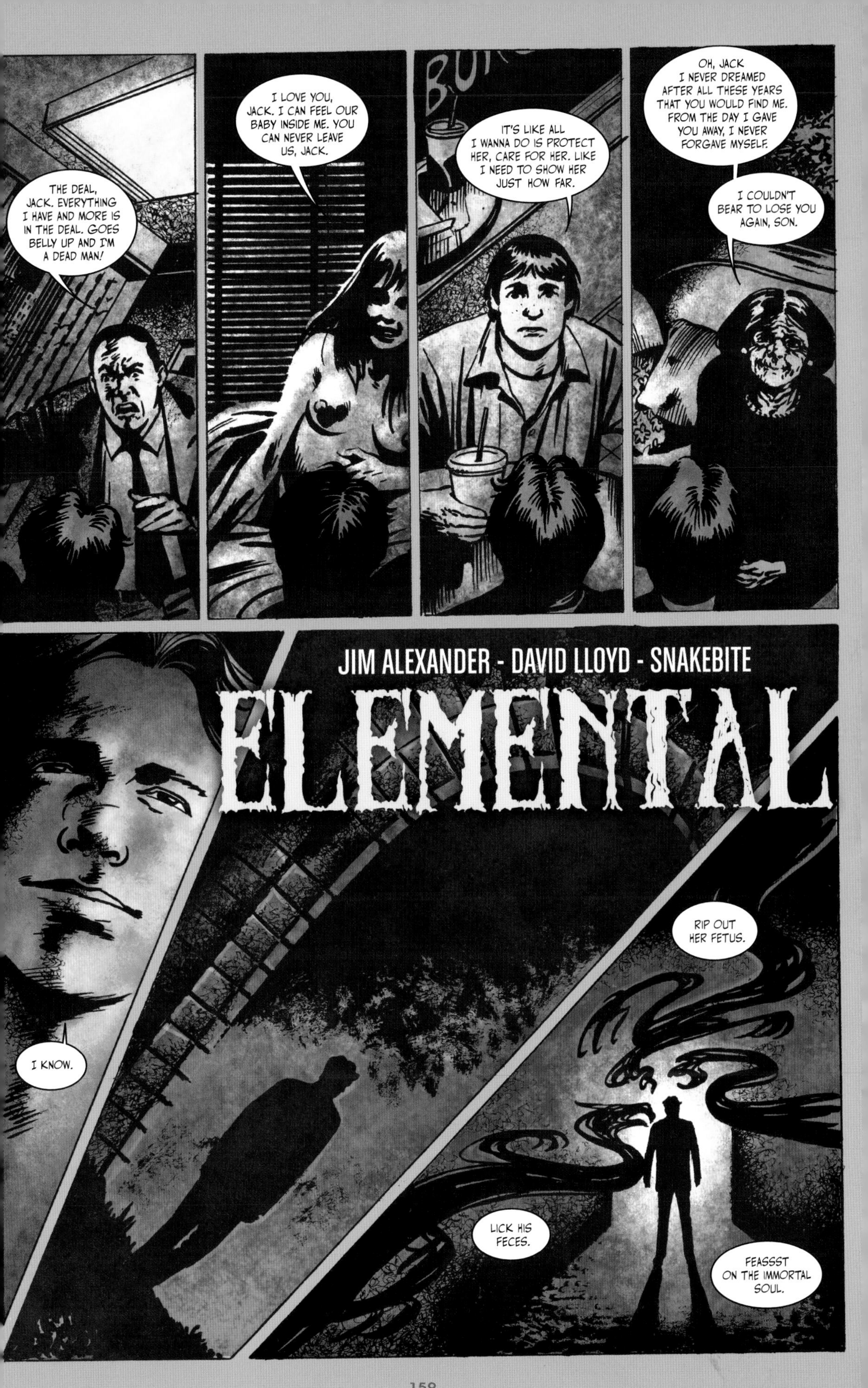
THE DEAL, JACK. EVERYTHING I HAVE AND MORE IS IN THE DEAL. GOES BELLY UP AND I'M A DEAD MAN!
I LOVE YOU, JACK. I CAN FEEL OUR BABY INSIDE ME. YOU CAN NEVER LEAVE US, JACK.
IT'S LIKE ALL I WANNA DO IS PROTECT HER, CARE FOR HER. LIKE I NEED TO SHOW HER JUST HOW FAR.
OH, JACK I NEVER DREAMED AFTER ALL THESE YEARS THAT YOU WOULD FIND ME. FROM THE DAY I GAVE YOU AWAY, I NEVER FORGAVE MYSELF.
I COULDN'T BEAR TO LOSE YOU AGAIN, SON.
JIM ALEXANDER - DAVID LLOYD - SNAKEBITE
ELEMENTAL
I KNOW.
RIP OUT HER FETUS.
LICK HIS FECES.
FEASSST ON THE IMMORTAL SOUL.

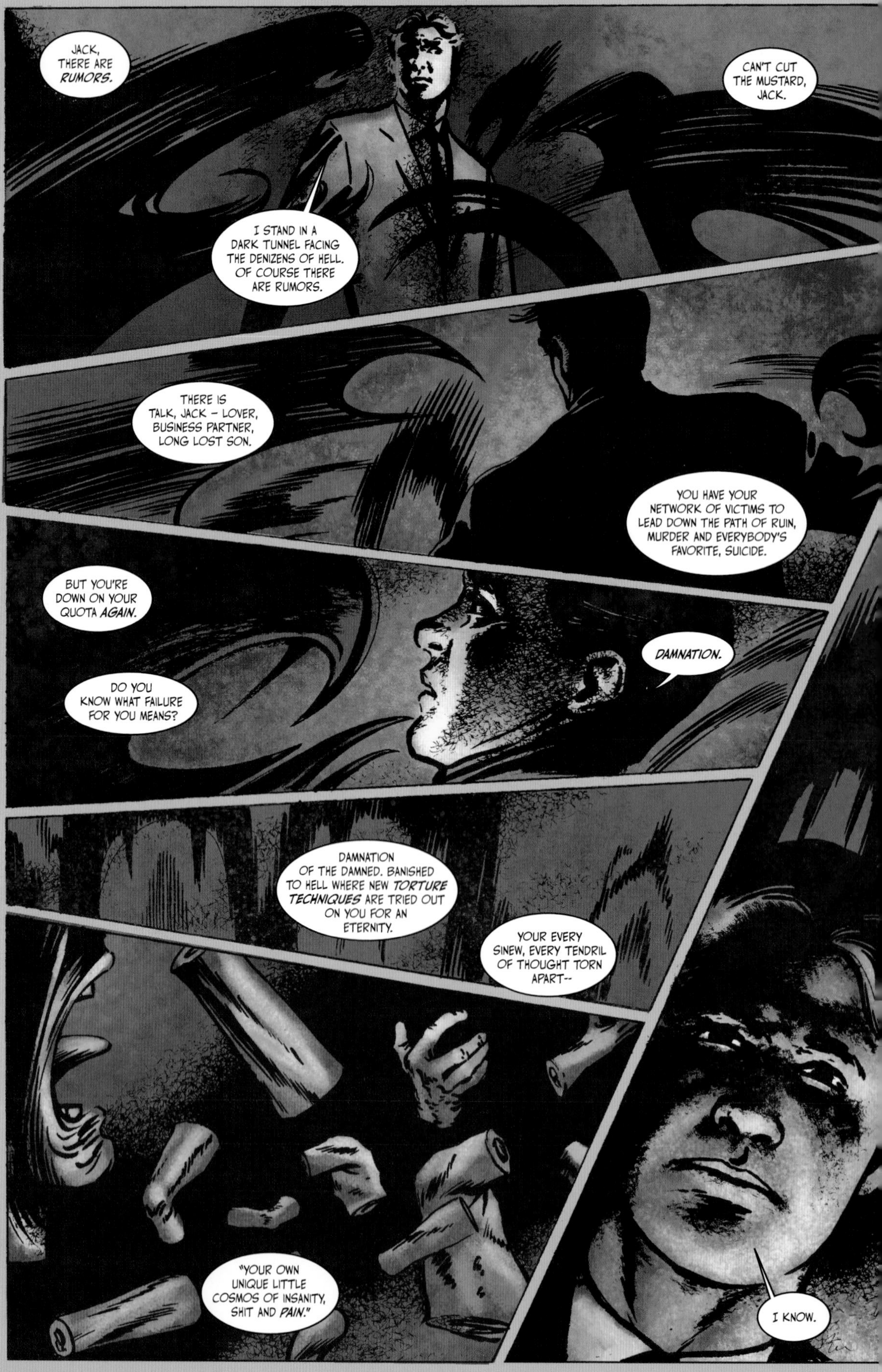
JACK, THERE ARE *RUMORS.*
CAN'T CUT THE MUSTARD, JACK.
I STAND IN A DARK TUNNEL FACING THE DENIZENS OF HELL. OF COURSE THERE ARE RUMORS.
THERE IS TALK, JACK – LOVER, BUSINESS PARTNER, LONG LOST SON.
YOU HAVE YOUR NETWORK OF VICTIMS TO LEAD DOWN THE PATH OF RUIN, MURDER AND EVERYBODY'S FAVORITE, SUICIDE.
BUT YOU'RE DOWN ON YOUR QUOTA *AGAIN.*
DO YOU KNOW WHAT FAILURE FOR YOU MEANS?
DAMNATION.
DAMNATION OF THE DAMNED. BANISHED TO HELL WHERE NEW *TORTURE TECHNIQUES* ARE TRIED OUT ON YOU FOR AN ETERNITY.
YOUR EVERY SINEW, EVERY TENDRIL OF THOUGHT TORN APART--
"YOUR OWN UNIQUE LITTLE COSMOS OF INSANITY, SHIT AND *PAIN.*"
I KNOW.

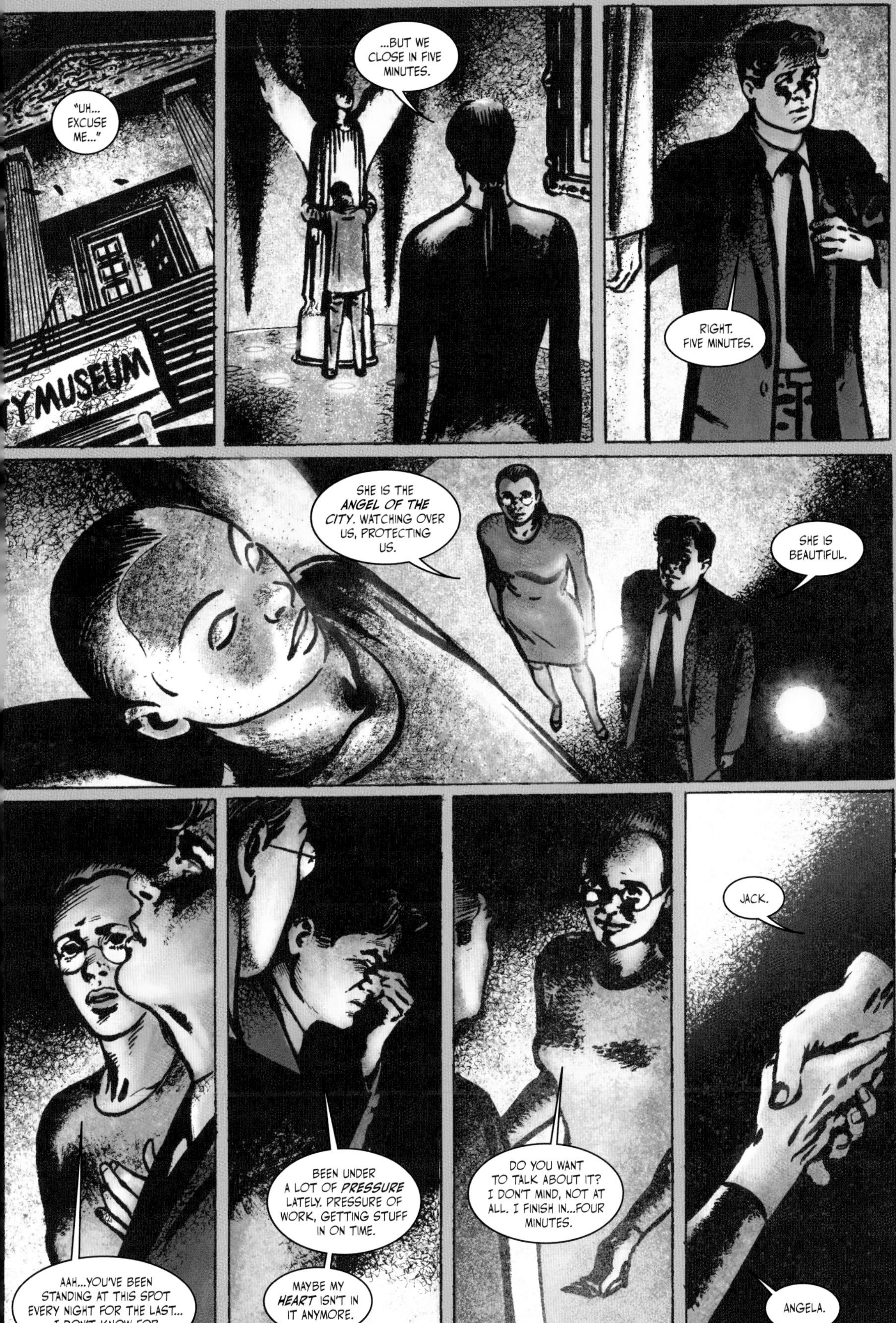

"UH... EXCUSE ME..."
...Y MUSEUM
...BUT WE CLOSE IN FIVE MINUTES.
RIGHT. FIVE MINUTES.
SHE IS THE *ANGEL OF THE CITY*. WATCHING OVER US, PROTECTING US.
SHE IS BEAUTIFUL.
AAH...YOU'VE BEEN STANDING AT THIS SPOT EVERY NIGHT FOR THE LAST... I DON'T KNOW FOR HOW LONG.
BEEN UNDER A LOT OF *PRESSURE* LATELY. PRESSURE OF WORK, GETTING STUFF IN ON TIME.
MAYBE MY *HEART* ISN'T IN IT ANYMORE.
DO YOU WANT TO TALK ABOUT IT? I DON'T MIND, NOT AT ALL. I FINISH IN...FOUR MINUTES.
JACK.
ANGELA.

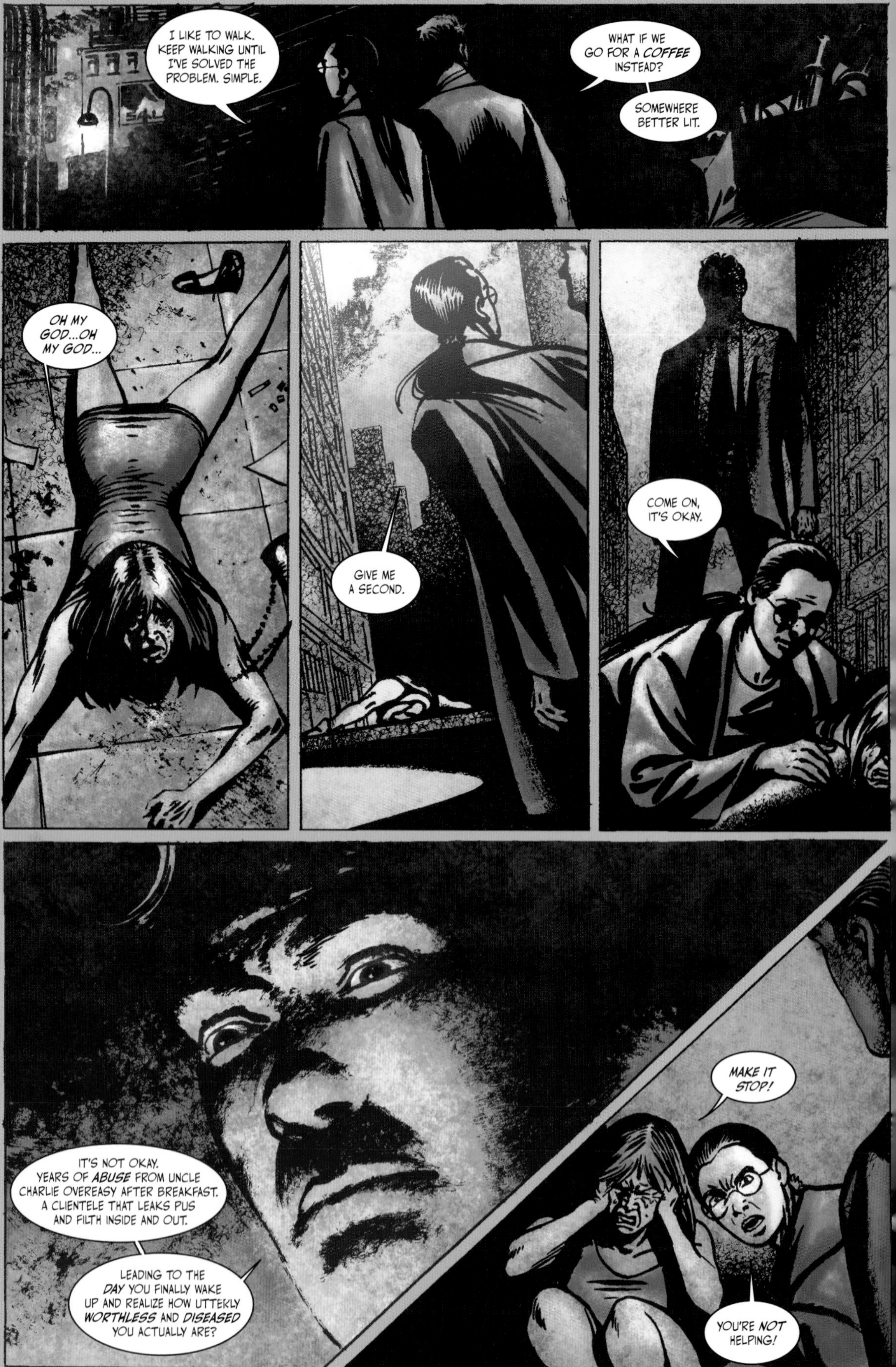
I LIKE TO WALK. KEEP WALKING UNTIL I'VE SOLVED THE PROBLEM. SIMPLE.
WHAT IF WE GO FOR A *COFFEE* INSTEAD?
SOMEWHERE BETTER LIT.
OH MY GOD...OH MY GOD...
GIVE ME A SECOND.
COME ON, IT'S OKAY.
IT'S NOT OKAY. YEARS OF *ABUSE* FROM UNCLE CHARLIE OVEREASY AFTER BREAKFAST. A CLIENTELE THAT LEAKS PUS AND FILTH INSIDE AND OUT.
LEADING TO THE *DAY* YOU FINALLY WAKE UP AND REALIZE HOW UTTERLY *WORTHLESS* AND *DISEASED* YOU ACTUALLY ARE?
MAKE IT STOP!
YOU'RE *NOT* HELPING!

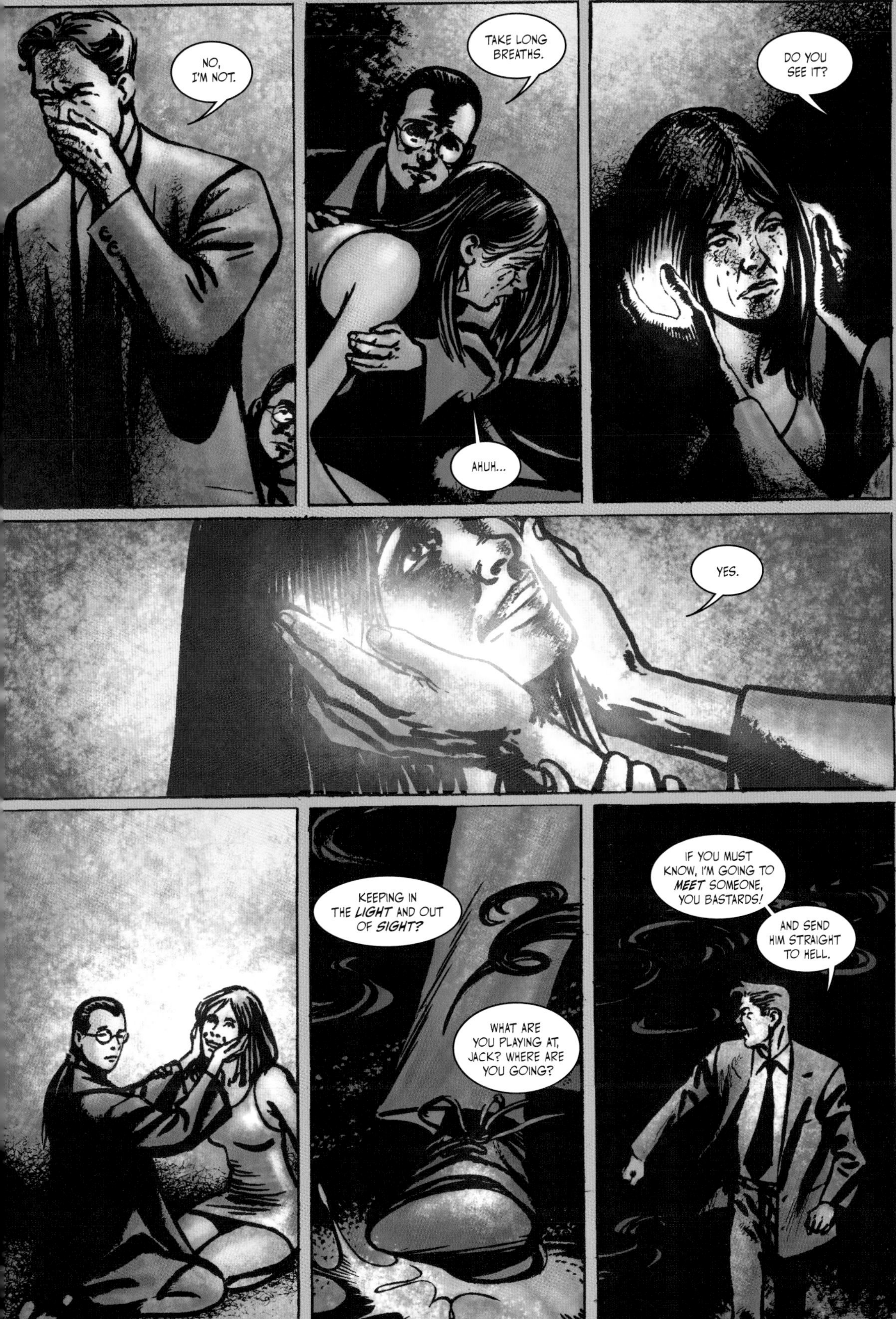
NO, I'M NOT.
TAKE LONG BREATHS.
AHUH...
DO YOU SEE IT?
YES.
KEEPING IN THE *LIGHT* AND OUT OF *SIGHT?*
WHAT ARE YOU PLAYING AT, JACK? WHERE ARE YOU GOING?
IF YOU MUST KNOW, I'M GOING TO *MEET* SOMEONE, YOU BASTARDS!
AND SEND HIM STRAIGHT TO HELL.

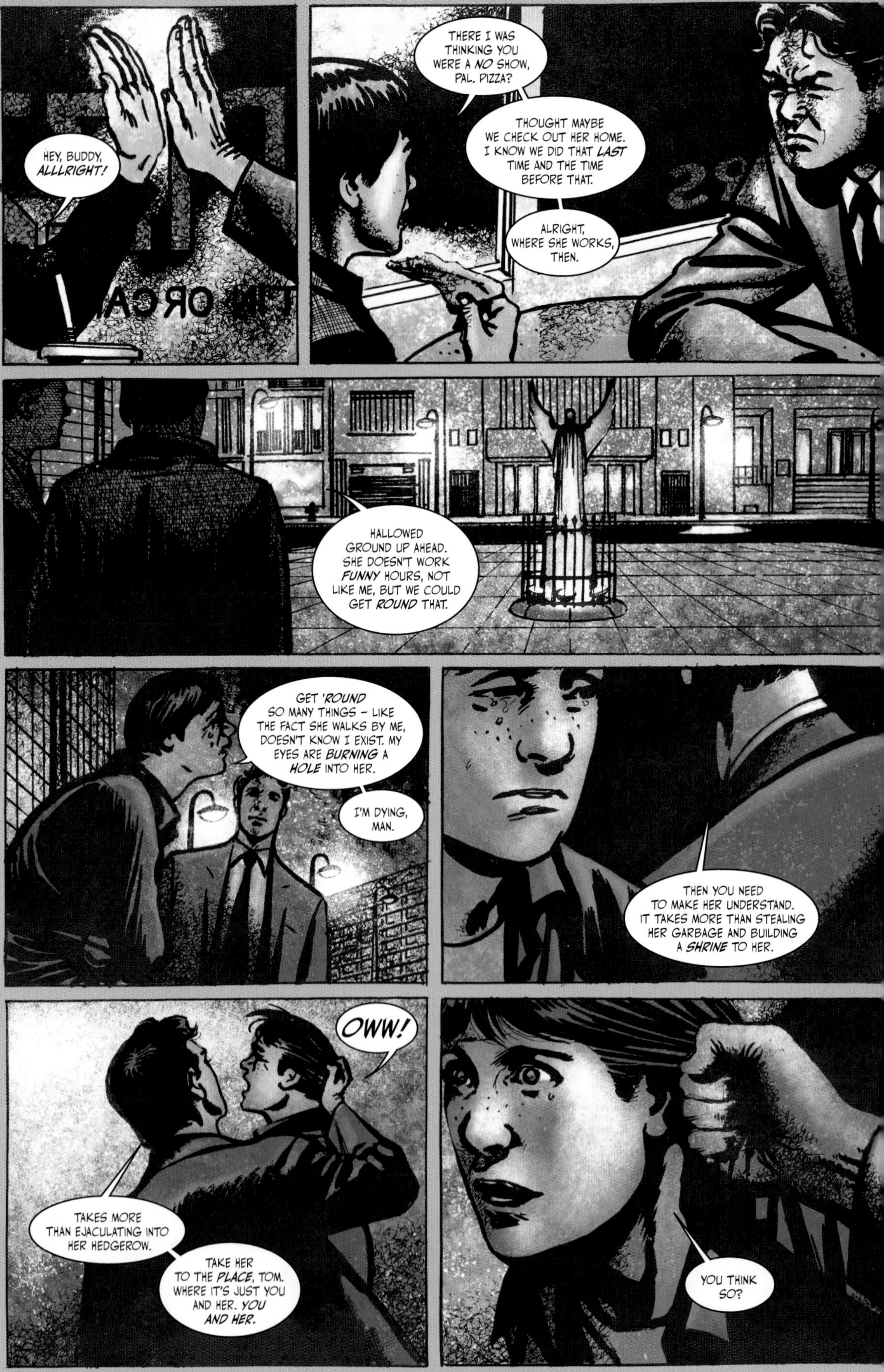
HEY, BUDDY, ALLRIGHT!
THERE I WAS THINKING YOU WERE A NO SHOW, PAL. PIZZA?
THOUGHT MAYBE WE CHECK OUT HER HOME. I KNOW WE DID THAT LAST TIME AND THE TIME BEFORE THAT.
ALRIGHT, WHERE SHE WORKS, THEN.
HALLOWED GROUND UP AHEAD. SHE DOESN'T WORK FUNNY HOURS, NOT LIKE ME, BUT WE COULD GET ROUND THAT.
GET 'ROUND SO MANY THINGS – LIKE THE FACT SHE WALKS BY ME, DOESN'T KNOW I EXIST. MY EYES ARE BURNING A HOLE INTO HER.
I'M DYING, MAN.
THEN YOU NEED TO MAKE HER UNDERSTAND. IT TAKES MORE THAN STEALING HER GARBAGE AND BUILDING A SHRINE TO HER.
OWW!
TAKES MORE THAN EJACULATING INTO HER HEDGEROW.
TAKE HER TO THE PLACE, TOM. WHERE IT'S JUST YOU AND HER. YOU AND HER.
YOU THINK SO?

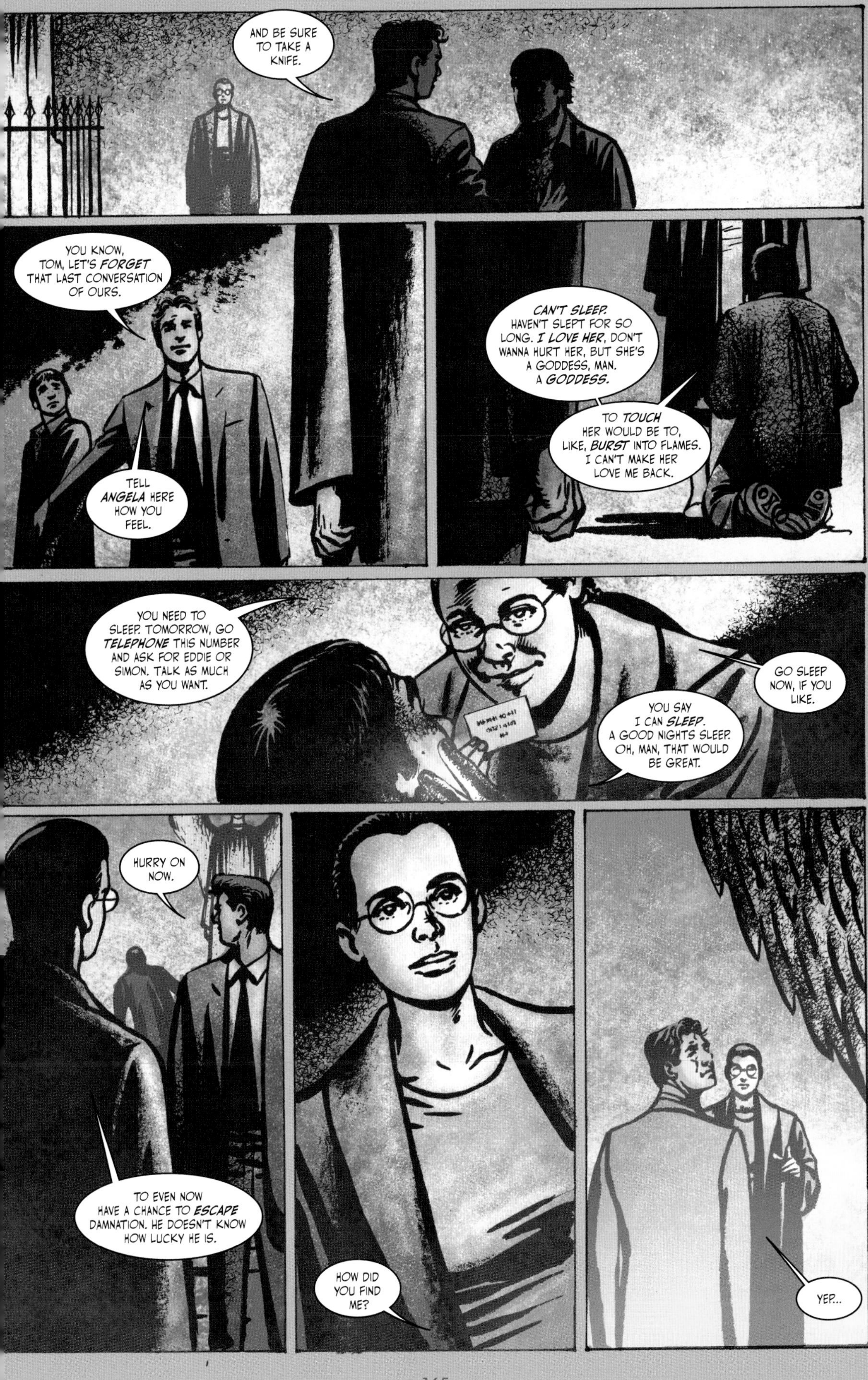
AND BE SURE TO TAKE A KNIFE.
YOU KNOW, TOM, LET'S FORGET THAT LAST CONVERSATION OF OURS.
TELL ANGELA HERE HOW YOU FEEL.
CAN'T SLEEP. HAVEN'T SLEPT FOR SO LONG. I LOVE HER, DON'T WANNA HURT HER, BUT SHE'S A GODDESS, MAN. A GODDESS.
TO TOUCH HER WOULD BE TO, LIKE, BURST INTO FLAMES. I CAN'T MAKE HER LOVE ME BACK.
YOU NEED TO SLEEP. TOMORROW, GO TELEPHONE THIS NUMBER AND ASK FOR EDDIE OR SIMON. TALK AS MUCH AS YOU WANT.
GO SLEEP NOW, IF YOU LIKE.
YOU SAY I CAN SLEEP. A GOOD NIGHTS SLEEP. OH, MAN, THAT WOULD BE GREAT.
HURRY ON NOW.
TO EVEN NOW HAVE A CHANCE TO ESCAPE DAMNATION. HE DOESN'T KNOW HOW LUCKY HE IS.
HOW DID YOU FIND ME?
YEP...

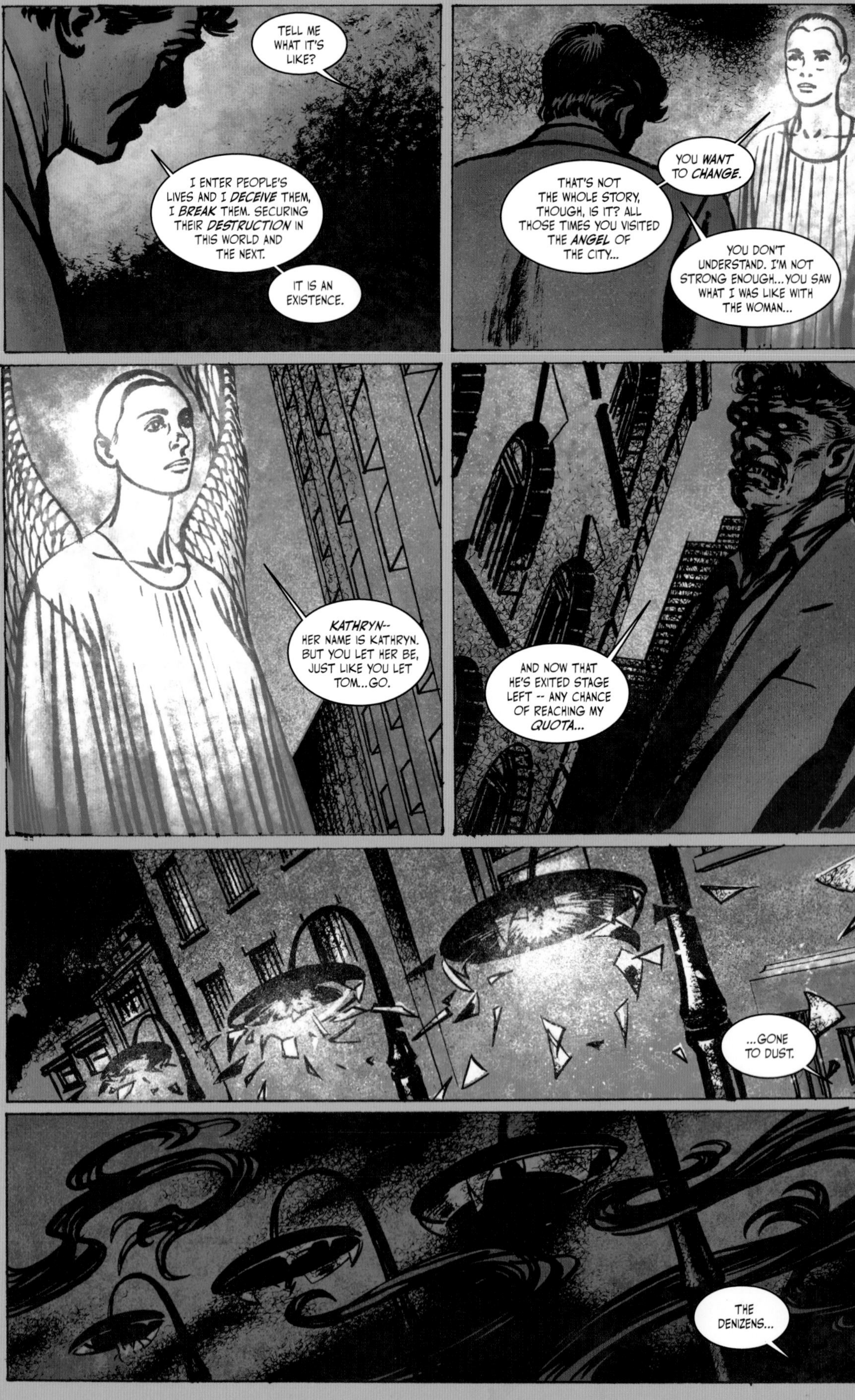
TELL ME WHAT IT'S LIKE?
I ENTER PEOPLE'S LIVES AND I *DECEIVE* THEM, I *BREAK* THEM. SECURING THEIR *DESTRUCTION* IN THIS WORLD AND THE NEXT.
IT IS AN EXISTENCE.
THAT'S NOT THE WHOLE STORY, THOUGH, IS IT? ALL THOSE TIMES YOU VISITED THE *ANGEL* OF THE CITY...
YOU *WANT* TO *CHANGE*.
YOU DON'T UNDERSTAND. I'M NOT STRONG ENOUGH...YOU SAW WHAT I WAS LIKE WITH THE WOMAN...
KATHRYN-- HER NAME IS KATHRYN. BUT YOU LET HER BE, JUST LIKE YOU LET TOM...GO.
AND NOW THAT HE'S EXITED STAGE LEFT -- ANY CHANCE OF REACHING MY *QUOTA*...
...GONE TO DUST.
THE DENIZENS...

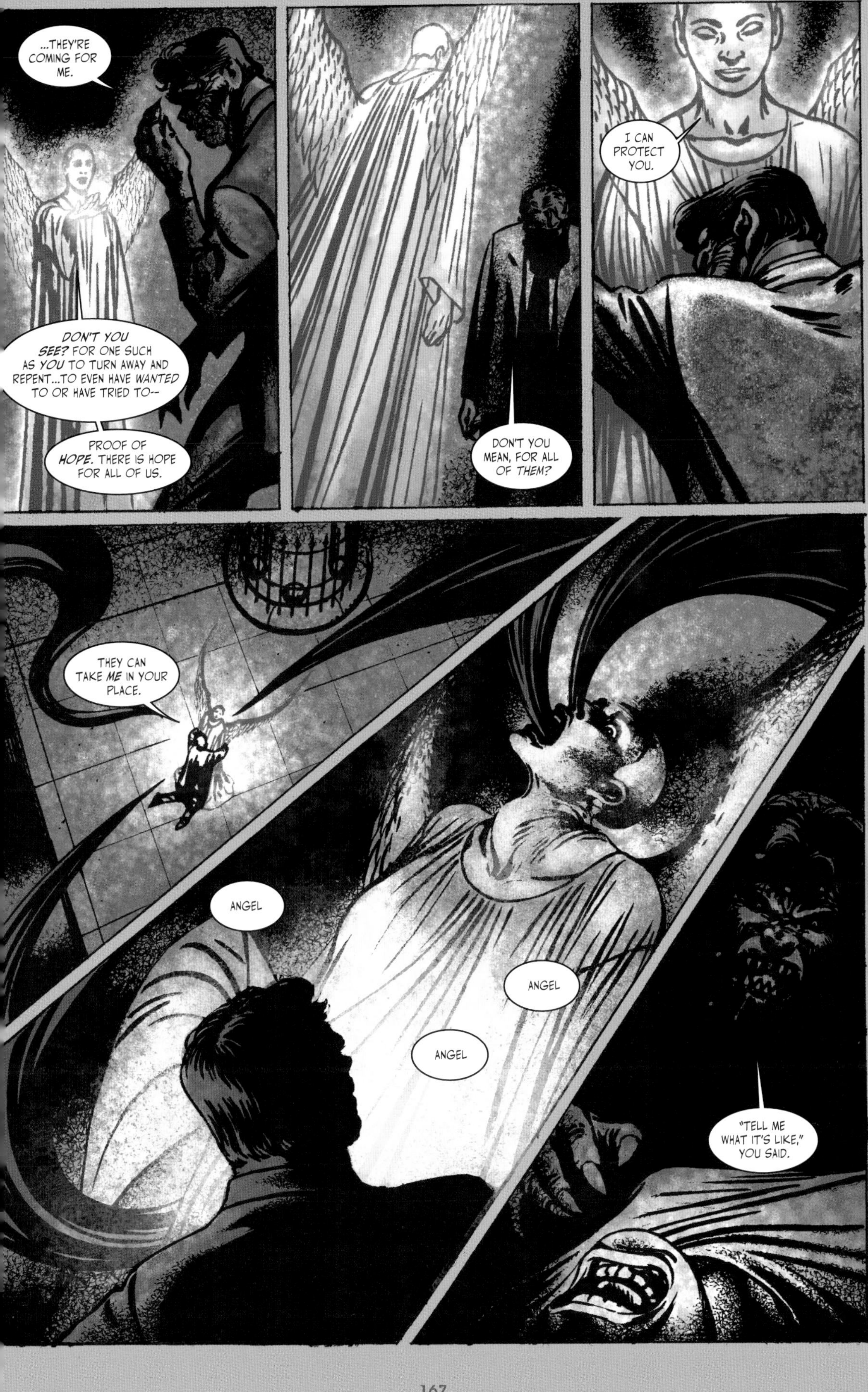
...THEY'RE COMING FOR ME.
DON'T YOU SEE? FOR ONE SUCH AS YOU TO TURN AWAY AND REPENT...TO EVEN HAVE WANTED TO OR HAVE TRIED TO--
PROOF OF HOPE. THERE IS HOPE FOR ALL OF US.
DON'T YOU MEAN, FOR ALL OF THEM?
I CAN PROTECT YOU.
THEY CAN TAKE ME IN YOUR PLACE.
ANGEL
ANGEL
ANGEL
"TELL ME WHAT IT'S LIKE," YOU SAID.

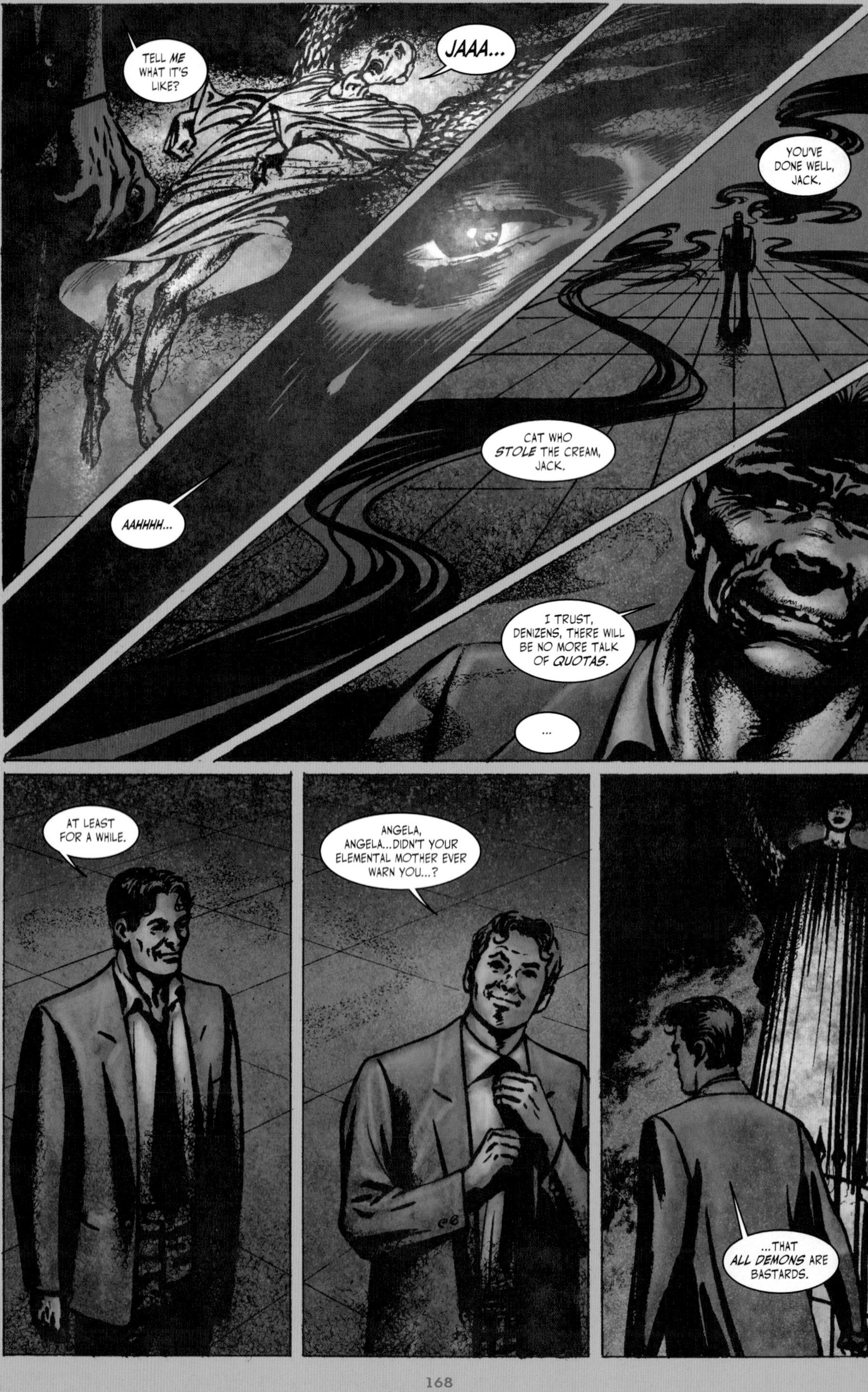
TELL *ME* WHAT IT'S LIKE?
JAAA...
AAHHHH...
YOU'VE DONE WELL, JACK.
CAT WHO *STOLE* THE CREAM, JACK.
I TRUST, DENIZENS, THERE WILL BE NO MORE TALK OF *QUOTAS.*
...
AT LEAST FOR A WHILE.
ANGELA, ANGELA...DIDN'T YOUR ELEMENTAL MOTHER EVER WARN YOU...?
...THAT *ALL DEMONS* ARE BASTARDS.

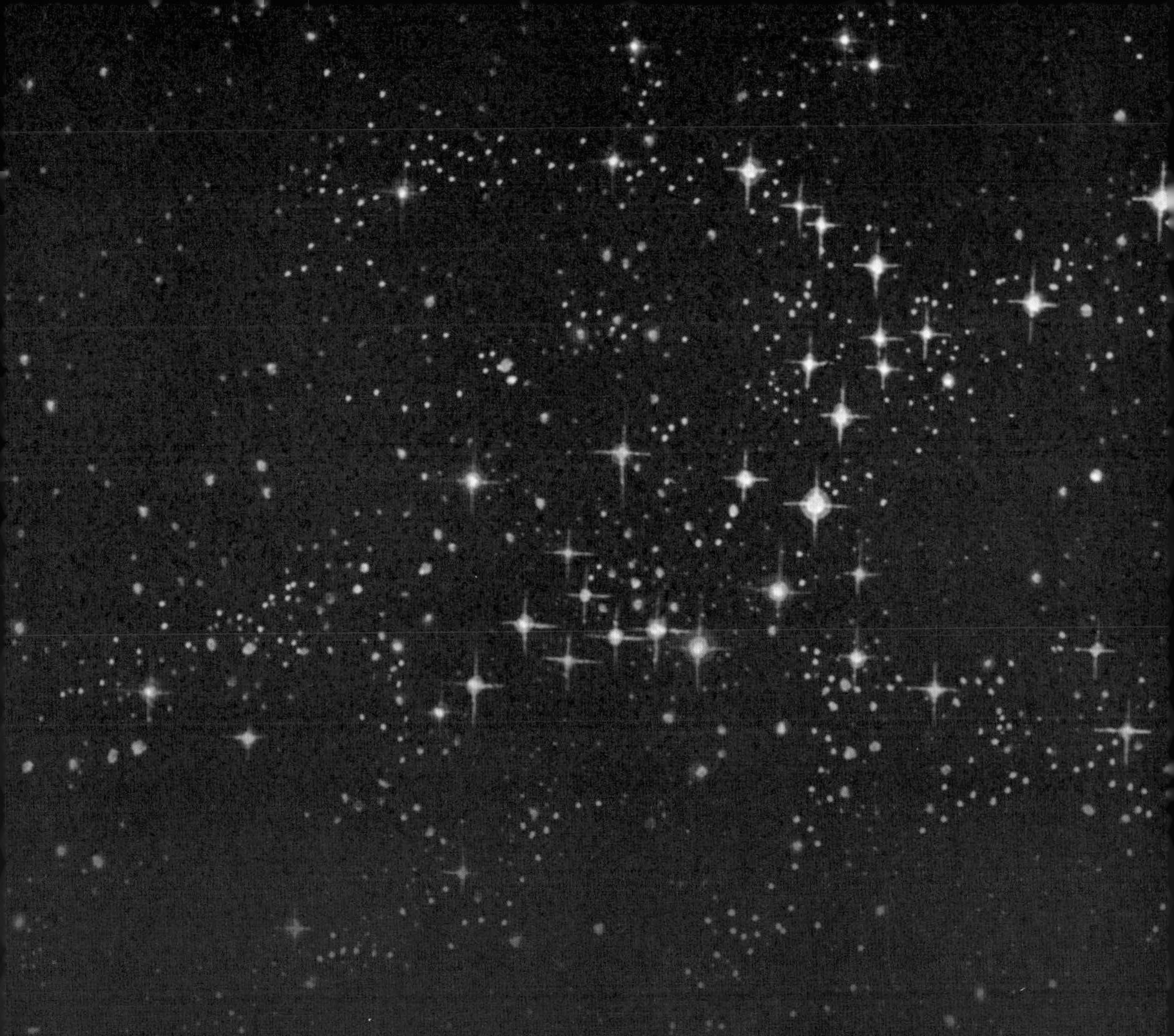

WHISKY IN THE JAR

Story by JIM ALEXANDER
Art by GERALD PAREL

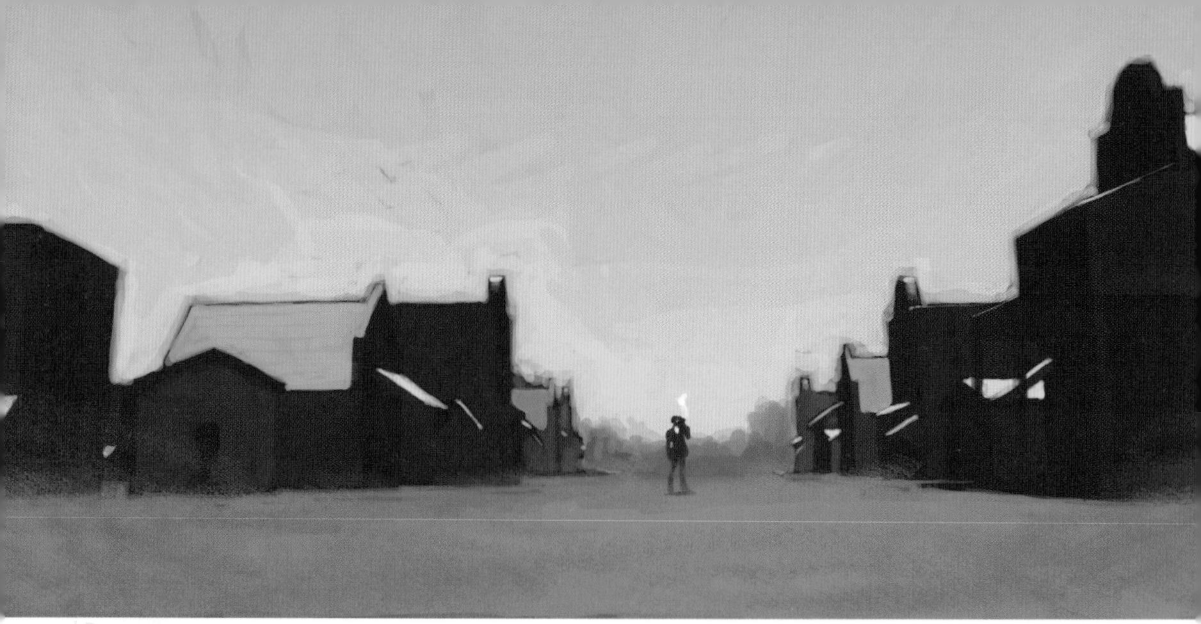

WHISKY IN THE JAR

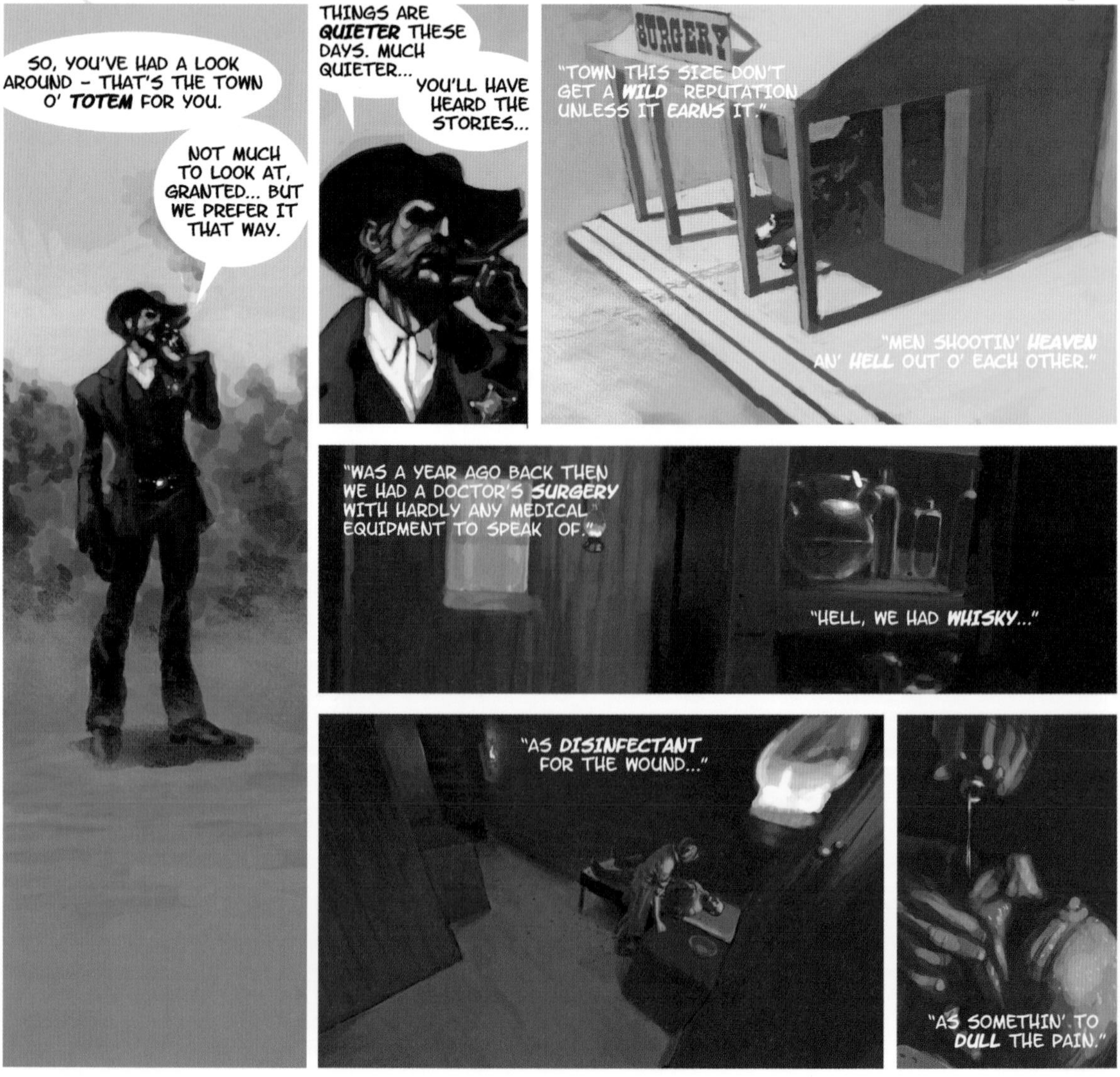

SO, YOU'VE HAD A LOOK AROUND - THAT'S THE TOWN O' TOTEM FOR YOU.
NOT MUCH TO LOOK AT, GRANTED... BUT WE PREFER IT THAT WAY.
THINGS ARE QUIETER THESE DAYS. MUCH QUIETER...
YOU'LL HAVE HEARD THE STORIES...
SURGERY
"TOWN THIS SIZE DON'T GET A WILD REPUTATION UNLESS IT EARNS IT."
"MEN SHOOTIN' HEAVEN AN' HELL OUT O' EACH OTHER."
"WAS A YEAR AGO BACK THEN WE HAD A DOCTOR'S SURGERY WITH HARDLY ANY MEDICAL EQUIPMENT TO SPEAK OF."
"HELL, WE HAD WHISKY..."
"AS DISINFECTANT FOR THE WOUND..."
"AS SOMETHIN' TO DULL THE PAIN."

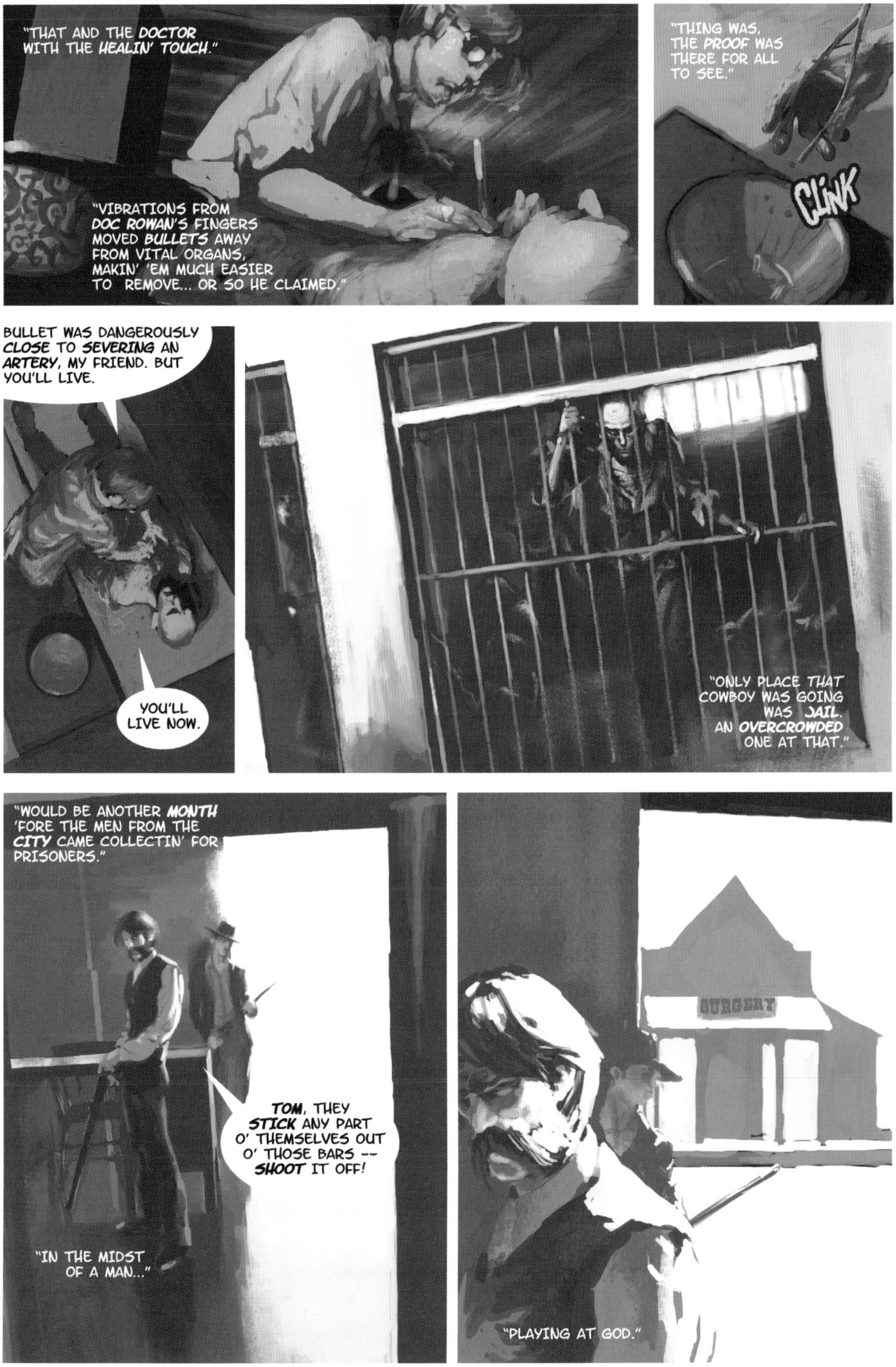
"THAT AND THE DOCTOR WITH THE HEALIN' TOUCH."
"VIBRATIONS FROM DOC ROWAN'S FINGERS MOVED BULLETS AWAY FROM VITAL ORGANS, MAKIN' 'EM MUCH EASIER TO REMOVE... OR SO HE CLAIMED."
"THING WAS, THE PROOF WAS THERE FOR ALL TO SEE."
CLINK
BULLET WAS DANGEROUSLY CLOSE TO SEVERING AN ARTERY, MY FRIEND. BUT YOU'LL LIVE.
YOU'LL LIVE NOW.
"ONLY PLACE THAT COWBOY WAS GOING WAS JAIL. AN OVERCROWDED ONE AT THAT."
"WOULD BE ANOTHER MONTH 'FORE THE MEN FROM THE CITY CAME COLLECTIN' FOR PRISONERS."
TOM, THEY STICK ANY PART O' THEMSELVES OUT O' THOSE BARS -- SHOOT IT OFF!
"IN THE MIDST OF A MAN..."
SURGERY
"PLAYING AT GOD."

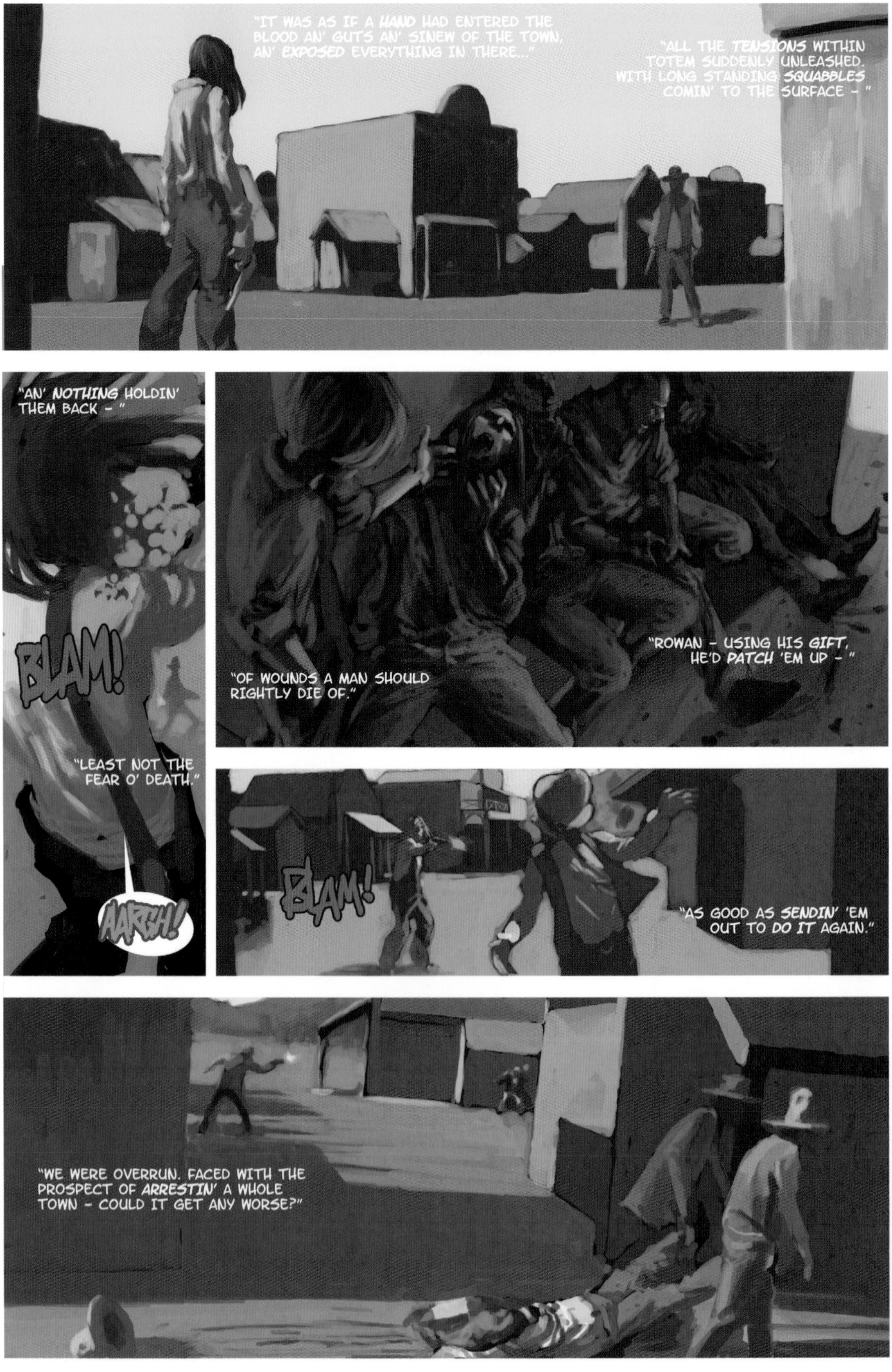
"IT WAS AS IF A HAND HAD ENTERED THE BLOOD AN' GUTS AN' SINEW OF THE TOWN, AN' EXPOSED EVERYTHING IN THERE..."
"ALL THE TENSIONS WITHIN TOTEM SUDDENLY UNLEASHED. WITH LONG STANDING SQUABBLES COMIN' TO THE SURFACE - "
"AN' NOTHING HOLDIN' THEM BACK - "
BLAM!
"LEAST NOT THE FEAR O' DEATH."
AARGH!
"ROWAN - USING HIS GIFT, HE'D PATCH 'EM UP - "
"OF WOUNDS A MAN SHOULD RIGHTLY DIE OF."
BLAM!
"AS GOOD AS SENDIN' 'EM OUT TO DO IT AGAIN."
"WE WERE OVERRUN. FACED WITH THE PROSPECT OF ARRESTIN' A WHOLE TOWN - COULD IT GET ANY WORSE?"

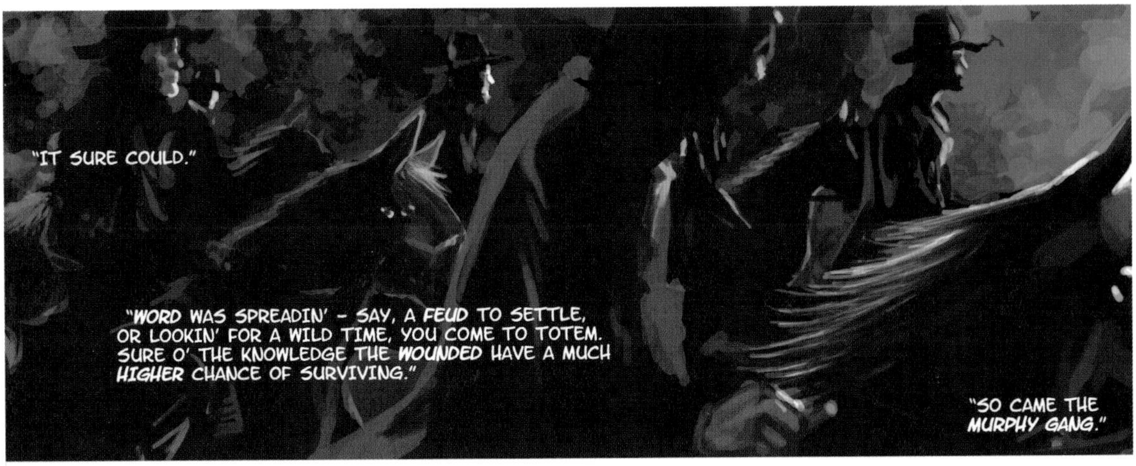
"IT SURE COULD."
"WORD WAS SPREADIN' - SAY, A FEUD TO SETTLE, OR LOOKIN' FOR A WILD TIME, YOU COME TO TOTEM. SURE O' THE KNOWLEDGE THE WOUNDED HAVE A MUCH HIGHER CHANCE OF SURVIVING."
"SO CAME THE MURPHY GANG."

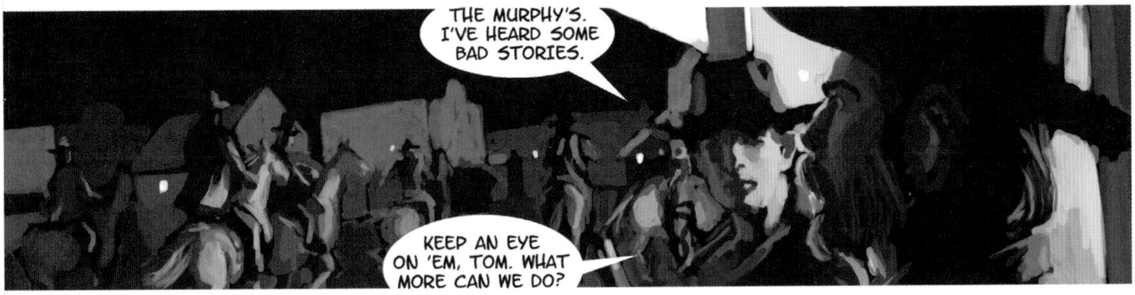
THE MURPHY'S. I'VE HEARD SOME BAD STORIES.
KEEP AN EYE ON 'EM, TOM. WHAT MORE CAN WE DO?

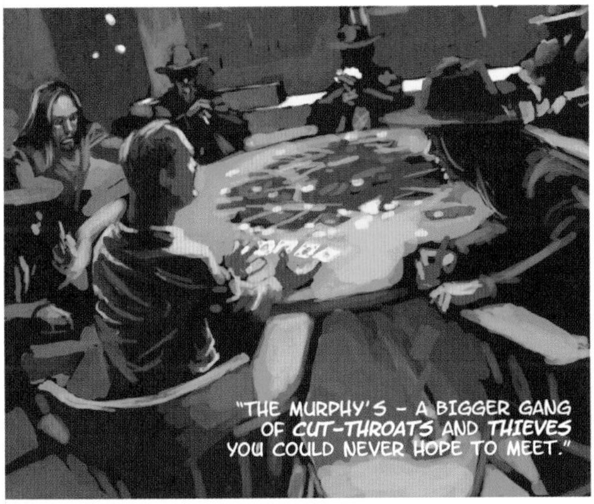
"THE MURPHY'S - A BIGGER GANG OF CUT-THROATS AND THIEVES YOU COULD NEVER HOPE TO MEET."

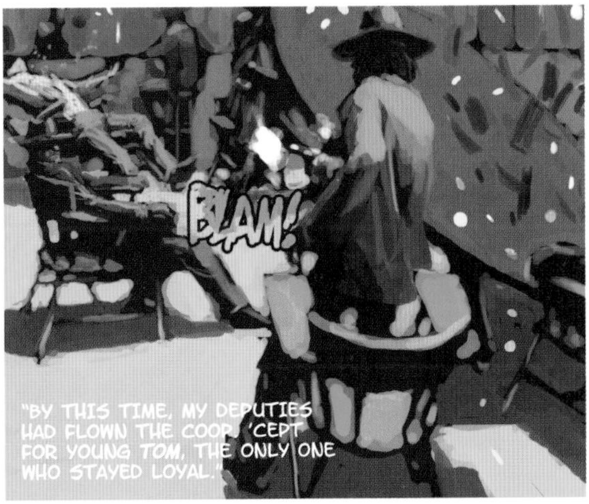
BLAM!
"BY THIS TIME, MY DEPUTIES HAD FLOWN THE COOP, 'CEPT FOR YOUNG TOM, THE ONLY ONE WHO STAYED LOYAL."

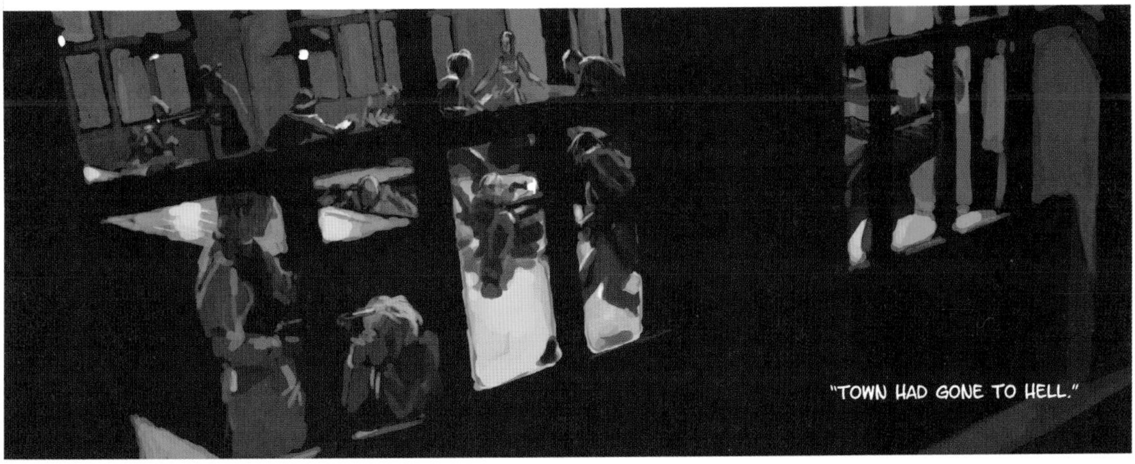
"TOWN HAD GONE TO HELL."

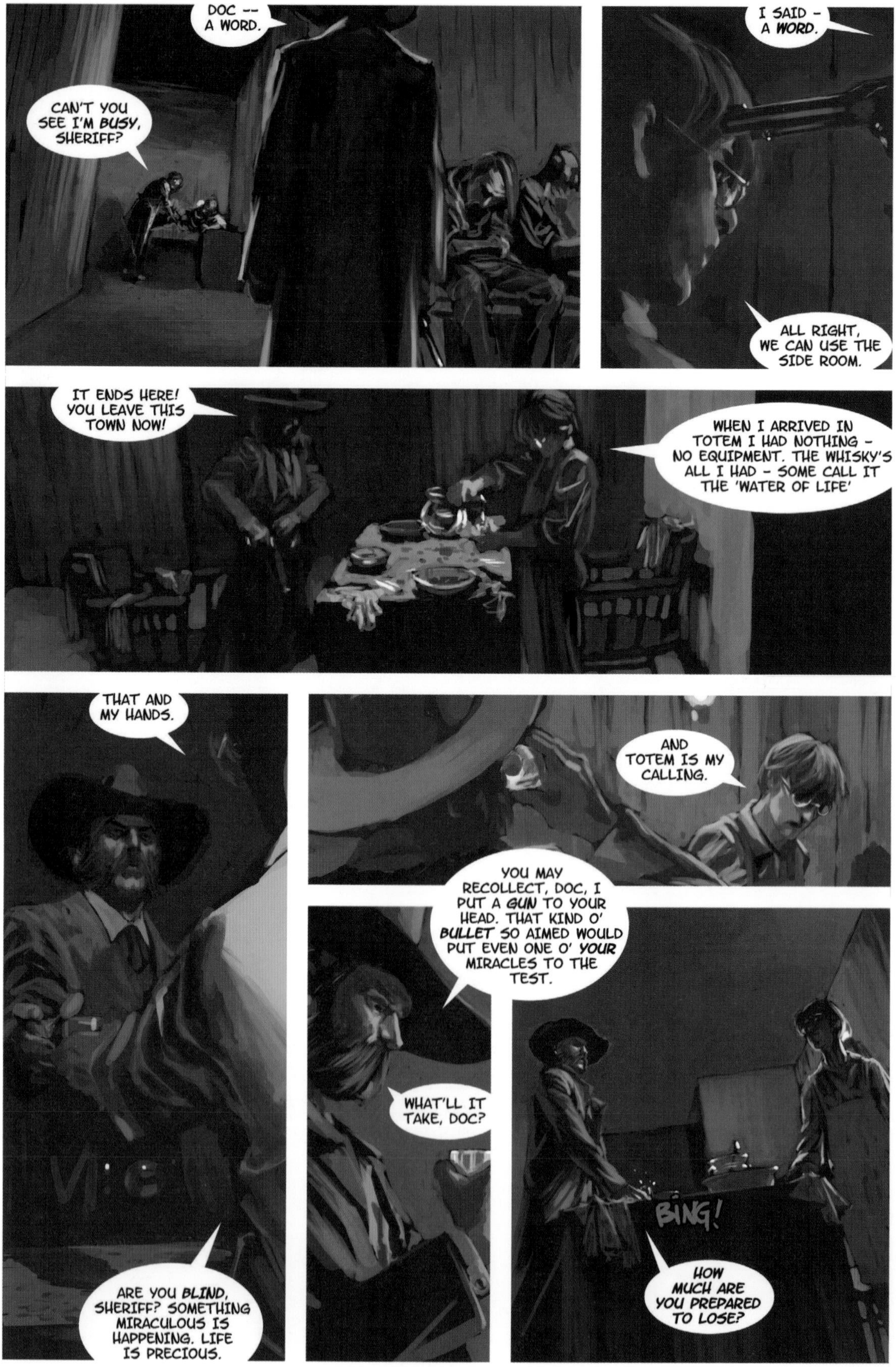
DOC -- A WORD.
CAN'T YOU SEE I'M *BUSY*, SHERIFF?
I SAID - A *WORD*.
ALL RIGHT, WE CAN USE THE SIDE ROOM.
IT ENDS HERE! YOU LEAVE THIS TOWN NOW!
WHEN I ARRIVED IN TOTEM I HAD NOTHING - NO EQUIPMENT. THE WHISKY'S ALL I HAD - SOME CALL IT THE 'WATER OF LIFE'
THAT AND MY HANDS.
ARE YOU *BLIND*, SHERIFF? SOMETHING MIRACULOUS IS HAPPENING. LIFE IS PRECIOUS.
AND TOTEM IS MY CALLING.
YOU MAY RECOLLECT, DOC, I PUT A *GUN* TO YOUR HEAD. THAT KIND O' *BULLET* SO AIMED WOULD PUT EVEN ONE O' *YOUR* MIRACLES TO THE TEST.
WHAT'LL IT TAKE, DOC?
BING!
HOW MUCH ARE YOU PREPARED TO LOSE?

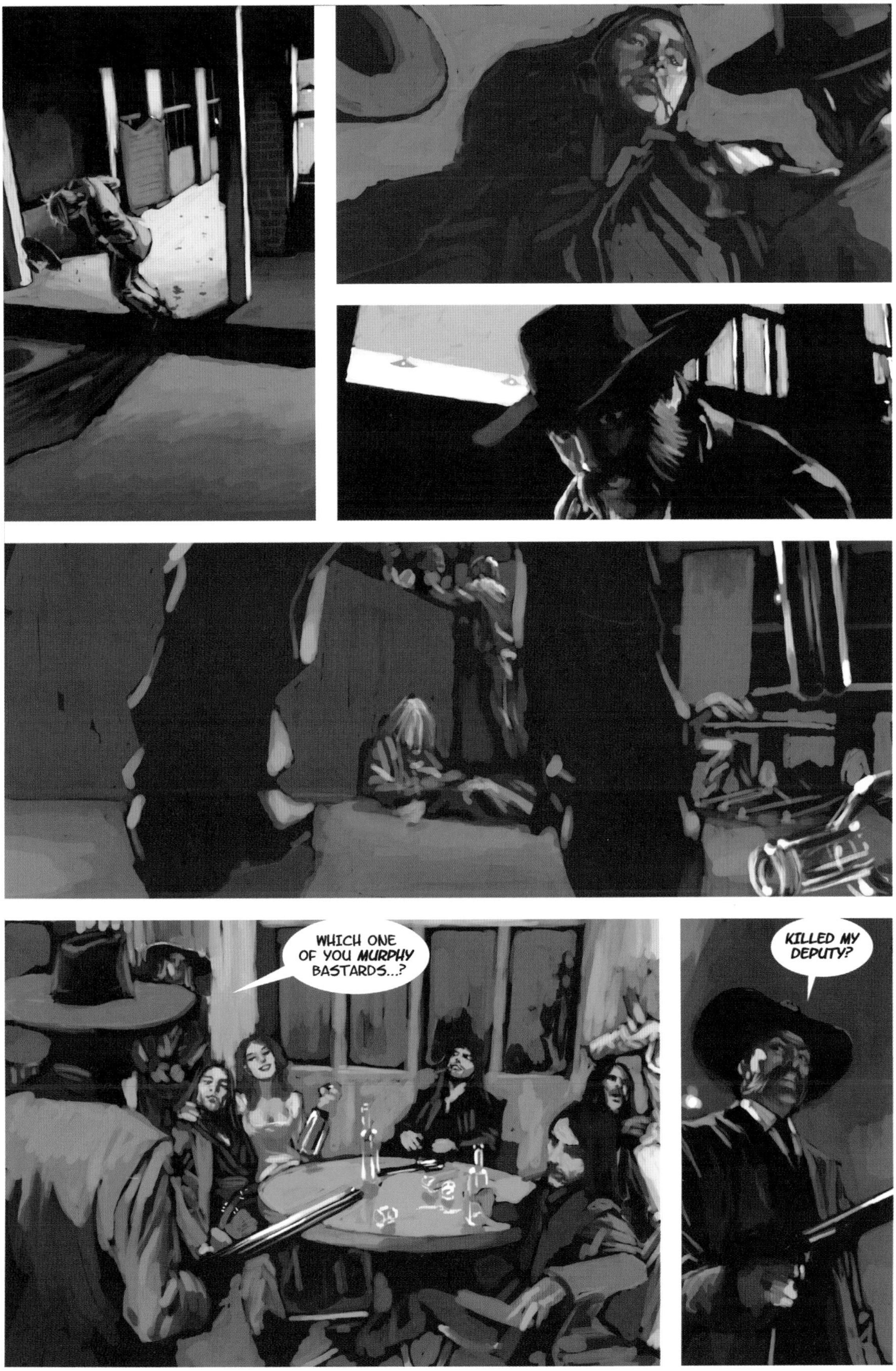
WHICH ONE OF YOU MURPHY BASTARDS...?
KILLED MY DEPUTY?

"TOO MUCH ANGER. HANDS SHAKING. NEVER HAD A CHANCE."

"TASTE OF BLOOD AN' WHISKY IN MY MOUTH."

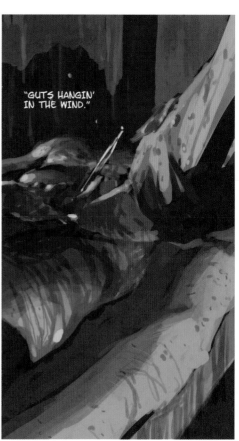

"GUTS HANGIN' IN THE WIND."

BULLET IS WEDGED DEEP, SHERIFF. TORN A HOLE RIGHT THROUGH YOUR STOMACH.

NORMALLY TOO DIFFICULT TO REMOVE. NORMALLY YOU'D BLEED TO DEATH.

BUT YOU'RE IN MY HANDS NOW.

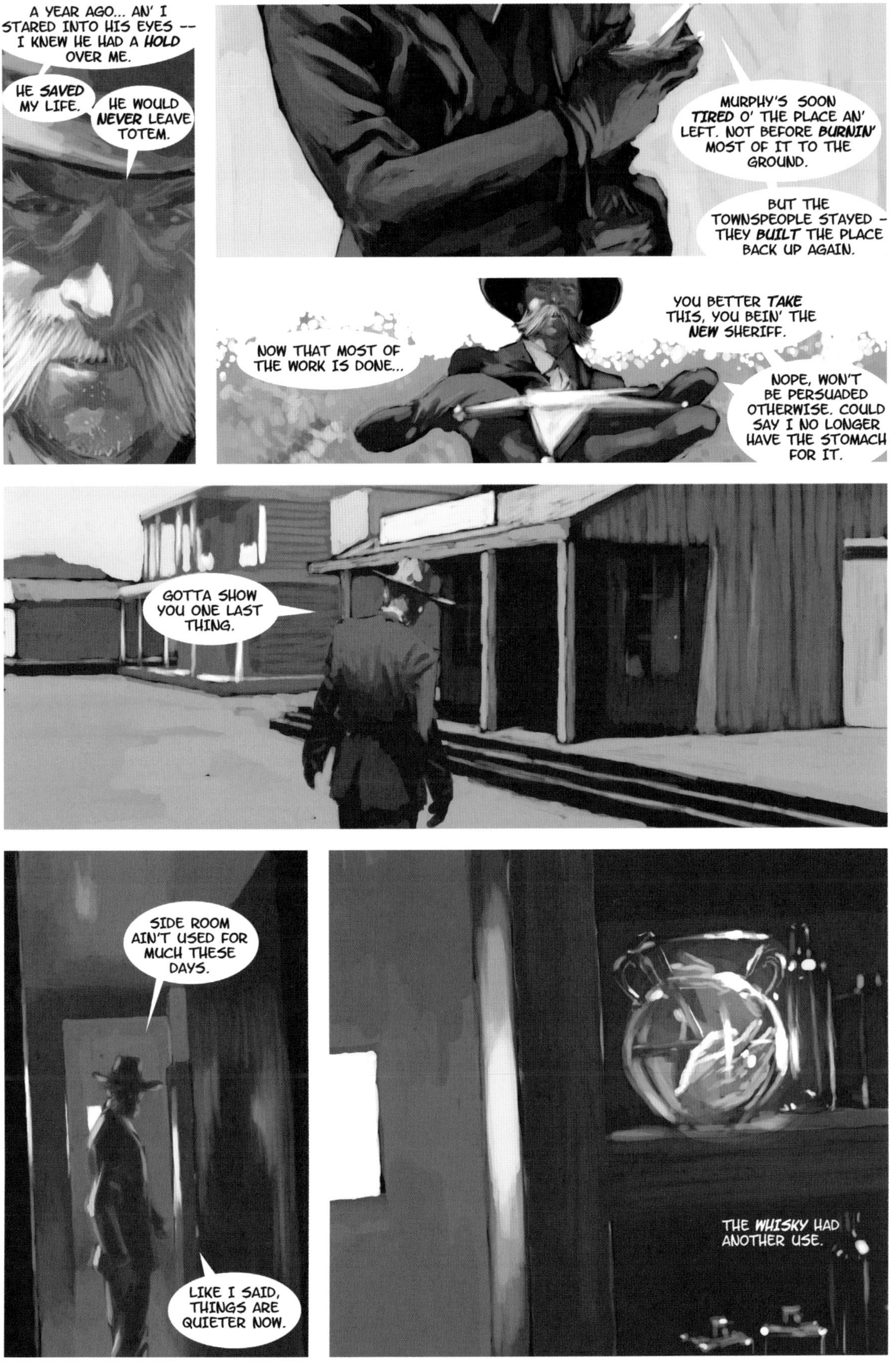
A YEAR AGO... AN' I STARED INTO HIS EYES -- I KNEW HE HAD A HOLD OVER ME.
HE SAVED MY LIFE.
HE WOULD NEVER LEAVE TOTEM.
MURPHY'S SOON TIRED O' THE PLACE AN' LEFT. NOT BEFORE BURNIN' MOST OF IT TO THE GROUND.
BUT THE TOWNSPEOPLE STAYED - THEY BUILT THE PLACE BACK UP AGAIN.
NOW THAT MOST OF THE WORK IS DONE...
YOU BETTER TAKE THIS, YOU BEIN' THE NEW SHERIFF.
NOPE, WON'T BE PERSUADED OTHERWISE. COULD SAY I NO LONGER HAVE THE STOMACH FOR IT.
GOTTA SHOW YOU ONE LAST THING.
SIDE ROOM AIN'T USED FOR MUCH THESE DAYS.
LIKE I SAID, THINGS ARE QUIETER NOW.
THE WHISKY HAD ANOTHER USE.

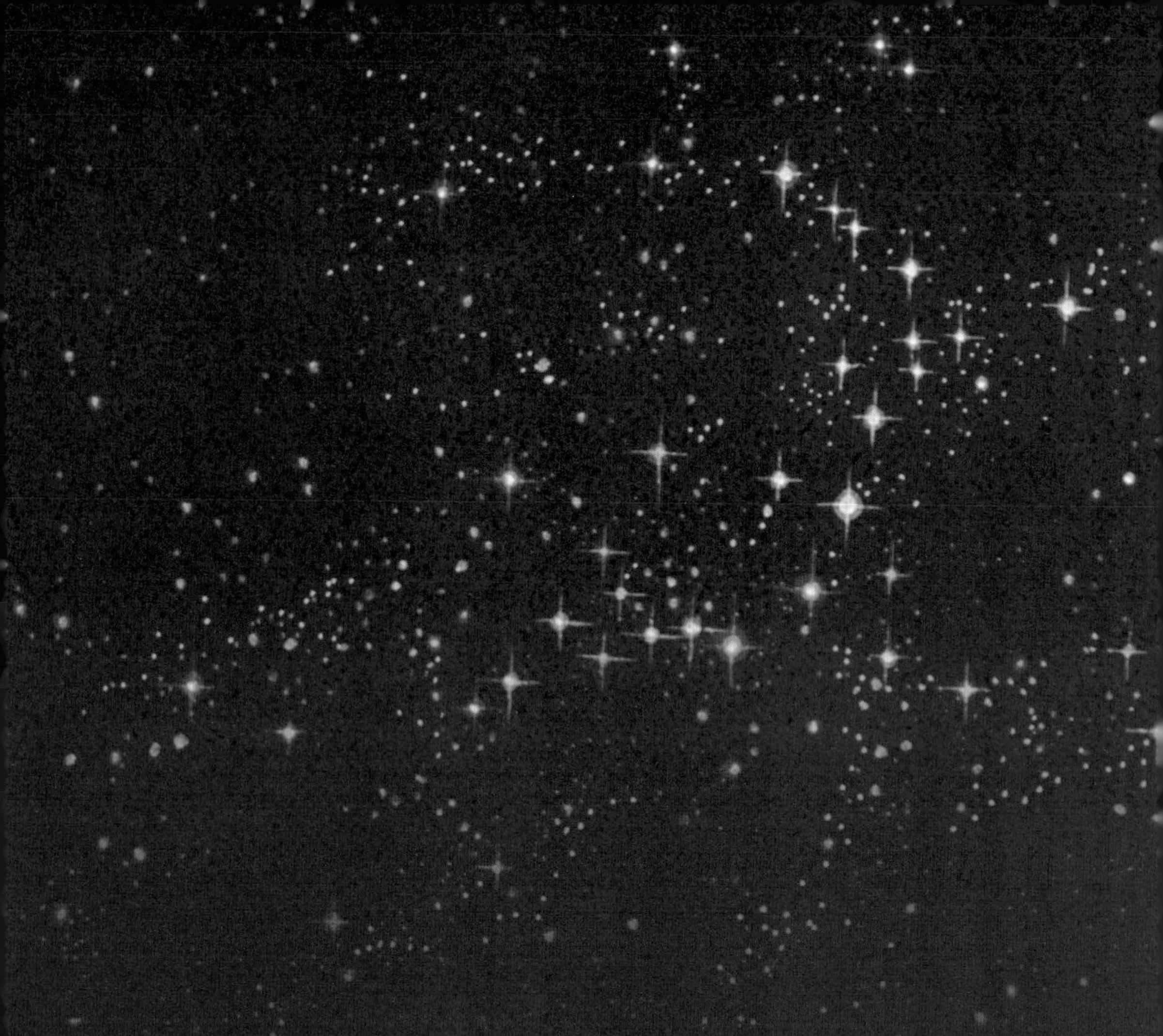

KING'S CROWN

Story by JIM ALEXANDER
Art by RICHARD CORBEN
Colors by DAN BROWN

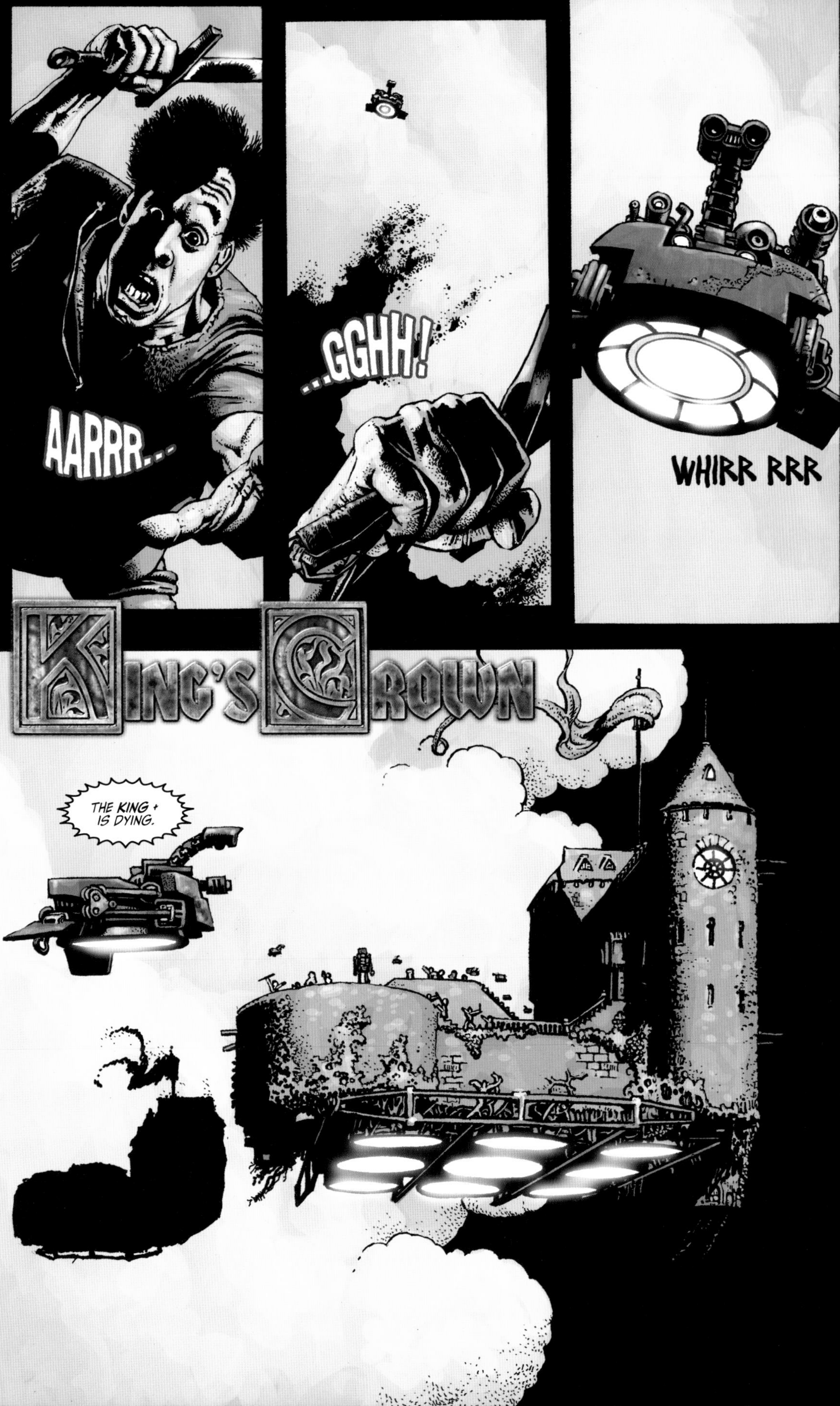
AARRR...
...GGHH!
WHIRR RRR
KING'S CROWN
THE KING + IS DYING.

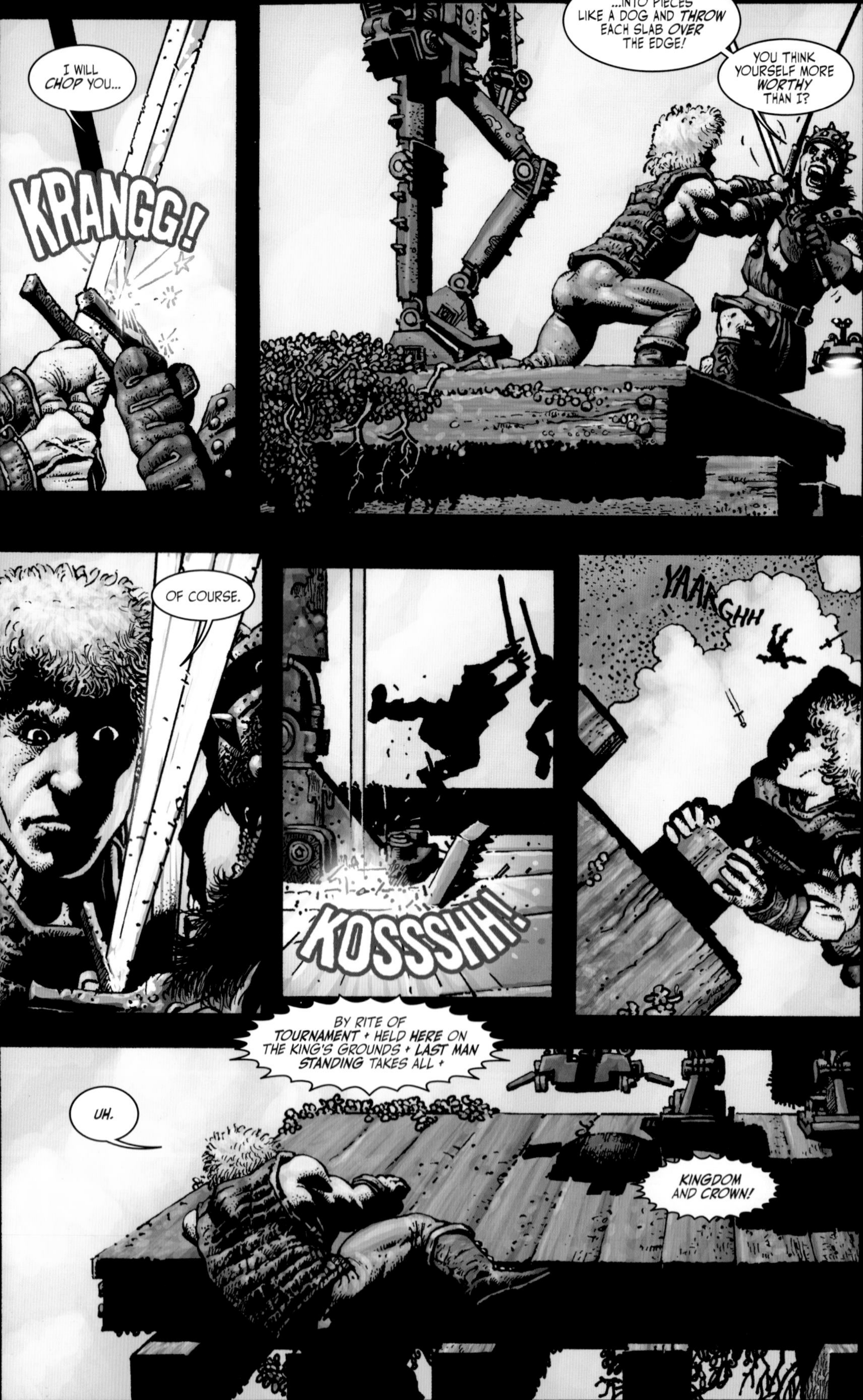
I WILL CHOP YOU...
KRANGG!
...INTO PIECES LIKE A DOG AND THROW EACH SLAB OVER THE EDGE!
YOU THINK YOURSELF MORE WORTHY THAN I?
OF COURSE.
KOSSSHH!
YAAARGHH
BY RITE OF TOURNAMENT + HELD HERE ON THE KING'S GROUNDS + LAST MAN STANDING TAKES ALL +
UH.
KINGDOM AND CROWN!

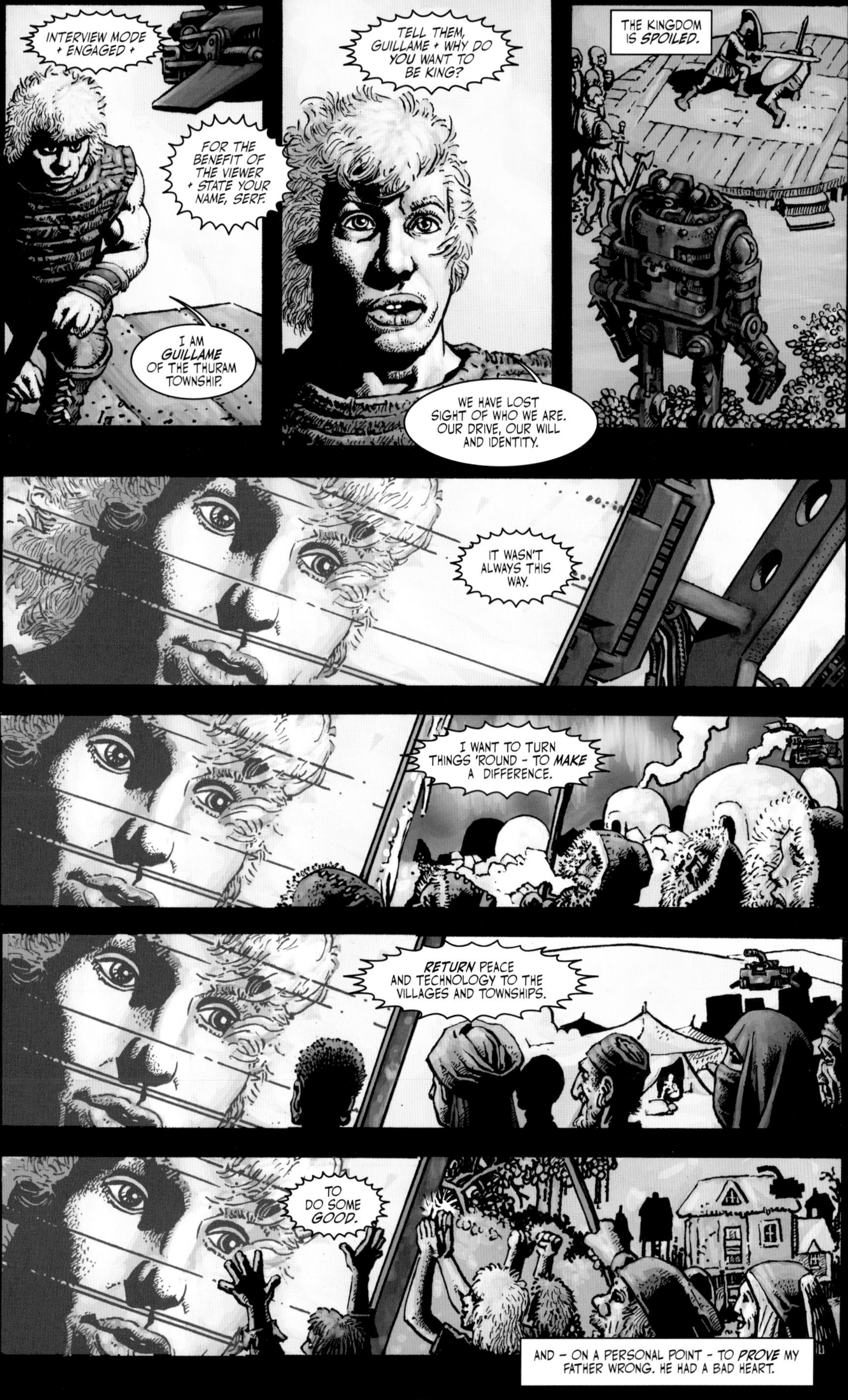

INTERVIEW MODE + ENGAGED +
FOR THE BENEFIT OF THE VIEWER + STATE YOUR NAME, SERF.
I AM GUILLAME OF THE THURAM TOWNSHIP.
TELL THEM, GUILLAME + WHY DO YOU WANT TO BE KING?
WE HAVE LOST SIGHT OF WHO WE ARE. OUR DRIVE, OUR WILL AND IDENTITY.
THE KINGDOM IS SPOILED.
IT WASN'T ALWAYS THIS WAY.
I WANT TO TURN THINGS 'ROUND - TO MAKE A DIFFERENCE.
RETURN PEACE AND TECHNOLOGY TO THE VILLAGES AND TOWNSHIPS.
TO DO SOME GOOD.
AND - ON A PERSONAL POINT - TO PROVE MY FATHER WRONG. HE HAD A BAD HEART.

CEASE YOUR YOWLING...

...AND DO SOME *FIGHTING!*

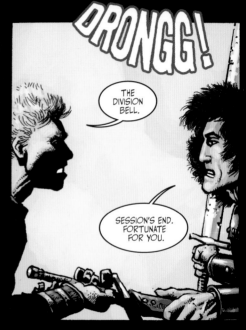

DRONGG!

THE DIVISION BELL.

SESSION'S END. FORTUNATE FOR YOU.

MY FELLOW PLAYERS... AS WE PUT *HOSTILITIES* TO ONE SIDE FOR *BOISTEROUS EXCESS* —

I, *TEAGUE* OF LANDRAU, BEG OF YOU SOME MOMENTS OF YOUR TIME.

LET ME TELL YOU ABOUT THE KING *BEYOND* THE ROYAL PROPAGANDA.

THE *KING* HAS GROWN *CORPULENT* ON THE *TRIBUTES* HE DEMANDS SO REGULARLY FROM A POVERTY STRICKEN POPULATION.

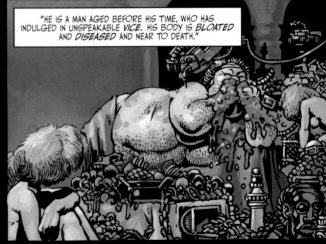

"HE IS A MAN AGED BEFORE HIS TIME, WHO HAS INDULGED IN UNSPEAKABLE *VICE*. HIS BODY IS *BLOATED* AND *DISEASED* AND NEAR TO DEATH."

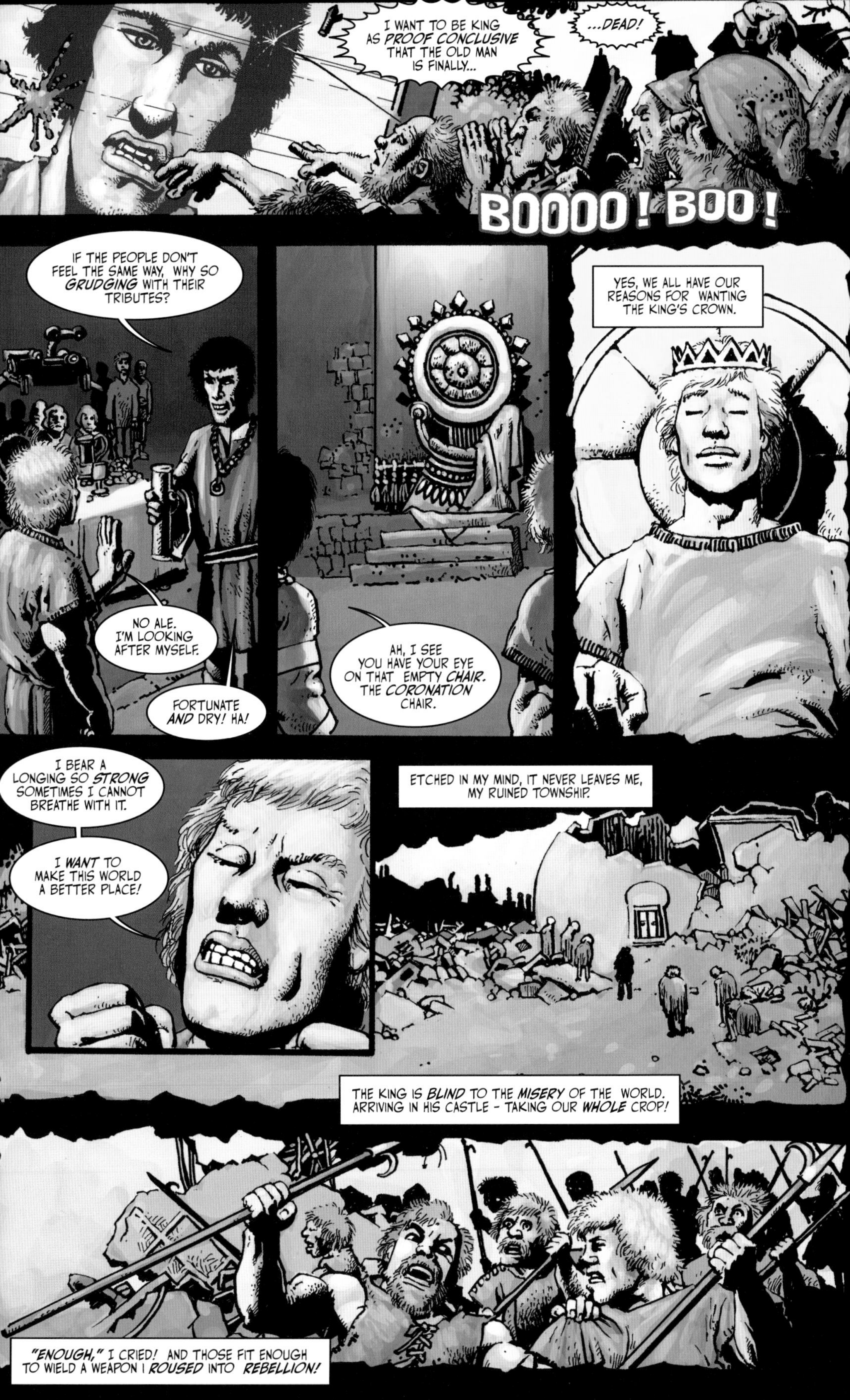
I WANT TO BE KING AS PROOF CONCLUSIVE THAT THE OLD MAN IS FINALLY...
...DEAD!
BOOOO! BOO!
IF THE PEOPLE DON'T FEEL THE SAME WAY, WHY SO GRUDGING WITH THEIR TRIBUTES?
NO ALE. I'M LOOKING AFTER MYSELF.
FORTUNATE AND DRY! HA!
AH, I SEE YOU HAVE YOUR EYE ON THAT EMPTY CHAIR. THE CORONATION CHAIR.
YES, WE ALL HAVE OUR REASONS FOR WANTING THE KING'S CROWN.
I BEAR A LONGING SO STRONG SOMETIMES I CANNOT BREATHE WITH IT.
I WANT TO MAKE THIS WORLD A BETTER PLACE!
ETCHED IN MY MIND, IT NEVER LEAVES ME, MY RUINED TOWNSHIP.
THE KING IS BLIND TO THE MISERY OF THE WORLD. ARRIVING IN HIS CASTLE - TAKING OUR WHOLE CROP!
"ENOUGH," I CRIED! AND THOSE FIT ENOUGH TO WIELD A WEAPON I ROUSED INTO REBELLION!

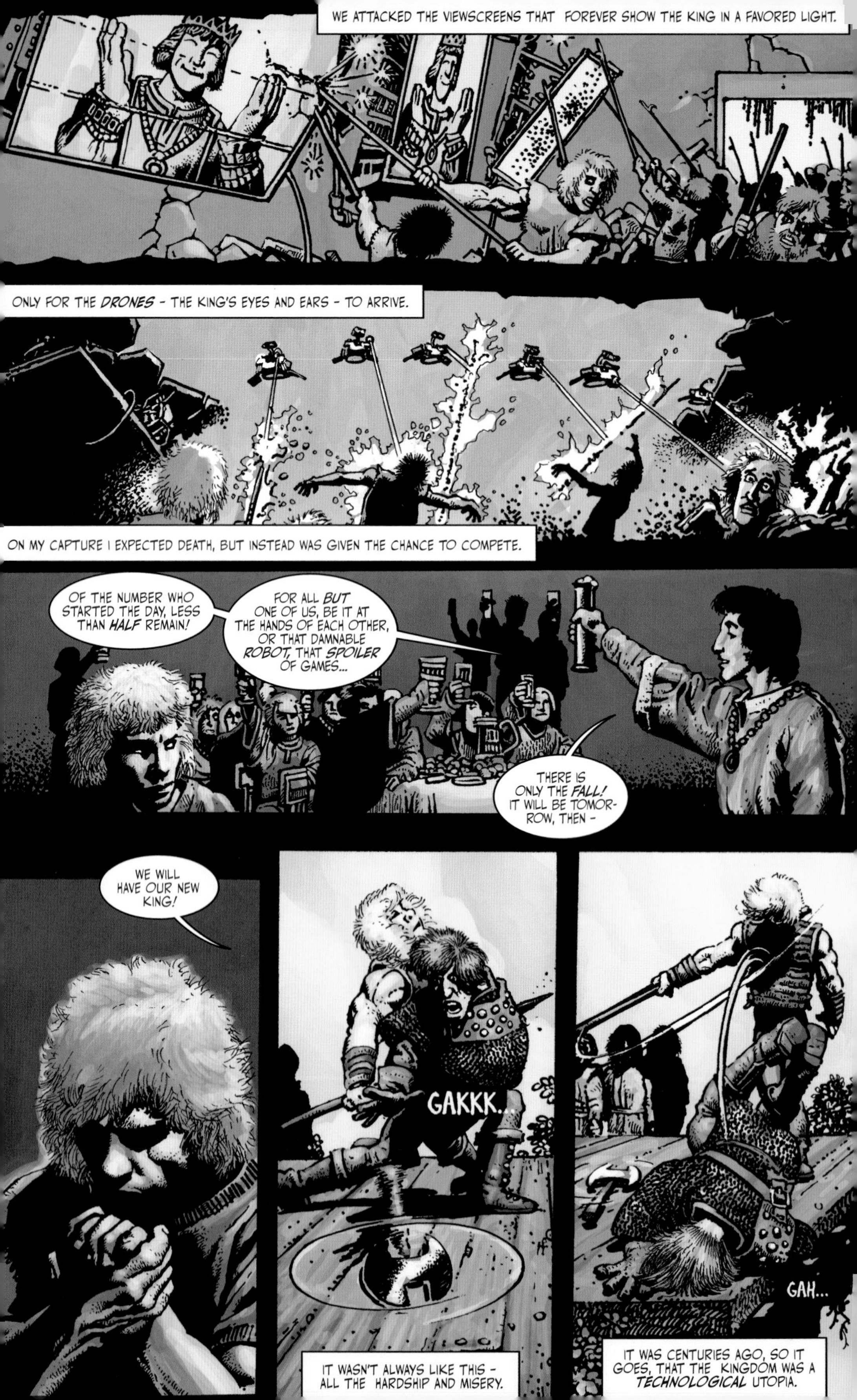
WE ATTACKED THE VIEWSCREENS THAT FOREVER SHOW THE KING IN A FAVORED LIGHT.
ONLY FOR THE DRONES - THE KING'S EYES AND EARS - TO ARRIVE.
ON MY CAPTURE I EXPECTED DEATH, BUT INSTEAD WAS GIVEN THE CHANCE TO COMPETE.
OF THE NUMBER WHO STARTED THE DAY, LESS THAN HALF REMAIN!
FOR ALL BUT ONE OF US, BE IT AT THE HANDS OF EACH OTHER, OR THAT DAMNABLE ROBOT, THAT SPOILER OF GAMES...
THERE IS ONLY THE FALL! IT WILL BE TOMORROW, THEN -
WE WILL HAVE OUR NEW KING!
GAKKK...
IT WASN'T ALWAYS LIKE THIS - ALL THE HARDSHIP AND MISERY.
GAH...
IT WAS CENTURIES AGO, SO IT GOES, THAT THE KINGDOM WAS A TECHNOLOGICAL UTOPIA.

No one wanted for anything.

It was the *king* of the time that ended it —

SWIPE!

Asking 'What good a kingdom if not based on sufferance?'

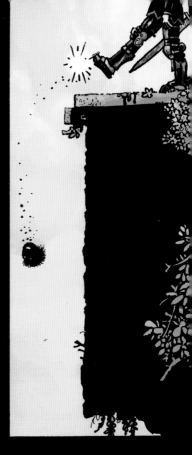

As he forbade it to others, so the king *kept* the technology for himself.

And here...

We are.

Ah, fortunate *Guillame*. All others have taken the *fall*. Destiny surrounds us like a cloak.

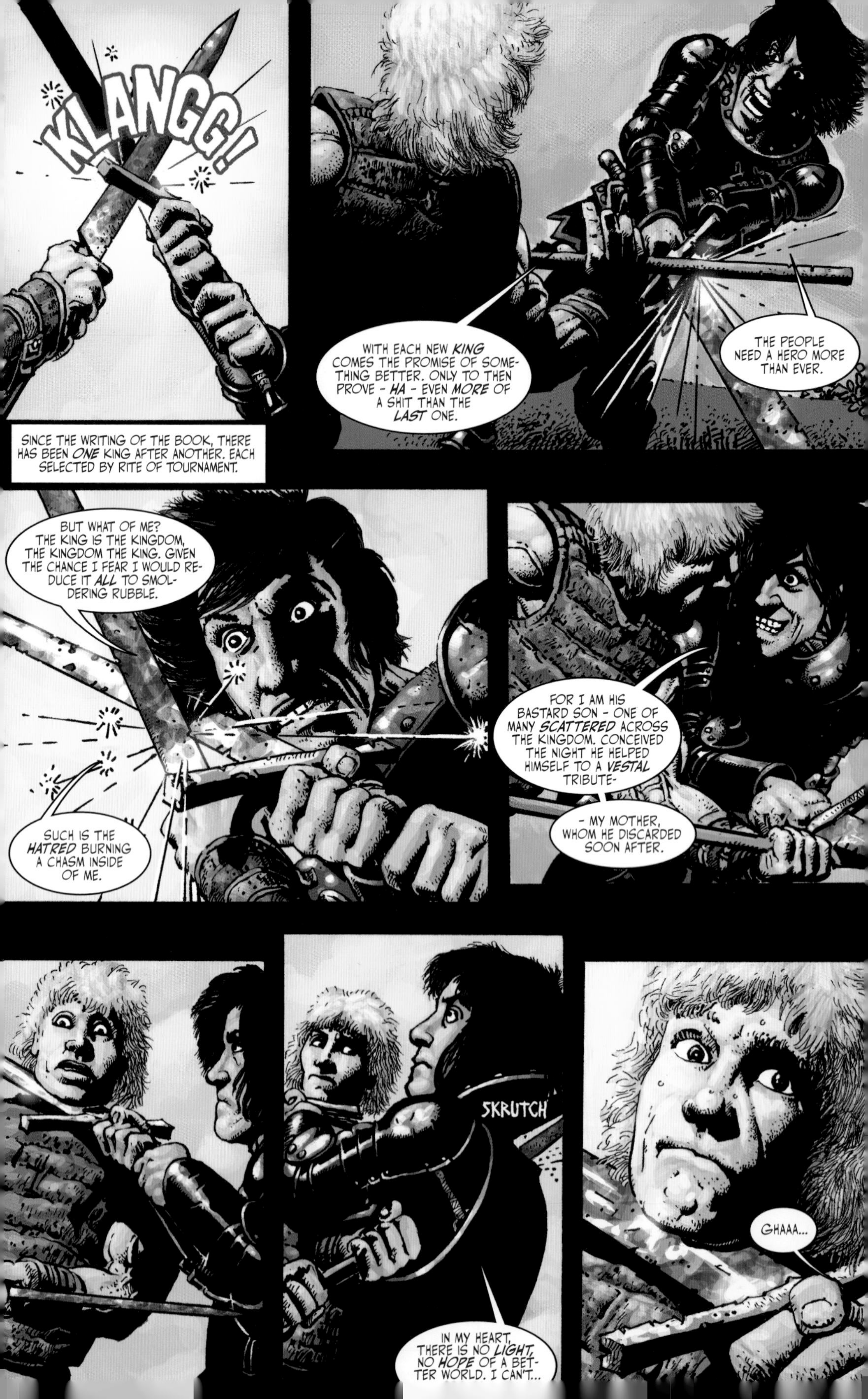
KLANGG!
SINCE THE WRITING OF THE BOOK, THERE HAS BEEN ONE KING AFTER ANOTHER. EACH SELECTED BY RITE OF TOURNAMENT.
WITH EACH NEW KING COMES THE PROMISE OF SOMETHING BETTER. ONLY TO THEN PROVE - HA - EVEN MORE OF A SHIT THAN THE LAST ONE.
THE PEOPLE NEED A HERO MORE THAN EVER.
BUT WHAT OF ME? THE KING IS THE KINGDOM, THE KINGDOM THE KING. GIVEN THE CHANCE I FEAR I WOULD REDUCE IT ALL TO SMOLDERING RUBBLE.
SUCH IS THE HATRED BURNING A CHASM INSIDE OF ME.
FOR I AM HIS BASTARD SON - ONE OF MANY SCATTERED ACROSS THE KINGDOM. CONCEIVED THE NIGHT HE HELPED HIMSELF TO A VESTAL TRIBUTE-
- MY MOTHER, WHOM HE DISCARDED SOON AFTER.
SKRUTCH
IN MY HEART, THERE IS NO LIGHT, NO HOPE OF A BETTER WORLD. I CAN'T...
GHAAA...

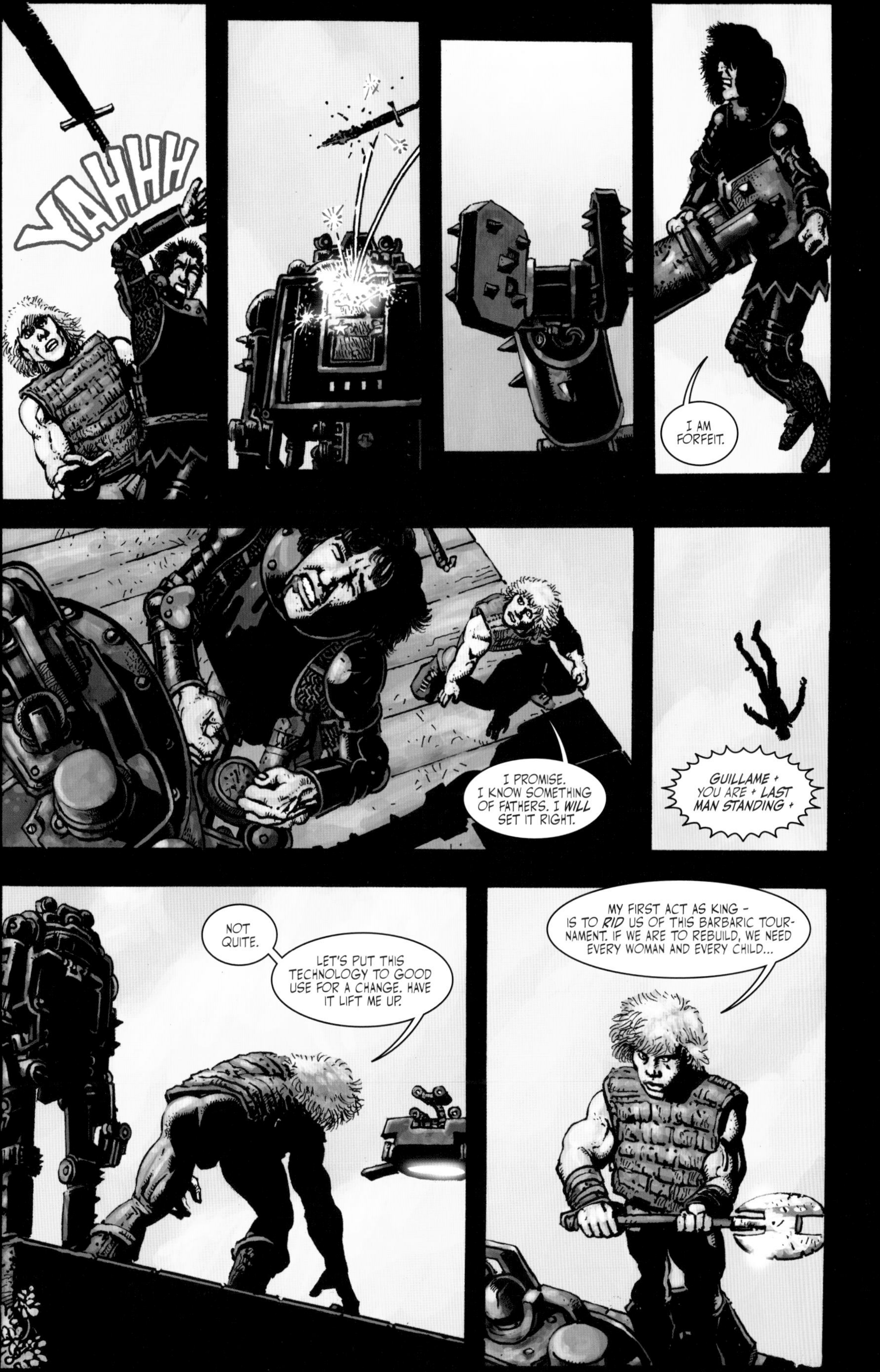
YAHHH
I AM FORFEIT.
I PROMISE. I KNOW SOMETHING OF FATHERS. I WILL SET IT RIGHT.
GUILLAME + YOU ARE + LAST MAN STANDING +
NOT QUITE.
LET'S PUT THIS TECHNOLOGY TO GOOD USE FOR A CHANGE. HAVE IT LIFT ME UP.
MY FIRST ACT AS KING - IS TO RID US OF THIS BARBARIC TOURNAMENT. IF WE ARE TO REBUILD, WE NEED EVERY WOMAN AND EVERY CHILD...

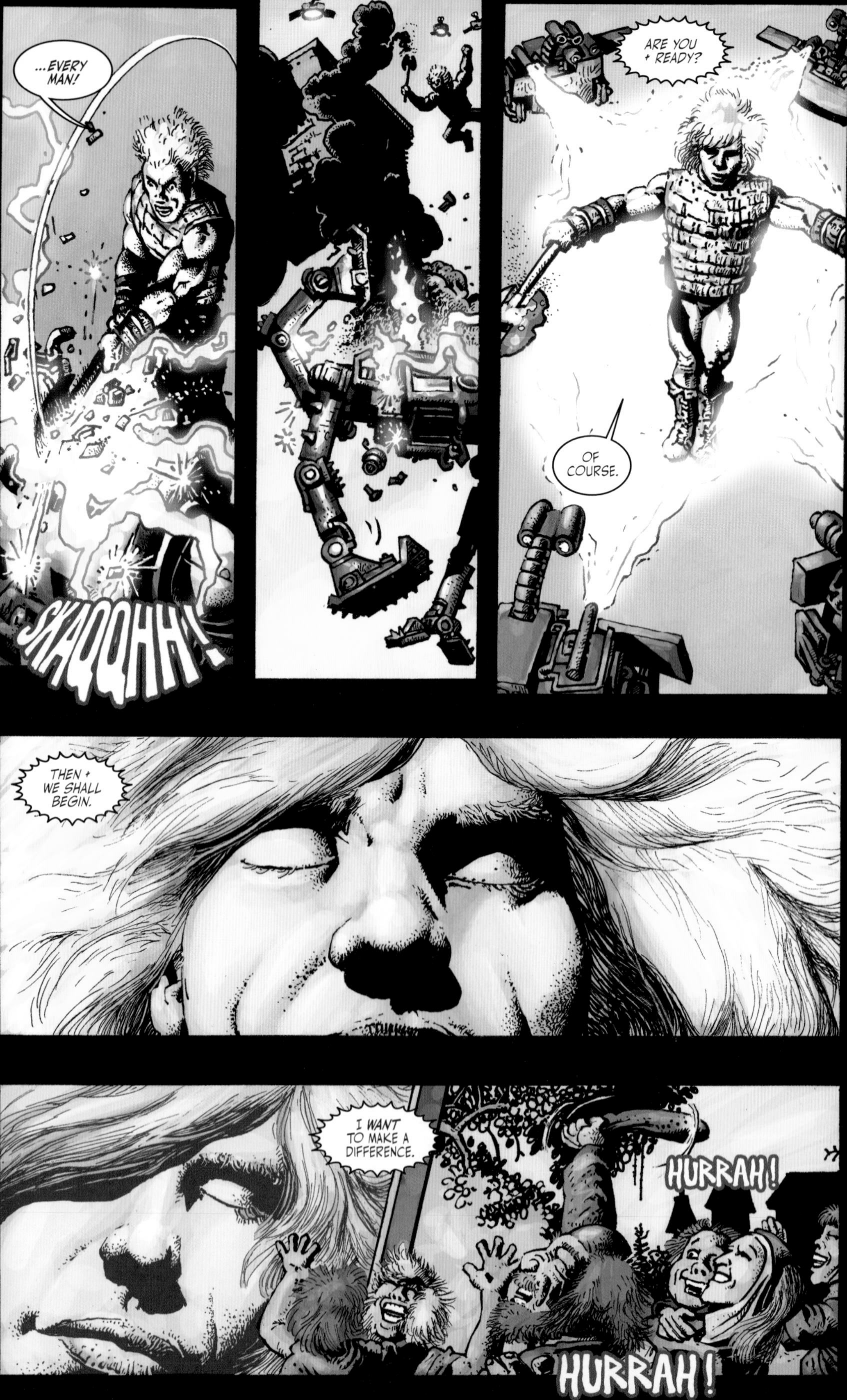
...EVERY MAN!
SKADOHH!
ARE YOU + READY?
OF COURSE.
THEN + WE SHALL BEGIN.
I WANT TO MAKE A DIFFERENCE.
HURRAH!
HURRAH!

THE KING
+ IS DEAD.
+ INITIATING
CORONATION
SEQUENCE +
NOOOO!
TRANSPLANTING
+ NOW!

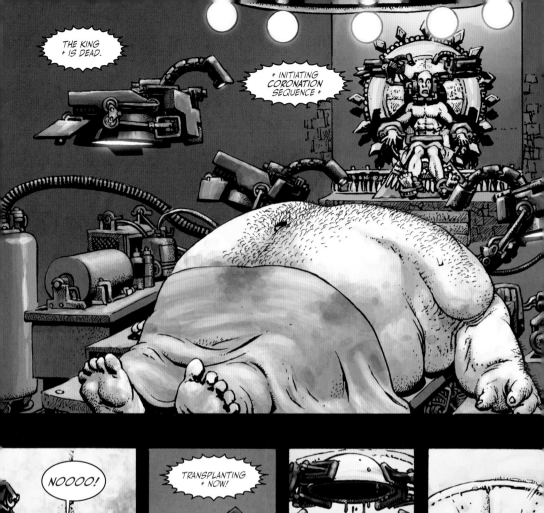

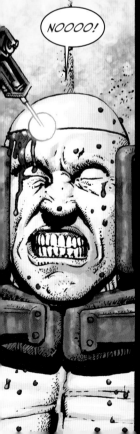

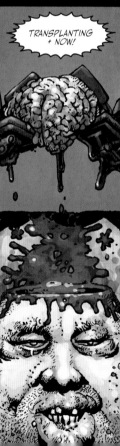

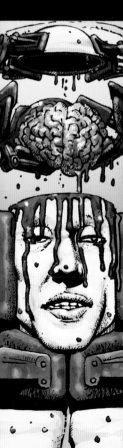

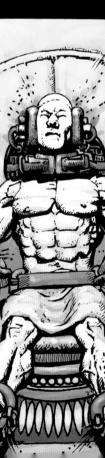

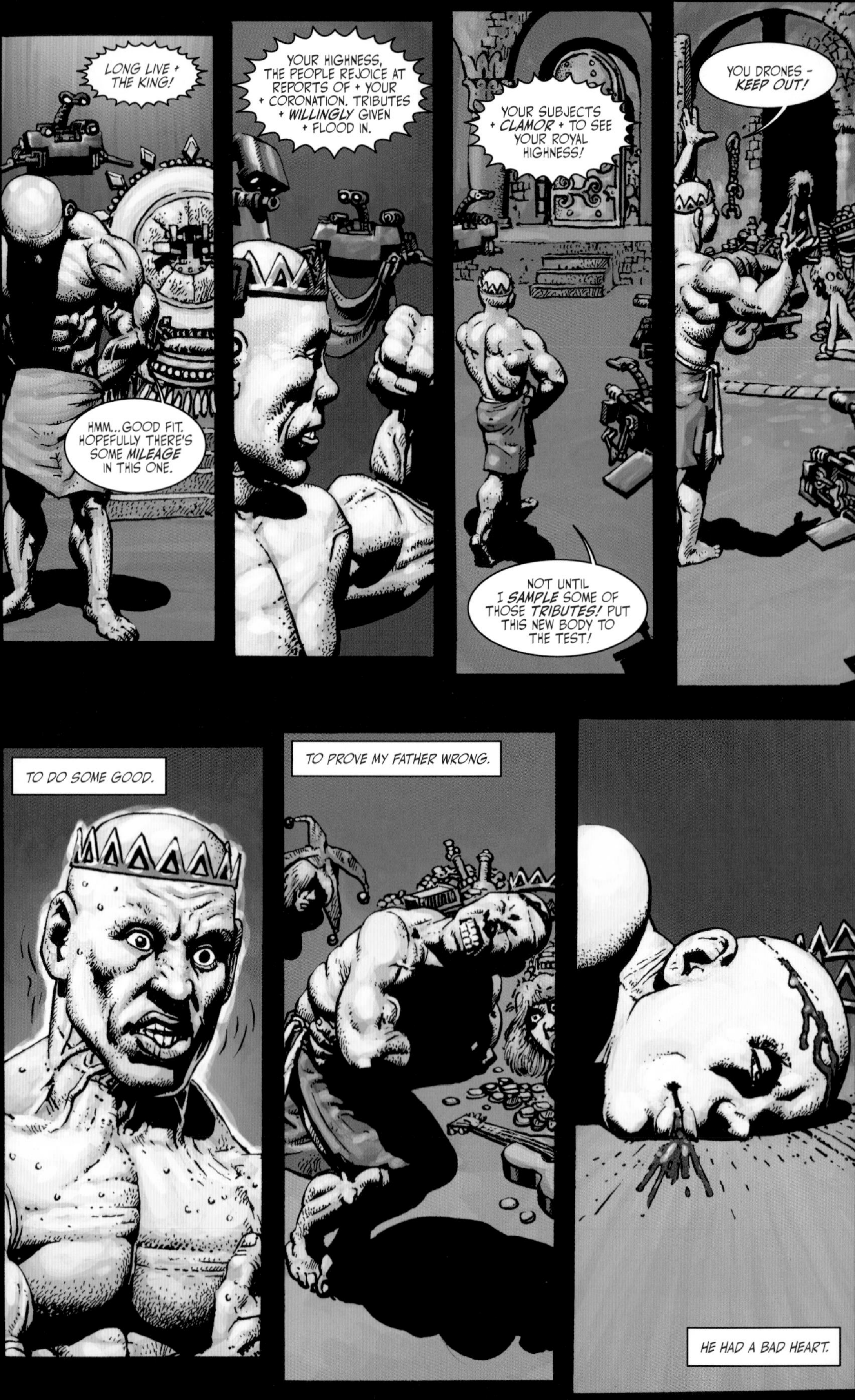
LONG LIVE + THE KING!
HMM...GOOD FIT. HOPEFULLY THERE'S SOME MILEAGE IN THIS ONE.
YOUR HIGHNESS, THE PEOPLE REJOICE AT REPORTS OF + YOUR + CORONATION. TRIBUTES + WILLINGLY GIVEN + FLOOD IN.
YOUR SUBJECTS + CLAMOR + TO SEE YOUR ROYAL HIGHNESS!
NOT UNTIL I SAMPLE SOME OF THOSE TRIBUTES! PUT THIS NEW BODY TO THE TEST!
YOU DRONES - KEEP OUT!
TO DO SOME GOOD.
TO PROVE MY FATHER WRONG.
HE HAD A BAD HEART.

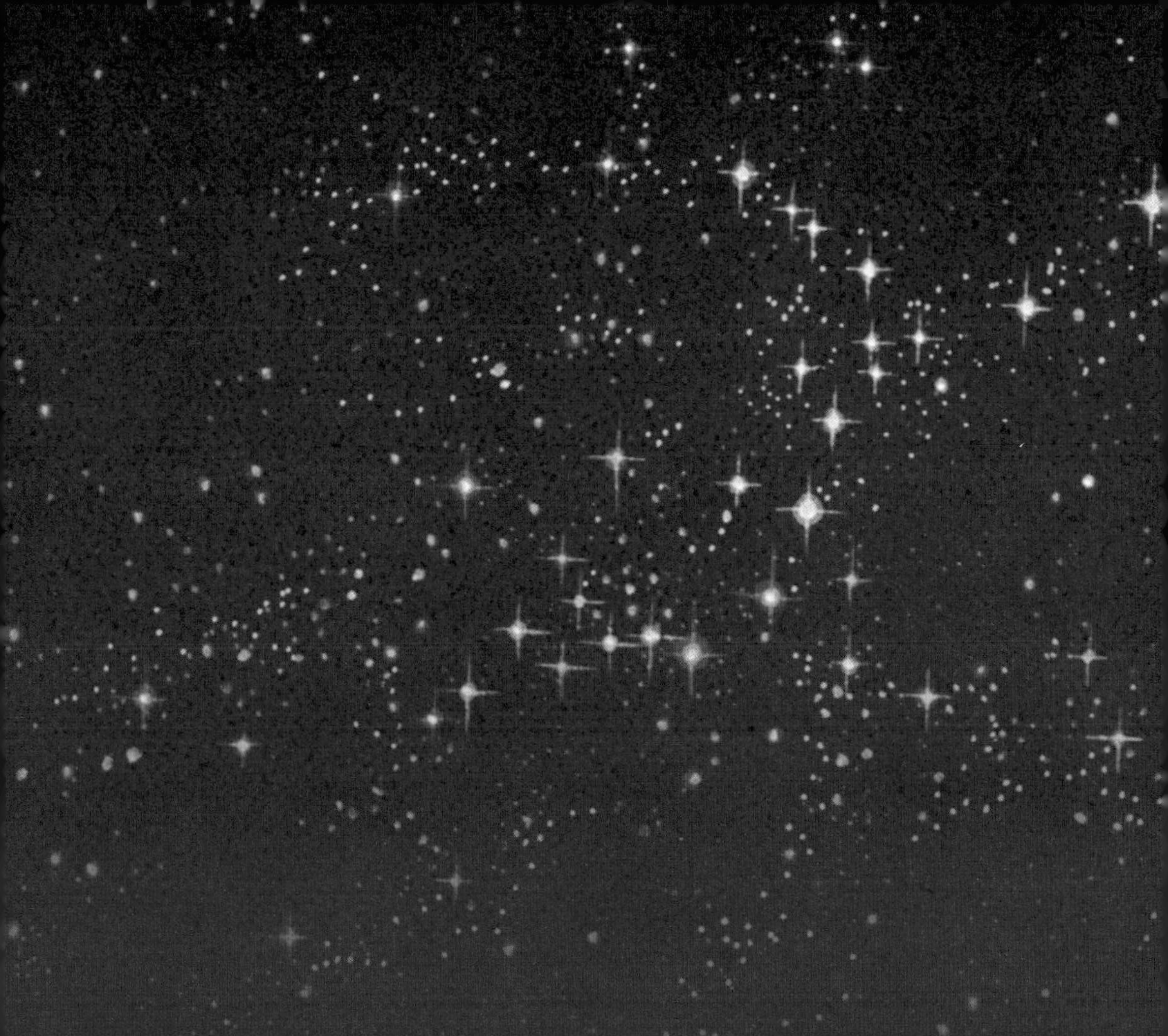

TWENTY TO ONE

Story by FRED LE BERRE
Art by CORENTIN

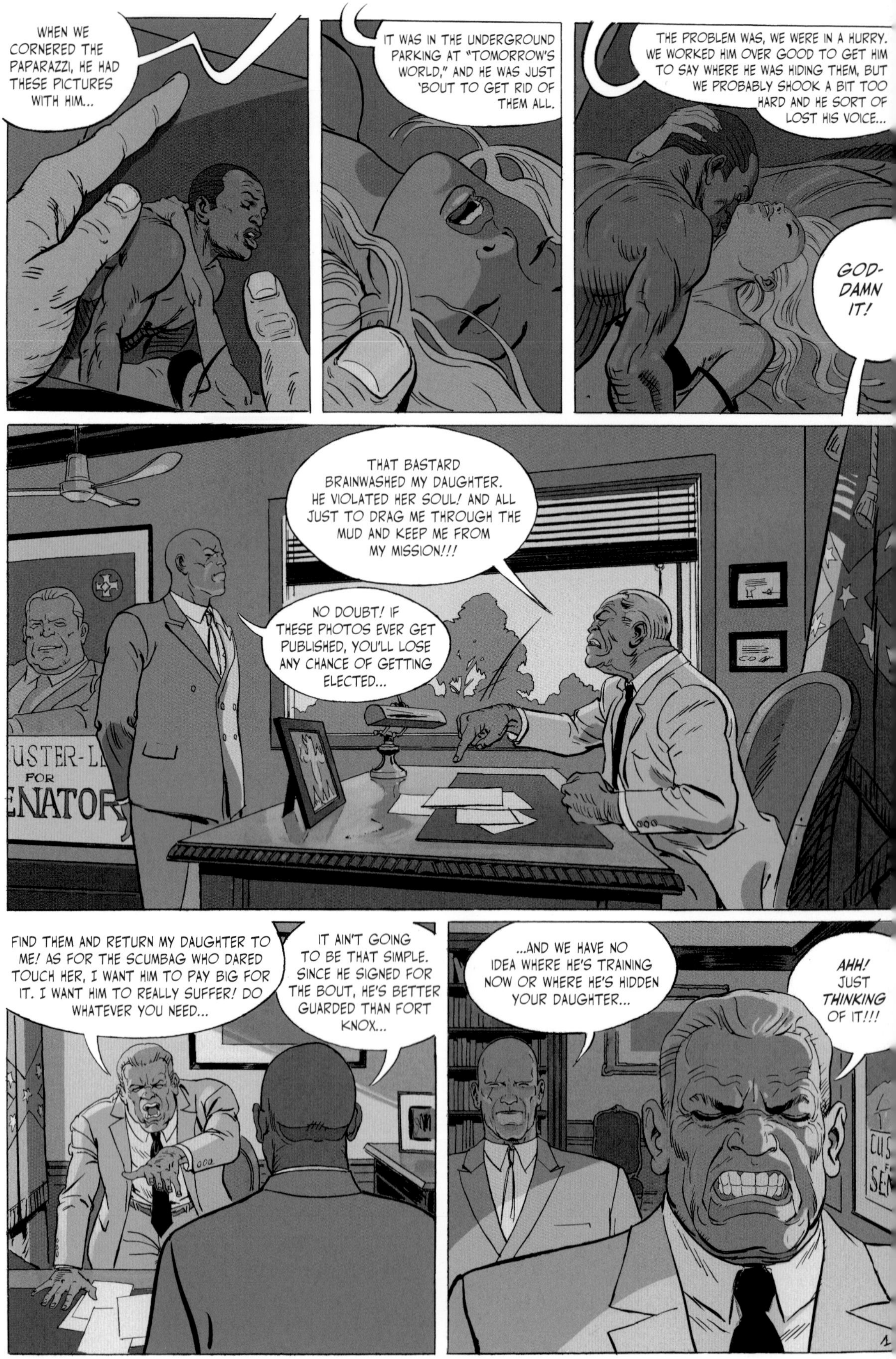
WHEN WE CORNERED THE PAPARAZZI, HE HAD THESE PICTURES WITH HIM...
IT WAS IN THE UNDERGROUND PARKING AT "TOMORROW'S WORLD," AND HE WAS JUST 'BOUT TO GET RID OF THEM ALL.
THE PROBLEM WAS, WE WERE IN A HURRY. WE WORKED HIM OVER GOOD TO GET HIM TO SAY WHERE HE WAS HIDING THEM, BUT WE PROBABLY SHOOK A BIT TOO HARD AND HE SORT OF LOST HIS VOICE...
GOD-DAMN IT!
THAT BASTARD BRAINWASHED MY DAUGHTER. HE VIOLATED HER SOUL! AND ALL JUST TO DRAG ME THROUGH THE MUD AND KEEP ME FROM MY MISSION!!!
NO DOUBT! IF THESE PHOTOS EVER GET PUBLISHED, YOU'LL LOSE ANY CHANCE OF GETTING ELECTED...
USTER-LE FOR ENATOR
FIND THEM AND RETURN MY DAUGHTER TO ME! AS FOR THE SCUMBAG WHO DARED TOUCH HER, I WANT HIM TO PAY BIG FOR IT. I WANT HIM TO REALLY SUFFER! DO WHATEVER YOU NEED...
IT AIN'T GOING TO BE THAT SIMPLE. SINCE HE SIGNED FOR THE BOUT, HE'S BETTER GUARDED THAN FORT KNOX...
...AND WE HAVE NO IDEA WHERE HE'S TRAINING NOW OR WHERE HE'S HIDDEN YOUR DAUGHTER...
AHH! JUST THINKING OF IT!!!
1

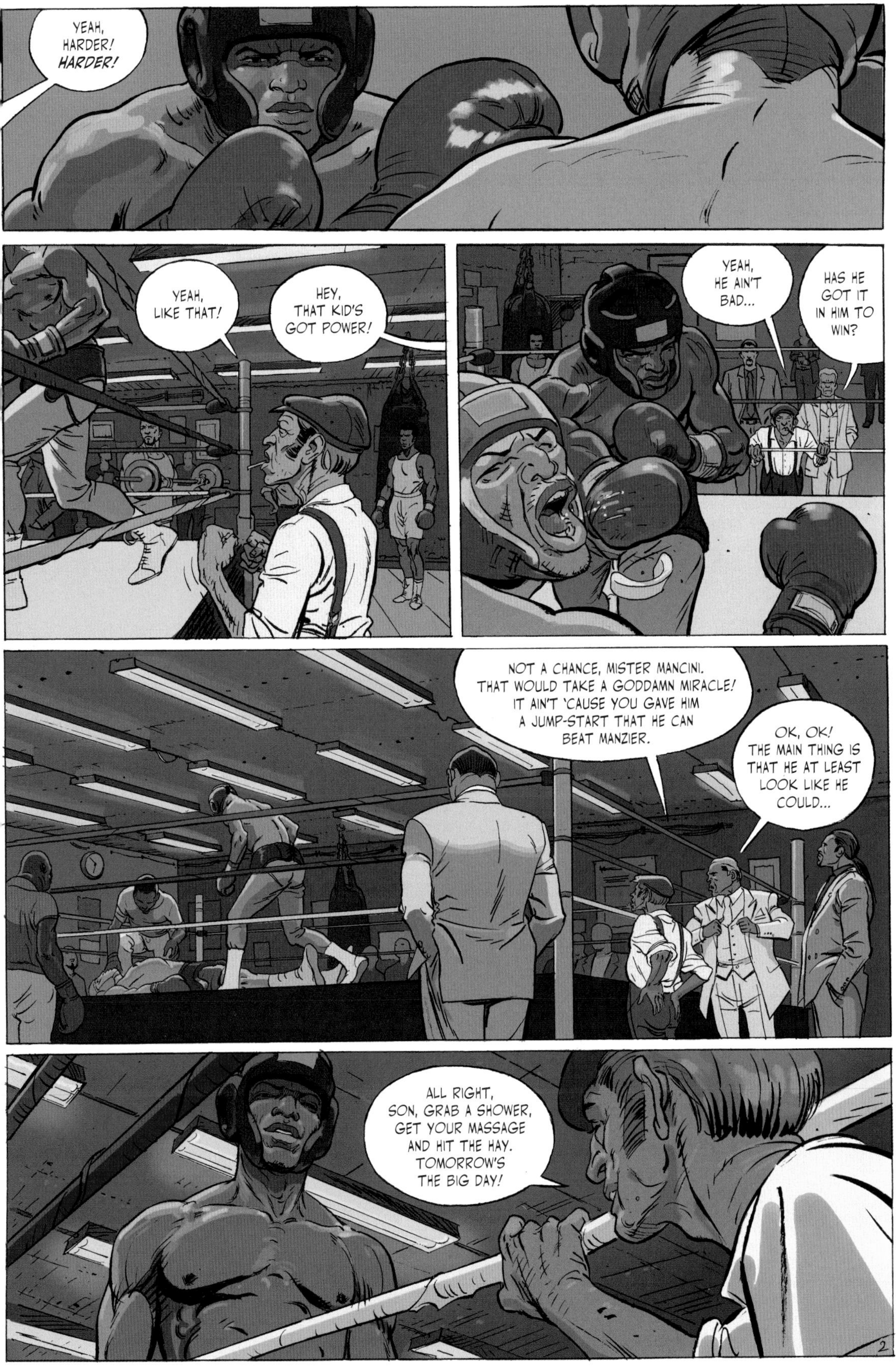
YEAH, HARDER! *HARDER!*
YEAH, LIKE THAT!
HEY, THAT KID'S GOT POWER!
YEAH, HE AIN'T BAD...
HAS HE GOT IT IN HIM TO WIN?
NOT A CHANCE, MISTER MANCINI. THAT WOULD TAKE A GODDAMN MIRACLE! IT AIN'T 'CAUSE YOU GAVE HIM A JUMP-START THAT HE CAN BEAT MANZIER.
OK, OK! THE MAIN THING IS THAT HE AT LEAST LOOK LIKE HE COULD...
ALL RIGHT, SON, GRAB A SHOWER, GET YOUR MASSAGE AND HIT THE HAY. TOMORROW'S THE BIG DAY!

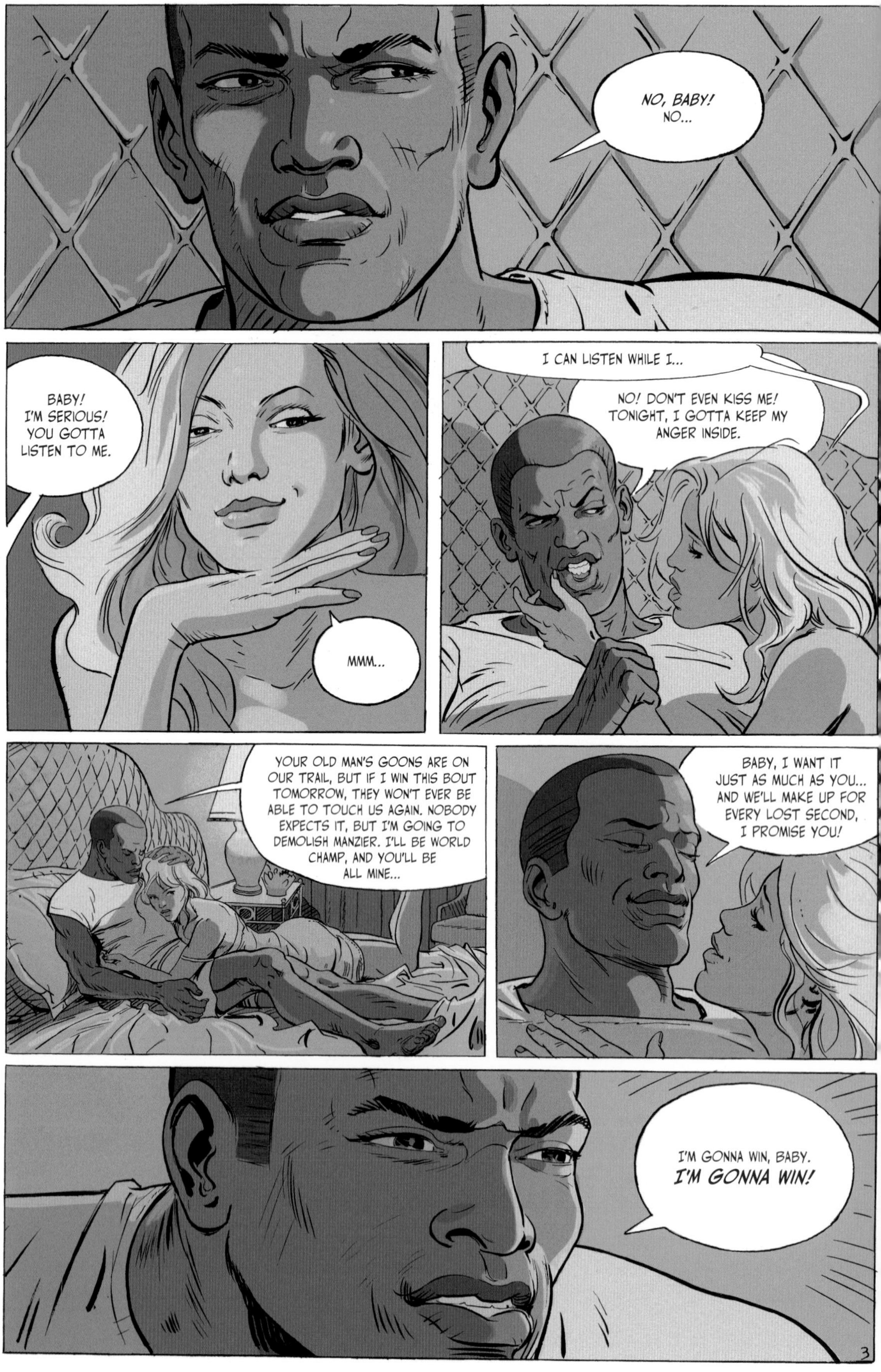
NO, BABY!
NO...
BABY! I'M SERIOUS! YOU GOTTA LISTEN TO ME.
MMM...
I CAN LISTEN WHILE I...
NO! DON'T EVEN KISS ME! TONIGHT, I GOTTA KEEP MY ANGER INSIDE.
YOUR OLD MAN'S GOONS ARE ON OUR TRAIL, BUT IF I WIN THIS BOUT TOMORROW, THEY WON'T EVER BE ABLE TO TOUCH US AGAIN. NOBODY EXPECTS IT, BUT I'M GOING TO DEMOLISH MANZIER. I'LL BE WORLD CHAMP, AND YOU'LL BE ALL MINE...
BABY, I WANT IT JUST AS MUCH AS YOU... AND WE'LL MAKE UP FOR EVERY LOST SECOND, I PROMISE YOU!
I'M GONNA WIN, BABY.
I'M GONNA WIN!
3

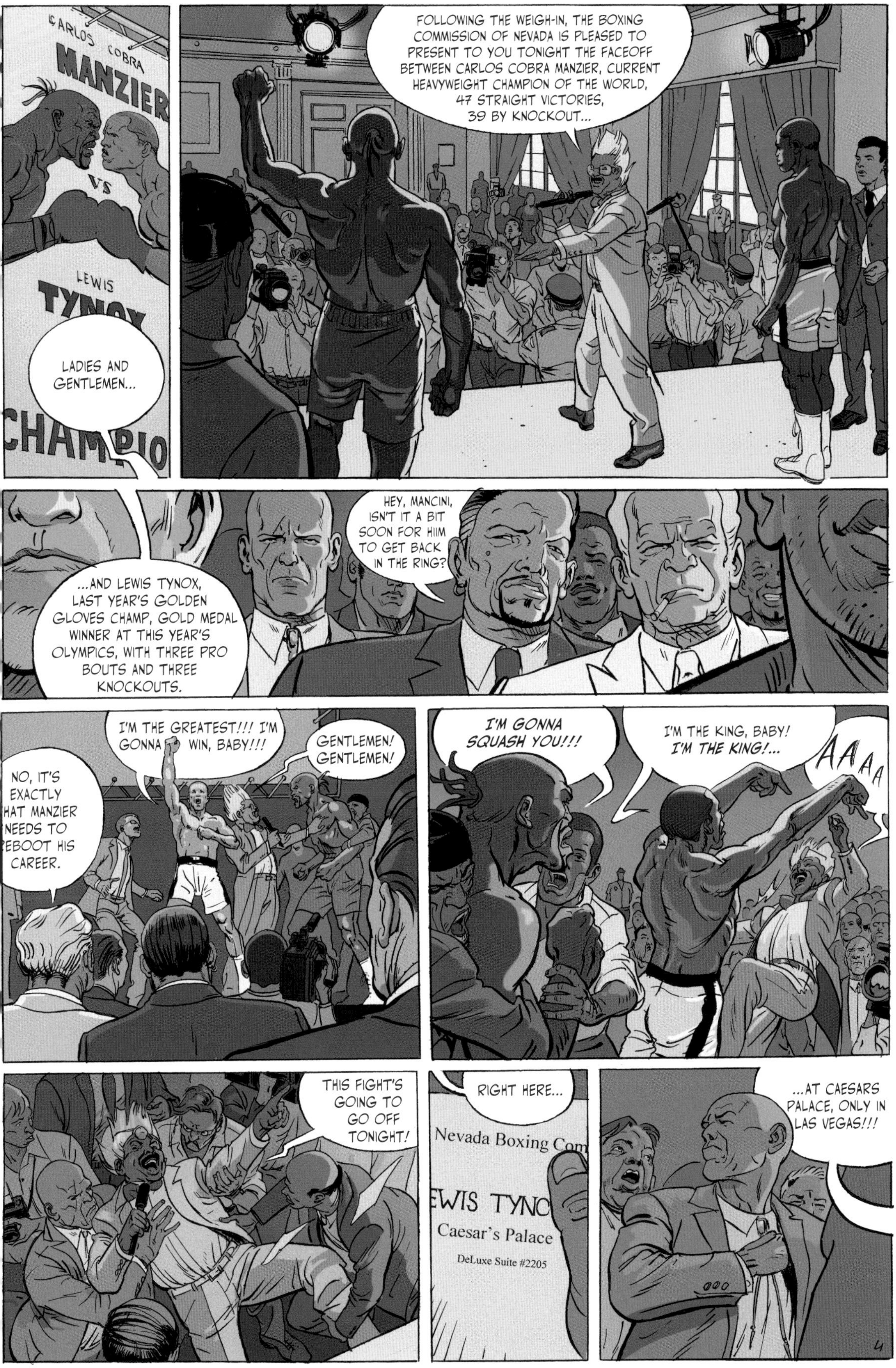
CARLOS COBRA
MANZIER
VS
LEWIS
TYNOX
CHAMPIO
LADIES AND GENTLEMEN...
FOLLOWING THE WEIGH-IN, THE BOXING COMMISSION OF NEVADA IS PLEASED TO PRESENT TO YOU TONIGHT THE FACEOFF BETWEEN CARLOS COBRA MANZIER, CURRENT HEAVYWEIGHT CHAMPION OF THE WORLD, 47 STRAIGHT VICTORIES, 39 BY KNOCKOUT...
...AND LEWIS TYNOX, LAST YEAR'S GOLDEN GLOVES CHAMP, GOLD MEDAL WINNER AT THIS YEAR'S OLYMPICS, WITH THREE PRO BOUTS AND THREE KNOCKOUTS.
HEY, MANCINI, ISN'T IT A BIT SOON FOR HIIM TO GET BACK IN THE RING?
NO, IT'S EXACTLY HAT MANZIER NEEDS TO EBOOT HIS CAREER.
I'M THE GREATEST!!! I'M GONNA WIN, BABY!!!
GENTLEMEN! GENTLEMEN!
I'M GONNA SQUASH YOU!!!
I'M THE KING, BABY! I'M THE KING!...
AAAA
THIS FIGHT'S GOING TO GO OFF TONIGHT!
RIGHT HERE...
Nevada Boxing Com
EWIS TYNC
Caesar's Palace
DeLuxe Suite #2205
...AT CAESARS PALACE, ONLY IN LAS VEGAS!!!

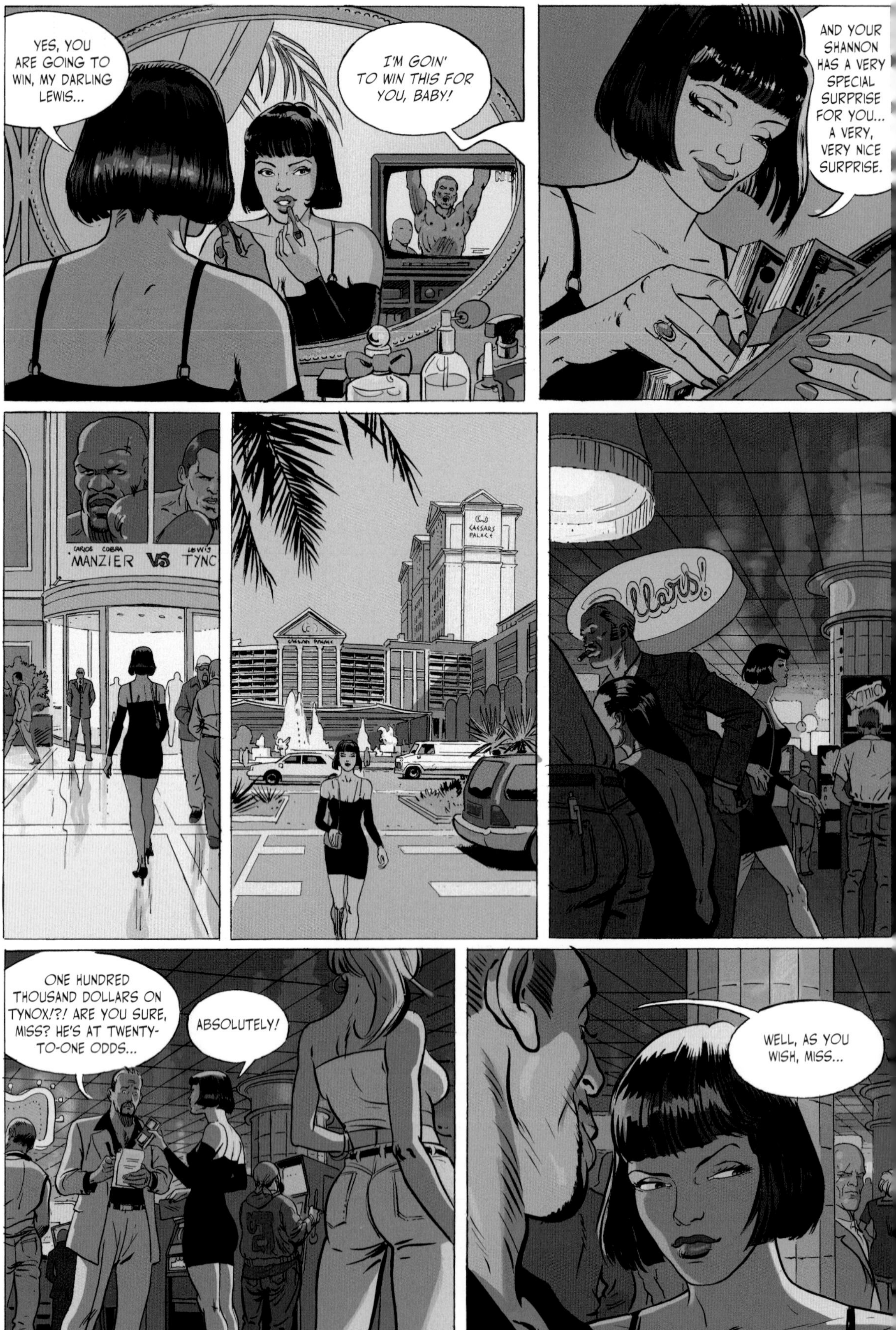
YES, YOU ARE GOING TO WIN, MY DARLING LEWIS...
I'M GOIN' TO WIN THIS FOR YOU, BABY!
AND YOUR SHANNON HAS A VERY SPECIAL SURPRISE FOR YOU... A VERY, VERY NICE SURPRISE.
CARLOS COBRA MANZIER VS LEWIS TYNC
CAESARS PALACE
ONE HUNDRED THOUSAND DOLLARS ON TYNOX!?! ARE YOU SURE, MISS? HE'S AT TWENTY-TO-ONE ODDS...
ABSOLUTELY!
WELL, AS YOU WISH, MISS...
5

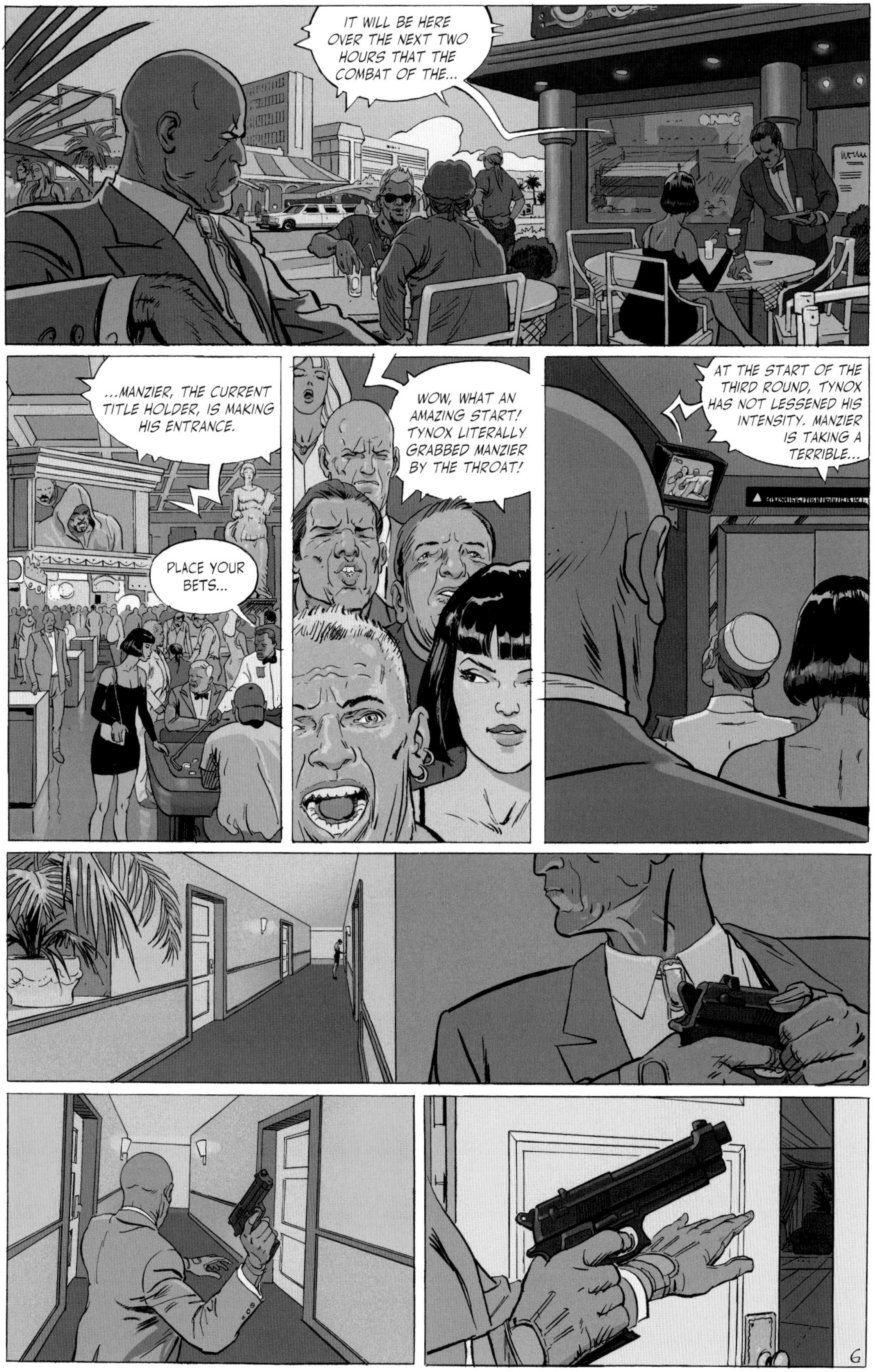
IT WILL BE HERE OVER THE NEXT TWO HOURS THAT THE COMBAT OF THE...
...MANZIER, THE CURRENT TITLE HOLDER, IS MAKING HIS ENTRANCE.
PLACE YOUR BETS...
WOW, WHAT AN AMAZING START! TYNOX LITERALLY GRABBED MANZIER BY THE THROAT!
AT THE START OF THE THIRD ROUND, TYNOX HAS NOT LESSENED HIS INTENSITY. MANZIER IS TAKING A TERRIBLE...
6

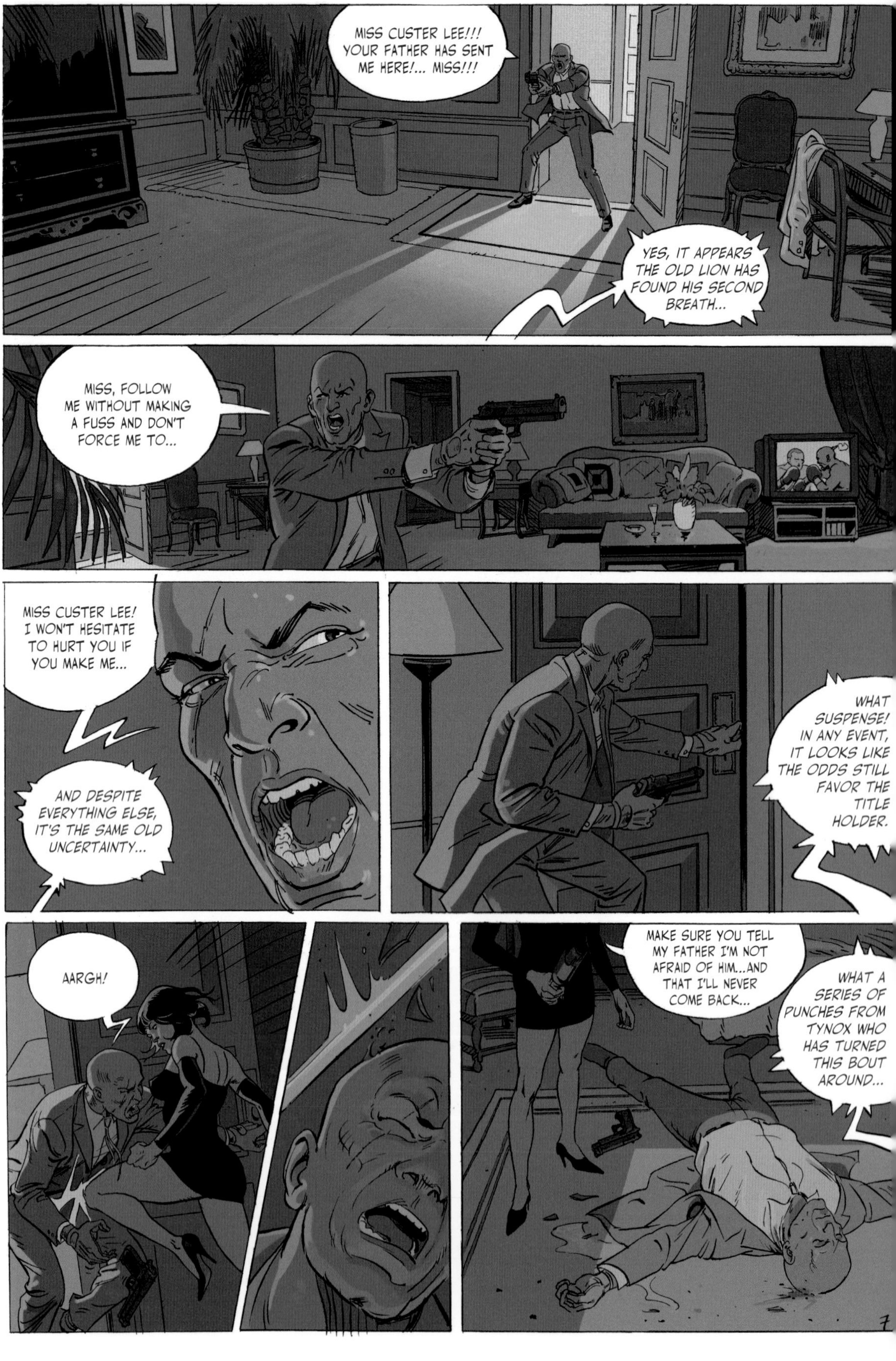
MISS CUSTER LEE!!! YOUR FATHER HAS SENT ME HERE!... MISS!!!
YES, IT APPEARS THE OLD LION HAS FOUND HIS SECOND BREATH...
MISS, FOLLOW ME WITHOUT MAKING A FUSS AND DON'T FORCE ME TO...
MISS CUSTER LEE! I WON'T HESITATE TO HURT YOU IF YOU MAKE ME...
AND DESPITE EVERYTHING ELSE, IT'S THE SAME OLD UNCERTAINTY...
WHAT SUSPENSE! IN ANY EVENT, IT LOOKS LIKE THE ODDS STILL FAVOR THE TITLE HOLDER.
AARGH!
MAKE SURE YOU TELL MY FATHER I'M NOT AFRAID OF HIM...AND THAT I'LL NEVER COME BACK...
WHAT A SERIES OF PUNCHES FROM TYNOX WHO HAS TURNED THIS BOUT AROUND...
7

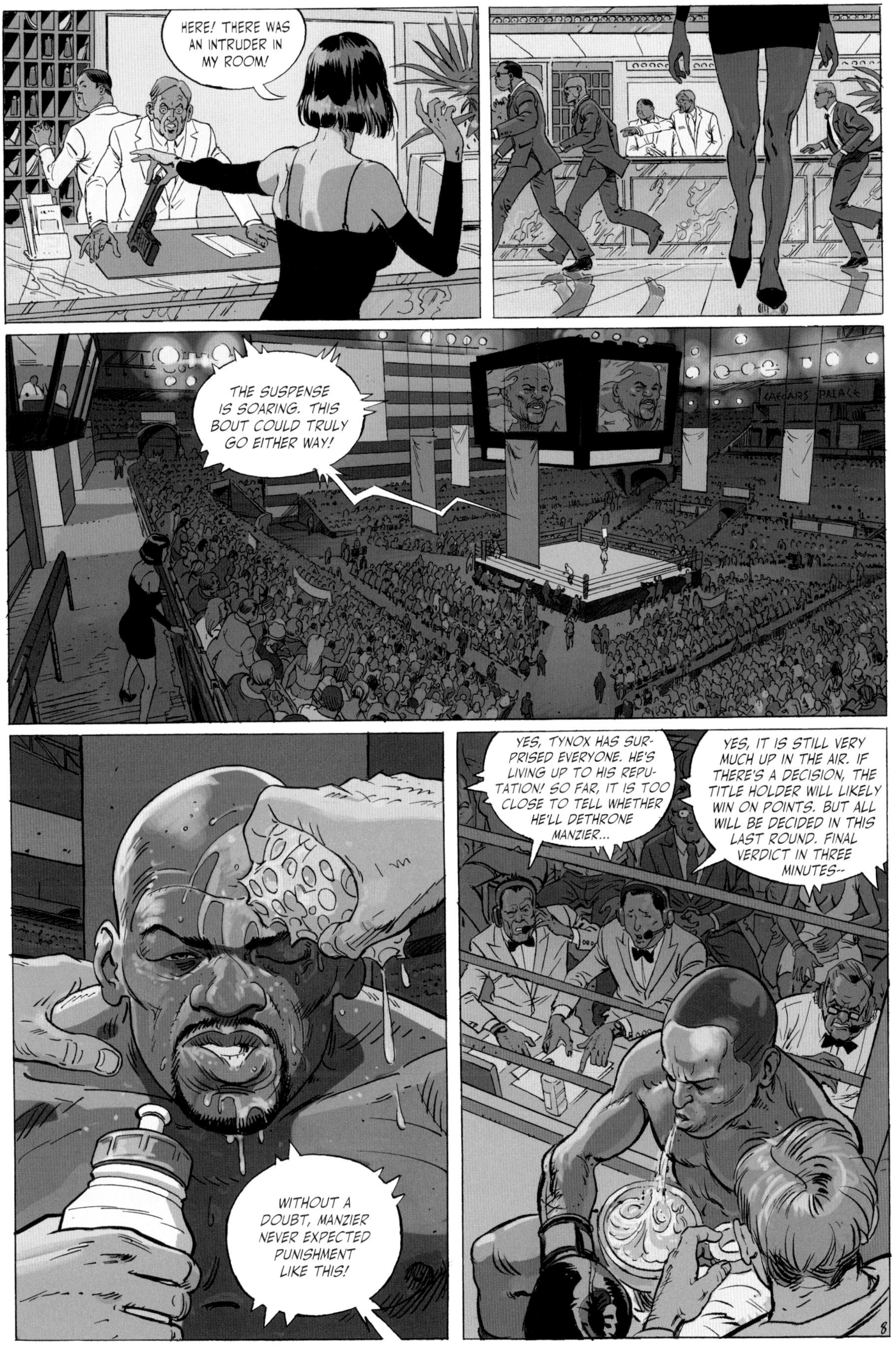
HERE! THERE WAS AN INTRUDER IN MY ROOM!
THE SUSPENSE IS SOARING. THIS BOUT COULD TRULY GO EITHER WAY!
WITHOUT A DOUBT, MANZIER NEVER EXPECTED PUNISHMENT LIKE THIS!
YES, TYNOX HAS SURPRISED EVERYONE. HE'S LIVING UP TO HIS REPUTATION! SO FAR, IT IS TOO CLOSE TO TELL WHETHER HE'LL DETHRONE MANZIER...
YES, IT IS STILL VERY MUCH UP IN THE AIR. IF THERE'S A DECISION, THE TITLE HOLDER WILL LIKELY WIN ON POINTS. BUT ALL WILL BE DECIDED IN THIS LAST ROUND. FINAL VERDICT IN THREE MINUTES--

TYNOX IS RIGHT BACK IN ACTION. HE'S GIVING IT EVERYTHING HE HAS!!!
THIS YOUNG MAN IS REALLY A RAGING BULL... CAN YOU SAY WHETHER THAT WILL BE ENOUGH TO TOPPLE MANZIER?
OH, YES!!! FANTASTIC!!! TYNOX LANDS A BLOW TO MANZIER'S LIVER...
THE OLD LION IS INJURED! MANZIER IS SUFFERING BAD...
CAN THE OLD WOUNDED KING OF THE JUNGLE STILL BE DANGEROUS?
AND THAT DOES IT! MANZIER HAS BEEN KNOCKED OUT!
THE UNBELIEVABLE HAS JUST HAP-PENED! TYNOX IS NOW THE UNDIS-PUTED CHAMPION... OF...THE... WORLD!!!
WOW!!! WHAT MADNESS!! TYNOX, CHAMPION OF THE WORRRRLD! A STAR IS BORN!!!
I'M THE CHAMP, BABY!!! KING OF WORLD!!!

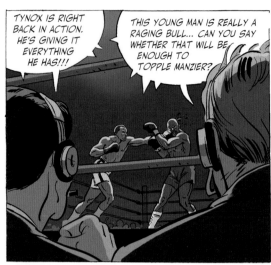

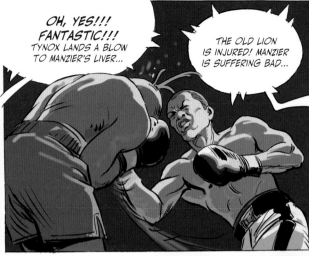

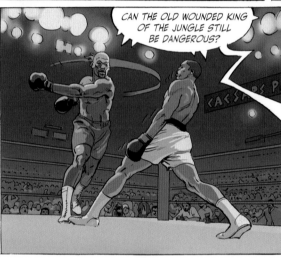

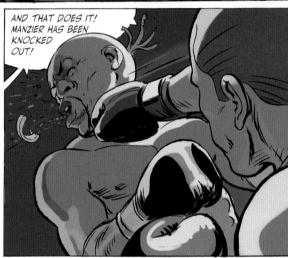

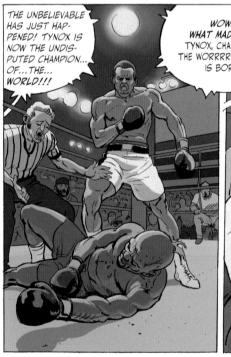

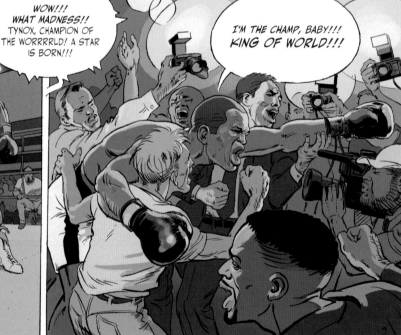

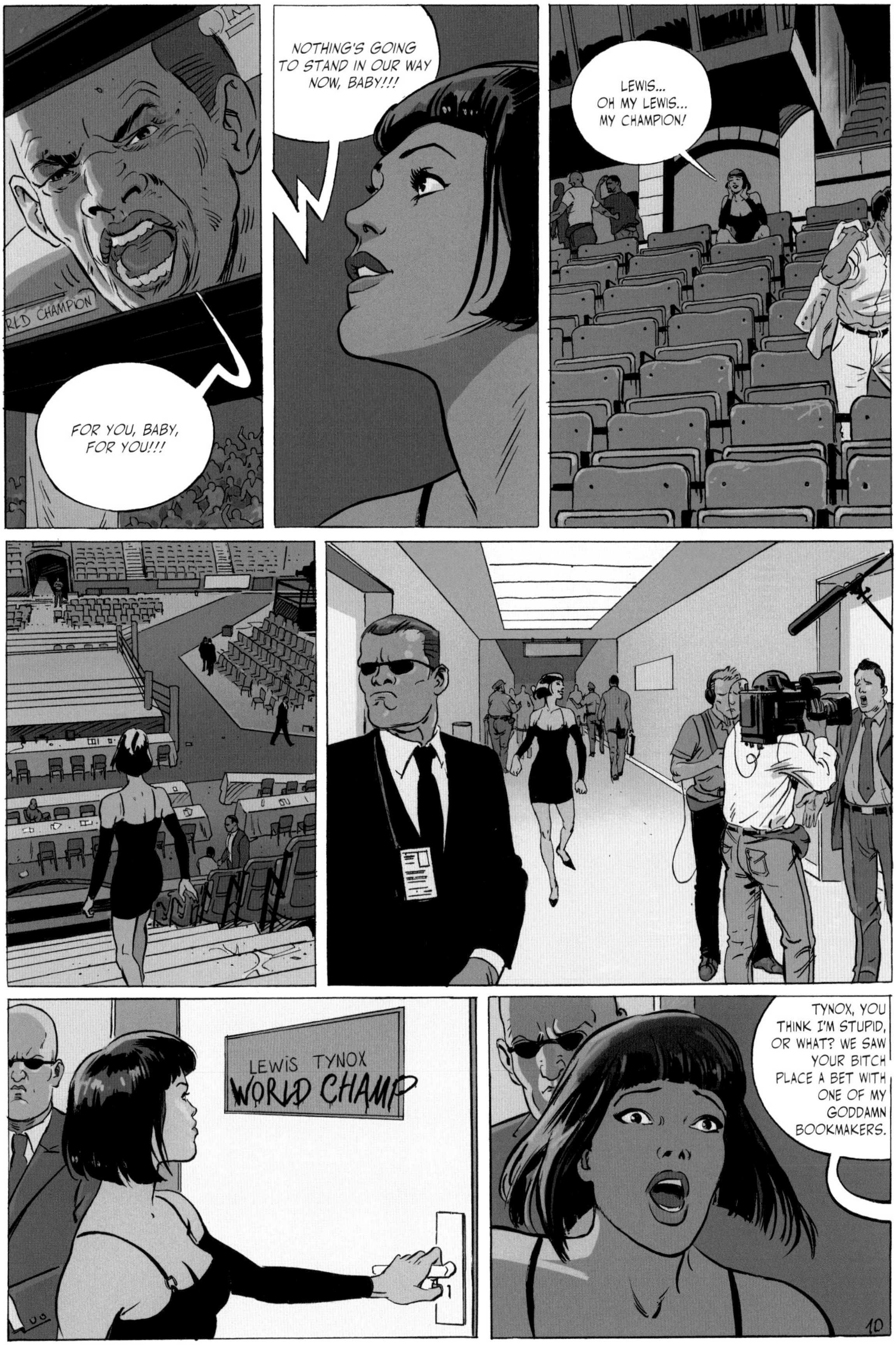
WORLD CHAMPION
FOR YOU, BABY, FOR YOU!!!
NOTHING'S GOING TO STAND IN OUR WAY NOW, BABY!!!
LEWIS... OH MY LEWIS... MY CHAMPION!
LEWIS TYNOX
WORLD CHAMP
TYNOX, YOU THINK I'M STUPID, OR WHAT? WE SAW YOUR BITCH PLACE A BET WITH ONE OF MY GODDAMN BOOKMAKERS.
10

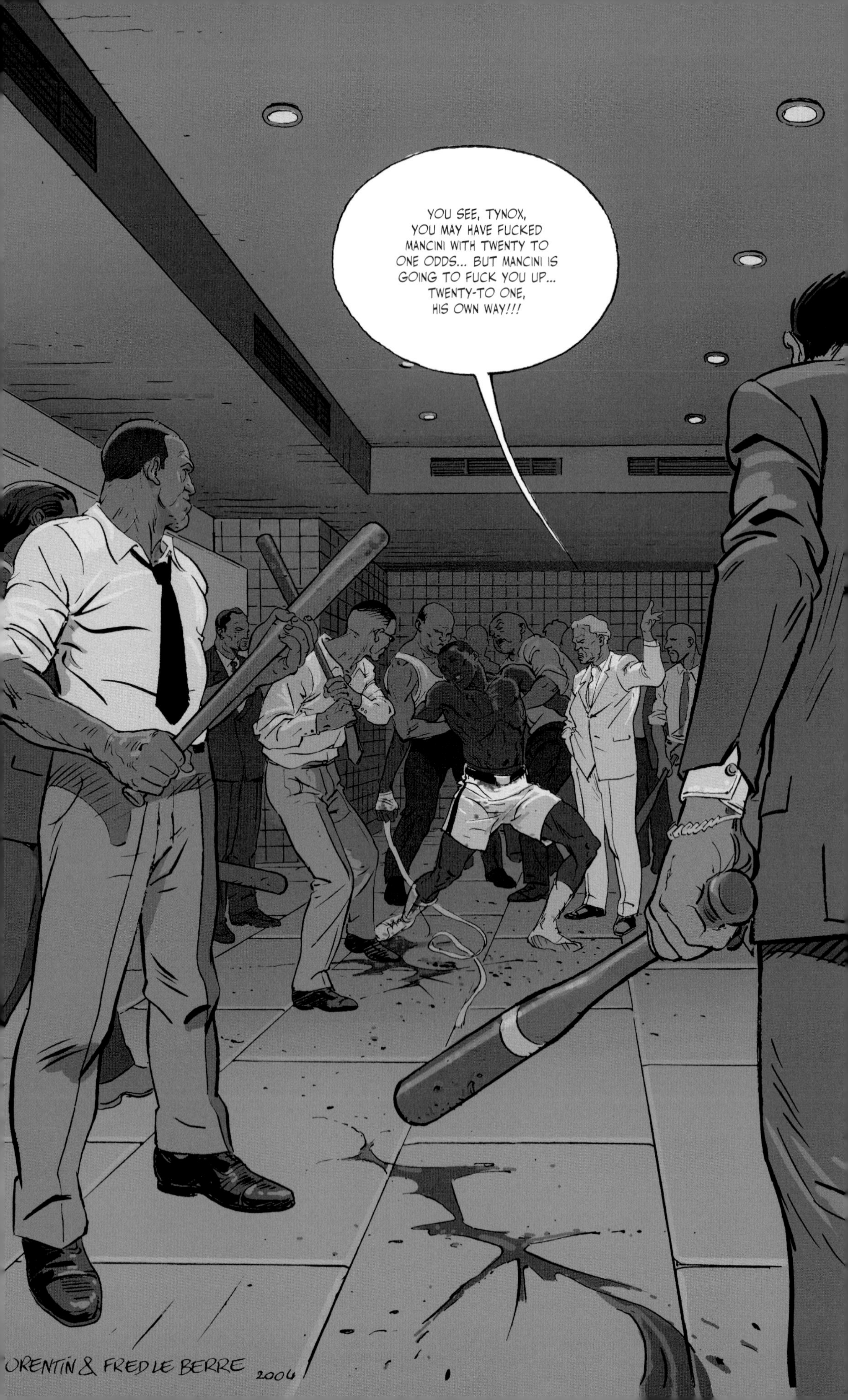
YOU SEE, TYNOX, YOU MAY HAVE FUCKED MANCINI WITH TWENTY TO ONE ODDS... BUT MANCINI IS GOING TO FUCK YOU UP... TWENTY-TO ONE, HIS OWN WAY!!!
ORENTIN & FRED LE BERRE 2006

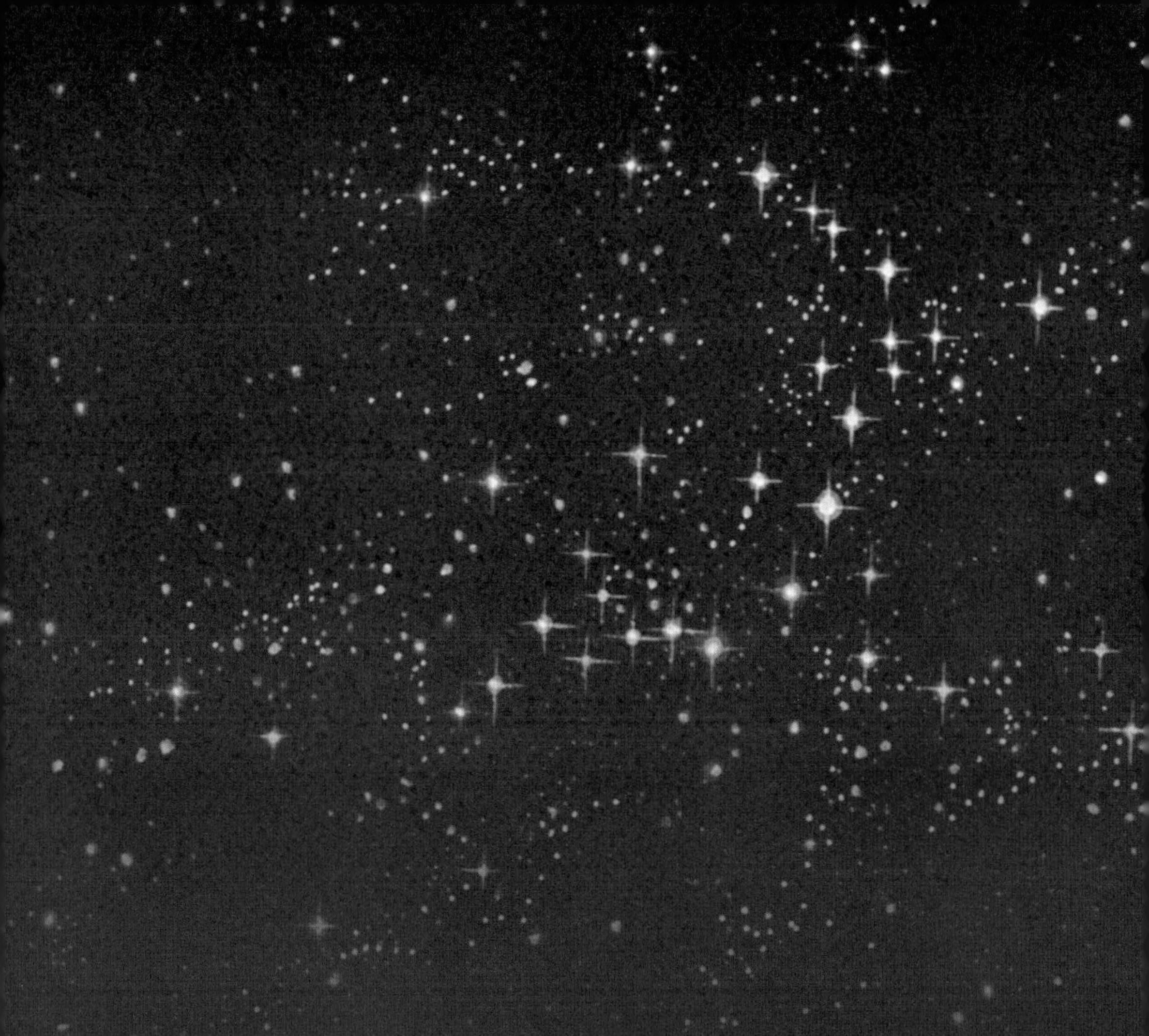

SHELTER ME

Story by DAN WICKLINE
Art by MARK VIGOUROUX

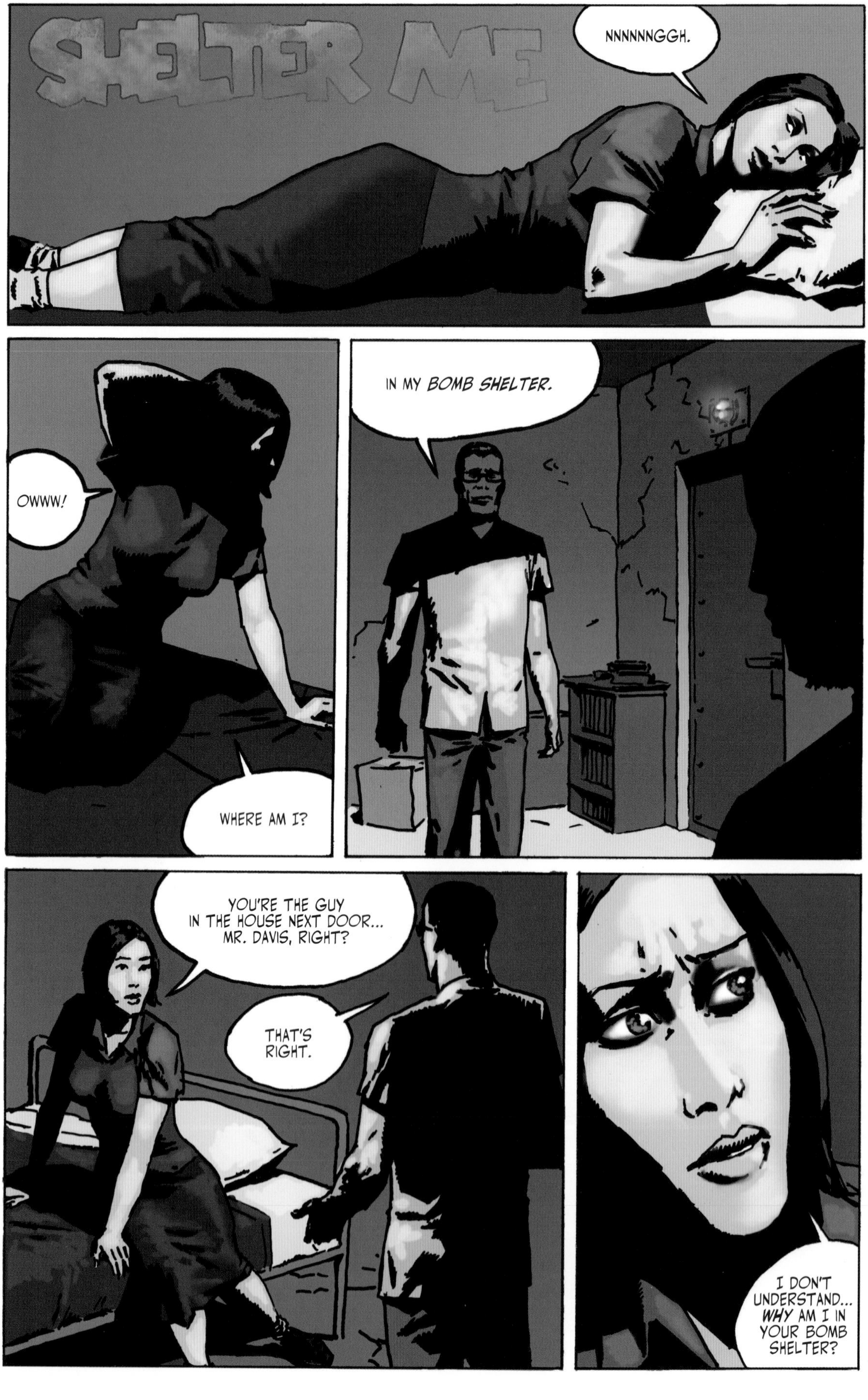
SHELTER ME
NNNNNNGGH.
OWWW!
WHERE AM I?
IN MY BOMB SHELTER.
YOU'RE THE GUY IN THE HOUSE NEXT DOOR... MR. DAVIS, RIGHT?
THAT'S RIGHT.
I DON'T UNDERSTAND... WHY AM I IN YOUR BOMB SHELTER?

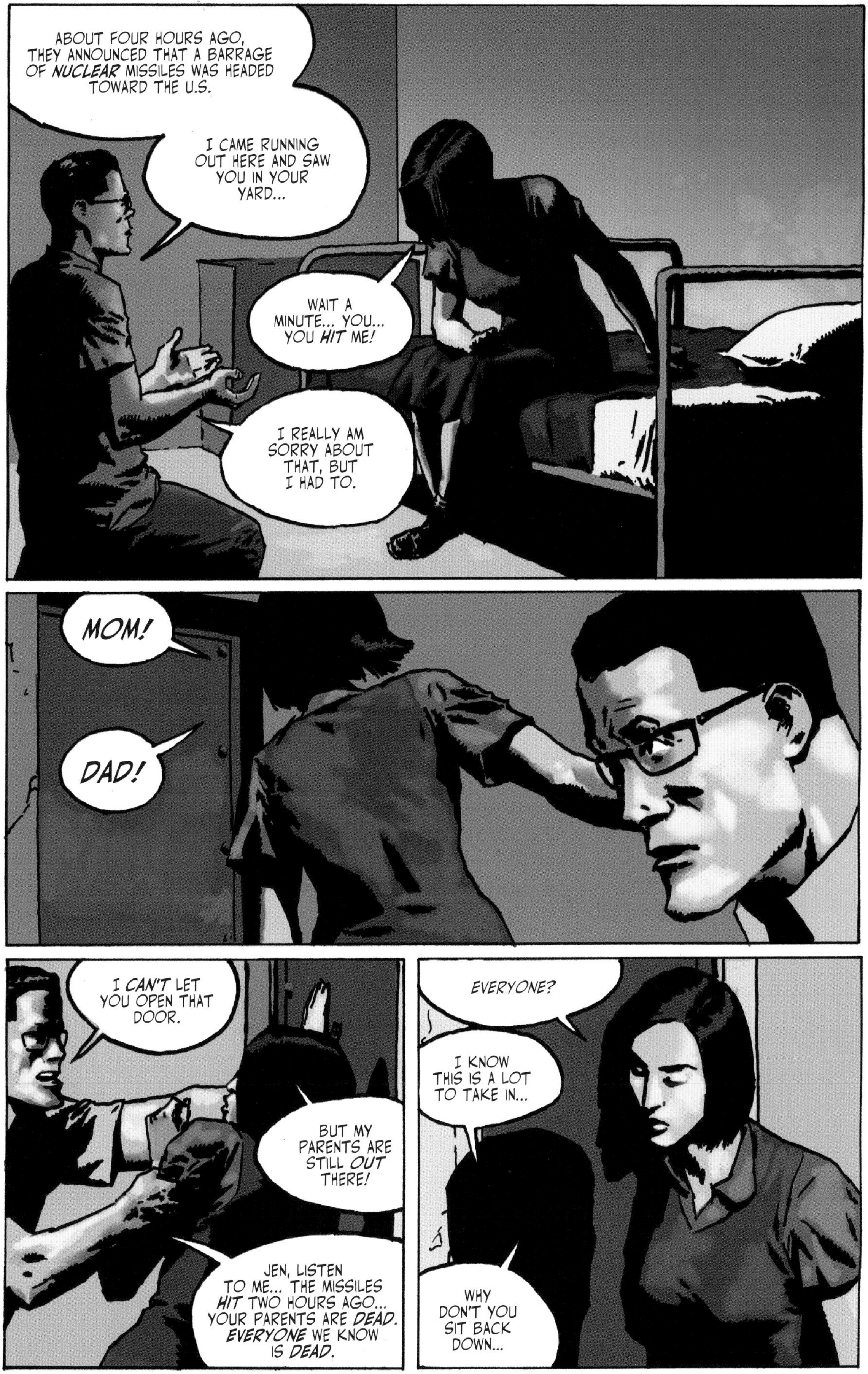
ABOUT FOUR HOURS AGO, THEY ANNOUNCED THAT A BARRAGE OF *NUCLEAR* MISSILES WAS HEADED TOWARD THE U.S.
I CAME RUNNING OUT HERE AND SAW YOU IN YOUR YARD...
WAIT A MINUTE... YOU... YOU *HIT* ME!
I REALLY AM SORRY ABOUT THAT, BUT I HAD TO.
MOM!
DAD!
I *CAN'T* LET YOU OPEN THAT DOOR.
BUT MY PARENTS ARE STILL *OUT* THERE!
JEN, LISTEN TO ME... THE MISSILES *HIT* TWO HOURS AGO... YOUR PARENTS ARE *DEAD*. *EVERYONE* WE KNOW IS *DEAD*.
EVERYONE?
I KNOW THIS IS A LOT TO TAKE IN...
WHY DON'T YOU SIT BACK DOWN...

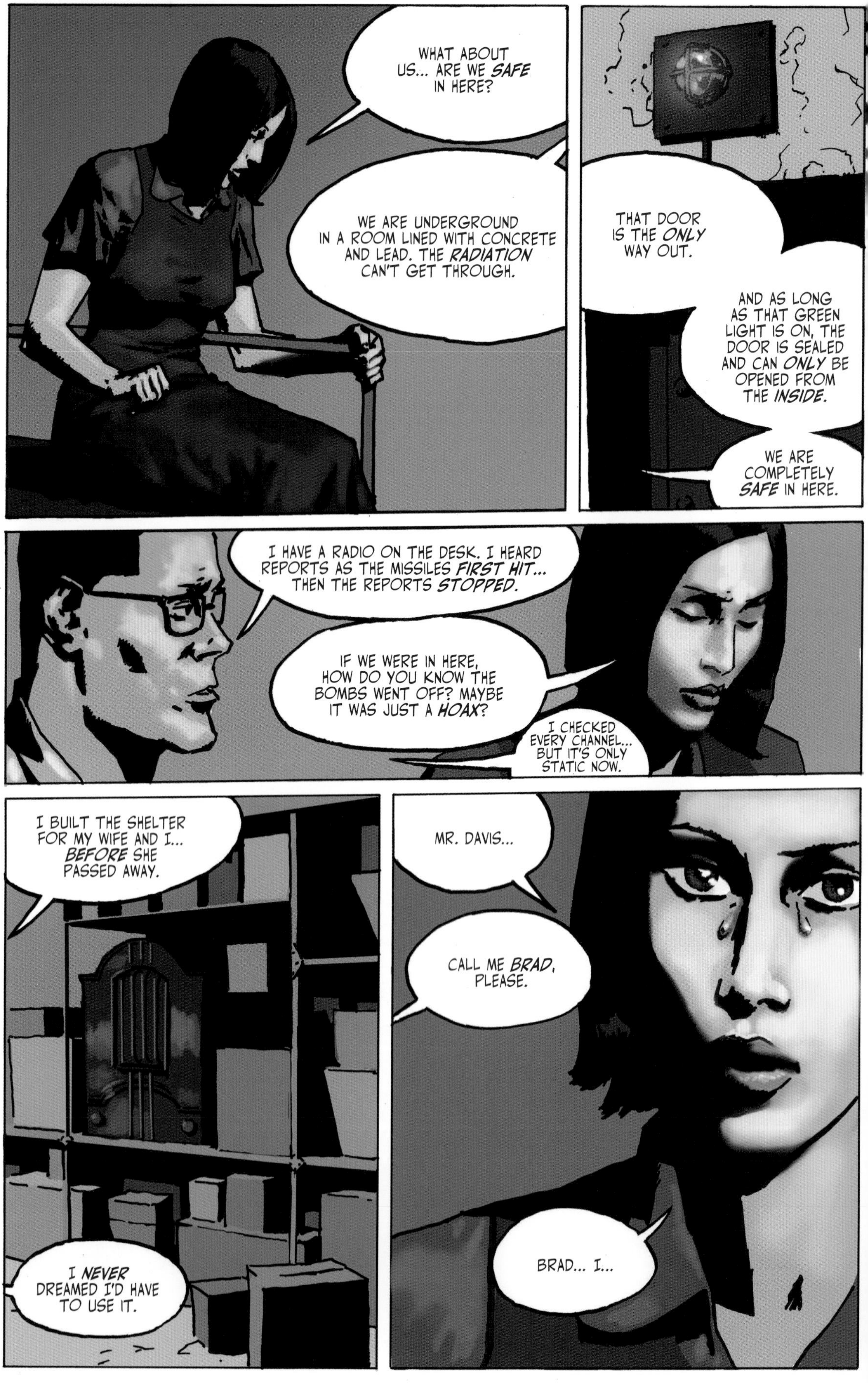
WHAT ABOUT US... ARE WE SAFE IN HERE?
WE ARE UNDERGROUND IN A ROOM LINED WITH CONCRETE AND LEAD. THE RADIATION CAN'T GET THROUGH.
THAT DOOR IS THE ONLY WAY OUT.
AND AS LONG AS THAT GREEN LIGHT IS ON, THE DOOR IS SEALED AND CAN ONLY BE OPENED FROM THE INSIDE.
WE ARE COMPLETELY SAFE IN HERE.
I HAVE A RADIO ON THE DESK. I HEARD REPORTS AS THE MISSILES FIRST HIT... THEN THE REPORTS STOPPED.
IF WE WERE IN HERE, HOW DO YOU KNOW THE BOMBS WENT OFF? MAYBE IT WAS JUST A HOAX?
I CHECKED EVERY CHANNEL... BUT IT'S ONLY STATIC NOW.
I BUILT THE SHELTER FOR MY WIFE AND I... BEFORE SHE PASSED AWAY.
I NEVER DREAMED I'D HAVE TO USE IT.
MR. DAVIS...
CALL ME BRAD, PLEASE.
BRAD... I...

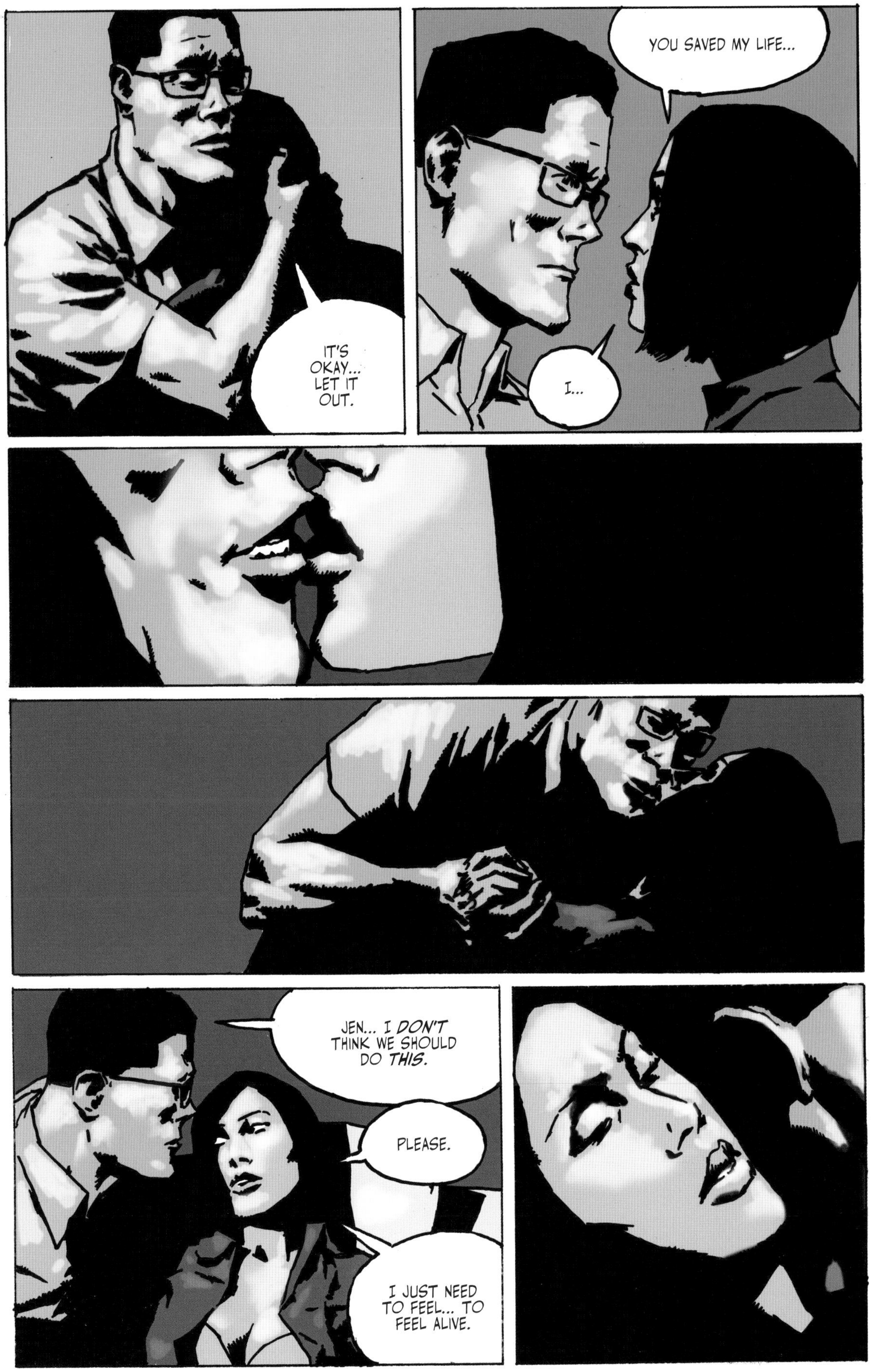
IT'S OKAY... LET IT OUT.
YOU SAVED MY LIFE...
I...
JEN... I *DON'T* THINK WE SHOULD DO *THIS*.
PLEASE.
I JUST NEED TO FEEL... TO FEEL ALIVE.

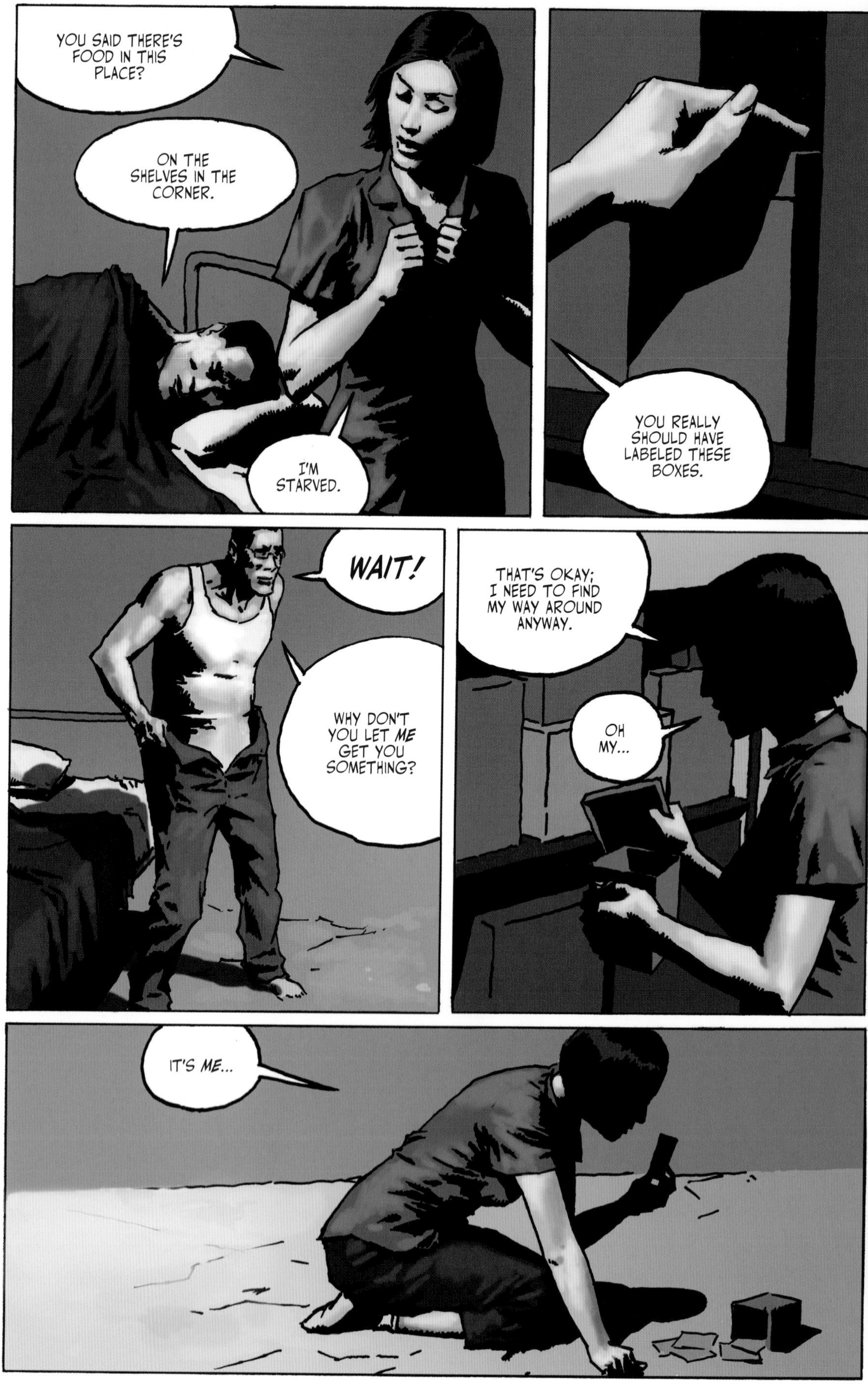
YOU SAID THERE'S FOOD IN THIS PLACE?
ON THE SHELVES IN THE CORNER.
I'M STARVED.
YOU REALLY SHOULD HAVE LABELED THESE BOXES.
WAIT!
WHY DON'T YOU LET ME GET YOU SOMETHING?
THAT'S OKAY; I NEED TO FIND MY WAY AROUND ANYWAY.
OH MY...
IT'S ME...

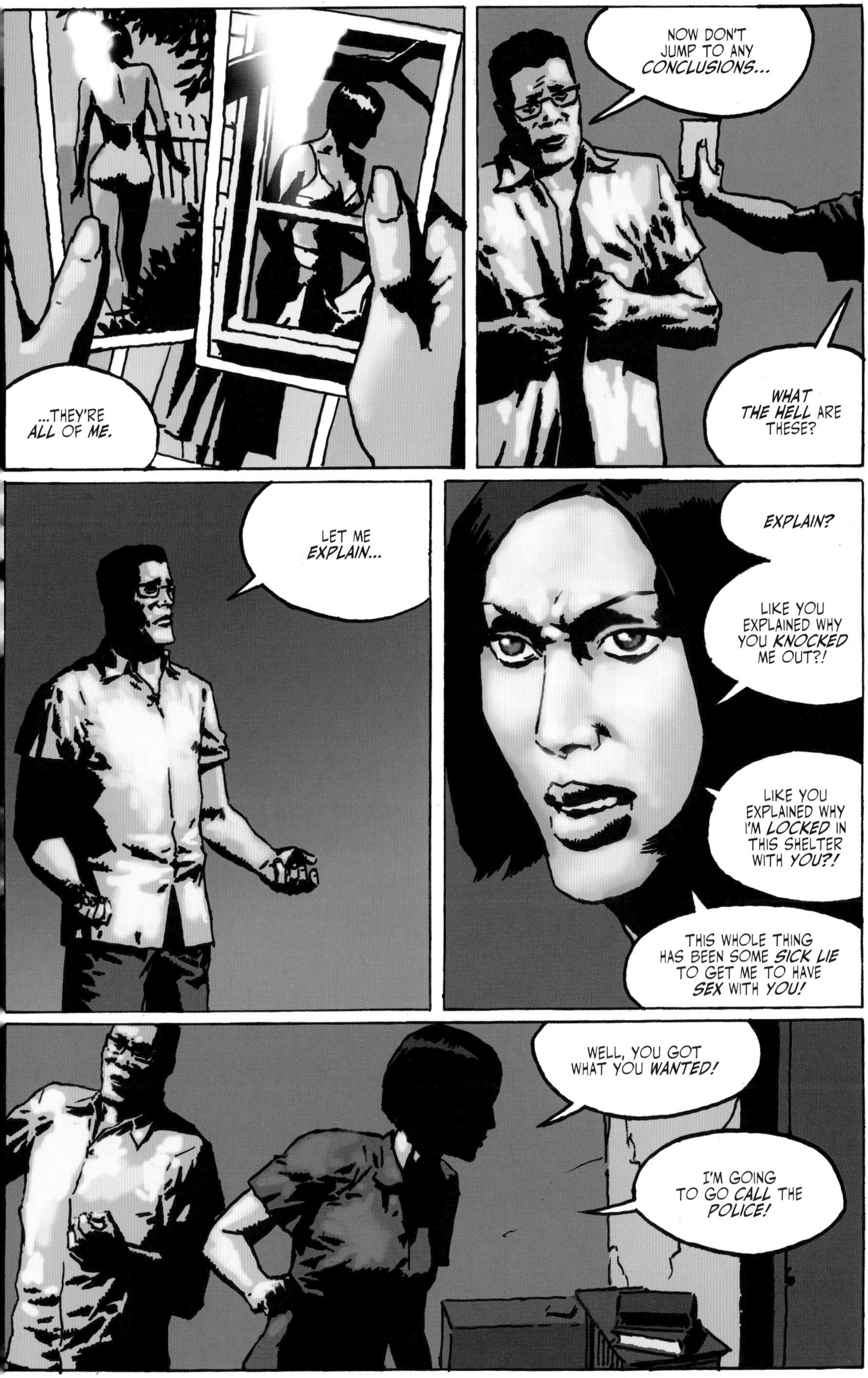
...THEY'RE ALL OF ME.
WHAT THE HELL ARE THESE?
NOW DON'T JUMP TO ANY CONCLUSIONS...
LET ME EXPLAIN...
EXPLAIN?
LIKE YOU EXPLAINED WHY YOU KNOCKED ME OUT?!
LIKE YOU EXPLAINED WHY I'M LOCKED IN THIS SHELTER WITH YOU?!
THIS WHOLE THING HAS BEEN SOME SICK LIE TO GET ME TO HAVE SEX WITH YOU!
WELL, YOU GOT WHAT YOU WANTED!
I'M GOING TO GO CALL THE POLICE!

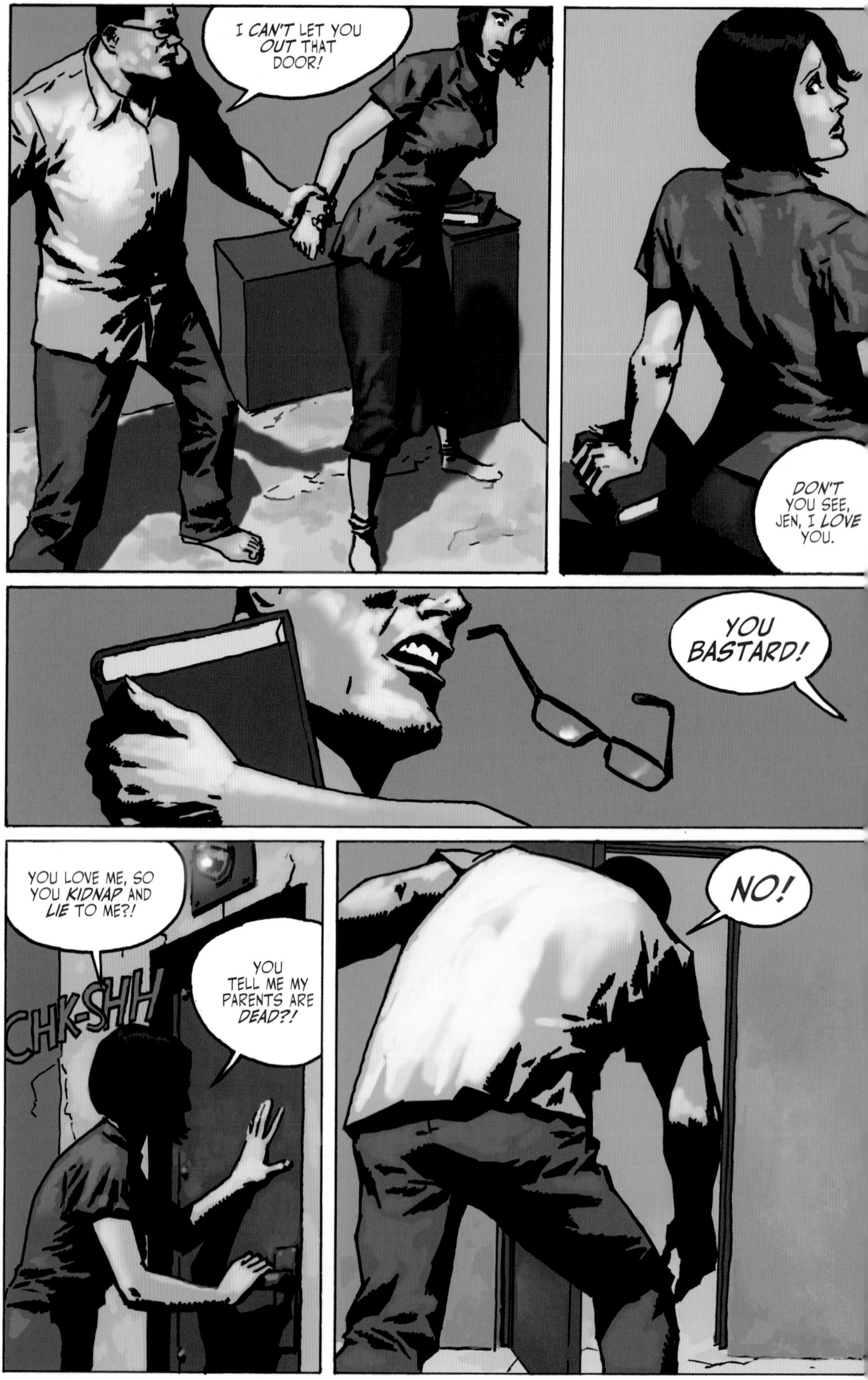
I CAN'T LET YOU OUT THAT DOOR!
DON'T YOU SEE, JEN, I LOVE YOU.
YOU BASTARD!
YOU LOVE ME, SO YOU KIDNAP AND LIE TO ME?!
CHK-SHH
YOU TELL ME MY PARENTS ARE DEAD?!
NO!

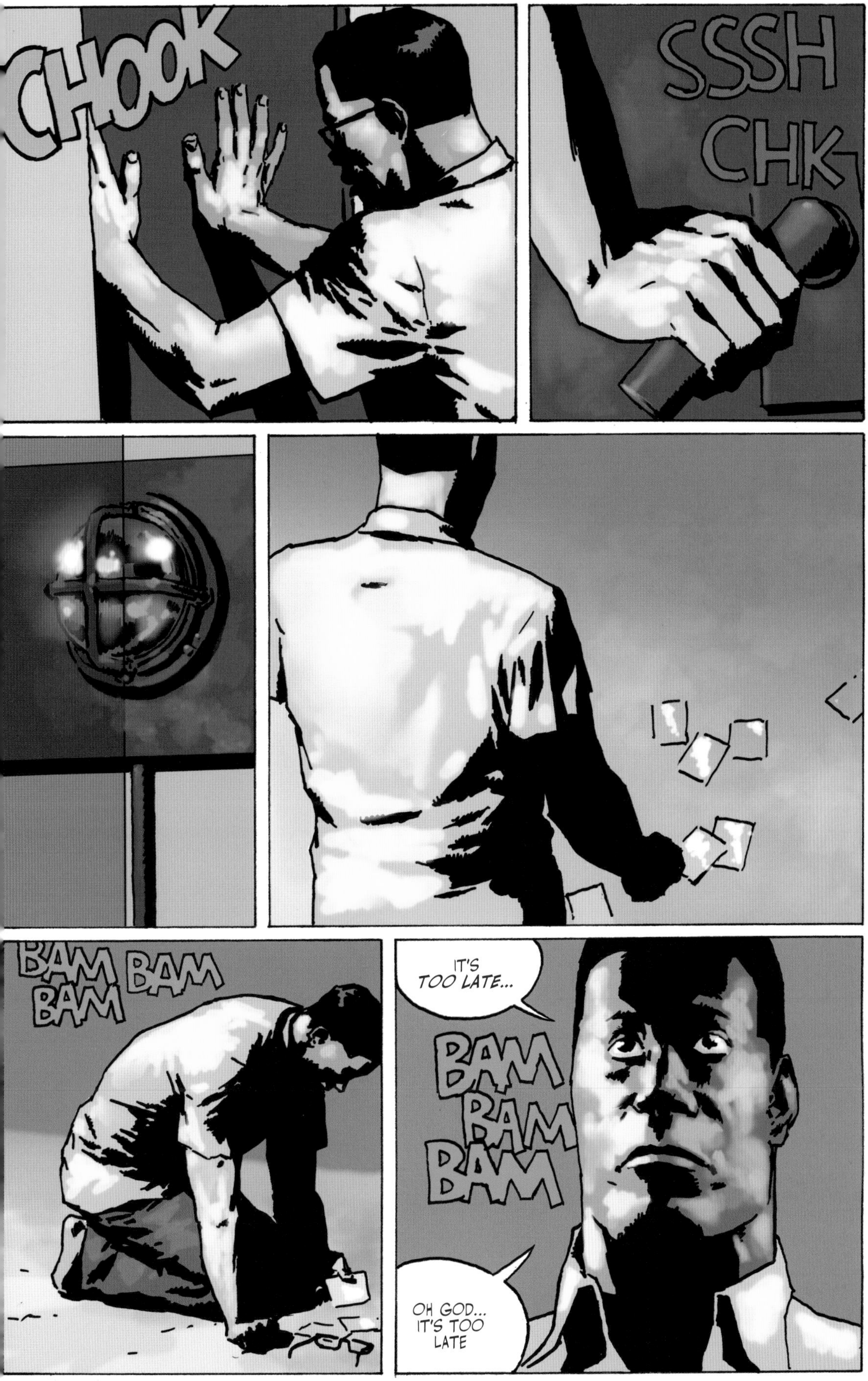
CHOOK
SSSH
CHK
BAM BAM
BAM
IT'S TOO LATE...
BAM
BAM
BAM
OH GOD... IT'S TOO LATE

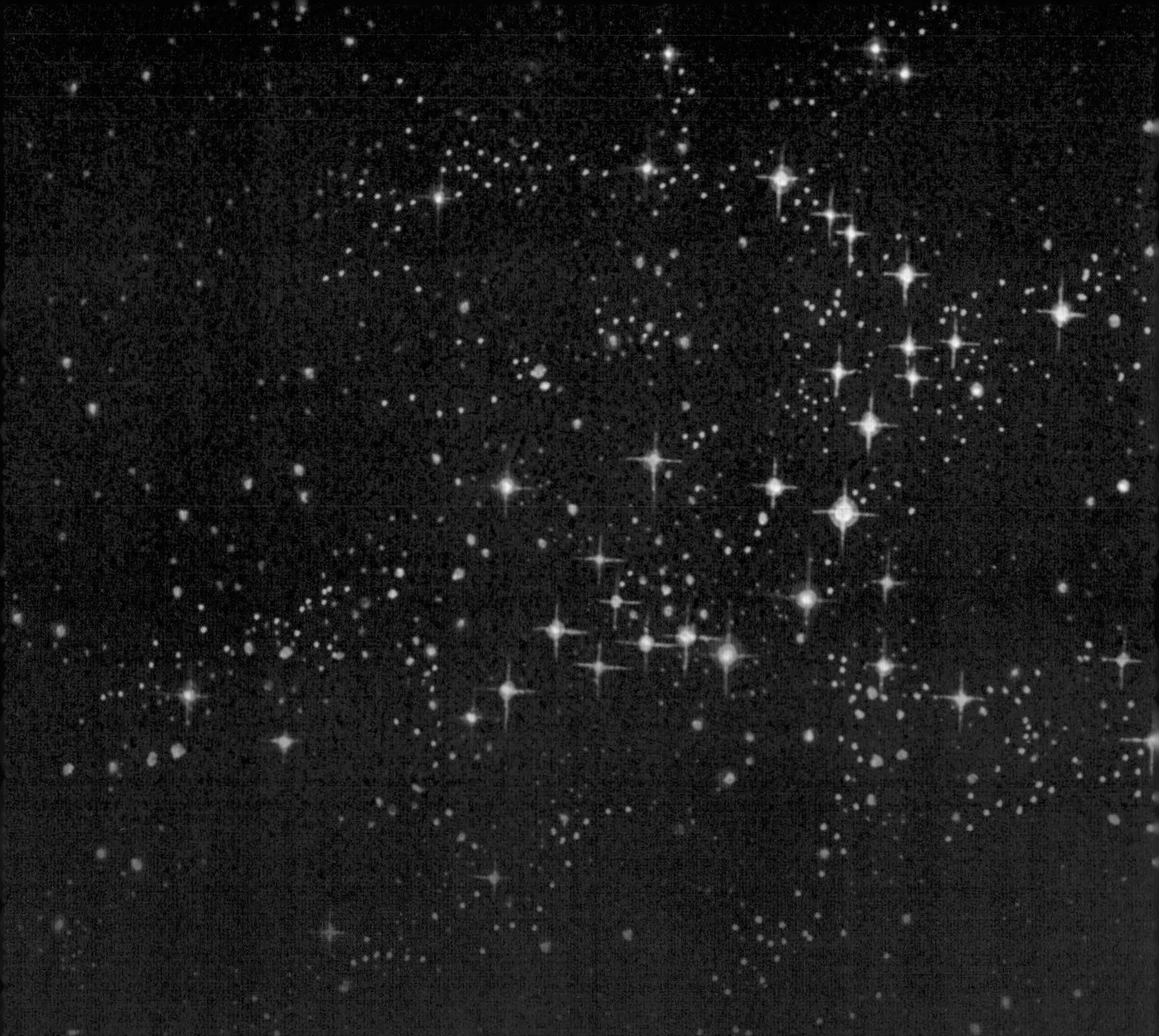

LAST MISSION

Story by SEBASTIEN GÉRARD
Art by IVAN GOMEZ

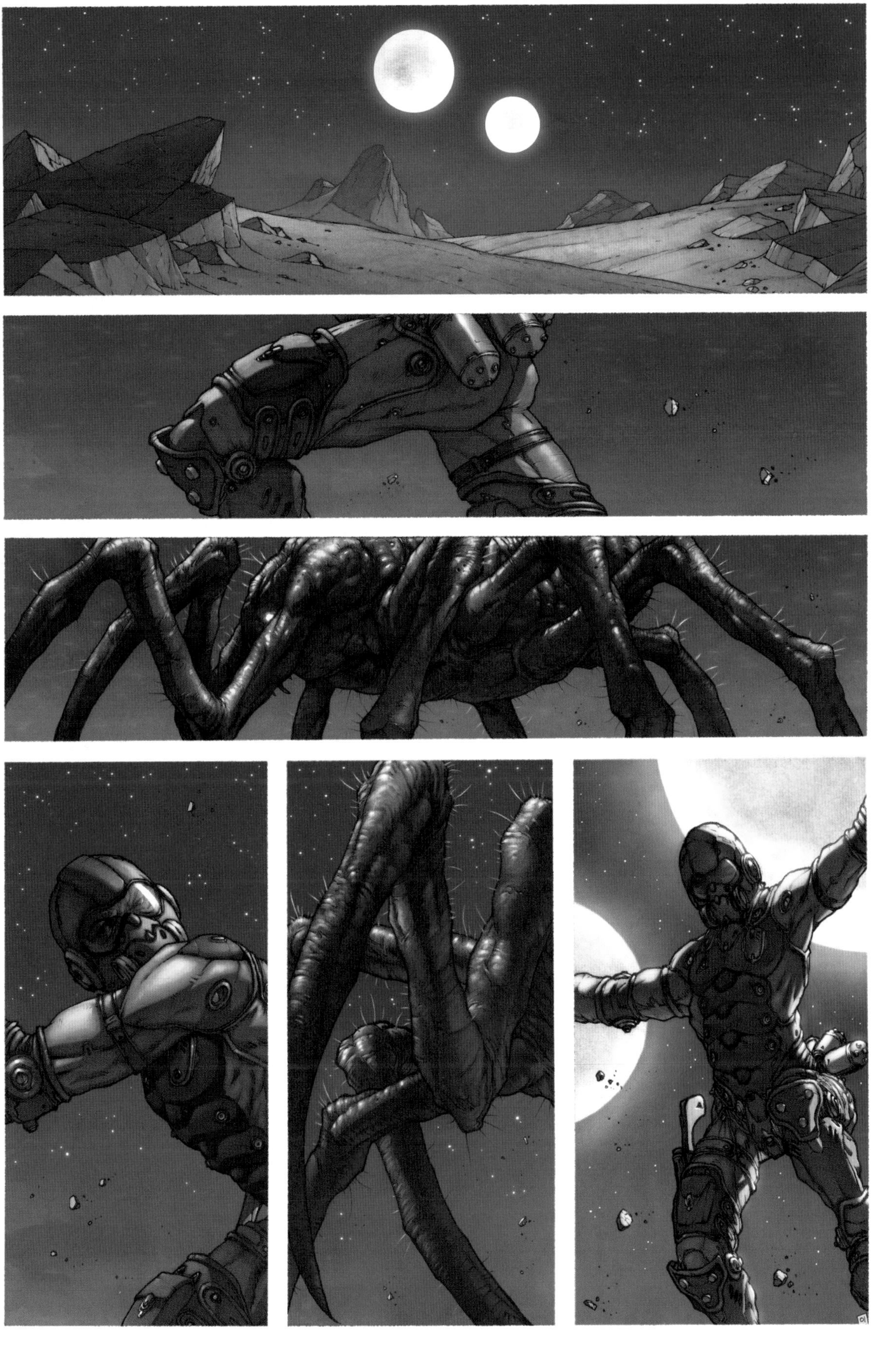

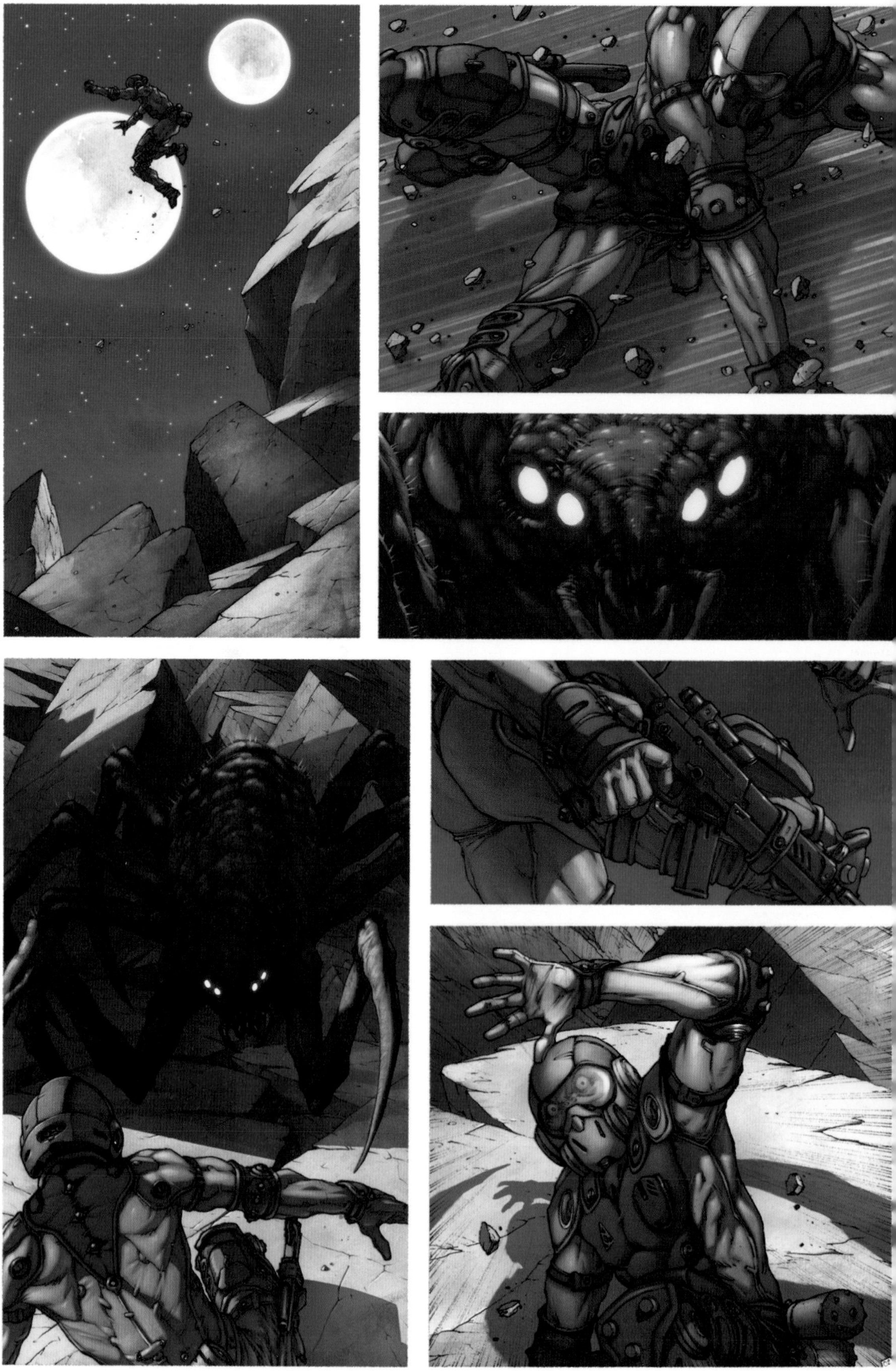

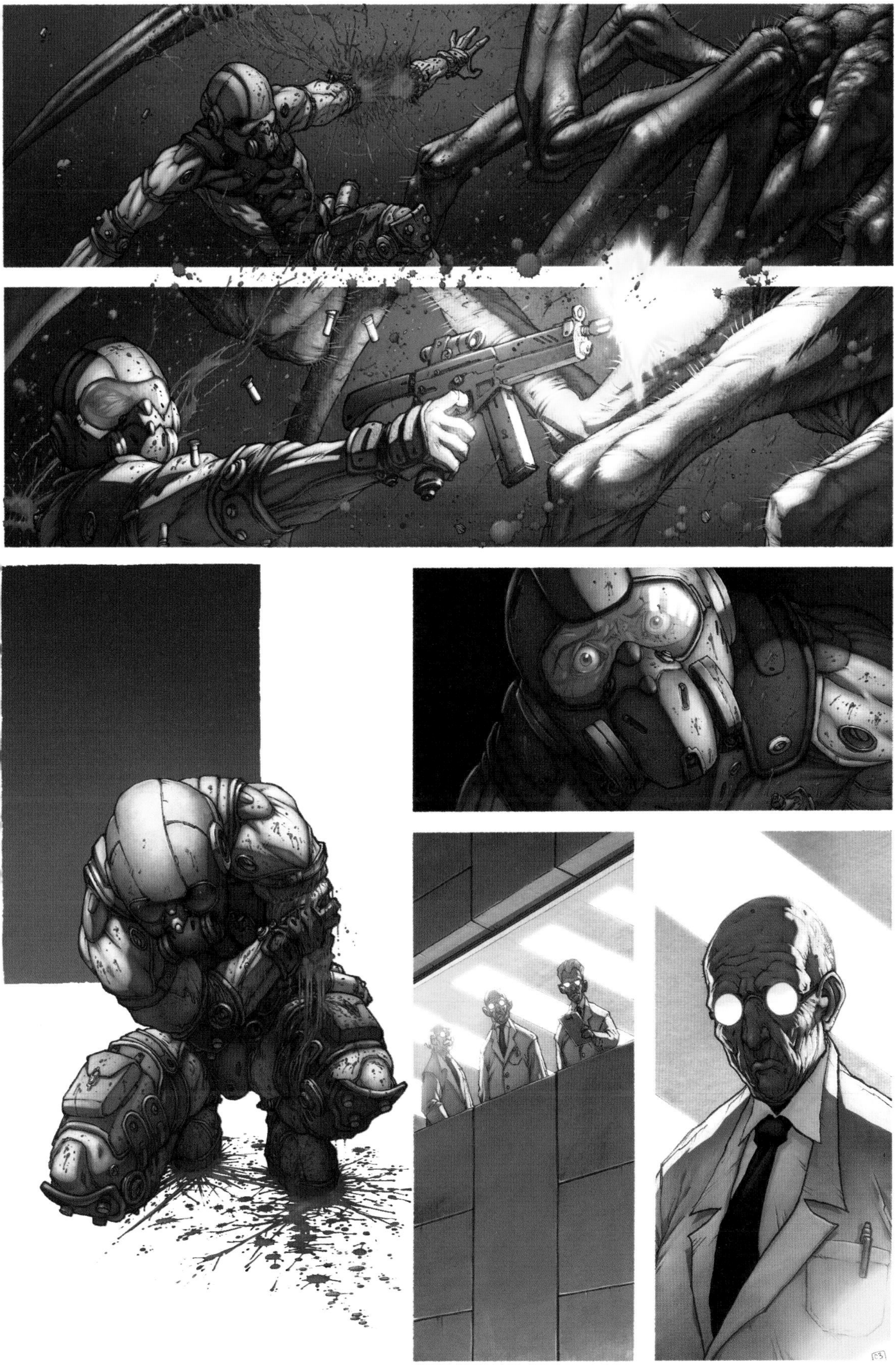

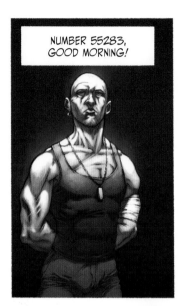

NUMBER 55283, GOOD MORNING!

HOW IS YOUR ARM?

GOOD, SIR, THE REGENERATION WORKED.

VERY WELL, SO YOU ARE FULLY READY TO DEPART...

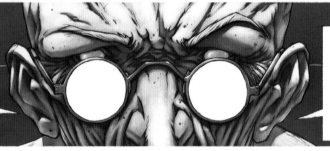

THE PARALLEL WORLD WHERE WE'RE GOING TO SEND YOU TODAY SHOULD BE A TAD LESS HOSTILE...

HOWEVER, I ADVISE YOU TO STAY AWAY FROM ANY NATIVES THAT YOU MIGHT COME ACROSS...

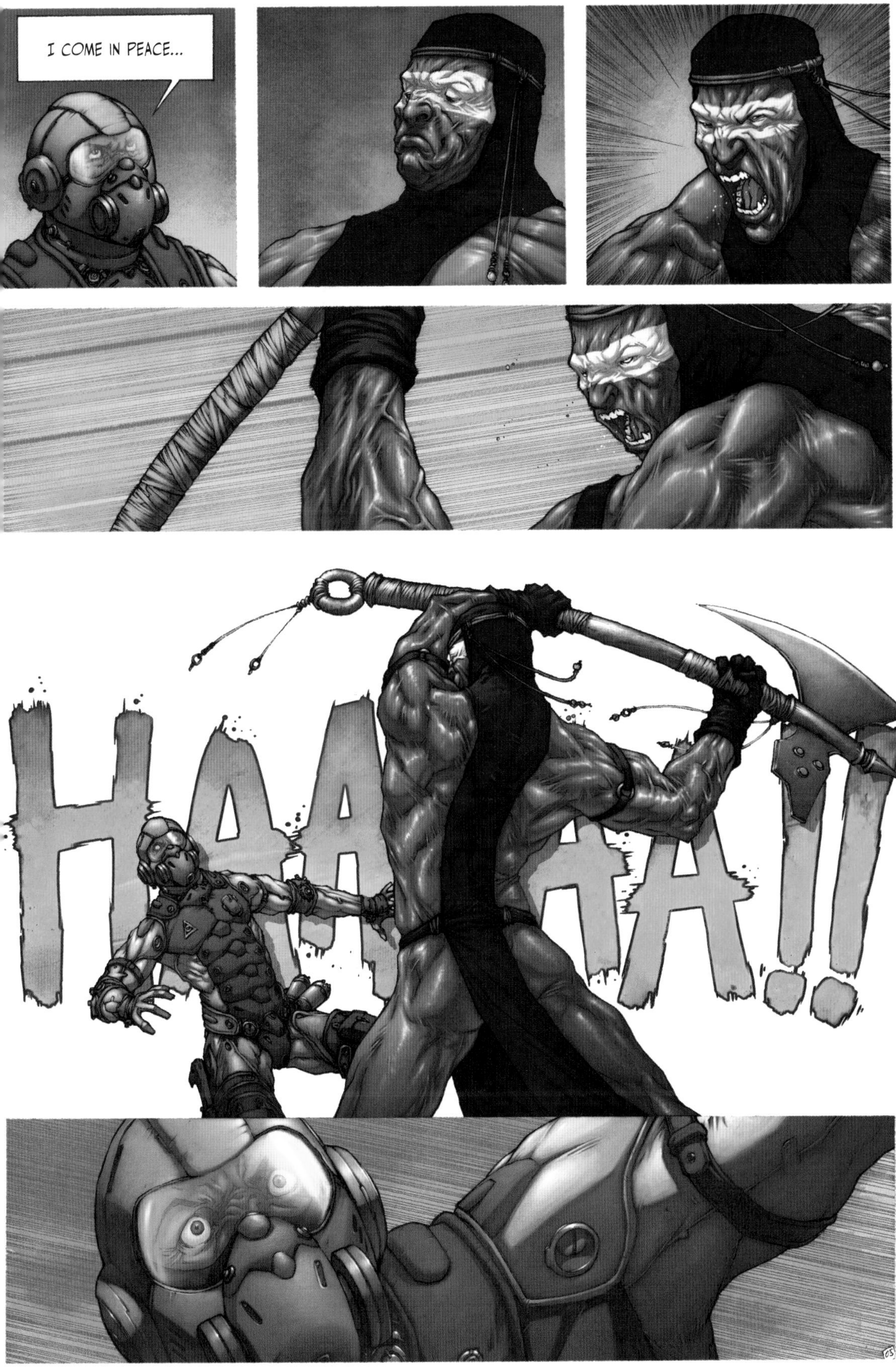
I COME IN PEACE...
HAAAA!!

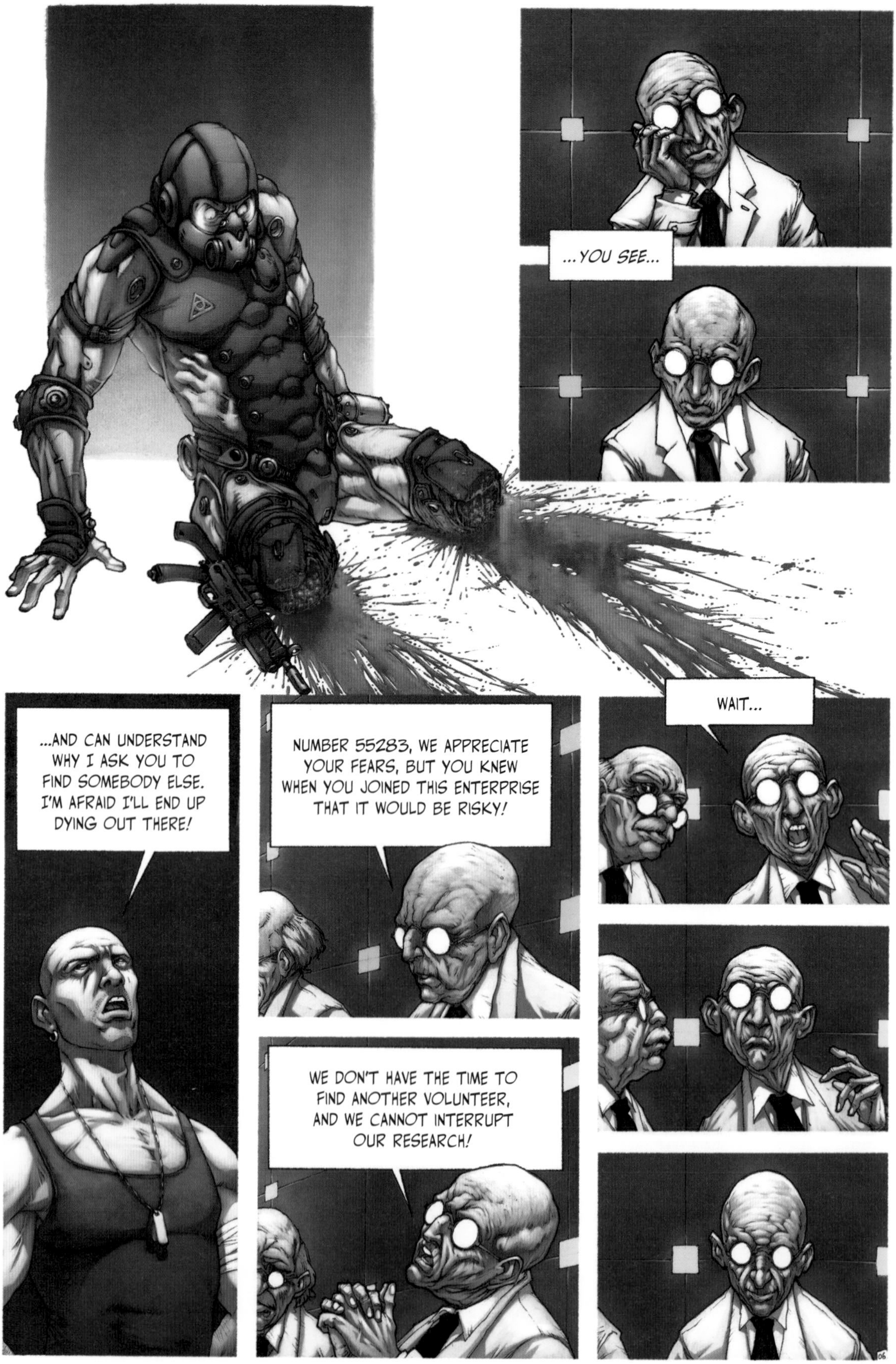
...YOU SEE...
...AND CAN UNDERSTAND WHY I ASK YOU TO FIND SOMEBODY ELSE. I'M AFRAID I'LL END UP DYING OUT THERE!
NUMBER 55283, WE APPRECIATE YOUR FEARS, BUT YOU KNEW WHEN YOU JOINED THIS ENTERPRISE THAT IT WOULD BE RISKY!
WE DON'T HAVE THE TIME TO FIND ANOTHER VOLUNTEER, AND WE CANNOT INTERRUPT OUR RESEARCH!
WAIT...

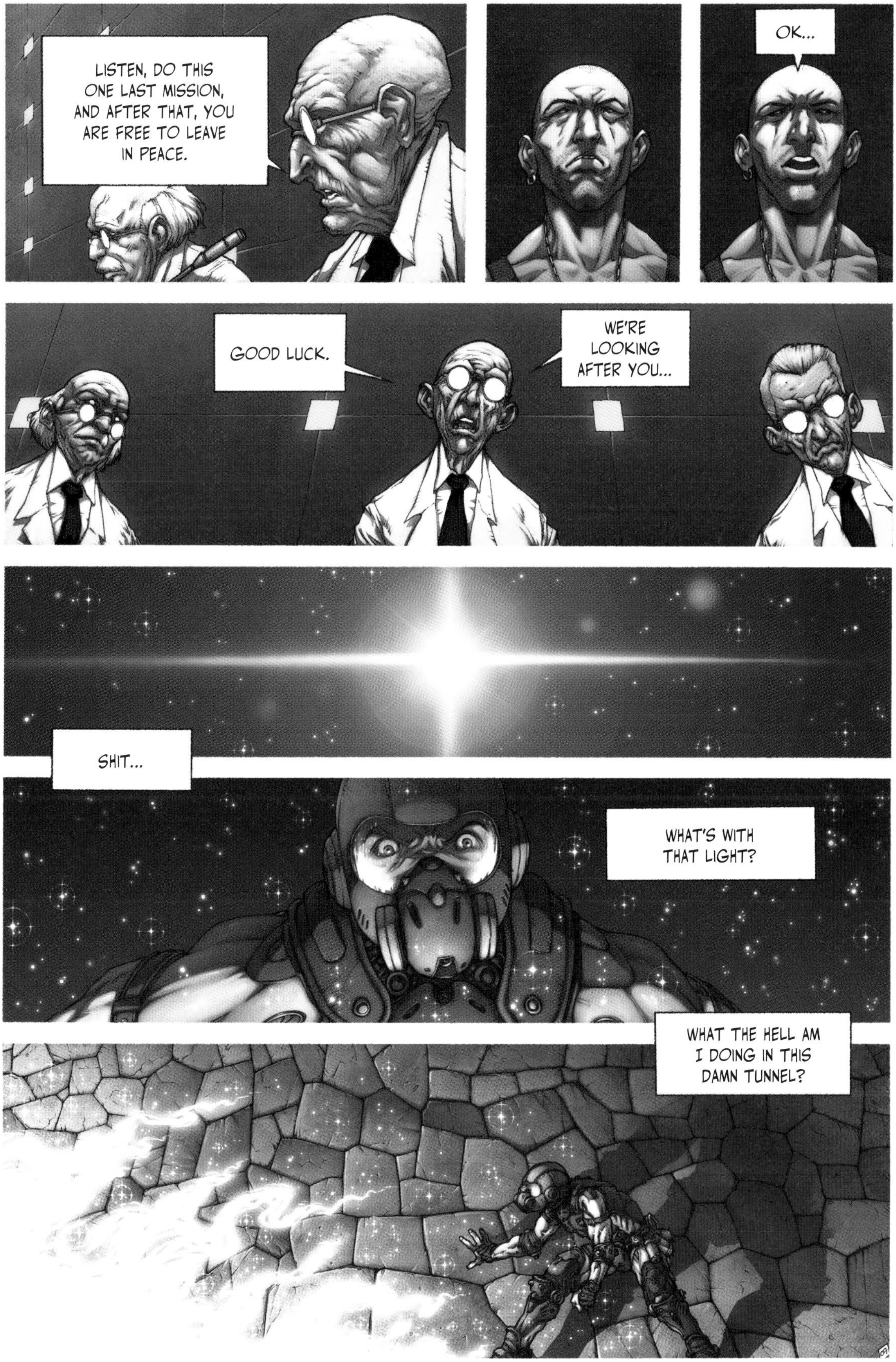
LISTEN, DO THIS ONE LAST MISSION, AND AFTER THAT, YOU ARE FREE TO LEAVE IN PEACE.
OK...
GOOD LUCK.
WE'RE LOOKING AFTER YOU...
SHIT...
WHAT'S WITH THAT LIGHT?
WHAT THE HELL AM I DOING IN THIS DAMN TUNNEL?

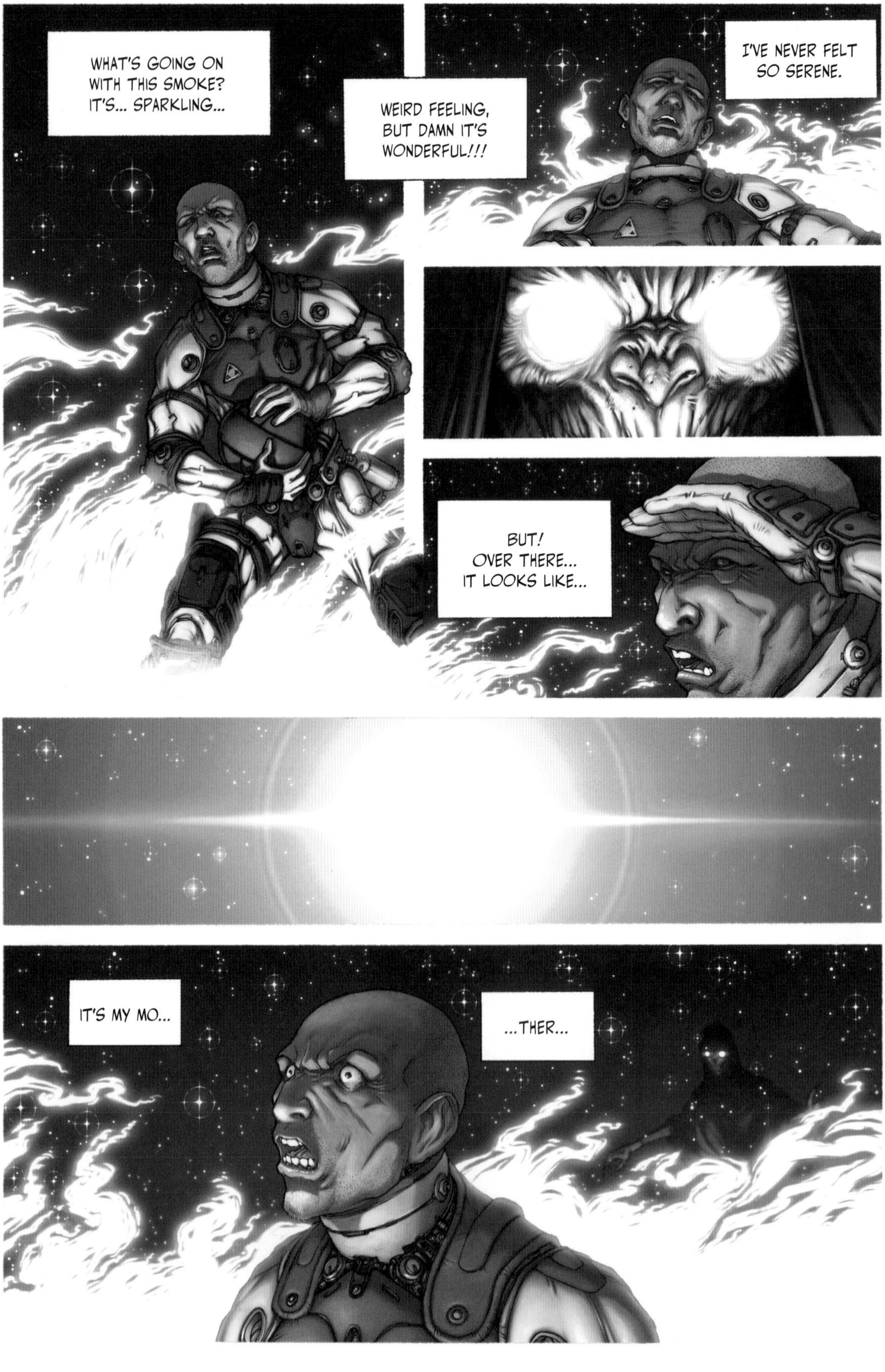
WHAT'S GOING ON WITH THIS SMOKE? IT'S... SPARKLING...
WEIRD FEELING, BUT DAMN IT'S WONDERFUL!!!
I'VE NEVER FELT SO SERENE.
BUT! OVER THERE... IT LOOKS LIKE...
IT'S MY MO...
...THER...

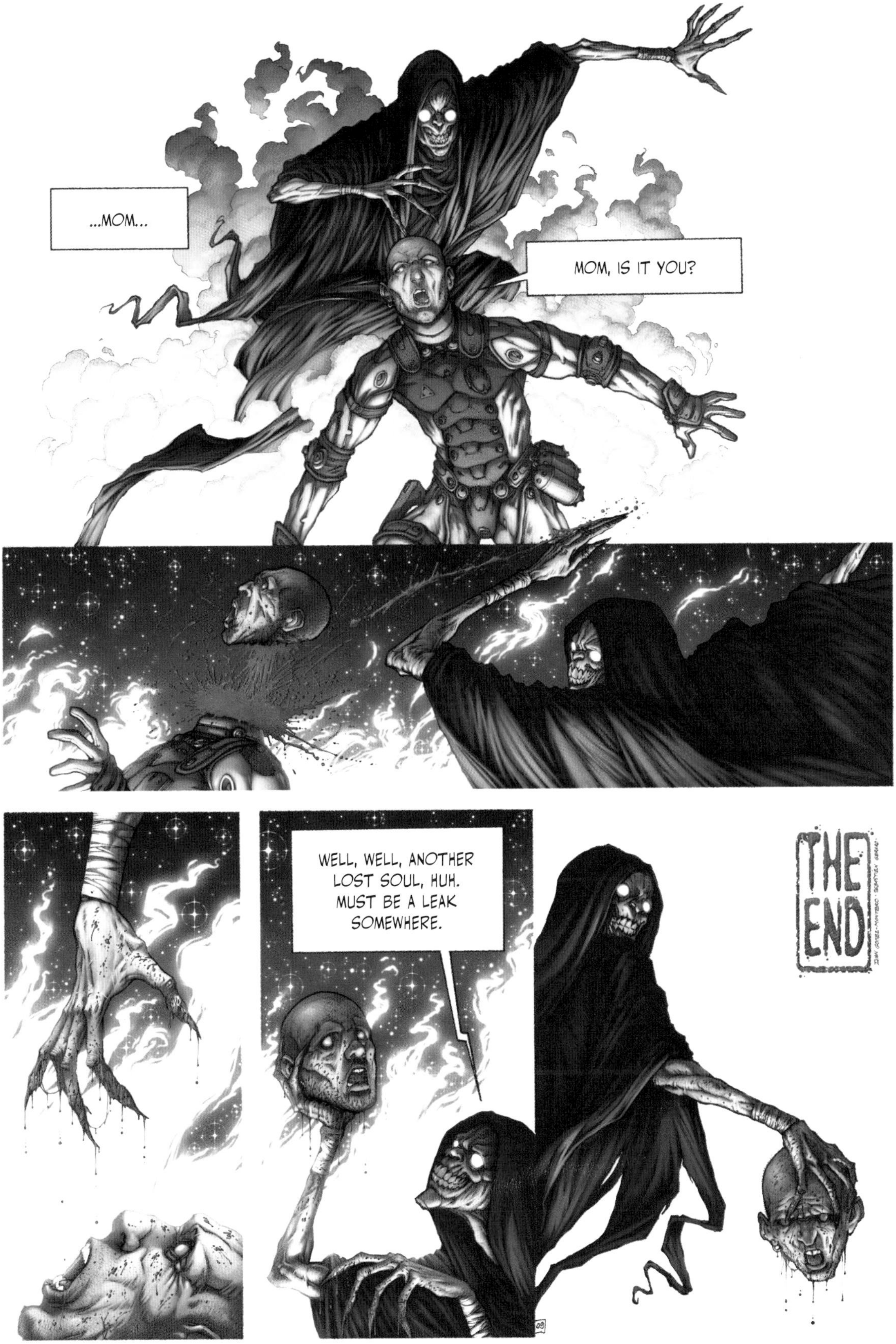
...MOM...
MOM, IS IT YOU?
WELL, WELL, ANOTHER LOST SOUL, HUH. MUST BE A LEAK SOMEWHERE.
THE END

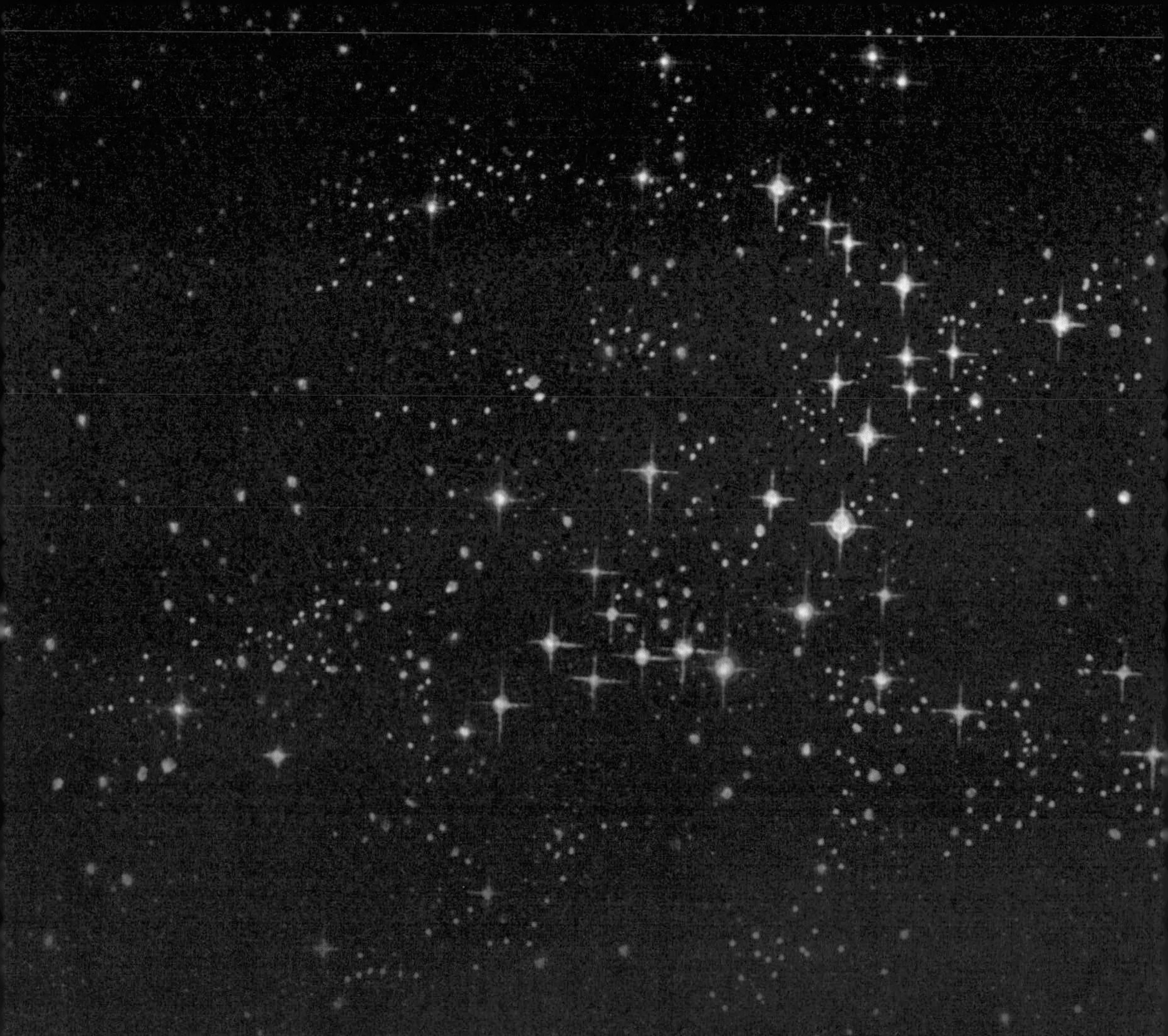

COLD HARD FACTS

Story by R.A. JONES
Art by MATT COSSIN

IN LEGEND AND IN FACT, IT IS CALLED **METAL HURLANT** –

THE LAST FRAGMENT OF A ONCE LIVING PLANET. ITS **BODY** WAS BLASTED INTO DUST BY THE MADNESS OF ITS OWN INHABITANTS –

WHILE ITS **ESSENCE** WAS CURSED TO ROAM AIMLESSLY THROUGH TIME AND SPACE - SCREAMING IN PAIN AND SORROW.

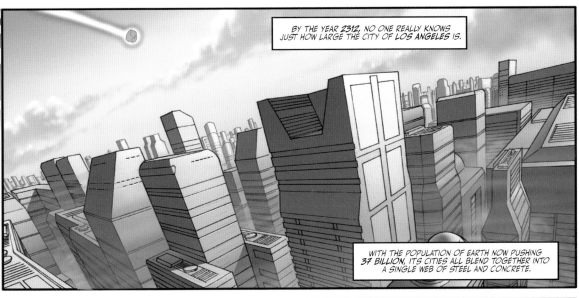

BY THE YEAR **2312**, NO ONE REALLY KNOWS JUST HOW LARGE THE CITY OF **LOS ANGELES** IS.

WITH THE POPULATION OF EARTH NOW PUSHING **37 BILLION**, ITS CITIES ALL BLEND TOGETHER INTO A SINGLE WEB OF STEEL AND CONCRETE.

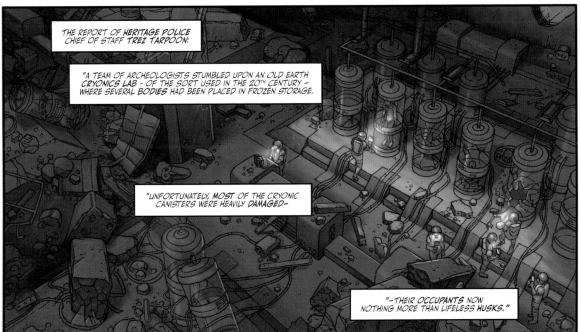

THE REPORT OF **HERITAGE POLICE** CHIEF OF STAFF **TREZ TARPOON**:

"A TEAM OF ARCHEOLOGISTS STUMBLED UPON AN OLD EARTH **CRYONICS LAB** - OF THE SORT USED IN THE 20TH CENTURY – WHERE SEVERAL **BODIES** HAD BEEN PLACED IN FROZEN STORAGE.

"UNFORTUNATELY, **MOST** OF THE CRYONIC CANISTERS WERE HEAVILY **DAMAGED**–

"–THEIR **OCCUPANTS** NOW NOTHING MORE THAN LIFELESS **HUSKS**."

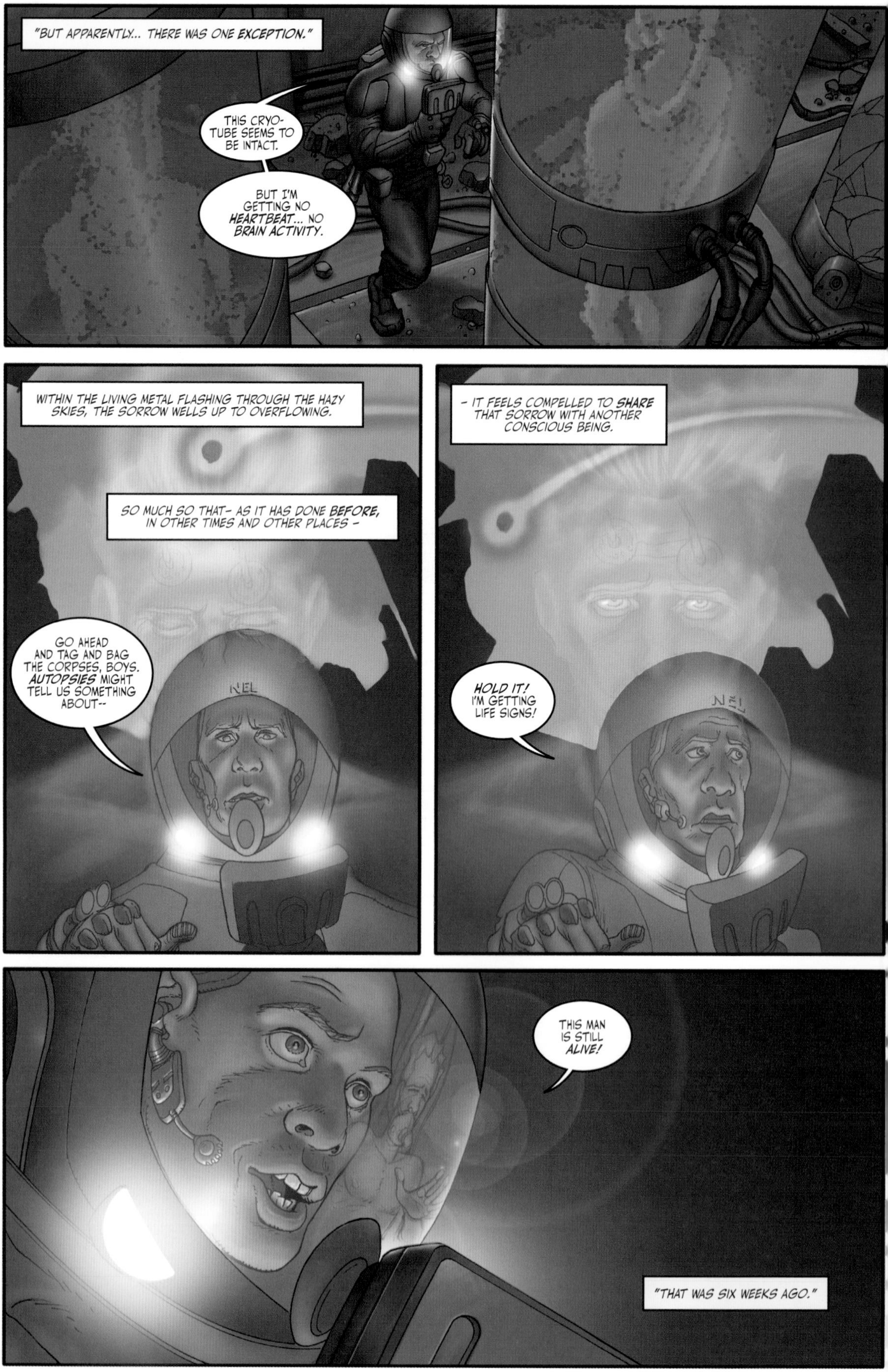
"BUT APPARENTLY... THERE WAS ONE EXCEPTION."
THIS CRYO-TUBE SEEMS TO BE INTACT.
BUT I'M GETTING NO HEARTBEAT... NO BRAIN ACTIVITY.
WITHIN THE LIVING METAL FLASHING THROUGH THE HAZY SKIES, THE SORROW WELLS UP TO OVERFLOWING.
SO MUCH SO THAT- AS IT HAS DONE BEFORE, IN OTHER TIMES AND OTHER PLACES -
GO AHEAD AND TAG AND BAG THE CORPSES, BOYS. AUTOPSIES MIGHT TELL US SOMETHING ABOUT--
NEL
- IT FEELS COMPELLED TO SHARE THAT SORROW WITH ANOTHER CONSCIOUS BEING.
HOLD IT! I'M GETTING LIFE SIGNS!
NEL
THIS MAN IS STILL ALIVE!
"THAT WAS SIX WEEKS AGO."

WE HAD NO TROUBLE *REVIVING* THE MAN —

AND A FEW SIMPLE INJECTIONS *CURED* HIM OF THE *DISEASE* THAT LED HIM TO BE FROZEN IN THE FIRST PLACE.

AHH — MODERN MEDICINE. IT ALLOWS PEOPLE TO LIVE AND BREED FOR *AGES*.

MOLAN DROOG

NO *WONDER* THE WORLD'S IN A STATE OF SOCIAL *MELTDOWN*.

I SUPPOSE OUR *ICE MAN* IS IN PERFECT HEALTH NOW?

NOT *EXACTLY*, SIR. SOMETHING HAS ... IMPAIRED HIS *MEMORY*. HE CAN'T EVEN RECALL HIS OWN *NAME*.

WHAT MEMORIES HE *DOES* RETAIN HAVE BEEN DULY RECORDED AND STORED.

BEYOND THAT—

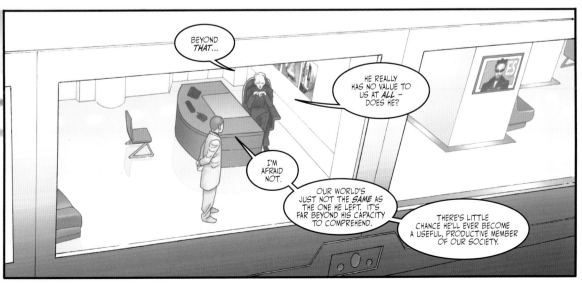

BEYOND *THAT*...

HE REALLY HAS NO VALUE TO US AT *ALL* — DOES HE?

I'M AFRAID NOT.

OUR WORLD'S JUST NOT THE *SAME* AS THE ONE HE LEFT. IT'S FAR BEYOND HIS CAPACITY TO COMPREHEND.

THERE'S LITTLE CHANCE HE'LL EVER BECOME A USEFUL, PRODUCTIVE MEMBER OF OUR SOCIETY.

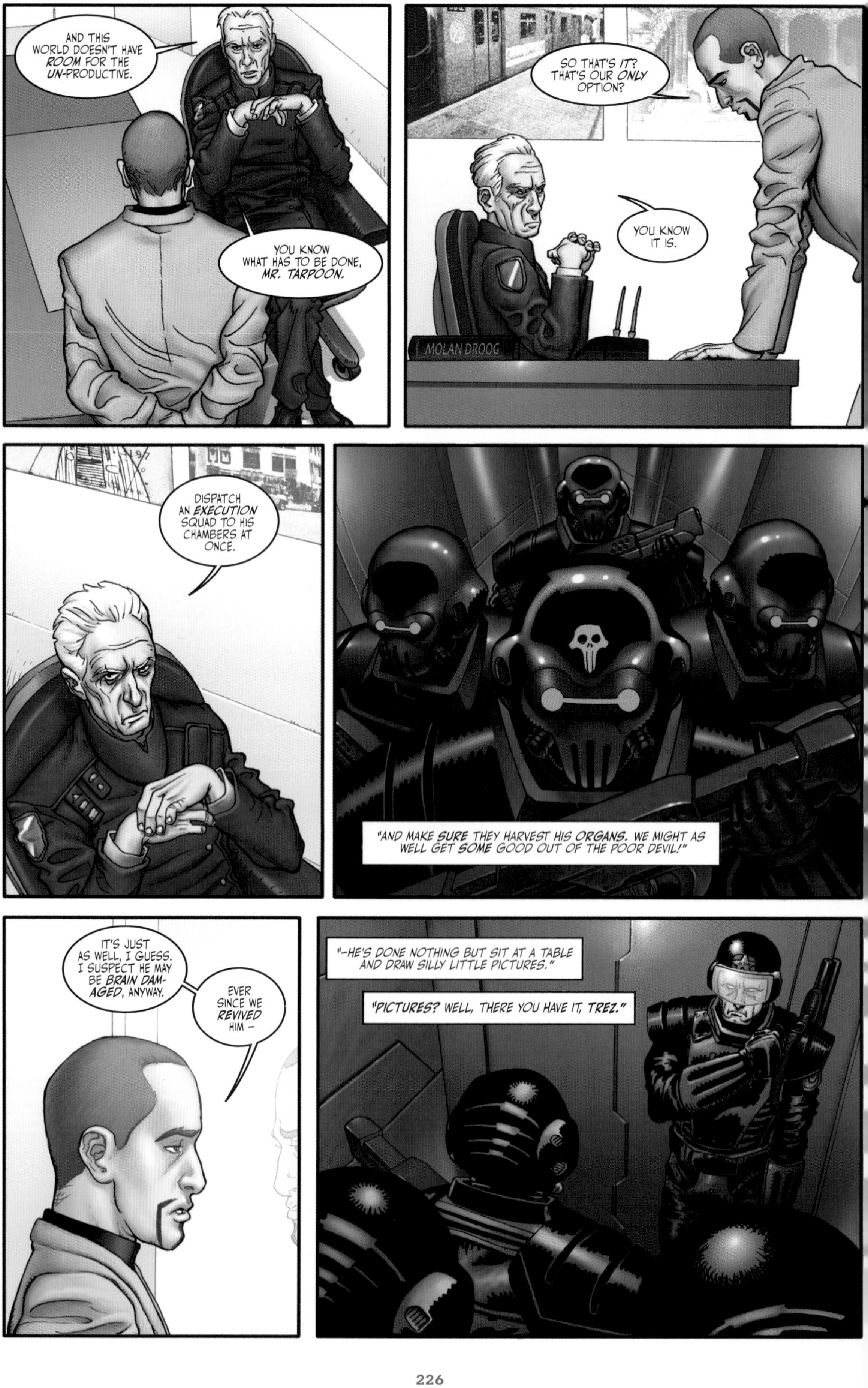
AND THIS WORLD DOESN'T HAVE ROOM FOR THE UN-PRODUCTIVE.
YOU KNOW WHAT HAS TO BE DONE, MR. TARPOON.
SO THAT'S IT? THAT'S OUR ONLY OPTION?
YOU KNOW IT IS.
MOLAN DROOG
DISPATCH AN EXECUTION SQUAD TO HIS CHAMBERS AT ONCE.
"AND MAKE SURE THEY HARVEST HIS ORGANS. WE MIGHT AS WELL GET SOME GOOD OUT OF THE POOR DEVIL!"
IT'S JUST AS WELL, I GUESS. I SUSPECT HE MAY BE BRAIN DAMAGED, ANYWAY.
EVER SINCE WE REVIVED HIM –
"–HE'S DONE NOTHING BUT SIT AT A TABLE AND DRAW SILLY LITTLE PICTURES."
"PICTURES? WELL, THERE YOU HAVE IT, TREZ."

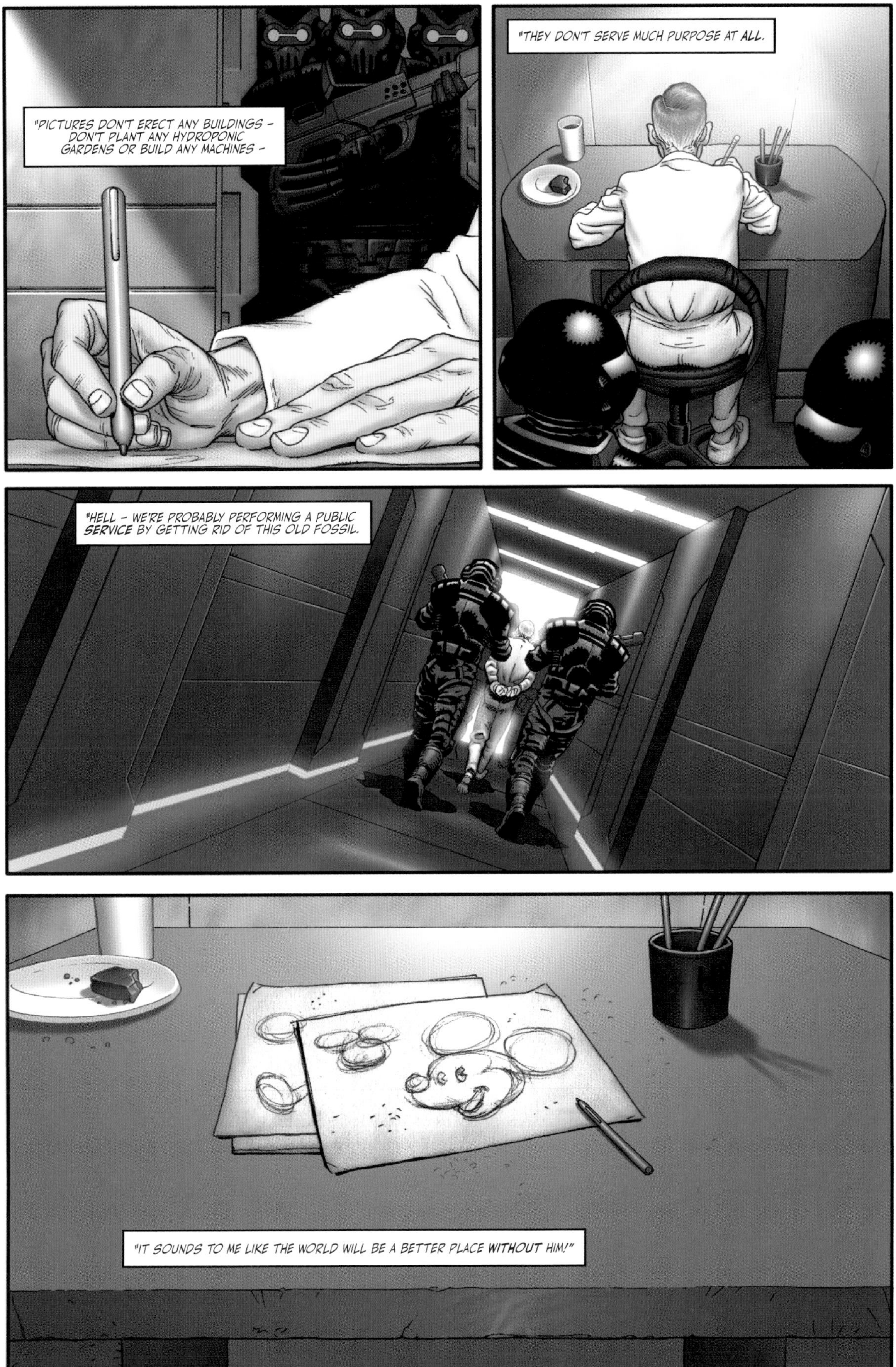
"PICTURES DON'T ERECT ANY BUILDINGS - DON'T PLANT ANY HYDROPONIC GARDENS OR BUILD ANY MACHINES -
"THEY DON'T SERVE MUCH PURPOSE AT ALL.
"HELL - WE'RE PROBABLY PERFORMING A PUBLIC SERVICE BY GETTING RID OF THIS OLD FOSSIL.
"IT SOUNDS TO ME LIKE THE WORLD WILL BE A BETTER PLACE WITHOUT HIM!"

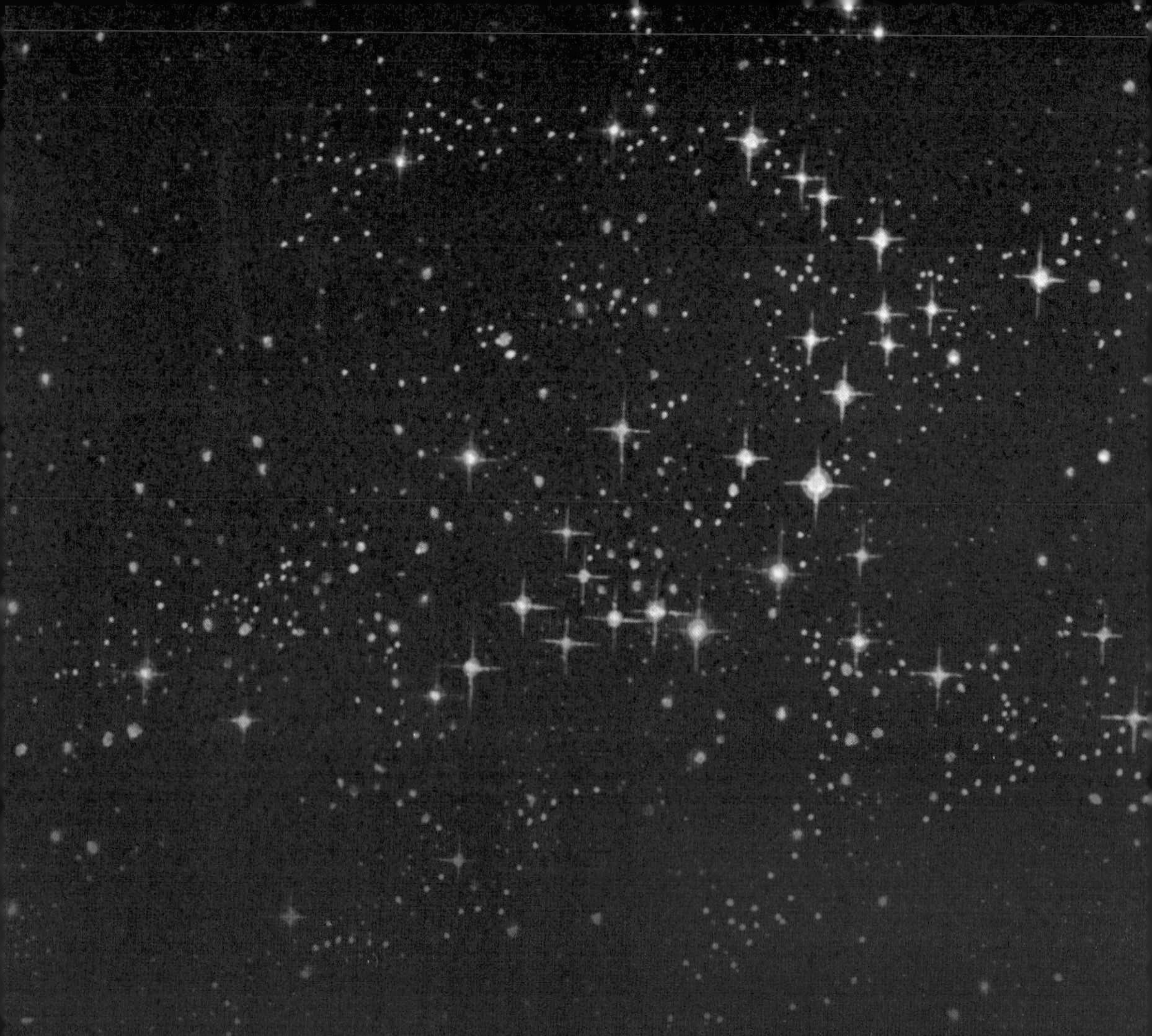

PEACE!

Story and Art by CAZA

PEACE!

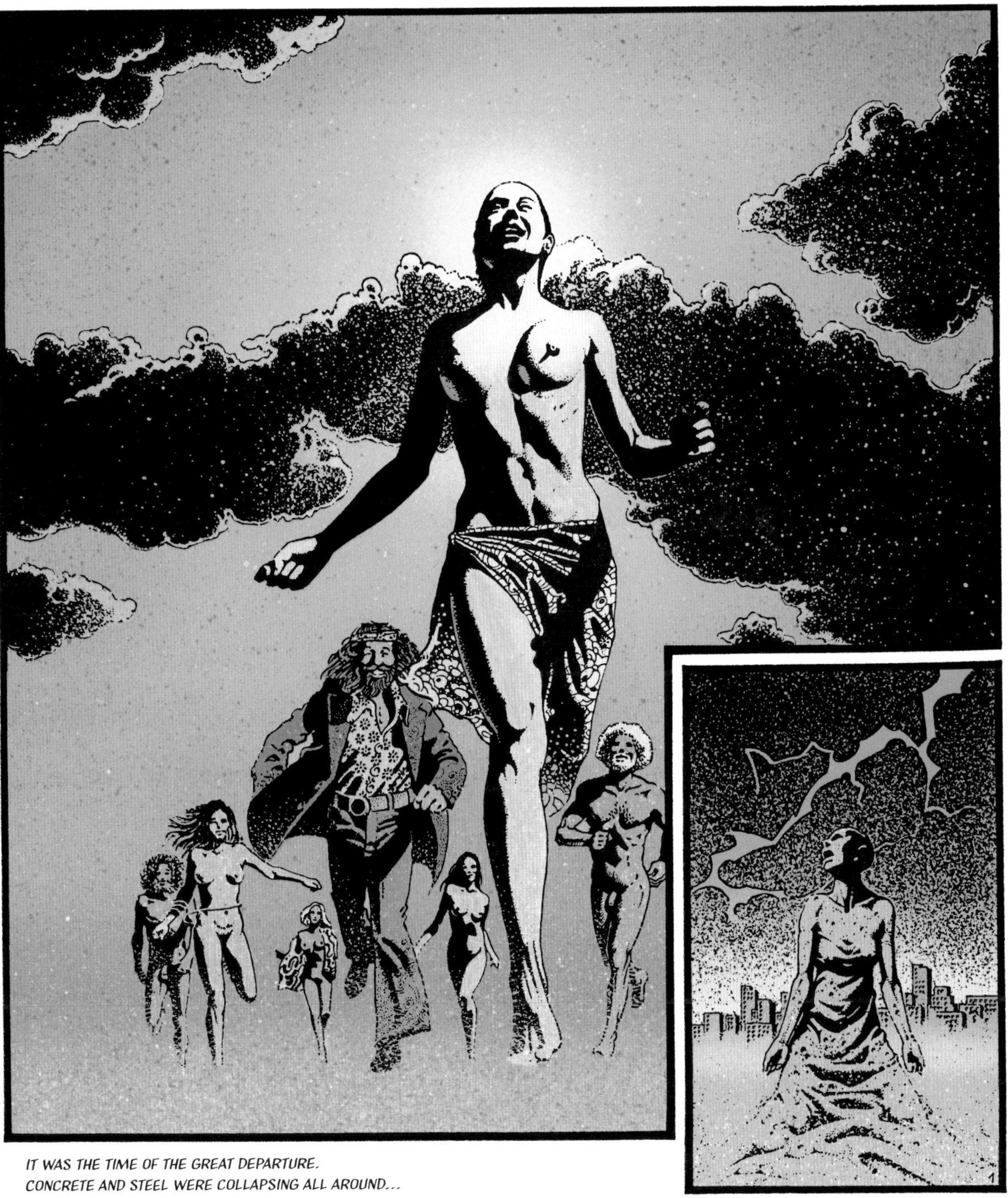

IT WAS THE TIME OF THE GREAT DEPARTURE.
CONCRETE AND STEEL WERE COLLAPSING ALL AROUND...
THE RATS WERE LEAVING THE SHIP...
IN GROUPS, AS COUPLES, OR ALONE.
TAKING ONLY WHAT THEY HAD WITH THEM,
THEY FLED. STRAIGHT AHEAD.

AND WHOEVER LOOKED BACK
INSTANTLY TURNED
INTO A STATUE OF SALT...

I CHOSE TO STOP HERE...

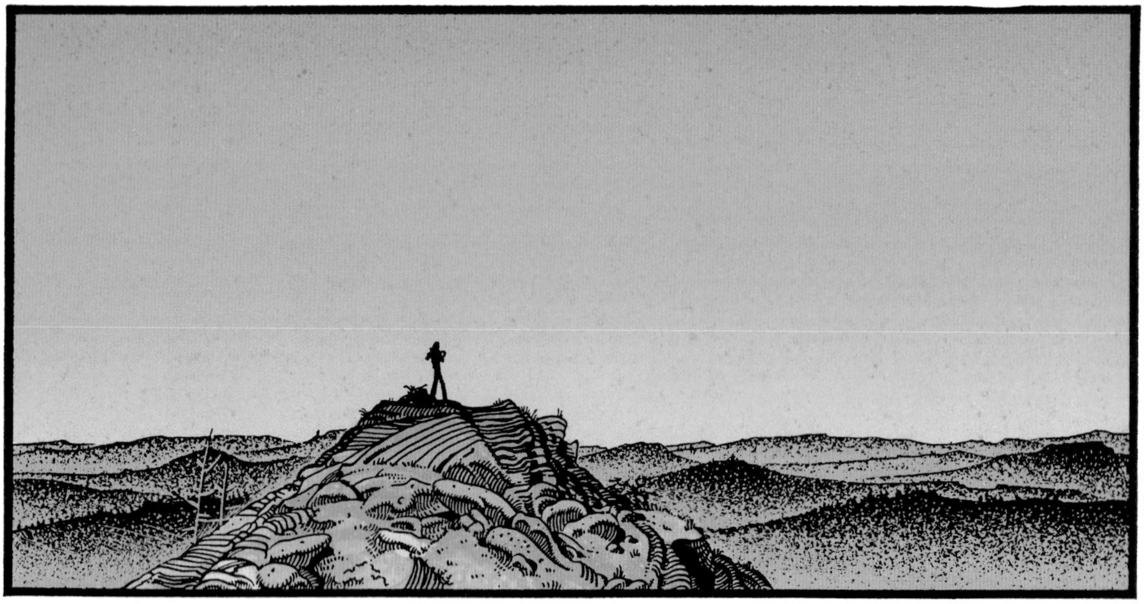

AND I CEASED TO MOVE.
FOR GOOD.
SO, VERY SLOWLY,
I TOOK ROOT...

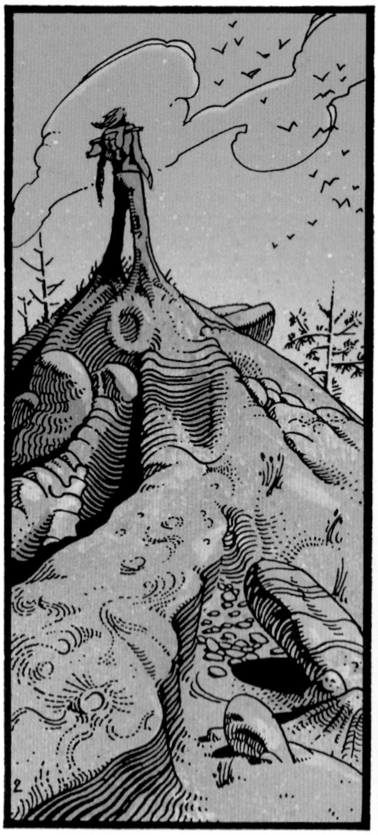

SAP, ENERGY,
TELLURIC CURRENTS,
FLOWED THROUGH ME.
I GREW, I BLOSSOMED...

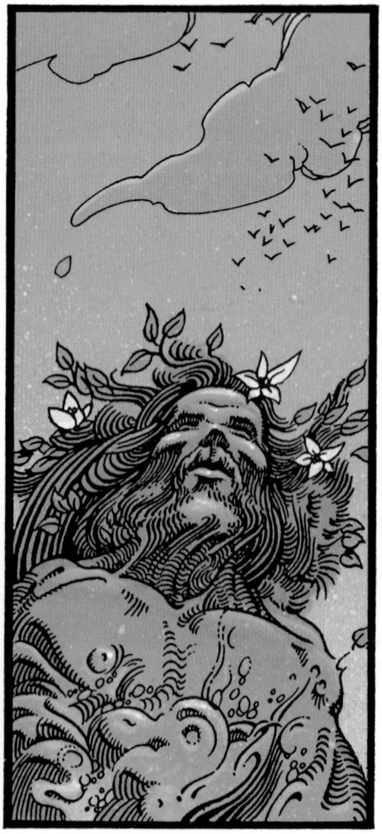

EFFORTLESSLY, MY FEW
POSSESSIONS ABANDONED ME,
WORN OUT AND BLOWN AWAY
BY THE WIND...

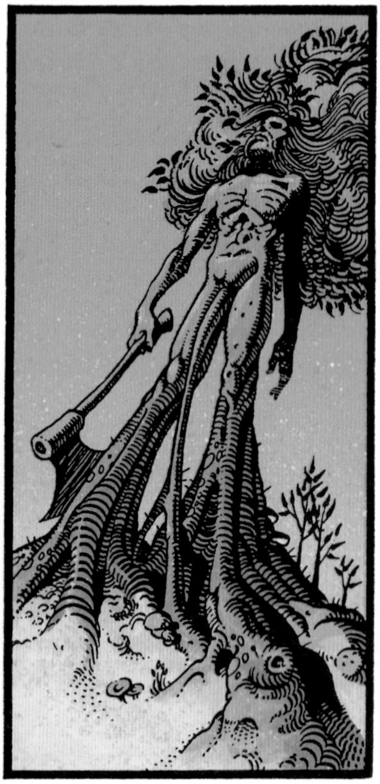

I KEPT ONLY MY AX.

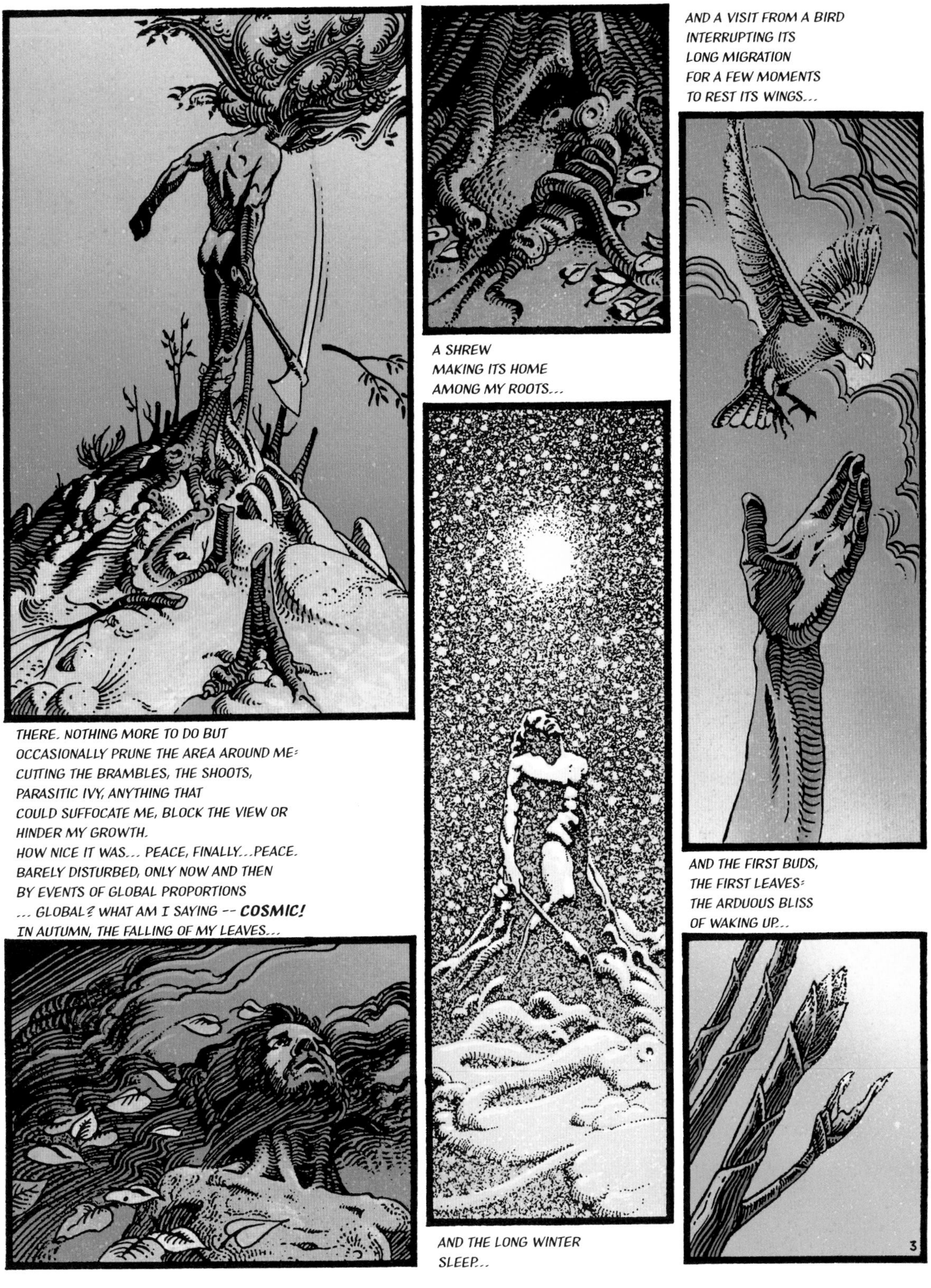
THERE. NOTHING MORE TO DO BUT OCCASIONALLY PRUNE THE AREA AROUND ME: CUTTING THE BRAMBLES, THE SHOOTS, PARASITIC IVY, ANYTHING THAT COULD SUFFOCATE ME, BLOCK THE VIEW OR HINDER MY GROWTH.
HOW NICE IT WAS... PEACE, FINALLY...PEACE. BARELY DISTURBED, ONLY NOW AND THEN BY EVENTS OF GLOBAL PROPORTIONS ... GLOBAL? WHAT AM I SAYING -- COSMIC!
IN AUTUMN, THE FALLING OF MY LEAVES...
A SHREW MAKING ITS HOME AMONG MY ROOTS...
AND THE LONG WINTER SLEEP...
AND A VISIT FROM A BIRD INTERRUPTING ITS LONG MIGRATION FOR A FEW MOMENTS TO REST ITS WINGS...
AND THE FIRST BUDS, THE FIRST LEAVES: THE ARDUOUS BLISS OF WAKING UP...
3

AND, EVERY MORNING, THIS...

EVERY EVENING, THIS...

TWO HUNDRED AND FIFTY SIX
SHOOTING STARS
IN THE AUGUST NIGHT SKY...

AND THE MOON,
ALWAYS
RENEWED...

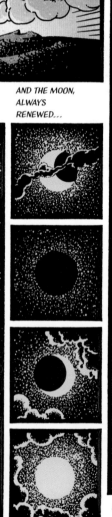

AND SUMMER!

THE SUN!

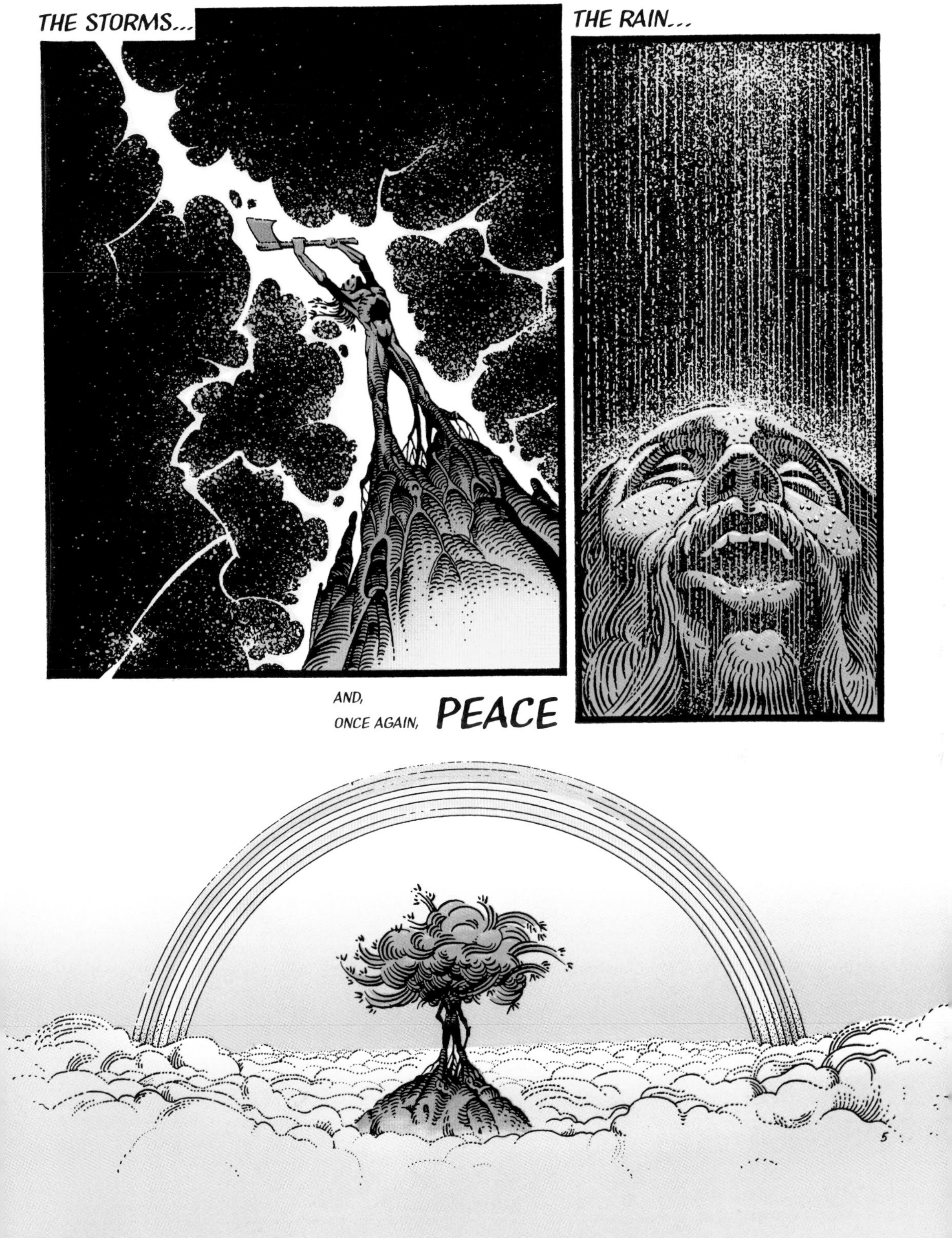
THE STORMS...
THE RAIN...
AND,
ONCE AGAIN, PEACE
5

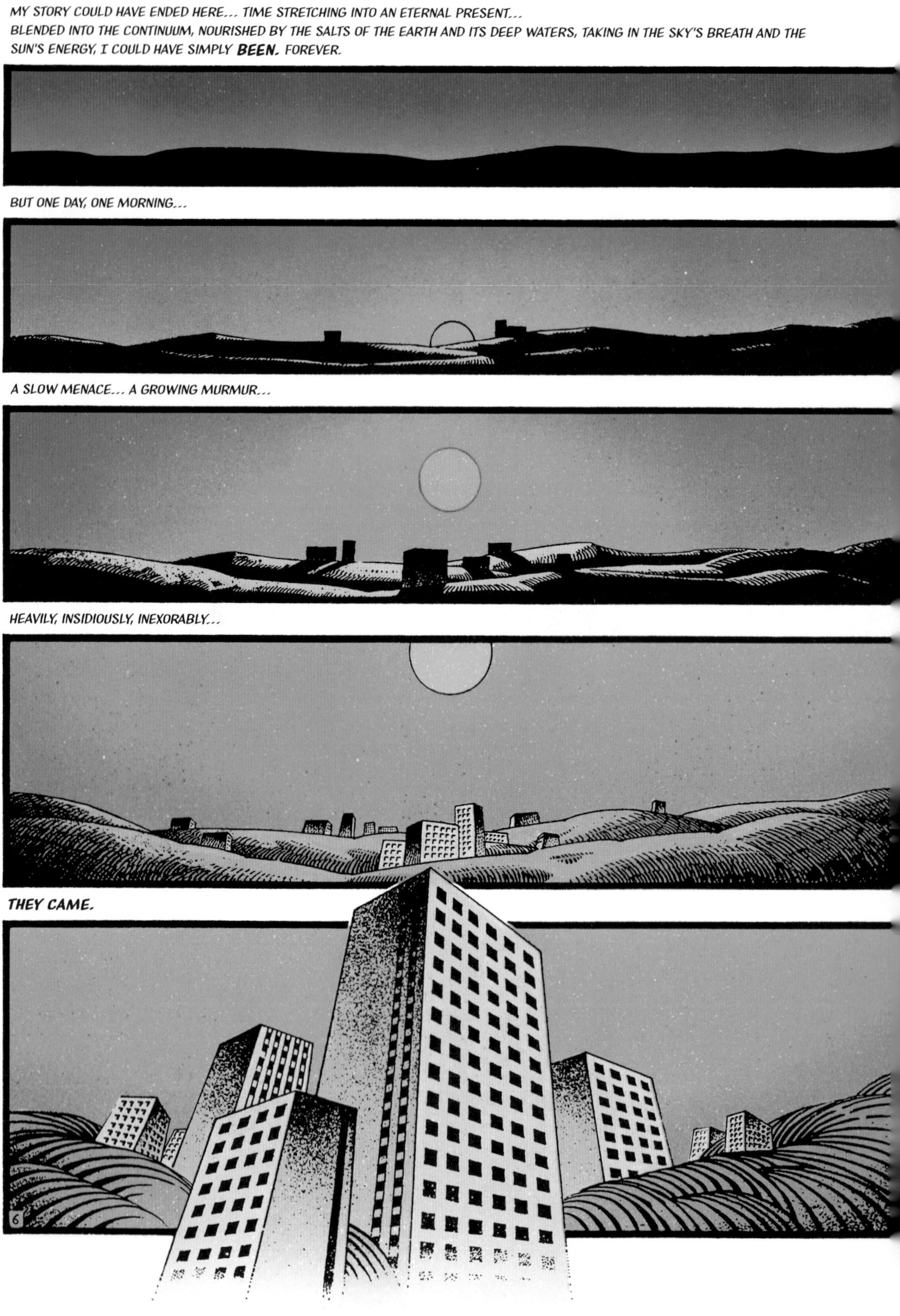
MY STORY COULD HAVE ENDED HERE... TIME STRETCHING INTO AN ETERNAL PRESENT...
BLENDED INTO THE CONTINUUM, NOURISHED BY THE SALTS OF THE EARTH AND ITS DEEP WATERS, TAKING IN THE SKY'S BREATH AND THE SUN'S ENERGY, I COULD HAVE SIMPLY BEEN. FOREVER.
BUT ONE DAY, ONE MORNING...
A SLOW MENACE... A GROWING MURMUR...
HEAVILY, INSIDIOUSLY, INEXORABLY...
THEY CAME.

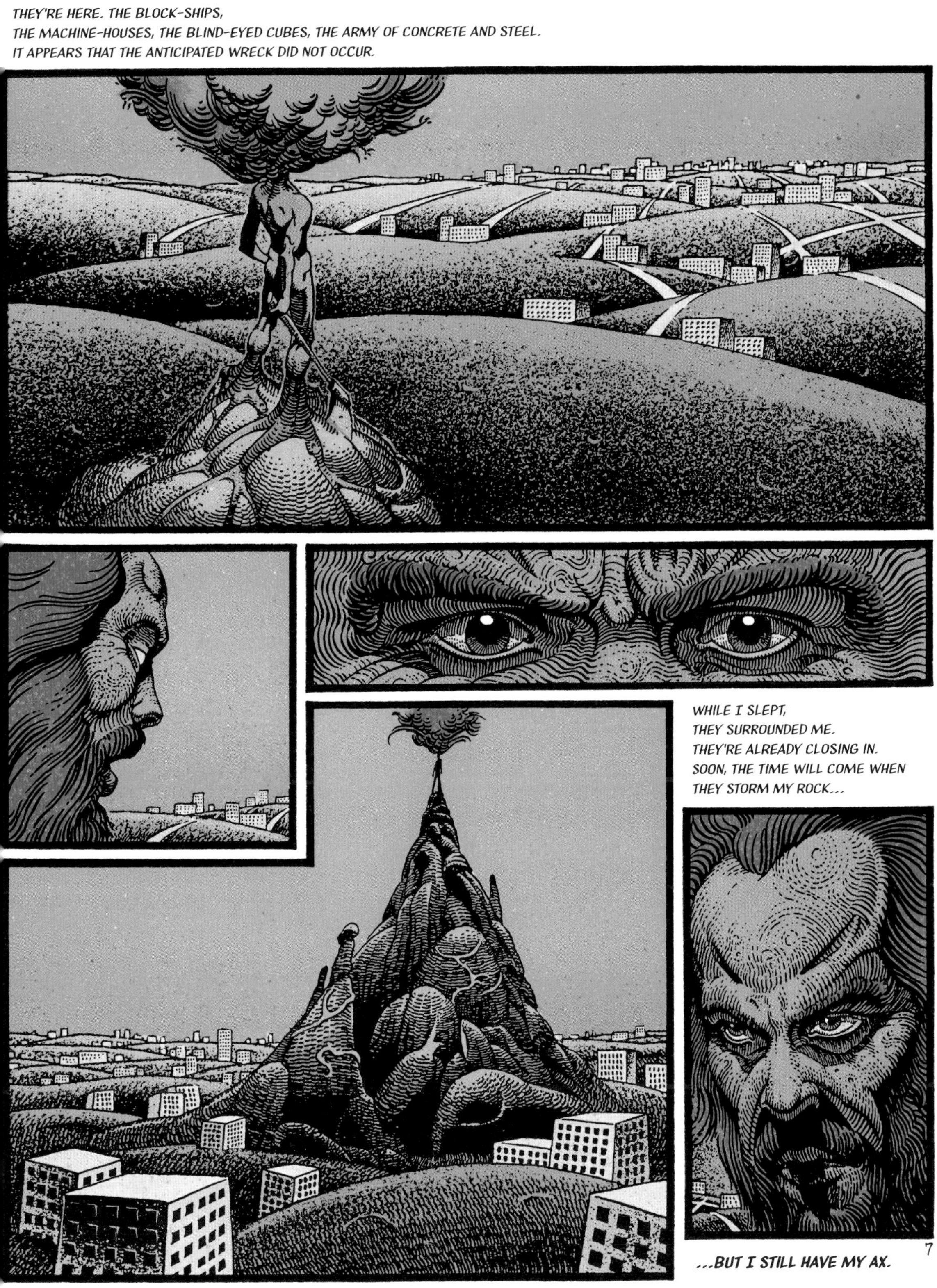
THEY'RE HERE. THE BLOCK-SHIPS,
THE MACHINE-HOUSES, THE BLIND-EYED CUBES, THE ARMY OF CONCRETE AND STEEL.
IT APPEARS THAT THE ANTICIPATED WRECK DID NOT OCCUR.
WHILE I SLEPT,
THEY SURROUNDED ME.
THEY'RE ALREADY CLOSING IN.
SOON, THE TIME WILL COME WHEN
THEY STORM MY ROCK...
...BUT I STILL HAVE MY AX.

7

SO, BY MY OWN HAND,
I CUT MY BRANCHES.
I CUT MY ROOTS.

AND
I GO DOWN THE MOUNTAIN.

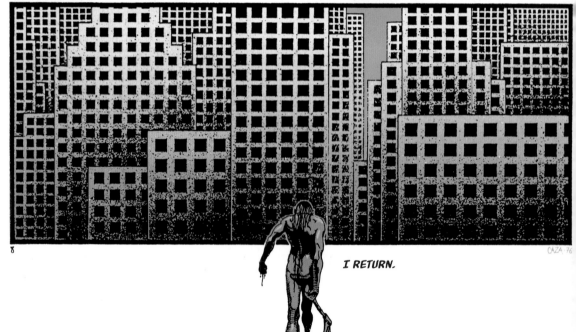

I RETURN.

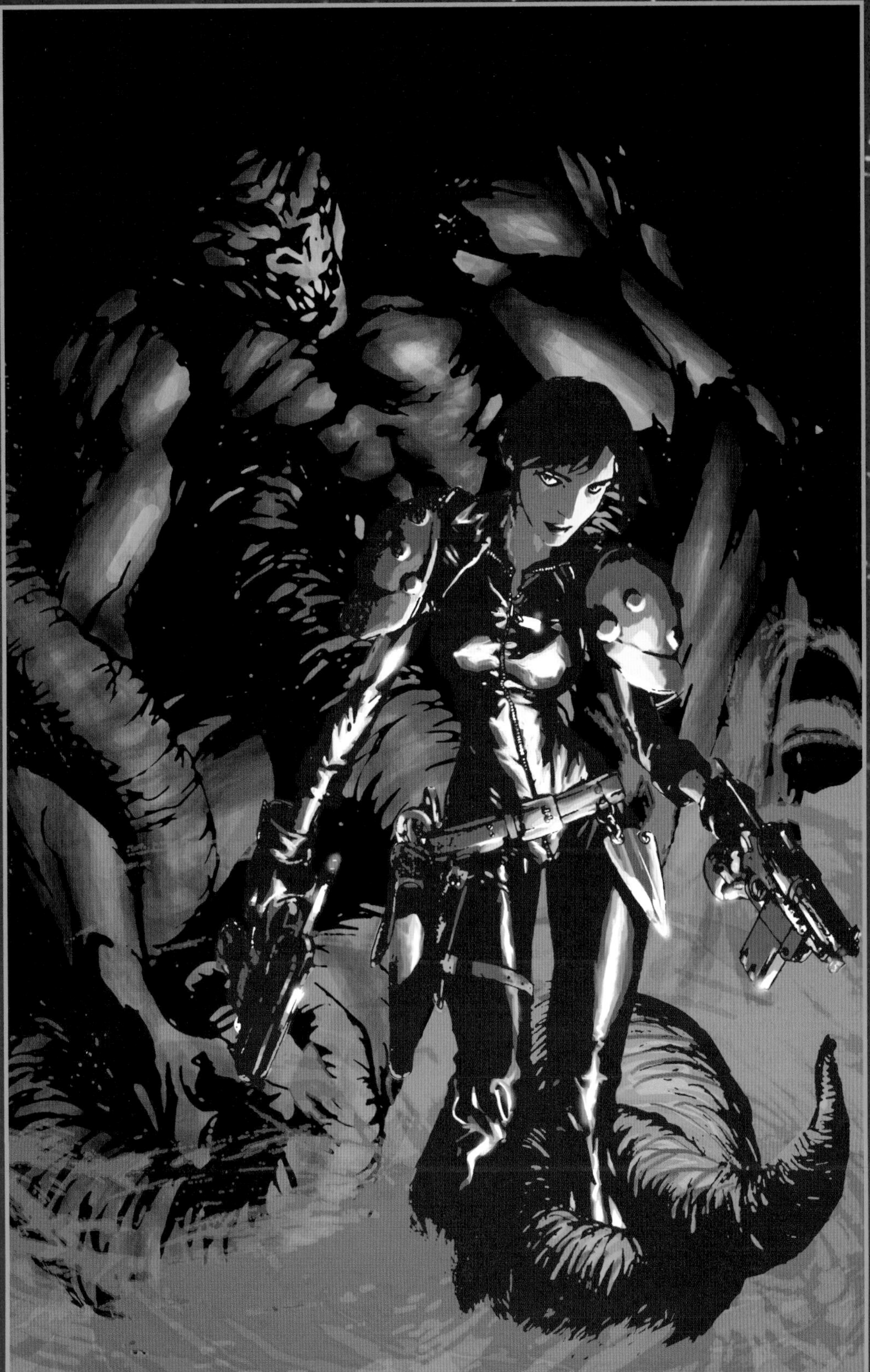

Cover of Issue #3 - Art by Gerald Parel

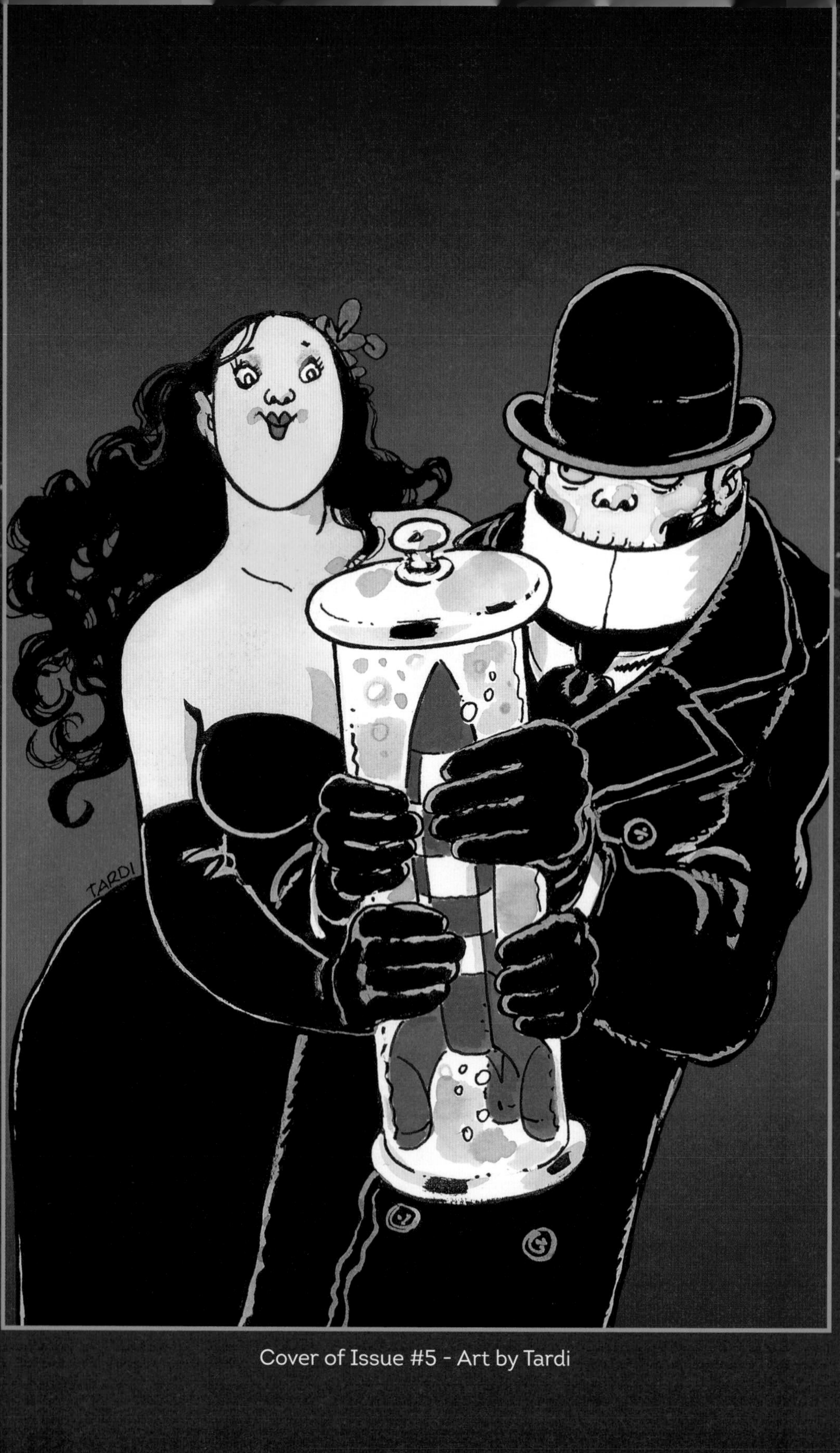
TARDI

Cover of Issue #5 - Art by Tardi

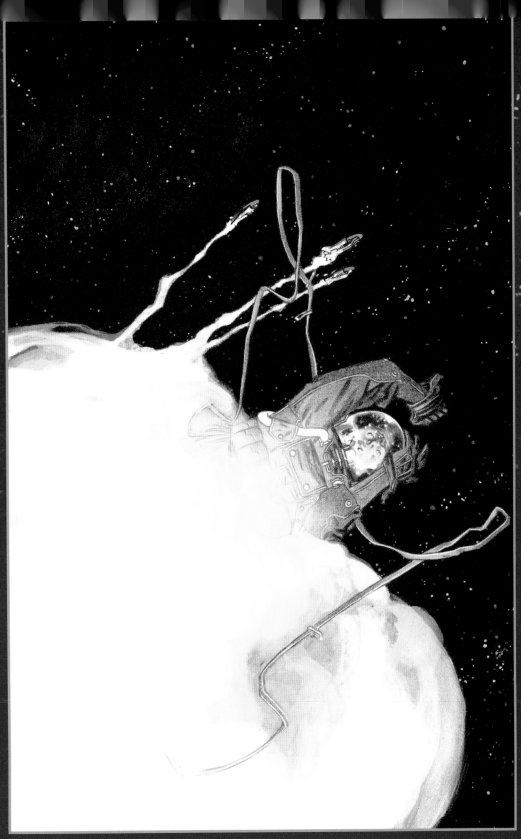

Cover of Issue #6 - Art by Ryan Sook

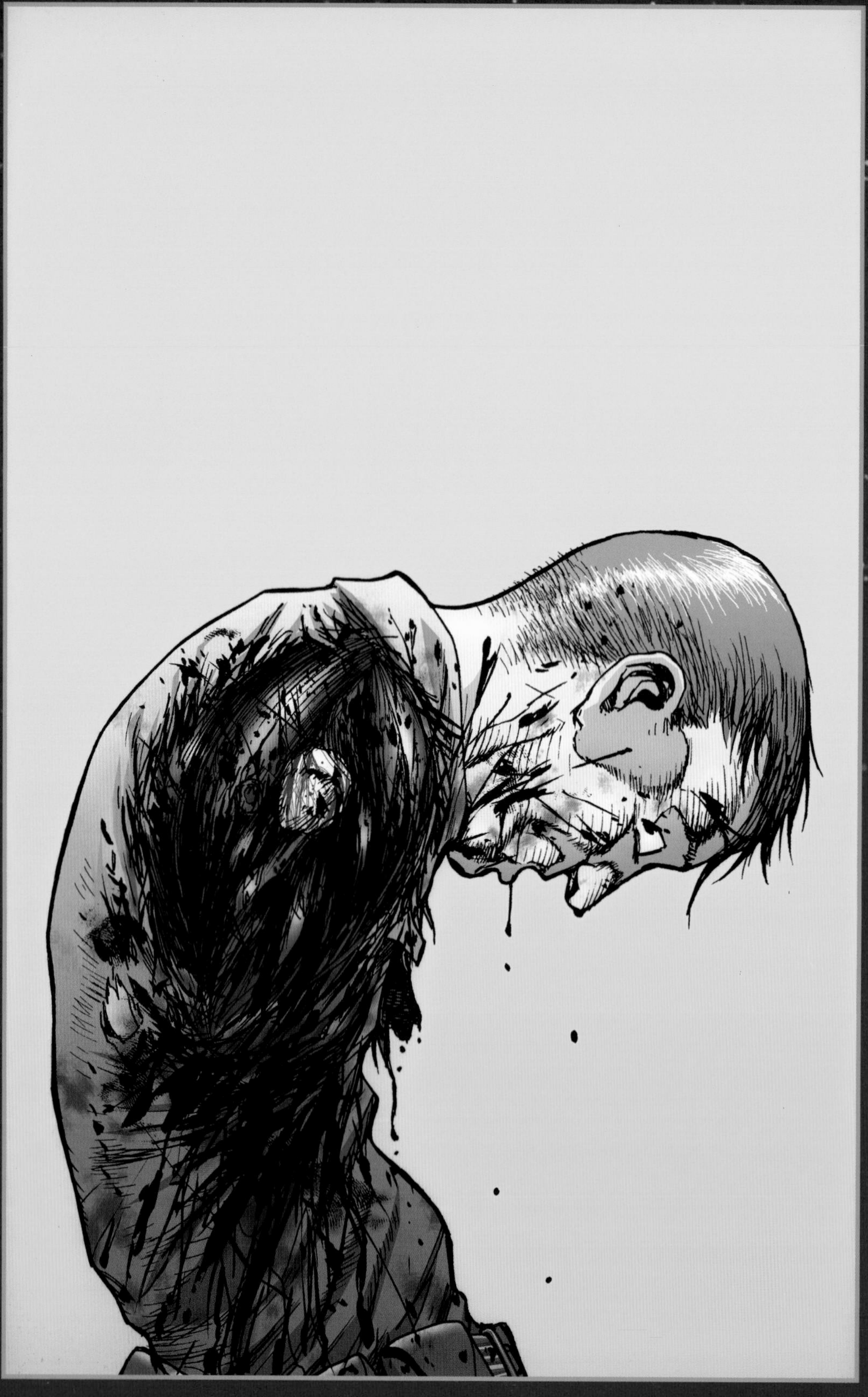

Cover of Issue #12 - Art by Rob G.